Shiny Scissors

By
Lawrence Bell

CHAPTER ONE

Another day...another year...

Well, in point of fact, no it wasn't.

To be realistic, I knew something was going to happen, it happens to everybody I suppose but I just hadn't made any plans. Well, nothing definite anyway.

You see, this was going to be 'the year'. Unbelievably, it was at last going to be my final year, and then I would be done. Frighteningly, and also very, very quickly and to my complete amazement, retirement was finally approaching and with just another month to go. I would be done and dusted and I could finally hang up the old scissors.

Let me explain what I do for a living. I'm a hairdresser, or should I say that I'm actually now a barber. Years ago I used to be a ladies hairdresser, but when my mental capacity could take no more, I jumped ship and opened a barbers shop. That was about twenty five years ago now, and it all seems to have somehow passed in a flash.

And today is Tuesday. Tuesday morning to be precise, and as usual with every working day, I'm walking up the road to my barbers shop, as I do every morning.

Repetition, I suppose is a fact of life, whether you like it or not, and funnily enough, I think that I actually do.

I know that the general public have mixed views on the hairdressing trade, but I'll tell you something, it's actually a great job. Hard work it certainly is, but it has to be said, it's the people that you meet that colour your day.

And every day I open up the shop, and I raise the shutters, and unlock the door, then turn off the alarm and turn on the T.V. I fill the kettle, fill the till, and make a brew. I mentally count to ten and then open the appointment book and see who's going to entertain me today, and vice versa of course.

Unfortunately, this morning seems like it's going to be a quiet one, and that doesn't really suit me because I like to be busy, busy makes the clock go faster.

As a result, there's no hurry, and so eventually I sit myself down, brew in hand, and I put my feet up and have a look out of the window. It's a beautiful sunny day and as I glance down the road, I suddenly wonder how many times I've actually walked up that same road to get to work.

This is all a bit pathetic, and I have to control the urge to get out my calculator and work it all out, because I've just realized that its 25 years times 365 days, less weekends.

And I think to myself...'Oh hell', because that's just the walk here, there's the walk back home as well.

This is not good.

Anyway, I sit there and I look down the road, and I start to consider things, well my life really, and the assorted ups and downs of it all, and the people that I have met and dealt with and listened to over the years and the stories that I've been told. There are extraordinary reminiscences of people that I know and have known, it's remarkable really. And as I sit there looking down the road, a memory comes back to me, and a number, a figure...and that figure is '300 yards'.

Strange as it is, it's a figure that always sticks in my mind, and it makes me think. It's only a short distance, '300 yards', a short walk maybe, but for me it does have some significance.

Fifteen, twenty years ago, I forget exactly when, but I used to have a neighbour who lived just two houses up from me. His name was Harold Moors. When I first met him he was elderly and retired and when I think about it now, he never actually changed, it's strange but Harold Moors was an old man, white haired and thin, for the twenty years that I knew him. There was another thing about Harold; he was a true gentleman in every sense of the word.

Married to Florrie, his wife, who was originally from Yorkshire, Harold, a Lancashire man 'born and bred', he used to joke that she was the only good thing to have ever come out of Yorkshire, much to Florrie's great annoyance.

I was fond of Harold, in a way he reminded me of my own grandfather. He was of a generation, he'd seen two world wars and hunger and hardship and the changes in the social life of this country, but he still hung on to the old values of being neighbourly and kind hearted and caring.

Life for Harold was his family, who were all girls, his wife, daughters and granddaughters. He was a happy man and he made the best out of the life that was his.

My barbers shop is just a short walk away from my house, walk up through our estate through a winding walkway and past the 'over 50's' flats, and there sits my barbers shop. Almost every day Harold and Florrie would walk past and wave to me through the shop window as they went shopping at the local supermarket. I think it was something of their generation that they bought their food every day, as opposed to the usual 'weekly buy in'.

Harold was a regular customer and when he needed a haircut, it would always be Florrie who rang to make his appointment. It would normally be around eleven in the morning, and the conversation was always the same.

She would ring me and say "Hello, it's Florrie, yes it's me...and how are you? We're just having our first drink of the day". She would then continue "I'm on gin and tonic, and Harold's having a whiskey. Now then, can he have his haircut tomorrow please?"

I would chuckle to myself, there's one thing about alcohol, it does seem to keep the old folk going.

As he sat in my barber's chair, conversations with Harold would generally relate to his past, his life and the war, which for many of his generation was something that they would never get over, let alone forget. With the outbreak of the First World War, Harold aged fifteen, lied about his age, and along with many of his pals, he joined the army.

I once asked him why on earth he did this; to me it seemed sheer lunacy.

"Ah" he said "you wouldn't understand, you see, things were different in those days. You had to do the right thing and you were expected to be in uniform, you had to fight for 'King and Country'. There was talk...talk about the German soldiers, molesting and raping women and children all across Europe That's what we were told anyway, and we were worried for our mothers and sisters, worried about what could happen. They were different times back then, there was no radio or television in those days, just newspapers and talk...plenty of talk.

If you weren't wearing a uniform, people would actually stop you in the street, and they'd ask you questions,

"Where's your uniform, why aren't you signed up"...and even "are you a coward?"

That's the way it was, they were just different times".

He told me quite a few stories about life during the first and second world wars, but there was one thing he once said that struck me.

"The great war, the first world war, was absolutely terrible. There was no one that it didn't affect. In many cases it took out a whole generation in towns and villages all over England, the local men folk were simply wiped out. We though, and we eventually knew, that it was the war to end all wars. The price we paid was terrible. But, if you had told us back in 1918 that in another twenty years we would be at War again, and be fighting the Germans again" Harold would shake his head "We would have never believed it"

I have always thought about what Harold said, and understood what he meant. The stupidity of mankind in trying to destroy his perceived enemy, his fellow man, is something peculiar only to the human race. We seem to exult in the wilful killing of our own species.

It's something I'll never understand.

Anyway, as they say...I digress.

Strange things go on in wartime, and Harold once told me about something that happened in Bolton during the Second World War, something that was hushed up and never reported.

It's the story of a soldier, a Bolton man, who'd been away for over three years, fighting the War in France and Italy. He'd been involved with the Americans in the hard campaign to retake central France and then onwards to Italy where he fought at the infamous battle for 'Monte Casino', which turned out to be one of the hardest sieges of the war. He was given leave, just a couple of weeks to return home before eventually being called back to fight.

It was only a short time, but he'd not been home or seen his young wife for over three years. There had been letters of course, but the war was not a good postman and he'd been constantly fighting at the front.

Travelling by a series of overcrowded trains that were full of desolate refugees, and by the constant use of various army supply trucks, the soldier slowly traversed Europe. He finally got himself to Calais where he handed his leave papers to the navy, who then got him on a boat and shipped him back across the channel. Another series of supply trucks got him to London and from there on an overnight train, he travelled up to Manchester and then another train and on to Bolton.

And so on a cold, dark morning, the soldier got off the train at Bolton station. He stood for a moment and he looked around at the once familiar sights. All he carried with him was his rucksack and his rifle. The two things he'd carried for nearly three years, the two things that had kept him alive. In his rucksack were rations, water, bandages and cigarettes, and in his rifle were three bullets.

It seemed a long time ago, but when the soldier had received his call up papers at the beginning of the war, he had been ordered to an army recruitment camp near Reading for a month's basic training. From there, he and the other young raw recruits would be sent off to the killing fields of Europe. That first day, as he along with others entered the camp gates, he suddenly stopped and took out his papers and again read them. They simply stated that he was to be private. 796721 and that was it.

And so hesitantly, as he stood there at the camp gates, he made a decision.

"I am no longer myself, I am now a number, I am private. 796721 and this is the only way I will get through this war. I must forget my home, my wife and my family. Thinking about them won't do me any good, all I am now is private.796721. I am a soldier now and forget everything else".

That first night, as he lay in his camp bed listening to some of the other young men sobbing, lonely and lost, he knew that he'd made the right decision.

And so, three hard years later, he stood there on Bolton railway station. Leaning over, the soldier picked up his rucksack and rifle and walked off into the dark morning.

He lived a mile away, just the other side of the town centre. As he walked, he smiled to himself, he had ten day's leave, he was back home, and for ten days he would not be private. 796721, he would be himself again for a short time, and he thought about his young wife and he smiled again.

He walked his usual walk home through the town and nothing seemed to have changed much. It was still dark and had just started to rain. He walked down the familiar back street to his house and opened the door to the back yard. Nobody ever locked their doors in those days and he quietly opened the back door and immediately breathed in the wonderful smell of home. The thought of his wife upstairs in their warm bed stirred him. And he walked through the kitchen and up the stairs, smiling as he walked into their bedroom. His wife lay in bed asleep, her dark tousled hair across the pillow, still beautiful, so achingly beautiful.

And at the side of her lay a blonde man, asleep, his hand across her breast.

The soldier just stood there, in front of the bed, their bed, and he looked on in disbelief.

His wife moved, and then she suddenly opened her eyes and stared at the soldier in her bedroom.

And then she saw his face and she gasped. The blonde man stirred slowly and looked at the woman whose bed he was sharing. He saw the look on her face and then he turned and saw the soldier, still standing there, watching them both naked in bed.

The blonde man, somewhat affronted and now angry, said to him

"What the bloody hell do 'you' want soldier?"

The soldier simply dropped his rucksack to the floor, and then he spun the rifle in his hand and in one practiced movement brought the weapon to his shoulder.

The blonde man was dumfounded. What was going on?

The soldier's wife just whispered "My...my husband"

The blonde man's eyes widened, now understanding, he'd always known that she was married.

And without another word spoken, the soldier shot him in the head and shot him in the chest.

The soldier's wife sat in their bed, now spattered with warm blood, she sat there petrified.

The soldier slowly turned and pointed the rifle at his wife. There was just one bullet left.

She sat there in bed and started to shake, she couldn't utter a single word, she just looked at the soldier, her husband, and a tear slowly formed in her eye.

The soldier looked down at his wife, and her beautiful face. She was everything to him. She was the only thing, the only reason for him to come home, because he loved her.

And he thought of everything he'd been through, everything, and now this.

He took one last look at his wife, at the beauty and the fear and he knew that he was lost and that she was lost...lost to him. Nothing could ever be the same again, he was heartbroken.

His finger was tight on the trigger, but suddenly, the rifle started to shake in his hands.

Standing there in silence, the soldier understood. He loved her, and because of that he knew he couldn't kill her. He just couldn't.

So he turned and walked out of the bedroom, then he went down the stairs and walked out of the house for the very last time.

Standing in the back yard, he began to breathe more slowly as he calmed himself down. He stood there and quietly lit a cigarette, and watched as it shook in his slightly trembling hand. Cool drizzling rain ran down his face and as he blinked the water away, he made yet another decision.

He finished his cigarette, and then he straightened up and walked straight out of the yard and back into the street, then made his way back down into the town centre. Once in town he headed for the Central Police station. He entered the police station and marched straight up to the reception and stood to attention as he saluted.

On duty that morning was Police Constable Reg Gregson. He sat at his desk and looked up as the soldier approached. Something was not quite right.

"Can I help you soldier?" said PC Gregson.

The soldier, still at attention, arm still raised in salute, snapped it out.

"Private. 796721 reporting sir. Reporting that I have just killed someone sir, a civilian, I have just shot and killed him."

And then he lowered his salute.

"Oh Christ" said P.C Gregson.

The policeman immediately stood up.

"Don't move" he said to the soldier, and he went to find help, this was going to be a problem.

Detective Sergeant John Adler was immediately called out of his office, and he and PC Gregson took the soldier into the Interview office where they questioned him and learned what had happened.

Detective Adler then stood up and went back into his own office, he picked up the telephone and asked the operator for the Ministry of Defence. Ten minutes later he put the phone back down.

He went back into the Interview office and took PC Gregson to one side.

"Get two of your best men and find a van..." he said..."Now"

And that was it.

The body disappeared, and so did the soldier's wife. She was resettled somewhere in Southern England, never to return to Bolton. The few people, who knew about her and her boyfriend, simply thought that they had run off together.

The soldier was taken straight back to his camp, where he was spoken to by his Colonel and a man from the ministry. A decision was made.

That evening, the soldier was put on an aeroplane and flown back to his company on the French and German border were the fighting was ferocious.

Nothing was ever heard of the soldier again, whether he was killed or he survived the war, nobody ever knew, he just never came back, a casualty of war...a number.

The Colonel and the man from the ministry parted with a nod and a handshake. They were in agreement. British soldiers had been through a long, hard war. Winter was coming and the fighting in Europe was at its worst. It was a simple decision really. British soldiers did not need to know that their wives and girlfriends, waiting back home, were possibly screwing somebody else. It wasn't good for morale.

Life goes on.

Harold once told me a story about his best friend's son, a young man, whose name was Jonathan Harris.

Harold and Jonathan's father 'Peter' went to secondary school together and then worked in the same engineering offices until the First World War interrupted things. After that war, although they both went their separate ways, they always remained good friends.

Peter Harris eventually got married and he and his wife had their only child, Jonathan.

Jonathon inherited his father's love of engineering and ended up working for the same company that employed his dad. They both had a single passion, and that was motorcycles, in particular Triumph motorcycles .They each owned a big 500cc machine which they loved to ride around Harwood, the village where they lived, situated on the outskirts of Bolton.

At the age of twenty, Jonathan ended up in the army, by then World War Two was in full onslaught. He was newly married, just twelve months, and then he had two passions in his life, his wife Joanne, and his beloved Triumph motorcycle.

Two years into his war and Jonathan came home on leave, and on the first Friday night he went out with his dad and met up with Harold at their local, 'The Nab Gate pub'. Something that the two older men had done for years.

Sitting at a table away from the bar, the three of them discussed Jonathan's war.

Jonathan, who had arrived home only two days before, was quite restrained. Several pints of bitter were consumed, and Peter, trying to brighten up the mood of the evening, started to buy large whiskies, almost as a form of indulgence.

It was then that Peter asked his son about his colleagues in the army

"What was the lad called that you met on the first day. Eddy...Eddy something?"

"Eddy Armitage" replied Jonathan.

"Yes that's him. You two hit it off from the first day didn't you, he was a motorbike enthusiast too, wasn't it Norton's that he was interested in, they're good motorbikes..."

Jonathon looked at his dad strangely, and then he bit his lip and put a hand over his eyes and then slowly, he started to sob.

Peter and Harold were taken aback, and they looked at one another. What on earth was the matter?

The whiskey, of course had begun to take its toll.

Peter gently took his son's arm "What is it Jonathan, what's happened son?"

Jonathan reached into his jacket pocket and took out a handkerchief and rubbed his eyes and then blew his nose, it was a gesture to hide any embarrassment caused.

Harold, who up till now had been silent, put his hand on Jonathan's shoulder.

"We were in the last war son, we know what it's like, so don't ever be ashamed of crying. I've cried for twenty years, I don't think I'll ever get over it."

Jonathan straightened up and tried to pull himself together, and then he concentrated, and he looked at the other two men and started to speak.

"I can't believe what's happened dad, I just can't..." he said "...from the first day I joined up, me and Eddy were mates. We stood in line together to sign up, we got talking and that was it. We ended up being best mates, talked motorbikes, shared cigarettes and shared rations. Hard times and better times, we'd been through it all....all the fighting and all the fear. When you've shared that fear with someone and got through it, you're as close to that person as you can ever be."

Peter and Harold nodded, yes, they'd been to war and they'd had to fight for their lives too.

Jonathon continued "We're on the Dutch and Belgian border at the moment, the fighting is horrendous, one week nothing at all happens, and the next week it's slaughter.

Eddy had been on leave, ten days welcome break from that hellhole, he'd been back to see his wife and his family for the first time in nearly two years. Like me, he was only just married when he got called up, and then was sent off to fight. Eddie's a character, always good natured, but when he came back to camp, there was something different about him. He was quiet, and a bit sullen. I put it down to him having to return to camp, we all did really.

Our camp is rough, and as rough as it gets, we can't get regular supplies and the weather's turned, there's rain and mud everywhere. Anyway a few days passed and he was still very subdued and a bit distant, I thought I'd maybe upset him, I don't know why. On the third day he missed the evening meal and so I went to find him. He was sitting in our tent, just staring at the floor, so I coughed loud enough, and then went inside.

He looked up at me, expressionless.

I said to him "Come on man, I'll buy you a cigarette" and I held out my hand and I pulled him up. He gave me a sort of restrained look and half heartedly walked out of the tent with me. We strolled up the hill in silence, away from the mess tents and the other men and up to a line of trees which gave us some shelter. We stopped under an old elm tree and I pulled out two cigarettes and handed him one. Then I pulled out a match and we lit up. In the glare of the burning match, I looked directly at him.

"What's up Eddy?" I said.

He looked back at me.

"Come on Eddy" I said "what's wrong"?

He blew the smoke out slowly, and said "Everything...everything's wrong" and he shook his head.

"What is it?" I asked him "...is it me?"

"No...No, it's not you mate"

"Well...if it's the war, and I know it's bloody awful here, but..."

"My wife's pregnant" he suddenly blurted out.

And there was a silence as my stupid brain tried to take this in.

"What do you mean pregnant?"

"My wife...Margaret, my fucking wife, she's pregnant"

He was shaking now, and angry and upset.

And all I could manage was "Oh Christ Eddy...No"

"Yes...Oh Christ, fucking yes" and he turned and spat on the floor with contempt.

We just stood there in silence, and he swayed slightly as he shook his head in misery.

"What the hell's gone on Eddy?" I asked.

He took a long draw on his cigarette and slowly blew out the smoke, and I saw his hand shake, and then he told me...

"I went home on leave, I got back home about a week ago, it was Friday. I only had three days and then I would have to make my way back to this bloody place. I'd gotten a last minute notification about leave, so it was all a bit of a dash, nobody back home knew I was coming. I just rolled up at our house, walked down the garden path and opened the front door.

I walked into our front room and through to the kitchen. The house was silent, and at first I thought that Margaret was out and then I walked into the kitchen, and I stopped dead. There she was, standing at the kitchen sink...the sink, full of plates and pans and hot soapy water, and she was just standing there looking at them, nothing else, she just stood there, staring at the plates and pans.

I smiled as I watched her, my god she was bonny, with her beautiful brown hair tumbling down over her shoulders.

"Hiya darling" I said gently.

Her eyes widened as she spun around in astonishment.

"Hey" I said "...It's me, I didn't mean to frighten you. I'm home love...surprise!"

But she was still in some sort of shock, and I moved towards her, ready to put my arms around her.

I laughed and said "Come here love and give us a hug".

But she didn't move, she just stood there with a look of horror on her face. I was puzzled, I didn't understand, and she just kept staring at me, totally silent. And then she slowly raised her hand to her mouth and bit her knuckle, and I saw it in her face...she was terrified.

We both just stood there facing each other, and she started to shake, and then she said.

"Oh God...No"

I moved towards her, but she held up her hands to make me stay where I was.

"What the hell's wrong Margaret?" I said "It's me...me..."

She just said "Oh god Eddy...oh no..." and then she started to cry.

I went to put my arm around her, but once again she fended me off.

"No Eddy...No..."

So I took hold of both her wrists, she was beside herself now.

"What's the matter?" I said...I couldn't understand what was happening.

She just looked up at me, almost dutiful, and then she said it, she just blurted it out.

"I've just found out, I'm pregnant Eddy, it's by another man...it was all a mistake, I'm so...so sorry Eddy" and her voice just trailed away and then there was silence.

And I felt as though I'd been hit by an axe.

I just looked at her. I know I should have been mad, and I felt like going crazy, this couldn't be happening. But she just stood there...she was so beautiful to me.

All I could say was "Margaret, what the bloody hell have you done?"

She blinked and began to wipe a tear from her eye.

"I went out, six weeks ago with my friend Shirley. She was fed up and so was I, and there was a dance on at the Town Hall on the Saturday night. So we decided to go, it was just a one off...I don't go out, honestly I never go out. But on that Saturday we went to the local pub for a few drinks and then went down into the town centre. We were in one of the pubs in town and we got talking to some American soldiers who were on leave. They took us around the pubs, we had a lot to drink and then we all went to the dance together. I ended up talking to this American lad, his name was Jerry and we carried on drinking, then we ended up coming back here, I don't really remember, but in the morning I woke up and we were in bed together. When I realized what had happened I started to cry, and he woke up and just said that he was sorry and he got dressed and then he left".

I closed my eyes and I thought about her with another man, together in bed, my pretty wife with another man...and I went sick.

And then she started to sob.

"I didn't think you'd be back for another year. I...I was going to go down south to my aunts and have the baby there and have it adopted, and then come back home and nobody would know"

I looked at her "Well, you'd got it all planned hadn't you. Very nice Margaret, very nice...well done".

And I turned around, and I picked up my kit and walked out of the house, and all I could hear was her behind me, crying.

I walked off down the road, and as I passed my local pub, two blokes that I know came out of the door and got hold of me. They pulled me into the pub and it was full of people that I knew, and they all cheered when they saw me. We had a celebration because they thought I was only back for a day. Somebody joked that I'd only come home to 'sort out' my pretty wife and then I'd sneak off again, probably back to some French girl.

I gave them all a daft grin "Yes, something like that" I said...and I drank...I drank myself stupid.

I woke up the next morning, on a bench at the bus station, I was a mess. I had to sort myself out, but from there I made my way all the way back here to camp".

"So there you have it Johnny boy" he said. "...I've come back to this hell hole, and I just hope that some bloody German put's a bullet through my head and then all this would be over"

I looked at Eddy. "Don't say that mate" I said.

"I mean it, I fucking mean it, I don't bloody care anymore"

We stood there in silence and I lit two more cigarettes and handed him one.

"What are you going to do Eddy?" I said.

And as we both stood there, I made the decision for him.

Quietly, I said to him "Do you still love her Eddy?"

"Yes" he said, and then he looked at me and he slowly started to weep.

I gave him a couple of minutes and then I put my arm on his shoulder.

"We've got to do something about this Eddy, we've got to sort this out"

He turned to me "What on earth can I do, there's not a damn thing I can do about it".

"Well" I said "You have two choices. We have to stay here and fight. Now whether or not we survive this war is in the lap of the gods, but after the war 'you' will have nothing...nothing at all to go home to, and you won't even be able to go home because of the shame. And Margaret might not even be there, she may have left by then, and then you'll never see her again. Yes, it's a disaster alright, but if you still love her Eddy, and you do, well for god's sake put this behind you. I know the silly stupid girl got drunk, but we've both been drunk and you know as well as me that anything can happen. She didn't go out looking for another man. She's young and just wanted a night out dancing. It happened and now she's heartbroken."

"But she's having a baby"

"Well, let the baby be your baby. Be a father to the child, the child's innocent, so be a husband and be a dad. Eddy, don't ruin your life because of a stupid, drunken mistake"

"But people will know"

"No they won't, nobody knows what's happened and if she's pregnant they'll all put it down to the leave you've just had. People aren't that good at dates and that's what they'll think, they will, believe me"

Eddy looked at me.

"Eddy" I said "Listen to me and listen good, because I'm going to tell you the truth. If for any reason this had happened to me, to me and Joanne...I'd forgive her".

"You would?"

"Yes" I said "I would, and just like you I wouldn't be happy, but that will pass and eventually it'll be forgotten. What I would not do is destroy my life and lose everything, and lose the woman I love. I'd accept it for what it was, a mistake, and I'd get on with my life...

Nobody else needs to know, and you'll have more children and they'll all be brothers and sisters together, they'll all be your kids Eddy"

Eddy looked down at the ground, and then he said "But I just walked out...out of the house, I just walked away, what can I do...I've left her"

I thought about it for a moment. "I know what we can do" I said "one of the lads who works in the telegrams office owes me a favour or two, I'll get hold of him. Let's see if we can send your Margaret a telegram."

Eddy gave me a silly smile "If a bloody telegram arrives at home, she'll think I've been killed"

"Serves her right" I said, and I punched him on the shoulder and laughed.

So we sent the telegram.

It said...'Everything is alright...don't worry...everything is alright...don't have our baby till I get back home...love you very, very much...Eddy.

No more misery and the despair, Eddy got to grips with the situation and accepted it, and we all got on with the war.

About a month later, we were fighting at the front, it was heavy fighting and the tank division had been called in. The weather had turned really bad, there was heavy rain and the wind was blowing hard and cold. Me and Eddy had just come out of a forested area into a clearing at the bottom of a small hill. We'd just had a crafty smoke and decided it was time to move forward. But as we entered the clearing we saw that there were two of our tanks there, they were parked about 200 yards apart. There was an officer with an umbrella with a small group of men, they were standing in the rain about 20 yards away from the nearest tank. It was a massive green machine with bits of camouflage stuck all over it. As we approached them, the officer called us over, he wanted to know who we were and what we were doing. We briefly told him some sort of vague story which didn't really add up, and Eddy, who was standing slightly to the side of the officer, kept giving me one of his daft grins.

"Right" said the officer, who was actually only about the same age as us "Right, I am commandeering you two, we are a man down in each of the tanks and the gunners need assistance. So the pair of you, I want one of you in each tank now...go!" and he spun on his heels to talk to the other men.

Eddy continued with his daft grin "Here we go again" he said merrily and then he laughed at me because I was far from happy, I didn't like tanks, not one bit, and he knew it. I cursed him as I walked over to the tank. I'd only walked seven or eight paces and the next thing I knew I was stumbling and ended up flat on my face.

Eddy had tripped me up, and as he trotted past me to get to the nearest tank he laughed and shouted back "You can have that one over there, you can get wet Johnny boy" and when he got to the tank, he jumped onboard and turned to give me the V sign, and then he laughed as he descended into the tank with a wave.

I got up off the floor, wiped my face, and thought about what I would do to him later when I got hold of him. So then I had to jog the 200 yards over to the other side of the field, to the other tank. It was pouring with rain and I was soaked. I climbed into the tank, sorted myself out, and got my instructions from the gunner as the tank suddenly set off.

Basically, I had to pass the gunner the shells as quickly as possible, for him to load into the gun muzzle and fire.

I asked the gunner what was the plan...

He told me that we were driving over to the other tank, and then together we were going over the hill to face "Germans...bloody loads of 'em, and armed with god knows what!"

I shuddered at the thought of it.

We set off, and trundled over to meet up with the other tank, we were about 30 yards apart as we topped the crest of the hill, and then all hell broke loose. The Germans had heavy artillery, which was aimed directly at us.

The first shell exploded about a hundred feet in front of us. The second shell was a direct hit on the tank that Eddy was in and it took them out completely. The tank turned into a fireball and the blast and the force of the explosion rocked and blistered our tank. Our driver responded immediately, and threw our machine into reverse, and that action saved our lives.

Our gunner had been knocked unconscious, and I climbed over him and grappled with the turret door until I got it opened, the heat from the explosion was turning our tank into an oven. The driver had the tank flat out in reverse and was driving blind as we smashed back into the forest. A hundred yards in and finally under cover, we stopped and I dragged the gunner out through the turret door of the tank. The driver and gunner collapsed in the dark shelter of some oak trees, and then I set off running...running back up to that bloody hill. I came out of the forest and the shelling had stopped, but there it was, the utter carnage, the blazing remains of what was left of the tank.

I ran up to the tank and I just stood there, about twenty yards away from that terrible heat. I simply couldn't believe that inside that tangled mass of red hot burning metal was my best mate. I couldn't help it...I screamed at it in despair.

All that we had been through, everything...everything, was gone.

I slumped to the ground, devastated, and I knew...knew that if he hadn't tripped me up and hadn't been the joker that he was, I would have been in that tank and I would have burned to death. And I thought about his wife, and I thought about my own wife, I'd lost my best mate, and I turned on my side and vomited.

I lay there and I cried. The guilt, the fear and the horror of it all...it was just too much.

Jonathan looked up from the table full of beer, looked at his father and at Harold. "I'll never forget him dad, he was a true mate".

Peter and Harold sat there, astonished, as Jonathan finished telling them his story.

It was Harold who spoke first "You've lost a friend, but a friend you were true to, and you were there for him when he thought he'd lost everything, nobody could ask for more. Just remember the good times that you both had, I'm sure that's what Eddy would have wanted."

His father turned to him "It's terrible son...and war's terrible, but for your mother and I, just the fact that you're still alive, you know what I mean. You're everything to us, and to Joanne, she's missed you so much".

"I know dad" he said "I know".

"How long have you got back in England?" asked Harold.

"Another three days, I was given compassionate leave. I'm going to go and see Margaret, to talk to her and explain that Eddy really had forgiven her, she has no family down there you see. I just need to talk to her, to put her mind at rest...if that's possible."

So after three days, Jonathan went back to fight in the war. It was a war that would only last another six months, and by the end of the year he was sent home, his fighting was over.

He arrived home early on a sunny Saturday morning. He opened the front door, walked into the kitchen and took hold of his startled wife and hugged her till she gasped. He told her he loved her and they went upstairs to bed.

Later that morning they both sat at the kitchen table grinning at each other. Joanne had made them some breakfast...an egg, with a sausage and some good bread, and a proper cup of tea.

"So what else are you going to do today 'husband'?" and she smiled at him "Well it is the weekend, so enjoy yourself, and then on Monday you can start back at work" and she laughed out loud.

"Well my beautiful wife, today I shall take out the other lady in my life"

"Oh, you mean 'Miss Triumph', your darling Motorcycle"

"Yes" said Jonathan "she needs a run for her money as well"

Joanne threw a piece of bread at him with a mock scowl and she giggled.

Jonathan smiled back at his wife "I'll get the bike out and go down to the paper shop for some cigarettes, and then I'll ride round to mum and dad's and give them a surprise."

So he got changed and walked down to the garden shed with great anticipation. He opened the door to the shed and there she was...his cherished Triumph.

Peter Harris had promised to maintain his son's motorbike throughout the war, and as Jonathan pressed the kick-start and the bike burst into life, he knew that his father had been true to his word. He put the machine in gear and set off slowly up the lane which led onto the main road.

He felt the power of the engine and rode on confidently. 'some things...you just never forget', and then he thought about his wife, and he laughed over the noise of the engine.

He turned onto the main road and went through the gears. It was a warm sunny day and it felt great to be back on his motorbike. As he sped along and felt the wind blowing through his hair, he felt as free as a bird. It would be great to see his parents, and he had a surprise for his father, because he had plans for a business, plans for the future which involved the both of them. And as he rode along in the sunshine he thought about Eddy and all the upset and tragedy. But now he had his own life back, his own future, yes he had lots of plans and he'd decided that he was going to talk to Joanne about having children...and starting a family.

Then straight out of a side road came a truck, the driver didn't even see the motorbike and he hit it head on...

Jonathan was catapulted off the bike and he smashed into a stone wall, his skull was crushed and he died instantly.

In a moment...it was over.

Back at home, Joanne hummed to herself, she was making plans too. Yes, they should think about having children. Now that all was well.

One morning as I was getting ready to go to work at my barber's shop, there was a knock at my front door.

I opened it to find Florrie, Harold's wife, standing there in front of me, and she was in some considerable distress. She just stood there and cried.

"Florrie" I said to her "what on earth's happened?" This was obviously something serious.

"It's Harold" she sobbed "he's had a heart attack, he was rushed into hospital last night, he's not well, it's not good" and then a flood of tears.

For two days, Harold lay unconscious, his family constantly at his bedside, then he finally passed away.

Later, I spoke to Florrie, and in her true stoic Yorkshire fashion she said

"It was for the best in the end, I couldn't bear to see him ill and suffer everyday".

And I suppose, she was probably right.

The funeral was a small affair. Harold had always been involved with the church, all his life really, and for years he had played the church organ and the piano.

He was very well thought of.

I suppose being elderly, a lot of the people that you have known in your life, whether it be friends or family, will have passed on. A few of the neighbours attended the funeral service and afterwards Florrie thanked us for being there.

It was during the service, that the Vicar said something curious, it just caught my ear as I sat there, half thinking about Harold, and half daydreaming.

Harold had two daughters, I knew them both well. But the vicar suddenly spoke about Harold's children, and he said something about "a son and two daughters", though at the time I must admit I only caught half the sentence.

I thought about it and just dismissed the subject. Maybe at sometime Harold and Florrie had a son. Anything could have happened to him, anything from childbirth through to the war. People still remembered their children, whether dead or alive and no matter what their age.

But in all the years I'd known them, they'd never mentioned a son, and I certainly wasn't going to start asking now.

Weeks passed, and by then it was summer and Florrie had gotten on with her life, helped along with the support of her family and us, her friends. We had fond memories of Harold, and Florrie was openly glad to talk about him. She seemed pleased that he was not going to be forgotten, not by us anyway.

When they were younger, Harold and Florrie had a busy social life through the Church, and the Church became something that they were both very involved with. Harold had played the church organ and the piano, he was actually very musically gifted, a talent that he passed on to his granddaughters in later years.

One Sunday afternoon, I was actually on the roof of my house, fixing some tiles and guttering. I was working away quietly and concentrating on the job in hand, when suddenly I heard a knock on somebody's door and when I looked down I saw that there was someone at Florrie's house, it was a man.

I called down to him "She's out...I think she's gone to her daughter's for Sunday tea"

And the man standing there at the door looked up at me and smiled and waved, and I suddenly recognised him, he was a customer of mine...David.

David lived with his wife in the 'over 50's' flats at the top of our estate, they're next door to my barber's shop. I'd cut his hair for about twenty years and I saw him most days, him and his wife, going to the shops. They were both retired and were lovely people, and if ever I was doing some job outside the shop they would stop for a chat.

"Oh, it's you David" I called back, though I was a bit curious to see him at Florrie's house, I didn't even know they knew one another.

Anyway, David called up to me "I've got something for her" and he waved a carrier bag at me.

"Leave it at my front door David, I'll take it round to her later" I called back.

So David put the bag on my front door step, and with a wave, he walked back up the road and out of the estate.

An hour or so later when I'd finished repairing the roof, I came down the ladder and started to tidy up. Then I remembered the bag with something in it for Florrie, so I went around to the front door and picked it up. I looked inside the carrier bag, and in it was a large one litre bottle of Gordon's Export Gin.

'Nice one' I thought to myself, and I took it into the house. David must have been on holiday and brought it back for her, and I did remember him saying something about 'Minorca' when he last had his haircut, but I didn't know that he knew Florrie, he'd certainly never mentioned her.

Later that night, I looked out of the front window to see Florrie standing at her front door. She was waving to her daughter, who was just driving away in her car.

'Ah'...and I remembered the gin, and so went into the kitchen and picked up the carrier bag and went across to her house and knocked on the door.

The front door was quickly opened by an ever smiling Florrie.

"Hello love" I quipped "Here's your medicine. David up the road left it for you" and I laughed.

"Oh" she said, grinning "I know what this is, he said he would bring me some gin back, he's been on holiday to Minorca"

"Yes, a bottle of Gordon's finest" I said, and then "I didn't know you knew David?"

Florrie gave me a curious look "Have you got twenty minutes to spare?" she said to me.

"Yes of course I have"...and I wondered.

"Come in" she said, sort of casually "I've something to tell you"

So I followed her into her house and as we stood there in the front room, she turned to face me, and gave a curious smile.

"Do you know who David is?" she said.

"Well" I replied "I've cut his hair for twenty years and I know he lives in the flats next door to my shop, but more than that, not a lot really"

Florrie just looked at me, grinned, and ever so slightly tilted her head.

Then she spoke "David...is Harold's son" and her words hung there for a moment.

"What!" I said. I was astounded. "But...how?" and then I suddenly remembered the funeral, and the vicar and the mention of something about a son, and I realized that I'd not misheard.

"Let me tell you something" she said slowly "Harold was married before...before he ever met me, he was only a young man at the time and it turned out to be a bit of a disaster"

I was amazed. "I never knew, Florrie" I said "I just always just thought of you two, well 'forever' sort of'.

Florrie smiled "I'll tell you a story, and it's a strange one. Well, it's a long time ago now I suppose, a lifetime really, but when Harold came back from the war, the 'Great War'...he was young and lonely, and upset. Things had happened to him during the war that he would never talk about, and things that he never forgot and it troubled him all his life. The slaughter that he'd witnessed, friends blown to bits and friends mowed down, row by row by the machine guns. When he finally came back home from the war, he got a job straightaway at the local co-operative, he was in the grocery department and dealt with the dairy produce, eggs and bacon and butter, that sort of thing. Rationing was on and food was in short supply and very expensive. A lot of people were surviving on potatoes and cabbage back then, and getting enough food for a family was a daily struggle.

Harold used to call in at the local pub on his way home from work, and when it was discovered that he could play the piano, the landlord offered him a couple of shillings a week to play in the pub on Friday and Saturday nights, plus a few pints of free beer.

And it was on one of these nights that he met...'Ivy'.

Because he was the main source of entertainment in the pub, Harold quickly became the centre of attention, and Ivy saw the opportunity and made a bee line straight for him.

She just wouldn't leave him alone and, well, she was young and attractive, dark haired and slim, and sticking close to Harold gave her free drinks all night.

Harold was flattered by the attention...all this was a different world to him, different from the trenches and the mud and horror of France. He was popular now, he'd made new friends and people liked him in this busy comfortable pub, and well, now there was 'Ivy' and free drinks, and before long he was getting very comfortable with her, and she was very accommodating.

She lived in a little rented terraced house that had seen better days, and living with her was her elderly mother who was bedridden. They had to survive on what money Ivy could earn in the local mill, where she worked as a weaver. But Harold worked at the Co-op, and he handled food, and before long he was supplying most of the food in Ivy's house, free food.

So Ivy was getting her eggs and bacon, and Harold was getting his oats, so all seemed well.

Two or three months quickly passed, and then one tea time, Ivy walked into the pub where Harold was standing at the bar with friends, having a pint of bitter.

He looked up and smiled at her and said "Hello love, are you having a drink"?

She simply stood there and said "Outside...now" in a tone of voice that Harold had never heard before, and with that, she walked out of the pub.

Harold stood there, mystified. What was wrong, she sounded angry, but there was also something else there in her manner. It was 'indifference'.

There were raised eyebrows as Harold dutifully put down his pint and followed Ivy out of the pub. When he got outside, she stood there facing him, her hands on her hips, and somehow defiant, and the look on her face was somewhere between a smirk and distain.

Now, Harold was concerned, more than that, he had a slight feeling of alarm. He'd never seen her like this, she was normally so cheerful, and always most compliant, in fact they'd never had a cross word between them. Ivy had seen to that.

So, with a strange feeling of dread, he stared at her and quietly said "What's wrong Ivy?"

She looked straight at him and she just rolled it out, tight lipped and not a hint of a smile.

She simply said "You've got me pregnant, I'm having a baby and it's yours".

There was no happiness, no joy, not even concern. It was a statement, delivered in some way like a threat.

She just stood there, and he looked at her and he knew something had changed.

This was a different Ivy, and it was an Ivy who had the upper hand, calculating and hard.

"What are we going to do?" Harold said, stupidly...as it turned out.

"We" she retorted "We, will be getting married, that's what 'we' will be doing".

And Harold gasped.

He liked Ivy, well he liked the sex...and sex whenever he wanted it really, she never said no.

And she'd told him "Not to worry", she couldn't get pregnant because she'd had Scarlet Fever as a child, and Harold had believed that little tale too.

"I thought you couldn't have a baby"

"Well now I can" she said "and it's yours, and you'll have to do the right thing by me".

So there it was, and Harold was stupefied.

"We need to talk about it" he said, he was flustered now. Marriage was something he hadn't contemplated, well certainly not to Ivy.

And then she spat it out "Now you just listen, because I'm doing the talking now. I'm expecting your baby, you've got me pregnant, and 'you will' marry me" and she continued.

"Tomorrow, we'll go and buy an engagement ring, I'm coming with you, and then we'll go to the church to see that Vicar of yours. We'll tell him exactly what's happened, the truth, and we'll get him to marry us quick. He'll do it, you're the church organist for god's sake, he won't want any scandal" and with that, she actually grinned, "Now, you'd better go home and tell your family what's happening, they can think what they like, I don't care, and also between now and the wedding, we'll have to find a house..."

"What?" gasped Harold, again?

"Yes, a bloody house, are you stupid, we're going to need somewhere to live. We can't live with your family, there's no room, and anyway I'm not living under their bloody roof, not with that sanctimonious lot "

She had only met his parents once, they didn't approve.

"We need a bigger house, there's the baby, and there's my mother" and she stared at Harold, daring him to say anything "she can't live on her own, she's bedridden and I can't just leave her".

All of this was like a bomb going off in Harold's head.

"You had better go home now and tell them what's happened, and then come over to my mother's house. We've things to sort out."

Harold dutifully obeyed and went home to drop his own bombshell. He left home an hour later, his father ranting and his mother in tears.

That night at Ivy's house, plans were laid and the orders were given. Harold had no say in things whatsoever, it was like being back in the army, in fact, he wished he was.

So eventually, things went to plan, well, Ivy's plan.

They got married. The Vicar came up trumps on that score. There was talk of course, and a lot of nudging and winking, but like most scandals, after three or four weeks everybody knew and there was nobody left to tell.

And then Harold found them a house.

He knew a 'Mr Claude Atkinson', he was one of the senior managers at the Co-op. He had a property that had been left to him by a late uncle and he was prepared to rent it to Harold at a reasonable rate.

"Working for the Co-op is like being in a large family" said a condescendingly righteous Mr Claude Atkinson, as he gave Harold the key, and Harold gave him the rent.

And so they were very quickly married and moved in. Their new house, Number 30, Temple Street, was an ample and pretty little three bedroomed terraced. It was quite nice, and for Ivy, very nice.

For the first time in quite a few months, she actually started to smile again, and Harold inwardly gave a great sigh of relief. The sex sort of returned as well, but only on Saturday nights after an evening in the pub, when piano playing Harold could supply all the free drink that Ivy could get down her neck.

And Ivy's mother wasn't complaining either, she knew which side her bread was buttered, and since Harold supplied all the butter they needed and much more besides, she too was more than happy.

But, as always, human nature is never satisfied and people get greedy, and Ivy and her mother were definitely in the latter category.

Time passed by, and as a family they were now quite settled, well as settled as they were ever going to be. The baby was due, and Ivy was well, very well. Harold was working at the Co-op and getting decent wages and now he entertained at the pub five nights a week, he was popular, the pub was busy and the landlord knew his worth. So there was steady money coming in, along with Ivy's wages from the mill. However, in addition to this, Ivy had started her own little business, a sideline.

It all started off quite casually, with just a simple conversation really. Ivy was at work at the mill, she worked in the number four weaving shed, along with a gang of several other women. One day she was talking to her friend Peggy, who was complaining about the price of butter.

Of course, there had been the war and rationing was on, so good food was scarce and expensive, and it was very hard to make ends meet.

But for Ivy, who already had two cupboards full of butter, life was a little different, and so she mentioned to Peggy, 'rather vaguely' of course, that she may be able to get Peggy some extra butter at 'about half price' and that it was 'something of a staff bonus' that Harold got for working so hard.

Peggy nearly snatched her hand off.

The other girls in the weaving shed soon got to know about the cheap butter, Peggy could never keep her mouth shut, and before long Ivy was supplying them all with cheap butter. Then, she began to sell them eggs, and quickly moved on to cheese and then bacon. Since Ivy was getting all this for free, she was suddenly in the money. It was all profit.

Before long, there was food hidden all over the house. There was tinned food under the bed, condensed milk and tinned fruit under her mother's bed, cheese in the baby's cot, and several cases of eggs stored under the stairs. She even had a large wooden trunk in the backyard that was locked up tight, it was full of bacon.

Ivy started to hide her money in a pair of her old boots in the bottom of the wardrobe, and when Harold was out playing at the pub, she would tip all the money onto their bed and count it, and smile with glee at the accumulation of her cash. Every week there was more and more money, lots of money, and Ivy was amazed. She'd always had to struggle to earn her money, and now she gloated at her unexpected success, and of course, she wanted even more.

She had always pushed Harold into bringing home more and more food from the Co-op warehouse where he worked, and Harold, to keep the peace, had done just that. It was stealing of course and Harold knew it was, but in his mind he had downgraded it as petty pilfering, almost a perk, and he justified this to himself because most of the other staff were 'pilfering' too, all the way up to senior management, and that also included the high and mighty Mr Claude Atkinson. They were all helping themselves to the 'perks' and Harold had quickly understood all this, he was an industrious worker and he had a keen mind, yes he saw what went on.

In those days, huge amounts of produce passed through the Co-op, and in between it being delivered and distributed, and sorted and sold, there was room for Harold to manoeuvre, and he quickly realized that it would be very difficult for the Co-op to keep a check on everything, in fact, it was an impossibility.

On most days, Harold would be the last one at night to leave work, and he was soon given the responsibility of locking up every evening, simply because everyone else wanted go home as soon as possible, so he was quite willingly given the keys. He would go into work early, carrying a rucksack which contained a lunch bag with his lunch, and another large folded canvas bag. At night he would leave work with the rucksack, the lunch bag and the canvas bag, all full of groceries, and this would happen five or six nights a week.

One night, it was on a Thursday evening, and as he was ready for leaving the Co-op, Harold walked through the warehouse switching off all the lights, then he made his way towards the butter and cheese counter. He stopped there and put down his bags, and he was just about to open his rucksack and take out the other two bags and start to fill them with cheese, when suddenly he got the strangest of feelings, something was not quite right. He felt uneasy, and something, just something, didn't feel right. And then he had a moment of comprehension, it was something that later he would look upon as some sort of almost religious experience. In that one strange moment, he suddenly understood exactly what this was, it was guilt, simple and utter guilt. And with that, the realization that he was stealing, and he'd become a thief.

He stopped dead in his tracks and looked down at the floor, and as he stood there he considered 'what on earth' was he was doing? He had always accepted that he was doing a 'bit of pilfering', and he had tried to dismiss it as something trivial, but no, this was theft, and it was so simple, Ivy had made him become a thief. He bristled at this and he felt angry, but he couldn't dismiss the truth, this was merely an attempt to shift the blame elsewhere. But the blame was his and his alone, he had become weak and now he was nothing more than a common thief, and more than that, he was all at once disgusted with himself.

Harold bit his lip hard, and under his breath he quietly said to himself "No more".

So he picked up his rucksack and slung it back over his shoulder and turned to go...and in complete astonishment, he almost walked straight into Mr Claude Atkinson, who had been standing right behind Harold and had been watching everything and every move that Harold had made.

Harold jumped back and visibly gasped with shock.

"Just leaving are we Harold?" said Atkinson with a somehow knowing and uneasy stare.

"...I...I...err...I thought everybody had gone" replied Harold as he tried not to choke.

"Mmm, oh really" said Atkinson with a perceptible sneer "Well you can go now, I'll finish off here" and he just stood there looking at Harold, he hated Harold.

Harold nodded, quickly turned and left, and hoped to God that his shaking hands would not give the game away. As he made his way home that night, he considered the events and thought about it. 'Lord' he'd been lucky, thank goodness he hadn't taken anything and he'd not been caught, and as he walked home on that dark night the same thoughts kept going over and over in his head. 'This was a warning, 'surely' this was God warning him', and once again he said to himself "No more".

Claude Atkinson watched Harold walk away. He had actually been watching Harold for over an hour. He'd stood in the shadows and watched Harold finish in the office and gather his belongings, and that rucksack. He had watched Harold switch off the lights and walk down to the butter and the cheese department, and then stop and put down his bag.

This was it...this was the moment, the moment that Claude Atkinson had been waiting for. Yes, he'd been watching Harold, watching him for some weeks now, and he'd waited... Because Claude Atkinson had his own plans, yes he did.

Every Friday afternoon, at around five o' clock, Claude Atkinson would call at Harold's house at 30 Temple Street, for the rent.

Ivy would always answer the door, yes beautiful Ivy, and Claude would just stand there in the doorway, staring at her and feeling stupid. But she never once invited him in.

In fact, she would hardly speak to him, but there was just 'something' about her, and he tried to make light of the situation, he would even try a bit of humour or even a joke sometimes, but Ivy, the gorgeous Ivy, would just dismiss him and go upstairs for the rent money. Always up those stairs, and Claude Atkinson would watch those lovely legs sweetly bounce all the way up there, and only wish and hope that he could follow them, and his mouth would go wet at the thought of it.

Claude Atkinson, for a long time he'd made it his business to find all and everything about Ivy, and from the rumours he'd heard, Claude knew exactly just how Ivy had trapped her stupid husband...stupid Harold.

And she'd had a past, 'oh yes' she'd had a past and Claude knew that she was definitely up for it, when it suited.

So the fascination with Ivy began, and he'd started to watch Harold, and for a reason. There was something not just right, why was it that Harold was always the last person to leave the Co-op every night?

And so, that Thursday night Claude had stayed late. He'd stood in the shadows and observed the goings on, and for a brief moment he thought he had Harold in his grasp, almost.

When Harold had stopped with his rucksack at the cheese counter, he thought that was it, and Claude Atkinson was ready to pounce and catch him in the act. He would reprehend Harold, and then call the police and have him arrested.

It was Co-op policy to prosecute all thieves, and Harold would go to prison.

Yes, he would pounce on Harold, and then he would pounce on Ivy. Claude knew that with no money coming into the house, Ivy would be poor again, and what would she do for free rent, god only knows?

But, it hadn't happened, Claude had watched him. He'd seen Harold stop, and he'd seen him stop by the cheese with his rucksack. He was sure, so sure...but then nothing. The stupid man had just stood there for a few seconds, and then walked away, he'd just walked away.

Claude stood there silently and he thought about it.

'He must have seen or heard me, after all why did he stop, why did he stop there by the cheese?'

Then in anger, he spat out his hatred "I'll catch you...you little bastard, I'll bloody well have you"

And with that, Claude Atkinson walked into one of the large meat fridges and picked up the box of stolen chickens that he'd hidden away, as he did every Thursday. He carried the chickens outside to his car and put them into the boot. On his way home he would drop the stolen chickens off at Gresty's Butchers on the High street and Mr Gresty would pay him cash, as he always did, every Thursday.

As he walked home from work on that cold dark Thursday night, Harold pondered on his decision to stop stealing from work. And the more he began to think about it, the more he realized the extent of his thievery. He had stolen a lot, well more than a lot, he and Ivy had accumulated a huge quantity of groceries and dairy produce.

Once home, Ivy took control of it all, he never really saw it again, but he knew exactly what she was doing. She went off to work every morning with a couple of shopping bags, full shopping bags. And of course, she'd told him some story about how girls at work were struggling to make ends meet, and how she couldn't 'just let them starve' could she?"

There was of course no mention of money, though it was quite obvious that they were all paying Ivy. However, Harold had decided to turn a blind eye to all this 'to keep the peace' and that's all he wanted really, for too late he had found out that his wife had a terrible temper, and bringing home regular supplies seemed to keep her reasonably happy, and quiet.

And too soon, the baby would arrive, and then Ivy would have to stop working. So whatever money she was making now, would help when she finished at the mill.

Walking home, Harold began to wonder how on earth he'd gotten himself into this situation. One minute he was 'happily' playing the piano in the pub, and now he was somehow 'unhappily' married, and a baby on the way. He had an awful home life, living with a bad tempered wife, along with a rotten old mother in law, and he was working every god given hour, and the thieving and the lying. And all the money that he was earning from working and stealing just seemed to disappear into Ivy's purse. He saw none of it.

Actually, the only time money was ever mentioned was on a Friday, when she always had to inform him that..."That dirty old bastard Atkinson had been round for his rent, dirty bastard always looks right up my skirt when I go upstairs for his money"

Harold had always wondered why she didn't just leave the rent money downstairs in a drawer. After all, Atkinson called around at the same time every Friday. But that suggestion had every possibility of turning into a row, and so Harold decided to keep his mouth firmly shut, as always, but not tonight.

As he walked down Temple Street, Harold took out his key as he approached their house. He was resolute, there would be 'no more stealing'. His mind was made up, but he knew there was going to be trouble, Ivy would go mad.

He put the key in the door and walked in to pandemonium.

The first thing he heard was terrible screaming, it was coming from the kitchen, loud wailing and howling, then he heard something on the stairs directly in front of him, and he looked up to see that it was Ivy's bedridden mother. She was trying to slide down the stairs on her backside and unfortunately her nightdress had run up to her waist.

Harold gasped...it was a sight he never wanted to see again.

He realized that the screaming coming from the kitchen was of course Ivy. Harold dashed in there to find Ivy on the floor, propped up against the kitchen sink.

"Ivy" said Harold.

"Aaaagghh"...screamed Ivy, in reply.

"Are you alright?" asked Harold.

Suddenly, between contractions, Ivy felt she could speak.

"What! ...no, I'm not alright, I'm having the bloody baby, where the hell have you been?"

"Well, you said you needed cheese and I..."

"Aaaaghhh "screamed Ivy, again.

"Well, you did say you needed cheese" said Harold as he tried to justify his timekeeping.

"Stuff the bloody cheese. The baby's coming, do something for Christ's sake" and then she screamed "Ooowwhh...Waaahh"!

Harold went white and felt a bit dizzy.

Ivy, once more between contractions shouted "Bloody hell Harold, go to Mr Johnston's and get the bleedin' van. Owwhh...Waaahh...'oh mother of god'..."

Harold ran out of the kitchen and headed for the front door, trying not to look at his semi naked mother in law, who had by now managed to slide half way down the stairs.

He shouted at her "Get back upstairs mother, and cover yourself up for God's sake"

Harold ran out of the house and up the street to Mr Johnston, who owned the Ironmongers shop and who also owned a small van

Harold was quite friendly with Mr Johnston and Ivy bought all their coal and paraffin from him...a lot of coal and paraffin actually. They were good customers and Mr Johnston was appreciative. In truth, Harold had always wondered just how Ivy paid Mr Johnston, nothing was ever said, but he got the feeling that Mr Johnston was another recipient, whose name was on Ivy's 'butter list'.

Anyway, during past conversations, Mr Johnston had told Harold that when the baby decided to arrive, he would run them down to the Hospital in his van.

That time had now arrived.

Harold ran to the Ironmongers shop and knocked ferociously on the door, he was now in a bit of a state. Within half a minute, the shop light came on and Harold heard someone banging about inside. Then the door was unlocked and finally opened by Mr Johnston, who was eating a large bacon sandwich. Harold's first thought was that the bacon probably came from Ivy...'good god' she must be supplying half the neighbourhood. Then Harold remembered his predicament, and he blurted out about Ivy's condition and the state she was in.

Mr Johnston jammed the rest of his bacon sandwich into his mouth, and through the spit and crumbs, told Harold to get into his van which was parked outside the shop. They quickly drove down the street to Harold's and ran into the house. The first thing Mr Johnston saw was Ivy's mother's huge flaccid naked backside, now on full show as she attempted to crawl back up the stairs.

"Bleedin' hell" said Mr Johnston in horror, and he backed out of the door and then tactfully added "I'll wait outside with the van"

Harold gave him a knowing look and nodded.

Well they managed to get Ivy into the van and off down to the hospital, and on Friday morning at exactly ten past six, eight pounds and two ounces of baby 'David Jacob Moors' was born.

Three days later, they left the hospital, and Ivy and baby David came home.

The next week saw an endless stream of visitors as everyone wanted to see the baby. The girls from work, friends from the pub, and even Harold's parents, who now had to bite there lip because Ivy now had the upper hand, and they would have to dance to a different tune if they wanted to see their grandchild. 'Oh yes', she had the advantage and they knew it...it was all false smiles and stilted conversation between them, and when they finally left the house, there were sighs of relief from both sides.

But, babies can be wonderful peace offerings. The family decided that a fresh start was called for, after all, this concerned was their son and their grandson, and it was plain to see that baby David was the apple of Harold's eye. He simply adored his little son, so if Harold was happy, all was well.

Two or three weeks passed by, and as things started to settle down, they'd all got into a routine of sorts. Harold was always at work and Ivy had the baby to look after. People were constantly coming round to the house, they still wanted their butter and other stuff of course, and this suited Ivy down to the ground.

No longer did she have to do any carrying, people now came to her. It was just like having her own shop.

Every morning, before work, she would have Harold put different provisions on the kitchen table so that they would be on hand when her 'customers' called round.

Well, she had a baby to look after.

One lunch time, Ivy's friend Peggy along with another girl from the mill called round to see Ivy, and the baby of course. But while they were there, they asked if they could both 'just' have half a dozen eggs?

Chatting away, Ivy passed baby David to the enthusiastic Peggy, and went into the kitchen for the eggs. To her surprise, there were none, not on the table anyway. So she looked in the cupboards and under the stairs and then all the other usual places. There were none, none at all, and there was something else, something was not quite right. She went upstairs to look under the beds. There were no eggs, but there was also very little else, and that was when she finally realized, all the cupboards downstairs empty, and upstairs hardly anything. Where was everything, everything had gone?

She stood there in the bedroom and suddenly felt quite hot and flustered. Something had happened, something was wrong, very wrong, and it was something to do with Harold, it had to be.

Ivy went back downstairs and put on a breezy smile.

"Oh well, it looks like we've run out of eggs love" she said, in a matter of fact sort of way.

The two women looked back at her.

"Run out?" said Peggy "what do you mean?"

"Hmm...err, I don't know, I'll have to ask Harold"

"When will you be getting some in?" asked Peggy.

"Err, I'll have to ask Harold" and suddenly Ivy felt flushed, and awkward.

Peggy, now less enthusiastic, looked at the other woman and then back at Ivy.

"Bloody hell Ivy, my husband's expecting egg and chips for his tea, if all I give him is a plate of chips he'll go mad."

"I'm sorry Peggy...I don't know what's happened"

"Have you any baked beans?" asked Peggy again "I'll have to give him chips and beans"

"I'll have a tin as well" said the other woman quickly.

Ivy went back upstairs to check what was under the beds. Not a lot.

She came back down "All I've got is condensed milk" she said, a bit apprehensively.

"I can't put tinned milk on chips can I, oh bloody hell Ivy" Peggy was now definitely upset.

Suddenly Ivy came up with an idea. She had no other choice really.

"I'll get you both some bacon" she said.

Peggy almost choked "I haven't got that sort of money Ivy, not 'bacon money' it's the middle of the week, I'm broke"

"Don't worry" said Ivy "we'll sort something out" and with that she turned and hurried off down the backyard, leaving the two women whispering to each other.

Ivy took the key off its hook and went down the yard to the large wooden trunk, her 'stash'.

Her hands shook awkwardly as she put the key into the lock, and she had a strange feeling as she clicked open the lock and lifted up the large lid of the trunk. Then she gasped out loud, it was empty...of course it was.

When she went back into the house, empty handed, there wasn't a lot that she could say.

Peggy handed back baby David rather too quickly, and both women made their excuses and left almost immediately.

Ivy just stood there, slowly rocking with the baby asleep in her arms. She had to think, she had to sort this out, what on earth was happening? Harold had never mentioned anything, and he'd never said that anything was different regarding the supply of food. But when she started to think about it, Ivy realized that lately she had not really been keeping an eye on Harold. He always came home from work late or he was entertaining at the pub, and often he would eat at the pub and that suited her fine. In the mornings, he would stack all the groceries on the kitchen table for her, so that all she had to do was sell them on. Then he would play with the baby before he went to work, and that was about it really.

So what the hell was going on? Ivy was getting angry...Ivy needed a plan.

Harold came home from work that evening and to his surprise, the baby was still up and awake. He walked into the kitchen and there stood Ivy with baby David in her arms. She rocked him gently side to side as the baby chuckled and gurgled, and the sight of him made Harold smile with joy. Then he looked at Ivy, and he stopped smiling. Because she just stared back at him, in silence.

'Oh God' He knew this moment would come, he just wasn't expecting it tonight.

"Are you alright love?" he asked, almost submissively. But he knew she wasn't.

There was a silence, and it was awkward, but it was planned to be awkward.

Calmly, she said to him "What's going on Harold, what's exactly happening?"

"What do you mean?" he said nervously.

She took a sharp intake of breath, and still rocking the baby gently in her arms, she stared ruthlessly at him as she spoke.

"I don't know what you're up to, you stupid, stupid bastard, but you've let the food run out, and now there's hardly anything left, so I'll ask you again, tell me why...why...you bloody idiot?"

Harold stood his ground, he knew this was going to happen and he was ready to explain and try to reason with her.

"I know I should have told you before Ivy, I know I should, but that night we had to take you to the hospital to have the baby, well that night I nearly got caught. Atkinson nearly caught me stealing, he was watching me and he was waiting, I'm sure he suspects something."

"Rubbish" spat out Ivy "he would have sacked you if he'd suspected anything".

"I said he 'nearly' caught me" Harold continued "I was lucky, more than lucky, it was only by an act of god that I got away with it, and after...after that, I started to think about it, and I realized that I've become a thief. What I'm doing, and what we're doing, is wrong. You know what it says it in the bible 'Thou must not steal' and I've decided Ivy, I've made up my mind, I'm not stealing anymore food and that's it."

There, he'd done it, he'd finally stood his ground and he'd got it off his chest.

Ivy just stared at him and then she spoke, cold and hard.

"So that's it, that's what you think do you Harold? You think you're going to stop, just like that? No, No Harold, you're not going to stop and I'll tell you why"

And she breathed and seethed "I've got a good little number going on here and I'm making good money, very good money. It's all profit, all that food you get from work, I sell most of it and I've made a lot of money, I've got nearly a thousand pounds tucked away"

Harold's eyes widened "What...a thousand...a thousand pounds!" it was unbelievable.

"Yes, I've a thousand pounds, hidden away, all safe and sound and 'my' money'."

Harold was dumbstruck. He couldn't believe it, a thousand pounds.

A thousand pounds was a small fortune, a thousand pounds could buy you a house outright, it would easily buy the house that they were living in.

"Oh my god Ivy" said Harold, shaking his head.

"Yes, oh my god Harold" she retorted.

"But, if we get caught...all that money"

"Never mind the money...I'll take care of the money".

Harold shook his head "No Ivy, good god no. I can't carry on like this. If I get caught I'll end up in prison. Oh my lord, all that money"

"I've told you Harold, I'll take care of the money."

"No Ivy" Harold was adamant now, he was going to stand his ground "No more, I'm not stealing anymore. It's over and it's finished".

Ivy was incensed, she wasn't putting up with this, not from him, and now it was time for her to stand her ground. She had to manipulate him and above all, she had made him see sense.

"No it's not over, it's far from 'over' Harold, so you just listen to me. I've never had money before, not like this, I've had to struggle all my life to get by, and I've always had to look after my mother, all alone with no help, just me. And now for the first time in my life I'm in front, I've finally got something, I've got cash. I've thought this through and I've got plans, big plans. Another twelve months of this and I'll enough money to buy a shop, and pay for it cash, no bank loan or anything like that, and I'll have enough money to stock it, and stock it well. The money won't be a problem and I'll trade like any normal shop, but anything surplus that you can get from the Co-op, well that will be 'all' profit, I'll make a fortune."

Harold was mesmerised, she had it all planned out, and he also noted that she kept saying the same words...'I'...and 'I've'.

Harold ploughed on "No Ivy, I can't carry on, Atkinson's on to me I'm sure he is, and eventually he'll catch me"

"No he won't Harold. You see, that's where you need to get clever, you've got to start watching him, you need to watch him like a hawk and you've got to follow him around and watch his every move. He's a man of habit is Claude Atkinson, and I'll bet he does the same thing at the same time every day. Christ, he rolls up here every bloody Friday on the dot, always dead on five, just to look up my bloody skirt"

Harold couldn't take all this in.

She continued "If I made him a cup of tea and talked to him, he'd stay an hour, he'd stay all bloody night if I gave him half a chance, he fancies me, he just stands there at the door with his tongue hanging out"

And then her eyes brightened "You know what, we should buy a car like Atkinson has. If we had a car, every Friday I could keep him here talking and you could gets loads of stuff, you could fill the boot"

Harold snapped "A car...a car Ivy, have you gone mad, people like us don't have cars, not on my wages. Folk would talk, and people would want to know where we've got the money from. And Atkinson, what about Atkinson, he knows how much I earn, he knows I can't afford a car."

Ivy thought about it a moment "Mmm, you might be right, we'll have to think that one out"

"We'll think nothing out, it's over Ivy. I've told you, I'm not stealing anymore".

"And I told you Harold, I've got plans" and she lifted baby David in her arms and kissed his forehead, and whilst still looking at the baby, she spoke to Harold over her shoulder.

She'd tried manipulation, and she'd tried to make him see sense, but that wasn't going to work. So now it was time for her to play her 'Ace in the hole'. It was time to be cruel.

"I knew something was going on Harold, you've let all my stocks run down and now I've hardly anything left"

And she turned around to face him, little David in her arms, the baby was smiling at his daddy.

And then she delivered the coldest ultimatum "I'm going to tell you something. I'm not going back to being poor and having no money, and I'm not going back to work in that bloody Mill, never again. I've got some money now and I plan to make plenty more. But you...you weak bastard, 'Holy bloody Harold', you just can't see farther than the end of your stupid nose. You're the weak link in the chain. I can't stand your weakness and I can't stand you, I've put up with you, but if as you say, you're going to stop bringing home the goods well okay, stop, if that's what you want to do" and as she spoke she reddened with anger, and then she took another breath of contempt and continued.

"But if you do stop I'm telling you now, I'm going and that's it, I'm off. I'm not staying around here anymore, I'm leaving and I'm leaving you, and I'll be taking this baby with me"

Harold gasped "What?"

"Oh yes, it's like I said...I've got plans"

"What do you mean you're going? Going where?"

"Going where you won't find us, and you'll never see this baby ever again"

"You can't do that Ivy" it was an imploring statement from Harold.

"Yes I can" and she leaned her head towards him, facing him now, up close "Yes I can and I will, believe me I will. I've got money now and I can go where I want, I'll go somewhere down south where you can't find us, I'll make sure of that" and then she smirked as she held out the baby "And you Harold, you'll never see this little lad ever again" and she pulled the baby back into her arms and cuddled him. Baby David gurgled with pleasure.

Harold just stood there in shock, and he slowly realised that everything he'd worked for, absolutely everything, was about to disappear, and the only thing he really loved, his little lad, was going to be taken away from him.

He implored her "No Ivy, please"

But she just shrugged...shrugged her shoulders as spoke to him, very cold and very calculated "You know I'll do it"

And he knew she would.

"You'll come home one day, and we'll be gone, and that'll be the end of it."

Harold looked at his son and gulped down a deep breath, there was pain and upset and he felt a tear form in the corner of his eye, and he was angry at his own weakness and his own fear and stupidity. He knew he was beaten...the price of course, was too high.

Ivy looked back at him in disgust, and with sheer contempt in her voice she just said. "Get those cupboards filled up again" and she turned and walked away.

She'd won.

So that was it. Things went back to normal, or whatever normal was in that house.

Harold went back to stealing, and now on a fairly regular basis. He did however take Ivy's advice seriously and he began to watch Claude Atkinson's every move. And her observation on Atkinson's habits turned out to be absolutely right. Mr Claude Atkinson it seemed, lived his life by the clock and the calendar.

The man was almost obsessive about his timetable at work. He would have a cup of tea brought into his office every forty minutes, on the dot. And on the hour, every hour, he would walk around the Co-op building to inspect what was going on. He would take a different route every time, but those routes would always be taken in the same order, even a visit to the toilet had to work in with his inspections. Harold simply made a diary of Claude Atkinson's comings and goings, it was quite fascinating really, that a man could lead such a repetitive life. Yes, the clock and the calendar.

Harold continued to watch him and he wrote it all down, the days Atkinson came in early and the days he came in late. The long lunch, the short lunch, and of course more importantly, the times that he left at night. Even this had a twist. Sometimes Atkinson would 'pretend' to leave, usually early, but then an hour later he would suddenly return and try to find out if anyone else had left work early, or was stealing, or simply just sat around doing nothing. He would continually sneak back and try to catch the staff breaking the rules. But Harold soon noticed that if Atkinson left early and he didn't take his briefcase with him when he left his office, well, he always returned.

If however, Atkinson went home and took his briefcase with him, he never came back. It was as simple as that, no briefcase...no Atkinson.

The man lead such a repetitive lifestyle, that very soon Harold had nothing else to put in his diary, and before long, Harold, just by memory and looking at what time it was, would know exactly where and what Atkinson was up to.

He also discovered Claude Atkinson's other little perks.The stolen chickens that went to Gresty's butchers every Thursday was only one of Atkinson's little enterprises. Harold soon realised that Atkinson was supplying various shops around the town with cases of tea and sugar. Butter was another prized commodity, along with other canned goods, such as corned beef and tinned fruit.

Harold almost had to laugh. When it came to 'theft', Claude Atkinson was wholesale, and Ivy was retail.

And again, Harold would dwell on Ivy. Claude Atkinson might be predictable, Ivy was not.

And there was also that thing about Atkinson going round for the rent every Friday and looking up his wife's skirt, Harold was not entirely happy about that either, he remembered what Ivy had said about Atkinson fancying her.

The more he watched the man and found out about him, the more Harold began to hate Atkinson, the money, the deceit and the power, and above all the hypocrisy. And though Harold was stealing too, in his mind he was now stealing from Atkinson, it was Harold's way of justifying things. He was a thief, stealing off another thief.

Misguided...but there it was.

The months passed quickly by, and things had sort of settled down. Number 30, Temple Street was again packed to the gunnels with groceries, and quietly, quietly, Ivy was doing well, very well.

And 'quietly, quietly'...suited Harold down to the ground.

But all was about to change.

Friday came around once more, and Claude Atkinson looked at himself in the mirror as he combed his hair and smartened himself up. It was Friday afternoon, his favourite day, and in half an hour he would be out of work and round to Temple Street, to see Ivy.

Oh yes, beautiful Ivy. It was the highlight of his week, six or seven brief minutes of heaven.

Well heaven for Claude anyway. By now Claude, in his misguided thoughts, had decided that Ivy's total indifference to him was actually a cover, and it was really the misery and the loneliness that made her look so unhappy. She must be so depressed, living with bloody little Harold Moors, no wonder she couldn't bring herself to smile, how terrible for her.

Claude Atkinson was unmarried and he lived on his own and had done for years, after the eventual passing away of his parents. Claude had never had much luck with the ladies and was woefully inexperienced when he was around them. For Claude, women fell into two distinct types, there were the ugly and uncouth who were in his view 'just common', and then there were the attractive good looking girls...girls with a hint of intelligence. And that was what Claude dreamed of, a beautiful, clever wife.

Unfortunately for Claude, he was certainly no oil painting himself. He was tall and thin and miserable looking, he was a man who did not smile easily, if at all. He also had a personality that could only be described as 'dour'. There wasn't a lot of humour in Mr Claude Atkinson, not one bit.

So on that Friday afternoon, his hair combed and his best tie straightened, he left the Co-op building, got into his car and drove over to Temple Street. He parked as always, right at the end of the street and then would just sit there for five minutes, as he did every Friday. During those five minutes he would practice his lines, the lines that he had gone over again and again, lines he would use to try to get Ivy to talk to him, lines of possible dialogue.

He'd tried chat and humour, interests, the weather and the baby, and even her mother's health. In fact, he'd tried anything and everything. Any one thing at all that could possibly get some sort of conversation started.

He even had three of four 'witty' jokes that he had stamped into his memory, just in case one day he could get Ivy to talk and he needed to make her laugh and feel more at ease with him, in fact, he'd do anything to make her realize what a good chap he really was.

He wanted her to be interested in him, and more than that, he wanted her to want him.

But what Claude Atknson really wanted, was to control her, to totally dominate her and to make her do anything he wanted, that was his dream.

And so he would sit in his car and think about Ivy's beautiful legs, and he would close his eyes and privately dream his dreams.

And once again it was Friday afternoon, and the ever hopeful Claude Atkinson once more got out of his car and walked down the street and knocked on the door at Number 30.

At that same time, Ivy was having a really bad day. Her mother had become hard work of late, it was the beginnings of dementia really, and today, all day long, she had continually called down to Ivy, sometimes screaming at her for attention. Like a child with a cold who was bedridden and bored, she would shout downstairs with the same high pitched wail.

"I'm thirsty Ivy...I'm hungry...what time is it, are you there Ivy, I've wet the bed, are you there Ivy, I want the toilet...are you there? ...Ivy...Ivy...Ivy...?"

On top of this, baby David, now several months old was teething and he was howling with pain. Ivy had him in the pram downstairs in the kitchen with her and she was trying to get him to sleep while she sorted out her 'stock'. The house was absolutely full with groceries, and she had no more space in her cupboards, Co-op butter was piled high on the kitchen table and she didn't know where to put it.

She'd boiled a large pan of water and poured it into the kitchen sink with some soap, and she'd just started to wash the pots and plates in the hot lathered water when there was a knock at the front door. She brushed a soap filled hand through her hair, and cursed. Then she turned around and with wet hands she went through to the front door and opened it and was more than slightly startled when she saw Claude Atkinson standing there.

"Oh, oh is it...is it five o'clock already?" she asked him, and she was flustered.

"Yes, and its Friday" he said, and he smiled and tried his best not to look at her breasts, as he did every Friday.

"I didn't know it was so late, I...I'll get you your money" and she pushed a wet tendril of hair out of her eyes with her soapy hand, and Claude Atkinson was mesmerized.

At that moment, there was a loud bang and a scream from upstairs.

"Oh god, my mother's fallen out of bed" and Ivy turned around quickly.

"Can I help?" Claude asked.

"No" said Ivy sharply, and she grabbed her skirt and dashed up the stairs.

Claude watched her go and this time he saw more of her legs than ever before.

"My God" he said to himself quietly.

All of this commotion suddenly woke up baby David, who felt the treacherous ache in his gums and teeth, and immediately started to cry.

Claude saw the pram through the kitchen doorway and heard the baby crying.

Little David, now howling, turned in his pram and sat himself up. He expected attention and when there was none, he cried even more and then crawled towards the edge of his pram.

Claude watched in horror as he saw the crying toddler emerge and then start to lean over the edge of the pram. The baby was going to fall, Claude knew nothing about babies but he couldn't just let it fall out of the pram, could he? Well no, he couldn't.

And so he dashed towards the kitchen door, and as he did, the thought struck him that if he saved the baby, well, this heroic act could put him in good favour, Ivy would surely be grateful and he may have finally got 'his foot in the door'.

He managed to grab little David just before the child toppled out and onto the floor. It was a close one. He then held little David in his arms and he did the rocking motion that he had seen women do, and to his amazement it started to work, the child began to suck its thumb and stopped crying and just stared hypnotically as Claude continued to rock him to and fro in his arms.

"Piece of cake this" thought Claude, and he absent-mindedly wandered into the kitchen.

It was then that he stopped dead and nearly dropped the baby. Claude Atkinson stopped absolutely dead in his tracks, because in front of him, piled high on the table were blocks of butter, lots and lots of pristine yellow blocks of butter...Co-op butter.

As he stood there, his astonishment turned to slow anger. He was stunned. And with the child held in one arm he started to look around, and he went over and opened one of the cupboard doors. It was packed full of sugar. Then another cupboard, filled with packets of dried peas, and another...tinned fruit, and then corned beef, and tins of custard and sauces, and tea and salt. And all were the Co-op Brand.

Under the sink, there were trays and trays of eggs, and then in one of the drawers he found blocks of cheese, and in another, bacon and sausages, all wrapped up neatly in little parcels of grease-proof paper and tied with string.

Claude Atkinson stood there trying to take it all in, and then under his breath he whispered

"You thieving little bastard...you thieving 'little' bastard"

Then he suddenly had a thought, if this was the kitchen, what was in the rest of the house? There must be hundreds of pounds worth of stolen food here, all stolen, and stolen right from under Claude Atkinson's nose.

His thoughts were now hard and calculated, 'That little bastard must have been laughing at me behind my back' and Claude went red and hot with anger He began to pace up and down, and then he stopped, once again he stopped dead and he stood there, and he thought a little bit harder.

'Think Claude...think' he said to himself as he stood there in silence. And then suddenly and slowly, he began to smile.

"Got you" ...he said out loud.

He walked over to the kitchen table and quietly pulled out a chair and sat down. Little David was now asleep in his arms and so he sat there and waited and listened as Ivy finally came back downstairs. When she got halfway downstairs he heard her stop. There was a silence. In fact, there was a minutes silence as she stood there on the stairs and realised that something was wrong...very, very wrong, in truth, it was her worst fear.

Claude just sat there in the kitchen, analyzing what thoughts must now be running through Ivy's sweet head, and yes, he would have the upper hand now, and he would have the power, and finally things were going to change, because Claude had plans.

He heard Ivy mumble something, it could have been a curse, it probably was.

She slowly walked down the rest of the stairs and quietly closed the front door and then walked into the kitchen.

She stood in the kitchen doorway, for some reason she couldn't go in any further. And she looked at Claude, who unblinkingly stared back at her.

"Well then, what's all this Ivy?" he said almost casually, as he nodded towards the Co-op butter that was stacked high on the kitchen table "We've been busy little bees haven't we?" he continued as he sat there with little David comfortably asleep in his arms.

"I've had a look through your cupboards too. You've got half the Co-op in there. God only knows what's in the rest of the house, and 'oh yes' and by the way Ivy, 'the house', this house...'my house' Ivy".

And his mouth smiled, but his eyes didn't.

Ivy couldn't speak, fear and guilt, and she knew she was trapped, she'd been caught.

It was a maternal thing, but all she could do at that moment was to walk over to Claude and take her child from him. It was as though her little boy was in some sort of harm's way and somehow Claude Atkinson was dangerous, a threat, and she was almost right.

She put the sleeping child gently back in his pram and then because she had nothing else to do or say, she couldn't face Atkinson, and she couldn't deny anything, so she went over to the kitchen sink and silently started to wash the pots.

Claude Atkinson sat silently watching her, he was intrigued. How different this was, he now held the power, he was the cat and she was the mouse. It felt so, so good.

He sat there and he watched her, with her wet hands and arms elbow deep in the white soap suds, and her dark hair falling over her silently beautiful face, and he watched her motion and her movement. He looked at the back of her slim neck and then down her back to her waist, and then at her shaped bottom and all the way down to those beautiful, beautiful legs, and his breathing changed its pace.

Ivy was in silent panic, what could she do, she had to find some sort of excuse, but what?

She was caught, and she knew it, she knew she was stuck but what on earth could she do, she just stood there with a feeling of total despair, it was hopeless, and it was over.

But Ivy was a smart girl, resourceful, and suddenly in an instant her panicking brain finally, finally, began to work, and suddenly, in that absolute instant, she saw a way out.

And so, with a gentle little sigh, so gentle...Ivy quietly started to sob.

And she let the tears trickle slowly down her cheek and she gave a little sniff, almost childlike, an innocent sobbing as she continued to wash the pots in silence.

Claude just sat there entranced, and she took her hand out of the soapy water and ran it through her hair and then across her cheek to wipe away a tear, and it left a delicate line of foam across her cheek and down to her mouth, and her hair was wet, tendrils of dark wet hair.

Claude gasped. He slowly got out of the chair and walked up behind her. He took a deep breath as he reached out and put both his hands on her waist and then leaned forward and gently kissed the back of her neck, and she let him. And he kissed her again, longer this time, and she silently stopped washing and slowly turned around to face him.

"I didn't know what to do Claude "she whispered "you don't know what he's like"

And then she gave another almost imperceptible sob.

"I know Ivy, I know. I've always known" said Claude, as he looked down at her beautiful face. Ivy lifted her warm wet hands to his face and drew him to her and she kissed his lips.

Claude Atkinson nearly melted. For over a year he had fascinated over this woman, he just could not get her out of his mind, and now he was kissing her and she was kissing him.

Oh lord, it was wonderful.

Then Ivy leant back against the kitchen sink.

She gasped "I've had no 'tenderness', for over a year now, no love at all"

She stared at him and then slowly reached up and undid the top button of her blouse, and then the second, and suddenly as he looked down, he could see the top her breasts, then she undid the third button and displayed her cleavage. Claude gasped again as Ivy undid the last two buttons and shed her blouse completely. It dropped silently to the floor. Claude gently put his hands on her shoulders and took down her bra straps and then rolled down her bra to get his hands onto her breasts.

Oh god, it was an intimacy he'd never known, and he nuzzled her and sucked her as he took in the wonderful taste and smell of her body.

Ivy began to moan and Claude was urged on by her response. She then reached down and grabbed hold of the buckle on his belt and undid it, and then her expert fingers quickly unbuttoned the front of his pants and she reached in and took hold of him. Claude had never known pleasure like this, and then her hands went to work on him, expert hands, and now it was Claude who was doing the moaning.

Ivy inwardly smiled, she almost laughed, it was that simple.

'Men, stupid bloody men, once you have their dick in your hands, you can rule them, you can make them do anything you want'

And with that thought in her head, she suddenly saw another possibility, and another future, and all of a sudden everything dropped into place. She now had plans, new plans, it was time to change track.

Ivy stopped what she was doing, she had to get Claude's attention, but Claude was in a trance. She stopped and stepped back against the sink. Claude suddenly blinked. He didn't want her to stop, ever. She slowly lifted her head and looked directly into his eyes.

"I've always respected you Claude, you're a good man, and I've had to try and hide my feelings"

"I know, I know" he said. He would actually have said anything to get her to carry on what she'd just been doing to him.

"Oh God Ivy, don't stop" he implored.

She gazed at him and then, decision made, she stripped off her skirt and the rest of her clothes and stood totally naked in front of him.

He looked down at her body, the perfectness of it, her dark pubic hair against that pale white skin, she was the most beautiful thing he had ever seen, and he wanted to touch every part of her.

Ivy pulled him towards her and took hold of his pants and slid them down, then she ran her hands over his buttocks and slid off his underclothes, then she reached down and took hold of him once again.

Claude groaned with the pleasure of it as she started once more. And then she opened her legs and pulled him into her, her expert fingers led him in. She put her hands around his backside and put her mouth to his ear and kissed it.

"Fuck me" she whispered "fuck me"

And Claude did exactly as he was told.

Twenty minutes. Twenty minutes of lovemaking that Claude Atkinson would remember for the rest of his life.

Though for Ivy, it was ten minutes of sex and a lot of performance, but she'd been there before and could carry it off.

They lay on the floor, both naked, and she leant over him and ran her hand through his hair, lovingly of course.

She smiled down at him "What am I going to do with you Claude Atkinson?" she asked playfully.

"What do you mean, love?" he said

He had just called her 'love' and Ivy knew she was on a winner.

"I can't go on like this. I can't live my life like this anymore, not with Harold. You don't know what I have to put up with, all this stealing, I knew he'd get caught one day, he's got me selling all this stuff to people, he sends all sorts round to this house for cheap food. I don't know what he does with the money, we never see any of it, and we never see much of him really. He just comes home from the pub at night usually drunk, and then the arguments start, and then the violence"

Claude immediately looked up at her "What violence?"

"You don't know what he's like Claude, he has a terrible temper, he thumps me in the back so that nobody ever sees the bruises, I've been black and blue but nobody knows. The other week he kicked me and I couldn't walk properly for a week"

Claude was incensed "The rotten little bastard, I'll have him Ivy, I'll not have him hitting you, the bastard"

The fact that Claude had just seen every inch of her naked body, and that there was not one mark on her, completely passed him by.

"No Claude, there's only one way out of this for me"

His eyes widened with hope "What's that?"

"I'm going to go away, me and the baby. I'm going leave and I'm not coming back, I 'm going to get well away from him, somewhere he'll never find me".

And a small tear welled up in the corner of her eye, small, but effective.

"Oh hell, no Ivy"

"I can't go on like this, especially after what's just happened, you know, me and you"
She gave him a resigned look, with just a hint of finality.

This unsettled Claude, he'd just had the sexual encounter of his life and he certainly
didn't want it to be his last.

She continued "I'm not going to have an affair with you Claude...I'm not that sort of
girl. What we just did was wrong, I'm not going to lead you on or give you any false
hopes, it just wouldn't be fair, and it wouldn't be fair on you and it wouldn't be fair on
me. I'm not being somebody's knock off, I won't be something to brag about to your
mates"

"I'm not like that Ivy, honestly, I wouldn't say anything" said Claude earnestly.

For a moment she thought her plans had gone astray, just how committed was he?
And so she leant over and kissed him fully on his mouth. He felt her beautiful breasts
on his chest and suddenly he was aroused again, and he reached up for her, but she
pulled back.

"No" she said, and then giggled as she tactically slapped his lower stomach.

"What are you like Claude Atkinson? You're an animal" and she gave him her best
smile.

Claude liked the sound of that, it made him feel powerful. My god, she was so bonny.

Baby David turned in his pram and made a sound, and Ivy looked over and then
stood up.

The spell was broken and the moment was over. And Claude Atkinson's heart sunk.

She picked up her clothes and looked at the clock and then at Claude.

"You'll have to go...look at the time, Harold will be on his way home soon"

And suddenly Claude felt his nakedness. He was suddenly uncomfortable and felt he
was a thief in somebody else's house. And this confused him, because this house and
this woman, well it was his house, he owned it, and for a brief moment he had owned
this woman too, and the mention of Harold's name angered him. She'd said "Harold
will be on his way home soon", as though little Harold Moors was some sort of threat
that he should frightened of.

Claude put his clothes back on, but he didn't speak. Ivy could see that he was angry
and embarrassed but she didn't speak either, and when he was finally dressed and he'd
put his coat on, she went to him and started to button up his coat...almost motherly.
Then she looked up at him with a lost smile and a look of finality.

"Don't be angry" she said.

He looked at her face and all the emotions came rushing back.

"Ivy, I don't want it to end like this."

She gave him a hug.

"Claude Atkinson, you're a special man, you're so good and nobody knows what you're really like, but I do. I wish I'd never met Harold" and she stood back and looked at him, a look so sad. Then she said "If only I'd met someone like you first".

And with that, she almost hustled him out through the front door and immediately closed it behind him.

Claude stood there, alone on the pavement. He felt like a man who had just won a million pounds and then lost it. He slowly walked back to his car, he was in some sort of daze, it was dark now and cold and he was confused and somewhat mystified. What had just happened? Well he knew what had happened, he'd just been closer to someone than he had ever been in his life, he'd just been shown a kindness and an intimacy that he had never known, and now it was supposed to be over as though it had never been. He sat there in his car in the dark, trying to think, and he closed his eyes and thought about her, and he could smell her neck and her body and then he remembered the softness of her beautiful skin.

What was he going to do? He had to see her again, because all he wanted to do was be with her. He just couldn't stand being on his own again, living that lonely life. No, not after this.

Claude started the car and drove home, and that night he emptied the whiskey bottle.

As soon as she'd got Claude out of the house, Ivy leaned back against the door.

'Thank god he's gone" she thought to herself, and then she smiled as she thought about it. 'That was a good job done', and she'd hooked the bugger, she was sure she had, and now she would have to wait and see. She wondered 'if or when' he would be coming back, back and knocking on her door. And she thought about it, if it was Monday or Tuesday, he would be coming for her, if it was Friday, he would be coming for the rent. And she was in trouble because there was still the matter of all the stolen food in the house, and she knew that he wouldn't let 'that' go. It was a simple fact, Mr Claude Atkinson, senior manager at the Co-op, would now hate and absolutely despise his assistant, Mr Harold Marsh, and all hell was about to break loose.

Yes, what would happen now?

Ivy decided that the next day she would go out and buy a suitcase, and while Harold was at work, she would pack some clothes for her and baby David. She would also pack all her money, which was now a considerable amount, almost two thousand pounds, and that would take her anywhere. At the first sniff of trouble, be it Claude Atkinson or the police, she would be off like the wind. She considered her mother, well...she would have to sort that problem out at a later date, and anyway, whatever happened, somebody would have to look after the old woman, and the more she thought about it, she'd had a lifetime of looking after the old cow and she was sick of it.

Yes, she could run if she had to.

It was a long weekend for Claude Atkinson. He hadn't been to bed at all. He'd sat in the chair in his front room all weekend, trying over and over again in his head to think what on earth he was going to do. The whiskey hadn't helped, his thinking had gone from rational to the irrational and back again, and the lack of sleep didn't help either.

He finally went to bed on Sunday evening and lay there for hours, looking at the ceiling.

She was something he could not get out of his mind. Those twenty minutes of lovemaking   had unforgettably had a dramatic affect on him. He knew that she had been wayward in the past and he could forgive and forget that, and he would make her the better woman if only he could have the chance. But how would he get that chance, she was married with a child, yes married and married to that 'bastard'.

And what would he do if she ran away. He'd never see her again, and he knew she was capable of doing that, she'd told him exactly what she'd do.

There was also the matter of all the produce that Harold had stolen from the Co-op.

Claude was now party to that knowledge and he had to do something about it. If he didn't say or do anything he could get implicated, simply by doing nothing. What if Ivy turned on him and defended her husband, and said that Harold and Claude were both in it together, simply to get herself out of trouble, after all she did have a baby to look after.

And did she really want him? What had she said ...'If only she had met me first'...she must want me, we'd been so passionate, surely she must love me after what we did.

Oh God...think man...think.

At four o'clock in the morning he got out of bed, sleepless and weary. He went down stairs and boiled the kettle and made a mug of strong sweet tea.

As he sat there, stirring the hot brew, he thought about Harold, bloody little Harold Moors. He was the root of the problem, of all the problems. And then suddenly, a thought struck him, a possible solution, it was all so obvious. 'Harold Moors'...get rid of him, get rid of Harold and the field was clear, and for a brief moment he even considered murder, but no, that was the whiskey talking. There were other ways, and then suddenly, Claude had a plan.

Monday came around, and Harold was the first into work as usual. He went about his jobs, listing what was coming in and what was going out, all the usual stuff, he could have done it with his eyes shut. Within the hour, the rest of the staff had arrived and finally, and dead on time, Mr Claude Atkinson came into the building and walked straight faced, straight into his office. Harold watched him through a gap in the shelving and noted that Atkinson looked quite pale, was he ill?

As the morning passed, Harold noticed that Atkinson was doing nothing as to his usual routine...

No strutting around, no spying, not even a trip to the toilet, and then he saw Atkinson's secretary coming out off his office with a full cup of cold tea, it hadn't even been touched.

Harold spoke to the secretary and she just shrugged her shoulders "He's in a right mood" she said, somewhat exasperated.

At eleven o'clock, Harold took his lists into Atkinson's office and as usual tapped on the glass door and walked straight in.

"Here are the lists Mr Atkinson" said Harold cheerily.

Atkinson looked up at Harold, and it was a look of complete hatred.

It made Harold jolt.

"Get out" said Atkinson, in a voice that put the fear of god into Harold.

He didn't have to be told twice.

Half an hour later, Claude Atkinson walked out of the building, it had never been known.

He simply got in his car and drove off.

Harold watched him go. 'There's a man with problems' thought Harold, little did he know.

Claude Atkinson drove straight round to Temple Street and parked the car in the usual place.

Before he got out he collected his thoughts. He had to be decisive, he had to take control of the situation and he was going to have to be strong because he'd made a decision. He simply had to know if Ivy loved him and was prepared to be with him. If she was, he would talk to her about his plans because he had the answer to all their problems. If not, well at least he would know, and then he would have the police arrest Harold for theft and have him sent to prison, and then for free rent and keep, he would keep hold of Ivy like a caged bird.

He got out of the car, took a deep breath, and walked down to Ivy's house and then without any hesitation, knocked stoutly on the door.

Within a minute the door swung open and she was stood there in front of him, he was back.

And Ivy was taken aback.

She wasn't expecting this, she thought it was a customer, truth be known...it was.

She didn't expect Claude Atkinson on her doorstep that Monday morning, and she took one look at him and realized that she would have to have her wits about her, because this was the moment, she would either win or lose everything, it was sink or swim.

Claude looked directly at her, and was lost.

"Ivy....I just need to know..." he said quietly. It was almost a plea.

And that was it, just those few little words and she knew she'd won. She had him, and all the way to the bank. And now her plans could start to work too.

She took his hand and pulled him through the doorway and quickly closed the door.

"Oh god Claude" she purred "I've missed you so much, I thought you were never going to come back" she lied.

And with that, she put her arms around him and kissed him passionately.

"I can't live without you Ivy" he said desperately, it was almost childlike and Ivy had to bite her lip to stop herself laughing at the sad bastard. Claude just didn't see it, he thought she was just being emotional.

She took hold of his arm. "Come on" she said and she led him to the stairs and up to her bedroom.

Half an hour should do it, she thought.

Twenty minutes later, Claude finally rolled off her. He lay there breathless...it just got better and better.

She gave him a few minutes to calm down and then turned to him and leant on his chest.

It was time to talk...

"What are we going to do Claude?" she asked him.

Claude looked at her and smiled "I'll tell you exactly what we're going to do Ivy" he said, and then he told her his plans. And as she listened, her eyes widened, she could have possibly misjudged Mr Claude Atkinson.

It was Thursday morning, and before he went into work, Claude drove to Whitehurst's Agricultural Stores on the edge of town, and purchased two sizable tarpaulins. He packed them into his car and then went off to the Co-op. That night Claude stayed at work late, as he did every Thursday.

Harold left work that evening, empty handed, as he also did every Thursday. He knew that tonight was Atkinson's night for stealing the box of chickens that would be delivered to Gresty's butchers shop .

Atkinson watched him go and grunted and shook his head. He had things to do before he called round at old man Gresty's.

Harold arrived home from work, and to his surprise, Ivy had a hot meal waiting for him.

Meat pie with roast potatoes and peas, he was shocked but pleased. Maybe she was having second thoughts. The conversation at the table that night was stifled, if not a little awkward.

They did'nt have a lot to talk about these days, but she was being more pleasant than usual and Harold appreciated it.

"I think I'll come to the pub with you tomorrow night" she said... "its ages since we've been out, I could do with a change".

Harold was quite surprised.

She continued "I've organised a babysitter, Peggy from work. She said she would do it 'for a favour' Harold"

"What favour?" he said cautiously, and he inwardly sighed.

"Well, she's having a birthday party for her sister this weekend, and she wondered if we could get her some tins of luncheon meat and tins of boiled ham for the sandwiches?"

"Oh Ivy, I don't know" He wasn't entirely happy about this.

"Please Harold, just this once" she asked nicely, "and I'll tell you what, since we've got loads of stuff in, it doesn't matter if you don't bring anything else home for a week or two. How's that sound?"

He was stunned, she must have gone off being so bloody greedy or she really, really wanted a night out. Then again he considered, a drunken Ivy was someone you could have sex with, and with that thought, the deal was sealed.

"Okay then" he conceded.

"About fifteen tins will do it" she said casually.

"How many! Oh god Ivy" and he stared back at her, he'd fallen for it again.

She turned to him "You heard me, fifteen, and I'm going to bed. I've got a headache" and off she went.

On Friday, Harold went off to work early as usual, and as always he was the first man in.

He wandered around the storeroom and noticed that stacked in a corner, were a large pile of boxes, and when he examined them, he found that they were all full of co-op tinned meats. Well, what a stroke of luck, easy pickings for him to take home tonight, simple.

Claude Atkinson came into work at his normal time, but once again he broke his routine and left again at eleven o' clock, taking his briefcase with him.

Harold watched him go and smiled, this was a new routine for 'old Claude', and so Harold decided that for once he would also finish early tonight, for a change.

Atkinson could get stuffed, the thieving bastard.

Claude never came back, and at four o' clock Harold had a word with one of the other staff who was willing to lock up for him And with that, he set off for home with a rucksack full of tinned meats that he'd pilfered during his lunchtime.

It was good to finish early for once, he would be able to have a sleep before he went to play the piano in the pub.

And he thought about Ivy, them both going out together would be a nice change, and there was always a chance of, well...who knows what.

When Claude left work at eleven o' clock that morning, he drove straight round to Ivy's.

And Ivy had been busy. She had listened, and waited for the front door to shut, as Harold went off to work, then she'd got out of bed and dressed quickly and then started to empty the house of everything that Harold had stolen.

She carried all those groceries into the backyard and stacked them up against the back wall.

Claude arrived and parked his car at the back of the house and together they emptied the house of everything that had been taken from the Co-op, and that was a considerable amount. Claude looked on and wondered how on earth he had not seen all this happening.

It was unbelievable.

He took the tarpaulins from the back of his car, unfolded them and then covered up the stacks of groceries.

Then he took Ivy to bed.

Twenty minutes later, of course, he left the bedroom, left the house and drove round to the local police station.

Harold wandered home in an amiable sort of fashion, there was no rush. On his way home he stopped and chatted to a few different people. Locally, he was a bit of a celebrity, and everybody knew him from church or from the pub, or both. He almost considered calling in for a quick pint on the way home, but a rucksack full of clanking tins was a bit noticeable, so he decided to carry on walking back home. He strolled down Temple Street, opened the front door and walked into his house.

And then he stopped dead in his tracks.

Standing there in his front room and waiting for him were two policemen, along with Claude Atkinson, and Ivy.

Harold's legs nearly buckled 'Oh Jesus Christ no'. All his worst fears had just arrived home with him.

He couldn't speak, his mouth just gaped open as he just stood there looking at them.

The leading policeman broke the silence.

"Harold Moors?"

"Y...Yes..." stuttered Harold.

The policeman continued "We are here, following enquiries about a theft or multiple thefts from the Co-operative Building in Bolton. We have reason to believe that you are involved with these thefts and we have been asked by Mr Claude Atkinson here, the

Co-op's senior manager, to inspect your premises. Last night, goods were stolen from the Co-op, the gates and the rear doors had been unlocked with keys, and the thief never relocked those gates and doors, or he forgot to. Mr Atkinson here, informs us that the only persons with keys to the building are himself and you, and before we go any further Mr Moors, we have to inform you that we have already spoken to your wife.

Harold looked at Ivy, and Ivy looked away. Harold's stomach turned and he began to feel sick.

"Would you follow us into the backyard please Mr Moors..."

Harold followed them through the kitchen and into the backyard, He was now frightened, he felt a numbness, but strangely he still wondered what they wanted in the backyard. When they got outside Harold was surprised to see the tarpaulins.

The policeman went over and then lifted back the tarpaulin covers, to reveal all the stolen groceries, all stacked up and hidden underneath. Harold's shoulders sagged as everyone once again looked at him, but still in the back of his mind, he couldn't work out why everything was out there in the yard.

The policeman spoke again "Harold Moors, I am arresting you in relation to the theft of a large quantity of goods from the Co-operative Building, Bolton" and they charged him.

The policeman then instructed his associate policeman to handcuff Harold. To do this, they had to ask Harold to take off his rucksack, which he dropped to the floor with a metallic clunk.

The policemen both looked at one another and one of them opened up the rucksack, it was of course filled with cans of Co-op Brand tinned meats. The leading policeman looked at Harold and shook his head.

"Not a lot more to say, is there son?" he said.

They led Harold back into the house and they all stood there in an awkward silence as the other policeman went for the police car, which had been tucked away around the backstreet.

Harold looked across at Ivy, but she wouldn't look at him. There were things here that he didn't fully understand. He glanced warily at Claude Atkinson, who gave Harold a curious sort of look, it was somehow disgust, but there was something else there too, a sort of smirk, it was almost glee.

As they were leading Harold out of the house, handcuffed, Harold suddenly turned and spoke to one of the policemen.

"Please, could I just have a word with my wife, we have a child you see"

The leading policeman nodded, Harold was handcuffed, he wasn't going anywhere.

Harold stepped back into the front room were Ivy stood, now on her own.

He faced her "What's going on Ivy. Why is all that stuff in the backyard?"

And at that moment Claude Atkinson emerged from the kitchen. He walked into the room and went to stand right behind Ivy, up close, and as he looked directly at Harold he slowly slid his hands around the front of Ivy's waist and then reached up and began to fondle her breasts. Ivy smiled as she lifted up her arms to accommodate him, and then she reached up a hand to touch Claude Atkinson's cheek.

Harold stood there, transfixed, and in total shock of what he was seeing right in front of him.

"You!" was the only thing that Harold could manage to say to Atkinson.

"Yes" replied Claude, staring back at him "...and 'You' can get out of my house you thieving piece of shit"

Harold was taken to the police station, charged, locked up and then convicted. He was sent to prison for three years.

In those austere times, the theft of large amounts of food was looked upon as a serious crime.

Florrie was now so sad, and looked at me and as she finally finished her story.

"He had a terrible time in prison, it broke his spirit. He'd lost his little lad you see, he loved that little boy. Ivy of course divorced him, which he expected, but the rotten bitch just had to keep turning the knife. She wrote to him just once whilst he was in prison, just one letter telling Harold all about her antics with Claude Atkinson, and not one mention of baby David. Then Harold's mother died, she caught pneumonia and passed away and Harold always burdened himself with guilt over that, he wasn't even allowed to go to her funeral.

When he was finally let out of prison he went over to Yorkshire to find work, that's when he met me.

My family were Church people too, that was where we met, all those years ago.

Harold would always volunteer to play the church organ if ever the regular organist couldn't attend.

We would talk, we talked a lot, and I really liked him but he always had a quiet side. There was always something a bit secretive about him and I could never get him to tell me much about his past. Then one day after church, as usual he asked if he could walk home with me, we would always stroll back home through our local park. Of course I said 'Yes', and as we casually ambled along, he suddenly turned to me with a desperate sort of look on his face, and then so very serious, he told me that he needed to talk to me about something.

"You need to know about me Florrie" he said"you're a lovely girl and there's something I have to tell you, and when I've finished, it's up to you whether or not you want to speak to me again. I'll understand"

We were passing a park bench and he sat me down there, and looked directly at me as he gathered himself.

Then he told me the whole miserable tale, he told me everything, all about Ivy and Claude Atkinson, and little David, and Prison...and the thieving and the lying and the deceit. We sat there for nearly an hour as he told me the whole awful story, every word and syllable, and when he'd finished, I burst into tears.

I flung my arms round him and whispered in his ear "I'll never let you down Harold, ever"

The silly man held me in his arms and said "Will you go out with me then?"

I could have hit him.

I've remembered that Sunday and that walk home all my life. Harold wanted to start off right you see, no secrets. We've never had any secrets, ever.

When we got to my house, we went in to see my parents. Harold asked to speak to them privately. He told them everything, as he had told me. My parents were good Christians, good people, they listened to him.

My father though shocked, he admired Harold's honesty. My mother was a little more worried, in fact, she was very worried, but they were staunch Christians and the Christian ethic is to forgive, and they did, and they eventually welcomed him into the family. My father later managed to get Harold a job at the engineering firm where he worked.

Three months later we got engaged, and a year later we were married.

We were living in a little terraced house that we rented off a friend of my fathers .We were as poor as, well as church mice. We had been married about a year by then, poor but happy, when I found out I was expecting. The family were overjoyed and I felt in my own way that this might compensate somehow for little David, you see Harold never went back home after prison, never went to see David, never wanted to see Ivy. He said that after all this time the little boy wouldn't know him and there would be a lot of upset if he just turned up. Better if he stayed away. He wrote occasionally to his own father, but they had become distant, Harold said that he'd let both of his parents down.

But, Harold was doing quite well a work. He had a natural ability for engineering and had a leaning towards numbers and measurement, and then he enrolled for day release at college where he took a course in Technical Drawing. His employers were pleased with his progress and very soon he was taken off the shop floor and moved into the drawing office. His ability began to shine, Harold had found his niche.

Then one Friday afternoon as I was making our tea, there was a knock on the door. I had stopped working by then because the baby was due, and when I heard the door I shook my head, thinking that Harold had forgotten his key again. But when I opened the door, there were two policemen standing there. And I froze.

"What's wrong" I blurted it out. I was instantly worried over my family, was it an accident, or was it Harold?

"Mrs Moors?" asked one of the policemen "Mrs Harold Moors?"

Yes that's me" I said, I was really worried.

"Could we speak to Mr Moors please?"

"What for?" I said, and I said it a bit too sharply, but in my mind I thought that this was something coming back to haunt us, something from Harold's past, an intrusion into our now happy lives.

"Mrs Moors, we really need to speak to Mr Moors personally. Is he in?"

"I...well, he'll be home any minute actually" and I realised my ridiculous stupidity.

The policemen glanced at each other, and then they both gave me the look of the obvious.

I relented, and said to them "Would you like to come in, do you want a cup of tea?"

"Oh yes please" and in they stepped.

I left them in the front room and as I came back in with two mugs of hot tea, the front door rattled and opened as Harold finally arrived home. As he walked into the front room he was confronted by the two policemen standing there, and for a moment I thought Harold was going to collapse, the nightmare was repeating itself.

He stood there rigid, as though waiting for the inevitable. He simply said "Yes?"

"Ah Mr Moors" said one of the policemen, as he shot a quick look across to his associate.

"We're sorry to interrupt you" he continued "but we're from Bolton Central Police Station in Lancashire. We've been sent over here to contact you, and...err, I'm sorry Mr Moors, but we're here to inform you that unfortunately your father has died."

Harold just looked at the policeman, and blinked.

Whatever Harold had expected the policeman to say, it wasn't this, and for a moment he didn't comprehend what was being said to him.

"I'm sorry Mr Moors, are you alright?" asked the policeman.

Then suddenly, Harold shook himself out of it and he glanced at me, and then for a moment he stared open mouthed at the police, and finally he spoke "Oh dear god. No"

I put down the tea and went over to him and held his arm for reassurance.

"When did Mr Moors die?" I asked. It felt strange to use the name.

"It was five days ago actually. We're sorry, but it's taken us this long to trace you".

"What happened?" I asked again.

"A heart attack apparently, a neighbour found him, looked through the front room window and saw him in the chair, he'd just passed away as he'd sat there. When we got into the house, he was in his armchair, the radio was on, and there was a cup of tea at the side of him. He'd been reading the paper.

Harold gave a stifled smile, and then started to cry.

He had to return to Bolton to sort out his father's affairs, there were no other family, just Harold.

A week later and after the funeral, he returned home, and then fate took a turn.

Harold was called into work to see the manager. The firm owned an associate company in Bury in Lancashire and there was a new opening in their design office. They needed someone who was bright and they needed new ideas. It was a promotion, and Harold's name was put forward.

I remember us sitting at the kitchen table and talking about it, our plans and our future.

Bury is a small town, the next town to Bolton. We had a house in Bolton, Harold's father's house. Yes, we already owned a house in Bolton so there was no rent and no mortgage.

This was a big step forward, but for Harold of course, it was also a step backwards.

But we looked at the bigger picture and decided to give it a go, and if things didn't work out, well we could always sell the house and find something else, somewhere else.

And then a week later, I gave birth to our daughter.

Within a month, we moved to Bolton, lock, stock and barrel. And life went on.

I never once asked Harold if he had ever been around to see Temple Street, and he never, ever spoke about it.

Harold worked in Bury for three years and then left and went to work as Chief Engineer for Bridesons Ltd, a Bolton Company. By then we'd had our second daughter.

And as I said, life goes on.

Several years seemed to pass quickly, and they were happy times. Then one day Harold came home from work and we all sat down around the table for our tea as usual, but on that day he was unusually quiet. After we had eaten and the girls had disappeared, I started to clear the dishes.

He looked over at me and said "Would you sit down love please, I need to talk to you"

I was a bit apprehensive, and I had a feeling that something was troubling him. So I sat down, and as we sat there across the table, Harold continued.

"I want to talk to you about David, remember David?"

I nodded.

"He's approaching fifteen, I've never encroached on his life Florrie, I've never even seen him, but I do have a responsibility. At the end of the day, he's still my son.

I bit my lip at this, seven years and suddenly Harold felt responsible. I felt a bit uneasy about this, and wondered what was coming next.

He swallowed "I've found out where Ivy lives, through the Town Hall. I can't approach him, not now, not out of the blue. For all I know, he may not even know about me. I can't go and see him Florrie, it's too late for that, but I deal with the Town Hall through work and I've spoken to some people. There's an opening in the surveyors office, a job opening for a junior and, well it would be a start for him, a good start."

Inwardly, I sighed. I suppose I knew that this would never really go away. It was always there in the background, my private fear. It was the only thing we never spoke about. Buried, but never forgotten.

I held my breath, this was dark territory for me, and I suppose for Harold too.

I just said "Yes", and I'd said it straight out, almost carelessly "whatever you think is right Harold"

"You're sure?" he asked.

"Yes" there was nothing else that I could say, and I got up from the table.

"I'd better wash the pots" I said to him.

And as I stood at the kitchen sink, I knew he was watching me and the back of my head felt hot as I imagined him continuing to look at me.

I lay in bed that night, and it was stupid I know, but I kept worrying and thinking about the threat from the past. Yes, it was stupid because Harold and I, well we were husband and wife, till death us do part, I knew that but still it troubled me.

The next day at teatime, me and the kids and Harold were all of sat around the kitchen table.

I suddenly said "I've been thinking about David" and I said it out loud, sort of out of the blue.

Harold looked up, a little too quickly "Oh, right" he said.

"We need to talk about this" I said, somewhat directly.

I suppose this was the Yorkshire in me, straight talking, it was how I was brought up, how we were all brought up. I had lain in bed that night worrying, and I'd finally come to a conclusion, I had to go with it. Whatever was going to happen, it would be better for us to face it together. And in my heart, I knew we were unbreakable.

We then told the girls all about Harold's son, and that they had a brother. Typically of children, they thought it was all very funny and quickly disappeared into the front room to play.

We were left on our own...

"I know we need to talk about it" he said, and he gave a deep breath "I was thinking about writing a letter to Ivy, to tell her about the position, and if it's okay I'll organize an interview for him, and we'll go from there. It'll be nothing to do with me and I won't be involved. The thing is Florrie, it would be a start for him. I've never given him anything, but he is my son Florrie, he is my son".

The next day Harold wrote the letter.

Harold's firm, 'Brideson's', were one of the town's most prestigious companies. Not only were they engineers, they were also manufacturers and were also heavily involved the construction industry. They handled a substantial amount of the town's civil engineering and building work. In those days, deals were done and hands were shaken.

Harold was constantly involved with the Planning Department and the Town Hall, and he was well known and respected. Getting David the job would be a mere formality. So he wrote the letter.

We waited, but we never got a reply, ever.

Months passed, and we never spoke about it, until one Sunday afternoon after dinner, we were both washing and wiping the pots when Harold broached the subject.

He simply said "He mustn't want to know"

And that was the end of it, we never mentioned David's name ever again.

I looked at Florrie.

"And that was it?"

"That was it" she said.

"And he never contacted David, ever?"

"Never ever" she replied.

I was still amazed "the funeral" I said "he was mentioned at the funeral"

"Yes, well we'd always told the girls, they were old enough to understand, they'd always known they had a brother somewhere. We decided to be open about it, no secrets you see. And when Harold died, the girls took the decision to find David and let him know, let him know about his father.

Unfortunately, by the time they found him and contacted him, the funeral was over.

"What a damn shame" I said, a comment that was worthless.

Florrie shrugged her shoulders and smiled "And now you know everything"

And I thought about it all for a moment

"But Florrie" I said "You and Harold have both walked up and down the road past my shop for over twenty years"

"Yes, I know"

"And David and his wife have done the same, for twenty years"

She nodded "Yes"

"You must have walked past each other countless times, hundreds of times"

"Yes I know" she said again.

"And you never knew"

"We never knew"

I shook my head, "Unbelievable" I said

Florrie looked at me, bittersweet "If only, if only we'd known. It would have changed Harold's life, and it could have answered a few questions, I just don't know"

"It's strange, and I suppose that's life Florrie, but my god it's hard to take in"

"It is" she said and she shrugged, "Now I think I'll have a gin and tonic, after all that" and she laughed again, in fact she almost giggled with relief.

I gave her a peck on the cheek and left, I went home slightly spellbound I must admit, I suppose it's just the way life throws the dice.

Two days later, I was outside my shop, sweeping up or cleaning the windows or whatever. Anyway, I looked up and walking towards me was David. As usual, he was on his way to the shops.

He walked up to me and smiled, "I believe you've heard all about it" he said. He'd obviously been in touch with Florrie .

"Yes David, I have" I said "and I can't believe it. The number of times you must have passed each other on the street, it's unbelievable, and you never knew"

He looked wistful "I know, it's a shame but no, I never knew him"

"Well David" I said "I did know your father, and I knew him well. I've known him for twenty years and I'd like to tell you something. You're dad was a great man, I had a lot of time for him, he was the kindest person you could ever wish to know."

"Thanks for that, I appreciate it I really do" he said, and he sighed "My life could have been a lot different if I'd known him, you know he did actually write to me once, he tried to get me a job with the council, I was about fifteen at the time."

"I believe so" I said.

"I never got the letter"

"You didn't?"

"No, I never got the letter. My mother probably ripped it up"

"Why on earth would she do that?" I asked him, I was a bit mystified.

He took a deep sigh "I'll tell you why" he said, "Because my mother was a bitch, she was a bloody awful 'bitch' of a woman, that's why. She didn't give monkeys about anybody else but herself and she gave me and everybody else a dog's life, and that's why she wouldn't have given my father the satisfaction of seeing his son do well. That's the sort of vindictive woman she was, a vicious, nasty piece of work. That was my bloody mother, the rotten, lousy cow".

He was suddenly embarrassed at his own anger.

I steered the conversation on with a question.

"Can I ask you something David?" I asked him cautiously "Did Claude Atkinson bring you up as his son?

"Claude Atkinson!" David sneered at the mention of his name.

"Claude Atkinson, I'll tell you about Atkinson, that bastard. He ended up in prison too, just like my father. Atkinson and my mother were together for about five years, after my dad went away. Atkinson and my mother eventually got a shop on the other side of town, it was all run on stolen goods, all pinched from the Co-op. But Atkinson had got himself in deep, too deep, and he'd made a few enemies at work. Somebody informed the chief executive at the Co-op about Atkinson and what he was up to, and they in turn put somebody to work in the Co-op to keep an eye on him and find out what exactly was going on. By the time the police were called in, the bosses at the Co-op knew everything, down to the last bag of sugar. Atkinson was arrested and got five years. My mother got away with it by the skin of her teeth, she begged the judge and told him that she had a child and a bedridden mother to look after, she was bound over and had to serve some sort of probation. When she came home from court that day, she apparently laughed at her sentence.

For years I had a succession of different fathers. Temple Street was hell for me, a chain of drunken men and a drunken mother. And always, there was the violence.

It must have been five years later, because one Saturday morning Claude Atkinson just walked in through the front door, completely out of the blue. He must have finally been let out of prison. He walked in and went straight upstairs to find my mother in bed with some man, they were both drunk.

He hit the man with a bottle, then dragged him downstairs and threw him out of the house. Then he went back upstairs and started to beat my mother. She was in a state of drunken shock, well she hadn't seen him for years, she never ever went to see him in prison.

I was only about ten or eleven years old, and when I heard all the shouting, I ran into the bedroom to find Atkinson kicking my mother as she lay on the floor screaming. I lunged at him, trying to get him to stop, but he grabbed me by the ear and punched me right in the side of the face and knocked me out. I was only a kid.

When I came 'to' on the bedroom floor, Atkinson had already dragged my mother down the stairs by her hair and had thrown her out onto the pavement. When I opened my eyes, I was groggy and sore. Atkinson was throwing all my mother's clothes out of the window. The neighbours were all out, some of them were laughing, some jeering. My mother wasn't liked, she hadn't a good word for anyone and she hadn't done herself any favours with the other residents on Temple Street.

Atkinson heard me move and he turned around. I just looked up at him and he came at me again and kicked me right in the face. I sprawled back on the floor, screaming and crying, he'd really hurt me.

He reached down and once more grabbed me by the ear and pulled me up to him, right up close to his face, and it was then that I smelt the whiskey on his breath.

He snarled at me "Get out of my fucking house or I'll kill you, and your fucking mother too"

His eyes were all bloodshot, I was terrified of him and even though my face was throbbing I ran, ran for my life, down those stairs and out of the house. The whole of my face and my eyes were purple and black for a month. We never went back there.

The next few years were filled with different houses and different men, and with basically the same results. We just moved on.

I was told that Atkinson eventually sold up everything and moved away. At seventeen I did the same, I'd nothing to sell of course, I just packed a bag and moved out of where we lived at the time, I couldn't stand it anymore. Eventually I got a job in the mill, I was on the shop floor, and I worked there all my life, then at sixty I got made redundant and that was my working life over, it's always been a struggle. And now I find out that things could have been so different, if only I'd got that letter I could have had a good job. I could have made something of myself and had a different life. But no it wasn't to be, all because of her, that rotten cow."

David was again moved with anger, it was in his eyes.

"What happened to her?" I asked.

"I don't know. I can only suppose she died. I never went back, I bloody hated her"

And the moment passed and David calmed down and began to breathe a little more easily.

He shook his head slowly.

"Well" he said wistfully "that's life, and we'll just have to get on with it. I've got to go now and do the shopping, I'll see you later pal"

And with that he walked away, off to the shops.

It's a strange thing, but after that conversation, even though we did speak regularly, he never broached the subject of his father with me ever again, and for that reason, neither did I.

But that same evening as I closed the shop and walked home, I thought about Harold and about David...David, the son that he had loved and had lost. And the real tragedy was, living so close to one another for all those years and never knowing it. He was just moments away from the son he'd felt he had to walk away from, rightly or wrongly.

I can only suppose that they were different times back then.

As I walked home from work that night, I began to count my footsteps. My stride is as near as matters, a yard in length, and I counted my footsteps all the way home to Harold's house.

It was just 300 steps...just 300 yards.

It's a distance that sticks in my mind, always.

CHAPTER TWO

The next morning...and its Wednesday...

Another day of course and the same routine, once again I've walked up to the shop, raised the shutters, unlocked the door and sorted out the alarm. Then I've switched on the T.V, filled the kettle, filled the till and made the brew, etc, etc.

Yes, I know, all very boring.

It was around lunchtime, and I was having a laugh with one of my long serving customers, about the ups and downs of life, as you do. I'd just finished cutting his hair and as things drew to a close, I reminded him of an old expression, it was actually an old 'saying' that I'd heard years ago, and the expression was 'If you want to make God laugh, tell him all your plans'

It's an amusing sort of phrase and the customer agreed with me wholeheartedly, then we went on to have a short discussion on the meaning of life, and there you go.

As he left the shop, I bid him farewell and once again filled the kettle for the umpteenth time.

And as I sat there, drinking a mug of freshly brewed coffee, I once again started to think about the phrase, 'If you want to make God laugh, tell him all your plans', and with that thought still running through my head, I started to remember the antics of another long serving customer, a customer that I'll definitely never forget. His name was 'Derek', the one and only, the indefatigable Derek.

Now there was a man who God had unquestionably decided to have some fun and games with, and the more I thought about him, the more I just had to smile.

Let me explain.

Derek bless him, was a complete and utter computer nerd.

Well, when I say nerd, I mean it with the best possible intentions. He wasn't odd, not strange or even boring, in fact Derek was a lovely, lovely man. Aged around forty-five, he was tall with both wiry build and wiry hair, and a beard that would have done a Viking proud.

I only used to cut Derek's hair about three times a year. He had hair as thick as carpet and he was one of those blokes that only had his hair cut when it was too, too long and was beginning to become an embarrassment, both for him and for me.

I used to say to him "I hope you never tell people that you come here for your haircut, because Derek, you're not really a good advert"

He would chuckle, and then talk away nonstop.

Derek had two loves. One was computers, and the other was his wife.

Derek worked for a computer company who knew his worth. He was a 'company' man through and through and I don't think that he ever gave a thought to working for anyone else. His firm would send him all over the world to sort out different problems with companies' computers and programmes and software and all that sort of stuff. He used to tell me in great detail, where he'd been and the problems he had fixed, half the time I didn't understand a word he was wittering on about, but the places he'd visited were always interesting, so at least we had some common ground.

As to his wife Jill, well Jill suffered from bad health. She had kidney problems, which had become increasingly more serious over the years. So Derek had problems in both of his worlds. Computers he could fix, his wife he couldn't.

I met Jill quite a few times, she usually delivered Derek to my shop and then had to collect him again after his haircut. She was a lovely woman whose true beauty lay in her personality. Jill cared...cared about people, she was thoughtful and kind without making a fuss, and she never ever, discussed her illness. And Derek told me never to ask her.

I remember them taking a long awaited holiday to Egypt. They didn't really do holidays, Derek was always on a plane flying all over the world, and for him a holiday was being comfortable at home, relaxed, and with Jill. And for Jill travelling was a problem because she was on a dialysis machine and it meant dragging the machine along with them, or finding access to a machine wherever they went.

So holidays were never really top of their list.

Anyway, Derek came into the shop, very excited, telling me all about their proposed trip. Jill had just been through a bad spell, very bad, she was quite weak and she needed to convalesce. It was a very cold January, and so Derek had decided to take her to Egypt for some sun and warmer weather. It was to be a cruise down the River Nile. He had amazingly organised the trip, so that dialysis machines would be made readily available at the various stopovers during their cruise.

They had a wonderful time, and spent most of the trip sitting at back of the boat, talking and just idly watching the beautiful green banks of the Nile slowly pass by. They came back from the holiday relaxed and tanned, but Jill was still weak and not really well. But in their own way they had never been happier or closer.

Five weeks later my phone rang and it was Derek, his voice so quiet. Apparently two days earlier he had come home from work to find that Jill had died.

"She just sat on the sofa watching the television and passed away, so peaceful, so quietly. No fuss, just like Jill to do it that way" he said, and his voice cracked with grief as he took a breath.

There was a funeral of course, which I went to. The whole service was small and sad, they didn't have a large circle of friends and the family consisted mostly of the elderly. Derek stood alone, no real emotion, no outpouring of tears, he just stood there on that breezy grey morning looking completely lost and not really understanding what had happened.

Quite a time passed. It was probably around three months later when Derek finally came into the shop for his haircut. As he walked through the door I looked at him, he was thinner and although he had never really carried a lot of weight, it was his face that struck me. The strain in his face was one of sorrow and loss.

"Hi" he said.

"Hi Derek, how are you?" I replied, and I was concerned.

He sat down in the chair, and began to talk as I cut his hair. He'd let his hair grow nearly twice as long as it's usual overgrown state, and his beard was now nearly spreading onto his chest.

"Sorry it's got into such a mess" he said quietly "I'm afraid I've let it overgrow a bit, Jill used to always remind me to have it cut and well..." and his voice trailed off.

"Well you're here now" I said, trying to put some balance into the conversation.

He began to talk and he started to open up bit by bit. We spoke about grief and about loneliness...

I just rolled along with him, he needed to talk and I just nodded in response. He certainly didn't need someone to lecture him on what he should do, or how he should start living his life.

Derek wasn't looking to any sort of future at that moment, and he didn't actually want to move on anywhere. He wanted to live life as it had always been, with Jill. But deep inside, he knew that wasn't possible anymore.

Yes grief, deep grief.

And so a year, and possibly longer passed by, and Derek would come in for his regular and irregular visits for a haircut. He had slowly come to whatever terms he could find to handle Jill's death. And as I always knew he would, Derek threw himself totally into his work.

He would disappear to parts all over the world for months at a time, and instead of coming home to nothing, he would simply fly onto the next job, somewhere else to fix yet another company's computer problems.

I'd actually not seen him for well over two or three months, when one morning the phone in my shop rang, and it was Derek.

"Hi" he said "It's me, can you book me in for a haircut please?"

I replied "Okay, tomorrow at eleven suit you?"

"Yes, that's fine" he said "but you may have to help me through the door"

"And why's that?" I asked.

"Because I'm on crutches"

"What?"

"I've broken both my legs"

"How on earth?"

"Don't ask" he replied "I'll tell you all about it tomorrow."

And with that, he started to laugh. Well no, he actually started to giggle.

And I thought to myself, 'Mmm, something's different here.'

So the next day, I think it was a Wednesday morning, business as usual, and a black taxi cab rolled up outside the shop, engine thumping and lots of black smoke. The rear door swung open and out he almost fell, all crutches and hair, and its Derek.

Using one crutch to hold himself up and another firmly wedged under his arm, he hopped around to the driver's door to pay his fare. He has a short, lively conversation with the driver, laughing and smiling, and then the cabbie drove away leaving Derek standing in the middle of the road, all very jovial and waving a crutch in a farewell salute.

You'd think it was Christmas.

He turned, and grinning from ear to ear, he put his crutches under his arms and hobbled towards the front door of my shop, which I opened like a smiling butler.

"Hi there" he said as he negotiated the step.

I offered a hand, and with a bit of backward and forwards manoeuvring and a couple of near misses, Derek finally almost fell through the door and into the shop.

"The eagle has landed" I ceremoniously quoted, and we both laughed as I got him sat in the chair. I put a cape on him and a towel around his neck and we went through the usual formalities, and then I looked at him through the mirror, and suddenly I realized that the Derek of old had returned and I smiled, and I actually gave a sigh of relief. It made me feel good.

"Well, what the bloody hell have 'you' been up to?" I said, grinning.

Derek, as usual, started to wave his hands about "Where do I start?" he said, and then he shook his head at me "Have I got a tale for you...you won't believe it".

"Really" I said "well, go on then"

He concentrated for a moment, and then with a wry smile he looked up.

"I know" he exclaimed "Marbella, I've been to Marbella"

"And what were you doing in Marbella?" I was a bit surprised, this was not like Derek.

"Oh, I was over there on a contract with work" he said breezily "just outside Malaga actually, a software company we deal with called 'Stalla Software Inc'. Their computers were having a bit of a funny turn, and they're important customers so my company flew me out there straight away to try and sort things out."

"And did you?" I asked him, and that was a stupid mistake.

"Oh yes" Derek replied "there was a binary malfunction that caused a glitch in their input data coding, so the function ability and re-formatting capability were impaired and..."

And on he rambled like this for the next several minutes. I of course hadn't a clue what the hell he was going on about and I promptly forgot anything that he'd said, more or less 10 seconds later.

"And so, what happened then?" I prompted him, once the technical talk came to some sort of conclusion.

"Oh yes well, once the job was done they, the company of course, put me in a taxi and take me to a hotel for the night, and then I would usually fly out the next day"

"Usually?" I enquired.

"Err...yes" and he looked at me and rolled his eyes.

"And?" I said. Strewth, getting a story out of Derek was like pulling hens teeth.

"Well" he continued "I got a taxi and I finally arrived at the hotel, it was called 'The Hotel El Florres'. It was actually quite a way out from Marbella central, in a town called Fuengirola, it's a holiday resort really, and it took over an hour to get there. Why they booked me in there I couldn't understand, until the receptionist let it drop that the owner of the hotel, a 'Mr Hernandez' was related to 'Miss Hernandez', and she ran the personnel office at Stalla Software. So, any bookings made through 'Stalla' were given favourable 'dees-count'..."

Derek said the word 'discount' in his 'mock' Spanish accent and grinned enthusiastically.

I just groaned.

Then he continued "So I booked myself in and collected the keys for the room, then I had to carry my bags up three flights of stairs because the lift's call button wouldn't respond, why I don't know?"

"Probably the computer" I said, but Derek didn't quite pick up on the irony of that one.

"So I went into my room" he continued "it was quite nice really, basic but okay, and it had a lovely balcony facing out to the sea. Fuengirola is quite a touristy place you know, and it was quite busy for the time of the year. Well it was about five o' clock and it had been a long and hot day, so I thought that I'd have a shower to freshen up and then, as usual on these trips, I would order food from room service, eat in my room, read a good book and then early to bed and off to the airport next morning. However, just as I started to run the shower and began to get undressed, there was a knock on the door. So I wrapped a towel around myself and called out "Come in" The next thing I know, the door swung open and in walked a waiter holding a tray, and on it was a bottle of champagne in an ice bucket.

"Ah, good evening sir" said the waiter "Eez compliments of the hotel" and he nodded at the bottle. "Cava sir" he said.

"And Cava to you" I replied, my Spanish isn't very good, then I said "thank you very much, how very nice of you, a bottle of champagne, lovely"

The waiter then frowned slightly "No sir, eez not champagne...eez Cava!"

"Ah" I said, and then I realized...Cava must mean "Champagne" in Spanish.

"It does to some people" I said, and that comment went right over his head as well. I sighed and continued cutting his hair.

"So" continued Derek, unperturbed "the waiter put the bottle of Cava on a table on the balcony, and then with an 'efficient' smile, he said "Enjoy 'eet sir", and then he left the room.

Well, I had a shower, and then changed into my comfortable clothes and then went to sit on the balcony. It was about six o' clock, early evening, and I just sat there staring into space, and when I looked up, there was nothing to see but clear blue sky, there wasn't a single cloud, and the sun was just beginning to turn and there was a low red glow out to sea. It was just beautiful.

And I thought of Jill and how she would have enjoyed this moment. We would have just sat there too, the both of us enjoying a glass of wine, and I smiled.

I looked across at the bottle of Cava, and I thought "Well love, I'll have a glass just for me and you" and so I opened the ice cold bottle with a loud 'pop'.

I poured myself a glass, and I sat there in the warm sun drinking the chilled fizzy Cava, it tasted wonderful.

I sat there for the best part of an hour, thinking about life, or really the unfairness of it all. The way my life had turned out, it shouldn't have been like this. Jill was a really good and wonderful person, and I have always done the best I could to be a decent human being. And as I looked out over the balcony at the beautiful sea and sky, I thought to myself 'Where am I actually going with the rest of my life'?

And I poured the last of the Cava into the glass and drank it in one go.

Well, I'm not very good with drink, it makes my mind wander. And as I sat there looking out over the balcony, I eventually looked down and started to watch the small crowds of people strolling by. And as I watched and listened, I saw happy people talking and smiling, they were on holiday of course and were enjoying themselves. Yes, people sitting down in restaurants, ready to dine, all dressed in bright holiday clothes, all smiling with anticipation. And as I looked around at the restaurants, I saw other people already eating their meals, and I saw delicious food and I watched conversations over glasses of deep red wine, and it all looked so good. Suddenly, I felt hungry too, and as I looked to my empty glass I realized that I really, really wanted to go out and try a glass of that deep red wine.

The Cava had done its job, and now I craved food and drink, and truthfully more than anything, I wanted company and conversation, and I wanted to be out there with those people. In fact, I wanted to be out there with anybody because in some sort of instantaneous revelation, I suddenly realised that I was so damn lonely, and I was absolutely sick off it.

Yes the Cava had really done its job. I began to smile to myself and then I just burst out laughing, the feeling of release was wonderful.

And with that, I stood up and walked from the balcony and back and into my room.

I opened the wardrobe and picked out a pair of slacks and my coolest tee shirt. I quickly changed clothes, slipped on my sandals, sprayed on loads of aftershave and then virtually skipped out of the apartment.

"Sod the lift" I said to myself as I bounced down the stairs, two steps at a time.

Then I walked straight past reception and outside onto the lively street that only five minutes ago, I had gazed down at and wondered at.

This was one busy street, and was full of people. I looked around and noticed that across the road was the restaurant that I had been watching from the balcony. It had a bar that people were sitting and enjoying their drinks. Full glasses and full on conversations.

The entrance was a rustic brickwork arch that led into the restaurant and on this arch was a sign, in stark black lettering, it read 'The Los Varaderos-Bar-Restaurant'.

'Well' I thought, 'that looks like a good place to start', and as I strode across the road I had to dodge out of the way of a Spaniard on a scooter who very nearly put an end to my evening out.   The idiot nearly killed me. You know, I've always wondered about driving on the wrong side of the road, it's dangerous...

"Derek, for god's sake" I said, we were rapidly going off track here.

"Oh yes sorry, where was I?" he said apologetically.

"Scooter, road and the bar" I reminded him.

"Ah yes" and his eyes lit up and he smiled as the story returned "Well I crossed the road, 'just' and then I strolled into the bar. It was 'buzzing', this was the place to be all right. There were three barmen busily serving drinks. Some of the customers were sitting there waiting to dine and were casually talking as they studied glorious menus, which were large parchment affairs with curious orange lettering.

There were other customers there too, who were just there to drink and talk, it was all, very cool.

I pulled up a barstool and sat myself down and took in the atmosphere, it was a great place. The barmen were so totally professional. They served booze with a passion, pouring drinks from high, into tall glasses. They mixed the drinks with attitude, tossing lumps of ice into shiny chrome cocktail shakers and then with an almost 'act of reverence', they shook them like a set of maracas. It was all a 'full on' performance to entertain the customers.

On the bar there were small terracotta bowls filled with pistachios and salted cashew nuts along with small 'tostas' and other little salted snacks. Stuck in between these tasters, were small framed cards, placed into individual card holders that were actually made from twisted forks, the cards announced in large green letters that tonight was 'Mojito Night' and that they were serving their speciality, the 'Varaderos' Mojito Especials.

As I looked around, I noticed that most of customers were indeed drinking the infamous 'Los Varaderos' Mojitos Especials...and they looked really, really good.

Much, much later, I discovered that these things could be used to kill Bulls.

Anyway, behind the bar was a large shiny bucket that was filled to the top with the key ingredient, fresh mint leaves. They obviously sold a lot of these things.

As I stood there, the barman turned to me and "Signor?" he asked.

I pointed at the bucket and said "It would be rude not too", I was trying a bit of humour.

"Signor?" he said again, now with a little more urgency. He wasn't getting the 'humour bit' at all.

"Err...can I have a Mojito please, an "Especial" and I pointed to the card.

"Okay signor" he replied, then nodded and turned away.

Well I suppose they 'were' busy, but frankly I'd met friendlier bus drivers.

Anyway, I watched as he poured some stuff into the cocktail shaker, along with ice and mint, and then with great flourish, he shook it as though he had his mother-in-law by the throat"

Derek laughed at his own joke, we both did, that line was actually funny.

"Nice one Derek" I said, he was definitely back on form, and I smiled.

"The next thing" he continued "the barman returned and with one hand he threw a coaster in front of me and with the other he presented me with a tall full glass.

"Ey...'Los Varaderos' Mojito Especial,Signor. Si, enjoy" he said.

And with another nod, he quickly turned to another customer.

'Jolly chap' I thought, and with that I picked up my drink.

"Away-we-go...mo-hee-toe" I said to myself, rather too loudly, as I raised my glass and toasted, well, toasted myself actually.

Some of the people around the bar heard me and burst out laughing, and one guy called out "Here's back at you", then another couple raised their glasses and added "cheers" and several more glasses were raised in agreement.

"Are we all drinking these?" I asked.

There was laughter as the glasses were raised again, and a red haired lady giggled and said

"It would be rude not too" and we all laughed as I realized they'd been listening to my conversation with the barman.

"Here goes" I said out loud, and I took a drink and 'Oh...my...God'

"Oh lord" I said out loud again "these are bloody wonderful"

"Aren't they just?" replied the red head.

And so the night began.

It turned out that 'the gang' in there drank Mojitos at the Varaderos most nights, whether it was "Especial" night or not.

I ordered a second, and the barman almost smiled.

"Is he ill?" I asked, more laughter, and then one chap called Alan, told me that the

Barman, 'Jimmy', this was not his real name, but something that had been thrust upon him a couple of years earlier by a gang of Scottish women who were on a hen party, somehow the name stuck and had just stayed with him. Anyway, Alan then told me that Jimmy is a great barman, he just has to get to know you.

"And how long will that take?" I asked.

"About two years" belched Alan, and that sort of set the tone for the night.

We continued to drink and talk and midnight came and went. We all drank loads of Mojitos, and then we drank Mojitos with Cava chasers, or was it the other way about? Anyway, we then went on to challenge Jimmy's bartending skills by asking him for the most obscure cocktails ever known to man. Pure liquid exotica, with names like 'the Bullshot' and 'The East Indian', there was the 'Egg Nog Nashville' and the 'Bosom Caresser', and a strange drink named the 'Mayan Whore', and then he produced something awful called a 'Monkey Gland'.

But to give him his due, Jimmy could concoct every drink that was ordered, and he did this with great flair and expertise, after which he was applauded and cheered. And with time, even 'old Jimmy' started to lighten up a bit and laugh, but in a macho way that only Spanish men can do.

At one point we got onto Flaming Sambucas, which is a liqueur that you set fire to, not a wise move, anyway on the third round of these we accidentally managed to knock them all over. Several glasses of Flaming Sambucas were spilt, and these then set fire to the bar.

'Jimmy' had a Spanish panic attack.

Alan thankfully, was quickly at hand and put the fire out with a bottle of Cava.

And so the night rolled on.

At one point I got into conversation with a Belgian guy whose name was Gerry. He was a tall bloke, all dark haired and tanned, he looked a bit like an aging male model, and on most nights he was also a regular at the bar. It turned out that he owned some villa somewhere outside of town. Anyway, somehow we got talking about the Grand Prix and Formula One motor racing. I've always followed Formula One and so had he, and we ended up discussing the next Grand Prix and motor racing in general. Now we were very drunk, and we got into an intricate debate about team tactics and the merits of the various drivers. God only know what we were dribbling on about.

At around two o' clock, Gerry introduced me to the sophisticated delights of coffee and cognac.

"This will help you to sober up" he drawled in his strange Belgian accent, which to me sounded like a Frenchman trying to talk like an American.

"Doesn't the brandy cancel out the coffee?" I enquired drunkenly, but he deemed to ignore that question.

Coffee and cognac consisted of a cup of wonderful Spanish coffee and a huge brandy glass, half filled with Spanish 'Fundador' Brandy, an enormous measure. You then proceeded to drink the coffee whilst permanently topping it up with the brandy. When the coffee has gone, you drink the remainder of the brandy, and in our case, in one go, and then you order another.

We drank several of these over the next hour and they did actually start to work as a slow paralysis set in.

It was now past three in the morning and the bar was beginning to empty as the remaining customers staggered off home.

"Come on" said Gerry as he toppled off his bar stool "we'll go back to my place for some drinks and something to eat, some breakfast, isn't that a good idea?"

"Yeh, great" I said, and something in my memory reminded me that I had actually come to the 'Varaderos' to wine and dine, and what with all the drinking, I'd forgotten about the dining bit, and suddenly I was starving.

"Come on, let's go" he said and we hailed Jimmy and thanked him for the evening.

"Thank you Meester Gerry" called back Jimmy.

I put my hand up to Jimmy to wave him goodnight, but he'd disappeared.

So I shrugged my shoulders and followed Gerry out of the bar.

We walked down the street a short way, and then turned left and went down and around the back of the restaurant where there was a car park.

There was only one car parked there. It was a bright Red Ferrari.

Gerry staggered towards the car, fumbled in his pocket, and produced a set of keys.

"Is this yours?" I said, trying to see straight.

"Yeah" he replied.

"It's a Ferrari" I said stupidly.

"Yeah"

"It's a Ferrari Testarossa" I said, trying to sound knowledgeable.

Gerry turned to me "For fucks sake Derek, get in the fucking car"

"Okay" I said dutifully, and I opened the door and got in.

Then Gerry started up the car.

"Are you alright to drive?" was my next stupid question.

"No problem, I do this all the time" he said, and he hiccupped.

So off we went, out of the car park, through Fuengirola town centre, and onto the Marbella highway.

Now let me tell you something, the Marbella main highway basically runs from Malaga Airport, through Marbella and all the way down to Gibraltar. It is regarded as one of the busiest and most dangerous stretches of road in Europe, and is known locally as the 'highway of death'.

And now, two very drunken idiots were driving along it in a high powered sports car.

It struck me that we probably had more fuel in us than the car did.

The road was empty and Gerry hit the accelerator. The car shot off so fast that my neck cracked.

"Jesus Christ" I said, and I meant it.

We were going at a blistering speed, and I rather nervously asked Gerry how far we were going.

"Oh not long, it's near Marbella" he said "I'll crank her up, it takes less than five minutes once we hit around...220"

"Miles an hour?" I gasped.

"No you dick, kilometres" and he laughed at me over the noise of the engine.

"Oh" I said, slightly pacified "how fast is '220' in miles per hour?"

"About a 140 mph" he replied.

I think I felt a bowel movement.

"Give over worrying, we'll soon be there, I do this run all the time" he said as the car hit warp speed. I just clung to my seat.

"You know" he continued "'The Varaderos, what a great place. I love going there, what a bar, and what about that Jimmy. 'Man' he must know every cocktail ever invented, and what a great gang they are down there. Do you know how I met Alan? I was once...WHOOPS!"

And Gerry immediately stopped talking.

He stopped talking because at that moment, he'd hit the brakes and then turned a sharp right, sending the Ferrari into a sideways skid.

We were doing about a 100 mph at the time, and suddenly most of my internal organs were being shoved to the left.

He simply flicked the steering wheel left and right, and unbelievably gained full control of the car as we shot through a huge stone-pillared gateway.

I gave Gerry an astounded look and he laughed "Sorry about that" he said, and then he laughed again "I nearly missed my fucking house"

"You nearly missed fucking Marbella" I replied.

He looked at me as I shook my head, and then we burst out laughing.

Gerry thought this was great and he grinned as he steered the car with one hand.

"We need a drink" he said.

"We do" I agreed.

With that, and at a respectable 30 mph, Gerry drove the Ferrari up the quiet and dark winding road. Suddenly the road opened up, and there in front of us was a beautiful, huge white house. It was three stories high, all pillars and large shuttered windows.

We pulled up on the gravel driveway and stopped outside the house, then we got out of the car.

I was amazed "Some villa" I said. This was not what I had imagined.

Gerry just shrugged his shoulders "Come on" he said and we went into the house.

It was truly beautiful, and was without doubt the most beautiful house I have ever been in.

The décor and the furnishings were exquisite. And suddenly I realised that Gerry was actually a very wealthy man.

We went into a large sitting room that was all cream furniture and gold fittings, and we sat down on two of the opulent cream leather sofas. Gerry reached over to a glass coffee table, picked up the phone, and pressed one of the buttons.

I heard him say "Ah Silvee" and then he broke into Spanish and I realized that he was asking for some food. He looked at me and said "What do we drink, oh I know, Bloody Mary's" and he nodded at me for agreement. Then he spoke down the phone again, this time in English "and Silvee, a pitcher of 'Bloody Mary's' please."

Gerry put down the phone and continued "Bloody Mary's are like food when you've been drinking, they'll straighten us up".

By then, I didn't care what they did. I had been drinking for about six or seven hours by then, and my brain was living in a body that it no longer understood.

Within ten minutes, Silvee arrived. A silver haired lady in her late sixties and dressed all in black, she came in through a set of double doors, pushing a gold coloured glass trolley.

"Ah, Mr Gerry" she smiled "You are home. Finally"

"Hi Silvee" he replied, he said something to her in Spanish and then he introduced me.

"This is Derek, a friend of mine from England".

I said "Hi" to Silvee and she nodded back at me and smiled.

Gerry laughed "Silvee never goes to bed until I come home, she stays up all night sometimes. She's like a Mamma"

At this, Silvee laughed too and ruffled Gerry's hair "You're a crazy boy" she said and she turned and left the room, shaking her head in mock disapproval.

On the top of the trolley, was a glass pitcher of Bloody Mary's. It was surrounded by plates of cold cuts of various mixed meats, salamis and sausages, along with chunks of coarse Spanish bread. What a feast. We set to it, first the booze and then the food. It was great.

Gerry and I got into conversation. It turned out that his family were quite successful industrialists and owned various businesses all over Europe. Gerry had another Villa at Cap Ferrat in the south of France, along with a yacht that he had moored down there. He'd done just about everything, from skiing to motor racing, hence his deft handling of the Ferrari when we almost missed the house. He talked about his life, and I told him about myself and my life and Jill. He understood.

"That's why I go to the Varaderos most nights, when I'm over here" he said "I have quite a lonely life really, it's the money you see. I'm just a rich man's son, I've been married twice and each time it was all about the money, the wealth. Whereas you Derek, you are a lucky man, you have actually known true love. Down at the Varaderos, most of them don't know I'm wealthy, I just go down there to meet normal people. Good conversations and good times.

We talked until daylight. And as the sun began to slowly enter the room, the phone started to ring with different calls for Gerry, and it was back to work for him and he suddenly became a businessman again. And I knew it was time to go.

Gerry rang for his driver to take me back to Fuengirola. As I got up to leave, he said "If you are ever in Fuengirola again, we'll have to meet up"

But we both knew that wouldn't happen, you just say these things and it was all becoming slightly embarrassing. Just as I was leaving the phone rang again, Gerry picked it up and as he broke into conversation, he gave me a cursory wave and looked away.

I turned and left, feeling as though I had just been dismissed.

I stepped out of the house and into the bright sunshine of a new day, and it nearly blinded me.

I just stood there pulsating with alcohol, half drunk and half hung over, this was definitely not good.

Then I heard the sound of tyres on gravel, and suddenly a huge white Mercedes-Benz sedan drove up to the front of the house. It stopped right in front of me and the driver, who was dressed in a smart grey uniform, got out and walked around the car and then opened the rear passenger door.

"Signor" he said flatly, as he looked at me.

I got in, just.

The driver got back behind the wheel and looked at me through his mirror, then said "Where to signor? I am to take you anywhere you want"

I was tempted to say "England".

But I told him "Fuengirola centre, the Hotel El Florres please."

Saying nothing at all, the driver turned the car around and drove all the way down the drive and back onto the Marbella highway.

The Marbella highway again, oh well, the trip back was certainly going to be a lot slower and uneventful, and it was. I sat in the back of the sedan, cruising along, and I lowered the window to let in the warm breeze, it felt so, so good. I thought about the evening and what a time I'd had and I smiled. I know it was the alcohol, but I felt some kind of release, and for the first time in a long time I'd been happy. And suddenly I realized something, now without any guilt, I could move on.

The Mercedes pulled up outside the Hotel El Florres, and the driver got smartly out of the car and opened my door. I climbed out and then I put my hand into my pocket and fumbled for some money, a tip or whatever, but the driver shook his head.

"No, No signor, is okay" he said, and with that he got back into the car and drove off, leaving me standing in the middle of the road. I turned to the hotel entrance and was just about to go in and go up to my room to pack, when I heard somebody shout out from behind me.

"Derek..!" It was in a long pronunciation and came out as "Daarr-ickk".

I turned around and was astounded to see that it was Alan, I couldn't believe it. He was still sat at the LosVaraderos bar and was waving at me, so I shrugged, grinned, and ambled back over.

Alan laughed when he saw the state I was in. He turned to the barman, who thankfully wasn't Jimmy, and said "You'd better bring another glass with that order"

"What's happening Alan?" I asked him.

"Breakfast, that's what's happening. Cava Bucks Fizz"

"Oh no"I said.

"Oh Yes" he said "Cava Bucks Fizz is the best thing there is for 'the morning after'.

"I thought 'coffee and cognac' was the best thing"

"No that's next" he said.

And with that, the bartender popped the cork off an ice-cold bottle of Cava and put it in an ice bucket in front of us. He then produced two large champagne glasses that were half filled with chilled fresh orange juice, along with a tall glass jug which was also filled with orange juice and slices of lime and lemon and topped with ice.

Alan ceremoniously topped up the champagne glasses with cold Cava and then he handed me a glass.

By then the dehydration had really kicked in and my mouth felt like a sweaty sock.

"Cheers, and down your neck" said Alan.

I took a long, long drink and then I looked back at him and said "god that's good"

"Isn't it just" he agreed "Now then, where did you end up last night?"

"I went back to Gerry's place in his bloody Ferrari. God almighty, he nearly killed us both"

Alan almost fell off his bar stool laughing "Yes I've done that run a few times with him, he's frightened the crap out of me too, but he's a brilliant driver, he could have got into formula one at one time you know"

I nodded and drank, as Alan continued.

"You're actually very lucky, you should thank yours stars that there wasn't a Grand Prix on somewhere this weekend"

"And why's that?" I asked.

Alan smiled "Well I'll tell you, the first time I met Gerry was here at the Varaderos, it's a couple of years ago now, but oh what a night that was. We went on a 'Bourbon extravaganza'. We drank just about everything, from Jack Daniels to Wild Turkey, and by the bottle. When I woke up the next day, we were in Brazil"

"Brazil. Do you mean Brazil, as in 'South American' Brazil?"

"Yes exactly, 'that' Brazil"

"You're joking" I was awe struck.

Alan poured more Bucks Fizz

"No I'm not joking" he said, "You see, we were really, really smashed, and we must have been talking about motor racing and 'old Gerry' gets it into his head that he wants to see the Brazilian Grand Prix, it was on that weekend. I thought he intended to watch it on the telly but, well Gerry's family are massively wealthy, they own some sort of conglomerate with huge businesses all over the place. And it seems they have a private jet at their disposal, it whisks them off all over the world.

Anyway, old Gerry only commandeers the damn thing, gets us both on it, and then orders the pilot to take us to Brazil so that we can both watch the bloody race.

I don't remember much about the flight, apparently we did Tequila Slammers for the first thousand miles and then passed out.

We woke up in a hotel in Sao Paolo. 'The Intercontinental' I think it was, anyway Gerry has contacts over there. Apparently he used to drink with Ayrton Senna or something, and well, one phone call and we suddenly have grandstand tickets for the race. So off we went to the Interlagos Circuit, we watched the race and had a high old time, then we spent the next two days in Rio.

It was absolute madness, and then we finally flew back. When we got home I slept for 48 hours"

Alan poured the last drops of the Bucks Fizz into our now empty glasses.

"My God" I said.

"My God indeed" said Alan "ever since then, if there's a Grand Prix on anywhere I disappear, and you my friend had a lucky escape. I'm not the only one that's ended up on one of Gerry's Formula One binges"

"Lucky for me, I'm flying home today" I said, and I looked across to the bartender "Can we have another of these please?"

He nodded as he turned and reached down into the chiller for more Cava.

I was feeling quite good now "You know, this stuff really works" I said.

Alan beamed "See I told you, it certainly does get you back on the straight and narrow. Now then, what time do you fly out?"

"The 6-00 pm flight to Manchester" I said as I looked at my watch "Christ, its only half past ten"

"Yes my boy its early doors, you've got plenty of time" he said appreciatively as the Bucks Fizz arrived.

Suddenly, a thought struck me.

"Maybe I should have something to eat with this, do you think they could make me some toast?"

"Toast?" said Alan "you can't eat that stuff"

"Why not?"

"Because it's too noisy"

And we both laughed.

"Don't worry" said Alan "when we've had our Bucks Fizz, I'll sort us out some breakfast" and with that he replenished our glasses "another hour and the gang will be here"

"The gang?"

"Yes" he said "the gang, from last night"

"Do you lot drink in here all the time?"

"Oh yes, this is our little oasis, I'll tell you something Derek, 'The Varaderos' is actually one of the best bars and restaurants on the Costa del Sol. We get all sorts of people in here and it's always entertaining. Well look at you, and you've only been here a day."

"Yes" I said "and that's nearly killed me. A week of this would have me in the crematorium".

I refilled our glasses again, "My God, we've nearly finished this bottle too" I said.

Then I looked across at Alan "didn't you mention something about breakfast?"

"Oh yes" he said, and he turned to the barman "Two pints of Guinness please"

"Guinness" I said, rather flabbergasted, now I was worried "Guinness, for breakfast?"

Alan grinned "Oh yes, Guinness, it's the staff of life, 'liquid steak', it's the best thing you can possibly have on an empty stomach"

Having drank nothing but ice cold Bucks Fizz all morning and now Guinness, I began to wonder how long it would be before my 'empty' stomach would start to empty itself.

So Guinness it was, and then we went back on the Bucks Fizz.

The "Gang" started appear in two's and three's and by one o'clock the place was buzzing, I certainly was. I was now drinking beer, in a misguided attempt to stay sober.

I was really having a great time, these people were brilliant, they certainly did have a different view on life and I got into several very different and intriguing conversations.

At three o'clock I decided to go to the hotel and pack my case. It had been decided by general agreement that I should bring my stuff back to the Varaderos Bar so that 'the Gang' could all see me off. So with a lot of effort, I climbed off the bar stool and staggered back across the road and into my hotel.

As I ambled back in there, a lady was already in the lift, she was English and was quite large and she held the lift doors open for me as I stumbled in past the reception. As I squeezed into the lift with her, I turned to thank her and smiled and started to make some inane conversation. She must have got the wrong idea and thought I was trying it on.

The lift doors opened and she told me to "Bugger off" as she pushed me out of the way, and barged out of the lift. I tried to somehow apologize, but the doors quickly closed behind her.

I just stood there for a moment, and considered that I'd had a lucky escape.

I got into my room after a bit of fumbling with the keys and simply threw all my clothes into my suitcase. Then I took the lift back downstairs, signed something at reception, and walked out of the hotel.

As I dragged my case and myself back across the road to the 'Varaderos' a cheer went up, and as I approached the bar there was applause.

"What a guy" said Alan "we've all been betting that you would have collapsed on the bed and missed your plane. Here, have a Jack Daniels and Coke" and he passed me the drink.

"Bastards" I said, and I drank it.

We carried on until four and then the barman dutifully rang one of his cousins, who luckily happened to own a taxi firm. When the taxi arrived, I was 'assisted' onto the back seat with an accompanying cheer from the 'Gang'.

The taxi door was slammed shut to more cheers, and calls of "Come back soon" and "all the best"

Suddenly the door whipped open again, and Alan stuck a bottle of Cava in my lap.

"For the trip home mate" he said, and he quickly shook my hand and waved me goodbye. The taxi u-turned in the road, scattering two Spanish women who had to run to get out of the way or be mowed down, one of them spat at the car. The driver laughed as he shouted something incomprehensible to them. It was all Spanish to me, I was drunk.

Half an hour later, I was ceremoniously dumped at Malaga airport, ticket in hand

and with the time ticking away.

I was already late for my flight, but somehow I managed to get through passenger booking and passport control by feigning flu. I held a large handkerchief to my face to hold back the alcohol fumes, and I answered any questions with a nod or a shake of my head and a variety of long and short groans...given the state I was in, the groaning came quite naturally. Nobody 'official' in Malaga Airport wanted what I'd got, and I was quickly ushered through.

When I eventually reached the terminal gate I was very late, but there were two flight attendants there and they rushed me down the boarding tunnel and onto the plane.

I was the last man on, late and holding up the flight. I was also staggering and had my face covered with a large handkerchief. You should have seen the looks I was getting.

The flight attendant guided me straight to my seat and immediately strapped me in. The poor couple who were sitting next to me looked worried, very worried. So I lowered the handkerchief, and gave them a smile and said "It's alright, I'm just a bit drunk that's all, I've had a bit of a weekend."

The 'couple', who turned out to be 'Ronnie and Eva', were in their early sixties and very suntanned. they just looked at me and then at one another, and then grinned and burst out laughing.

"Don't you worry" said Ronnie, husband of Eva "we're suffering a bit ourselves, we had a bit of a send off last night"

"Thank god for that" I replied.

They introduced themselves, and Ronnie said "We've just done two weeks in Torremolinos, it's been a full on 'all inclusive'. What a trip.

"Oh yes" said Eva "It's been nonstop party-party, never again. Well, not till next year, and she winked at me and she and Ronnie both laughed.

"Thank god this planes finally taking off and we can get some service" said Ronnie.

I glanced out of the passenger window to see that we were indeed moving. The flight attendant was going through her health and safety dialogue and we were actually about to take off.

Five minutes later and we took to the skies.

The three of us had been chatting about Spain, I was very chatty by now.

Eva started rummage in her hand luggage and produced two cans of beer and some plastic cups.

"Oh good" she said, we have enough cups"

"Nice one" said Ronnie, and he turned to me "we always carry something with us instead of waiting for drinks trolley, it can take ages".

"It can" I agreed, as Eva popped the two cans and poured beer into three plastic cups.

"You're very kind and very generous" I continued giddily "Cheers"

I think the change in air pressure was getting to me.

"Cheers" said Ronnie and Eva.

It seemed that they had just been back to Torremolinos for their tenth year, they had done different hotels, but always went back to Torremolinos.

"Why not?" said Eva "if you find somewhere you like, why go anywhere else?"

Ronnie nodded his head in approval.

"I'll drink to that" I said, and I did. We all did.

Cups now empty, Ronnie said "Where's that drinks trolley?" and we looked around to see that it was still loitering at the back of the plane.

"Oh for God's sake" he said.

"Hey, wait a minute" I said, and I reached down into my holdall and produced the bottle of Cava that Alan had given me as I left in the taxi.

Ronnie and Eva looked on.

"What have you got there?" said Eva with a smile.

"Cava, it was given to me by a friend as I was leaving and it's still cold, so pass the cups over folks"

I opened the bottle with a loud pop, and the people opposite gave us the 'disgusted' look as I poured out the Cava into the three plastic cups. It was a touch of class.

We said "Cheers" as we toasted ourselves and we raised our cups, and got more disgusted looks from people opposite.

"We normally only drink Lager or Gin" said Eva "but this is lovely" .

Ronnie totally agreed.

"Travel broadens the horizons" I stated, and in my case it certainly had.

The drinks trolley finally arrived and I asked if they had any Cava.

"Oh no" said the blonde flight attendant smartly "We only do Champagne" she said, with a touch of the aloof.

"I'll have two then"

"What?"

"Two" I repeated "bring us a couple of bottles of your Champagne, and do you have some nice glasses please."

For a moment she was flustered, and then with a "Err...I'll get you some" she regained her composure and flitted off.

A few minutes later, she was back with the Champagne and some real glasses.

I thanked her and paid with my credit card and a smile. She turned out to be quite pleasant really.

"Here" I said and handed Ronnie and Eva a bottle "We're flying back in style, Cheers"

"This is very generous of you" said Ronnie, with Eva nodding in agreement.

"No" I burbled on hazily "your warmth, friendship and your own generosity have been overwhelming, and I thank you both" and I raised my glass and continued "plus,

I could have been sat next to those two miserable gits opposite"

The miserable gits opposite looked away, but they were still disgusted.

I looked at Derek through the mirror.

"And that" he finally said to me "that was Marbella, what a trip"

I was amazed "Unbelievable, and your still alive and kicking, thank god"

He nodded and laughed.

"Well, you'll remember that trip" I said.

"Yes, I certainly will"

"Hey, hang on a minute" I said "what has all this to do with your broken legs?"

Derek grinned, and was hesitant for a moment "Oh yes, I fell off the plane"

"What?"

"I fell off the plane at Manchester Airport, onto the tarmac.

"Bloody hell, how?"

He looked back at me through the mirror and then with one hand, he rubbed his eyes.

"Well you see, by the time we landed at Manchester I was totally rolling drunk. I hadn't stopped boozing all day and I'd also been out all night. Anyway, the plane came in to land and finally rolled to a halt. The seat belts signs were turned off and we sort of stood up, we'd been sitting next to one of the exits and so we were the first off. At the top of the stairway as we were leaving the plane, I turned to thank the flight attendant for the Champagne and the lovely flight and well, I missed the top step of the stairway and somersaulted down the rest. I landed face down on the tarmac, legs askew."

"Good god Derek" I said "what did you do?"

"Well" he continued "Ronnie and Eva dashed down the steps to help me, followed by the flight attendant. It was all a bit of a commotion, I kept telling them that I was all right, but I was very drunk and I couldn't stop laughing.

Apparently, I kept shouting."Hey, I've just fallen off the bloody plane".

Ronnie and Eva thought it was hilarious, the flight attendant did not.

Anyway, Ronnie and Eva persuaded the flight attendant to get me a wheelchair, and told her that I was just drunk and that they would take care of me. The flight attendant, seeing a way of solving the problem without the chance of being sued, very smartly acquired a wheelchair. So there I was, inebriated and slightly concussed, being pushed along by a slightly tipsy couple into Manchester International Airport.

We must have looked a real sight.

Passport Control and Baggage was a bit of a haze, but we got through it and the next thing I know, we were outside at a Taxi rank. Ronnie and Eva got me into a taxi with the help of the driver, they managed to bundle me into the back seat and then they waved me goodbye. I told the driver to go to Bolton, and off we went.

Two miles down the motorway and things were not going too good. My legs had started to pulsate and began take on a life of their own.

I vaguely remember saying to the driver "Do you know were Bolton General Hospital is?" and then I passed out.

Remarkably, I actually woke up in Bolton General Hospital, 24 hours later.

The taxi driver, bless him had driven me straight there. He'd taken me at my word and thought that I'd just fallen asleep in the back of his cab.

When I awoke, I had a very bad headache and I had very bad leg ache, well two very bad leg aches.

As I lay there, with the hangover from hell, a nurse came over and seeing that there was still some life in me, she said "and how are you?"

I felt like I'd been hit by an axe, and then run over.

"Not good" I managed to reply.

"Well" she said "You've hit your head quite badly and you've also managed to fracture both of your legs, and you smell like a brewery" and she looked at me quizzically.

"Is there anything I can get you?"

"Water" I croaked.

She returned a minute later with a large glass of iced water.

I drank it slowly, "Nectar" I whispered to her.

"T'is better than the booze" she said, and as she spoke, I heard the accent.

"Where are you from?" I asked her.

"Ireland" she said, and she smiled.

"I was in hospital for another three days before they would let me out. It was all X-rays and crutches, but I finally got out and went home, that was about three weeks ago. Since then, I've been in recuperation".

"Well Derek" I said to him "I've got to say, for a man who's been through all that, you're in remarkably good spirits. Marbella's done you good, you're a changed man".

He looked back at me through the mirror and gave a curious smile.

"Ah well" he said "you see, it doesn't just end there"

"Oh yes"

"Yes" he said, and then hesitantly "I'm seeing a girl"

"Really, well good on you man".

Derek was quite happy with that, though he hardly needed my consent.

"And who's the lucky lady?" I said.

"The nurse" he grinned.

"The Irish Girl" I said.

"Yes" and he laughed and I smiled.

"She's been looking after me, it was during those three days in hospital, we got talking and became friends, sort of just hit it off. She's really nice and she's great to talk to. When it came to being discharged, I wanted to keep in touch so I gave her my address and my phone number. The day after she drove round to see me and ever since then, well it's been great.

"I'm really pleased for you Derek" I said "she sounds lovely".

"Oh she is, really lovely".

And I was pleased, genuinely pleased. It was so good to see him happy for the first time in a very long while, and for me, it was like seeing someone recover from a serious illness, and that was good.

Haircut finished and beard mown down, I rang Derek a taxi.

As he left the shop and I was helping him into the back of the taxi, I said "Good luck with everything buddy, I hope everything works out alright".

He turned to me as he got into his seat, then he nodded back and said "Don't worry, it will" and he waved to me out of the window as the taxi drove off down the road.

I watched the taxi slowly disappear into the distance, and I stood there contemplating Derek's story. As I walked back into the shop, I thought about his antics again and I laughed to myself as I picked up the brush and swept up an extremely large pile of hair.

Only five or six weeks later the phone rang, and it was Derek.

"I need a haircut" he announced.

"So soon?" I said. I was quite surprised, this was not like him, not at all.

"I'm under orders" he replied.

"Ah I see, so she's smartening you up then eh?"

He laughed "Yes, it looks that that way"

And with that, I knew things must be going well and that they were obviously still together. So he booked himself in for the next day, at one o'clock in the afternoon.

And like clockwork, at one on the dot the following day, Derek arrived in a taxi and this time no crutches. He was now on walking sticks.

I ceremoniously opened the door for him, and in he tottered.

I sat him in the chair and got ready to cut his hair, and after a "and how are we doing buddy?"

He looked at me through the mirror, swallowed, and said it straight out.

"I'm getting married"

"What?"

"I'm getting married"

I laughed out loud "What, to the Irish girl?"

"Yes"

"Really"

"Yes"

Then we both laughed and I shook his hand.

"Derek" I said "I am really so pleased for you, really pleased"

"Thanks" he said

"And when did this all happen?"

"Well you know we met in hospital and we just hit it off, and so we've been seeing a lot of each other, in fact" and he gave a sort of nervous grin "in fact, she's moved in to my place. Err... well it makes more sense" and he twitched slightly in the chair.

"Good man." I said to him, and that seemed to make him more at ease. You'd think we were living in the Victorian times.

He continued "Well, she was living in her flat and I was living in my house, which has loads of space. We'd talked, and we talked about our futures and you know, we're both adults, we're not teenagers anymore, and no responsibilities to anybody and no children. I'm on my own and she left Ireland a long time ago and has lost touch with any family she ever had over there, she's never been in contact with anyone for years.

And so we decided, well we talked about doing the right thing and getting engaged, and all of that just seemed a ridiculous waste of time. You get engaged to get married, we just wanted to be married, so why waste time. So we decided to get on with it, sort of take the 'bull by the horns' instead of dithering about."

"Well that seems fair enough" I said "what a good idea"

"Thanks, we thought so too"

"So what's the plan of attack?" I asked him

Derek beamed, with a smile that went from ear to ear "Barbados" he said "We're getting married on a beach in Barbados in exactly three weeks time" and he grinned at me.

"Three weeks, hey that's brilliant. So you didn't consider going back to Marbella and tying the knot over there with 'your mates', you know...'the gang'?" and I laughed at him.

"Not bloody likely" he said "my wife-to-be isn't going to let me anywhere near Marbella ever again"

"Yes" I said "or she could easily end up being a widow".

"Yes" said Derek "Anyway, three weeks from today and with a bit of luck I should be off these sticks and it's off to Manchester Airport and away we go".

"I hope you're using a different airline too" I laughed.

"Definitely" he said nodding his head "Definitely".

So we talked, and discussed his wedding plans, and eventually I finished cutting

Derek's hair. His taxi finally arrived, and after a bit of backslapping I tipped him into the back seat, wished him good luck and all the best, and then waved him off.

And I smiled to myself. It's funny how things work out.

About six weeks late, the phone in the shop rang, and it was Derek.

"Hello there you 'Married Man', and how are we?" I enquired enthusiastically.

"Great" he said.

"Did everything go okay?"

"Yes great" he said again, in a very businesslike manner.

I shook my head and thought 'Oh well, back to normal, 'one word' answers to everything, typical Derek'.

"I need a haircut as soon as possible, it's a mess and I'm really busy"

"Well my last appointment tonight's free" I said as I looked down at my appointment book.

"Good, I'll take it"

"My god" I said "you're in a rush"

"Oh, you won't believe what's happened since I last saw you"

"Why, what's wrong?" I asked him.

"I'll tell you later, I can't speak, I'm waiting for a phone call"

And with that, he put the phone down.

I just stood there, still with the phone in my hand, wondering what on earth had happened, And after quickly considering every option, starting with pregnancy and ending with death, I put the phone down.

I would just have to wait.

Evening arrived, and so did Derek. No sticks now and he's back driving, he has an old Nissan Micra, all red and rust. He jerked the car to a sudden stop, right outside the shop and came through the door like a whirlwind.

"Hi there" I said to him, a bit hesitantly.

"Hi" he said breathlessly, and he gave me a sort of weird smile.

And I thought 'Oh well, it can't be death then'.

"Are you alright Derek?" I asked him.

He immediately went over and sat himself in the chair. I was a bit taken aback, and then he turned and looked up at me.

"You're not going to believe this" he said, all wide eyed "What's happened is unbelievable"

I stared back at him, and took a deep breath. "Go on then" I said.

And he started to tell me.

"Our lives have been totally thrown upside down, I can't believe what's happened to us both"

"You did get married? I asked.

"Oh yes...yes we got married. We went off to Barbados, everything was great, we arrived at Manchester airport, the flight was on time and off we flew. We had a wonderful time, the food on board the plane, and the champagne, it was all brilliant.

We landed in Barbados and were chauffeured to our hotel 'The Fairmont Royal Pavilion'. What a place that is, our room led directly onto the beach, it was heaven. For three days we did nothing but relax. We just lay on the beach and had our food brought to us there in our room. Towards the weekend, we sorted out the arrangements for our wedding.

We had the ceremony on the Sunday afternoon. It was all very proper and we dressed up for the occasion, it was a beautiful day, there on the white sand. Just a simple ceremony, it was quite quick really. After the service, we had a meal on our own at a table on the beach at the water's edge. We took our shoes off and had the warm sea under our feet as we sat there, it was all very formal, she was in her wedding dress and I was in my suit. We had champagne and lobster, it was so romantic.

Then with another week to go, we explored the island. We found some beautiful secluded beaches and then we would go and find one of the local places for an entertaining lunch, usually washed down with some beers and the local rum.

We had a great time, it was unforgettable.

And then at the end of two brilliant weeks, we flew back home and landed in Manchester. It was raining as usual, but what the hell. We were married and had just had a fantastic honeymoon, we had the best of time ever, and my thinking was 'Well, let's get on with the rest of our lives'.

We'd been home, two days I think it was, and we were supposed to start work the following day, both of us.

It was late afternoon and the phone rang, and I picked it up, it was somebody phoning from Ireland and it turned out to be a solicitor, it seems he'd been trying to trace my wife. And so, a little mystified, I passed her the phone.

There was a fairly lengthy conversation, and at the end of it she simply put the phone down and turned to me.

Then she said quietly "We've got to go to Ireland, tomorrow. My mother's died and it's her funeral".

I was stunned. We'd talked about our past lives, obviously I'd told her all about Jill, and she'd spoken about her past life in Ireland, she'd left about fifteen years ago to come to England to pursue her career as a nurse. She had very little family left in Ireland, and in fact, the way she'd spoken gave me to think that her parents had died years ago. There'd never been any mention of her mother.

She looked at me in a very direct way "That was the family solicitor, he's been trying to contact me but obviously we've been away. She had a heart attack, the funerals tomorrow afternoon at three o'clock in 'Tullrooly', that's the town I come from. I have to go. He says that he needs to speak to me, something about tidying up my mother's affairs. I have to go, or..." and then she blinked and suddenly looked uncomfortable "I'll go on my own if you can't make it", and she said these last words slowly, and I knew that she really needed me with her.

"Hey" I said "You're my wife now, we'll both go."

She smiled back at me "Thank you love, I need some backup".

"Don't worry. So now then, let's get organized. You make dinner and I'll sort out the flights. Where are we flying to by the way?" I asked.

"Dublin"

"Dublin it is then"

An hour later, and with the flights booked, we sat down to dinner. I opened a good bottle of red wine that I'd bought especially for our homecoming.

We ate and we drank, and the wine mellowed us.

Finally, I just said it "So do you want to talk about your mother?"

She looked across the table at me, and then slowly said "My Mother?"

She was suddenly angry, no more than that, she was bitter, and for a moment she stared into nowhere, then she replied "Where do I start, God...my mother"

Then she looked back at me and sighed "Yes okay, I'll tell you all about her" and she leant back in her chair.

"It seems like a lifetime ago, well it is really. I left Ireland to come to England, you see I ran away Derek, I ran away from home, away from home and away from my mother"

She took a sip of wine "all my memories as a child are of my mother and father arguing, constantly arguing. He was a good-looking man and a gambler and I think other women were involved too. I remember, ours was a little terraced house, only small. I would have only been about ten years old, and one afternoon I was sitting on the sofa in our front room watching the television, my mother was doing the ironing. At one point, she asked me to go to the corner shop for a loaf of bread. I remember complaining that I would miss the programme that I was watching, but she insisted because my father would soon be home for his tea. She reached for her purse, and she opened it, and suddenly gasped, and then she cursed. She looked over to me and then told me not to bother. I told her that I would go but she just shook her head and continued with the pile of ironing, I didn't understand. Within the hour my father arrived home, he'd been drinking. As he walked into the front room, my mother simply picked up the hot iron and hit him in the face with it. He fell over onto the floor.

Then she pounced on top of him and leaned over him with the hot iron just inches away from his face.

She spat out her words "You've stolen my money for the last time you bastard", she was shaking with anger "you'll go now or I'll burn your fucking face off, I will, believe me I will"

He sat there on the floor, propped up against the wall, and I saw the fear in him.

"You'll go now, get to your fancy piece and live with her. You come back here, and I'll kill you, understand?" and with that, she touched his cheek with the edge of the hot iron. He screamed with the pain of it and he tried to back away, but she moved nearer to him, the hot iron clenched in her hand so he couldn't escape. He looked up at her and I knew in his face that he was beaten.

That was the last time I ever saw him. He just went, he never ever came back to see me, never.

After that we were both on our own, and my mother's character changed, she hardened.

Now she was on her own, she was stuck with me, and she had little or no money. She worked as a cleaner at different houses, and she would take in cleaning and do stitching and repairing people's clothes until late into the night.

My mother had no time for love, not for me or anybody else.

She never went out, never enjoyed herself. She'd always had a temper and now I felt the worst of it. She seemed to be forever shouting at me, there was no affection, not anymore If I did anything wrong, if I did anything at all to upset her, she would go to the sideboard in the living room and open the middle drawer and take out her hairbrush. She had this brush, it was oval in shape like a paddle and was made from dark, shiny mahogany with stiff black bristles. She would beat me with that brush, beat me badly. I can remember it, remember it all. You see Derek, I was terrified of her, absolutely terrified.

She was stuck in that awful house, and she was lonely and she was poor, and she was stuck with me.

By the time I was sixteen, I'd had a lifetime of it and I'd had enough. I enrolled to go to college and at the same time I started to work part-time in a care home, to bring in some money. I lied about my wages and I began to save. Eventually I had enough money, and then one day I simply packed a suitcase and left home. As I was leaving the house, I took the mahogany brush out of the drawer and placed it in the middle of the kitchen table.

It was a message, the only message I needed to leave.

I got a taxi to the docks, got on the ferry to Liverpool and started a new life. You see Derek, I always wanted to be a nurse"

She stopped talking and looked at me.

"So that was your Mother?" I said.

"That was my Mother" she replied, and she gave me the saddest of smiles.

Early next morning, we went to Manchester Airport to fly to Dublin and typically, there's a delay. An hour becomes two hours, then three, and by the time we got onboard and ready for takeoff, we were seriously late. We sat on the plane silent and stressed.

"Are you okay?" I said to her.

"Not really. I...I'm just wondering what sort of reception I'm going to get from my relatives, or anyone else who's there"

"And who'll actually be there?" I asked.

She shook her head "I don't know really, it's been over twenty years and I never kept in touch. I only remember a couple of aunties and uncles, they could have all died too. I don't know 'what' to expect"

"It'll be alright, you'll see" I said and I squeezed her hand. She smiled, but she was still anxious.

We eventually landed at Dublin and jumped straight into a Taxi.

An hour later, we arrived at the church in the small provincial town of Tullrooly, just ten minutes before the funeral was about to start. The weather was grey and dull, with all the signs of the looming Irish rain. There were only a few people there, they turned out to be an elderly aunt and uncle, 'Annie and Bill', and there were some cousins, and a couple of elderly ladies who were old neighbours, also turned up. To our surprise we were met with open arms, she was hugged and kissed and there was a lot of emotion, it was as if she was a long lost child. Well, she was really.

"I thought you wouldn't want to know me" she choked "I just left you all, I've never been in touch I know, I just couldn't".

Her aunty and uncle cried. She was hugged by all the family in turn, even the neighbours were in tears.

The funeral itself was a cold affair. A priest who had never known her, tried to speak about someone he never knew, it was all a bit of a nothing.

When the funeral was over, we all went across the road from the church to 'The Tullrooly Hotel'. Aunty Annie had organized something for us all to eat and drink after the funeral. We all had a large Jameson's Irish whiskey to toast her mother and then we tucked into the food, good meat on good bread, pies and salad. And oh yes, Guinness.

We were comfortable and everybody seemed at ease, conversations flowed, family history was discussed and finally we talked about her mother.

Some eyebrows were raised. Even the old neighbours had their say.

Uncle Bill took a drink from his glass of Guinness, paused a moment, and then spoke.

"Your mother was a difficult woman, we all knew that. She was always troubled, even when she was young, but your father brought out the worst in her. When they met, well your mother hadn't had much to do with men, it was her attitude, she would frighten them off. She was always very critical, nobody was ever good enough. And then along comes your father, a born liar, and that was the problem you see, he always had all the right answers for your mother. He was a good looking man and dark haired, that's where you get your colouring from"

Uncle Bill paused for a moment "He was handsome and could tell a tale, and of course he was much more experienced than your mother. And well, he threw money about, that was the gambler in him, he was always up and down with the money, but your mother couldn't see it. She just loved the bloody man, and that was it, there was the problem.

We tried, all of us, the family, her mother, all of us tried to make her see sense and see what a worthless bastard he was, but she just stuck her heels in, and in the end she fell out with us all. They both disappeared one weekend, and a week later they came back, married and honeymooned. Not long after that, she became pregnant with you. But they were never right, he was soon back out drinking and gambling, there was never any money"

"And the woman" suddenly Auntie Annie joined in.

"Aye" continued Bill "and always some bloody tart, and after she threw him out, and because of her stubborn bloody pride, she wouldn't come back to the family. She kept us all at arm's length, even her own mother. She didn't want to have anything to do with us, her and her foolish bloody pride. She had a hard life, cleaning houses and taking in the laundry and the stitching and the sewing. We tried to help out, we all offered to look after you when you were little, but she resented it, said we were interfering, and in the end she stopped us all seeing you altogether, it broke your grandma's heart. Your mother kept well away, just stayed in that house, alone with you. So, what can I tell you, the years rolled on, you're mother never let you out much and she was very controlling. Then we heard that you'd left home and disappeared, nobody blamed you love, I think we almost expected it. And then a strange thing happened, about a year after you left, an old man that your mother used to clean for, it was old Mr Caswell. Well he died, and in his will he left her everything, the house, the furniture, everything, and some money. I don't think it was a fortune or anything like that, but it was money. He didn't have any family, he had nobody really, and your mother had always looked after him. She would cook and clean for him and he must have felt she deserved it, so suddenly, there she was, with a spare house and some cash."

One of the ladies who had been an old neighbour, laughed.

"I remember that" she said "I remember her getting the house and that money, that was when she came to see me, she came round to my house, just knocked on my door one night. I opened the door and I let her in, she was all agitated".

"Why was that?" asked Uncle Bill.

"Because she had a plan" said the lady, her name was Mary, and she had been a neighbour for over forty years. She continued "She had a plan, and it turned out that I was going to be her stepping stone"

We were all intrigued.

"It was late one Friday night, I always remember that it was a Friday because that was rent night and 'Smedley', that money grabbing landlord of mine had been round for his cash. He owned most of the houses in the area and we all had to pay him rent. It was the rent that made us all poor you see, whatever money was left after that went on food, and that was about it. Well, your mother knocked on my door, and really, I was surprised to see her. We were sort of friendly but we were never close, but I'd done her a few favours, usually a bit of babysitting if she was very busy. She stood at my door and asked to come in, said she wanted to talk to me. I was a bit apprehensive because I knew what she could be like, but I let her in and put the kettle on. We sat at the table talking, with two mugs of sweet tea, and then she put a proposition to me.

"I'm going to Dublin" she said "I'm off"

"Are you really?" I said. I was surprised.

"I've got a plan, and if it works I could save you a lot of money Mary"

"Could you now" I said slowly.

"Yes" she said "I can change your life Mary"

Well, now she had my attention.

"I'm going to sell old Mr Caswell's house to Smedley, he says he'll buy it off me for cash and it's a fair price he's offering"

I wasn't impressed, that money grabber had enough property. He loved to own people.

"And how does that help me?" I said.

"My house is on a mortgage, I don't pay rent, I own it, and now I've nearly paid it off"

I looked at her, and I couldn't believe that she'd been able to manage it, I was astounded.

She said "I haven't scrimped and saved and worked like a slave all these years for nothing. Now listen Mary, this is what I want to do. I want you to move into my house, come out of this place and move into my house. I know what rent your paying and I'm prepared to charge you half that rent, and I'll fix it at that and never charge you a penny more, forever".

I was taken aback, if she really meant this it would mean that I could live an easier life. Half the rent, and forever. It was too good to pass, I couldn't believe it.

"Do you mean it?" I asked her straight out.

"Yes, but there's only one thing" she then said.

'Here we go' I thought, and so I asked her "Yes, and what's that?"

"If things don't work out for me in Dublin, I'll come back here and move back into my house, and before you start, just listen. Whatever happens, and if do have to come back, well you can stay here with me and live in the house 'rent free' forever."

I stared back at her "free...forever, really forever?"

"Forever, only 'if' I do have to come back"

"So I can't lose, either way" I said.

She nodded slowly "You can't lose Mary, either way"

"It's a deal darlin" I said quietly, and we actually shook hands on it.

"What will you do in Dublin?" I asked her

But she just stood up.

"I have plans" she said "I'll be in touch" and with that, she turned and walked out of the house.

Mary looked at us "Three weeks later I moved into your old family house. I've been there now for nearly twenty five years and true to her word, she never changed the rent."

Then Mary stammered a little and looked slightly embarrassed "It's only a pittance now"

"So she never came back?" I asked.

"I've never seen her since, not once in twenty five years"

"Who do you pay the rent to?"...Auntie Annie asked.

"Dooley and Breen, they're solicitors in Dublin, I send the rent to them".

My wife interrupted the conversation, "They're the solicitors that rang to tell me that my mother had died, we've got to go and see them tomorrow in Dublin to sort out my mother's affairs"

"I suppose that's my house" Mary said quietly.

My wife looked at her "Mary, nothing's going to change, you can stay in the house. It's like my mother said 'forever', and that was the deal"

Mary gave us a nervous smile "Thank you, thank you very much darlin."

Uncle Bill broke the moment "Dooley and Breen. I remember Dooley's solicitors, they used to be here in town, it was old Mr Dooley that handled your mothers divorce. Old man Dooley had a son that came into the business, he was very sharp, I think his name was Peter"

"Yes, that's who I spoke to, that's who we're meeting tomorrow", my wife looked at me and nodded in recognition.

Bill spoke again "When young Peter took over the business from his father, the firm grew very quickly, and the next thing we heard was that they'd bought into a partnership in large commercial solicitors over in Dublin. They closed up shop here and moved on, that was a few years ago now"

"Well" I said "We're going to go to Dublin tomorrow, and sort out Mary's house with this Dooley guy and then we've got to get back to the U.K. straight away, my boss has been on the phone to me and they want me back as soon as possible.

And with that, the conversation changed, the drinks were refuelled, stories were told and jokes were laughed at.

A few hours quickly passed and finally it was time for everyone to go.

Thankfully, we'd booked the night in the Tullrooly Hotel, and so we were staying there.

A minibus had been ordered for the relatives, and when it arrived we all filed outside to say our good-byes. We all promised that we would keep in touch, my wife was in tears, but as happy as I'd ever seen her.

Mary was one of the last to get in the minibus and she took hold of both our hands.

"I just want to thank you for your kindness, I've been really worried over what was going to happen to me"

We smiled at her, and my wife said it all "Mary, we've no plans for Ireland. I left a long time ago and was never for coming back, it's nothing but bad memories for me. My life is in England with this man, I've loved seeing the family but I don't think we'll ever be back, there's nothing for me here anymore. The house is yours, we're going to give it to you, I'll see to that tomorrow."

Mary burst into tears, and I nearly did as well but for different reasons. Christ, she'd just given a bloody house away!

They hugged and Mary got in the minibus and off they all went. We stood there and waved them off...

"Come on, let's have a nightcap before we go to bed" I said.

We went back to the bar, and sat on two bar stools and ordered two large Jameson's Irish. We sat there for a moment, quietly sipping the whiskey.

"Can I ask you something?" I eventually said.

"Yes" and she smiled, and there was a warm look in her eyes.

"Was it wise" and I tried to sound a little bit matter-of- fact, "err, was it wise just to give away a house just like that?"

And she pounced "Ha, I knew it, I knew it" and she laughed, thank god.

"I saw your face, ha...ha, 'money, money, money" and she rubbed her two fingers together in front of my face.

She laughed again "Order us two more Jameson's and I'll tell you something"

I did as I was told. The drinks arrived, and she faced me, smiling, and then she spoke her mind.

"Derek, I love you, but this is how it is. I never, ever want to walk back into that house. I hated it and I want nothing to do with it ever again. It's something from my past and I want to put it to rest. We have our own home and we don't need that one, we don't, do we?"

It was neither a statement nor a question, it was simply a fact.

"No" I said, and I saw the sense in it "we never owned it and we don't need it"

We touched glasses and went to bed happy.

The next day, we went Dublin.

In the morning we left the Hotel to take a taxi into Dublin, and in what should have been a leisurely hour's drive into the city, we did in just twenty-five minutes.

The Taxi driver turned out to be a lunatic.

We spent the whole trip hanging on for dear life as he dodged and weaved between parked cars and articulated wagons. In the end my wife finally started to scream as we dodged out of the way a low loader, which at the time was trying to avoid a milk float.

I grabbed our driver's shoulder, and began to shout at him.

"Bloody well slow down, you'll kill us all at this rate".

His reply "Oh, a fockin' English, go on yer soft man"

My wife retorted angrily "Hey I'm Irish, not English"

"Well, yer shouldn't have fockin' married one" he shouted, and then the bastard laughed.

We finally arrived, white knuckled, outside the offices of Dooley and Breen.

We got out of the taxi, shaken. I paid the idiot and he set off back to Tullrooly like Michael Schumacher.

As we stood outside I looked up at the Dooley and Breen Building, it was about twenty storeys high, all glass and steel.

"Impressive" I said "Young Mr Dooley's done alright for himself" and I laughed as we walked through the two sliding glass doors and into the entrance.

My wife smiled back at me "God, I don't think my mother's rent will have paid for all this" she said, and we chuckled like a couple of conspirators.

I looked around the building, it was 'very' stylish.

I said "I'll tell you something love, this Peter Dooley must be some really sharp guy, look at this place, it sure is all a bit 'wow'.

We went to reception and told a very efficient dark haired girl who we were, and that we had an appointment with Peter...Peter Dooley. She looked at her appointment list and then looked back at us and her eyes widened.

"I'll get him on the phone, right now" she said, rather too urgently.

I turned to my wife and whispered "He must be a real bastard to work for"

Anyway, two minutes later the chrome doors of the lift slid open and out stepped Mr Peter Dooley. He spotted us immediately, and came over, smiling like a car salesman. He was dressed in an immaculate dark blue suit and looked as cool as a cucumber.

'Bloody hell' I thought 'it's James Bond'.

My wife swooned.

Here we go. I had a theory, and we were going to get ripped off.

Peter Dooley was scrupulously charming, and my wife continued to swoon as I gave him my thinnest of smiles as he introduced himself and led us towards the lift.

Once in the lift, and as we shot forever upwards, my wife just kept nodding and saying "Yes" to everything he said.

I kept my distance, as you do when you think your wife could be contemplating having an affair. Anyway, we finally arrived on the top floor and were ushered into his office, it was absolutely stupendous, and I felt the noose tighten.

Peter Dooley's private office had a full 180 degree view of Dublin, it was a stunning.

"It's a long way from Tullrooly" I quipped.

Peter laughed "Not in my Porsche it's not. I'll order us coffee" he said, smiling at my wife.

Would nothing faze this man, if only I'd had a gun.

The coffee arrived via a very attractive blonde secretary, Peter smiled at her appreciatively.

"Ah Heather, thank you very much, and could you bring me in the papers and the will now please".

Heather looked at him and smiled back, and that smile was about three seconds too long.

I thought 'Yes, and there's the next Mrs Dooley, whether he's already married or not'.

We sat down as Heather went out of the office and then efficiently returned with the papers as required. She was very good. She laid out the papers out on the desk for Peter, just like the good wife she was going to be.

Peter walked over and sat on the edge of his desk to face us. Through the large glass windows behind him was the large expanse of Dublin City, and this guy looked like he owned it all.

He sat on his desk and simply pushed the papers that he had asked for to one side and dismissed them.

He looked at us both, paused for a moment, and then turned to my wife.

"What do you actually know about your mother?" he asked.

"I beg your pardon" she replied.

"I'm just asking, what do you know about your mother?"

My wife became flustered, and then a little angry, and then a little more than angry.

"What do you mean by that?" she shot back at him "are you here trying to prove whether or not I'm her daughter, because if so, you're barking up the wrong tree here my friend. I've only come over to Ireland out of respect for the rest of the family. Yes, I'm her daughter, and if you want to know what 'I know' about my mother, I'll tell you straight"

She was now getting really angry, and I secretly smiled, I'm a coward.

"My Mother was a bitch, a nasty, nasty piece of work. She beat me and she bullied me as a child and she hadn't a good word for anyone, so if you're looking for the doting daughter, just so I can get my hands on that old house you can forget it, and stuff the house. The only reason I've come here is to sign it over to the old woman who rents it. I don't want the bloody house, and do you want to know why, because for years it was my prison. So I'll tell you what, we're leaving and you can forget it, in fact send the bill for the rent to me and I'll pay it", and she nodded her head at me for us to go, and go at once.

"A Euro a year" Peter Dooley said, and then he laughed.

We stood there for a moment, and my wife said "What?"

"A Euro, the old lady, all she pays is a Euro. One Euro a year, that's the rent.

As we looked at him, Peter Dooley raised his hands, and shook his head and smiled.

My wife was now slightly confused "She only charges her a euro for a year's rent?"

"Yes, that's right" said Peter and he leaned forwards, with a look of anticipation.

We looked at one another and my wife spoke to Peter again.

"She only charges Mary one euro a year...only a euro for a year's rent, how could she do that..? How could she afford it, I mean, she still had to make a living, how could she survive on only charging a euro for the rent?"

"Ah" said the smiling Peter Dooley "and that's what I was coming to. So can I ask you again, how well did you know your mother?"

She looked straight at him "Besides her being a complete bitch, I know nothing about her, not after I left home anyway. You see, once I left, I was never going to get in touch with her, ever again. I've made a new life for myself in England"

"Okay" said Peter, and he paused before he spoke to us.

"Twenty five years ago your mother called at our old offices in Tullrooley. She came to see my father to tell him that she was going to Dublin. Before she went, she told him that she wanted us to collect the rent on her house, it was only in later years that she reduced it to a euro per year. She also wrote her will"

Peter picked up an old brown manila envelope with some faded handwriting on the front.

"This is it, her original will. She never, ever changed it, although at times we did advise her to update it. Your mother however, wouldn't change the wording or anything else, all she would ever say was "let it stand".

My wife stared at the envelope, and it was as though her mother had just entered the room.

"What's in it?" she almost whispered.

"I can tell you without reading it" he said "Your Mother, quite simply, left everything to you. It was her single wish. You were her flesh and blood, and no matter what had happened between you both, it didn't make any difference to her, that was how she wanted it. Whether it was to somehow make amends, I do not know, your mother was a very private person and very single minded."

"I...I don't know why me?" my wife shook her head "I hated her"

"People are strange" said Dooley "you'll never know what's going on inside someone's head, especially your mother's".

"You knew her well?"

"As well as anybody I suppose, but she was a closed book, she never let anyone into her thoughts or I think, her heart, it's possibly the old thing about never getting hurt again. She even left strict instructions about her funeral, nobody was supposed to attend. I know you went but she just wanted to be buried and that was that. No fuss at all"

My wife sighed "Well I suppose what's done is done" and she looked at me and at her watch

"So Peter, let's sort this house thing out. I don't want it, and we've decided to give it to Mary. We've got to get back to Manchester sometime today, Derek's company need him back at work".

Peter Dooley straightened up and said "I'm afraid it's not just as simple as that"

I suddenly straightened up too "Here we go" I said "it's the bill isn't it, we've ended up with the bloody bill"

Peter shook his head and smiled at us, and that worried me too.

"Just let me tell you a bit about your mother" said Dooley "Please, take a seat, and please, sit yourselves down"

We did as he asked, and then he told us a tale.

"Your Mother arrived in Dublin twenty five years ago, armed with the money from the sale of old Mr Caswell's house and a suitcase. It was a different Dublin in those days, the city was not spread out like it is today, there were just rows and rows of dilapidated houses and a lot of run down property, both in dwellings and commercial property. When she arrived, your mother rented a cheap house, and back then there were plenty of them. Then, for over a month, she simply walked around Dublin City. She walked everywhere, around the different streets and all the different areas of Dublin. And by doing that, she got to know the city, and got to know the feel of the city. In fact, she got to know it like the back of her hand.

She looked at houses, large and small, in all the different areas of Dublin, and she began to realize the possibilities.

Eventually, she bought her first property, well actually two properties. It was about two months later and she bought a pair of really run down terraced houses, very small, but very cheap. She put down a deposit on them both. My father handled it for her. She always used us and always trusted us. She then lived in one and had the other done up. The house was really rough, but she somehow lived in it while she got the builders to totally revamp next door. Then she moved into the modernised property and had them do up her remaining house.

With both properties now prim and proper, she put them on the market, six months later and they were still unsold. She was stuck, and she knew it, and her money was beginning to run out. Then she had a stroke of inspiration. She called the builders back in and had them knock down the interior walls that divided both properties, then she bricked up one of the front doors and jiggled about with the interiors. When she'd finished she was left with one big house. By joining the two properties together and making it one bigger house, she suddenly had something that was a lot more attractive, and it sold, it sold straight away, and more importantly she realized a decent profit.

Now that first project sort of 'lit a fire' under your mother. She'd finally made money, her own money. And from there, she began to buy very cheap terraced properties and do exactly the same thing. Adjoining properties knocked into one, all nicely done up and with plenty of space, and slowly but surely, she began to make a very good return on her money. She always used the same builder 'Jimmy Horan' she always paid him on time, although her no nonsense attitude kept him on his toes, she wouldn't put up with any mistakes or excuses. Horan's are in a big way today, they're one of Dublin's largest civil contractors.

Then she had a brainwave, it was so simple, but no one else had seen the opportunity.

She found a whole street of condemned houses, a full row and all of them empty. I think there were about twenty houses, and she bought the lot. People had left and slowly the whole street had become deserted, you couldn't sell any house on that street. She picked up the lot for a song, and then, the really clever bit.

She met up with Jimmy Horan up and gave him his instructions.

As she walked him down the empty street, she pointed to the first house.

"See that house"

"Yes" said Jimmy

"Knock it down" she told him.

"What" said Jimmy?

"I said, knock it down"

Jimmy took a breath, he didn't understand.

"See the second house"

Again Jimmy "Yes"

"Leave it up"

"Right" said Jimmy

"But the next one along, I want you to knock that down too, and then the next one, leave that one up, and carry on like that down the whole street. And what we're going to do Jimmy, is instead of having twenty terraced house, we're going to have ten detached houses. And in the spaces in between, we're going to use all the demolished spare brick to build a garage onto each house, and we'll extend at the rear and put on a kitchen extension with an extra bedroom over the top, and along with that, each house will have its own small garden. We'll do up the internals and put in a nice new bathroom, and then we'll give the outsides a good sandblasting and they'll look brand new".

And that's exactly what they did.

Half way through construction, she did another deal and bought all the houses on the opposite side of the street, she realized that people wouldn't buy a new house if it faced an empty condemned property. But in buying both sides of the street she'd created an area of affordable new houses and people liked them, they were stylish and smart, and people wanted a garage and a garden. And they sold, her project was a huge success.

Off the back of this, she bought adjoining streets and used the same approach, and slowly but surely, the whole area upgraded, and suddenly it was the trendy place to live, and by then she was in a position to rent or sell, and the money was rolling in"

We were both astounded, my wife certainly was.

"I can't believe it 'my mother' building houses and 'developing property'. I'm amazed, absolutely amazed"

"Your mother was very astute" continued Peter Dooley "she spent her life buying and developing property all over Dublin. Understand that this city has grown and has greatly expanded over the last twenty years, especially when we joined the EU and converted to the Euro. Things really took off then"

I looked at my wife and then at Peter.

"Well" I said "somebody's got to ask the question Peter. How many houses did she actually own?"

Peter Dooley did a quick mental calculation, and then he said

"Around two hundred"

"What!" We both nearly shrieked.

"Yes" said Peter "two hundred, two hundred and fifty, something along those lines"

For once, I was speechless.

He continued "But the houses are secondary really, they're only a small part of your mother's very extensive portfolio.

"Extensive portfolio?" my wife asked.

"Yes, she moved into commercial property"

"You mean shops?" I said

Peter frowned "Well she did buy some retail property, but it's mainly commercial office property."

"What does that mean?" I asked, now feeling totally out of my depth.

Peter Dooley looked at us both "Let me explain something to you" and he stood up and turned to look out at the view of Dublin.

"Let me give you an example" he said, and he pointed at the nearest office block, it was about the same height as the Dooley and Breen building, around twenty storeys, all black tinted glass and shiny stainless steel.

Peter nodded "See that building, well that's one of your mothers, and this place, the Dooley and Breen Building, this building belongs to your mother too, along with a dozen other similar high rise office properties situated throughout Dublin. There's also the retail side, several different malls and shopping centres, plus of course the houses, and in the last few years your mother bought substantial parcels of land all around the outskirts of the city. This land has already greatly multiplied in value as Dublin itself has expanding at a phenomenal rate. Over the years, for a percentage, she lent money at favourable rates to some of Dublin's most successful companies. She still retains substantial holdings in these businesses. She actually owns seventy-five percent of Horan Construction, and finally, she is, or was, a partner in this company 'Dooley and Breen'. She extensively invested in this company and provided the much needed cash which helped us grow into one of the biggest legal firms in Ireland"

Peter then looked at us earnestly.

"Your Mother was a very wealthy and successful woman. I can only estimate her wealth, but I think you could conservatively say that your mother was worth around several hundred million pounds, and that's just property. Put everything together, and your mother was probably well on her way to a billion."

All I could do was to turn and look at my wife. She just sat there, staring at Peter Dooley. She was sort of paralyzed.

Peter looked to her "Are you alright?"

She just looked back at him and silently shook her head, trying to comprehend it all.

Peter reached over and pressed the intercom button on his telephone.

"Heather, bring three cups of tea in here please, and bring the whiskey bottle too"

The lovely Heather arrived with the tea and a good bottle of 'Bells'.

Peter poured a large shot of whiskey into each cup of tea, and I never realized how good whiskey actually tastes in tea, it's wonderful.

"Get this down you" he said.

We were half way through drinking our tea, when my wife turned to me and said.

"What on earth are we going to do. We don't know anything about commercial property and things"

"I know…" I said dumbly…but I didn't know…

Peter Dooley tactfully interrupted "…Ah well…this is where 'we' come into the equation…or at least I hope we do…"

Peter leaned back against his desk and continued,

"When your mother suddenly died, we had to call an emergency board meeting. Your mother, her position in the company, and her business interests are quite pivotal to the financing of this firm. Any substantial withdrawal of specific funding could cause a lot of distress within the company and affect the credibility of this firm."

I heard what he was saying, and I suddenly realized his predicament.

"What you're saying Peter, is…don't rock the boat'" I said.

Peter looked directly at me "No, I'm not saying, 'I'm asking'. I'm asking you to work with us, and to help us get through this difficult period"

And in that moment I saw it, the mask ever so slightly slipped and I saw the strain in his face and for the first time I felt some concern for him. My wife saw it too.

She spoke to him "Peter, I still stand by my original principles, this was my mother's money, not mine"

I twitched for a moment. 'Oh my god' I thought, 'she's going to give it all away'

"However" she continued "we are no longer talking about one house here, and neither are we foolish. This is a life changing event and we are certainly out of our depth here. Derek and I will have to discuss the implications of it all, but from what I can see, you seem to be doing a great job. My mother worked with your father, and I think I can work with you" .

Peter Dooley exhaled, smiled and reached out to shake our hands.

"Thank you, thank you very much" he said

The mood lightened and Peter continued, "The thing is, we need you here for a few days. We need to sort out some legal stuff and now, if you're 'onboard' so to speak, we need to give you a fuller picture of the business. We can book you into our hotel and start to work things out from there"

"There's a hotel?" I asked

"Oh yes, I forgot to mention that, it's 'The Royal Dublin', five star 'all the way'. Also, we will transfer the monies from your mother's private account into an accessible account for you"

He looked at my wife "unless of course, you have a specific account?"

"I use the Post Office" she said.

"You may need something bigger"

"Why's that?"

"Your mother liked to have money readily available, just in case she spotted something she liked the look of"

"And" I said?

"Twenty million, she always had about twenty million in her private account. We can transfer that directly to you, and since we are the trustees, it could be done today"

At that moment, I wondered if I was actually dreaming all of this...

Peter Dooley continued "I'm going to play the honesty card here. The truth of it is very simple. Your mother left everything to you, 'everything', no fancy trust funds, no off-shoots, no complications, she left the lot to you, lock stock and barrel. If you were to pull the plug, for any reason, it would not only bring down Dooley and Breen, it would damage and possibly bankrupt some of the most important companies in Dublin, the repercussions of which would be felt all across Ireland. My father started this company from nothing, and together we built it up. I know you didn't get on with your mother, but my father was my best friend and he was so proud of what we had accomplished together. We are an ethical company, a major charity supporter and we are diverse. We do a lot of good, we're a good company"

"Don't worry Peter" my wife was resolute "we won't rock the boat."

"Hey" I said "we could actually buy a boat"

"No we can't" said the wife.

And Peter Dooley laughed with success.

I had to ring up my boss to ask for extra leave, he was far from happy. We were then booked into The Royal Dublin and it certainly was 'five star' all the way. Then for the next three days, we were given a crash course in business finance and the Law, and a guided tour of the extensive and varied properties that her mother had acquired. It certainly was an insight into the business heartland of Dublin.

We were then flown back by private jet into Manchester Airport on Sunday. It's all been a bit of a rush. I had to talk to my boss because Peter Dooley wanted us back in Ireland, and it was all becoming a bit of a strain. We needed to get back home and get our feet back firmly on the ground. We've been back three days, after the first day I just unplugged the phone.

I finally put my scissors down, haircut over, and Derek just sat there, staring into the mirror, with the blankest of expressions on his face, then he looked up at me.

"What do you think?" he said.

"What do I think?" I replied "Well Derek that is the most remarkable story I have ever heard, it's unbelievable. I don't know what you're going to do, but when your wife said that "this is life changing", she was right. This changes everything, and now your whole life is going to take a different path, like it or not."

"And that's the problem" said Derek "How much change do we actually want?"

We sat down last night for a late dinner and a bottle of wine. To be honest, we've both been a bit stressed. This is just a whole new world to us. We talked late into the night and came to a simple conclusion, basically that we know nothing about business, and in truth, we don't want to know or really get involved. There are other people who are more qualified to do that than us, and we really do feel that we can trust Peter Dooley to do the best for the company. It's in his blood, he's honest, he has integrity, and he's become a good friend.

So our decision is quite simple, obviously we have the money from her mother's private account"

"The twenty million" I said

"Yes, the twenty million", and he had to grin as he said it "Surely, we can live on that amount?"

"I would think so" I said, trying to sound casual.

"So" he said "we keep the twenty million and let Peter Dooley run the company, totally. We rang Peter to tell him our decision this morning. He thanked us for our confidence in him, and 'oh yes' he added, that if we did spend the twenty million, we were just to give him a ring and he would transfer some more funds into our account, just like that. It's bloody frightening."

"Yes, but bloody handy" I joked. And then "What are your plans going to be Derek?"

"Well, we've talked, and my wife has always wanted to live on a farm, just to be around animals. We don't actually want to be farmers. We just want to live on a farm and sort of have animals wandering about. She's even talked about starting a sanctuary for donkeys and ponies, that sort of thing. Peter says that it won't be a problem to find us something"

"So you're going to move over to Ireland?"

"Yes" said Derek "it's strange, my wife said she would never go back to Ireland, but all this, as you said is 'life changing'. It was never part of our plans, but I think going back to live there and more importantly, being in touch with her family again is giving her some sort of closure"

"And what are you going to do Derek?"

"What do you mean?"

"Well" I said to him "Computers have been your life. I mean, come on, you love the damn things"

He laughed at that "I know. I suppose I do really".

"Well tell me, is 'life on the farm' going to be enough for you?" I asked him.

"My boss said the same thing to me on the phone this morning"

"Yes, I'll bet he's a bit upset, you've been an asset to that firm. What did he have to say?"

"Actually" said Derek "he's come up with an idea"

"Oh yes?"

"Yes, and it might just work. You see he reckons, like you, that I will eventually start to seriously miss my job. So he ran this idea by me. He wants me to take a break, call it time off for personal issues. He wants me to take off as much time as I want and sort myself out, along with everything that's going on. And if I go to Ireland, and it looks like we definitely will, he wants me to work from over there, via the internet".

"Can you do that?" I said "I mean, can you do your job 'through' the internet?"

"Oh yes, nowadays we can just go online and hook up to the customer's computer, in most cases anyway. It works with all the latest tech, it's called 'Problem solving' online, and really I suppose, it is the way forward. Anyway, it would save me travelling all over the place, my boss is quite enthusiastic about it all, and it will probably open up a new division to the business. There will still be some jobs I may have to travel to, but I think I can manage that"

And that was that. 'Haircut done', Derek stood up ready to leave.

"Well all the best Derek" I said to him "and I really, really hope that everything works out okay"

We shook hands.

"I think we'll be alright" he said "and thanks for listening to me over the year. It's certainly been eventful" and then he laughed "and I'll tell you something else, it's a good job I met her before she got all this money"

"Yes, you're right there Derek" I said "and do you know something, but for 'Marbella', you two would never have met".

"Don't I know it" and he grinned.

So he left the shop, and then turned back and gave me one of his funny waves, he did sometimes have a strange way about him. He then got into his old Nissan and drove off around the corner.

I never saw Derek again, but I wish him well.

It's a strange thing, the nature of the hairdressing business, and there's nothing more entertaining than the people that you deal with. You see young men grow up, and old men grow older, and then you deal with a lot more in between.

Life, as they say is a tapestry.

As Derek disappeared around the corner, I considered his extraordinary tale, it was indeed remarkable.

And as I thought about it, something suddenly struck me. All the way through his story, he'd never, ever told me his wife's name.

Only that she was 'an Irish girl'.

Makes you think, doesn't it?

CHAPTER THREE

Thursday morning...

It's eleven o' clock in the morning and I've already had of a couple of customers in the shop.

The gentleman that I've just finished is someone whose hair I've cut for years, he's an elderly man and he's Polish by birth, his name is Harry.

Harry was originally a Polish refugee during the war, who met a local girl whom he married and then never went back to his native Poland, well not until years later anyway. Harry is now in his late eighties and is not good on his legs, and he now permanently uses a walking stick. Unfortunately, his wife passed away last year due to illness, and Harry is now beginning to struggle with his life. Harry's routine, is to always walk down the road to my shop, he always takes his time and sets off early. But these days, the walk back home has become too much for him, and now after having his haircut, Harry always has a taxi to take him home. I usually ring the taxi for him, we are quite well served in the area and I generally use the same firm. Within minutes, the taxi arrives and the driver gets out, he's a young man named Nilesh, and he comes into the shop to give Harry a helping hand. Nilesh is an Asian lad who I know quite well, in fact I know his whole family. He often picks up old Harry and he always comes into the shop to give Harry a bit of help and assistance and to get him safely into the taxi. He's a good lad.

Nilesh and his whole family have all been taxi drivers at one time or another, and I think that I've dealt with all of them over the years. So the three of us sit and have a chat, and I ask Nilesh how is family are doing.

He laughs at me "Hey, you know us all, from years back"

I have to agree.

Finally, we roll Harry into the front seat of the taxi, and with a fond farewell to both of them, off they go. As they turn the corner and set off up the road, I thought about Nilesh and his family, and yes he was right, I had known them all for years, his brothers and cousins, and his mum and dad, and also my very good friend 'Gupta', who was Nilesh's uncle. Gupta was the family legend, and the man who had started it all.

Back in the eighties, Gupta was 'our' taxi driver. Indian by birth, at the time he was one of the first Asian taxi drivers in our area. He was our local taxi driver all through the 1980's and 90's, a very popular man, he was well known locally by all, simply because Gupta, God bless him, would always get you home.

Small, robust and always busy, Gupta had the sort of accent that has all but disappeared. He actually reminded you of an Englishman trying to mimic an Indian accent in one of those old British comedies. He had a wonderfully enthusiastic, lilting voice that always, just made you smile.

Gupta used to drive up and down our road with the regularity of a bus, and we always wondered when he slept. To my amazement he once told me that he had two jobs, and that he also worked in a local Mill. I always wondered if he had a twin brother that he hadn't told us about.

He drove a series of absolutely awful, shaking and rusty Japanese cars. Datsuns and Toyotas from the Middle Ages with hundreds of thousands of miles on the clock. Whenever he passed you on the road, he would always honk his horn and wave, always. He was a very wise man, and he knew all of his regular customers.

Gupta was always laughing. Mind you he had a lot to laugh about. He was an astute business man and would never, ever, miss a fare wherever possible. And there wasn't shortage of customers either. Back in those wild and woolly days of the 80's god bless em, when my friends and I had decided to drink our way through the decade. They were good times back then, and in those days the beer was really, really cheap, plus the fact that my body, liver, and other internal organs were much younger and were in far better shape.

Anyway, that was Gupta, and he was 'our' man and our dedicated taxi driver and he was the man who got you home safe and sound. I would sometimes wake up in bed after a sensational night of drinking, and lie there not knowing what the hell had happened, but 9 or 10 hours later, I was usually fairly well recovered and was ready to 'fly the flag' once more. And so a shower and some clean clothes, and then ring a cab, and 'hey presto'. A smiling Gupta would be outside the front door in a jiffy, honking the horn and raring to go.

Once I was in the taxi, the conversation would go something like this.

"Hello Gupta"

"Hello my friend and how are you?"

"Not bad thanks Gupta"

"Oh bloody hell my friend, you were really drunk last night"

"Err, oh really Gupta. Did I see you?"

"See you. Oh yes. I take you home, you bloody pissed."

"Oh, right. Where was I?"

"You where asleep at side of road"

"Oh Christ"

"Yes I saw you, and I thought 'Oh bloody hell' he pissed again. So I stop taxi and I put you in back of the car and take you home and get you into house".

"Err, did I pay you Gupta?"

"No"

And then Gupta would laugh."But I know I see you tomorrow, so is okay".

"You're a good man Gupta, and thanks for that".

"No problem my friend"

And so you paid up and everybody's happy.

And that was it you see, the man would do that, it was part of the service. Gupta would get you home, he got us all home, and we were glad to pay him to do it.

Gupta was in my shop one day having his hair cut, when he told me a story. It turned out to be his story, the story all about him and his family. They were originally Ugandan Asians who had all been thrown out of Uganda by the president, the infamous General Idi Amin.

I was cutting Gupta's hair and chatting away as usual. He was my taxi driver and I was his barber, so the conversation came easy.

I have a television in my shop and the news channel is on all day long. Suddenly, something came on the T.V about Uganda. It was the announcement of General Idi Amin's death in Saudi Arabia. It seems that the General had been living in Saudi for years after eventually being ousted from power, apparently he'd fled there for his life. General Amin had been a ruthless and barbaric leader and if he'd remained in his homeland, he would have certainly had to pay the ultimate price for his past atrocities.

"I am from Uganda" Gupta said suddenly, and he looked up at me.

"I didn't know that" I replied. And I was surprised, in those days I presumed that all the Indians came from India.

"Yes, I grew up there, we had a large farm, generations of my family lived there. We had thousands of acres of land, we grew sugar cane."

I was slightly amazed, this was a bit of a revelation.

He continued "Our farm was a huge place, we used to employ hundreds of people, in fact we employed a whole village. They all worked for our family back then"

He stopped for a moment, and suddenly he looked sad and slightly wistful.

"The villagers that worked for us" he said "we looked after those people, we even had a school and a clinic".

He looked up at me again, as though he had to give an explanation.

"Everybody had a good life, we all worked hard and we were all looked after. Everyone was healthy back then and there was always enough food, enough for everyone. But we had to leave, not just my family, all the Asian families. We'd all lived there for years but we had to go. It was General Amin's orders"

I looked back at Gupta through the mirror and considered what he had just told me, and so I asked him what had happened, why did General Amin make all the Asian people leave Uganda, after all it was their homeland too, they had owned the farms and farmed the land there for generations past.

Gupta looked slightly distant for a moment, for a split second his mind was somewhere else, and then he spoke.

"I remember a story" he said "a story that was told about what really happened, it's a long time ago now, but it's supposed to be a true story"

I stood there and listened, curious.

He continued "You see, the Asian people in Uganda were very successful, we had farms and land, and shops and businesses. We worked and we were industrious, we all worked very hard to make a good life out there in Africa. But unfortunately, some of the Ugandan Africans, men who were in power at that time, they were envious of us and increasingly so. They were General Amin's men, and they thought that we were beginning to get too powerful, they were resentful of our wealth and suddenly, they began to consider us as a threat. These men were General Amin's advisors and fellow politicians, and they were also usually his fellow tribesman and that's how it works in Africa. They had the close ear of their General, he was their kinsman, and General Idi Amin held absolute power and had the total control of his country. He was a tyrant ruler, the 'all powerful', and he was a bully and a thug, and he was corrupt. His advisors and politician friends began to manipulate Amin because they wanted our land and our farms and businesses and they told him that we were a threat. They warned him that our wealth would one day give us political strength and that we would eventually 'buy' our way into power and ultimately get rid of the General and his cronies.

Now in southern Uganda there lived a very rich, very wealthy Asian business man. He had a huge farm up in the hills there that looked down onto Kampala and he had land that stretched east, all the way to Lake Victoria. He was one of the richest men in the country, and he was even wealthier than General Amin. This man owned several similar farms situated all across Uganda, and he owned many successful companies and had property all over the country.

He was a multi-millionaire.

And he also had a daughter, a very beautiful daughter.

Now it was commonly known by all, that General Idi Amin had a weakness. Simply put, he was a womaniser.

He was obsessed by women, and though he was a big ugly man, he knew that because of his status and his power, he could have and own any woman that he wanted, and what he wanted, he got.

There was a particular social occasion, a large function to which the General attended, along with the most important people in Kenya. And it also happened that the wealthy Asian business man and his family had also been invited. There were throngs of important people there, both from the African and Asian communities, and they all in their turn had to be introduced to the General. The rich business man and his family were eventually brought before General Amin for their turn at 'polite conversation'. They stood before the General, who turned to speak to them, and it was at that moment that General Idi Amin saw the rich man's daughter for the very first time. She was so incredibly beautiful, and Amin was totally fixated by her.

For a moment, the General couldn't speak, he just stared at the girl, and then he grinned stupidly at her and began to behave like some naive youth. After several minutes of awkward conversation, during which the General tried to be witty, humorous and charming, all of which he failed, the rich man finally managed to prise his family away, and away from the General, who they considered an arrogant oaf.

But it wasn't over. General Idi Amin was completely besotted by this girl, and that meant trouble. And it was not only her beauty that attracted him, it was also the fact that she was socially out of his reach, and he knew that. She was somehow, a class above him and he saw her as something exquisite and rare, and he wanted her.

A few days later, the rich businessman, the father of the beautiful girl, was duly summoned to the presidential palace for an audience with the General.

And so, hesitantly, the rich man went to see General Amin on the appointed day at the appointed time. What else could he do? General Idi Amin ran the country with an iron fist, and like all tyrants, he was all powerful. He totally ruled Uganda with an iron fist, and just his word could mean life or death.

The rich businessman was brought before a smiling Idi Amin and they sat and spoke for a while, and after a few drinks and pleasantries, the General informed the rich businessman of his plan, which simply was that he, General Idi Amin, President of Uganda, had decided that he would marry the rich man's beautiful daughter.

And to General Amin's delight and surprise, the wealthy business man's response was favourable and he immediately agreed to Amin's wishes. Had there been a different response, there was no doubt, General Amin would have had a different reaction altogether.

Amin congratulated himself on what seemed an effortless and amiable task and he instructed the girl's father to make all the arrangements. Absolutely no expense was to be spared. This was going to be a state wedding of huge importance, and for Amin, it would be the door into the high echelon of the powerful Asian society. In effect, he would finally be socially acceptable, and the door to both his worlds would open.

He would have a foot in Africa, and a foot in Asia.

The rich Asian businessman drove home, and when he arrived there he made one phone call.

Six hours later, he and his wife and his beautiful daughter were on his private jet on route to Canada.

They would never return.

You see, the businessman was a very clever fellow, and he'd already realized that Uganda under the rule of Idi Amin, was heading for financial disaster and that eventually the country's economy would fail.

So he had taken steps to secretly move huge amounts of his money to different parts of the world, in particular Canada, where he also had family.

It was two days later when the General found out what had taken place and he went berserk, totally berserk.

For years his word had been Law, never questioned, he could have anything or anyone at a whim.

It was his world.

And now unbelievably, he had been disobeyed, and even worse, he had been tricked and lied to. This simply did not happen to him, he was General Idi Amin, the 'President' and Ruler of Uganda.

The Men who surrounded General Amin realized that this was their moment. They played on his rage and they goaded him. They told him that everyone in the Asian community knew that the rich businessman was going to fly off to another country with his daughter, and that the Asian community knew that the General had been tricked and they were all laughing at him. In fact, they were now calling him General 'Idiot' Amin.

And the Presidents men, Amin's personal advisors, told him 'See, we told you not to trust the Asians, any of them. Look what has happened, they have made you look a fool'.

And with that, Idi Amin blew. He exploded.

He ordered that every Asian person, absolutely everyone, was to leave Uganda. And they had to leave their money, leave their property, their farms and businesses and all their goods. They had to leave everything and go, get out.

Gupta stopped for a moment and looked at me through the mirror as I continued cutting his hair.

"I will always remember the airport..." he said

"I was only a young boy. We, my family and our relations and our friends, and hundreds of other Asian families had to go to the airport. We had nothing more than a suitcase each, that's all that we were allowed. We were to be put on a plane and flown out, out of Uganda, our home."

Gupta then said to me "Do you know that in Asian families, the old folk have a saying.

'Always keep a suitcase packed'.

"Why's that?" I asked him.

"It's because of the experience and the feeling of loss at being thrown out of your home, and having nowhere to go and being homeless. It is never forgotten, it never leaves you. Losing everything you have ever had is something that you can never forget"

"And do you think that you or your family could ever get thrown out of England?" I asked him, I was actually a bit surprised.

Gupta shrugged "You never know"

"Gupta" I said "Don't ever worry, that will never happen, not here. England is still the safest place in the world to live, along with Canada of course" and I winked at him.

Gupta laughed "Good one" he said, and he laughed again.

"You were saying. About the airport" I reminded him.

"Yes...yes, the airport" he said slowly, and once again he returned to his past.

"I was only a small boy, I remember standing in a line, a long winding line of people all getting ready to board a large silver aeroplane that gleamed in the sun, hot and bright and shiny.

We had all been taken to the airport on trucks and led into a long wooden building and we were left there for hours, waiting for the plane. It was very hot and the children were crying, worried mothers hugged them and tried to be brave. Outside on the tarmac were armed soldiers, there were four of them, all in uniform, tall and slim and as black as coal. The soldiers were grouped together in conversation and were nodding in agreement with each other. Our fathers watched them and looked very worried, and glanced at one another and spoke very quietly, trying not to be too obvious, but we all knew that something was going very wrong.

Finally, we were paraded out of the building and were all standing in a line, ready to board the plane. Each of us was holding a suitcase, and that was all we were allowed, one suitcase. Then two of the soldiers came up to our line and one of them, a tall man, shouted out the orders 'that none of us were allowed to take any money or valuables with us, and anyone with money or valuables should hand them over immediately'.

Nobody moved.

Minutes passed, then the tall soldier issued orders to the other soldiers, and they came forward and grabbed the suitcases off one of my uncles and another man. They threw the cases on the ground, opened them and then tipped the contents onto the hot tarmac.

We watched as the clothes tumbled out, and along with the clothes there were bundles of money which spilled out onto the ground, bundles of money, all neatly tied up with white string.

I gasped when I saw the money, we all did, and I knew that my uncle and the other man were in trouble. The tall soldier started to scream at them both, I was only a boy, I didn't really understand. And then the tall soldier shouted out some orders and he and the other soldiers suddenly grabbed hold of my uncle and the other man, and they dragged them around to the back of the long wooden building and out of sight. Then we heard more shouting, followed by a moment of silence, and then suddenly the deafening explosion of gunfire.

'Oh my God!' We were absolutely panic-stricken, and the women started to scream because we didn't know what the soldiers were going to do next.

And at that moment, I realized that we were nothing. We had no rights and we were helpless, we were like cattle with no future, and now we were at the mercy of people who could do anything they wanted with us.

For a moment we all just stood there in shock, and then it was my father, he was the first to react. His brother had just been murdered and he realized what was happening, and what was about to happen. He suddenly picked up his suitcase and threw it as far as he could. As it flew through the air he screamed at us "Throw away your cases, get rid of them...now!"

And we did, everybody did, and the cases skidded across the tarmac as we all threw away every last thing that we owned.

Everybody realized that before the soldiers reappeared around the building, they had to get rid of their suitcases cases and their money, the money that they'd worked so hard to accumulate over the years, and the money that was now going to get them killed.

It was all worthless now.

The soldiers strutted back around the building, guns ready, eyes full of blood and lust and greed, they were ready to slaughter us now...now they had the excuse. Then they suddenly stopped...and stopped dead in their tracks. They stood there and looked at the pile of suitcases that were strewn all over the runway, and they looked and were puzzled for a moment. Then the tall soldier said something to his men and he laughed out loud. The soldiers looked at each other for a moment and then they started to laugh too.

Then the tall soldier turned to us all and shouted "Get on that plane now and go, get on it and leave quickly, or we will shoot all of you bastards"

And we did, all of us, frightened children and silent men, and shaking, weeping women.

But it was the right thing to do" said Gupta "My father was right. You see the tall soldier realized that each and every one of those cases contained money, lots of money, and in that great pile of suitcases heaped on the tarmac in front of them, there was a fortune. If they'd shot us all, well questions could be asked and if it was found that there was a huge amount of money involved, other people would want some, demand some, whereas the only people involved were the four soldiers. Once we were on the plane and gone, and gone forever, there would be no evidence. They would quickly bury the two bodies and then collect all the discarded suitcases and take them away somewhere and secretly count all the money. Then they could keep it for themselves, and no questions asked, nobody would know.

I looked at Gupta through the mirror "My god" I said "you must have been absolutely terrified"

"We were, it was terrible, really terrible. It's a long time ago now, but I still remember everything.

"What happened then?" I asked him.

"Then, oh then, oh yes well, we flew to England to try and start a new life. We worked hard and made new lives here, we got work and new jobs and we started new businesses over here with our families."

"It must have been hard, with no money" I said.

"Well, we did eventually get some money by selling our valuables, we did quite well really, and that got us started again."

"Valuables" I said "What valuables?"

"Jewellery"

"Jewellery..?" I was at a loss "but I thought you'd left everything in the cases at the airport?"

"Only the money" said Gupta.

"So how did you get jewellery out of the country?" I was mystified.

Gupta smiled at me, and then started to chuckle.

"The women" he said, and then he started to laugh "The bloody women. Their husbands made the women swallow their bloody jewellery"

"You are joking" I said, totally astounded.

Gupta now laughed out loud "While we were waiting to board the plane, while we were in the long building. The men made the women swallow all their jewellery, their gold rings and jewels. Why do you think the women were weeping and crying as they got onto the plane? They were worried that if the soldiers realized that there was no jewellery in the cases, and then figured out what they'd done, they would all have got their bloody stomachs slit open"

He rocked with laughter.

I shook my head and laughed with him, I'd never heard anything like it in my life.

"You're a bad man Gupta" I said smiling.

"Hey, it was our fathers, and times were hard"

I had to agree with him, and we continued talking.

As I finally finished his haircut I said to him "Did you ever think of going back to Africa, and back to Uganda?"

"Oh, I once did go back" he said "about ten years later".

"Oh right" I said to him.

"The then 'New' Ugandan government had put proposals to us, asking Ugandan Asians if we would go back and take up our farms again, we could have all our land back and start again.

It seemed that suddenly, they needed us again.

It was an appealing idea, we had owned thousands of acres of land. By then Idi Amin was long gone, and the country needed to recreate wealth again through farming and industry.

I was about seventeen years old by then. The family got together and it was decided that two of my older cousins would go out to Uganda to see how things were, both politically and socially, and to see what had happened to our old farms. I was invited along.

So off we went. We flew all the way to Kampala, I remember we landed at about ten in the morning and already it was 'so' bloody hot. I'd forgotten about the African heat, it's like the baking heat from an oven, overwhelming.

My cousins had sorted out a hire car, a four wheel drive Toyota with wonderful air conditioning. We went to a small supermarket and bought enough food and water for our trip. Then, armed with some old maps and a compass, we finally set off on the long drive.

The trip took us through our old lands...land that had once been good farmland, good agricultural land, there was acres and acres of it. But it had all changed, and in the ten years since we'd left, everything had turned back into bush and scrubland. It was unrecognizable. More than that, it was useless.

Late that afternoon, we eventually arrived at my cousin's old family farm. We drove the Toyota down the remains of a road and onwards to the once grand farmhouse and the remains of the surrounding buildings. We slowly got out of the Toyota to look at the ruin that was once my cousin's home. Half of the buildings had gone, disappeared completely, and some were just the burnt out remains of some past fire. The old farmhouse had mostly disintegrated and was basically a shell that was just rotting away. My cousin was very upset. He stood there and looked on in disbelief.

"Look at the house" he said "My home, it...it's gone" and he stood there and tried to remember the past.

He turned to us and spoke "There used to be people...people that we used to know, the folk from the village?"

He just stood there, quietly "All those people, they've all left...all gone"

We left him to walk around on his own, he was very upset, he had spent the first twenty years of his life here, he had more memories here than me. It had been his father, my uncle, who had been shot and killed at the airport when we were waiting to flee the country. He'd lost his father in Uganda, and left his father in Africa.

After half an hour, I went to find him. I carefully walked around the back of the old farmhouse, where there had once been a beautifully shaded garden. There used to be a large old Acacia tree there and I remembered when our families would sit under that tree in the shade, they were happy times. Our parents would sit there talking, and we children would play in the garden, they were carefree days, our life was good, and we were happy.

I finally found my cousin. He was standing there by the old Acacia tree. It was still there, almost as if it was waiting for us.

He stood there with tears in his eyes and with his arms stretched around the old Acacia. It was as though he was hugging an old friend that he'd just met up with. The Acacia was all that was left of the garden, everything else was gone. He just cried as he stood there hugging that old tree.

I quietly walked up to him and slowly put my hand on his shoulder. He turned to me, in despair

"I remember this, the old Acacia. It's like part of my family. I used to sit on my dad's knee here under this tree. It was the best place in the world. I would sit here on his knee in the shade as he talked to all our friends and family and laugh with the villagers, and now it's gone, all gone. This tree is my only real memory of him, and he's dead, he's gone, and I've lost him."

I looked at my cousin, he was so sad.

"Listen to me" I said "My dad says that you are only dead if you are forgotten, and we will never ever forget your dad."

I turned around and quietly walked away, there was nothing else for me to say.

I went back to my other cousin, who was standing by the Toyota, and we waited, we stood there in the heat and the buzzing insects, not speaking, just waiting.

Eventually, my cousin walked back from around the remains of the old farmhouse. He walked straight up to the Toyota and we all got in. No one spoke. He started up the engine, put it in to gear, and without a single glance back he turned the Toyota around and roared up the old farm road.

We drove until it was dark, then stopped and camped for the night. It wasn't safe to drive at night in the bush, the roads are particularly bad. The next morning we broke camp at about 9-00 a.m and set off in good time to get back to Kampala and the airport.

We'd been driving for about two hours, through some really dense scrub, when suddenly in the distance two policemen stepped out of the bush and onto the road. My cousin made some comment and started to slow down. I was in the back and I leaned over his shoulder to see what was going on.

The policemen, all sunglasses and relaxed, and dressed in khaki, just stood there in the middle of road in front of us, and as we came to a halt one of them raised his hand, just to his waist, just to let us know that we had to stop. It was a sign of control, very cool, very casual, from a man who was used to being obeyed. They walked to either side of the Toyota and motioned us to open both of the front windows. It was quite intimidating.

I jokingly said to my cousins "Hey, the cavalry's got us surrounded" and my cousin glared back at me through the driver's mirror.

The thing was, back then I was just a cocky kid, a smart mouthed seventeen year old who thought he knew it all, and then some. I had already had a few run-ins with the police back home, and I certainly wasn't going to put on by these jumped up, uneducated locals. So I opened my window so that I could hear what was going on. One of the policemen leaned on the driver's door mirror and peered in at us.

"Ah" he said slowly "So you're tourists"

And I thought to myself...'Brilliant deduction, you idiot'

The policeman then continued "And what are you doing in this area?"

My cousin explained the reason for our visit and that we were on our way back to Kampala and to the Airport.

"Mmm" said the policeman, and he casually took off his sunglasses and put them into his shirt pocket, then he took out a cigarette and slowly, very slowly began to light it.

I sat there in the back of the Toyota, as the lovely cool air from the air conditioning, got very quickly replaced by the searing African heat. And I began to get very pissed off, I think it's called 'attitude'.

The policeman lit his cigarette, took a long 'draw' on it, and slowly exhaled.

Before all the smoke had even left his mouth he said "You were speeding...you give me 100 dollars for fine, and I let you go"

Well, it was stupid of me I know, but I couldn't stop myself.

"You what" I suddenly demanded, all the way from the back seat "Speeding on these roads, you've got to be joking, there's 'no way' we were speeding" and then I blurted out "this is nothing but a bloody rip off"

There, I'd said it. And that was it, so what.

But I noticed that both my cousins had suddenly gone rigid in their seats, and the look of panic on their faces could have meant that maybe I'd overstepped the mark a bit.

The policeman just stared at me.

'Right' I thought, that's him told.

And then it happened.

In an instant, he spat out his cigarette and reached over to my window and grabbed me by the hair. He slammed my head onto the edge of the door and held me there with my face burning on the hot metal. I screamed and tried to break free, but he was too strong. I couldn't move an inch, I just howled in pain.

He hissed "Shut your mouth you piece of brown shit" and then, 'oh my god', he reached down and suddenly pulled out a handgun. He took the gun and pressed the steel grey barrel down into my ear so hard that I was paralysed.

He stared down at me, seething with anger "Am goin' to blow your head off boy...blow your cheeky fuckin' head off"

And then I heard the 'click' as he cocked the gun, and I realised I was going to die. And this was unbelievable and it couldn't be happening, but his finger was going to pull the trigger and blow my brains out, and suddenly I was frightened of what the pain would be like. I was terrified of the pain.

Then I heard some sort of noise, voices, they were my cousin's voices. I was nearly passing out, but suddenly the pressure of the gun barrel in my ear relaxed a little, and I remember thinking...'oh thank god'.

My cousins, I could hear them shouting "deal, deal, take it easy man, we can give you money, plenty money. You can have it all, take all our money, it's okay"

The policeman looked across at my cousins and then back at me, and then with disgust he slammed my head back inside the Toyota.

The policeman then pointed the gun at my cousins, and two full wallets were handed out through each window.

"And your watches..." he said, almost as an afterthought.

These were handed over too. Then the second policeman walked back round to his partner, he'd never spoken a single word, he just nodded to him and then sauntered back into the bush and disappeared.

The policeman slowly put his gun away and then he casually put his sunglasses back on.

He looked down at us and said "Don't ever come back". That was all he said, and he turned and walked silently back into the bush.

They were gone.

We just sat there in shock. The moment had passed, and we had kept our lives. I was shaking like a leaf, and I thought that my cousins were going to be furious with me for being so utterly stupid.

But no, they were concerned, very concerned that I was alright and that I was safe.

"We nearly lost you there little one" said my older cousin, and for an instant he was almost tearful, and there was still the memory from his past and the shooting of his father. He reached over and touched my chin, for just a moment.

We sat there in silence, and then my cousin looked at us both and gave a very deep sigh, and my other cousin looked back at him and smiled, and then he suddenly started laughing. We stared at him for a moment, and then we began to laugh too, it was almost infectious, and for some reason, probably a stupid, crazy sense of relief, we all just sat there giggling like three silly kids.

And at that moment, I truly realized what it meant to have 'family', the closeness and the caring, and that feeling has never left me.

We finally calmed down and as my cousin started up the engine, he turned to us and he said

"You know something, I hate this fucking country. There's nothing for us here" and he paused for a moment "Let's go home" he said.

And we did.

And that was it. That was Gupta's story.

That was his recollection of his early life in Africa, and his return there. And it fascinated me. It was an insight into the injustice and brutality that people all over the world sometimes have to endure.

Living in England, it is something that we will never experience...ever.

It was later that year, and Gupta walked into my shop for his haircut, and I looked at him and something was very wrong.

The haircutting business, you deal with people and you get to know them, and know them well. And sometimes when a customer walks through the door, you just know that something's not right. Something in their demeanour or the look on their face, but it's there, and it's a sense that all is not well.

And now Gupta had that look.

He gave me some sort of half smile and he croaked "How are you my friend?"

And his voice, 'oh my god' his voice...it was gone. That lyrical, resonating voice with that wonderful accent had turned into a grating and gasping rasp.

I looked at him, and I saw the weight loss, and his lined drawn face.

"Are you alright Gupta?" I asked him. It was such a stupid question.

He shook his head "No, my friend"

"What's wrong Gupta?"

He told me, straight out "I've got T.B...I've got Tuberculosis".

I was stunned "Tuberculosis, are you sure?" another stupidity.

"Yes" he replied "I'm sure"

"How do you know?" I was shocked, upset.

"Because I've seen it before" he said, and he gave a rasping, breathless cough "I've seen it before, in the old country, back in Africa. I know this disease, know all about it, earlier this year I went back to Africa, back to Uganda, to try and sort out some business, and when I got back home I started to feel ill. I must have picked it up from over there somehow"

He simply shrugged his shoulders and said "Africa got me in the end. Bloody country"

And that was it.

Three weeks later, Gupta died.

And we all attended his funeral.

He was a lovely man and a good friend, and I'll never forget him.

And I've always remembered his words

'You are only dead if you are forgotten'

Bless you Gupta.

CHAPTER FOUR

So that's the morning out of the way, and now it's Thursday afternoon and I've done a few more haircuts.

The phone has just rung, and it was 'Patrick', he's a customer from London, and he wanted to make an appointment. Patrick is a man who mixes business with pleasure, along with his haircuts, and he comes up to Manchester regularly with his work and he always comes to me to get his haircut, and I love the loyalty.

They say that 'life goes around in circles', well not always. Sometimes that circle turns out to be like a figure eight, sometimes it can end up being a complicated triangle, depending on where you're stood and in which direction you're looking. It can all be a bit complex.

And that is sort of what happened to Patrick. We have some sort of history, me and Patrick.

Something happened a while ago, something that made a customer, a very good friend.

But going back three or four years, I remember that it was a different story altogether.

It was the first week in February, and Christmas was definitely past, as I sat in the chair in my barbers shop, studying the painful awful grey of the New Year.

It was midmorning, when suddenly the door of my shop swung open, and in walked Patrick.

Yes Patrick, not Pat, and definitely not Paddy. But Patrick, and always Patrick. A small and smart sort of man, he always wore a really good suit, and he was also full of life. Good fun and good to talk to, that was Patrick. He was also a total music buff, and when he turned up, he usually always brought me in a C.D of some new music that he'd discovered.

Whenever Patrick was booked in for a haircut, I would smile when I saw his name in the appointment book, because I knew that I was in for an hour's easy conversation and no doubt, some amusing tale, well always an amusing tale, and hopefully a new C.D. He really did know his music and good music it was.

Things happened to Patrick, all sorts of things, and he would deal with the everyday problems in his life through humour. He would simply laugh things off with a shrug of his shoulders and make some joke or some hilarious comment. Whether he ever reflected on things, I never knew, but that was how Patrick seemed deal with life and the world in general. A barrel of fun was Patrick.

But not today.

He walked into the shop, and he looked at me and just said "Hi"

And that one word was the quietest that I'd ever heard him speak.

I studied him for a moment and saw the flat look in his eyes and his tired face, and I knew that something was not right with this man, definitely not right.

He walked over to my barber's chair and quietly sat himself down.

I looked at him through the mirror, and I paused for a moment. I was more than slightly concerned, and so I said to him.

"Are you all right Patrick?"

There was a second's silence.

"No, No not really" he replied slowly.

"Trouble?" I asked, cautiously.

And he just looked up at me and said "the worst, the worst trouble of my life" and he went quiet again and seemed to slowly fade in the chair, right in front of me.

There's something about my profession, the job's physical, and in dealing with people 'hands on' so to speak, you can judge the strength of a man through his head and through his shoulders. The strength is in the balance. And there are occasions, when someone is ill, or even ill at ease, it somehow shows in the neck and shoulders and it gives you a forewarning that something's wrong. I've dealt with very stressed people, who have had shoulders as rigid as wooden coat hangers, and necks set like coiled springs. And at the other end of the spectrum, illness or depression can sap the strength from a man so much that he may struggle just to keep his head upright.

Patrick slumped in the chair in front of me, and his shoulders sagged and his head tilted forward wearily. This wasn't good.

He suddenly started to speak again "I'm having a terrible time at the moment, things aren't good" he said, and he sighed deeply.

"What on earth's wrong Patrick?" I asked him, I was genuinely worried now, this was definitely not normal for Patrick, not one bit.

He looked up at me, contemplating the moment "Do you really want to hear this?"

I nodded slowly to him, and I wondered.

And with that, he began to tell me just what had happened.

"It all started the week before Christmas, it was on a Sunday morning and I was sitting in the kitchen, recovering. I had gotten up at around ten and I was on my second cup of coffee, it was reviving me and helping me to wash away the effects of the couple of bottles of wine that I'd drunk the night before. As I sat there, browsing the

Sunday newspapers, the same way I'd done on a hundred different Sunday mornings, my wife Ruby came downstairs and walked into the kitchen. She wandered past me and clicked on the kettle, she'd been out the night before with a group of friends from work, and I vaguely remembered that she had arrived home quite late, and was probably in the same condition as me, or so I thought.

She just stood there, with her back to me. I thought nothing of it really, and then she slowly turned around and leant back on the cupboard, and looked directly at me.

"Morning" I said, I was still slightly jaded, and then I smiled at her "have a good night then?"

She just looked at me, she was silent for just three or four seconds too long, and then she took a sharp intake of breath before she spoke.

"Listen" she said "I've got to tell you something"

"Yes" I replied, and I yawned as I started to slowly concentrate.

She continued "I've something to tell you, and there's only one way to say it"

And there was the briefest pause while she just stared at me.

Then she said it "Patrick. I don't love you anymore"

I looked at her for a moment, not understanding, and I thought that I mustn't have heard her right.

But then she continued "I just don't love you anymore, I've had enough. I want us to separate Patrick and I want a divorce, it's over Patrick, it's finished."

I just sat there, and my brain somehow wouldn't take it in.

And then in a rush of outpouring, almost as if to justify herself and to make me comprehend what was actually happening, she delivered the hammer blow and the words that would cripple me.

She then told me the truth "I've been seeing somebody else, somebody from work".

I sat there stupefied, and I blurted out "What, what do you mean?" It was all I could say.

But on she rolled, she couldn't stop herself now, and on reflection I realize that it was a prepared recording, all stored up and ready to play.

She continued "He's a married man and he's not happy with his wife, but he's got kids."

And she looked at me, and suddenly reflected "I wanted him to leave his wife but he says he can't leave his kids, and he won't leave her because of their children"

So there it was, and with that brief statement that probably only took a minute to deliver, and with those few short sentences, my whole little world came tumbling down.

Me and Ruby had been together for twenty five years, twenty five wonderful years, or so I thought.

We had two kids, two wonderful kids, and we had our own house, we'd worked hard and the kids were growing up, nineteen and fourteen, almost independent. And the mortgage on the house, almost paid, only another few years to go and then good times, and better and easier times, and the future to look forward to with grandkids and good holidays. That is what people did, people like us, you worked hard and you reaped the benefits. We had a great life and we were surrounded by friends and family.

Of course, there were people we knew who had got divorced, even some of our best friends had separated, but never us, never in the memory of man, not us.

We were a couple, Ruby was my best friend.

Was my best friend.

I gazed at her in disbelief, and her words kept spinning in my head. 'You don't love me' and 'an affair with a married man' and 'you want to separate'.

And from me, just one word "What?"

That was all I could say, and in my mind I kept on thinking that this couldn't be happening, it couldn't be true, not Ruby.

Then suddenly my brain presented me with a vision of her making love to another man, and I was nearly sick.

And I sat there and my face twisted, and a stupid tear ran down my stupid cheek. I was upset, and I just didn't get it, and how could she not love me anymore, she loved me last week, and last month, and for the last twenty five years. And I just didn't understand.

I looked up at her and started to say things like 'I don't believe you' and 'You don't mean it'. But she did mean it, and I felt very hot and confused. It felt like this was some sort of nightmare and that if I waited a minute or two it would pass, but it didn't.

I still didn't understand, had I done something wrong, what had I done?

"Whatever's wrong, we can work it out" I said, and pleaded.

She just shook her head.

I started again "I don't want us to break up, please Ruby, don't break up this family, please"

I almost begged, and then I did beg, and I tried to come up with every reason I could for us to stay together..

And I asked her again "Why?"

She just stood there and looked at me, and then in that instant it happened, there was change in her, a change in her personality and she suddenly gave me a look of total disgust, and then she said "You just don't get it do you...you stupid bastard"

I was stunned. 'Stupid bastard'...she'd never spoken to me like that before, ever.

She spat it out "Listen you clown, its bloody well over and that's it"

And suddenly, it was as if a stranger was talking to me, somebody I didn't know.

And from that awful tragic moment, our marriage and our life together very painfully began to wither and die.

It was the week before Christmas and normally we would have a big family meal and then a party afterwards. Everyone was invited, family and friends, every year, it was always an open house affair and lots of fun.

Then Ruby announced that Christmas was 'cancelled'.

She said "It will all be a sham. I just can't be bothered"

"What about the kids?" I said. I was desperate.

She just shrugged "It'll just have to be the four of us" and then she looked at me as though the words 'the four of us' had been something she didn't really want to say.

And I thought about the kids. 'Oh hell' what about the kids? They weren't going to have a Christmas, not the sort of Christmas that they were used to anyway. What on earth was she thinking of, did she not consider the kids?

So I rang around and told all our friends a lie. My family of course I had to tell the truth, and the truth, I didn't really know the truth but I had to tell them what had happened. They were all totally astounded. She was their daughter, their sister, their aunty. They couldn't believe what she's done, and what she was doing.

Our eldest child, our daughter, was aware of what was happening but our son failed to understand the situation. I was heartbroken as I realized that their lives too, were never going to be the same. The loss of security and their happy home, always safe with mum and dad ever on hand, that's what home was supposed to be for kids, and that's what parents do. Everything's for the kids.

Christmas Day desperately arrived. And for the first time in my life I dreaded it.

We woke up in the morning and Ruby just got out of bed and walked out of the bedroom, she didn't even look at me.

There was no "Good morning and Merry Christmas" and of course, no Christmas kiss.

And I lay there on my own and despaired, because I realized that this could possibly be the last Christmas that I would ever have with her and the kids as a family. I felt depressed. I felt weary.

Ruby and the kids were downstairs ready to open their presents, so I put on a smiling face and went down to join them. They opened their presents and gifts were exchanged, all so fast, too fast.

I'd bought Ruby some Christmas presents of course, some jewellery and her favourite perfume. She casually opened them and then turned to me and just said "Thanks" in a flat and conciliatory sort of way.

I sat there and watched them. I was never going to have another Christmas with my wife and kids, and it was awful, it felt like a terminal illness.

I didn't want that day to ever end, but it ran away like sand through my fingers.

We sat there with the television blurring through the programmes. The Christmas films, and the Christmas news and the Christmas shows, it was like time ticking away.

As usual, I cooked the Christmas dinner, as I do every year, and I got the wine flowing to try to ease things, and to a point it worked. I got Ruby into some sort of scant conversation, it was maybe a start.

We had our Christmas dinner, and we sat at the table with another bottle of wine. Then at around eight o' clock, our daughter decided that she wanted to go over to her friend's house and stay the night, so I took her there in the car.

Ruby was quite mellow by then, it was the wine of course, and she was even laughing. I'd hardly drunk a thing.

I dropped my daughter off, and then drove back home like a maniac. I wanted to get back, even then hoping that the wine would help us to talk and try to sort things out.

But when I got back, to my dismay I found that Ruby was no longer sat at the table, she'd left the wine, left everything and gone to bed.

Christmas Day, and it was all over and finished.

I went upstairs to our bedroom and I stood in the doorway looking at her, she was in bed and asleep. I got into bed with her, and suddenly on impulse, I leant over and put my head into her long dark hair, and it felt soft against my face. I could smell her hair, so clean, so lovely, and her perfume intoxicating and all the memories returned. I loved her and I put my hand onto her hip because I wanted to turn her to me and I wanted to kiss her, I just couldn't help it.

And then she murmured, and then she woke up immediately as she suddenly realized what was happening, and that it was me, it was me who was touching her.

She was startled, and then she was angry and she stared back at me in disbelief.

"No....No...Get off me" she said, and there was a threat in her voice.

I realized my mistake, and my stupidity.

I stuttered back "I'm so sorry, I'm really so sorry, it won't happen again I promise" and I felt stupid and guilty and hopeless.

She rolled over and turned her back to me in silence, a wall of silence.

And I lay there and stared into the dark, wondering about what had just happened, and what I'd just done.

Two days later, she informed me that she'd made an appointment to see a solicitor.

I felt like I'd been hit by a hammer.

I still even then, hoped in my 'naivety' that she would come to me and tell me it had all been a stupid mistake, and that we needed to talk, and needed to make a new start, and that we would try and make a go of it. And now, a solicitor.

Things were moving on, getting involved and getting complicated and I felt as though I was falling through some sort of trap door, and my whole life somehow became a little darker.

She came back from the solicitor's office, full of ideas. 'Oh yes', suddenly she was ready to talk to me, she definitely wanted to talk to me now, about how it would be simpler 'if' and how it would be cheaper 'if' and how much quicker it would be 'if'. And when I tried to explain to her that I didn't want this, I didn't want 'if'...she suddenly changed and began to shout and lose her temper.

I felt like the old car that you trade in for a newer model, you don't want your old car anymore, you want to get rid of it really, and once you've driven off in your shiny new car, you don't give the old one another thought, it's gone and it's forgotten.

The atmosphere at home was now terrible. The children were so quiet, the strain of it all was beginning to affect them.

I asked Ruby if we could please try to handle all this with some civility, but within a week curt replies were all I got to any of my pathetic attempts at conversation.

And then, all conversation came to an end when I arrived home after work and found that she'd moved into the spare bedroom. When I asked her why, she simply said that she had 'nothing at all to say to me'.

I lay in bed on my own that night after twenty five years, I lay there distraught.

My kids, I was worried sick about them both. What about the kids, they deserved the love and security that they'd always known, all of this was their life too.

Then one day in the car, my daughter quietly said to me "Our house isn't the same any more, is it dad?"

And I felt like I was being ripped in two.

My son just didn't understand what was going on, he knew that me and his mum weren't speaking and he'd slowly got used to that, but he didn't understand why.

My daughter began to be away from the house as much as possible, always 'round at her friends', and my son would just bury his head in those damn video games.

And I felt useless, because I was.

Work of course, began to suffer. I just could not concentrate on my job. I have the phone to my ear all day long, dealing with customers, but I couldn't be bothered listening. Their words just seemed to roll into a mass of inane moans and groans and endless bloody questions, and I just couldn't be bothered because I had my own problems, bigger than they would ever know.

My Boss began to notice, and finally I was called into his office. I tried to explain, but of course 'Mr Perfect', with his perfect family and his big salary didn't understand, didn't want to understand, all he wanted was results.

So we ended up having a row and I ended up with a written warning and the threat of suspension, and I just didn't care, and the boss realized that and I knew that it was probably going to cost me my job.

Then, Ruby started to go out in the evenings with her 'friends' from work.

As she got ready, she would sing away to her 80's music, which she played very loud. She would put on her makeup and some fancy outfit, get herself all dolled up and look absolutely gorgeous. Then she would skip out of the door and into the back of a waiting taxi and zoom off to god knows where.

And I would sit there and writhe with jealousy and wonder what she was up to, and who she was really seeing.

At night I would lie in bed, watching the hands of the clock go round, wondering what time she would come home, and I'd lie there, hour after hour...waiting.

Then a friend of mine rang me. He'd just heard about me and Ruby, and like everybody else he couldn't believe it. He suggested that we meet up and 'have a chat', maybe throw a few ideas together. He would be a shoulder to lean on, a well meaning and friendly ear. He said that we should have a drink, meet up in some pub and have a meal, or whatever. I told him that I hadn't been drinking at all since me and Ruby, well since Ruby announced that she wanted a divorce and that I probably wouldn't be very good company.

But he insisted "A night out would do me good, a quiet chat, nothing crazy"

So we met up in some pub that he knew. I ordered the drinks, him a beer, me a coke, and we found a quiet corner, it was a table near a lovely open fire, and it was cosy and comfortable.

We talked, we talked a lot, and then he went to the bar and came back with two pints of lager. I sort of protested, but he said that 'what I needed was a drink, it would help me relax, help me to chill out'.

And it did, and two or three pints later we decided to have a bottle of wine. My friend recommended a bottle of something Australian, he'd had this wine before and it was actually his favourite. When it arrived it tasted wonderful, deep plumy red and quite strong. It was so good to be in the pub, so comfortable and warm, and away from the grief at home and away from the grief at work.

Just being able to talk, to vent your anger and confront your fears, and listen to somebody else's perspective and of course he agreed with me."Yes, of course this was all Ruby's' fault" and "What on earth can she be thinking of" and "What a bitch for doing this to you", and what about the kids and the family, and the financial implications.

"She's bloody crazy" he said.

Of course she is.

By the time eleven o' clock came around we'd had another two bottles of his 'favourite wine' and we were both really drunk. It was now quite late, and having put the world to right and sorted out my marriage, my friend then rang me a taxi on his mobile phone. Although he lived just around the corner, he always used this particular taxi firm.

"They're brilliant" he kept saying as he tried to focus on his phone and press the correct buttons.

Eventually I fell into the back of a taxi and muttered my address to the driver. I spent the whole of the journey home in a drunken haze, with a taxi driver who was trying to maintain some sort of inane conversation.

I just kept answering."Yeh...yeh.." at the appropriate moment.

I finally arrived home and I paid the driver and then struggled noisily with my keys, and cursed until I eventually managed to open the front door.

Ruby had heard the commotion and was coming down the stairs to let me in, and as I opened the door and staggered in she gave me a look of disgust and pushed past me.

"Oh here we go" I said drunkenly "It's Mrs Bloody Ignorant."

She spun around and glared at me. "Shut up, you idiot" she said, and I heard the contempt in her voice.

"Oh fuck off" I said.

She retorted with "I wish that you'd 'just' fuck off ". That was her smart reply, and then she continued with "Yes, why don't you just fuck off and go...go and live somewhere else and leave us alone"

I glared back at her "So that you can move your boyfriend in, that's it isn't it? So that he'll leave his poor bloody wife and kids and then move in with you...you lousy bitch".

She turned on me, now wide eyed with anger and seething.

"It's nothing to do with you" she was shouting now.

I'd hit a nerve and I knew it, and the alcohol in me raged in my head.

It was my moment now and I began to shout "Nothing to do with me, you go screwing another man, you break up my family and you try to fuckin' ruin me, you are one fucking, lousy, rotten bitch"

And then suddenly, I started to laugh at her "And do you want to know what's really, really funny? Your clever boyfriend gets to fuck you, and he gets to fuck his wife at the same time" and I continued with drunken glee "Clever boy, he gets two for the price of one" and I just had to continue, I was on a roll now "And I'll tell you something else you stupid bitch, he'll never leave his wife for you, and do you know why? Because darlin', he knows that your just a fucking slag".

And with that, she totally erupted.

She came at me and snatched at my shirt, and then in temper she started to hit me in the face. I was shocked by the violence of it, and because of everything that had happened between us, it totally incensed me and I went mad. I grabbed hold of her hair to try to stop her from hitting me, but then I began shaking her violently and ended up banging her head against the wall.

Suddenly I could hear screaming, but it wasn't Ruby. No, it was my daughter, she was at the top of the stairs screaming at me to stop, she was crying and frightened, and it was me that she was frightened of. Yes me...her dad.

Oh dear god, what had I done, and my anger turned to despair. I let go of Ruby and I held my hands up.

"I'm sorry, I'm sorry. I didn't mean it" I shouted, and then I was in tears as I turned to my daughter and tried to explain "I'm so sorry, I just...I didn't mean it, I didn't."

Ruby screamed something at me as she pushed past and rushed to the phone.

And the next thing I heard was "Police".

And I gasped " Oh no, please no, don't do this"

But it was all too late.

I was arrested, and then taken to the police station and put in a cell to sleep it off. But I didn't sleep. They let me out the following day around tea time. I was given a 'caution' by the police and was informed that I was not to return to my house. Ruby had told them that she was frightened of the possibility of further violence. Apparently, I was unpredictable.

I rang up home but the phone was slammed down immediately.

It was the end, it was over.

From there, I slept on different sofas at different friend's houses for a few nights at a time. Then I went round to my house for some clothes. My keys wouldn't fit in the locks...the 'new locks'. They'd all been changed.

Within a few days I'd had an injunction served on me from her solicitor, via the courts.

It instructed me that basically, I was out of the house, due to excessive violence, and in front of the children.

And there it was, I'd truly lost everything that I had ever loved.

So I rented a bedsit. It was a flea pit, a ground floor affair, damp and mouldy, with a very used bed and crusty old wallpaper. And as for the bathroom, don't ask. The other residents seem to be permanently drunk or drugged, banging about all the time, and screaming and shouting at one another.

The rent is ridiculous, but it's all I can afford at the moment. I was suspended from work, due to what my boss called 'a lack of motivation' and also my 'possible effect on my work colleagues'. Apparently 'my attitude was disrupting the working environment'. Then a week later he asked me to come into the office and see him. With a sham of a smile, he informed me that business was bad, and so he was going to have to 'let me go'.

And no, he wasn't sacking me, I was being made redundant. 'So'...I'll get some money'.

Yeah...right.

He'd obviously made me redundant because it was a quick way of getting rid of me, and without any legal hassle. And then as a favour he informed me that 'Oh, and by the way', I didn't have to serve any notice or anything'. Still smiling, he said "and it would be easier if you didn't come back in" and "we'll pay you for your time, of course".

And that was that.

I finally got Ruby to answer the phone and I asked her if I could come round and pick up my remaining clothes.

"I'll pack them for you" she replied offhandedly "Ring me when you're coming"

I told her that I'd be round the next day, at around four.

When I arrived home or what used to be my home, it all seems strangely distant now but I turned up to find two suitcases left outside the front door, and that was it. I put them into the boot of the car and then I got ready to leave.

I sat there in the car, and though I'd promised myself I wouldn't do it, I just couldn't help but turn and look at my old home. Twenty five years, all gone.

I bit my lip at hopelessness of it all. I felt that this was the end, this was the last step and I was finished.

I started the car and began to drive away, and I'd only gone a short distance when I glanced in the mirror, and I inwardly gasped. My son had opened the front door and was running up the road after me.

Oh no, no, I didn't want this, I didn't want any last goodbyes and I didn't want any more upset, because deep down inside, I truly felt that I was deserting my children. My poor kids, I'd continually kept on worrying how all this was going to affect their lives, they were the innocents in all this they were the real victims, none of this was their fault.

So like an idiot, I put my foot on the accelerator and the car sped on. I thought he would stop, but he didn't, he kept on running after me and I just stared at him through the mirror, and he still kept on running.

And then it suddenly struck me. 'Oh my god', what on earth was I doing, what in god's name was I playing at. And I suddenly braked heavily and the car stopped dead in its tracks, and I opened the door and got out.

He ran to me and I had to face him, he's my son.

He was breathless, worry all over his face and somewhere a hint of tears.

"Where are you going dad?" he asked, desperate now and his eyes very wide.

"I...I've just picked up my stuff" I said "just the rest of my clothes"

"But where are you going?" he asked me again.

I had to explain things to him, and I said "I've got a new place to live at now"

He looked at me "Aren't you coming back?" he said desperately. And I wished I was dead.

I had to do something, so I put my hands on his shoulders and looked into those enquiring eyes.

"Listen to me" I said "I won't be far away, and me and your Mum are going to sort something out and I'm going to see you every Saturday or Sunday"

"Is that all?" he asked, and I had to take a deeper breath.

"Well" I said "I can ring you anytime, and you can ring me on my mobile whenever you want to". They were all hollow words, almost like lying, because that's what excuses are really, they're just lies.

"I'll always be here...I'm your Dad aren't I?" I said.

"But you won't be living with us anymore" and he just didn't understand.

"No, well your Mums decided its better this way, we've both decided".

"But why?" And there was the question that I couldn't answer.

I looked down at him "I don't know why pal, but it will be better...it will."

He suddenly looked tired, and resigned to it all, and in that face I had all the memories of him, from the wonderful moment that he was born and his first day at school, and on holidays and swimming pools and birthdays and Christmas's. And then this...this awful, bloody rotten Christmas.

He wasn't a man yet, and he wasn't a child, but he was someone who needed both of us and he didn't want things to change. It was a need for security, and he wanted his home to stay the same, the same comfortable place that he'd always known, and I suppose really, we both did.

I put my arms around him and hugged him, the most precious things I'd ever have were him and his sister.

"Come on ya' crackpot" I said with a false laugh" you'll be missing your TV programmes and your tea will nearly be ready, and I've got to go, I'll ring you tomorrow, I will."

I looked at him and then back to the house. Ruby was standing at the door watching us.

"I think your Mum wants you" it was an excuse to diffuse the moment.

He looked around to see his Mum.

"Yes, I think my tea's ready" he said.

"Right, off you go then or she'll be moaning that it's getting cold" and that was another excuse.

"You'll ring me then, promise?" he said.

"Course I will" I said "You'll be sick of me ringing you, and you'll be saying 'Oh it's the phone and Oh it'll be my dad 'again', and 'why' does he always ring when I'm watching my favourite programmes?"

And I pulled a funny face at him.

He smiled at me, he didn't laugh, but he smiled. And I'd got him through the moment.

"Okay" I said "I'll see you later"

"See you later" he replied, and he looked at me as though a decision had been made in his head, and he turned away and walked back to the house.

'Later' is a strange word. In truth, it means absolutely nothing.

Ruby just stood there and watched him walk back, and I wondered how she could put the children through all this. I would never know, I only thing I knew was how much she actually despised me. I didn't know where my daughter was, but she obviously wasn't at home and had probably disappeared to a friend's house so that she wouldn't have to be here for the 'final visit'.

So I got back into the car and drove away for the last time, knowing that I'd never live in that house again.

I reflected on how we started and I thought about the day we first moved in, it was a freezing cold January, twenty years ago now, and it was a brand new house, just built. I always remember our first night there because it was Ruby's birthday. We had no carpets, but we had central heating, and we'd never had central heating before. That first chilly night when I came home from work, Ruby had the house like an oven, and I went to have a bath that had a never ending supply of hot water and Ruby brought me up a can of beer to drink as I soaked and we laughed at the luxury of it all. I'd brought some wine home to celebrate Ruby's birthday, but we had no oven, so I ordered us some Pizzas which never arrived because we were on a brand new housing estate and the delivery man couldn't find the address. We drank a couple of bottles of wine and then finally gave up and sloped off to bed in our lovely warm, brand new house. I remember us happy and excited, and with so many plans and so looking forward to our future."

And that was it.

Patrick stopped talking and he looked at me through the mirror.

And as I stood there, I suddenly realized that I hadn't cut a single hair on his head. I'd just been standing there, scissors in hand and listening to him.

"Patrick" I said "I'm so sorry"

He gave me a weary sort of smile "thanks for listening, sometimes you just need to talk to someone"

"Well, that's what a good barbers for" I said, somehow trying to ease things.

He contemplated, and was silent for a second or so, then he said something.

"You know, there's one little thing that I keep remembering, something that happened. It's a while ago now, but it was just one of those 'moments'..

A couple of years ago we went to Liverpool for the day, just me and Ruby. I remember we went on the train. It was a lovely sunny day and we had lunch, we'd found a French restaurant on the first floor above a trendy boutique. It was a bustling, very busy place with loads of atmosphere. We had to wait to get a table, but the food was excellent and we sat there for over two hours, chatting over a bottle of good white wine. When we'd finished, I paid the bill and then we walked over to the Docklands. As we walked, not talking, just walking along, Ruby put her head on my shoulder and nuzzled my neck, and then she squeezed my arm tightly. It was just a moment, a wonderful moment, and I knew that she loved me, really loved me.

I'll always remember it, the feeling was so good. I don't think I'll' ever forget that day"

I just looked at him and I couldn't say a word, there was simply nothing left to say.

He took a breath and spoke again "I suppose I'll always be able to say that I've been loved. I've loved and been loved"

"Not everyone has had that Patrick" I said to him "You've had something that was special, very special"

He nodded back at me...

"I'll bet you think I'm pathetic" he said.

"Not one bit Patrick, not a bit. In fact, it all makes me very sad".

I looked back at him, I knew he was suffering.

"You're a good friend" he replied.

And with that I cut Patrick's hair, and we talked and still tried to make sense or reason over what had happened to him.

When I'd finished cutting his hair, and as he was leaving the shop, he turned to me and fumbled in his pocket and then pulled out a C.D.

"I always bring you some music" he said, and he stared down at the disc "I actually need to get rid of this, its wonderful music but there's too many memories, here, you have it" and he passed me the disc.

"Who is it?" I asked.

"Bonny Rait"

"Oh, thanks Patrick" I said "Cheers" and then I felt a bit stupid.

Patrick smiled, and as he opened the door to go he turned to me and said "Track number three. It says it all." and with that he left.

I watched him walk away, and I had strange feeling that I wouldn't see Patrick again soon.

I didn't know why, it was just the finality of our conversation, there was just nothing left to say. It was strange really.

I arrived home from work that evening, feeling slightly at odds with myself.

Patrick's story had stuck in my head and had stayed the day. I'd eaten dinner and then I went upstairs to catch up with my e-mails and do some work on my computer, just messing about really. And then I remembered Patrick's C.D. His choice of music was always good and it struck me that I could listen to it on the computer while I worked. So I went to retrieve the disc from of my coat pocket. I looked at the label on the disc and 'oh yes', that was it...

'Bonny Rait'

I went back and sat down at the computer and inserted the disc into the drive.

Patrick's taste in music had always been excellent, varied yes, but always quality. Over the years he had opened many 'musical doors' for me, and it had been an education. It had led me to listen and appreciate a host of different musicians and varieties of music that I would have never known, never even heard of for that matter.

The disc was in the drive and the player came up on the computer screen, along with the list of tracks.

Then I remembered, what was it Patrick that had said to me?

Oh yes, 'Track number three', and he'd mentioned the track had some meaning.

So I looked down to the third track, it was called 'I can't make you love me' and I sort of sighed and thought 'well, here goes' and I pressed play.

The music started, and I leant back, and I listened to it.

And then 'Oh my god' and I sat there and gasped. The music, and the sound of it, it just hit me. It was the most wonderful and the saddest song that I had ever heard, and it still is.

It was all there, all the pain...the pain and the heartbreak that Patrick had talked about, it was all there, still fresh in my mind. And I sat there so sad, and I actually cried for the man and I shook at the memory of it. Because I was Patrick, and you have been Patrick, and anyone who has ever loved...loved someone and lost them has been Patrick, and the heartbreak and the desolation and the loneliness is unbearable.

Time, it seems certainly does run away with you, and almost a year passed by.

It was one cold and cloudy, grey March morning and I was down in Bolton town centre. Actually I was just walking out of my local bank, and for an instant I stood there on the pavement and zipped up my jacket in an effort to try and stay warm. I was just about to cross over the road when a bus drew up and stopped right in front of me, it was picking up the people who were sat, cold and waiting, at the bus stop directly opposite. I stood there for a moment and waited for the bus to move away, I was in no hurry, and within seconds the bus revved up its engine and set off again. As it drove away, I noticed that it had left someone behind. It was a man, and he just sat there. He hadn't got on the bus. He just sat there on the cold bench, staring at the floor. And in that brief instant as I stood there, I looked at the man again, and to my utter, utter shock, I realized that I was looking at Patrick. I just stood there and stared in disbelief.

Yes, it was Patrick, and Patrick was broken.

He was wearing an old green parka and faded brown trousers. Gone were the smart clothes and the sharp suits. He sat there with the haze of alcohol about him, red eyed and worn out. His face was thinner, hair now longer, uncut for some time. He'd never come back for a haircut and now I knew why.

And as I stood there facing him, he slowly looked up and he seemed to look straight through me, there was not one hint of recognition, nothing, not even a second glance.

He was on his own, and in his own lonely sad world. Poor, poor Patrick, I looked across at him and I was saddened and dismayed.

For a moment, I thought about going to go over and speak to him, to ask him how he was. But no, I didn't. I turned and I walked away, to my shame, I just walked away.

And at the time, I felt that it was because I didn't want to embarrass him, I'd known what had happened to Patrick and I knew that he'd suffered and suffered badly. But really that was just an excuse, it was just another lie, and you can't lie to yourself because deep down inside, you know the real truth. And later on I realized why I'd walked away, it was because it had been 'me' who was embarrassed, that was the reason, and I considered it and was ashamed.

Patrick had opened his heart to me and told me everything, because he looked upon me as a friend, and now I too had deserted him.

And that was unforgivable.

And so, under the great scheme of things, the story ended there, or so I thought.

You tend to put events to the back of your mind and get on with your life, everybody it seems, is busy and we all have plenty of things to do. And I suppose the old adage 'out of sight, out of mind' is a fairly accurate statement, even though it's not very praiseworthy.

Well, that was how I'd left things, until about six months ago when the phone in my shop rang, and when I answered it...it was Patrick.

To be absolutely truthful, I was a bit stunned. His was a voice from the past, and in all honesty, I never expected to hear from him again, or that's what I'd thought. And once again I remembered what had happened that day, when I saw him sitting at the bus stop, despondent and alone, and the thought of it made me feel ashamed, and more than that, a little guilty.

"Hi there" he said "It's me 'Patrick'. Remember me?" and he laughed.

Slightly amazed and slightly shocked, I just blurted out "Patrick. I don't believe it"

He laughed again "I know, it's been a long time"

"How are you?" I asked him, and again I felt the tinge of guilt.

"I'm fine, I'm fine. Listen, I need to come and see you and get my hair sorted out"

"No problem" I said "tell me, when do you want to come in?"

So two days later, the door of my shop swung open, and in walked Patrick.

It was like 'déjà vu, everything was repeating itself again.

But I looked at him as he stood there smiling at me, and this was a slightly different Patrick.

Time stops for no man, and Patrick too looked that little bit older. There were a few extra lines in his face, and his hair, now quite long had acquired the odd fleck of grey.

Gone too, was the sharp business suit. He was actually wearing some 'good' blue denim jeans with a pair of grey sneakers and an open grey and white checked shirt with a 'Rolling Stones' t-shirt underneath.

And I have to say, he looked pretty cool.

"Yo" I said to him "look at you...you look well Patrick"

"Hi buddy" he replied "it's good to see you"

And we shook hands like a couple of old friends, and I felt better for it.

We stood there talking, and the first thing I noticed more than anything was the change in his demeanour, and his manner. There was a slight change of character, this was a more 'laid back' Patrick, and this was a man who seemed much more at ease with himself.

Very, very much different from the last time we spoke.

So I got him sat in 'the chair' and we discussed his haircut, and then I asked him the inevitable question.

"So what have you been up to?"

He looked at me through the mirror, and he thought about it for a moment, and then smiled.

"How long is it since I've seen you? A year...two years?

"Nearer two, actually it may be more" I said.

"Christ, time flies"

"Tell me about it" I answered with a grin.

"Well, the last time I saw you...things weren't too good"

"They certainly weren't" I replied "you were having a terrible time of it"

"No, it wasn't good, for over a year I struggled, and struggled badly. I was living in a crappy flat and I was out of work, I was unemployed and unemployable. I'd taken to drinking, and I was drinking a lot. Truth be known, I think I was heading all the way to being an alcoholic. I'd stopped seeing the kids on a regular basis, basically because just going around to the house to pick them up, well it totally depressed me. Ruby always made a point of answering the door, she was always dressed up and ready to go out, just as soon as she could get rid of the kids. Strangely, she'd started smoking and would always open the front door with a glass of wine and a cigarette in her hand. She would simply give me a look of disgust and turn away as she called to the kids. Then she would shut the door in my face.

I also stopped seeing the kids regularly because it would to stop to her from going out. It was one of the reasons anyway, and I knew it would annoy her.

This carried on for months, and then one Saturday afternoon I was in my flat watching the T.V when there was a knock at my door. I groaned as I stood up to answer it, thinking 'what now'?

But when I opened the door, standing there were my kids.

My daughter had tears in her eyes, and my son just stood there silent.

I looked at them both "What's wrong?" I asked, and my daughter started to cry.

So I ushered them both in and tried to calm my daughter. I sat them both down at the table as I quickly tidied up and boiled some milk to make three mugs of hot chocolate. That done, I sat down with them at the table and asked them again 'What was wrong'?

My daughter spoke for them both, she told me everything.

Ruby, it seemed, was going crazy.

I hadn't known what was going on at home, I'd tried not to think about 'my home ' anymore because I wasn't part of it...it was gone, I'd lost it. So I sort of put my 'head in the sand' and let them all get on with their lives, it was an excuse I know, but it was the only way I could handle things.

Anyway, my daughter started to tell me what was going on, and I couldn't believe it.

Ruby was now living a different life. She was going out most nights, she just wouldn't stay in with the kids and her excuse was that 'she had a life to lead'. So she was going out nearly every night, apparently to some pub where her 'gang' hung out, I think they must have been her workmates. She would apparently come home from work, make the kids their tea and then go upstairs with a bottle of wine and get ready for 'the pub'. By eight o'clock she was out of the house and off. She would arrive back home somewhere between eleven and twelve and stagger around the kitchen before finally going upstairs. The kids would be in bed but they could hear the commotion.

The weekends were the worst. After the pub, Ruby would arrive back home with some man in tow, or with her gang of friends along with some men. Everybody got drunk and rowdy, and on occasion they had even staggered into the kid's bedrooms as they stumbled around looking for the toilet.

It seems Ruby had lost interest in their schoolwork, she no longer helped them with their homework and didn't get involved with my son's school anymore, or my daughter who was at college. There was a strange change of attitude towards the kids, she always used to make them both a packed lunch every day for school, there was always something different every day. But all that had stopped, she would give them both money and told them to 'just buy yourself something'.

When I heard about 'the men' I felt angry, very angry. But it was more than just jealousy, I was angry for the kids. I knew Ruby didn't want me, and I'd sort of come to terms with that, but now it seemed to me that she didn't want our children either, and it was as though they were in the way, and all because 'she had a life to lead'.

The thought struck me that if she wanted to 'live the life', why hadn't she just left us. Admittedly, I wouldn't have been happy, but I would have looked after our kids better than this. All that upset, just because she wanted her 'freedom'.

Life's never simple, is it?

I made us three more mugs of hot chocolate and pulled out a packet of biscuits and a couple of bags of crisps from the cupboard. The kids devoured them, and that slightly worried me. And I wondered, just how often they were this hungry?

As we sat there at the table, I looked at my daughter and she was still very uneasy. My son was more contented. Crisps and biscuits were his heaven. But my daughter...no.

So I picked up the remote for the television and passed it to him and told him to put something on the T.V. I mentioned some DVD that I had and I knew it would suit him. When he finally got interested in the telly, I turned to my daughter.

"What's wrong love" I said.

She looked back at me with her deep brown eyes, so bonny, and she started to sob.

"Dad, I don't know what to do" she said, and then she started to cry.

I looked back at her.

"What's happened?" I asked slowly.

She gulped, and I reached over and gave her my handkerchief. And as she wiped her eyes I asked her again "tell me love, what's gone on?"

She sniffed as she dried her eyes and then she told me.

"It was this morning dad, one of mum's boyfriends"

I felt angry, but "Go on" I said, and I wondered, just what was I about to hear?

She continued "Mum...Mum went out last night, as usual. She came home at about midnight with her new boyfriend 'Mick'. I don't like him, he's weird and he always looks at me a bit funny. Well last night I heard them come in and they were both having some sort of argument, they were both drunk, and I heard Mum shouting about some woman called 'Tracey' who he'd been talking to.

At one point Mick came upstairs, I thought he was going to the toilet, but then he opened my bedroom door. I asked him what he wanted, but he just stared at me and said that he was just checking that I was alright. He was drunk, but then Mum shouted up to him and asked him what he was doing, and he shut the door and went off to the toilet.

In the end, I put on my headphones to drown out the noise and finally went to sleep as I listened to my music.

In the morning, I got up as usual and went downstairs to get a drink. I got some juice out of the fridge and sat at the table for a while, then I heard someone moving about upstairs and then coming down the stairs. I thought it was Mum, so I went over to the sink and was washing my glass when I heard the kitchen door open. I just said "Hi" over my shoulder, there was no reply, but the next thing I felt two arms go around my waist and somebody said "Hi darling" in my ear, it was her boyfriend 'Mick'. I could smell his breath, he stunk of drink"

She stopped talking and looked across the table at me, nervous.

"Carry on love" I said "go on, tell me"

"He...He groped me Dad, he ran his hands up to my boobs, I didn't know what was happening, I couldn't believe it. I spun around to stop him, I was frightened but he held onto my shoulders, and then he leaned forwards and I think he was going to try to kiss me, I could smell his stinking breath. Then suddenly there was shouting, it was my Mum, she was standing at the kitchen door watching us and she was shouting "What do you think you're playing at" and Mick let me go as he he turned around to face her.

But she carried on "I know your game, I knew there was something going on"

She stood there and looked at us both, and I realized that she was still drunk.

"I bloody knew it" she screamed, and she turned to Mick "You...you dirty bastard" and then she looked back at me "and 'you'...I've seen you looking at him, and walking around in your knickers all the time, do you think I'm bloody stupid?"

As we sat there, she looked up at me "Dad, I was wearing my pyjamas"

"I know love" I said

"And I hate him dad. I can't stand him".

I nodded "Go on love, tell me what happened" and I tried to keep calm, but inside I wanted to kill the bastard.

She told me that they'd all had a big row and she'd run upstairs to her bedroom. Downstairs in the kitchen the arguing continued, and then it went quiet, and the next thing a Taxi arrived and her mother and 'Mick' got into it and disappeared.

I shook my head and glanced across to my son, he wasn't listening to the television, he was listening to us, and he knew all about what had gone on. His face told a story too.

And as I sat there, I wondered what the hell was happening to my family.

Now my first instinct was to charge over to the house and get hold of this 'Mick', and then beat the crap out of him, that would have been easy, too easy. Or maybe I should have rung the police and got them involved, but that would also involve my daughter and I didn't want that. And in the end, the pair of them could just lie about what had happened, and the police would probably believe her mother. If I went round to the house and beat the guy up, well, Ruby would take great delight in simply ringing the police, and it would be all my fault again, and this time I could end up in prison.

No, I had to be positive, and I had to think what was going to be best for my children, because things just couldn't carry on like they were.

And then it all clicked together.

"Right" I said "both of you, listen to me because I want to ask you something"

I now had their attention, and I took a deep breath, because this was a jump into the unknown.

"I'm going to ask you both something and whatever your decision is, I'll be okay with it, alright? I want to know if you would both like to come and live here with me."

And that was it, I'd said it.

They looked at one another, and smiled, and then they grinned for the first time that day.

And 'oh yes' that's what they wanted, and for the first time in a long while, I had a purpose.

So we sat there and we talked and we made plans, it was exciting stuff. Later that day I rang their mother and explained that they were staying the night and that I was going to call round with them the next day. She had a hangover, she didn't care.

So the next day, it was Sunday, and I went around to the house at around lunchtime. Ruby finally opened the door and stank of booze. I just said that I knew there had been a bit of a falling out and that I would have the kids for a week or so, just until things calmed down.

She didn't want to stand there and talk to me, she just said 'whatever' and closed the door in my face, and that was that.

Me and the kids went back there that evening at about nine o' clock, we knew she'd be out.

We packed up most of their clothes and their personal stuff and took everything back to my flat. During the next week we went round there again several times, always at night, and we got everything.

Anyway, the next morning I got them both off to school and to college and then I set about my flat and made it decent. The first thing I did was to throw away the booze. I threw all of it into the wheelie bin. Then I went down to the social services and told them everything. I told them why the kids were living with me because I was worried about the possibility of abuse, or even worse. They liased with the council offices and I was told that I would go on 'the list' for better accommodation. It took two or three months, but I was persistent, 'bloody persistent', and eventually they found us a three bed roomed house, and that was heaven, and it was a start. During that time a mate of mine helped me get a taxi drivers licence, he was a taxi driver too and when I finally passed the test, he got me a job at his firm. That was great, I had a job at last, and it was very flexible. It let me work around the kids because I only drove during the day and sometimes did a couple of hours after our tea. I was always home for eight o' clock. I never did the late night thing.

The strange thing was that taxi driving actually found me a new future. One day I got a call to take some guy to Liverpool Airport, I picked him up at his house and he jumped into the back of my taxi and off we went. We got onto the motorway and in between his phone calls he started to listen to my music, I always had something playing away in my cab.

"This isn't bad" he said "Who is it?"

And that started a long conversation on music.

"You seem to know you're stuff" he said.

"It's been a lifelong passion" I explained.

Then he told me "I'm in the music business" he said. "Well trying to be"

It turned out that he'd been a D.J in the past and he was now producing and mixing dance music of his own. He was also trying to promote music by other like minded D.J's that he'd met on the club circuit. He was a busy man, and now he was trying to get some commercial work, and that's why he was going to the Airport, he was flying to London to meet some producer.

"You never know, I could just hit on a winner..." he said, and as he laughed, he introduced himself.

"By the way my names Paul Stacey"

"And I'm Patrick, your friendly, musical taxi driver" I replied, and we shook hands over my shoulder.

When we got to the Airport he paid me and then reached into his bag and produced a C.D.

"Here" he said "have a listen to this, it's something I'm trying to promote, and hey give me some feedback, I'd appreciate it, my web address is on the back of the cover"

I thanked him for the C.D and off he went, and so did I.

On the way back, I put his C.D into the player and listened music that I'd never heard before, and it gave me a 'buzz', it was something really different.

That night I got onto his website 'Meridian Music' and I checked out what he was doing. I'd been listening to his C.D all day and in all honesty, I was hooked. So I decided to e-mail him and gave him some positive feedback. A couple of days later he e-mailed me back, he appreciated my input and we got into a conversation. After a week of swapping various e-mails, he asked me if I would like to listen to some of the other stuff that he was trying to promote, and he asked me to come down to his studio, which I did, actually the next day.

The studios were in an old mill, which were rented out as various sized units and were used for recording and practice workshops by musicians and D.J's. It was all about the music.

The whole place had a brilliant atmosphere, there was music everywhere, both live and recorded, and I was in seventh heaven.

So I got involved, and me and Paul became good friends. He was renting one of the studios where he mixed and produced his own and other people's music, and I sort of got into it.

And suddenly, if I wasn't taxi driving or with the kids, I was at the studio. In the end the kids started coming with me, they loved it. We set up a computer at home and got some music software and started messing about ourselves. We would put some track together and then the three of us would dance around the kitchen, it was absolutely brilliant. I was hooked, my god I was hooked.

I used to be up till three in the morning, mixing and messing about with different tracks, I just loved it. Finally, I put something together myself and gave it to Paul to listen to, and he liked it. He educated me somewhat, my music...it wasn't on the edge, but it was good solid dance music and he told me to keep at it. Then a few weeks later he came up with something. Some contact that he had in London had been approached by an Advertising Agency, and they were looking for someone to put some music together for their 'jingles', that's the catchy music they use with the adverts. They wondered if he was interested and Paul had immediately said 'Yes', but he then told me that he just didn't have the time to do it.

"So...you can do it" he said, sort of out of the blue.

"Me?" I was surprised. I was flabbergasted.

"Yes you" he insisted "I've sorted it all out. And here..." and he reached down and picked up a keyboard which he passed over to me.

"And here, you need this too" and he stuck a C.D on top of it ". That's the production software, go home and plug the keyboard into your computer and download the software, and then have a go.

"But I can't play a keyboard" I said "I can't play anything"

He just laughed and said "With that software 'you can'. Believe me"

So that's what I did, and my god, I almost became a musician overnight. The software was incredible, it let you programme the keyboard into the computer, and after that you could never play a 'bum' note. Whatever you did, and whatever key or keys that you pressed, the computer would find the next compatible note or chord and play it totally 'in key'. So you simply could not play anything out of tune. It was brilliant. Me and the kids were almost fighting over the damn thing. Anyway I started, and things began to come together. I would come up with an idea, mess about with it and try to make it sound right, then I'd put the music into a file and e-mail it off to Paul at the studio. At one point he was getting some new music off me every couple of days. Some worked, some didn't, but 'hey 'that's the music industry. Eventually though, he did start to send some of my work down to London and they liked it, and 'hey presto' they used it, and we got a cheque through the post and that really made us buzz, because it was also really decent money. Me and Paul shook hands on it, and basically, he invited me into the business.

"You're ready for this" he said "and I need somebody solid like you to back me up".

So we became partners and I gradually cut down my taxi work and spent more and more time in the studio, and I learned my craft, and finally it all came together. All those years of listening to all kinds of music had turned my brain into some sort of musical reference book and suddenly, I could pull out sounds from anywhere. It was almost as if 'anything'...anything at all I wanted was all there in my head, I felt like a walking juke box. And I could use all those sounds because I'd learned my craft, and I could turn it all into dance music.

We were on a roll, and we started producing and manufacturing dance C.D's and now we're distributing them and it seems to be taking off, big time. We have dance music out there now that all the Club D.J's are starting to use, we've even got orders from Ibiza and Miami.

So its fingers crossed.

I stopped cutting his hair for a moment and stood back.

"Strewth Patrick, you never, ever cease to amaze me"

Patrick laughed "Thanks buddy, to tell you the truth I can't believe it either, I've sort of amazed myself. It's like 'riding the tiger'."

"So where are you heading with all this?" I asked him.

He looked up at me "London".

"Really?"

"Yes, me and Paul are moving everything down there. We've found some studios that we want to set up, and once we've done that we can make all our own contacts. Now we have a foot in the door and have some credibility, our music's in demand and our label is finally getting some respect"

"So you're going to live down there?"

"Yeah, I've found a place, a good sized flat just outside Notting Hill. Me and Andrea and the kids are moving in next month, we're all really excited about it".

"Whoa, stop right there" I said and I started to laugh "just back up a minute there pal... 'Andrea'. Who's Andrea? You never mentioned that bit of news".

And Patrick suddenly began to grin like a schoolboy.

He laughed "I was about to get round to telling you about that"

"Well" I said "go on then, tell all"

He smiled and took a deep breath. "Err...well it was about four or five months ago now.

One night and I was mucking about on the computer, I was checking my e-mails and doing the 'facebook' thing. I'd been putting the usual daft comments to the stuff on 'facebook' when suddenly a reply came back, it just said "Well I never" and it was from somebody called Andrea Berkley. I hadn't a clue who it was, so I clicked onto her name and her 'facebook' page came up, and her photograph. It was a girl I used to know years ago, but she used to be called Andrea Sutton then. She sort of 'went out' with a friend of mine for a while, and I used to go out with a friend of hers. We went out as two couples and used to go all over the place. We were a bit 'young and wild' but we used to have a right laugh. Anyway, I replied to her, I just wrote back "and where the hell have you been" and that was that, and it was also the start of things. We kept e-mailing each other for a couple of weeks, and finally we decided to meet up. To tell you the truth, I always did have a bit of a thing for her, she was gorgeous, and she always looked a bit 'Italian', a proper stunner. Back when we all used to go out, me and her used to always end up talking to each other, I often thought that there was 'something' there, but 'she' was going out with my mate and I was going out with her friend so it was all a bit too complicated, and of course we were young and very daft.

Anyway, we decided to meet up on a Saturday night at a local Wine Bar in the town centre. I sat there at eight o' clock, watching the door and as nervous as a sixteen year old on a first date. And then, in she walked, and I gasped. She took my breath away, she was as beautiful, and as beautiful as she ever had been, and I jumped up and just stood there with my mouth wide open. Truthfully, she looked better than I ever remembered.

She just looked at me, smiled and said "Hi stranger, how are you?"

"I'm a lot better now" I said, and I gave her a hug and a peck on the cheek.

We said our 'hellos' and then we went over to the bar.

"What would you like?" I asked.

She thought about it for a moment "Can I have a glass of Prosecco please?"

"Yes, and I'll have one too" I said, but as the barmaid arrived I changed my mind.

"Give me a bottle of Prosecco please, and sling it in an Ice bucket" I said to the barmaid.

Andrea looked at me, a bit startled "You're pushing the boat out"

"And you're worth it." I said to her, and she laughed again, and I was smitten.

The chilled bottle of Prosseco arrived in a cut glass ice bucket which was all very classy, and I picked it up along with two glasses and then led her over to a table in the corner. And then we just sat there and talked. There's a really clever thing about buying the bottle, you don't have to keep getting up to go to the bar. Anyway it must have worked, because we just sat there all night and talked to each other. I kept looking at her beautiful face, and lord, she just made me feel good. By the time we'd finished the second bottle I'd turned to her and kissed her and the deal was done, we were already a couple, it was that uncomplicated.

"My God Patrick" I said "You've won the bloody lottery"
Patrick grinned back at me "You're right there, and that's exactly what it feels like"
"How are the kids with it all?" I asked him.
"They love her to bits, they really do. Andrea never had any children of her own, just a bastard of a husband who used to hit her".
"Oh bloody hell" I said.
"Oh yes, he gave a hard time, and why I don't know, she's really lovely"
"Some blokes are like that" I said "it's probably the jealousy thing"
"I don't know, but anyway we've told each other everything, we both know each other's past and I think it's made us stronger. You know...'no secrets' and all that.
"Nice one" I said and yes, I had to agree with him.
"So we've been together nearly six months now and it's so easy, it's like she's always been there, she is my best mate without doubt. I love talking to her, we sit at the kitchen table with a bottle of wine and talk all night, it's really good, and I feel like I've got my life back"
"You 'have' got your life back Patrick" I said, and I looked at him through the mirror and I saw a happy man, and I was happy for him.
Then he laughed at me "My god man, you've really seen me through some crappy times"
"Yes I bloody well have" I said "and for a time back there, you had me worried pal"
"Yeah I know, it was awful, but you know what they say, 'time is a great healer'..."
"Yes that's true" I said "and I don't really like to broach the subject Patrick, but do you ever hear from your ex-wife?"
Patrick raised his eyes to the ceiling "Yes, from time to time. Every so often she meets up with the kids and drags them off to a pub for some food, no surprise there then. The last thing I heard was that she was going off to Greece for the whole of the summer. Apparently, 'now' she's going over there 'to find herself '. Which actually means that she'll be drunk for the best part of six months, or she'll run out of money and have to come back home" .
Patrick smiled at me "She always did fancy herself as some sort of 'Shirley Valentine'. Maybe somebody should have told her that it's just a bloody film".

He laughed, and I just shrugged in agreement. And that was it, I'd cut his hair and it was time to go.

We shook hands and he gave me a man's hug. It was a hug from a friend.

"Thanks buddy" he said "and when I'm back up here I'll be in for a haircut"

As he left, I wished him well. And I stood there and smiled as I considered his new life, and his old one.

And true to his word, he always does come back for his haircut, always.

The door 'does' still swing open, and of course...in walks Patrick.

CHAPTER FIVE

The stories told in my shop are a bit like a two way street. I listen to some and I tell some. Well that's what a good barber does. And over the years I've told many a tale about my father, a rather hilarious man who managed to get himself into all sorts of predicaments.

In many cases these stories involved me too, so really, it's a family thing.

My Dad, well where do you start? Firstly, we never ever knew his birthday. He was born somewhere around 1921, I say somewhere because unfortunately whoever signed the birth certificate back then put the wrong date on it. So his birthday was deemed to be 'sometime' in January. His mother, my grandmother, eventually picked out some random date, and everybody worked from there. One wonders, did they never own calendars back then?

Not the best of starts, but it does actually say something about our family. It seems that we,

'The family', have always been a bit blasé about the little things...'the fine detail of life'.

We tend not to bother about the mundane and everyday matters, and the infamous 'It'll be alright' or 'Yes, I'll get back to it' and the much celebrated 'Oh, it'll sort itself out' have always been staunch family mottos.

Anyway, my ancestors were all originally farmers, and apparently more than a century ago we used to farm in the town of Burnley in Lancashire. That was until my great-great grandfather was thrown out of town for marrying a young girl of the opposite faith. Whether the young lady was catholic or protestant I don't really know, because it seems that over the past decades we'd swopped sides a few times, backwards and forth, and always for the love of a younger woman. So nothing's changed there then either.

From Burnley, we silently immigrated to Bolton and bought a farm there. Thankfully there was no internet or telephone back in those days or we could have all been burned at the stake. Marrying one of the 'other lot' back then was not taken lightly. You could have a fling with a sheep, but kiss a Catholic and 'Oh my godfathers'. You had to get out of town, quick.

So we set up in Bolton, and we were doing quite well for about seventy or eighty years, then suddenly, things took a turn for the worse.

It was the Co-op.

My Grandfather was running the farm by then, it would be around the late thirties and we'd become quite successful. |My great grandfather and my grandfather had by then successfully built up the farm and we had a herd of over one hundred cows, it was actually the biggest herd in Bolton and this was at a time when farmers were the rich people of the town. It turns out that we had land all over the place, and money. My father was brought up in a house that had servants and as a child he even had a nanny.

Back in those days, the daily milk was delivered every evening by horse and cart. The farmer would pour his milk into several round metal containers known as 'kits', and then load them onto the back of the cart and go round the streets of Bolton, house to house, supplying the milk. Women would come out to the cart with a jug, and the milk would be ladled from the kit into the housewife's jug or pot.

That was how it was, always had been. And then, out of the blue, the Co-op arrived, and with it, the Co-op Dairy. Bugger.

And the Co-op had this brand new idea, they put the milk into bottles, and then as if that wasn't enough, they also decided to deliver the milk to your doorstep, in the morning, at the crack of dawn.

My god, they were almost cheating.

And so the local housewife only had to open her front door and the milk was there, waiting for her. How lazy could women get?

My grandfather, who was very single minded, just couldn't understand the wind of change, and refused to, and in fact famously said

"Eh don't worry, they'll always come out wit' jug for their milk"

Well they didn't. In fact, nobody did. And very quickly he had a lot of milk and not a lot of customers.

The family implored him to sign up with the Co-op dairy, and supply them with milk directly just as a lot of the other farmers had done. Or alternatively, buy a bottling machine and go it alone, as others were also doing, and then do the morning 'doorstep' delivery. But no, the foolish man would not change his ideas and his stubborn character would not let him change his mind, unfortunately, another family trait.

Things soon started to go wrong, badly wrong. Well, there was no money coming in and the bills were soon beginning to stack up. Then my grandfather came up with a solution, a master plan that would solve his financial problems. It was quite simple, every time a large bill arrived, he would sell a cow to pay off the debt. How clever.

This financial wizardry was akin to the ostrich that buried its head in the sand, and yes, as the bills rolled in, the cows rolled out. And so over a period of time the herd began to quickly and inevitably decline, and of course diminish, and then finally disappear altogether.

In fact, he was left with just one cow.

The family finally had to sell up and leave the farm.

They moved into a small terraced house nearby and they took the cow with them. Apparently they kept it in the back yard, the mind boggles. Grandfather resolutely refused to buy milk off anybody else because they'd been producing their own for generations.

It was a humiliation I suppose. He'd lost the family farm, the land and all the money, and was now reduced to living the same life as everyone else. The locals relished all of this of course, it was good gossip and as ever, people loved to see somebody else's downfall. So the terraced house it was, my grandfather and grandmother, my father and his three sisters, and of course the cow. Throw in a dog or two and a handful cats and you have a pretty full house. It must have been fairly noisy too, what with the dogs barking at the cats, the sisters barking at one another, and the cow having a right old moo. One could only feel sorry for the neighbours.

But the humiliation of all this spread to my father, he was ashamed of what had happened to them of course, and well, he was a young man by then and nobody likes being laughed at. In the end he had to get a job as a bus conductor, and then eventually, along came the war.

It's curious, my father and I would have long conversations on every topic under the sun, but he would never talk about his own father, it was a taboo subject and from a young age I subconsciously learned never to ask. On the two or three occasions that my father did ever mention him, I soon realised that my grandfather was a hard man to live with. There was no love, but there was definitely brutality. It seems that he was a very strict and humourless sort of person, definitely not the doting father, and I suppose those were different times back then. But my father once did tell me that 'they' the family, had implored my grandfather to go onto the bottled milk, my grandmother begged him to, she could see way things were heading.

As my father finished telling me this, he said "But no, the stubborn old bastard wouldn't do it, and we lost everything", and losing everything had affected his life.

In due course, I came to understand how much he hated his father, and also how much he loved me. And I realized how much he enjoyed the father and son bond that he had with me. It was something that he himself had never had.

The war arrived, and like a lot of other young men, my father was called up for service and he was enlisted into the army.

It was whilst he was away, fighting in Italy, that his father died. Coming home for the funeral was never going to happen, there was a war on so the possibility of being sent home for a funeral service was simply out of the question.

After the funeral, the first thing my grandmother did was to get rid of the cow. Well, who would want to have to milk a cow twice a day when you could have the milk delivered fresh to your door, every morning, in a bottle. It just made more sense.

My father fought the war, and spoke little about it. When I was a young boy, I once naively asked him 'if he had ever killed anybody'. He looked at me, and gave me the sternest look I'd ever had in my life, and he simply said "No"

And at that moment, I knew it was something that I should never ask him, ever again.

He did however, like to tell tales about some of the funnier things that happened during the war. He had a friend in the Army whose name was Harry Jackson, and my father and Harry thankfully served the whole of the war together and were the best of mates. According to my father, the war was something that you just had to try and get through. Nobody was an intentional hero, and most of the 'hero's' that he ever knew, were in most cases, in the wrong place at the wrong time, but managed to do something spectacular about it . Bravery wasn't really given a second thought...it was the sense of survival that saved the day. And it was Harry's and my dad's sense of survival that without doubt kept them alive. Their viewpoint on the war was 'Keep your head down, and for god's sake, never volunteer for anything'. And it was that attitude that got them through it, eventually.

There was also a lot of swearing, it's what happens when men get together, it goes with the territory and it also it goes with this story.

My father once gave me his thoughts on guns and weapons in general.

"Forget guns" he said in his wisdom "Waste of bloody time, you didn't need guns. No, it was a spade you needed, a good spade, a bloody rifle only got in the way."

"A spade..?"I said, slightly mystified.

"Yes lad 'a spade', it was part of your kit. A short spade, army issue, it was about two foot long. A great piece of kit"

"What did you do with it dad, throw dirt at the enemy?" I said with glee. He ignored the comment completely and continued.

"Oh no, with a good spade you could dig, and dig bloody quickly. When we heard them bloody German shells coming our way, me and Harry could dig a three foot hole and jump in the bugger quicker than the Germans could get the next round in. Dig a good hole, and you've got a chance of surviving. We used to sit in camp at night and all around us the other men would be polishing their rifles, daft sods. Not me and Harry, we used to sit there and sharpen our shovels, we had 'em as sharp as razors, Harry reckoned he could shave with his. We weren't daft, we knew what kept you alive, bloody rifles aren't much use when a sodding great tank's lobbing shells at you."

I took in what he said, and it did make sense.

He continued "I always remember when me and Harry got our big break, we couldn't believe our luck, they put us on stretcher duty. Well I'll tell you...that was just great."

"And why was that"? I asked.

He looked at me and shook his head, as you would, to an idiot.

I was chided, but puzzled.

He shook his head and continued "Think about it, if you had somebody injured on a stretcher, you didn't go over and show the Germans what a good job they'd done, you went back...back to camp or wherever. You went to first aid, you went anywhere, but you got yourself out of there and as quick as your bloody legs would carry you. In the end me and Harry left our rifles in a hole somewhere in Italy, we could manage better without them. When you've got an injured soldier on a stretcher, he takes some carrying, especially if you're trying to run like a bloody greyhound".

I could see where he was coming from.

"Me and Harry had it off to a fine art, if you got shot, we could have a bloody stretcher under you before you hit the floor" and he laughed.

"I'll always remember when Harry tried to get somebody to shoot him"

"What?" I said, and I grinned, I knew this would be good. Dad's tales were always good.

"He was trying to get away...away from the shelling and the bullets, stupid bugger".

He chuckled "Harry...what a card. Never a dull moment, bless him. Well Harry had got fed up, we'd had our share of near misses and he must have been beginning to wonder just how long our luck would last. Anyway, we'd arrived at some first aid tent somewhere in the hills at the back of beyond, with a soldier that was in a bad way. He'd had his arm nearly shot off and had some bad facial injuries, we'd had to carry him for over an hour, but the poor bugger died while the doctors were trying to save him. We were sitting outside the first aid tent with some of the other injured lads, having a breather and sharing cigarettes, when one of the doctors walked over to us and threw some papers into the face of one of the injured men who was sat on the floor.

"You've got your ticket" the doctor said, and he looked at the soldier with absolute disgust, then turned and walked away.

We looked down at the injured man, who was sitting there with his foot bandaged up, there was a wooden crutch on the floor at the side of him.

"What was all that about?" said Harry

The soldier with the crutch leaned down to pick up his papers and then with a bit of help, he stood up.

"I got shot in the foot" he said

"That was bad luck" said Harry.

"No, it was good luck" said the soldier "it was good luck, now I get to go home, for good" And then he turned away and without further a word, he limped slowly off.

I looked at the rest of the soldiers "What was that all about...with the doctor?" I asked them.

One of the soldiers looked at me "We think he shot himself, shot himself in the foot. Now he can't walk and he can't run, he's no use to the army now so they ship him back home and that's it."

We all stood there in silence, smoking our treasured cigarettes. Nobody spoke, and I looked across at Harry, who was just staring at the soldier who was hobbling back to his tent, and for once, Harry had nothing to say. He just stared at the injured soldier.

About a week passed, it was an afternoon and we were all having a rest. There'd been no fighting for a couple of days and I was lying in the grass, just on the edge of camp. I'd been having a snooze in the afternoon sun and I was looking up at the blue sky and thinking about life and things. You know something, Italy is so beautiful, even with the war going on it was such a beautiful country. The fields, all so green or full of yellow corn, and the buildings, pale grey stone, or pink and orange brick with terracotta roofs, all sort of rustic, they were just lovely.

Anyway, somebody kicked me in the leg and I looked up and it's Harry, all smiles and cigarettes.

"Hi" he said and he passed me a ciggie as he squatted down at the side of me.

"Thanks for spoiling my bit of peace" I said.

"We're at war pal, there's no time for peace" and he thought that was funny and he laughed at himself...that was Harry. He took a long drag on his cigarette and slowly blew out the smoke.

"I've had an idea" he said.

"Oh god, here we go" I said, and I lay back on the grass and shook my head.

Harry's ideas were legendary, and they usually got us into trouble. He once did a deal on a case of stolen rum. We sold some of it, but drank the rest, and we got so drunk that we actually fell over the side of a stone bridge as we staggered back to camp. A passing platoon found us the next morning, very badly hung over and stuck in the mud under the bridge. We were floundering about like a couple of drunken fish, some state we were in 'and' I'd managed to knock my front teeth out. Anyway that got us three days in the glass house, and after that a trip to the army dentist for some false teeth.

Harry continued "Listen" he said slowly "I need to talk to you about something"

He was suddenly serious, and that was worrying.

"Go on" I said, a bit apprehensively.

"It's like this. I want out, I've had enough."

I just looked at him "What do you mean you want out. Christ man, I know you want out, we all want out, but we're at war...remember?" and I tapped my forehead.

"No" he said "I mean it".

"Oh bloody hell Harry" and I lay back on the grass and looked back up at the sky.

"Please don't tell me you're going to desert. If you do a bunk, they'll catch you and bloody well shoot you"

"No, it's nothing like that, no I've been thinking. Do you remember that bloke, the other week at that camp up in the hills, the bloke who shot himself in the foot and got himself sent home?"

I put my hands over my eyes "Oh strewth Harry, you're not thinking of shooting yourself for Christ's sake" I moaned "You can't do that"

"I know" he said "You're right, I couldn't shoot myself. So I've been thinking, and I want you to do it".

"You what" I said, and with that I sat back up quickly "What...me, shoot you?"

"Yes"

"And you can sod off" I said. I couldn't believe it, and then of course, I could.

"Harry, you can 'bugger off. There is no way that I'm going to shoot you, not a chance, no way".

"Only in the foot" he exclaimed, and to my amazement, he was quite taken aback by my refusal to blow his foot off.

"I am not shooting you in the foot, or anywhere else for that matter. Christ man, we spend all day picking up men who've been shot, you've seen what damage a bullet can do."

"Could you not just shoot off a toe?" he said.

"No I could not"

"Well, some bloody mate you are" he said "well don't bother then, and thanks for nothing" and he turned to walk away, he was in a right old temper.

He shouted back "Don't you worry, I'll get somebody else to do it, I've got other friends that will shoot me"

"Carry on like that and I'll do you a favour, I'll just bloody club you to death" I called after him.

"Get stuffed" he replied and stamped off.

Now I was laughing at him, and I shouted "Why don't you go and have a chat with the Germans, they'll help you out".

He shouted something back, it sounded like 'Fuck off'.

By the following week Harry had asked to several of the lads to shoot him, they all refused of course, and they came straight round to me to let me know what was going on.

Eventually, the penny dropped, and he finally came and found me and we had a chat.

"Nobody will do it" he said, he was a bit downhearted.

"What do you expect?" I said "The lads are here to shoot the enemy, the bloody Germans. They won't shoot another English soldier"

Harry shrugged "Some of them said they'd gladly shoot that 'git' of a sergeant"

Our sergeant was not a nice man, he was from Cardiff, had red hair, and shouted at us all the time.

"Yes" I said "But he's Welsh, and yes I'd personally grenade the bastard myself"

We laughed and lit up some ciggies. We were mates again and that was good.

But Harry was Harry, and he just wouldn't let things go. A week later he got hold of some whiskey and he then announced to us all what he was going to do.

Five of us were sitting around the campfire one night, as he told us his plan.

"Listen, I've got this whiskey, and on Friday night I'm going to have a good drink and then I'm going to shoot myself"

"In the foot or through your thick stupid head" I asked him.

I looked at the other lads "Here we go again" I said.

Harry continued "In the foot of course, it'll be alright. I'll say it was an accident, I did it while I was drunk"

"Really" I said.

Suddenly the lads around the campfire decided that this could be good sport.

"Can we watch?" they asked enthusiastically.

"Course you can" said Harry with a bit of bravado.

And suddenly, the lads all decided that they'd all take bets on the result.

I just sat there knowing the result, it would be another disaster.

So eventually Friday night arrived, and by now half the camp had heard about Harry's plan and had decided to make a night of it. It was decided that the deed should be done in the mess tent, which was quite large and would accommodate an audience. To give them their due, all the lads who turned up brought some booze with them with the idea that they could help Harry along by getting him drunk, and there was so much surplus alcohol about that a bit of a party started. The fact that everybody was having such a good time began to worry me a bit, if things got out of control with the booze, and some of the other lads decided that foot shooting was the way to go, half our platoon could end up legless, in more ways than one.

Harry was loving it of course, he was the centre of attention, laughing and joking, and there was plenty of back slapping. Everyone was offering him a swig from their bottle, to help him on his way, which it was.

Within an hour he'd drank his own bottle of whiskey and was half way through another. He'd also had a lot of swigs from a lot of other bottles too, in fact, he was pissed.

It was decided, that Harry should shoot himself whilst standing on top of a table so that everybody could see. Everyone was in full agreement, a lot of money had changed hands by then and the betting was rife. The moment had arrived and a flushed and staggering Harry was finally led to the table, accompanied by a lot of cheering. The lads lifted Harry onto the table with even more cheering, but it was quickly realized that the drunken sod couldn't stand up, in fact he couldn't get up off his knees. There was a bit of consternation, 'the show must go on' and all that, plus the betting. So it was decided that Harry should shoot himself whilst lying on his back and that he could prop his foot on top of a beer crate so that he would be able to see his 'target'. So they rolled him over onto his back and the beer crate was acquired.

Harry lay on the table laughing and repeating the words "I'm gonna do it, I'm gonna do it"

Then, grinning stupidly, he suddenly propped himself up on one arm and shouted out

"I need a fucking gun"

We'd forgotten about that.

One of the soldiers dashed out and returned a couple of minutes later with a loaded rifle. He gave it to Harry and everybody decided to stand back a bit. Harry lay there on his back and started to take aim at his left foot. It was then that some idiot shouted out that he should take his boot off, obviously this fool liked the sight of blood. That started a huge discussion and continued with arguments as to how the deed should be done, 'boot on or boot off'.

As the dispute continued, there was suddenly a loud crash, and we all looked round to see that Harry had rolled off the table, along with the rifle and the beer crate. Two of the lads dashed over to check Harry, three of them went to check the rifle. Anyway the rifle was okay and Harry, along with gun and the beer crate, was put back on the table. It was finally decided that he should shoot himself with his boot on, since this was going to be reported as an 'accident', even the more intoxicated realized that the chances of somebody wandering about with one boot off, and then shooting themselves in that same foot, was pretty slim.

Harry bless him, was now past caring, he'd have shot his mother.

He was very drunk by then, and it was decided that things would have to get a move on because there was a serious chance of him passing out.

So, Harry was lying on the table with his foot on the beer crate and somebody once again gave him the rifle. Harry looked confused, and then he suddenly remembered what he was there for and he went into action. Settling the rifle butt against his shoulder he proceeded to take aim. However, having consumed the equivalent of two bottles of scotch and more besides, his aim wasn't that steady. He was also having great difficulty in focusing on his foot, he pointed the rifle in the right direction, but it kept swaying about from side to side. The lads who were standing in the area down from

Harry's foot quickly moved out of the way, they realized that with the present amount of 'sway' , they were in great danger of getting blasted too .

Finally, Harry got some sort of control and wedged the end of the barrel directly onto his boot. There was a hushed silence as everybody suddenly realized that this was the moment, and then somebody called out

"Do it Harry" and then the rest of the lads began to shout "Come on Harry"

And with glazed eyes, Harry looked at his foot, and pulled the trigger.

There was an ear shattering bang as the gun went off. Some of the lads actually ducked as the noise from the gun resonated around the enclosed area of the mess tent.

"Oh Christ" I said "he's bloody done it"

And I looked across at the table. Harry lay there unconscious as his left boot smouldered and smoked, and then it caught fire.

There was a mass scramble to the table, half the lads thought Harry was dead and the other half were throwing beer over his flaming foot.

"It's alright, he's alive" I shouted as I slapped his face from side to side and cursed him

"You stupid bugger"

And as his boot was finally doused, I instructed the lads to revive Harry by pouring the surplus beer over his head.

It was an act of mercy.

Half a dozen pints in the face later, Harry came to.

The first thing he said, well he didn't say anything really, he just screamed.

He screamed just like a pig being slaughtered, and he howled too, but at least he was alive. Although just what state his foot was in, inside that smouldering boot, God only knew.

We lifted him onto a stretcher and then me and another lad ran him round to the medical tent. Harry moaned in agony and vomited all the way there, a stomach full to the brim with whiskey and a throbbing burnt foot with a bullet hole through it was not a good combination.

We ran him into the tent where a doctor and nurse were in attendance.

"Emergency" I shouted as we ran through the tent flaps "Bullet wound in left foot sir"

The Doctor and nurse went into action straightaway.

"What happened?" asked the doctor as he rushed over to examine Harry.

"Err, this is Private Jackson sir, we were having a bit of a celebration and whilst private Jackson was cleaning his gun sir, it accidentally went off, sir"

The Doctor looked up at me over a pair of horn rimmed spectacles.

"So you're telling me that Private Jackson was in the habit of cleaning his gun whilst it was loaded?"

"Yes sir"

The doctor leant over Harry and was immediately hit by the smell of whiskey and vomit.

"Good god" he gagged "and was this man in the habit of cleaning a loaded gun while he was drunk?"

"Yes sir, it was because he was drunk that the gun remained accidentally loaded. It was probably carelessness sir"

"There's a lot of it about" replied the doctor with a raised eyebrow and some scepticism.

I realized that he knew all about 'carelessness'.

"We'll take it from here soldier" he said. "Dismissed"

We saluted, turned sharply, and did one.

Forty eight hours it took, eventually forty eight hours later I was allowed in to see him.

I was finally given permission to go into the medical tent to see how he was doing.

Well, my god, you should have seen the state of the man. He was still lying on his bed, still hung over even after two days, he was a wreck. His left foot was a mass of bandages and he just lay there and watched me walk up to the bed through his matching bloodshot eyes.

"And how are we"? I asked jovially.

He stared up at me "What happened?" he croaked.

"Well, you managed to shoot yourself you bloody idiot, that's what happened"

He put his hand on his forehead and slowly rubbed his eyes.

"I've got the hangover from hell, and my foot's bleeding killing me, it feels like it's on fire."

"It was" I said.

"What?"

"It was on fire, we had to throw beer on it to put out the flames. You nearly burned your bloody foot off".

Harry looked at his bandaged foot and shook his head "This had better be worth it 'Jesus Christ' its sore" and he groaned again.

He looked really rough, well he was, and so after a short stay I left him to sleep it off.

It took another two days before I could get back to visit him again. I walked into the medical tent and spotted Harry straightaway, he was now sat on the side of his bed and he did not look happy.

"Hi ya matey, how's it going?" I said.

I looked at him and 'oh dear no', he wasn't happy, not one bit. In fact he was mad, angry and mad.

"What's up?" I said.

"What's up, I'll tell you what's up. That bloody doctor came to see me this morning, and I'm expecting him to tell me that my foot's so badly injured, that I won't be able to walk or run properly again and here's my ticket home, and 'Bobs yer uncle' and I'm out of here.

But 'Oh bloody no'! It seems that I haven't shot myself in the foot at all, I bloody well missed, and the sodding bullet went right between my toes. My big toe's got third degree burns and it's killing me, but that bloody rotten doctor says that 'with three weeks' and a lot of antiseptic cream, he'll have me skipping about again like a gazelle. What a bastard!"

I completely fell about laughing.

"Oh, I knew 'you'd' find it funny. Bloody hilarious, thank you very much"

And that was that, a month later we were back on stretcher duty. Every so often Harry would have a moan about his 'bad' foot and walk about with an exaggerated limp as he complained about his famous injury, but he fooled no one.

Strangely though, he was always remembered by everyone for that night's entertainment, and for all the wrong reasons, he became a bit of a legend.

It was a good story, and we both laughed. My dad loved telling stories about the funny things that happened in the war. I think the humour was used as a compromise, something to keep your spirits up as you lived with death, fear and danger.

"Did you ever get any medals, you and Harry?" I asked.

My dad burst out laughing "Medals, no lad, we didn't get any medals. You had to be running at the Germans to get medals, me and Harry were busy going the other way. And I'll tell you something else, it was only a couple of months after Harry's foot got better that we got into some real trouble and ended up in the glass house again. We got locked up big time, and this time it was serious".

"Why, what happened" I asked.

"We killed the Major's dog".

"What?"

"We killed his dog. It was an accident really, but Christ, at the time I thought we were for the firing squad"

"Did you shoot it or something?"

"No, it was nothing like that. It all started one morning when me and Harry had gone for one of our 'walks'. We used to disappear, it was easy really, both of us would set off somewhere in a hurry carrying our stretcher. It looked like we were actually doing something, and so nobody questioned what we were up to. If an officer appeared, we just put on a bit of a dash and they presumed we were either going off for someone or had just brought somebody back, and it usually worked.

So there we were, strolling back to camp for a brew, when suddenly a grey staff car went past us and slowed and then stopped. Somebody got out of the back of the car and started waving at us to come forward, it was an officer, we immediately thought 'Jesus, what now' and so we quickly trotted up to the car and saluted. A tall thin, moustached officer saluted back.

"I'm Lieutenant Ormrod" he said "can I ask you both what you are doing?"

We were trained for this, and we both blurted out "Nothing Sir".

And then Harry realized that 'doing nothing' could actually be a way of volunteering to do something, and he instantly went into action.

"We're scouting sir. We're searching for the injured and the dead, we always do that sir, just in case anyone's been missed"

Since all the fighting, shooting or shelling that was taking place, was actually several miles to the west of us, the chance of finding anybody, writhing in agony and only 500 yards from camp, was pretty slim.

"Oh really" said the Lieutenant, with a bit of a smirk "So you're not busy at the moment?"

This was not a question, it was a statement.

Harry quickly replied "Not at this 'actual' moment sir, but we could get busy after lunch"

I closed my eyes, 'god' you'd think we were playing cricket.

"Ah good" said Lieutenant Ormrod, after completely dismissing Harry's bullshit.

He then continued "Sitting in the back of the car is Major Duggan, he would like to speak to you both"

We went to the open door of the car and saluted "Sir!"

In the back of the car, Major Duggan acknowledged us. He was a rather plump man, in his mid sixties, with silver hair and a silver moustache. On his lap was a small black and brown Yorkshire terrier which immediately started to snarl at us.

"Gentlemen" he said to us "This is Smokey" and he looked down and affectionately stroked the little dog "We shall be stationed at this camp for approximately two months and I need someone to look after my dog. He will need feeding, walking and regular exercise in the mornings, at dinners and at early evening. Once he's been fed and watered and has had a little walk, you will bring him back to my tent"

Then the Major leaned forward and looked for his Lieutenant, then barked "Ormrod"

'Ah' I thought 'Big dog, little dog'.

Lieutenant Ormrod nearly jumped out of his boots at his master's call.

"Yes Major" he replied as he leant over to look into the back of the car.

The Major was attaching a thin brown lead to Smokey's collar.

"Ormrod, give the dog to the men" and he once more lovingly stroked the terrier and then passed him over to the Lieutenant.

The dog snarled and yapped and tried to bite the Lieutenant's hand. 'Smokey' didn't like the Lieutenant, however we were soon to find out that Smokey didn't like anybody, except of course the Major.

The Lieutenant placed the growling little dog on the ground and passed me the lead, I noticed that he wore leather gloves, and maybe that should have been a clue.

The Major turned to us "Have him back at my quarters in an hour" and then he looked down at his little dog, "Bye-bye Smokey, have a nice walk" he purred, and then he spoke to his other dog.

"Right Ormrod, let's go" he growled.

Lieutenant Ormrod calmly turned to us and spoke quietly from under his moustache.

"Look after the little bastard" he hissed. "Cock this up, and I'll have you strangled and buried in a hole".

And with that, he turned, smiled, and got into the back of the car with the Major.

We stood there and watched the car drive off, kicking up dust as it went, and then we looked down at the dog which was attacking the bottom of my trouser legs and trying to shred my turn ups.

"Oh for Christ's sake" I said, and I tightened the lead to try to pull the dog off my pants. The terrier didn't like that at all and it immediately jumped up my leg and attacked me as I tried to fend the bloody thing off.

Suddenly, Harry went into action. He skilfully grabbed snarling little Smokey by the scruff of its neck and shook the dog, and then he held it at arm's length and looked at it.

"You little piece of shit" he snarled back, and then he shook the dog again.

Smokey wasn't used to this sort of treatment, and the dog looked at Harry and slowly curled back its lips and bared its teeth. And right away you could see the hatred. That dog, really, really didn't like Harry.

We went off to the mess tent and Harry carried the dog all the way there by the scruff of its neck, then we tied it to a tent pole outside while we went and got some food. Everyone was on sausage and mash that day, and so we got an extra sausage for the dog, then we went back outside to sit down. Harry threw the sausage at the dog, it hit Smokey on the top of the head and the dog yelped.

"Shut up you little git" said Harry. Smokey growled back in reply.

The dog sniffed the sausage, looked up at us, and then just sat down, waiting.

"Don't you think we should cut it up for him" I said.

"Bollocks" said Harry "the bloody thing will eat it when it's hungry, look at the damn thing, its 'half dog, half bloody rat' that's what it is, it's a disgrace to all other dogs."

Smokey growled again, he didn't like being called names, but within ten minutes its interest in the sausage returned, and resentfully the terrier started to eat.

"Told you" said Harry triumphantly, and he looked down at the little terrier "that bloody dog's been spoiled, haven't you Smokey, you little twat".

I laughed my head off "He's a stubborn little bugger Harry, he's a lot like you really"

"Oh yes?" said Harry "Well he'll get my boot up his backside if he carries on"

The next morning we were back on 'dog duty'. We were once again given Smokey, who was again attached to his lead. We smiled, saluted, and off we went.

The dog had forgotten all the previous day's training and once more tried to attack us. So Harry got hold of a length of cord and he tied it to the dog's collar. Harry held the cord and me the lead and we walked along with the dog suspended between us. If we kept the cord and the lead tight enough, it couldn't get near either of us. We just walked around the nearby field with Smokey in the middle. The dog wasn't entirely happy with this and every so often he would try to break free, but we would just yank both the leash and cord tight and Smokey would shoot into the air and summersault like a spinning top, then we'd dump him back onto the ground. The dog didn't like this, but by the time we were half way round the field, he'd learned to calm down.

The thing was, the next day, breakfast, dinner or tea, we would have to go through the whole performance again. That dog would simply not remember things.

We went on like this for about two weeks, and nothing changed, except that Smokey could now devour a full sausage unaided. He loved the bloody things and after his meal he would sit there panting until he finally managed to give a little belch.

Harry had by now christened the terrier 'The rat'

"Look at the fat little swine" he would say.

And indeed, Smokey 'was' putting a bit of weight on.

Then one morning after the walk, and after the three of us had just had 'breakfast', me and Harry went for a stroll and a ciggie. We'd left Smokey tied to a tent pole as usual to sleep off the sausage, but when we got back he was gone. He'd disappeared.

"Oh Jesus" said Harry panicking "the rat's done one"

We both looked at each other and remembered Lieutenant Ormrod's warning. 'Oh crap'.

So we rushed around the camp asking everyone if they've seen the dog, but no they hadn't, nobody had seen a trace of him.

And then 'oh lord', we ran straight into Lieutenant Ormrod. He saw the panic on our faces.

"Where's the dog?" he asked immediately.

I spluttered "We don't know sir, we tied him to a tent pole but when we returned he wasn't there, we're looking for him now, sir."

Harry tried to diffuse the moment

"He can't be far sir, he's just had a sausage and..."

"Shut the fuck up Jackson" shouted the Lieutenant.

I thought he was going to have a heart attack.

Lieutenant Ormrod began to panic slightly "Oh Christ. Right, listen you two idiots, alert the camp, every available man is to look for that dog. Major Duggan has gone up to the front to meet up with a visiting Yank Colonel and is inspecting the troops or something, he won't be back until tea and that gives us some time".

Then he looked at us very seriously "If anything happens to that dog, I will personally see to it that you are sent to the Russian front, and while you are there I will have you fucking shot."

And he meant it, oh god, he meant it.

And then he started shouting at us. "What are you standing about for, go and find that bloody dog, you idiots!"

We alerted the whole camp and everybody who could, was searching for Smokey.

Then Harry came up with an idea.

"What if the dog's seen the Major's car drive off and he's chased after him?"

I just shrugged, I didn't know, I was on the edge of blind panic. I didn't want to end up shot in Russia.

"Listen" said Harry "everybody in camp is looking for the 'rat', there's nothing more we can do, and we've already looked everywhere. Let's go down the road and look for him there, that little git can't run all the way to the front, it's miles, he's probably sat at the side of the road somewhere, knackered, the fat little bastard"

It made sense, so off we went.

"You know we're in big crap over this one" I said to Harry.

"Yes" he said "I know, and that's why we need to get out of camp, coz' I'm telling you, if they don't find that dog I'm not coming back, and neither are you".

"What do you mean?"

"That Ormrod meant what he said" and Harry looked at me "I'm telling you mate, you and I are not going to freezing, bleeding Russia to get shot. If I'm going to get shot, I'll have it done here in sunny bloody Italy"

"What are we going to do?"

"We my friend, are going to go down this road and look for that bloody dog, and if we don't find it 'we' are going to keep going, even if we have to walk all the way to the front. If and when we get there, we'll stay there and stick with the troops, and when they move on, we'll move on with them. We're stretcher bearers for god's sake, we do our job, keep our heads down and stay low key. We've disappeared, but we haven't deserted, we're just doing our job and we've got caught up with things. 'Christ', there's a war going on and all sorts of things can happen, but just remember this, we haven't bloody deserted. Just think about it, we're in trouble. There's that bastard Ormrod, and don't forget Major 'bloody' Duggan, who by the way looks upon that dog as his long lost child. Let's just say, we don't want to be there"

"You know Harry" I said "your right, we can't go back", and we both knew we were in the shitter.

So we set off down the road heading all the way to the front, we'd made up our minds and we didn't care anymore.

We walked a mile in miserable silence, but finally I stopped, I needed to say something.

"Harry" I said "when we get to the front, would you consider shooting me in the foot please, because I want to go home."

He stopped, and stared at me "You clever bastard" he said, and we both burst out laughing. We sat down at the side of the road and lit a couple of ciggies.

I sat there and considered our situation.

"Why does it always happen to us Harry?"

"I don't know" he said "we're cursed, just when things were going right and now this"

He bit his nails for a moment "If we ever find that fucking dog, I'll kill the little bastard."

Harry didn't see the irony in that.

So we started off again, not caring, past caring actually, we were simply on our way to something new. That's how the war was I suppose, nothing was ever going to be simple. Anyway, about a mile and another twenty minute later, a truck rumbled towards us, it was full of soldiers, none injured thank god, they were just on manoeuvres. So we waved them down, and as the truck trundled to a halt, the driver leaned out of the window.

"Hi buddy" said Harry "I know this is a stupid question, but have you seen a little dog anywhere, a little terrier, a black and brown thing, size of a rat?"

"Yes" said the driver.

We went rigid.

"What!" said Harry, astounded?

Where was it mate?" I asked quickly.

"Five minutes back down the road, it's chasing some cows around a field, stupid little bugger, if the farmer sees it he'll shoot it".

"Oh Christ" I said "Come on Harry, quick"

We set off at a pace. And five minutes down the road we arrived at the farmer's field. There were no cows, but there was a terrier, and he was on his back rolling about in cow shit and hadn't a care in the world. Not only was he rolling in cow shit, he was caked in the stuff, head to toe. Why do dogs do that?

We jumped over the fence and chased after him. Little old Smokey saw us coming and immediately tried to bolt, but he was so weighed down with cow muck, he could hardly run.

Harry quickly caught up with the dog and kicked him straight up the backside. When Smokey landed, Harry swiftly trapped the dog under his boot. Smokey, who was covered in cow muck and now was trapped under Harry's size nines, immediately surrendered.

"Got you...you little bastard" said Harry.

I caught up with them and looked down at the little crap covered creature.

"Look at the state of him Harry, what are we going to do with him, 'oh strewth' he stinks".

Harry considered this for a moment and then said "Give me your boot laces"

I took off my laces and so did Harry, Smokey was beginning to squirm and growl a bit, but Harry tied the laces together to make an improvised lead and then tied it to Smokey's collar.

Harry lifted up his boot and the dog jumped up and shot off, only to be to be somersaulted into the air as Harry yanked him hard on the makeshift lead. The dog yelped as it hit the ground, but the acrobatics did manage to knock off some of the accumulated shit.

So we set off on the long walk back to camp, and every so often Smokey would get second wind and try to play 'silly buggers', but Harry would give its lead a really hard yank and the dog would once again fly through the air. In the end the terrier saw the sense in behaving, and for the last half mile we almost had to drag the muck caked little shit.

We walked wearily into camp, only to be met by Lieutenant Ormrod who had been informed of our return.

"Thank god you've found him" he said, and then he looked down at the dog "Oh good god, look at the state of him"

The Lieutenant looked hurriedly at his watch "The Major will be back in an hour, can you get him cleaned up by then?"

"We'll have him cleaned, fed and watered, sir" said Harry confidently, he trying to get us back in the good books.

"Major Duggan must not find out what's happened" said the Lieutenant

"Leave it to us sir" Harry quickly replied.

"I already did Jackson" and the Lieutenant gave us a cynical look that carried a hint of a threat, then he strode off.

"Whew" I said, and Harry rolled his eyes.

We retrieved the dog's lead and then retrieved our boot laces, and then we went to the mess tent and commandeered a sink. It was the middle of the afternoon, and the soldiers on camp had been fed and so the kitchens were pretty empty. We got some hot water and soap and filled the sink to the brim, and then we set about washing the muck off the dog. What a job that was, it took ages because the muck had dried into the dogs coat. So we decided to leave Smokey in the sink and let him soak for a while and let the warm water soften off the crap.

"I'm bloody starving" said Harry.

So was I, with all that had happened we'd missed our dinner, so I had a quick rummage around the kitchen and found the remains of some half warm stew that had been left in one of the ovens. I managed to get nearly two full plates out of it and some for the dog.

"Nice one" said Harry, as he tied the dog's lead to the tap and we went outside to eat and have a smoke.

We sat there in the sun and ate the stew, it tasted good and we were hungry.

"Thank god we found the little sod" I said to Harry.

"You're right there, we couldn't have come back you know, old Duggan would have blown a fuse and that bastard Ormrod would have put all the blame on us, just to save his own skin"

"Yes I know"

Harry lay back on the grass and lit another cigarette.

A couple of soldiers that we knew came up to us and they were laughing.

"So your back, you made it, along with the dog" they said.

I grinned "Yes we made it, just"

One of them said "We were all taking bets that you'd do a runner"

"You nearly won" said Harry from under his smoke.

"That Lieutenant Ormrod's been going frantic while you've both been away, he must have thought you'd done a runner too, he's had the whole camp looking for that dog, and you two as well. He's been screaming at us all bloody day, he's had the camp upside down, the bastard."

"He's shit scared of old Major Duggan, that's what it is, the arse wipe." said Harry.

We passed around the cigarettes and told them what had happened.

As they stood up to leave, one of the lads threw us a packet of ciggies.

"Here" he said "you've earned them".

We lay there another five minutes, and finally I said to Harry "Come on let's get finished, we'll rinse the dog off and then we'll get him fed and back to the Major, and then the jobs done."

"Right" said Harry "and thank god this day's over, I've got a bottle of red wine hidden in the bottom of my rucksack, I think we'll drink it tonight"

And so we stood up and walked back into the mess tent. And we stood there. And we went rigid with shock. Oh fuck!

We'd left the stupid dog tied to the tap, but it had decided to jump out of the sink and had throttled itself on its own lead.

It was dead, stone bloody dead.

Harry looked on in total disbelief "Oh no. No...No not this"

We looked at the bedraggled terrier, slowly swinging as it hung over the side of the kitchen sink.

"Are you sure it's dead?" I said quickly.

"Course it's fucking dead" snapped Harry "Look at it for Christ's sake. Oh shit...shit"

"What are we going to do Harry"?

"What are we going to do, fucking shoot each other, we might as well. 'Oh Christ' we are truly fucking screwed now" and he looked around desperately "What can we do, what can we do?"

He quickly paced over to the entrance of the mess tent. I suppose to see if anyone was about.

"Oh no!" he suddenly shouted, and he put his hands on his head "Oh Christ, the Major's back. His car's following two trucks up the road. Oh bloody hell no!"

"What are we going to do Harry" I spluttered, again.

"I don't know, I just don't know. Oh shit"

And then he suddenly looked at me and shouted "Get out of my way".

Then he ran back to the sink and quickly untied Smokey from the tap, he then ran back to the tent entrance and stood there with the dead dog dangling in his hand.

The two trucks and the Major's car steadily approached, and as the first truck passed us, Harry lobbed the dead dog straight under the back wheels, Smokey was mangled.

Harry then dashed out in front of the next oncoming truck and flagged it down to stop. He was jumping up and down shouting "Stop, stop. Accident...Accident!"

The truck and the Major's car stopped immediately, and the Major, along with the driver and some other soldiers, all got out to see what the commotion was.

Seeing the Major approach, Harry ran to him and stopped him from coming any further.

"Sir" Harry stammered "there's been a terrible accident. Its little Smokey sir, he...he ran out, and he ran right under the wheels of the truck sir. He's been killed".

The Major visibly slumped and Harry grabbed his arm. Then Lieutenant Ormrod arrived on the scene, he walked quickly towards the truck, he wanted to know what was going on.

I followed at a safe distance, then suddenly the Lieutenant stopped and looked down at the dead dog, and when he realized what he was looking at he started to wretch, a burst dog is not a pretty sight.

I quickly walked past him, to give Harry some back up. Harry was now holding up the Major who was very distressed. He kept repeating the words "Are you sure...are you sure?"

"Please don't look sir" I said sympathetically "it will only upset you"

Harry just looked at me, wide eyed.

Then the Lieutenant came running up, he was wiping his mouth with a handkerchief and he looked at us both with murder in his eyes.

But first he spoke to the Major "Are...are you alright sir?"

It was a stupid question.

Harry replied for him "The Major's upset sir".

"Shut up Jackson" seethed the Lieutenant "I don't know just what's happened here sir" he continued, "but..."

"It's Smokey, Ormrod. The poor little thing's been run over. Oh dear, oh dear me" the Major was now close to tears.

"I think we should get the Major to his quarters, sir" I said to the Lieutenant and it struck me, that me and Harry needed to get away from Lieutenant Ormrod.

"Yes" said Harry, catching my drift. He too realized that if the Lieutenant was going to try and murder us, we needed the Major as an ally, and quickly.

"Come on Major" crooned Harry "let's get you to your quarters, you've had a terrible shock. We'll take you back, you need to lie down and then we'll make you a mug of tea"

The Major leant on Harry's arm and said "Thank you men, it...it's been a bit of a shock, poor little Smokey. Oh dear me, yes your right I think I need to lie down, I'm feeling a little queasy"

And with that, we both quickly led the Major away.

Lieutenant Ormrod just stood there, open mouthed.

We didn't look back. We were sticking to the Major like glue.

For the next twelve hours, we were never out of earshot of Major Duggan. Ormrod kept coming around to try and catch hold of us, but we manoeuvred things so he couldn't get near without the Major being present.

Lieutenant Ormrod was beginning to fidget. He knew that when the Major had sufficiently recovered, questions would ultimately be asked. The Major would want some sort of enquiry to find out what had actually happened and who was to blame, because the Major was a fussy old bastard, and not only that, he was a 'ruthless' fussy old bastard, he was from the 'old school' and he was a man who would have no qualms at all in regards to stripping a man of his rank and position.

Lieutenant Ormrod was a worried man. He could be in trouble, if only because of the chain of command. He was in charge of the two men, who were in charge of the Major's dog. And those same two gits were now sucking up to the Major, and god only knew what trickery, lies and deceit they were using to get into the old man's head.

However it had to be said, Harry and me were pretty worried too. At some point, when the Major's brain began to work again, we knew he would ask the question.

'Who was supposed to be looking after his dog?'

And then the crap would definitely hit the fan, we knew we had to come up with something, but what? Though, I suppose anything would have been better than the truth. The truth could get us both shot, and possibly even worse.

But, as thing often do, events quickly came to a head.

The next morning, we presented the Major with a light breakfast.

"You have to eat something Major" we insisted as we passed him a large mug of tea. But just as we were about to butter his toast, the tent flap was pulled back and in marched Lieutenant Ormrod.

Without breaking stride he immediately spoke out "How are we this morning Major, a little better I hope, sir."

The crafty bastard, he was taking control.

"I'm a little better thank you Ormrod. It's been a terrible shock you know, little Smokey has been with me for years, got him when he was just a pup, wonderful little chap".

The Major's eyes suddenly started to glaze over again as he remembered his little dog.

"Yes Major" said Ormrod in a businesslike fashion, he needed the Major to snap out of it.

He then continued "I'm just looking into the incident sir, to find out who was to blame, sir".

"Blame" said the Major, blinking "What do you mean?"

"Well, somebody should have been looking after the dog, sir".

And the bastard glanced at us and gave a perceptible smirk.

We were sunk.

The blood ran back into the Major's face, and he went from pale to burgundy.

"Who...who the hell was it?" And he began to get louder and rather agitated.

"Ormrod, I want you find out who the hell was responsible"

And suddenly, out of the blue, somebody spoke.

"It was us sir" said Harry quietly "it was us".

The three of us looked around at Harry. I was astounded, we were all astounded, and all for different reasons, but we were definitely astounded.

Me, well I thought he'd lost his mind, and the Major was flabbergasted and for a moment he couldn't speak, but Ormrod's eyes nearly popped right out of his head. He was expecting lies and denial and a host of other excuses, yes he was ready for that and prepared, and he was in for the kill. But suddenly this, Harry's immediate and complete admittance, well it totally caught him off balance, and he was speechless.

Before anybody could say a word, Harry turned to the Major.

"Major, sir, may I speak?"

The Major was so taken aback, that all he could do was nod.

"Sir, for the last two weeks, we have looked after your little dog 'Smokey'. Three times a day, for the last two weeks we have fed and watered him, and we've walked him through the fields and over the hills. We've all had a great time and Smokey got fitter and better with all the exercise we gave him and he had actually put on a bit of muscle. He was well, really well, and he was in good condition. All in all, sir, I feel he was a happier and better dog at the end than he was when he first arrived. He really loved his walks and we would always get him a special treat from the kitchens when we got back. He really looked forward to that, sir"

I began to bite my bottom lip, smooth Harry, very bloody smooth.

Ormrod just stood there, he was sort of hypnotised.

Harry continued "The thing was sir, if ever you left camp and went off in the car, the dog would go mad. He'd kick up a right commotion, dog's are like that you see sir, they do sense things about their masters"

"Yes" said the Major sympathetically, and he nodded his head in agreement.

Ormrod just closed his eyes.

Harry never missed a beat "And the same thing would happen when you used to return sir, the 'little bloke' would go crackers, jumping up and down, he used to get over excited.

Well, yesterday sir, we'd been out for a lovely walk with him and we were all back at the mess tent, he was having some lamb stew with us, then suddenly he must have heard your car sir, and in a flash he just dashed out to meet you, and he ran right out in front of the truck. The driver couldn't do a thing sir, honestly. You can't blame the driver sir, he was terribly upset, we all were, we thought the world of little Smokey."

Nice one Harry, blame somebody else and then try to defend them, clever boy.

Harry nodded towards me "We're both devastated sir, we spent a lot of time with Smokey, he was like a little mate to us".

Harry then took a deep breath "All I can say sir, is that he didn't suffer, honestly he didn't. It was all very quick, he never knew what hit him."

'Yes' I thought, only because he was already bleedin' dead.

 I just stood there in complete silence, and wondered 'What now?'

It was the Major who spoke "I thank you for your honesty soldier. Who are you again?"

"He's Jackson sir" interrupted Ormrod, suddenly coming back to life.

"Ah yes, Jackson. Well thank you, both of you, for looking after my 'little man'. He was happy, and you're right, he had put on some weight, as you say some muscle. Thank you both for everything."

"And the truck driver sir, he wasn't to blame sir, honestly"

Nice diversion Harry, and stupid me, I almost grinned.

"Yes" said the Major "I can see that it was an unfortunate accident, however tragic".

Harry looked sympathetically at the Major "I know how you feel sir. I have my own pet back home, his names Whiskey"

Now he really was taking the piss, and I had to cough to stop myself from laughing out loud.

Even Ormrod caught that one, and he stared at Harry in disbelief.

"We'll bury the dog for you sir" Harry continued "and we'll let you know where the grave is".

The Major nodded "Thank you Jackson, you're a good man. That would be very nice".

Then he turned to Ormrod "Please dismiss the men Lieutenant"

We left the Major's tent under the direct glare of Lieutenant Ormrod.

It was a matter of one down, one to go.

We walked away from the Major's tent rapidly, but twenty five yards out and Lieutenant Ormrod called out after us.

"You two, get here. Now"

We trotted back to him and he directed us away from the Major and down between some tents where nobody could hear us.

He stood there, facing us for a moment. He was so angry that his moustache twitched sideways.

Then he started "Right, you two smart arsed imbeciles. You think you're clever don't you, trying to take the 'Mickey' out of me and the Major. And you think you've got away with it, don't you?"

"No sir" we both said immediately.

"No sir indeed, listen you two, I want to know exactly what happened to that bloody dog?"

"Nothing sir" I tried to explain "As you know, he went missing, and then we found him again and we took him to the mess tent and washed him and then fed him, and like we said sir, he heard the Major's car and he ran out in front of the truck, sir".

"And how did he run off?"

I looked back at the Lieutenant "He just ran off sir, heard the car and ran right out of the tent"

"So he wasn't on his lead then?"

"Err, No sir"

"So tell me, why is it that over the last two weeks, and since the moment you took charge of the Major's dog, the whole of the time, you have had to have it on its lead to stop the bloody thing from running away. It ran off yesterday morning, but miraculously by the afternoon, you were all sat around a camp fire together, 'eating lamb stew' with 'our little mate'. What a load of rubbish. Do you think I'm stupid, I've watched you two through the binoculars as you walked him 'through the fields and over the fucking hills', what a load of crap. You dragged the little bastard around that bottom field and kicked it's arse all the way back, that fucking dog hated you, and that's why it ran off this morning. So, I am asking you both again, what bloody well happened?"

"Your right sir" said Harry immediately. He obviously didn't want me to open my big mouth again.

"The dog slipped its lead 'again' sir." admitted Harry "just as we were about to feed it...it just ran straight out of the mess tent and ran right under that truck, honestly sir".

"How unfortunate" said the Lieutenant as he stared at us?

"Well maybe not sir" said Harry

Ormrod looked at Harry, and I looked at Harry. What the hell was he doing?

"And what exactly do you mean by that, Jackson?" asked Ormrod.

"Well sir, I suppose we won't have to waste our time looking after that dog anymore, any of us, you included sir. We know you're very busy sir, and also, the 'accident' wasn't anybody's fault and 'now' the Major realizes that. So I suppose we can all just get back to normal, would that be right sir?"

I swallowed.

The Lieutenant just stared at Harry, and then spoke slowly to him.

"Very clever Jackson, very clever, you're very, very good, you lying, scheming bastard".

And then suddenly he paused, just for a moment, and he started to think about what Harry had just said, and he abruptly stopped twitching and almost smiled.

"However, on this occasion you may actually be right, that dog was a bloody nuisance and I am quite happy to see the back of the nasty little swine"

Then he put his 'official face' back on.

"But, there is a call for 'dereliction of duty' here. I feel that you neglected your orders, in that you did not look after that dog properly and you showed a complete lack of care. You also tried to take the piss out of me, and I am nobody's fool, do you understand?"

We both glanced at each other and "Yes Sir" we both replied smartly.

"You will both be put on a charge, see me tomorrow morning at nine hundred hours... Dismissed"

We saluted and buggered off for a moan and a whinge, 'bloody army'.

The next day we were put on a charge and ended up in the 'glass house'. It turned out to be a barbed wire compound somewhere in Italy, for three weeks. It wasn't that bad really, well at least nobody was firing bullets at you".

My dad would tell these tales about the army and the war, and I often wondered that if the Germans had really known what was going on, they might have tried harder.

My dad came out of the army when the war finally came to an end.

He used to say that "All we came home with, was a demob suit" which was a suit of clothes given to every soldier to wear as he returned to civilian life. And civilian life for him was any job that was available. He did a month down in the coal pits as a coalminer and walked out in disgust at the conditions the men had to work in.

He often said "It wasn't a fit place for the pit ponies, let alone men"

He told me all about what it was like to work down the pit, and it has always given me the greatest of respect for the coal miners of the past, and present really. The price of coal in terms of human toil, illness and human life was much too high.

My father was of course a farmer's boy and he was always used to being outside and working in the open air, and I think that working under the ground, in the dark, and enclosed and cramped, must have been his own personal hell.

From there he went onto do various jobs and eventually ended up back on the buses, working as a conductor. It was during this time that he met my mother. She used to catch his bus on the way home from work and my dad took a shine to her and vice versa. My mother used to tell me that she would wait for hours until my dad's bus would finally come along and that she would jump on it just to see him 'as though it was a big coincidence'. When it came to her stop, my dad would hang off the back of the bus and waive her goodbye, all very cavalier, obviously his time spent in Italy during the war had rubbed off on him and he'd gone a bit 'Latino'. Well, it worked for the Italians, and it worked for my dad, because my mother started going out with him and of course, they eventually got married.

There was a ten year age gap between them, and it seems that and both sets of families were not impressed. With one lot, he was too old and with the other, she was too young, so they got married anyway and at the wedding both families pulled their faces, except of course when they were in front of the photographer.

Their first house was a dilapidated, old stone farm cottage that my dad rented off a farmer that he knew. It was apparently in a right old state, there were holes in the roof, holes in the floor and half the windows missing, but it was cheap, very cheap, and it was a start. Christmas arrived along with my mother getting pregnant and my parents decided to throw out the hand of friendship and invite my mother's parents around for Christmas dinner. My mother's father, my grandfather, was still reeling from the shock that his daughter was pregnant, and he'd made up his mind that this was more or less rape.

So my dad was not 'top of his list', as they say.

Anyway Christmas arrived and so did my grandparents. Nobody had cars in those days and because it was Christmas there were no buses of course. So they had to walk all the way to my parent's cottage, which was a distance of about four miles. Unfortunately, the cottage was slightly 'out in the wilds' and was situated half a mile down a twisting rough path, a dark meandering lane that ran down from the main road.

It took them nearly two hours in the freezing winter cold to walk to the path's entrance, where they were met by my father who guided them carefully down the now, dark lane. By the time they finally arrived, they were very cold and not very happy and definitely not in the Christmas spirit. Neither were they impressed by the 'rustic and cosy' cottage that their daughter had described to them.

It was no 'Shangri-la', in fact it was a dump, but because it was made out of stone and was stuck in the middle of a field, it was looked upon as 'quaint'. Things never change, do they?

My mother's parents were also quite dismayed when they sat down at the dining table, and as they looked up, they could see the stars in the evening sky, through a large hole in the ceiling which corresponded directly with the larger hole in the roof.

My dad, who had called in at the local pub in the afternoon and had been there till tea time was several pints to the merrier, and he just laughed a lot and took it all with 'a pinch of salt'. However, my mother was understandably nervous, especially when he produced a case of beer from under the sink and then proceeded to pass the bottles around the table. One look from my grandmother, and my grandfather knew that his first drink would be his last. Things didn't get better when my grandmother mentioned that she was a little chilly, due to the big hole in the roof, and she must have thought that my dad would put some more coal on the fire. Unfortunately, he produced a bottle of Rum and then offered it to them both to 'kill the chill'. They declined, and then were slightly taken aback when my mother, their pregnant daughter, had to go outside to the coal shed for some more coal, and my dad who was by then more than a bit tipsy, called out to her 'nice one love'.

Things finally came to a head when it started to snow. The turkey had been eaten in a stilted silence that my dad was totally oblivious to, but as they sat there, ready to eat their Christmas pudding, it started to snow heavily and the snow fell through the large hole in the roof and began to land on the table and then on top of their heads.

My father tried to seize the moment "Bloody hell, it's snowing, we're going to have a white Christmas, Cheers everybody" he called out as he drank his fourth glass of rum.

Suddenly, my grandmother started to cry. Oh dear me, things were not going well at all.

It was at that point that the turkey, the beer, and the rum, all started to do the dance of death in my father's stomach. He slowly stood up, swayed and belched and said "Excuse me folks" and then he went outside into the cold night air to throw up, repeatedly.

My grandparents turned to my mother, my grandmother in tears, and they pleaded with her.

"Come home love" they said to her "come back home with us, he's an idiot, you've made a mistake. You can't live here like this"

My mother of course refused and my grandparents decided to leave.

As they walked back up the path towards the main road they passed my father who was by then on his hands and knees. Disgusted, they ignored him, but as they walked away they heard him shout "Oh Bugger, I've lost my false teeth"

Nice one dad, nice one.

Time is a great healer and the birth of my sister unquestionably helped things along. About a year later my parents decided to move, this time into a nice terraced house on a main road, and not out in the wilds of the countryside.

'Moving day' was going to be on a Saturday morning and my dad had gone off somewhere to organize the furniture removal. My mother and her mother were going up to the 'new house' on the bus to get things ready. They were sitting on the bus, which had somehow got stuck in some huge traffic jam, and my mother was beginning to panic.

She said to her mother "The removal men will be there and they won't be able to get into the house".

"Why not?" asked my grandmother.

"I've got the door keys and they won't be able to get in, 'Tommy' (my dad) will go mad, he say's these removal firms charge a fortune".

My grandmother quipped "Well there's nothing we can do about it, it's this bus's fault, all the traffics held up, anyway the removal people will probably be held up too".

This calmed my mother down a bit and they just had to sit there as the traffic moved slowly and ever onwards.

Eventually, the bus got going and an elderly couple who were sitting at the front of the bus spotted the problem and took it upon themselves to inform the rest of the passengers.

"It's some gipsies" they told everyone "with a horse and cart, they're blocking up the road".

Everyone looked over to get a better view, and there was a lot of moaning and colourful comments, but finally the bus managed to get past the horse, which was pulling a large, over laden cart and had been causing the traffic jam. It was being led onwards by a small, scruffy looking man who was wearing a cap and a long coat, and who was slowly leading the horse on by its bridle.

Everybody on the bus groaned and the bus conductor began to moan about 'how the bus would now be behind schedule all day'.

"Bloody gipsies" said the conductor "they're always a damn nuisance, and always up to no good, look at the state of that one"

Everyone looked out of the window at the gipsy, who was leading the horse.

My grandmother commented "Fancy having to live like that, all your belongings on the back of a cart" and she spoke just loud enough for everyone to hear, she liked to impress people, and the other passengers nodded and muttered in agreement.

The bus conductor continued "They're all a bunch of bloody thieves, just look at him, he'll have been up to no good"

And as the bus slowly drove past the horse and cart, the gipsy glanced up at the passengers, and then he looked directly at my grandmother and suddenly whipped off his cap and started to wave it at her.

Then he shouted to her "Alright mother, I'll see you up at the house!"

Aboard the bus, there was complete silence.

Yes, it was my dad.

Both my mother and grandmother sat there open mouthed as all the other passengers stared back at them.

My grandmother just put her hand over her eyes and said quietly "Oh for god's sake, I don't believe it."

My mother looked down at my dad, who was still waving his cap and grinning, and she burst out laughing.

"Oh bloody hell Tommy" she said to nobody in particular, and then she got the giggles, then she started to laugh out loud, and that was it.

They both got off at the next stop.

We lived in that house for four years, while my father did various jobs. Then finally he came home one day and announced to my mother that he had got a stall on Bolton Market, selling dairy produce.

My mother had her reservations about this, but once he'd got an idea into his head there was no stopping him, so that was that. Bolton Market it was, and once he started, his little stall began to flourish. His principle was simply to buy it right, stack it high and sell it cheap. From there he finally went on to acquire another two market stalls in other outlying towns, but before that we had to move house again. He quickly realized that he required more room than his terraced house would provide, and he needed space for some large fridges and for storage, and so he went out and bought a farm.

I look back now and I still wonder how on earth he managed to finance it all, but somehow he did and good on him. I always wondered if he had possibly never gotten over the stigma of his father losing the family farm, but now he was back and back with a purpose, and the memory of what he managed still makes me proud.

And so, that's how I was brought up. I too was a farmer's boy.

Our Farm, what a legend, it can best be described as a place of organised mayhem that ever awaited the next disaster.

We seemed to have just about everything. There were chickens, turkeys and pigs, and goats and geese. It was a mad menagerie of animals.

Farming is a strange old game, something died every week, or ran off, or just disappeared. Some of the poultry that disappeared probably ended up on somebody's kitchen table, along with potatoes, carrots and gravy. But, that was life and it was all a bit hectic. My dad bred flocks of chickens and turkeys for the Christmas markets along with a large herd of pigs.

All of these, along with the goats and geese, used to wander freely about the fields, and every so often they would break out, and for some strange reason it always seemed to be on a Sunday. Are pigs religious? I just don't know.

Anyway, generally Sunday would arrive, and we would get a knock on the front door by somebody, telling us that the pigs had broken out and were on the main road and heading for town, or that the turkeys had invaded the local housing estate and were frightening the children. Our goats would regularly wander into the pub across the road and start eating the customers cigarettes and crap on the carpets, and every so often the geese would wander off and get into somebody's house and attack their dog and also crap all over the carpet, mind you, the dog was probably doing a bit of crapping as well .

We used to have to dash out and herd these wayward creatures back home. The pigs were a bad tempered bunch, and used to act like a load of moody teenagers and whinge all the way back to the farm. Turkeys on the other hand, are just plain stupid and simply cannot walk in a straight line. Turkeys all follow one another, and when the one at the front suddenly realizes it has no one else to follow, it has some sort of panic attack and shoots off to the left or right in an effort to try and find out where everyone else has gone, and of course all those behind it follow, so it's all chaos and commotion.

It was a case of the blind leading the blind.

The goats used to like to nip into the local pub and socialize, and no matter what, my dad would not go in there to get them back, he would send me, always. I remember having to go and get them one afternoon, yes it was a Sunday of course, and the landlord had rung us up complaining that the goats were in the pub, again.

I walked in there all bright and breezy, as though this was an everyday occurrence, well it almost was. The goats were always in there, they loved the damn place.

The pub was at a standstill. The locals were all a bit nervous of farm animals and everyone was standing in a corner, sort of paralysed.

I looked around, to see that one of the goats was on top of the bar, drinking somebody's pint of bitter. Another was wandering around the pub with a packet of 'Woodbine' cigarettes in its mouth, which it was trying to eat, and the third was confronting a pensioner, who was an elderly man that the goat had pinned into a corner, the goat was standing in front of him, waving its horns about.

Oh Jesus!

The beer sodden locals looked on in some sort of awe, nobody moved.

The Landlord broke the spell when he saw me walk through the door.

"Get these bloody animals out of my pub" he shouted.

I nearly foolishly replied 'and what about the goats?' but then thought better of it, this was probably not the right time or place. Well, I was only twelve.

"Right" I said, and I went up to the bar and grabbed the first goat by its collar and pulled it off the top of bar and onto the floor. Goats aren't daft and they knew that the game was up. It bolted off through the pub door, followed by its mate, which still had the packet of cigarettes in its mouth, and it sort of waved the captured 'Woodbines' at everyone as it left. The third goat, now disheartened, gave up on the pensioner and quickly about turned, then it ran off and followed the other two straight out of the pub door.

I turned to the old pensioner "Sorry about that mister" I said.

He was still a bit startled, and he said " The bloody thing were trying to eat me' cap, look at it...it's all chewed up".

And indeed it was. The goat had apparently snatched the cap off his head as he was playing dominoes, and the old man had managed to snatch it back but in the ensuing tussle the goat had got carried away.

"Bloody vicious, them goats" spouted the landlord "and what about all that shite?" he grumbled as he pointed at the floor.

"I'll go and get a bucket and shovel" I said apologetically, as I tried to leave.

"Tell your dad I need to have a word"

"I will" I said, and I dashed off, only to return five minutes later with a bucket and shovel and a pound note from my dad.

"It had better not happen again" said the landlord, but as long as the pound note always arrived, he seemed to have a very short memory.

Over the years, we had a series on run-ins with some of the local neighbour's dogs. Dogs, by their nature will chase any animal that will run away from them. It doesn't matter what size the dog is, big or small, their natural hunting instinct has never left them. If you are ever attacked by a dog, never run, that's the thing that a dog expects and is comfortable with, it's what it wants you to do and if you run it will attack you from behind. Just watch a wolf chasing a deer, a dog will do the same and it's always better to stand your ground and face the dog up. Most dogs are actually cowards and their bark is usually worse than their bite. However, I do have to admit that if a great big savage Rottweiler with large teeth came charging at me, I'd be off in a flash.

It's a strange thing, but dog owners could never believe that their 'Rover' or 'Fluffy" could ever be capable of chasing farm animals, but they do and I've seen the smallest terrier chase a cow right through a barbed wire fence and rip half of the cow's udder off. In times past, I've caught hold of many of the local dogs and returned them, bedraggled and full of cow muck, back to their owners, only to be met with disbelief and denial and then have the front door slammed firmly in my face.

I remember at one time, we were beginning to have a problem with one of the local dogs.

He was a large brown mongrel, who had started to come round almost daily and was chasing everything in sight. He was having a wonderful time of it, full of the joys of spring he was, but as time went on he started to bite and he was getting more and more vicious with the animals as his confidence and exuberance grew. It was in the dog's nature to hunt things down of course, but we knew that it would only be a matter of time before the dog killed something, as they say 'there is a wolf in every dog'. My dad had chased it off a few times, but the dog would return the next day and run the poultry and the pigs far and wide. He was starting to attack them too, and some of the chickens and turkeys were beginning to show the tell tale bright red blood stains on their white feathers. Then one day, one of the smaller pigs had all the back of its legs badly bitten and its ears were ripped and bloody.

My dad spoke to me about it, he said "That bloody dog is going to kill something, and we're going to have to do something about it"

And eventually, we did.

It is, or was a fact, that if a farmer caught a dog attacking his flocks or cattle, he could either shoot the dog or have the dog destroyed. Well, my dad didn't have a gun, and neither did he have the heart to kill somebody's pet, but we knew that we had to do something.

My dad came up with an idea, it was simple really. We dragged an old chicken hut into the field and tied some string to the door and arranged it so that when we pulled the string, the door would slam shut, then we ran the string all the way back to the farm, it was about fifty yards in total. The dog would always come around in the early afternoon, so at lunchtime my dad got out the frying pan and lightly fried some liver, into which he dropped some generous slices of corned beef. He put this warmed meat into a small bowl and we took it down the field and placed it inside the chicken hut

It smelled delicious. I could have eaten it myself.

"Dog's can't resist the smell of liver" he said wisely, and he carefully pushed the bowl into the middle of the hut.

I could smell the liver too. I was beginning to realize how the dogs felt.

"Right" he said, as we walked back to the farm "go and find yourself something to sit on and keep your eye open for that dog. With a bit of luck, it'll smell the liver and go into the hut, when it does, pull the string and we'll have the bugger. Let's just hope its hungry"

Well it was, and luckily for me, after only thirty minutes the brown mongrel arrived. It slid easily under the fence, and wagged its tail as it surveyed the field and the flocks of poultry and the pigs, and it was just about to set off and have some fun, when suddenly it lifted its nose into the air and visibly twitched.

Mongrels do tend to be very clever dogs, and though they may not be as intelligent as sheepdogs, they are actually the survivors of the dog world. A mongrel has no designated job, fancy breeding or pedigree to keep it going, and unless it had a particularly kind owner, they tended to have a bit of a tough life. Back before the days of the 'pooper scooper' and the dog fouling laws, stray mongrel dogs could be seen everywhere, roaming the streets and looking for food. It was survival of the fittest, and it made them ever resourceful. These dogs were always on the lookout for food, and this one was no exception.

The dog stood at the top of the field and lifted its nose into the air and almost swooned.

It moved its head from side to side, its nose trying to seek the whereabouts of the warm liver, and then its natural radar kicked in and it turned and trotted straight towards the chicken hut. Once it got there, it put its head through the doorway and saw the delicious food, then it suddenly pulled back and looked around, checking that the coast was clear and that everything was okay.

'Clever boy' I thought.

The dog was almost grinning with enthusiasm, and it looked left and right and then in it went.

Bingo!

I pulled the string, the door slammed shut and we had him. I jumped up and ran to the hut and locked the door, and I could hear the dog banging about inside as it ate the bowl of liver. If that dog thought for one moment that it was the 'condemned man', it was making damn sure that it was having its last meal.

I ran to tell my dad and he came back down to the hut with me, with a length of rope in his hand.

"What are we going to do with it dad?" I asked him.

"Well" he said "We don't know who owns the bloody thing, so there's nobody we can take it back home to".

Then he continued "But I've just read an article in the 'Farmers Weekly' it was about sheep farmers in Australia and how they deal with problem dogs".

The 'Farmers Weekly' was a popular farming magazine at the time, which most farmers read and used like the bible.

"So what do they do dad" I asked him, again.

He said "When a farmer catches hold of a dog that's been chasing the sheep, they take hold of it and then they tie it to a large Ram, and then they let them both go. Well, the Ram batters the shit out of the dog, and since it's tied to the Ram, the dog can't run off. It ends up well battered and also bloody terrified, and it never wants to go near a sheep ever again, so problem solved."

"But dad, we haven't got a Ram"

"I know" he said "we'll tie it to a pig"

I looked at him "A pig. Are you sure?"

"Well it's no use tying it to a bloody turkey, it'll run off with it and eat the damn thing and then we'll never get rid of the bugger"

So he opened the door to the hut and snatched hold of the dog, who I have to say, seemed a bit surprised about all the fuss. We tied a long length of rope to its collar and then we walked the dog up to some pig pens that led onto the field. Locked in one of these pens was a very large sow, it was a huge, bad tempered thing, the height of a man's waist.

"Stand behind that door with the dog" he said to me, and he took the rope which was tied to the dog and made a noose out of the other end.

He slowly opened the door to the pen, and as he did he pulled some potatoes out of his jacket pocket and started to call the pig over.

"Here pig, pig" he called out, and he threw it a couple of small potatoes.

This got the pigs attention straight away, and it quickly started to eat them. Then he slowly lured pig towards him as he threw it more food. He dropped a large potato at his feet and as the pig came forward to eat it, he neatly slipped the noose over the unsuspecting animal's head.

As the pig munched away, totally oblivious to what was happening, my dad slipped into the pen and got behind it, and then he stepped back and took a run at the pig and booted it right up its backside. The pig screamed, and spat out a mouthful of potato as it shot out of the open door.

It set off down the field at a gallop, and the rope was ripped out of my hand as it dragged the dog off behind it. The dog was in a state of shock as it was bumped along behind the stampeding pig and it kept trying to get back on all four feet but was having great difficulty.

Then it started to howl.

Well the pig must have thought we'd set a pack of wolves on it, because when it heard the dog howling away behind it...it started to scream loudly and then it began to run in small circles. The dog was now spinning around like a top as it was dragged round and around by the pig. Then the pig suddenly stopped and whipped around. It had either decided to face its 'enemy' or it had stopped to get its breath back, I think it was getting a bit dizzy. As it stood there panting, it heard the dog growling behind it, and when it turned its head and saw the dog, the pig went mad.

It charged at the dog, who immediately realized it was in trouble because it couldn't get away, and so it to went a bit crazy and it barred its teeth viciously and barked and howled back at the pig.

Finally, they both set about one another. This was now getting nasty and the huge pig was beginning to get the upper hand, then suddenly the dog bit into pig's cheek and hung on there for grim death. This must have really hurt the pig because it went completely berserk.

It shook its head madly from side to side but the dog had locked on and wasn't letting go.

So it set off running and screaming and dragged the dog along with it, it was going at a hell of a pace and there was no stopping it as it reached the perimeter fence and smashed straight through it, and then headed for the main road.

"Oh Jesus, no" groaned my dad as he watched his pig and the dog crash through the fence.

Then, the reality of it all dawned on him, there was a pig now running down the main road with a dog stuck to it.

"Come on, quick" he shouted at me as he set off running after the two crazed animals.

I knew all along that this had been a bad idea.

So we set off after them. By the time we'd got to the fence, both the dog and the pig had got onto the road and were causing absolute mayhem. Cars screeched to a halt as a large screaming pig with a dog hanging onto it, weaved in and out of the busy traffic. Drivers were then further amazed when a small man and a young boy, both wearing wellington boots, ran down the middle of the road at full pelt, chasing after the stampeding animals.

Finally the pig ran into the small front garden of a terraced house and tried to bury its head in the privets. We chased in after it and closed the garden gate to stop it escaping, but that pig was going nowhere, it was exhausted and it just stood there breathless and whining with its head jammed in the privet fence. The dog was still locked onto its cheek and was still growling.

The old lady who lived there opened the front door and peered out.

"What's going on?" she said.

"Go back inside love" said my dad straight away "we've got dangerous animals here".

She took one look at the size of the pig and said "Oh 'eck" and quickly closed the door.

A minute later she was peering out at us through her net curtains.

My dad undid the rope that tied both the dog and pig, but the dog wouldn't let go, it just hung on for grim death and continued to growl a lot. He shook the dog and then slapped it, but no, that dog was not for turning.

"What are we going to do dad?" I said, once again.

"I'll sort it lad" he said, and he leaned over and grabbed the dog's ear and started to twist it.

Well, almost immediately the dog stopped growling, in fact it nearly stopped breathing as it started to feel the pain caused by someone trying to pull its ear off. And suddenly it forgot all about the pig, it forgot about a lot of things really, except its ear, and it must have decided that the pig wasn't worth the trouble anymore because now its ear seemed to be an altogether bigger problem.

With a quick howl, it let go of the pig's cheek and tried to bite my dad, who was ready for it and simply pulled the dog back by its collar.

"Got you...you bloody thing" he said, and then he reached down and picked the dog up and with a good heave, he slung it over the privet fence. As it flew through the air it made some sort of howling noise that I can't even describe.

It landed on the other side with a heavy bump and a yelp, and I looked over the fence and watched as the shocked and shaken animal got to its feet. It shook its head and slowly staggered off, somehow slightly sideways. In a way, it looked like it was drunk.

I watched it go and I didn't think it would be coming back soon, and it never did.

The pig however, was another story.

We eventually persuaded it to get its head out of the privets, my dad kept hitting it with a stick until it finally gave up and pulled its head out of the foliage. Then we managed to walk it cautiously back home and into its pen.

"That buggers not happy" said my dad, as he prodded it with his stick.

I wasn't surprised.

Anyway, later on he took it in some potatoes as a goodwill gesture, but the pig just turned away with its head to the wall, it was sulking. Then suddenly it turned and charged at him. Luckily he saw it coming and he got out of the pen sharply and whipped the door shut behind him. The pig, in frustration, then started to give the door some form of punishment.

"Christ" said my dad, and he gave me a sort of 'worried' look.

I think at that point, we both knew that we could have a bit of a problem here.

From then on, the pig became insufferable, and if anyone went anywhere near it, the damn thing would attack you. So in the end we just threw its food over the door of its pen and let it carry on, we couldn't go in there, it would have eaten us too. And when the time came to clean out its pen, we would simply open the door and run for it. The pig would immediately charge out, looking for someone to bite, and after finding no one available it would wander off down the field on its own. It didn't like the other pigs either, they all kept out of its way too. At night it would simply wander back into its pen were it knew there would be food waiting for it.

Unfortunately for us, the pig was a breeding sow, and it was supposed to produce the piglets which we bred for the market. And so at some point we had to take it to the boar, which it was supposed to mate with it. On our farm we had our own boar, which lived in its own pen and led a fairly easy and solitary life. So when 'our' pig came into 'season', my dad decided that it was time for it to go and visit the boar.

I really, really was not looking forward to this, and I don't think the pig was either.

So my dad devised a plan. We had a load of corrugated metal sheets on the farm and he decided that we would make a 'run' out of these, a fenced path from the sow's pen all the way to the boars' pen. Sounds simple doesn't it.

"We'll just open the door" said my dad "and when it comes charging out, I'll get behind it and keep hitting it with something and with a bit of luck, it'll keep on going straight up the run and go straight into the boar pen"

He told me that 'my' job was to stand at the entrance of the boar pen and open the gate when I saw the pig coming.

"Right dad" I said, hopefully.

So off we went, my dad and I constructed the 'run' from the corrugated sheeting and made it secure. And the following day we went into action.

Just as we planned, my dad went to let the pig out, he whipped open the door of its pen and then quickly hid behind it. Within seconds, the pig came charging out like a train and my dad jumped from behind the door and chased after it, hitting it relentlessly over the backside with a length of fencing pole. The pig screamed loudly and ran on, and my dad too was going hell for leather behind it, and continued to batter the pig nonstop with the pole.

As they both very quickly approached me, he shouted "Open the bleeding gate"

Which I did, and the pig shot straight into boar's pen and I slammed the gate firmly behind it before it had realized what had happened. Success!

Dad ran up to me "Nice one lad" he said, as he stood there trying to get his breath back.

We then turned to look into the boar pen to see how the pig was getting on.

All that noise and commotion had woken up the old boar, and he popped his head out of his pen to see what all the fuss was about, and that was when he saw the pig. He immediately realized that a new sow had entered his domain and he was instantly aroused and awake.

Love was in the air and he sniffed the breeze, and suddenly his ears stood up, and then so did he, and he started to make quick grunting noises as headed directly for the sow He was a boar and he definitely knew what his job was, unfortunately the sow did not. She straightaway realized his intentions and was simply having none of it. She took one look at him and bellowed and then charged at him, head on.

The poor boar, the sexed up animal didn't know what hit him, and he was knocked straight off his feet and for a moment he lay there, winded on the floor. The sow then spun around and charged him again, and this time she bit his thigh.

He didn't know what the hell was going on, but he definitely didn't like it.

I heard my dad shout "Oh Christ...no"

And we looked on as the sow then chased the boar around his pen, trying to gnaw the back of his legs.

It has to be said, at that moment, sex was definitely off the menu

After he'd been chased around his yard twice, the boar had had enough and headed for the exit, and at full steam he simply smashed through the gate and ran off down the field with the sow chasing after him.

Eventually she gave up and went off for a wander, but by then the boar had got in with the rest of the herd of thirty sows and was running sexually amok. It took us the best part of two hours to finally get the sex crazed animal back into his pen.

As we looked down the field at the lone sow wandering about, my dad shook his head and said "That pigs got to go. I'm sick of the damn thing".

And I remember thinking 'Thank god for that'. Little did I know that unfortunately, the fun and games were far from over.

At that time, my mother had discovered all the joys of foreign holidays, and she and my dad had started, whenever possible, to fly off to Spain for the occasional week or two. I would always know when holidays were being planned because I would arrive home to find the holiday brochures spread out all over the kitchen table. And it was around this time that I came home one afternoon to find my mum and dad both sat in the kitchen, holiday brochures in hand. My mother announced that they were going to the Costa Brava for a couple of weeks. She then showed me the 'Thomas Cooke' brochure which read 'Benidorm' for just £25, which was actually a fair amount of money at the time.

While they were away on holiday I would stay at home with my sister, and my grandparents would move in. I would keep an eye on the farm, and my grandparents would of course, keep an eye on us...

So that was it. I had been informed.

My dad put down the brochure and then turned to me and smiled.

"And guess what?" he said "I've sold that bloody pig"

I looked at him "Honestly?"

"Yes" he said, and he grinned.

"Who to?" I asked.

"John the bread man" he replied, and he smiled.

'John the bread man', was a local purveyor of anything and everything. He'd acquired his nickname because he used to sell breadcrumbs to farmers, which they used as animal feed. The breadcrumbs were actually the waste cuttings from the sliced loaves of bread, produced in the town's local bakery, it was a huge place and still is, and back then John must have had the contract to remove their waste bread.

John was a strange sort of bloke, a large jovial man with curly dark hair. He was also a bit effeminate and had the habit of occasionally squeezing your bottom in a friendly sort of way, and not just me, most of the young lads who came on the farm got a friendly squeeze too.

It was only years later that we realized just where he was coming from, but in those days we were all a bit naive and we just thought he was being sociable. John always wore a pair of very worn old wellington boots and shabby old farm clothes, and usually some threadbare old jumper.

Curiously though, he also always wore a brightly coloured yellow cravat, a strange flamboyance, but I suppose it went with the territory.

John kept a smallholding, a rundown sort of place which always seemed to be knee deep in mud. He kept a few pigs, and some chickens, and he also kept his stock of breadcrumbs there, stored in a shed in large sacks, ready for him to deliver to the local farmers in his old blue transit van. He was a real character, and though he struggled to make a living he was poor, and poverty will either beat you down or keep you persistent.

Anyway, that was John.

And so, back at our kitchen table, and my dad announcing that we were finally getting rid of 'The pig'.

"John the 'bread man" I said "what does 'he' want it for?" I was a bit surprised.

My dad suddenly looked a bit vague "Err, I've told him it's 'in pig'", which meant that it was pregnant, "and I've told him we're a bit short of space at the moment".

"But it's not 'in pig' dad, it wouldn't let the boar anywhere near it".

"Yes, I know" he said "but John doesn't know that and by the time he does, it'll be too late. I'll tell him we must have made a mistake, I'll tell him the old boar must be knackered or something"

Well actually the old boar was, after the attack it hardly came out of its stall anymore.

"Anyway" my dad continued "he thinks he's getting a bargain, he's giving me £25 for it".

'Ah' I thought '£25', that's handy, and I looked at the Thomas Cooke brochure

"Yes" said my dad as he tapped the brochure "that's half our holiday paid for, and we get rid of that 'bloody thing'. "Two birds with one stone"

"Nice one dad" I could see his logic. Yes, 'nice one'.

"He's coming for it on Monday afternoon, so 'we'll' have to sort something out".

My heart sunk, I'd heard the word 'We' before.

"Right" I said, a bit apprehensively.

But my dad was enthusiastic "We'll make up another 'run' out of those corrugated sheets, and I'll make a 'ramp' out of some railway sleepers. We'll back John's van up to the ramp, I'll open the pen door and the pig will come charging out and go down the run, then up the ramp and right into the back of John's van, and 'bingo'!"

So that's what we did. Monday afternoon arrived and so did John in his van.

My dad greeted him like a long lost friend.

"Hello there John, how're you doing?"

"Oh Lovely" said John as he fluffed up his cravat.

"It's a lovely day" said my dad.

"Oh yes, it's lovely" said John

My god, I was only thirteen at the time, but even I shook my head. It's true, you can smell bullshit.

Anyway my dad told John to turn his van around and back it up to the ramp.

"It'll be easier John" he said.

'God help us' I thought, with a feeling of impending doom.

So John reversed his van up to the ramp and he opened the rear doors as my dad gave me the 'nod', and then he picked up a steel yard brush as he headed for the pig's pen.

John bless him, in his innocence had straightaway handed over the twenty five quid to my dad, so now it was just up to the pig.

My dad walked straight up to the pen and quickly whipped open the door, and within seconds our psychotic swine charged out, looking wildly from left to right, it's mouth wide open, it was grunting manically and looking for something to bite.

I cringed and took a step back.

Suddenly, my dad leapt behind the pig and started to pound the unsuspecting animal with the yard brush. This surprise attack caught the pig completely unawares, having its arse battered with a steel brush was a bit of a shocker and it squealed loudly and set off running like a bat out of hell. Down the run it charged, and when it got to the ramp it just carried on and ran straight up into the back of the van. I couldn't believe it.

My dad following closely, smartly slammed the van doors shut behind it. We could hear the pig bouncing about in the back of the van as it turned this way and that. It was trying to figure out what was going on, but we had it, a job well done, a problem well and truly sorted.

My dad gave me a knowing look and smiled, and then he turned to John.

"Nice one John" he said confidently "Good pig that, pity we couldn't keep it but we need the space".

"Oh lovely" said John.

But inside the van things were getting a little noisier as the animal realized it was trapped. It was a big pig and it suddenly found that it didn't have a lot of room to manoeuvre. My dad, hearing the increased activity, decided to walk John around to the front of his van to try to bid him farewell and get him on his way.

"Yes" continued my dad "She's always had large litters has that one, probably give birth to ten or twelve piglets. She's a good sow, a good breeder".

"Oh good" said John "that will be lovely".

"Yes, you'll make good money on that one, anyway we'd better get on John, we've other pigs to sort out" said my dad as he tried to bring things to a conclusion "We'll see you again then John, okay"

"Yes." said John "lovely to see you" and he opened the door of his van and climbed in.

We watched as he put the keys into the ignition and then stared in horror as a pig's head suddenly appeared over the passenger seat. It took one look at John, screamed, and then launched itself over the front seat to try and attack him. Thankfully it could only get halfway over, and so with its head and front feet hanging over the seat it began to snap savagely at John's head.

John, on hearing the screaming pig glanced sideways, only to see the massive head and snapping yellow teeth trying to get at him. John was a big rotund sort of man, but he was out of that van in a flash.

"Oh Jesus Christ" said my dad, and he put his hand on his head.

"Oh dear me" said a breathless and very alarmed John "Its mad Tommy, that pigs mad, it's vicious".

Things were no longer lovely.

Then John turned to my dad and said "I don't think I can handle it Tommy, it's a dangerous animal, I don't think I want it."

The look on my father's face, well, and the thought of handing back the money...'money' that was now designated for 'Benidorm', it was half the cost of the holiday. Oh dear me.

"Oh no John" said my dad, trying to sound casual "it's just a bit nervous that's all, it'll calm down once you set off"

My dad was now a bit nervous himself.

"I don't know Tommy" said John, who was now more than a little unsure.

And then the pig started to bang about in the back of the van again and John's eyes widened and he began to shake his head, and my dad suddenly realized that something had to be done.

"Just stand there and keep your door shut John, I'll sort it out" he said.

Then he walked around to the back of the van, and I dutifully followed. He looked around and there on the floor in the doorway of one of the sheds, was a steel bucket containing a large hammer and some nails that we'd been using it to repair some fencing. My dad reached down for the hammer, and then he picked up the bucket and tipped all the nails out onto the floor. He walked to the back of the van and stood there for a brief moment, then he turned and looked at me and he took a deep breath.

"Right" he said, and he steadied himself, then he wrenched open the van door and with a rush of momentum he jumped into the back of the van with the pig.

I was horrified...

The pig, hearing the van door open suddenly turned to see what was going on, and as it did, my dad jammed the steel bucket over its head. The pig was shocked, suddenly it couldn't see a thing and it moved its head from side to side, but that didn't help at all. Then my dad swung the hammer and started to pound and pummel the bucket with all his might. The pig staggered sideways as my dad continued to pound away like a jack-hammer and by the sixth strike the pig collapsed to its knees, another couple of strikes and its head dropped as it keeled over.

My dad removed the bucket and the pig just lay there cross-eyed, not even a grunt. I think it was punch drunk.

"Right" said my dad, getting his breath back "that's sorted that bloody thing out" and he cursed some more as he climbed out of the van.

It was all over and done in less than a minute really, and suddenly John appeared around the back of the van to find his new pig all sedated and quiet, he was a bit amazed.

"What did you do Tommy?" he asked.

"Oh, I just calmed it down John, it'll be alright now. No problem" said my dad casually.

"What was wrong with it" asked John again...

"Oh, it just got over excited John. Pigs do that, they're not used to riding about in vans"

My dad looked at me and rolled his eyes.

'John the bread man' must have been bloody stupid, because he actually did believe this.

And so we closed the doors and my dad walked and talked John around to the front of his van and bid him farewell. John got into his van and reversed out of the farmyard, and drove off.

And for us, that was the end of that.

However, it wasn't the end for poor John.

He'd got about a mile and a half down the road and was heading for town, when the pig suddenly stood up. It now had a bad headache and was in a bit of a mood, being in the back of a moving van didn't help either, it unsettled the pig and it was still a bit dizzy. It started to give a low threatening grunt. Hearing this, John glanced into his rear view mirror and he became rather anxious when he saw that the pig was now standing up again. He gulped, and was slightly concerned. But he was even more concerned when the pig suddenly raised the tempo of its grunting and started to head towards him, chomping its teeth. In a moment of anxiety and panic, John realized that he was about to be attacked again and he suddenly made a split second decision. He looked out of the van window and spotted a turning on the left, a side road, and so he immediately whipped the steering wheel hard to the left and the van screeched around the corner, it was nearly on two wheels. The pig did a sideways summersault in the back and bashed its head on a steel toolbox. It lay there groaning, momentarily stunned. John quickly looked round at it and then took the next right and then left and got himself back onto the main road. He then made a conscious decision, this pig was dangerous, he'd bought the damn thing and already he'd had enough of it. He knew it was going to be trouble, and he also knew my father, if he took it back my dad wouldn't have it, and neither would he give him back his money.

'Sold as Seen', as they say.

So he decided to cut his losses, there was only one solution, and so he took the next right turn, and headed directly for the local slaughterhouse.

But getting there proved to be more difficult than expected. The pig 'recovered' several times on the way, and every time it managed to stand up it headed towards John, grunting loudly and once again snapping its teeth. And every time this happened, John had to repeatedly take a sharp left or sharp right turn, to again knock the pig off its feet. So he was continually heading in the wrong direction, plus it seemed that the pig was now learning to handle corners better, and when John turned the van quickly left or right, the pig learned to lie down quickly, this way it only rolled over instead of being thrown about. John had to change tactics and the next time the pig stood up and charged towards him, John slammed on his brakes hard, and the van stopped dead in its tracks. The pig once again screamed as it was catapulted down the length of the van, it dropped on its knees as it slid along the floor and ended up with its head jammed under the passenger seat. It didn't like this at all, it still had memories of the 'bucket incident' and this wasn't helping.

By the time it had dislodged itself, John had got another mile nearer the slaughterhouse, and so by using the technique of sharp left, sharp right and slamming on the brakes, he finally managed to arrive at his destination. Anyone following John's van must have wondered what on god's earth was going on.

A ten minute journey had taken nearly half an hour, and it was a sweating and thoroughly exhausted John that drove his van through the slaughterhouse gates like a madman. He screeched to a halt, and then almost fell out of the van as he slammed the door shut.

As he walked towards the company office, two of the slaughter men appeared at the door to see what all the fuss was about.

"Bloody Hell John, you're in a hurry" one of them said "Where's the fire?"

He walked straight past them, breathing hard and wiping the sweat off his brow with his cravat, he called out to them without even looking back.

"There's a pig in that van. Kill it".

"And where are you going John?"

"To find a pub" said John, and he walked off rather shakily, and out of the yard.

Farms and farmers always have a dog, and we had many that we were very fond of, but the most favourite dog and the love of my father's life was without doubt his Doberman.

For many years, I could remember my father mentioning that he'd always wanted a Doberman dog, I can only assume that he had possibly seen them during the war in Germany. But one day, out of the blue, he told me that at the weekend we were going over to 'Westhoughton', a small town on the outskirts of Bolton. We were going to go and see about a dog, a 'Doberman, that he had seen advertised 'for sale' in the local newspaper.

All he said about it was "It's not a bad price" and so I just guessed that he must have been looking for a Doberman for some time.

Weekend arrived, it was a Sunday afternoon, and off we went to 'see a man about a dog'. The people selling it were actually a security company, 'A1 Dog Security', and my first thought was 'Oh hell, what are we getting into now' and I had this vision of some massive snarling beast that would attack you just for blinking.

So off we went. I drove us there in my dad's van, with an increasing feeling of trepidation and doom.

We finally found 'A1 Dog Security' it was a right turn off the main road and down a narrow lane. We arrived to find that the business consisted of an office building with a large compound attached to it, and behind that were several long sheds which must have been the kennels because we could hear a lot of loud and mixed barking coming from there. On the front of the compound was a large white sign with black lettering that read...

'A1 Dog Security...Guard Dogs and Attack Dogs...Trained and Supplied' and under the lettering was drawing of a snarling Alsatian dog.

I looked at the sign and thought 'Oh bloody hell'.

So we parked the van and walked over to the office and knocked on the door. A large man with a shaved head slowly opened the door and looked out at us.

"Hello there" said my dad jovially "I rang you up midweek, we've come to see about the Doberman"

"Oh" said the man, still staring at us "Right, you'd better come in"

Not the friendliest of people.

We entered the office and to my surprise , it was quite an efficient looking place with photographs of different breeds of large dogs on the walls, plus a host of timetables and booking sheets with days and dates written all over them, it seemed that this was quite a busy firm. There was another man in the office who he was sitting behind a typewriter, drinking a cup of coffee.

The big man introduced himself "Hiya, I'm Ron Stanton" and he leant forward and shook my dad's hand "and this is my brother Derek". Derek nodded back as a reply.

I was completely ignored, nothing new there then. So I just sort of nodded to everybody, but was still ignored.

Ron continued "Right, so you've come about the Doberman" and he looked across to his brother "Derek" he said "could you go and get the dog for us please".

"Okay" said Derek, putting down his cup, then he stood up and left through the back door.

"We'll go into the compound" said Ron, and he opened a side door and led us both through.

Once we were in the compound, Ron closed the door and turned to my dad.

"Can I ask you..." said Ron to my dad "what you actually want this dog for?"

"What do you mean?" asked my dad.

Ron sort of smiled and grimaced at the same time, he looked almost apologetic.

"Well it's like this" he said "do you want this dog as a guard dog, or a pet?"

"Oh" said my dad "as a pet, it's going to be a farm dog, I don't want something that's dangerous"

Ron seemed to brighten at this "and you do know it's not a puppy?"

"Yes, I know" said my dad "how old 'is' the dog?"

"It's about twelve months old" said Ron "it's what we call 'a juvenile'..."

My thoughts were that we were going to get some four legged skinhead from 'dog borstal'.

Ron continued "Let me just tell you something about this business" he said to us confidentially "What we actually do here is take dogs and train them up, we have to train them to be savage and to attack people, and to do that we have to roughen them up. We take dogs and we're brutal with them, it's hard, but it's our job to turn out that sort of animal. There's a huge demand in the commercial world for this sort of dog. Dog security is a growing market" Ron then rubbed his chin "and that's where we have a problem with this particular dog"

"Why's that" asked my dad, he was now looking a bit worried.

"We can't do a thing with it" said Ron "the dogs un-trainable"

"What do you mean" said my dad.

"Well it's like this" said Ron "We've hit it, beat and kicked it, we've tied it to a chain and dragged it around the compound, we've teased it and we've slapped it, and we've done this week after week, but we just can't get any response from the dog. No reaction at all, not even a growl"

"Is it mental or something?" asked my dad.

"No" said Ron "it's just bloody daft".

And at that moment we heard the compound gate open as Derek released 'the dog'.

And in it ran, well I say ran, no actually in it bounded with a sort of skipping motion, full of the joys of spring and 'woofing' loudly as it ran. It cantered around the entire compound three times like this and every so often it would stop and spin in a circle trying to catch hold of some imaginary tail.

Ron just shook his head.

I burst out laughing with relief, this dog was funny "My God, it's Scooby Doo" I said.

"It's a bloody joke" said Ron, and he turned to my dad "and that's the problem with it, all it wants to do is play, it's the giddiest dog I've ever known, not got a bad bone in its body, it couldn't even bite itself".

My dad didn't say anything, he just watched the dog lope happily around the compound.

But I knew my dad, he had a way with animals, dogs and horses, he could handle them all, it was a gift, and he turned to the dog as it skipped past and gave a low whistle. The dog slowed and looked round at him.

He put out his hand "Come hear bonny lad" he said to it softly, and he stretched out his hand.

The dog stopped and looked at him, and then suddenly it walked towards him. When it was within reach, my dad leaned forward and began to stroke the dogs head and rub its ears as he continued to talk to it, then he moved closer and got hold of the its collar, and pulled the dog to him and hugged it like a child.

I think that was the first human kindness that the dog had ever known, physical kindness, and the dog twitched with the excitement of it. My dad stood up and stepped back, and the dog looked up at him and then jumped up and licked his face. It was love at first sight, and with that one act, the dog would love my dad till its dying day.

We bought the Doberman.

Derek handed my dad the lead and both brothers looked relieved.

"It's called 'Taurus' said Ron.

"Isn't that the name of a bull" I joked, and then wished I hadn't.

As usual, everyone ignored me, but I suppose there wasn't much humour in a place where they beat up dogs for a living.

So we put 'Taurus' in the van with us and went home.

When we got back to the farm my dad immediately fed him, the dog was ravenous and we began to notice how thin he actually was. Though he was a big boned dog, Taurus had ribs sticking out of his skin that you could count.

"I'm going to take the dog for a walk and then I'm going to feed it again" he said.

"Watch it doesn't run off" I said to him "maybe you should keep it on its lead"

My dad smiled "Feed a dog, walk it and look after it, and it'll never run away"

He set off down the field with Taurus on the lead, and within fifty yards he reached down and unclipped the lead from the dog's collar. Taurus immediately ran off...off and away, and I thought to myself 'well that's it, that dogs gone'. Then suddenly, it turned around and ran all the way back to my dad. Then it ran off again, and again returned, then he ran around in wide circles, and then back and forth, and I watched them go easily across the fields.

My dad was right, that dog wasn't going to go anywhere.

Taurus soon became a firm member of the family. Full of energy and fun, that dog just couldn't sit still. He was like a kid on holiday, I suppose that's what he was really, he'd never had freedom, love or attention, and now he had it all in one big dollop and he thrived on it. It was a life that had suddenly become wonderful, and for Taurus it was a bit like winning the lottery.

Mealtimes became a whole lot more entertaining. The family would sit at the table in our large farmhouse kitchen, and this crazy dog would run round and around the table nonstop.

It drove my mother mad, it drove us all mad, except my dad who just laughed. He thought it was all hilarious. Then when the dog finally tired of this, he would go and lock his jaws onto the table leg and try to drag the whole table across the kitchen floor. We would just lift up our knives and forks as the table and our food moved a foot to the left or to the right. And believe me, it was a big, heavy farm table, this was one strong dog. My dad, of course, thought that it was all wonderfully funny and the dog picked up on this, and so he continued.

Mealtimes became slightly surreal. A family sitting there, the four of us trying to eat and chat, as a large black dog ran aimlessly round and round the table, and then every so often the table would move, jerked erratically, food sliding about and drinks knocked over, and we the family, carrying on as though this was normal.

Thank god we didn't have many visitors.

Mother was not impressed.

My dad would say "He's only young, he'll grow up" and of course he was right.

A year later, Taurus was a different dog. For a start, he was well fed, very well fed.

Besides having the farm my dad also ran market stalls which sold dairy produce and all sorts of cooked meats and hams. All the off cuts and trimmings were saved for the dog, so he had a daily diet of roast beef, roast pork, ox tongue and turkey breast. That dog ate like a king. Taurus never ever had tinned dog food once he came to the farm, and he actually became quite a fussy eater. If there was any fat in his food, he would simply eat around it, however, he did have one weakness, and that was 'corned beef'. That dog would sell his soul to the devil for corned beef. He even learned how to open the kitchen fridge, and if there was corned beef in there, the dog would pinch it and run off.

And he did get quite 'picky'. If you threw him some titbit of food to 'catch' and it was not up to standard, he would simply spit it out, give you a look of complete distain and then walk away with a very haughty attitude.

As time passed by, the dog got bigger and fitter and put on a lot of muscle. He matured and took on dominance and eventually he ruled every dog the area. Very soon, no dog ever came around to chase the livestock.

I remember one morning looking out of the kitchen window, to see some witless dog saunter around the corner of the farmhouse looking for plunder, its nose in the air, sniffing for opportunities.

Suddenly Taurus came out of an adjoining shed. He looked directly at the dog and then slowly and steadily strode towards the intruder. I was fascinated. The unsuspecting dog saw Taurus approaching and just froze, its eyes widened and it stood there in terror and for some reason, it didn't have the sense or the will to run. Taurus approached the dog with menace, and his black fur stood up along the whole of the length of his back and his neck, and his ears bristled. The intruder immediately rolled over onto its back, it was an act of total submission, to show the dominant dog that they know who he is and respect him.

As he got to within a couple of feet of the dog, Taurus started to snarl and he curled back his lips and fully bared his front fangs as he closed in on the poor animal.

I couldn't believe what I was seeing. Our soft and loving pet had suddenly transformed into some sort of wolf and I had visions of him simply ripping this poor dog's throat out.

The dog lay there on its back and started to shake as Taurus stood right over it with his snarling fangs and he actually dripped saliva onto the other dog. It was a moment of tension and terror. Slowly, he lifted his large clawed paw and then unbelievably, stamped on the dogs throat. I'd never seen anything like it. This broke the hypnotic spell and the dog spun on the floor and jumped to its feet and ran like it had never run before. It shot off down the back street, and it must have thought that Taurus was in pursuit because it never looked back or slowed or stopped, it just rapidly disappeared around a corner way in the distance. But Taurus just stood there and watched the dog run off, and then I saw his short stubby tail wagging and suddenly I realized that this was all an act, a performance, and he had no intention of chasing that dog down the street, and what for?

He'd simply given it the message 'Don't come round here'.

He turned and skipped into the kitchen and almost smiled at me, his wagging tail was always a giveaway.

"Here" I said, and I gave him a piece of chocolate.

"Well you got rid of that one didn't you" I said to him.

He wagged his tail some more and I gave him another piece.

"That's your lot" I said, and I shook my head. With that he turned and strolled back outside, he was back on patrol and he was doing his job. He was of course protecting his territory, which was the farm. He was working the partnership that man and dog have forged for thousands of years, from sheepdogs to police dogs, and rescue dogs and 'dogs for the blind', even your domestic pet. It's a unique relationship and the wonder of it never ceases to amaze me.

In our own home, the dog and his master relationship between Taurus and my dad never faltered. Every night after work when my dad fell asleep in his favourite chair, Taurus would lie there with his head on my dad's feet, he was the most faithful dog I've ever known.

Being a farmer meant that my dad was up every morning at around four o' clock, old habits die hard. He would get up very early and the first thing he would do was light the coal fire in our kitchen to warm up the house. To rush things along he would build up the fire in the hearth with newspaper, wood and coal and then light it. Then he would go outside to where we had a large diesel fuel tank installed, and he'd pour a pint of diesel fuel from the tank into a tin jug. Then he'd go back into the kitchen and throw the diesel onto the burning fire, and 'Whoosh'...the fuel would ignite and start a roaring blaze. Unfortunately, on a few occasions he overdid it a little, and the flames would blow back out of the hearth and set fire to the fireplace. It was a dodgy thing to do, but my dad always reckoned he'd got it off to a fine art.

My mother however, who had to continually scrub the blackened stone fireplace clean, didn't agree.

Also and unfortunately, old Taurus, who wasn't at his sharpest first thing in the morning, sometimes got caught in the middle of all this. He would sit there dozily, as suddenly my dad would proceed to do his 'flamethrower' bit.

Dad would give the dog a last minute warning.

"Aye up!" he'd shout as he launched the fuel onto the fire. Regrettably, the dog sometimes wasn't quick enough to get out of the way, and on several occasions he got caught in the flame and got his whiskers burnt. The dog would howl and run out of the house in panic.

A smouldering Doberman is best avoided.

Eventually however, the dog started to associate the smell of diesel with possible cremation, and he learned that when diesel was around, it was a wise decision to get out of the way, and rapidly. And being a wise old dog, that was just what he did, if he ever smelled diesel fuel, he would quickly dash off.

The thing was that this was a period when commercial vehicles were all converting to diesel power as petrol became more and more expensive, and all of the delivery vans that came to the farm were suddenly diesel fuelled. This threw the poor dog into turmoil and every time a van pulled into the farmyard and he smelled the diesel, the dog would run off down the field and wouldn't come back until the van had gone.

There was some sort of logic to this. It's called self preservation.

We've always been a family of habit, and each and every morning the 'ten o' clock brew' was something that was fairly sacred to us.

But one morning, my dad stormed into the kitchen and made a shocking announcement.

"Somebody's stealing our bloody milk" he said angrily.

"What...what do you mean?" asked my mother.

"Our milk, somebody's pinching it...it keeps disappearing".

"How do you know?" she said.

He sighed "Because...it's not there"

"Is it not the milkman? My mother asked "he might have forgotten us"

My dad shook his head "Jimmy wouldn't miss us"

'Jimmy Roberts' had always been our milkman, he had the farm a mile up the road from us and he'd delivered our milk for as long as I could remember. As farmers, we'd worked and farmed together for years and were more than just friends and neighbours, we were almost family and still are.

I had to agree with my dad on this one, Jimmy had always delivered the milk to our front door, every morning like clockwork, there was to be no mistake.

"It's not every day, it's every other day" said my dad "a pint keeps disappearing, but this morning it's all been pinched, all three pints. We've no bloody milk at all".

And no milk meant 'no' brew, no precious mug of tea. This was serious stuff.

My dad put on his serious face "Whoever it is, I'll catch him, just you watch" and he said this with all the conviction of a driven man. I'd seen all this before, and felt like going back to bed and let him sort it out.

'Here we go' I thought. 'Trouble'

It took four days, but my dad nailed the bastard, and he was a bastard, he was a young gentleman called 'Eric Naylor'. But he was known locally by his nickname...The 'Nail'.

The 'Nail' was the local 'Teddy boy', and he was a bully and an all round nasty piece of work. He was a tall, red haired lad, he had long wavy hair, quaffed up with Brylcream, and worn in the 'D.A' style, which in those days was a sort of stylistic 'rocker' look. He would have been about nineteen at the time and he always wore a black leather biker's jacket and he would strut around the village along with his little entourage of followers, hurting people and causing trouble. Vandalism, bullying and minor theft, usually from minor victims, were his personal trademark.

He made our lives a living hell, and I now consider the possibility that there was something of the psychopath about him.

I remember as a young lad, I was sitting in the local barbers one afternoon, waiting for a haircut. It was during the school holidays and I had gone there early in the afternoon because at that time it wouldn't be busy and I wouldn't have to queue for the usual boring hour and a half. When I'd arrived, one man was just leaving and another, an elderly pensioner was just sitting down in the barber's chair. Thankfully, there was no one else was in the shop.

'Great' I thought to myself, 'no queue' and I could get done quickly and then go and catch up with my mates, who had all gone off to the local park for a game of football.

Mr Forrester, our local barber was about sixty years old, and was possibly the most miserable man in the world. I sat there that afternoon and watched as he put the cape around the pensioner's shoulders and customarily tucked it into his neck. Then he turned to his customer and uttered his famous phrase "I see the Wanderers lost."

This was one of the only two phrases that Mr Forrester ever uttered to his customers. There was the "I see the Wanderers lost " or conversely "I see the Wanderers won".

Both comments were in reference to our local famous football team 'The Bolton Wanderers'.

Mr Forrester, a thin bespectacled man who always wore a drab white nylon coat, was without doubt the most miserable man in the history of hairdressing. He had no conversation at all, he would never ask a customer what sort of style they wanted because he only did one haircut, and that was the 'short back and sides'. It turned out that when he was younger he was originally a barber in the army and that was the only style that they ever did.

If you ever walked around our village, you would immediately notice that we all looked the same, it was as if we were all related. Every man and boy had the same haircut, except of course, the 'Nail'.

Old man Forrester would sit his customer in the chair, mention 'the Wanderers', and that was it, they would have to talk to themselves after that. There was however one an exception, and that was if you were a 'kid'. He hated kids. He never, ever spoke to kids. If you were under the age of twelve he would sit you in the chair and two or three minutes later you were done and ejected from the barely warm seat. I have been a barber for over forty years and to this day I still don't know how he could cut my hair so quickly. However, looking back at old family photographs of myself, it has to be said that my haircuts did actually look like they'd been done with an axe.

I came to realize in later years, something that was quite obvious really. Mr Forrester, without doubt hated his job, and being a barber must have been something he'd been pushed into doing when he was young, and then he was stuck with it.

I remember he once cut my ear rather badly, he was rushing because there was a long queue of customers waiting, and they were starting to moan. He slashed the side of my ear with the scissors and I started to bleed like a tap. Misguidedly, because of that I thought I'd be getting a free haircut. But he stuffed a piece of cotton wool in my hand and knocked me a penny off the price as he pushed me out of the shop door, what a miserable twat.

Anyway, there I was, sitting in Forrester's barbershop and Mr Forrester was just finishing off the pensioner's haircut when the door swung open, and in walked the 'Nail'. Oh hell.

Well the first thing that went through my mind was could I manage to hide my money down my sock without the 'Nail' noticing.

No money meant no haircut, and try explaining that to my mother.

The 'Nail' just stood there, looking at himself in the mirror and smirking at his own self importance, then he turned to Mr Forrester.

"I need a haircut. Now." he said, and he shook his head and ran his hand through his long red hair. "I want it trimmed and styled" he continued "and listen, I don't want it cutting bloody short, you hear me?"

It was a demand, and it was rude.

He glanced down at me and then back to Mr Forrester, and I realized that the 'queuing' system had just been shot to pieces.

Mr Forrester looked back at him, open mouthed, he was out gunned here, he knew that he couldn't possibly style, let alone trim the Nail's hair. He only knew one bloody haircut and that was 'The Forrester special'. He could do that with his eyes shut, and probably did.

Anyway, at some point in his life Mr Forrester must have heard the motto 'Never defend... always attack', because he suddenly came out of paralysis and gave the 'Nail' an absolute look of disgust.

Then he replied "And what do you expect me to do with that?" he sparked back at the 'Nail' and he nodded towards the Nail's greased and moulded head of hair.

He bravely continued "I'm not touching that greasy bloody mess, you can bugger off, go on ...get out" he retorted. It was an insult inflicted with derision, it was also self defence.

I grimaced, and 'Oh hell' I thought again.

For a split second the 'Nail' was stunned, and then he was insulted, and then he was mad.

He suddenly sneered "You cheeky old bastard" and then he grabbed hold of Mr Forrester, snatching him by the lapels of his white nylon coat. I can still remember one of the buttons being ripped off and bouncing across the red tiled floor.

Then everything happened in a instant. The 'Nail' swung Mr Forrester around like a rag doll and then incredulously, he head butted him straight in the face. It was a noise like someone slapping a pillow.

Mr Forrester gave out a howl and then a groan as he slumped to the floor, his face all covered in blood from his splattered nose.

I was stunned and shocked at the violence of it all, I'd never dealt with anything like this before, it was raw human violence and I've never forgotten that moment, and the fear of it sickened me.

I watched, almost in awe and totally helpless as the 'Nail', his face red with temper, stepped back and started to swing his leg. He was going to kick Mr Forrester in the face, and I went sick.

At that moment the pensioner, the elderly man who had just had his haircut pushed himself between the 'Nail' and Mr Forrester.

He started shouting "Stop it...stop it, you're going to kill him. I'm going to ring the police, do you hear. I know who you are, I'm ringing the police"

And this offensive or maybe the mention of the police, turned off the switch in the 'Nails' brain, and suddenly the anger was gone and he looked at us in strange amazement, as if trying to understand himself 'what' had just happened. Then the realization of his actions suddenly registered on his face and his expression changed, he immediately looked uneasy and a bit worried. And then he spun around and grabbed the door and bolted.

Poor Mr Forrester, the 'Nail' had really hurt him and he was bleeding and upset. We helped him shakily to his feet and the pensioner asked if he should ring an ambulance or the police. But Mr Forrester declined and simply asked us to go. He said that he would be alright and that he was going to close the shop for the rest of the day.

I felt so sorry for him. He was only slightly built and was a private sort of man and totally defenceless.

All this violence was of course, nothing more than the cruel act of a bully.

Anyway, back home, and the 'great milk theft'.

Oh dear me, my dad was now on one. He'd sat there morning after morning, day after day. For four days he'd waited and watched the pattern of the thief, and it was the 'Nail'.

On observing the theft, anybody else would have jumped out of the front door and apprehended the culprit, but no, not my dad.

The next morning he woke me up early, very early.

"Come on lad" he said to me "Get yourself up. We'll catch that bugger today"

And I realized...he had a plan.

So I got up and dressed and we went downstairs .We sat there in the hallway at a small window at the side of our front door. We sat there for about fifteen minutes, and then like clockwork, the thief, 'the Nail' silently appeared. He stood on the main road at the corner of our house for a moment or two looking around, and then he turned and walked casually down the path which went past our front door. As he strolled by, he nonchalantly stooped down and picked up our bottle of milk, and on that morning strangely, it was the only bottle of milk.

We watched silently as he walked past our window and then turned right, to walk down the backstreet opposite.

"Come on lad" said my dad as he grabbed my shoulder "Come on", and we quickly went out through the kitchen door and outside through our backyard. There was just the two of us, and the dog, who followed enthusiastically.

We just stood there staring down the backstreet, as the 'Nail' walked away. I couldn't understand why we hadn't reprehended the thief, and I thought that at least my dad would have confronted him.

And then...

"Watch this" said my dad.

"What?" I replied.

"Just watch lad"

"Watch what...watch him drink our milk" I said, I was a bit annoyed by now.

"It's not milk" said my dad smiling.

"What do you mean?"

"It's not milk" he said again.

"It's not milk. What is it then?"

"Paint"

"Paint" I said?

"White paint" and he smiled.

I was a bit surprised.

And then he said "I've sorted it out with the milkman, 'Jimmy'. He's been bringing 'our own' milk round to the back door for the last few days"

And then he grinned "I've been waiting for this, just watch".

And I turned to see the 'Nail' confidently strolling down the backstreet, the bottle of milk in his hand, wearing that same old biker jacket, and the back of his head, that red hair styled in a 'D.A', the Teddy boy style. I remember it well.

Suddenly he reached down and ripped the silver foil cap off the top of the bottle. He threw the cap away and then in one beautiful moment, he raised the bottle to his mouth and glugged down the milk. I suppose it was the momentum of the physical act of drinking, but for a split second, nothing happened, and even from a distance, you could see that he'd drank almost half of the bottle . And then, oh dear me.

The 'Nail' suddenly went rigid, it was like a spasm, and then he immediately started to convulse and shake about. He screamed something like "Gaahhh" as he threw his head back, and then he vomited, and the vomit went all over his face and in his hair. He dropped the milk bottle, which smashed and then he collapsed to the ground and started to thrash about.

'Oh my god'

Personally, I thought he was going to die.

He rolled over onto his hands and knees and he continued to vomit violently, unfortunately he rolled onto the broken glass from the bottle he'd dropped and then he howled, screamed and vomited all at the same time as the glass slashed his hands and stuck into his knees.

My dad reached down and took hold of Taurus's collar. The dog had already been watching the Nail's antics with some curiosity.

As he held the dog's collar Taurus looked up, he knew what to do.

In a low, hard voice, my dad said urgently "Go on lad...Get him."

Taurus gave a deep growl and pulled forward, he started to bark but my dad held him back for just long enough, just a second or two, and then he released the dog.

Taurus charged off down the backstreet, and as he closed in on the 'Nail' he started to bark viciously like some mad dog. The 'Nail' momentarily turned and stared in shock and horror as the barking and now snarling Doberman headed directly towards him. As Taurus rapidly drew nearer, he continued to snarl manically, and then he opened his jaws and curled back his lips to bare those full, large white fangs. The wolf was back.

Even in the state he was in, the fear of what was happening made the 'Nail' get to his feet and he staggered backwards against a garden wall.

The dog ran straight at him and then jumped up at the 'Nail', knocking him over and back on the ground. The 'Nail' fell over with a howl, and then the dog tried to bite him in the face, his fangs snapping and snarling just inches away from the 'Nail's' head.

I was getting worried now, this could be a disaster. We could end up having to ring for an ambulance or the police, or even an undertaker. Things were beginning to get out of hand.

The 'Nail' once again got to his feet and backed away screaming as the dog kept bounding up at him, barking viciously.

Pinned against the wall, his face and hair full of white paint and vomit, the 'Nail' suddenly started to cry. He stood there with his arms stretched out, trying to fend the dog off, and now he was simpering and crying like a baby.

It wasn't a pretty sight. I think he'd possibly crapped himself.

"Dad" I said urgently "I think the dog's going to kill him".

There was no answer, and when I turned to look at him, to my amazement I found that he was in hysterics, and unlike the 'Nail', my dad was 'crying' with laughter.

He pointed as he laughed "Look at the dickhead, not 'the big man' now is he, the sad git".

"Dad, if the dog bites him we'll be in trouble"

"The dog won't bite him" he said and he smiled "the dog won't bite him, it's all an act"

And he put his two fingers to his mouth and gave a sharp whistle.

Down the backstreet, the dog's head spun around. He stopped the attacking, glanced back at the 'Nail' and then simply turned and trotted back to us, tail wagging, and smiley faced. What a clever boy.

Yes, that's what it had all been 'an act'. What a clever boy indeed.

The 'Nail', seeing the chance of escape, hobbled and staggered off.

I'll always remember him, his red hair dripping with white paint and vomit, it gave me a sort of warm glow. He really was a bastard.

"He won't be back" said my dad as he rubbed the dog's head.

"No, he bloody well won't" I replied.

"He's had it coming for a while" my dad continued "everybody knows what he did to old Mr Forrester, the rotten bastard. And it's not over yet, there are others around here that are waiting to catch up with 'him'. He's been up to no good for a while now and he's pushed his luck, throwing his bloody weight about, and then he goes and batters old man Forrester, the poor bugger, he's never done anyone any harm and he works so bloody hard in that shop".

And then it suddenly struck me, every man in the village went to Mr Forrester to get their haircut, so of course everybody knew what had happened, and word had gotten round.

And suddenly, I began to realize that even though Mr Forrester was very miserable with us kids, he did do an important job within the community, and he had the respect of the men in the village.

And life unexpectedly began to change for the 'Nail'.

Standing in the busy bus queue one morning, the bus arrived and just as the 'Nail' was about to get on it, he was elbowed in the face and knocked to the floor. The people getting on the bus just stepped over him.

And then one evening as he was coming home from work, again on the bus, he was pushed down the steps and he fell from top to bottom and smashed his face on a safety rail, apparently nobody saw what happened

Suddenly, he seemed to get tripped and pushed all the time, yes word had got around.

He had an accident in the toilet of one of the local pubs one night, when his head was accidently jammed down the loo by some bloke, and then flushed.

And his entourage, his little band of followers, the other smaller bullies who had stood behind him and backed him up, well they all disappeared, quickly. Yes, word had got around.

He was on his own, and suddenly the 'Nail' found he had no friends.

Then there was a story, 'a rumour', that the 'Nail' had come out of the local chip shop late one night, and that Mr Forrester's nephew, a wagon driver from Wigan, had been standing outside watching and waiting. And when the 'Nail' came out of the 'Chippy' the nephew followed him, then pushed him down a suitable backstreet and introduced himself. He then apparently gave the 'Nail' a very severe beating, and then pinched his fish and chips.

The 'Nail' left the village shortly after, nobody knew just when or even where he'd gone.

He simply wasn't around anymore.

Years later, I was in some pub in Bolton and I ended up having a conversation with someone who had lived in our village all those years ago. His name was 'John'. I'd forgotten his last name and I only vaguely remembered him, but he remembered our farm and apparently he only lived about a mile or two further down the road from us.

As we sat there recounting past memories, the story of the 'Nail' and him having to leave the village came up in conversation. We both agreed that he had been 'a right piece of work' and an all round bully, but then 'John' told me something.

Apparently the 'Nail' only lived a couple of doors up from his house. They were neighbours.

"He never bullied me" said John "Never bothered me at all. If he ever saw me out or about he would just nod. He would never speak to me, but he always left me alone".

I was surprised "Why was that?" I said "he had no qualms about giving everybody else a hard time"

John just gave me a quizzical look and raised an eyebrow.

"Well we were neighbours, and we knew about his mother, and so I think he must have been a bit embarrassed".

"Why was that?" I asked.

"Because of his mother, she was a prostitute"

"What?" I answered, in total disbelief.

John nodded "Yes she was a prostitute, she was on the game. Don't you remember her? She was a very slim woman. She had bleached blonde hair and always wore loads of makeup, even during the day. She always had her cheeks rouged bright red, she looked like she was wearing a mask, all the local kids used to laugh at her. Every night at around seven o' clock she would go and stand at the bus stop and make her way down town, the women in the village would just stare. None of them ever spoke to her".

Something clicked in my mind, I did remember her. I think it was all that make up and the reddened cheeks, she used to remind me of a circus clown, and there was something about her, that white blonde hair.

"My god" I said "I never knew. I do remember her now, I used to always see her coming out of Howcrofts Butchers, just down the road"

"Yes" said John "she was knocking him off"

"What?"

"Oh yes, we all knew about it. Mr Howcroft would always close his shop at one o' clock for lunch, and at ten past one she would roll up and knock on his side door. Half an hour later, and she would leave with a carrier bag full of meat"

"Bloody hell" I said, and I grinned.

"We all knew what she did, and the 'Nail' knew that we knew. He was probably embarrassed and a bit ashamed, but they had no money. His dad, old man Naylor, had disappeared years before and had left them destitute and that was the only way she knew how to earn some cash. The thing was, she was never at home at night and when he was young, 'Eric'...the 'Nail', well he started going out all the time and was getting himself into trouble. He was running wild and I don't think she took much care of him.

She was always out till late at night and I can remember that my own mother used to say that 'she never got out of bed till dinner time' and so I think he sort of 'went off the rails'. I suppose he was angry and a bit humiliated, he probably thought that people were laughing at him, and his mother"

"They probably were" I said "Well, it was a village and everyone knew everybody else's business, you remember what it was like".

"Yes I know" replied John.

"I just wonder" I said "I wonder whatever happened to him. He was a strange lad, sort of driven towards violence and theft and robbing people, everything he did was wrong."

"It was simply his background, I think" said John "things went wrong from an early age and it was his way of fighting back"

John finished his drink and then stood up, he was ready to leave.

"Well" I said smiling "he's most likely to be in prison...or in business" and I laughed.

John turned to me and said "Oh no, he's probably a politician".

And he walked away chuckling to himself.

And he was probably right.

Over the years, most of our farm dogs had always slept outside, usually in the barn or in an outhouse. The exception of course was Taurus, who slept in our warm kitchen from day one. My dad would have it no other way. He even bought the dog a large pint pot, and in the morning, once 'the fire lighting' was over and done with, he would make them both tea and toast. They would sit there in front of the roaring flames and the dog would have his own pint pot of hot sweet tea put in front of him, along with a plate of buttered toast, and the pair of them would sit like this for half an hour, before my dad went out to work.

The dog had eventually got older, I suppose a decade had passed and old Taurus had got a bit slower and he slept a bit longer. Then one day my mother commented about the strange smell that was emanating from the kitchen.

"There's something a bit whiffy in there" said my mother, slightly concerned.

"Oh" said my dad with his usual concern, 'none', and then he lowered the newspaper that he was reading.

"I hope the dogs alright" he said.

She looked at him rather pensively "I think 'it' 'is' the dog" she said.

My dad looked straight back at her "No, it can't be" he retorted, with a bit of a huff "there's now't wrong with that dog"

"Well something's not right in there" she replied.

"Have you tried 'hoovering up'..." he said mistakenly, and then "or try using more disinfectant when you mop up" he continued, very mistakenly.

I thought she was about to clobber him.

"Right." said my mother, now annoyed "that's it, get yourself into that kitchen and we'll find out what the smell is. Come on. Now"

So my dad sighed as he put down his paper and followed her dutifully into the kitchen.

"I can't smell anything" he said.

"No, you 'wouldn't'. I'm telling you, it's the dog."

The dog stirred, he'd been asleep in front of the fire and now he looked over at them. Poor thing, he'd been disturbed.

"See" said my dad "you've woke him up now"

The dog yawned, and sighed.

My dad went over to Taurus and stroked his head, and the dog rolled back onto the carpet, exhausted.

My mother shook her head, and sighed. Then she leant over the dog and tried to examine it to see if it was the cause of the elusive odour.

"It's not the dog" said my dad defensively. He was starting to take this personally.

Then my mother got onto her knees and started to go round the kitchen smelling the carpet.

My dad looked across at me and winked and then with a smile said "woof, woof...good girl".

She actually did growl at that comment.

What a family.

Then suddenly my mother pointed to the Yucca plant. It was in a large blue and cream ornamental Chinese vase in the corner of our kitchen and had been there for as long as I could remember.

"That's it" she said "that's where the smells coming from" and she hovered closely over the plant and pulled her face.

"Oh god, it reeks"

"I'll throw it out then" said my dad. Problem solved.

"No, it's not the plant you idiot, it's the dog, he's been peeing on the Yucca".

"Never!" said dad "why on earth would he do that?"

"Because he's getting old and needs to pee in the night, that's why".

She looked down and tapped the dog on the head. Taurus woke up again, with bit of a start.

She looked at him and pointed at the yucca.

"Have you peed on that plant?" she demanded.

The dogs face said it all. He looked away and sighed, and then he slowly stood up and went over to the open kitchen door. Filled with guilt, he looked back at us and then slowly walked out of the house.

Caught, convicted and now completely miserable, he left the scene of the crime.

My dad put his hand over his eyes and said "Oh bloody hell"

My mother was on a roll now, for once she had the upper hand and now vindicated, she was on a mission.

"That dogs going to have to sleep outside" she said. It wasn't a statement, it was a demand.

My dad was horrified "But, he's never slept outside in his life. He's not used to the cold"

This was true, if the weather ever turned inclement, the dog would scuttle back into the kitchen and head for the open fire, and if it was ever frosty, he would refuse to leave the house.

It is a fact, Dobermans are definitely not Huskies.

"I don't care" replied my mother "I'm not having the house smelling of dog pee"

She did have a point.

"You'll have to get him a kennel" she retorted.

"A kennel!" my dad nearly reeled at the suggestion "he can't go in a kennel, it'll bloody kill him. He's used to being warm".

I heard a creak and I looked up, only to see the end of the Taurus's nose pushing through the door, he seemed to be listening while my dad was fighting his 'corner'. He obviously knew the game was up and was trying to stay out of the line of fire.

Mother rolled on "He needs to go in a kennel and well, you'll have to make it warm for him. Put some blankets in it or something".

And that was that, discussion over.

My dad looked at me for support. I just shrugged my shoulders. On occasions such as this, I always felt that neutrality was the way to go, I have always admired Switzerland.

So that was it, the next day my dad started planning some sort of construction.

"I'll have to build something" he said "I've seen those kennels that they sell in pet shops, they're crap. The dog wouldn't even fit into one of those bloody things".

He was right there of course, the kennels that were being marketed at the time were definitely not built for an overweight Doberman. If Taurus had have ever managed to climb into one, he would have never been able to get out.

My dad came back from the builder's yard later that day with a load of assorted wooden planks, piled high in the back of his van. Armed with a hammer, a saw and a bucket of mixed nails, he set to work.

The kennel was to be built inside the large open fronted shed which was directly opposite our kitchen window. We sometimes used for storage and sometimes as a garage for the car.

My dad decided to build the kennel against the back wall of the shed "away from the draught" as he put it. It did make sense.

Three days later, and the kennel was finished. It was a masterpiece.

"Come and look at this" he said proudly to me as I got home from work that evening.

I walked into the open garage to see how he had got on. And my god, it wasn't a kennel, it was a bungalow. It was huge, made from double cladded planks of wood, it was all varnished and sealed.

"Insulation" explained my dad.

"Strewth dad" I said "it's big enough".

"Yes I know" he said enthusiastically "just look at this" and he pointed to the entrance of the kennel, which had a multicoloured plastic fly screen attached to it.

"It'll be like a home from home for him" he said. Then he looked over his shoulder and said secretively "have a look inside...but don't tell your mother" and he gave me 'the nod'.

I pulled back the fly screen and peered inside the kennel. He'd put a wide plank of wood across the base of the entrance and you had to sort of step over this as you bent down to see inside.

Well, it was amazing. The interior was a foot deep in straw and blankets, there were even some pillows in there too , and to top it all, on the wall he'd actually fitted an electric radiator, I couldn't believe it. It was so hot in there, it was like a sauna. And lying there in the middle of all this extravagance was a blissfully happy Doberman. Taurus lay there, stretched out in total luxury and comfort, he lifted his head to acknowledge his 'visitors ', and he wagged his stumpy tail and then rolled back over to get comfortable again. It was without doubt, doggie heaven.

"He'll be alright in there" my dad said confidently.

I was seriously considering asking the dog if he would like to swap bedrooms.

Anyway, a family balance was reinstated. Both parents were happy, the dog was happy, ecstatic is probably closer to the truth, and I was happy because everybody else was.

Equilibrium had been restored.

Taurus really enjoyed living in his semi-detached, and every morning when he heard my dad get up he would get up too, and stroll into the kitchen for his breakfast. That dog loved a cup of tea.

My mother was stood at the kitchen sink one night, washing the pots and plates after our dinner, and she kept peering through the window, then finally asked me.

"What's that red light in the garage, I've noticed it a few times, what is it?"

It was of course, the power indicator light on the electric radiator in the dog's kennel.

"Oh that" I said casually, and I sort of squinted, as though trying to make it out "Oh it's just one the lights from the fridges in the back shed". And I held my breath.

"Oh…right" she said "I wondered what it was" and she carried on washing the pots. And I began to breathe again.

My mother was a bit of a fanatic for not wasting electricity, and she would spend half her time continually go around the house turning all the lights off. I think my sister and I spent half of our childhood in darkness. However, she never, ever twigged that there was the radiator in the kennel. And that radiator was never turned off for three years, winter or summer. I kid you not.

A few years passed by, and then one day I had to go over to the farm. My dad had rung me and asked me to come over. I was married by then and had moved into my own home some time before.

"There's something wrong with the dog" he'd said quietly "I've rung the vet"

So I arrived and we both went to the kennel and my dad leaned in and softly called the dog. There was a shuffling and some movement and finally Taurus appeared at the entrance of his kennel and he slowly stepped out into the yard. I was a bit taken aback when I saw how old he'd become. I suppose I'd been busy getting on with my life and I hadn't seen a lot of him for the last couple of years. He was now much thinner and had lost a lot of his stature, and his face had turned grey in what was once, dark black fur. But there was also something else, something different in his face, and as I looked down at him I realized that there was a change in the shape of his nose. The nose that was once pointed and sharp was now swollen towards the end and this somehow changed the dog's appearance. We walked him into the house and I noticed that every so often he would stop and shake his head. We sat down at the kitchen table with a cup of tea and the dog just lay down in front of the fire.

Finally the vet, 'Mr Allanson' arrived. Anyone who has ever lived on a farm knows that the vet is a regular visitor. Livestock gets ill all the time and the vet, just like the family doctor, tries to get your animals back to health. Farming is at the end of the day, a business, and healthy stock means healthy profits. We'd dealt with Mr Allanson for years and he'd become a family friend. He would come and tend to the stock and then we would always go into the house for a cup of tea and something to eat. We would hear all the gossip from him and the local farming news, he was an interesting and intelligent man, and very likeable.

When he arrived, he came into the house and sat down at the table and then reached over to the dog. Slowly, he ran his experienced hands over the dogs face and nose.

"Hmmm" he said and he let the dog go. There was a brief silence, and then my dad spoke.

"What is it?" he said.

"The dog has a tumour in its nose Tommy" said the vet.

"So what do we do?" asked my dad.

"Well" he said, and he took a deep breath and frowned "it's like this Tommy, I could operate on the dog, we could do the operation and it could be a success, or it might not be. Nobody knows which way these things will go, but I have to tell you one thing, a dog's nose is the most sensitive part of its body and that operation, whatever happens, will put the dog through agony".

My dad twitched.

"I don't want that" he said quietly.

"I know you don't Tommy, how old is the dog?" asked the vet.

My dad thought back "fourteen, maybe fifteen"

"It's a good age" said the vet "and he's had a good life, I know he has. It's kinder to put the dog down Tommy".

My dad blinked.

"I know" he said.

There's a simple rule about farming and keeping livestock. It's a farming rule, but it works. Simply put...'nothing suffers'. If an animal is ill, it doesn't matter whether it's a chicken or a horse, if it's ill and nothing can be done, it's never left to suffer, it's put down and that's it.

And it is a kindness.

At that moment my mother came in to make us some tea and a sandwich. She brightened the moment and the conversation changed. We talked about farming and discussed something about some new vitamin injection for pigs that was new on the market. As we spoke my mother laid out the cups and plates and Mr Allanson opened his leather bag and produced a syringe. While we were talking he leaned over and pulled the dogs fur behind his neck and injected him with painkillers or something. Every time he came to visit a sick animal, he would always give them some sort of injection, everything from painkillers to vitamins.

We just sat there talking. I'll always remember the old farmhouse, it was so comfortable.

The hot coal fire in the hearth and my mother fussing about and bringing in the plates of sandwiches and biscuits, all helped along with easy conversations, and I looked down at Taurus who just yawned, he'd seen it all before and he yawned again and lay down in front of the fire and went to sleep. As I sat there, I looked down at him and remembered what a magnificent animal he had been, and how full of life he'd been when he was in his prime.

He was part of this family and he was a true character, and now he was at the end of his life. And I too was a farmer, and I realized that we had to do the right thing by him.

And it struck me that time stands still for no one, and that things can never stay the same.

My parents were getting older, my life had changed, and it made me wonder what the future would hold for us all, good or bad, and I realized that this kitchen had been my comfort zone for years. It was my home, full of happy memories and laughter and sometimes tears.

It was as they say 'the best of times' and something never to be forgotten.

My thoughts were suddenly interrupted, as Mr Allanson finally put down his cup and slowly gathered up his leather bag, he was ready to go.

My dad looked at the vet and then he looked down at Taurus, asleep in front of the fire. He knew what had to be done, he was a farmer.

"What do we do about the dog?" he said "do we bring him down to the surgery?"

Mr Allanson looked at my dad and spoke softly "the dogs dead Tommy, I put him to sleep while he lay there in front of the fire"

My dad looked down at his favourite. "He's dead?" he asked quietly.

"Yes, it's the best way. A dog is always more at ease in its own home".

My dad just blinked "I can't believe it, he just went to sleep, and he just lay there so peaceful.

"Yes, I know" said the vet "it's painless, and it's an easy way to end it".

My dad was silent for a moment, and then he reached down and ran his hand over the dog's head and rubbed his ear fondly for one last time.

Then he spoke "Why on earth can't we do the same thing for human beings, for people who are dying and are in agony?"

Mr Allanson stood there and shook his head "I don't know Tommy, I just don't know".

A year earlier my dad's sister, my beautiful aunty, had died of a cancer. She suffered terribly and was the bravest woman that I have ever known. Her death shook my father, and it shook all our family and our families. We were devastated. And at that moment my dad saw the unfairness of it all, and how people had to suffer the insult of pain, when it was possible and it was a kindness, to let your loved ones go with dignity and in peace.

He'd once said to me "We all have to die, that's part of life, it's 'how' you die that matters".

And it made me stop and wonder, and contemplate my own mortality.

It was time for Mr Allanson to leave, and as he left he shook my father's hand and gave him an understanding smile. Yes, Mr Allanson knew all about life, and the worth of it.

We walked him out to his car and watched him drive away.

There was a moment of silence between us both, there was nothing to say.

Then my dad turned to me "I'll bury the dog" he said.

"Do you want me to give you a lift?" I asked him.

"No, I'll be alright. I'll bury him there at the top of the field just outside the farm gate, that's where he used to like to run" and he turned to me "thanks lad" he said.

There were things I could have said but didn't, and I think he was thankful for that. We were farmers and it was back to business. There would be better times...times to laugh and remember old Taurus, and tell the tales. Of course there would.

A couple of days later, I went around to the farm, but there was nobody in. When I looked in the garage, the kennel was completely gone. Dismantled, and I found out later, burned.

There were to be no reminders. It was over.

After Taurus we had other dogs, but dogs were just dogs again for my dad. He looked after them of course, but none of them had the character of his favourite Doberman.

I remember his last dog, an old brown Labrador whose name was Toby. He got this dog a couple of years before he retired, and when my parents finally sold the farm and moved into a nearby bungalow, the Labrador of course went with them. My dad never really walked dogs, we used to have a farm so you just opened the back door and let the dog out and it would exercise 'itself'. Anyway, they all moved into the bungalow, and because of my dad's past feeding regime, the Labrador became grossly overweight. The dog was so obese, that it began to resemble a baby seal. It became fatter and fatter, and appeared to have no neck at all. And things did not get better, the dog could no longer manage to go out for a walk and so it put even more weight on, in the end it almost gave up moving completely. It would go outside in the morning for its ablutions and then stagger back into the house and into the kitchen for its breakfast. Then with one huge final effort, it would drag itself back into the front room and collapse in front of the fire and sleep there till lunch.

Things went from bad to worse, and the dog finally got so overweight that it could no longer see its own feet. So it continually tripped over obstacles and fell over. In the end, the fat thing couldn't get itself back into the house because it couldn't get over the front step. So to get it back in, my dad had to lift up its front paws one at a time to get the dog halfway in, then he would give it a push and have to lift up its back paws to finally get it through the door.

In the end of course, the dog had a heart attack and dropped dead. What a surprise.

To my complete amazement, my dad wrapped its body in some black plastic bin liners, and then stuffed the dead dog into a wheelie bin.

"Well" he said "I'd nowhere to bury the bloody thing".

Yes, spoken like a true farmer.

As well as the farm, we also had market stalls, and my dad worked constantly to keep both of these businesses going. On the markets we employed staff. The farm however, he ran himself, with a bit of help from me, and it struck me in later years just how hard he had to work to make a living. Besides pigs, we also bred and reared Turkeys for the Christmas trade. This was in the days before mass refrigeration and frozen Turkeys, and the market and the weather set the trend, and the price. If the weather at Christmas was mild, the turkeys had to be killed and sold quickly, there would always be a certain amount of panic and prices usually fell dramatically. However if it was cold, better still freezing, the turkeys could be easily stored and it gave you more time to deal. Prices could be volatile because in those days the whole of the country went out to buy its Christmas turkey only one or two days before Christmas day. There wasn't the luxury of a fridge or a freezer in every household as there is today.

Sometimes there would be a glut, which was a disaster, and I remember one year on Boxing Day, my dad and myself driving two overloaded vans, stacked full of unsold turkeys, to the local cold store. That was a bad year for us and there wasn't much to celebrate that Christmas. Other years of course were better, and that was life's little bit of trickery.

One particularly year, a good year, it was freezing cold and it was Christmas Eve. We came home from the markets having sold everything, there was not one single turkey left. As always on Christmas Eve, we left everything in the vans overnight, and then my dad and I would unload them and sort everything out the next morning, Christmas Day morning.

This allowed my dad to swiftly get out for a few pints on Christmas Eve, and the next day it kept us out of my mother's way during the Christmas day family preparations.

It was Christmas Day, and about ten in the morning. We were in the dairy unloading the vans and packing all the produce into our large walk-in fridges, when suddenly, Mr Bates arrived.

Mr Bates was a well known character who lived locally. He was a rather stout man, in his late fifties, who liked to drink and loved to gamble. He used to come to the farm at weekends to buy bacon and sausages and whatever else took his fancy. He would usually turn up wearing the same beige cap, a rather loud check jacket and yellow scarf, and he wore gold rimmed glasses which had a piece of adhesive tape permanently holding one of the hinges in place.

Mr Bates's face could be anywhere from flushed to burgundy, depending on the amount of booze he'd consumed the night before. His breath was always a giveaway.

Mr Bates, and I never knew his first name, but he had an up and down sort of life, I suppose it went with the territory really. He was either a flushed with money, or he was potless and broke.

He would generally arrive at our farm on Sundays, and if he'd had a good day at the bookies on the previous day, he would buy bagfuls of the best. However, if the horses had come in unfortunately in the wrong order, and he had drunk himself stupid to contain his gloom and then subsequently run out of funds, he would 'throw himself' on my dad's good nature in order to obtain his groceries and then have to owe us the money.

He would usually turn up the following week with the cash and pay us, and for some strange reason, my dad liked him.

One day I asked my dad about Mr Bates, and the money.

My dad laughed "I once met his wife" he said, shaking his head "that bloke needs all the help he can get. That woman would frighten a horse"

"Oh, right" I said "that bad eh?"

"If I was him, I'd emigrate" he continued "it's no wonder he drinks, the best thing he could do is go to the pub and never come back"

Then he looked directly at me "and I'll tell you something else son, and listen to me because this is important. In life there is no quicker and easier way of losing money than gambling. It makes rich men poor and poor men desperate."

I nodded as he continued.

"And there's one thing that all gamblers have in common?"

"What's that" I asked.

"They only tell you when they've won"

It was good advice, and to this day I think I have only ever been into a bookmakers twice, although I have spent many a boring night in Casinos with friends, watching them and everyone else lose their hard earned cash.

Anyway, it was Christmas Day and Mr Bates has just arrived.

"Well hello there Mr Bates" said my dad jovially "and a 'Merry Christmas' to you. I didn't expect to see you this morning"

Mr Bates just stood there, and he didn't look in the Christmas mood at all, in fact he looked particularly dire.

Red in the face and breathing whiskey fumes, he was actually sweating even though there was a good frost on the ground outside.

"I'm in trouble Tommy" he said immediately.

My dad just stood there, holding a large tray of sausages, and he frowned.

"What's up?" he asked.

Mr Bates gave a deep breath, and then looked directly at my dad "I haven't got a Turkey" he said.

"What" said my dad, it wasn't a question, it was more of a surprised answer.

"I've not got a Turkey and I'm in lumber, it's the wife you see..." and his words trailed away.

"Oh bloody hell" said my dad.

Then I remembered his description of Mr Bates's wife, and yes, things could indeed be grim.

"I can't believe what's happened" said Mr Bates hurriedly "You see, I went out yesterday with strict instructions from 'the wife' to pick up a Turkey. I was going to call in at Bolton Market on my way home from town and get one from there. I do the same thing every year. Anyway, while I was out I called into at couple of pubs and then I met up with some of my friends and we carried on drinking, and then we headed for the bookies. One of the lads is 'connected', he knows somebody who knows somebody who works at one of racing stables. Well, one of the lads gave me the nod on a couple of 'horses' that were on form for winning, sort of a 'sure thing'. So 'top and tail' of things, they both came in, along with some other horses that I'd backed and I was on a roll, race after race, I just couldn't lose. And then my last horse scraped in at third and I knew my luck was turning, so I pulled my winnings and left. I went back to the pub and celebrated with the lads, I was there till late, then at eleven o'clock when they'd called 'last orders' and finished serving, me and a friend of mine went over to his cousin's pub and we carried on celebrating".

As he told the tale, Mr Bates started to breathe heavily and he took out his handkerchief and started to wipe the sweat off his now, very red face.

I looked at him and wondered if he was going to have some sort of seizure.

"Are you alright Mr Bates" asked my dad, he was obviously a bit worried too.

"I'm sorry Tommy" he said "I'm just a bit flustered, I only woke up an hour ago. The cleaner arrived at the pub this morning and 'she' woke me up. Me and my friend were collapsed on the floor. God only knows what time we were drinking to. The first thing I knew was when a wet mop hit me on the back of my head, and when I opened my eyes, this old woman was leaning over me.

She just said "Shift, I've got work to do" and then she continued to mop around me.

"I managed to get to my feet, god I felt rough. Then I looked down at my friend, and he was out for the count, you could have hit him all day with the mop, she probably did. Anyway, I got up and staggered to the door, and the cleaner just stood there and watched me go. She was shaking her head and cursing us under her breath, and I knew it was time for me to leave.

Then suddenly, I realized where I was, and that I'd not been home, and I groaned out loud because along with my hangover I knew I was in trouble .

And as I was walking out of the door, the cleaner called out "Bye Bye you drunken sod"...the old witch.

"Yeah, see you" I said groggily as I shuffled through the door.

Then suddenly, she shouted "...and Merry Christmas"

And I stopped dead, I had to pause and think for a moment, and then it suddenly hit me, and I went sick. It was Christmas day and I hadn't been home "Oh bloody hell!" and I leant on the door and tried to collect my thoughts and tried to remember what had happened. I knew that that I'd been in town, and I remembered being in the pub and meeting some friends, then we went to the bookies, and I'd won...won a lot. So I went back to the pub and celebrated, and celebrated a lot. But in my mind, there was something missing. Why...why had I gone to town?

And then I suddenly remembered 'Oh god no, the Turkey...the bloody Turkey. I should have bought one from the market and I'd completely forgotten about it. What was I going to do? And I stood there thinking 'It's Christmas day for Christ's sake and all the shops are shut, no where's open, and I'm a dead man. I can't go home".

Mr Bates suddenly focused and looked at my dad.

"And then it struck me Tommy, if I got myself up here quick, I could get a Turkey off you, problem sorted. Thank god you're here."

He began to breathe a bit easier and he wiped his flushed face again and actually began to smile.

"You'll have saved my bacon" he said, and he chuckled "and I'll tell you what, I'll have some bacon as well while I'm here, and some sausages" and he stood there smiling in semi-drunken innocence.

My dad just looked at him, almost embarrassed, and then he said "Mr Bates, I'm sorry but I haven't got a turkey, I haven't got any turkeys. We've got none left, we've sold them all. It's been a really busy Christmas".

Mr Bates visibly staggered. For a moment his mouth open and closed, but no sound emerged.

And then finally he stammered "What...what do you mean?"

My dad shook his head and repeated himself.

"We've nothing left Mr Bates, every Turkey we had has been sold, and we've sold the lot"

Mr Bates suddenly panicked " Oh for god's sake no, I can't go home without one, have you not got one knocking about that you could just kill?"

He was desperate now, and my dad gave me a sort of wide eyed 'look'.

My dad tried to soften the blow.

"Look" he said, and he pointed to the back of the fridge "I've got some really large chickens left, they're almost the size of a small turkey. Why don't you take a couple of those, they'll do"

"You don't understand Tommy" said Mr Bates, and now he was becoming a bit agitated, "You see, it's my wife, only a Turkey will do. We've got relations coming round for Christmas dinner, it's family and she's very fussy, she has to do things 'just right' or she can be awkward, very awkward. I don't know what to do. I've not even been home".

That was when my dad tried to help "Why don't you make up some story, you could tell her they'd sold out, or you could say you'd ordered one and they'd made a mistake and sold it to somebody else".

Then he came out with a classic "Tell her that you've been robbed, and somebody stole it off you"

My God, even I thought that one was rubbish.

But Mr Bates was no longer listening to my dad, he wasn't even looking at him, he was just staring over my dad's shoulder, gazing at something. He seemed to be slightly mesmerised and I thought we'd sort of lost him for a moment. My dad noticed this too, and he realized that he was talking to himself. So he stopped talking, and we all just stood there for a moment in silence. Suddenly, Mr Bates broke out of his semi hypnotic state and he slowly lifted his hand and pointed his finger over my dad's shoulder.

"What's that Tommy?" he said, and his eyes widened, bloodshot as they were.

My dad looked at him curiously, and he turned around to see what Mr Bates was pointing at.

"What?" said my dad.

"That" said Mr Bates.

And Mr Bates stretched his arm over my dad's shoulder and pointed "That...that's a Turkey isn't it?"

And there, on the shelf behind my dad, was indeed a turkey. It was a 20 pound Norfolk bred, corn fed, dimple breasted beauty. It was absolute perfection, and was ready to be stuffed and then cooked and be basted golden and presented to the table on Christmas Day.

My dad looked around to see what Mr Bates was pointing at.

"Oh that" he said.

"Yes that. I'll buy that" said Mr Bates hurriedly, and he looked back at the turkey as though it was a long lost child.

"Oh" said my dad, slightly embarrassed "Oh that one, oh I'm sorry Mr Bates but that's ours, It's 'our' Christmas turkey, it's for the family".

Mr Bates visibly twitched.

He swallowed, and then he swallowed again as he took a deep breath, and then he took hold of his tie and jerked his head slightly, he was going to say something, and it was as if some monumental decision was about to be made.

"Tommy" he said, and he looked my dad straight in the eye "I'll give you fifty quid for that turkey".

Now, just let me tell you what fifty pounds meant in those days. I have already earlier told you that fifty pounds would pay for a fortnight's holiday in Spain. Well besides that, just two weeks previously, my dad had purchased a shiny black Rover saloon car, I don't know how old it was, but it was in good condition and I knew that he had paid £50 for it off a local car dealer. More of that later, but yes, fifty quid back then would buy you a car.

So back to Mr Bates, and the fifty quid turkey.

My dad just stared at Mr Bates, and his mouth fell open. He continued to stare at Mr Bates and I saw the look on his face. Yes...'Fifty'...Fifty pounds' for a bloody turkey.

My god...

It is a fact of life, and it's simple but it's true. Every man has his price, and I mean every man.

My dad turned around, reached up, and picked up our prized turkey.

Then he turned back to Mr Bates and said "Here...it's yours, give us the money"

And with that, he handed our family's Christmas dinner over to Mr Bates.

We watched as Mr Bates sauntered out of the farmyard with our Christmas turkey under his arm. A happier, if not wiser man.

My dad stood there with the fifty wonderful pounds in his hand, and then he looked at me.

"Come in here" he said firmly, and he walked back into the dairy.

I followed him in.

He stopped, turned and stood there in front of me, then he spoke and I just listened.

"I've just got us fifty quid for that turkey" he said "fifty bloody quid...for a bloody turkey".

He was quite astounded, and so I just replied "Yes dad".

"Now listen" he continued "I'm now going to have go into the house, and I'm going to have to tell your mother some pile of crap about how we've made some great 'cock up' and we've mistakenly sold our turkey to Christ knows who. And I'm going to get loads of ear ache and grief, but I don't bloody care. We've just made fifty quid...fifty 'bloody' quid, so I need you to back me up and keep your mouth shut. Okay?"

"Yes dad" I said.

And even as I followed him into the house, I knew he was right and I inwardly smiled. He'd done the right thing, of course he had. Even I knew the value of fifty pounds.

And at that moment, like many other times and many other moments in my life, I admired him for his common sense values. I also admired his bravery and tenacity in facing my mother with the 'bad news'.

My mother played holy, holy hell. In fact she went absolutely ballistic. We were all 'useless idiots' of course, and 'she didn't know why she bothered'.

Well obviously.

My dad shrugged, apologized, remonstrated and finally capitulated. What a performance, it was worthy of the stage. And when she slammed out of the kitchen, cussing him repeatedly, he simply looked at me, winked and grinned from ear to ear, and then we both fell about laughing. It was a memorable moment for me...me and my dad.

We eventually had Christmas dinner, we had two large cooked chickens and my mother lambasted us both relentlessly for our stupidity.

After Christmas dinner, my dad sat down in his favourite chair, the dog at his side, a large glass of whisky in his hand and a smile on his face. Yes, it really had been a good Christmas.

The next day of course was Boxing Day, and it was a family tradition that we all went to my grandparent's house for our tea. They were my mother's parents and they lived in lovely stone cottage in Harwood, a village situated on the outskirts of Bolton. We always used go over there in the afternoon, after we'd seen to the farm and fed and watered the stock.

And we were as usual, late, generally due to my dad 'overdoing' it a bit on Christmas day with the whiskey. And because of that, things were not running smoothly and our efficiency levels were more than slightly jaded.

I've noticed in life, that anything you try to do when you have a hangover is three times harder and takes four times longer. It's just one of those a facts.

And so, it was Boxing Day and my mother was getting agitated. We were an hour behind schedule and so we, me and my dad, were ordered into the house to get washed and changed.

My mother was ranting, and we were in trouble. My sister, always the quiet one of the family, just sat there as usual reading a book, oblivious to everything and waiting for us all to sort ourselves out.

Nothing new there then.

Finally we came downstairs and my dad went outside to get the car, which had been parked in our hay barn. By then my parents weren't speaking. My dad was sulking silently and my mother had taken the 'huff'.

My sister and I of course had seen it all before, so we just kept silent and tried to stay neutral.

My dad backed the car out of the Hay barn a little too fast, and sat there revving the engine noisily as we all paraded out and loaded up the car with food and Christmas presents. Mother wasn't impressed by his lack of assistance, and I hurriedly got into the front seat of the car as my mother and sister sat in the rear, and off we went.

This trip was actually a big first for us. For as long as I could remember we had always had to go to my grandparent's house in my dad's old van. The four of us would be crushed up in the front cab and my mother would moan all the way there. In fact, we'd never actually owned a car before, so things were definitely on the up.

The car, a black Rover saloon, was a big old thing. I don't for the life of me know how old it was, but that didn't matter as much back then, when just owning a car was thought to be something. I think it must have been made sometime in the late forties or early fifties because it had smooth round mudguards with headlights the size of dustbin lids, and it had huge chrome bumpers front and back that could have knocked cattle out of the way. It reminded me of a 1920's American gangster's car, and when you sat inside, it had the delicious smell of leather and oil.

So off we went to my grandparent's house. With my dad driving, we turned left out of the farm and onto the main road.

We travelled the first mile in silence, and in the end it was my mother who was the first to speak.

"Well" she said, in her 'poshest' voice "well, this is very nice".

Nobody spoke, so she continued. "At last we can go out as a family in our 'new' car. Not a lot of people have a car, but at last we do and not just any old car either. 'We' have a Rover"

My dad sighed.

"What do you mean Mum?" asked my sister, quite innocently.

"Ah well" said my mother, and she gave a knowing smile "You see, there are cars and there are cars...and different people drive different cars. Very rich people drive Rolls Royce's, they're very big cars and are very expensive. Next along are the people who drive Jaguars, and they are usually very wealthy too. Then, there's 'the Rover'. Rovers are driven by people who are doing quite well for themselves, people who are on the way up".

My dad turned to me and gave me 'the look'.

I know we'd just sold a turkey for fifty quid, but we also had to muck out pigs morning, noon and night, and that definitely wasn't my idea of 'on the up'.

My dad looked back through the car's rear view mirror, and as usual, he was completely mystified by my mother.

"Bloody hell, it's only a car" he mistakenly responded.

She shot him a stony glance and replied tersely "No Tommy, it's not just a car, it's a statement. It's about 'what' the car means and it says something about 'us'. We now 'own' a Rover".

"Do you know how old this car his?" he continued.

And that was why the rows carried on. Neither of them would just let things go.

"I don't care how old it is" she snapped "it's a Rover, and people take notice of the people who drive Rovers. It means that 'socially', you've arrived".

My dad muttered something under his breath, something about 'talking crap'.

And as we drove on down the road, Mr and Mrs Parkinson, an elderly couple who lived just lower down from our farm, were walking up the road towards us. As we passed them, Mr Parkinson pointed at our car and his wife too looked up in our direction. My mother quickly leant over my sister and waved to them.

"See" she said triumphantly "the Parkinson's noticed our car, I told you didn't I, people do notice a Rover".

My dad sighed and sank in his seat. He'd been verbally beaten again.

But my mother just wouldn't let it go, and whenever we went past anyone, they all seemed to look at the car, and as they did, she would mention it with a haughty "there you go" and she would give herself a satisfied and knowing smile.

Now I know it was Boxing Day, and I know that there weren't a lot of folk about, but I began to watch the people that we did pass as we drove on. And well, people 'were' taking notice of our new car. We went through a fairly empty Bolton town centre, but anyone who saw us did seem to give us a second look. I sat back and considered that my mother could actually be right, and that somehow my dad had bought a posh car without knowing it. I also knew my dad, and the class and status thing went right over his head. He measured all social occasions on whether or not he would have to wear a tie, and that was about it.

We went through the town and rolled onwards onto the main road to my grandparent's house at Harwood. My dad became grumpier and more silent as my mother continued her dialogue on the benefits of 'Rover ownership'.

And as we travelled ever onwards, the few people that we did pass still gave us a second look and stared. I was beginning to feel a little haughty myself by now, could it be that at last, we were now a bit posh?

My grandparents lived in a row of stone cottage known as 'Ruins Lane' which was a long narrow lane off the main road that opened up to a row of several small cottages. It was, and still is a lovely spot. My dad clicked on the indicator and turned right into the lane, then drove slowly down towards the cottages. We finally arrived, to find both of my grandparents standing at their front door waiting to welcome us. As we rolled up, my grandfather pointed at the car and my grandmother simply stared back at us.

My mother beamed and said "Look at my dad's face, he's not seen our new car before".

And as the car stopped and we began to get out, I noticed that my grandfather was still pointing at the car, rather strangely I thought.

My dad frowned at him and wound down the window "What's up?" he said.

My grandfather, who was still pointing and looking rather quizzical, called back.

"It's your car Tommy. You've got a big bale of hay stuck to the front bumper!"

My dad got out and walked around to the front of the car, and there snared on the huge front bumper was a great big bale of hay. The front of the car looked like something that the cows would eat from. My dad stood there grinning as my mother arrived on the scene, and then he started to laugh.

"A bloody Rover" he said to her between the hysterics, and then he leant on the mudguard.

"Oh yes" he mimicked "We've socially arrived. Yes we've arrived alright, with a bleedin' bale of hay stuck on the front, no wonder people were looking at us all the way here".

I saw the joke, and so did my grandfather, and we to fell in with the laughter. The car looked ridiculous. It looked like something off the circus.

My mother was fuming and she gave my dad a look that made me glad we didn't own a gun.

Red faced and irate "Typical" she said angrily "Just typical, we can't do anything right in this family, I don't know why I bother" and she stormed off into the house.

We stood outside for a while and let her calm down, and also until my dad could control his laughter. Then we went in to eat and enjoy ourselves, and without doubt, definitely not mention the car, even though it was a Rover.

We used to have a market stall in Heywood, which is a small town just outside Rochdale on the outskirts of Manchester. This was a very busy stall, in fact it was my dad's busiest, and at that time it was the largest stall on old Heywood market, in the days before the supermarkets had arrived. He employed about fifteen women on the stall and we sold everything from chickens to cheese.

My dad's motto was 'If it was cheap...he could sell it'.

He became an outlet for various firms, and they would ring him up if they'd made too many pies or overproduced or overbought. Eggs, bacon, chickens, it didn't matter, if it was cheap enough my dad would buy it and sell it on at a good price. The stall had a good reputation.

We did, as others had famously done, 'piled it high and sold it cheap', and it worked.

I remember on one occasion, it was a very early Friday morning and the owner of a local meat company arrived at the market in his large refrigerated truck. He had his driver park up the truck, while he came to our stall to speak to my dad.

He introduced himself "Mr Bell, my names Harrison....Tom Harrison" he said. He was a tall, silver haired man in his early fifties, and they shook hands.

"I've been told to come and see you Mr Bell. We were wondering if you could help us out?" he said rather anxiously.

"What's your problem?" asked my dad.

"Well, it's like this, we've got a load of chilled imported sirloin steak in the truck, it's from Argentina. We bought it in good faith, but when it arrived yesterday and we checked it, it's nearly out of date. The actual 'sell by date' on the cases is this weekend".

Mr Harrison took a deep breath. He seemed to be a straight talking sort of man.

"It's like this Mr Bell, after this weekend we are obliged to hand it over to the dog meat people. In effect, it's worthless"

"What's your deal?" asked my dad. In business, he was a straight talker too.

"Sell whatever you can for us Mr Bell, 'at any price' and split the money with us, just give us 'some' sort of return".

There was a short silence, and then Mr Harrison looked directly at my dad.

"I'll be honest with you" he said "I'm in trouble with this one, the banks are chasing me at the moment and things are a bit tight. If I lose my money on this, it'll probably send me under".

He just stood there, he'd said it all and my dad admired him for it.

"How much meat have you got?" my dad asked.

Mr Harrison rubbed the side of his head, and it was a sign of anxiety.

"The trucks full...full to the top" he said "we've got about forty big cases of sirloins stacked in there".

He rubbed his head again "Is there any chance you could help us out, could you take some and try and sell it for us, just two or three cases, or anything at all?"

My dad looked at him and thought about it for a moment.

"Leave your truck" he said.

"What?" said Mr Harrison, he was almost dumbfounded.

"Leave your truck, give us the keys, and come back on Saturday night. We'll have a go, but it's got to be sale or return. Whatever we don't sell, you take back".

And that was that.

Mr Harrison gulped. He'd just been given a life line.

He called over to his driver for the keys and we walked out to his truck. Mr Harrison unlocked the large back doors of the refrigerated vehicle to reveal the cases of sirloins.

They were big, big cases, and I remember thinking 'Oh strewth', what the hell have we got ourselves into'. These were huge cases of meat, stacked high up to the roof of the truck. There was enough to feed an army, in fact a lot of armies. I looked across at my dad who was summing up the proportions of the job in hand, and strangely, he didn't seem fazed at all.

"Right" he said to Mr Harrison "Let us get on with it, come back tomorrow night and we'll see how we've gone on".

Mr Harrison was only half listening, he just stood there looking up at the mountain of meat and he started to rub the side of his head again. He was a man with problems.

We closed the doors of the truck and my dad took the keys.

"Away you go" said my dad "Come and see us tomorrow". He'd given them their instructions and Mr Harrison and his driver just glanced at one another, Mr Harrison was in some sort of daze. He simply shrugged and they walked away, to god only knows where.

As soon as they'd departed the scene my dad quickly re-opened the back of the truck.

"Climb in and break open one of those cases. Pull out a couple of sirloins and bring them into the cookhouse" he said.

The 'cookhouse' was a building at the back of our stall. It had a large walk-in fridge and a preparation area with a couple of bacon slicers and some scales.

I struggled, but I finally managed to open one of the cases and drag out a couple of the chilled sirloins of beef. They were thick strips of meat that seemed to be about two to three feet long, and as I looked into the back of that truck, I wondered if there were hundreds of them or thousands. Anyway I took the sirloins to my dad, back in the cookhouse. He put one of them on a wooden chopping block, picked up a large knife and cut it in half. Then he picked up one of the halves and put it onto the bacon slicer.

"Let's see what a decent steak comes out at" he said. He was talking to himself really.

He cut a few different widths of steak until he found the right thickness, then he cut half a dozen at that width. He then took the steaks to the scales and weighed each one as he wrote down some figures on a paper bag. It was a strange thing, but he seemed to do all of his calculations by scribbling on paper bags. It was an old habit, but tried and tested.

I just stood there and watched, this was all mystical stuff to me but let's call it 'part of my education'.

He turned to me and smiled "50p".

"What is?" I said, like an idiot.

"Fifty pence, that's what we can sell 'em at".

Now this was the 'seventies', and I know that things were cheaper in those days, but believe me, a fifty pence sirloin steak was a good deal, even back then.

"Right" he said, decision made "This is going to be your job for the day. I want you to cut steaks up at that thickness" and he pointed to the dial on the slicer "at that thickness, all day and nothing else. I'll put some large stainless steel trays out and put them right in the middle of the stall. You cut and stack up the steaks, and keep those trays filled."

And so that's what we did.

Markets, what wonderful things they were. If you had something to sell you could shout about it, you could tell everybody, and that was the name of game.

'Punting' as it was called, was about calling out to the passing public and telling everyone about the price or quality of your goods, and if you had a winner you could make a killing on the day.

So we started, and my dad immediately seized the day by punting the 'cheap' steaks.

'A sirloin steak for 50p ' and it worked and they sold, and we had fifteen staff behind that market stall, all serving away. And me in the cookhouse cutting up steaks like a man possessed.

Word got out in the town about the 'cheap meat' on the market at a 'giveaway' price and customers from all over started to arrive to buy the sirloin steaks. Six steaks, ten steaks, women were buying steaks for themselves, their mothers and their relatives. We were on a roll 'as they say' and my dad wasn't daft, he knew that while people were at the stall buying steaks, they also bought bacon, cheese and eggs and a bit of everything else that we sold. The stall was very, very busy and the atmosphere was brilliant, all very noisy and bustling.

My dad was in his element, 'punting' away, laughing with the customers whilst urging the staff on to get the never ending queue served as quickly as possible. What a performance.

One old lady, a regular and a real character, was standing in the long line of customers.

"Mr Bell" she shouted.

"Yes love" called back my dad.

"Are those steaks tender?"

"Have you got your own teeth?" my dad shouted back.

"No" she replied.

"Well don't bother love" he called out.

The whole stall fell about laughing...

"Never mind, I'll have six" she shouted back "if I can't chew 'em, they'll do for the cat".

Everybody roared with laughter, it was hilarious. They were great times.

And that was the market. I suppose you don't get the same atmosphere in today's large Supermarkets. Everybody seems serious and stressed, and in a bad mood as they try to manoeuvre around somebody's trolley or get stuck in some frustratingly long queue, waiting to get served.

There's nothing 'Super' about them at all really.

Anyway, back to the market and we're selling sirloin steaks like hot cakes. I'm back and forth and in and out of that refrigerated truck like a wasp, cutting open the cases of meat to get ever more sirloins to cut up.

Two days, two days we were at it, and I never stopped cutting up meat. By then we were selling bagfuls of steaks to people who had cafes and pubs and even restaurants, it seems that news travelled fast.

Saturday night eventually arrived, and the market finally came to a close. Our hard working girls, our staff, had all gone home and I was loading the remains of the day into our two vans.

My dad was at the till counting the money and scribbling away on pieces of paper when Mr Harrison walked into the market. He came over to our stall, and as he passed me he just nodded and said "Hello" in a quiet sort of way, that was all and he looked weary.

He walked over to our now empty stall and approached my dad, who was busily counting money and putting it into various bags.

"Hello there Mr Bell" he said in a subdued voice.

My dad turned around quickly "Oh, hello Mr Harrison. Come round...come round" he said and he pointed to the entrance to the stall.

Mr Harrison walked around the long counter and entered the stall. He was slightly strained and anxious, and you could tell that he was under some degree of stress.

My dad turned to him "Here's the keys to your truck" he said, and he passed him the keys.

Mr Harrison just stood there, keys in hand and waiting.

"How've you gone on Mr Bell" he said "did you manage to get rid of any?"

"Oh yes" said my dad.

"How much" he asked awkwardly.

My dad smiled at him "All of it, we've sold all of it"

Mr Harrison gasped "What?"

"Yep, we've sold the lot, your trucks empty" and he reached down and pulled out a bag full of money. It was stuffed with ten and twenty pound notes and my dad put the bag down front of him and the notes spilled out onto the counter.

"There's your money" he said smiling.

Mr Harrison was speechless, almost. He looked down at the money and then back at my dad, and for a moment he couldn't say a word.

Then he spoke "Thank you...thank you very much Mr Bell, you've just got me out of a load of trouble" and he reached out and shook my dad's hand.

"My dad grinned at him "The jobs right, we've both made a few bob".

I stood there in disbelief, 'a few bob'. We'd made a bloody fortune.

As they both stood there, chatting away, I thought to myself 'Oh, and by the way, while you two are slapping each other's backs and pinning medals on each other, what about a bit of praise for the young lad whose cut up every single one of those damn steaks. Two days nonstop, a bloody truck full, and the lad with frozen fingers who's now cutting up sirloin steaks in his sleep'.

But nothing, not a word, not even a note of recognition

It's great being invisible.

Mr Harrison bid my dad goodnight and thanked him once more, and then he left the stall.

As he left the market, he walked past me.

"See you 'cock' he said.

And briefly, I considered where I'd like to stick a frozen sirloin.

So, the day was done, and my dad turned to me casually and smiled.

"Did you cut up some steaks for home? he said to me.

"Err, no" I replied.

He frowned, and suddenly he wasn't smiling anymore.

"You what?" he said, now in a slightly louder voice.

"No...Err, I didn't think too" I said, again.

He looked at me, and suddenly he started to shake his head in disbelief.

"For Christ's sake lad" and then he started moaning at me "I don't believe it. We've got ten ton of bloody steak, we feed every bugger in town, everybody's up to their neck in best sirloin, and you, you've not got the bloody brains to cut some up to take home for 'us' to eat. You dim pillock".

And with that he walked out of the market, got into his van, and drove off. I just stood there on my own, thinking to myself 'When I get home I'm going to 'grass him up' and tell my mother how he once sold our Christmas turkey to Mr Bates for fifty quid'.

Talking of which.

Christmas came around again, as it does, and once again we stood the markets and handled the festive rush. It was as usual very busy, and on this particular year, it was extremely busy.

It was Christmas Eve on Heywood market and we'd done very good business and had basically sold most of everything. We had some 'bits and bats' left and there were still a few customers coming to the stall, but my dad had treated the staff, he'd paid the girls who worked for us and let them get off home early so that they could start their own Christmas celebrations. We were left serving and joking with the tea time customers who were either late or looking for a bargain.

In between cleaning up and serving the odd customer, I nudged my dad and pointed to the lone turkey that lay in the middle of the stall.

"That's the last turkey" I said, nodding at it. It was the last one ,and for some reason it was irritating me.

"Yes I know" he replied.

"Do you think we'll sell it?"

"Maybe" he said.

And then he suddenly gave me one of his daft grins.

'Here we go' I thought, 'what now'?

"I'll tell you what lad" he said with a big smile "the first one of us to sell that turkey can go home, and whichever one of us is left has to clean up and scrub down the stall, and then load up everything and lock up".

He gave me another cheesy grin. God he was infuriating at times, he was trying to wind me up. He was succeeding.

"You're on" I said, without actually giving it much thought.

He smiled and chuckled, and I read his mind, he was thinking 'Got you, sucker'.

I was about to be conned again, oh bugger.

And for the next half hour I tried my hardest to sell that turkey, but no one was interested and

I grew a bit disheartened. I even considered buying it myself. Maybe I could give it to someone for a Christmas present. 'Damn' and my dad just kept on with his silly smile.

I was only a young man at the time and all I wanted to do was get myself home, get washed and changed and charge off to the pub with my mates. 'Hey', it was Christmas.

And my dad knew it.

"Not sold it yet lad?" he kept saying, and he would laugh out loud.

God he could wind me up, he could be the most irritating man in the world.

The market began to quieten down as the day began to come to a close.

Then he said to me "Put the kettle on, we'll have a brew" and so I went into the cookhouse at the back of the stall. As the filled kettle was beginning to boil and the tea bags were put into mugs, I turned to see somebody walk past the door. I looked, and then I looked again.

The Right Honourable Mrs R. Fox-Braddock Q.C, the Lady Mayor of Heywood, had just entered the market.

For a brief moment, I almost stood to attention.

Mrs R. Fox-Braddock was the wife of Captain John Fox-Braddock, who was late of the Queens Royal Navy, very late. She was The Lady Mayor of the town and she did on occasion, give us a visit.

Usually, it was her good husband, Captain John (decorated / 2nd world war) who called at the stall for their groceries. My dad would always usher Captain Fox-Braddock to the side door and serve him personally. It was a strange thing, but when dealing with Captain Fox-Braddock, my dad started to speak with a slightly different accent, he seemed to suddenly go a bit 'upper crust'.

Captain Fox-Braddock had served in the Royal Navy during the war and took part in the dropping off of the allied troops in Italy, and my dad had been one of those troops. They ended up in the push north, which culminated in, well at least for my dad, the battle for 'Monte Casino', a particularly hard and crushing piece of the Italian offensive.

Strangely, and due to their joint involvement in the Italian offensive, my father and Captain Fox-Braddock had forged some sort of strange alliance. Listening to them talk, it was almost as though they'd carried each other up the beach, fighting off the enemy bare handed, a bit like 'Rambo'.

Anyway, as they stood together at the end of the stall, reminiscing about the 'Italian Campaign', you could almost see the bullshit accumulating.

But my dad was also canny and businesslike in every manoeuvre, and he'd turned this strange allegiance into a 'just and the good cause'. In effect, profit.

Because of his association with Captain Fox-Braddock, we now supplied the Town Hall and the local Golf Club with quality cooked meats for the buffets and sandwiches at all their functions. Yes, very handy.

But I also have to add, for good reason. It was a well known fact locally that our cooked meats were simply the best you could buy. And my father, even though he dealt with absolutely everything at a price, he did have one idiosyncrasy. He would only buy his cooked meats from one company. They were called 'Suttons Meats' and were a small local family firm who religiously hand cooked their meats to unsurpassed perfection. A trip to their factory was a joy to behold and we forged a close working relationship with that small company. Even to this day we are still firm family friends.

My dad would simply say "When they've tried our cooked meats, they won't buy any other", and he was right.

When we closed for holidays and then re-opened a week later, the customers would return with a vengeance and the general comment was "Thank god you're back, my husband's been going mad about the bloody rubbish I've been putting on his butties".

Well, at least my dad was right on that one.

So...The Right Honourable Mrs R Fox-Braddock Q.C, Lady Mayor and the Captain's wife, and she'd just entered the market. She marched in and strode forcefully up to our stall to confront my father.

Apparently, she was on a mission.

"Mr Bell" she called out.

My dad spun around like a top.

And instantly, with his best smile and false accent in place, he replied to her.

"Mrs Fox-Braddock, a very Merry Christmas to you. And how are we?"

Mrs Fox-Braddock just stood there in front of him, a look of complete despair written all over her face. Something was desperately wrong.

For a moment, I wondered if the Captain had finally 'popped his clogs', but no, it turned out that he was still alive.

However, here we had the Lady Mayor and she was definitely distressed.

"Oh Mr Bell, oh dear" she said to my dad "Oh Mr Bell...we're having a crisis"

"Why, whatever's wrong Mrs Fox-Braddock?" asked my dad, accent still intact.

"Oh Mr Bell, we were wondering if you could possibly help us out. We're having a dreadful time, it's a disaster".

'My God' I thought, this was serious, and I actually stopped stirring the tea.

With widened eyes she looked up my dad, and then suddenly she blurted out everything that had happened.

"We have friends" she explained "in the Lake District, in Grasmere, they're farmers" and then she took a deep breath "They supply us with 'all our meat and poultry', it's all top quality.'Organic' and 'Free range" and she waved her hands about a bit.

She then continued "They hand rear their own turkeys".

Now I ask you. How else would you rear them?

"They're simply wonderful" she bleated on "We have one of their Turkeys every year, they're all fed organically".

I will tell you something, whether a Turkey is fed on breadcrumbs, corn, crumpets or caviar, it will still taste the same, and don't believe the hype.

As my dad used to say "Put enough butter in your gravy and anything will taste good" and it's true, just ask the French.

Anyway, back to our Lady Mayor.

"Well, whatever's wrong Mrs Fox-Braddock?" asked my dad, again.

"You see" she continued "My husband was supposed to drive up there to pick up 'the Bird', but we've had so many social commitments that it just hasn't been possible. So, we of course rang them and asked them to deliver it to us, and they were supposed to be coming down today with our Christmas turkey. But now they simply can't get to us, it's a disaster. We've just had a phone call from Grasmere, and it's been snowing up there, badly. Apparently it's over a foot deep in places and they can't get out. Even their four wheel drive vehicle is stuck".

It had been a cold Christmas true enough, but amazingly, the only place in England that was experiencing deep snow at that time seemed to be Grasmere, how strange.

And as I stood there listening, I smiled as I thought to myself 'No, Mrs Fox-Braddock, what it is...is that they can't be bothered. Your Farmer friends aren't going drive a 180 mile round trip in their Range Rover, just to deliver a bloody turkey'. Dear me no.

Anyway, that was that.

"Right" said my dad sympathetically, and he nodded in acknowledgment.

"Well Mrs Fox- Braddock, don't worry about a thing, there's a turkey here on the stall that you can have. No problem" and he looked over to me and gave a small grin of success.

'Yes' and 'Ha-ha'. He had me beaten.

Mrs Fox-Braddock looked down at the turkey and suddenly seemed a little disenchanted.

"And what weight is it Mr Bell?" She asked.

"It's a sixteen pounder, a beautiful bird" he crooned and he reached down and picked up the turkey to show it off. He was in full 'sales mode' now and so he continued "It's free range of course, and it'll cook just lovely".

She suddenly broke in on his sales patter "I don't think that's going to be big enough Mr Bell" she said, with a look of deep disappointment.

But that was nothing like the look of disappointment that suddenly appeared on my dad's face. His shoulders sagged slightly and the word "Oh" was all he could manage to say.

She'd sort of taken the wind out of his sails, and his sale.

"You see Mr Bell, we have family coming for Christmas, and of course there will be some people from the Town Hall coming as well. We normally have something around the 'twenty' to' twenty five' pound mark. Do you have anything bigger?" she enquired.

My dad just stood there for a moment, staring at her, and a plan formed in his head and an immediate decision was made.

"I'll just have a look Mrs Fox-Braddock, I think we do have one left in the fridge in the cookhouse" and with the turkey firmly grasped in his arm, he set off down the length of the stall towards me.

He burst into the cookhouse and threw the turkey onto the chopping block.

"What are you doing dad?" I asked hastily "We haven't got another Turkey, you know we haven't. That's the last one"

"I know" he said "but I'll sell her this bloody Turkey if it kills me" then he winked at me. "Just watch your old dad...and learn a few tricks of the trade".

And with that, he grabbed hold of the turkey and straightened it up, and then he cut a long length of jointing twine and started to truss the bird. He wrapped the twine around the wings and then over its legs and then pulled back really hard, it was like pulling long shoe laces, and then he knotted and tied it at the back. The effect of this was that it made the turkey's breast significantly stand up and out, a bit like a good bra. Then he took some wooden skewers and inserted then strategically into the turkeys haunches, and that made its legs look like they belonged to a weightlifter. This was really clever stuff.

He spun the turkey around and inspected it.

"There" he said "a bloody masterpiece".

And indeed it was, that turkey was now 'muscle bound' and it did undeniably look a lot bigger.

He looked over at me and he said "You'd better get the mop out son, because it's you that going to be doing the cleaning up tonight" and with that he laughed as he scooped up the 'prized' bird.

He went back onto the stall, and once again burst into his sales patter.

"Ah, Mrs Fox-Braddock" he called out as he walked up the counter towards her "I've found it...the 'other' turkey. It was in the back of the fridge".

And with a mock effort, he sort of 'heaved' the turkey onto the counter in front of her so as to emphasise the weight of this, the 'heavier' bird.

"There" he said "Look at that beauty" and he gazed down at the turkey as though it was a new born child.

"Oh" said Mrs Fox-Braddock as she examined it "And and what weight is this one Mr Bell?"

"Err, roughly, about twenty pounds. It's a little bit more expensive, but it is a bigger bird than the other one" he said defensively.

What a salesman.

"Hmm" she said as she continued to examine it. "We really are having a lot of people over this year for Christmas dinner" she said as she gazed down at the turkey, and then she thought about it for a moment.

"And what weight was that other one?" she asked.

"Err, about sixteen pounds" said my dad, a bit apprehensively.

She studied the turkey for a moment, and then she looked up at him and smiled.

"I'll tell you what Mr Bell...I'll take both of them" she declared.

And as I looked at the stunned expression and the disbelief on my dad's face, I turned back into the cookhouse and spat my tea all over the floor. I burst out laughing, I nearly fell over.

And in a state of absolute glee, I grabbed my jacket and the van keys and walked out of the cookhouse.

My Dad was still standing there, still staring at Mrs Fox-Braddock, lost for words.

And she just stood there, looking back at him, sort of quizzical and smiling.

I broke the moment and shouted "See you Dad...Merry Christmas" and then I waved to him as I left the market. Yes, Merry Christmas indeed.

So, stories about my father, and there are a few.

He was a wise old bird and was always ready to give good advice if need be. He had his faults as we all do, but he was big enough to put up his hand if things went wrong.

He would share his lifetime of experience if it would help you on your way, usually assisted with a few good old fashioned anecdotes.

When I left school, I straightaway went to work in the chemical industry. It was deemed to be a very good job with good prospects and it was with one of the largest national chemical companies. I went to work in their laboratories, working with dyestuffs. It was going to be fascinating and interesting work. Well, actually no.

The truth was, that I totally and equivocally hated the place from start to finish, and it was without doubt the worst job that I have ever had in my life, and the reason why?

It was the totally tedious and unending boredom that I had to endure, each and every day in that awful, awful place.

I was only a young man. Seventeen years old, and I suppose I was full of life and wanted to do 'something' with that life. And that place was crushing me. After six months of repetition and boredom, my brain was beginning to twitch somewhat. I used to have to commute to Manchester every day in my car, in those days I owned a little red mini that used to rattle a lot. This was in the days before the motorways, and back then everyone who was travelling to and from Manchester was queued bumper to bumper on the busy main roads, and the rush hour was a nightmare.

And the same drive, there and back from Manchester every day, was total 'frustration on wheel's for me. The continual hold ups at the same junctions and at the same traffic lights at the same time, morning after morning, only to be repeated again in the evening, was brain numbing.

And then when I got to work, I was stuck in the laboratory all day, bored absolutely senseless and enduring the thankless luxury of repetition and exquisite tedium.

One grey and dull Monday morning, I was on my way to work and I once again came to the large, busy roundabout that took me into Manchester, and I just couldn't face it. I drove all the way around the roundabout, and when it came to my exit, I just couldn't bring myself to turn off and I went around the roundabout again, and then again, as I approached my exit, I just kept going and went all the way round again. In the end I went around that roundabout another four times and then in sheer frustration, plus a bit of youthful craziness, I came off in the totally opposite direction and I then drove all the way up to the Lake District where I spent the day in a hired rowing boat, pottering about on Lake Windermere and looking up at the sky. Strange one that, but on reflection, I was at a strange age.

Anyway, I was obviously not happy, and along with this, the family were beginning to feel the brunt of my frustrations. In effect, I started to become a complete and utter pain in the backside.

I suddenly began going out all the time and not coming home until three or four in the morning, sometimes sober and sometimes drunk, and these were in the days when all the pubs closed at eleven. I was constantly arguing and falling out with the family, and there was a continual air of strained silence as I skulked around the house.

I of course, was oblivious to all this. I was an idiot.

Then one night or morning, well it was after midnight anyway. I arrived home and was just about to go upstairs to bed when my dad called to me from the front room. He was sitting in his chair in front of the fire and had been waiting for me to come home.

I sighed, and expected once more to get a 'rollicking' for something I'd done or not done, and I thought to myself 'Here we go again'.

As I walked into the front room he looked up at me and asked me to sit down, which I did, and then he turned to face me.

"Now then" he said "Can you please tell me, what on earth is wrong with you?"

And he spoke to me in fairly neutral tones.

This was a new approach, I thought

"What do you mean?" I replied, and I gave him my 'confused teenager' frown.

Yes, at the time I didn't realize that I was being such a complete Pratt.

"Tell me" he continued "Why, are you giving us all so much grief?"

"What do you mean 'giving you grief?" I was slightly confused here. How could I give them grief, I never spoke to them.

"Well son, you go around the house just grunting, and you don't speak to anyone other than utter the words 'I don't know' and 'so what'. You're never in, and we don't know where you are or at what time or what day you'll be coming home. You're giving your mother hell, and in turn, I'm getting it in the neck".

Oh dear me.

"So" he said again "What the hell's up with you?"

"I don't know" I said, a bit mystified. But in truth, I didn't.

"Is it work?"

"What do you mean?"

"Is it work. Do you like where you work?" he asked.

I looked at him for a moment, and I had to tell him.

"Dad, I hate my work. I hate the place, it's bloody awful, and I hate every day that I have to go in there"

And from there I started to tell him what it was like. The boredom, and the clockwatching, and more boredom, and the commuting and the repetition of it all, it all just came tumbling out.

I told him "I stand in the laboratory hour after hour, and I play games with the clock. There's a large wooden clock above the door in the lab and I watch it go round all day long, and in the end I won't look at it, and I tell myself not to look at the clock for at least an hour. And I wait, and when I think an hour's passed and I look up, I usually find that it's only been about fifteen minutes, and I just can't believe it. And it's like that every day...day in, day out. So the answer to your question is. 'No dad', I don't like work. But then again, who does?"

He just sat there for a moment and he looked at me, and then said "Well I do".

There was something in his expression. It was a combination of confusion and concern, and also slight amazement.

"I need to talk to you son" he said "I never knew you were so unhappy".

And I just shrugged.

"No, no" he continued "Listen to me, if that's what you're doing every day, watching and waiting of the clock going round, well you're just wasting your life away and that's no way to live. I never watch the clock son. I chase the clock every day, for me there's never enough hours in the day".

So we both sat there and talked. We talked until the early hours of the morning, and we spoke as 'man to man'. And for the first time, he told me a lot more about his life, and his views and his plans, and plans that could become my plans.

He advised me to pack my job in. I didn't have to work in a lab if I didn't want to, it was that simple and it was my choice. And after our conversation that night and the advice that he gave me, the handcuffs were off and I was out of prison.

Life changed...and I changed.

I've looked back many times on what was always a memorable night for me, and I realize that after that night, my relationship with my Dad, had in some way moved on.

We were still the same father and son, but in another way, we had also become very good friends.

CHAPTER SIX

So onwards and upwards, and it's a Friday morning.

And of course, I'm in my shop as the weekend finally approaches.

Consider this if you will. 'Violence' is something that's a bit alien to me. You don't really put violence and hairdressing together, unless I suppose you did something diabolical to somebody's hair, and I've never done that, well not yet anyway.

But I do remember the one day, when violence of a sort walked into my shop.

It was one Tuesday, and it was a strange sort of day from the word go really, perhaps one of the strangest.

Like most people in the hairdressing business, I'm closed on Mondays. I open my shop and start my working week on Tuesdays. Tuesday morning, nine o'clock sharp. I've always joked with my customers when they come in and tell me how much they hate Mondays and the start of the week.

"You never get the Monday morning blues on a Tuesday" I always tell them, probably with a bit too much relish and also, probably a bit too often. Well we barbers are by nature a bit repetitive, and yes I know it.

So it's Tuesday morning, I've just opened the shop and I'm on my first cup of coffee when suddenly I was absolutely shaken by a blast of noise. It was the sound of the air-brakes on a large truck, and I recognised the sound of it, but it still made me jump and I spilled my precious first coffee all over the floor as the shock of it rattled me, along with the shop windows. I looked out of the still vibrating window to see an enormous green truck that had pulled to a stop, directly opposite my shop. As the truck's cab door swung open, I reached for the mop and started to clean up the spilled coffee. My first brew of the day, slung all over the shop floor is not a good advertisement. Out of the truck climbed the driver, he was a small man, in his sixties, and he energetically jumped from his cab and headed straight towards me. I looked across at him and suddenly my heart sank. Why? Because the driver was sporting the infamous 'comb over' hairstyle...the hairstyle that's the curse of all hairdressers. He also had a huge shaggy beard, and to add to the agony, his hair was a bright ginger red. He looked like some sort of rusty red foliage that could walk. As I continued the mopping the floor, I watched him walk towards my shop and as I looked out of the window and at that hair, I thought to myself 'Oh Christ. Here we go'.

Suddenly, it felt like Monday.

It's a strange and curious thing, but men with the 'comb over' hairstyle, are actually very hard work. They somehow fail to realize that they're bald. Everybody else knows it of course, everybody else sees it, but they don't, and for some strange reason they think that by cleverly spreading and gluing a dozen hairs across the top of their head, they can successfully deny the process. And they sit in my barber's chair and say and ask the most ridiculous things,

'What can you do with it?' is always a good one.

I feel like replying "Paraffin and a match". But you just can't...or can you?

Then of course, there's the equally ridiculous 'just thin it out' or even 'Err, don't cut my fringe too short'.

Well I never...what bloody fringe?

Anyway, I looked on as the ginger driver continued to walk across the road towards me.

Now I must tell you, that I only cut hair by appointment. I don't do the 'queuing thing'.

All of my customers have an appointment, it suits them, and it suits me and there's no waiting. But that particular morning, I didn't have a single customer booked in and so I was 'open' for business.

The driver stopped for a moment and stood there as he looked at the 'Appointments Only' sign that I have on the front of my shop door, and then he decided to take a chance.

"Do I need an appointment?" he said almost apologetically, as he popped his head around the door "I was just passing".

I put my best smile on "No problem" I said "I've nobody in, so I'll get you done".

And with that he came in and sat in the chair and I put a gown around him.

He sat there, a little uneasy.

"You local?" I asked him.

"No" he replied "I'm down from Preston, that's where I live. I'm down here with a load that I've just delivered, to the Paper Mill just down the road."

I nodded, I knew the mill well.

So I picked up my scissors and comb "Okay" I said "What do you want doing?"

He looked at me through the mirror and sighed, and then he said with complete honesty.

"Look at my hair, I need help". It was a moment of truce.

"Right" I said, looking back at him "tell me about it"

And that's what a good barber does, it's called communication.

He sighed "Look at me for god's sake, look at my hair. I'm bloody sick of it".

"I can see your point" I said, agreement is always the best way to go.

As all my customers can confirm, I am as bald as a badger, and quite happy with it. My hair decided to fly south for the winter when I was at the ripe young age of twenty one. I remember recognising the problem back then, with the help of a small mirror and I was in shock for about a week, before I took the decision to cut my hair very short. And that was actually the last time that I ever worried about it. For forty years I've had very short hair and nobody has ever known me any other way.

Hey presto, problem solved.

Anyway, back to my customer. "This hair" he said "is making my life a bloody misery, I hate it".

"I can see your point" I repeated myself, I often do.

"You don't know what it's like, having hair like this" he continued.

"No, I don't" I said.

"Do you know that every morning when I leave the house I have to check which way the wind's blowing? I have to either walk into the wind with my head down on one side, or walk away from it with my head turned completely the other way. It's like being at sea, I feel like I'm sailing a bloody yacht.

I nodded with sympathy, and managed not to chuckle. You have to remain very straight faced and professional at all times

He carried on "And you can forget looking up. If you have to look up at anything, the first thing you've got to do is hold your hair down, and then you look up. I once forgot to do it and all my hair fell off the back of my head, bloody embarrassing that was".

"Right then" and I tried to sound positive "let's see what we can do"

"Before you start" he said ominously.

And I thought to myself 'here we go...trouble'.

He looked back at me through the mirror "It's like this you see, I play snooker. I play at my local club, I'm in the snooker team and well, I'm in there all the time with the lads and at weekend it's our social club. All the wives are involved too, and the thing is that everybody there knows me, and if I turn up with a shaved head everybody will laugh at me. They'll take the Mickey 'big time' and I don't think I could handle it".

Well I stood there and I inwardly applauded the man's honesty.

"I know they probably already laugh at my hair" he said "and I know it sounds soft"

"No...No" I interrupted him "I 'do' know exactly what you mean, and I do think that I can sort you out".

He stopped talking for a moment and looked at me, a bit surprised "Oh, right" he said.

So I started to talk to him, 'educate' is a word that comes to mind.

"Listen" I said to him "It's not just your hair that's your problem, it's your beard as well, you're all out of balance".

"What do you suggest?" he asked.

"I'll cut your hair shorter, but I want to cut your beard short too, a lot shorter, like long stubble.

"Right, okay do it" he said immediately, he'd made a decision.

I got the clippers out and started on his beard."

"Do you know what's sparked all this off?" he said, as I worked away.

"No" I replied.

"My wife" he said

"Ah, it usually is" I again replied.

"We've just been to Lanzarote for two weeks, have you ever been?"

"No" I said "It's somewhere I've never been too"

"Oh it's brilliant. We go all the time. We've actually been going there for the last ten years"

"It sounds great" I said.

"Oh it is, it's lovely. But unfortunately for me, it can get a bit windy".

"Yes?"

"Yes, there's always a bit of a breeze".

He thought for a moment, and then carried on. "We were there two weeks ago, and the day before we came home we went down to the beach, it was late morning. We went down there and got ourselves a couple of sun loungers and got settled. The wife read her book and I slept off the previous night's beer. After an hour or so I woke up and it was hot, very hot. So I decided to go and get us a couple of ice creams from the stand further down the beach. I got up and I started to walk down the beach, it's about fifty yards to the ice cream stand. As usual, I judged the wind direction and set off. Halfway along, I walked past a load of young 'dolly birds', there were about ten of them, all stunners and some were topless, they were all laughing and having a good time. So like any bloke, as I walked past them I pulled in my stomach and tried not to look like such an 'old git', it's stupid I know. Anyway, I finally got to the ice cream stand and there was quite a long queue. It was scorching hot and by the time I'd got served I was sweating badly. It was so very hot and I ordered two very large cornets, smothered in raspberry flavouring. I paid, and I started to walk back down the beach. I was trying to get a move on because the ice cream was already starting to melt, but just as I was passing the 'dolly birds' again, the bloody wind changed direction. Instead of coming right at me, it suddenly started blowing sideways and it blew my hair completely off my head. My hands were full of bloody ice creams so the only thing I could do was swing my head about and try to 'hook' it back down, but it wasn't working. The ice creams were melting in my hands and I was swinging my head about like a madman, and suddenly all I can hear is laughing. I looked across to see the gang of young girls, all screaming with laughter. I'm jumping up and down with my bloody hair wafting about and they all think it's hilarious and are laughing their socks off. I took one last shot at it, and as I swung my head again, both my ice creams flew off the end of the cornets.

The girls went into hysterics, and the rest of the beach began to join in.

I stormed off back to the wife and had a tantrum. Then we had a row, and I got a 'rollicking' for my troubles. So I had a sulk, walked off, and went back to the hotel bar for medication and sympathy.

I was laughing, so was he, now.

"What happened?" I said.

"Well later, when I'd calmed down and the wife had calmed down too, we were in our hotel room and getting ready to go out for a meal. I was going through my usual ritual of plastering my hair down but this time I was moaning about it, and then my wife came up with a solution.

"What was that?" I said.

"She just looked at me and said "For god's sake, why don't you do something about it then. When we get back home, go and get it cut off".

"And that was two weeks ago?"

"Yes" he said "it's taken me two weeks to work up the courage, and then this morning I was passing your place and there was nobody in, so I sort of seized the moment".

"Yes" I said "and that's your beard done. How do you like it?

He stopped talking for a moment and he looked in the mirror and then looked back at me.

"My god, I'm a different man" he said...and he smiled as he ran his hand down his now short and very smart beard.

I was on a winner.

"It looks fantastic" he said.

"Now I'll cut your hair, and that'll be a piece of cake"

"Right" he said, now he was a more confident chappie.

"I'll tell you something" I said "In fact, I'll even bet money on it"

"What's that?"

"Next time you go to your snooker club, nobody will even notice you're haircut, but everybody will notice that you've had your beard cut shorter"

He laughed "You could be right there"

As I started to cut his hair, I asked him about his job "I suppose you've seen a few changes" I said.

"Yes" he replied "I've seen more than a few" and he sighed "my jobs changed completely over this last few years"

"How long have you been driving?" I asked him

"Over forty years now, in fact I've only got another couple of years to go and I can retire, and I can't wait".

"Is it that bad?"

"Yes, my jobs changed a lot. You know something, when I first started driving, I was only young and I used to love it. I'd get up very early mornings and climb into my wagon and be off. Those were great days. Early mornings, and I'd be on my way down to London or the south coast, sometimes over through to Wales. On other days I'd be off up north, up to Newcastle, or best of all Scotland. I used to get a run all the way up to Inverness, I loved that trip. I'd get up at the crack of dawn and set off really early, a thermos flask and a pile of sandwiches and my radio and I'd be off, it was freedom, total freedom. In those days all my mates used to work in factories, in the mills or in engineering, day after day stuck in the same place, and every day just the same. But me, I felt as free as a bird, I had no boss breathing down my neck, and every day I was somewhere different".

He smiled to himself as he remembered "Hey, and in those days the motorways were empty, not like today. Back then we had empty motorways where you could put your foot down. There were no speeding cameras or radar, and there were no restrictions, the roads were different then, now there's nothing but traffic lights and roundabouts and those bloody awful speed humps that they've put everywhere, they drive me mad. It always makes me wonder how fire engines and the ambulances deal with them in an emergency".

I'd actually never thought of that, but he was right.

"Yes" I said, and I had to agree with him "There's not much fun in driving these days, there's too many cars".

He nodded "Yes the roads are all full, so are the motorways, it doesn't matter what time I set off these days, day or night, the roads are constantly full of traffic. If there's an accident on the motorways the traffic backs up for miles. At one time you could come off and get onto the 'A' or 'B' roads and bypass the problem, but these days you can't, all the roads are full. If there are any holdups, we just have to stay in the line of traffic and keep going as best we can. We're instructed by the office, and you just hope that the tachograph doesn't run out".

"The tachograph, is that the clock thing? I asked him.

"Yes, we all have a tachograph in your cab. It registers how far you've travelled, what speed, and how long you've been driving. We're only allowed to drive for so many hours and then that's it, you're not allowed drive over your allotted time. So if you get stuck and run out of time you have to stop and the office has to send out another driver to take over your load. They're never happy, but what can you do, everybody's in the same boat. What with the tachograph, and now the wagons are fitted with trackers so they can see exactly where we are, and the damn phones. Now, you are always in contact with the office, and well, it's just not the same."

He looked up at me "To tell you the truth I'm sick of it, I'd finish tomorrow if I could. The freedoms gone and now it's all about delivery times and returns, it's all pressure and stress, but well, another couple of years will see me gone and I'm out of it".

I was just about to say something to him when the shop door swung open, and a man walked into my shop, straight in and in a hurry.

And I didn't realize it at the time, but my day was suddenly about to change.

He was youngish, probably in his mid twenties. Very slim, thin even, and very, very pale. And he had something about him, something not just right.

"Can you cut my hair now, right now?" he said straight out, and I sensed an 'attitude'.

And that was it. There was no "Hello" or "Hi, I was wondering if." It wasn't a question, it was almost a demand.

I glimpsed back at him, and I wasn't impressed "I'll be half an hour yet" I said casually "if you're in a rush there's a couple of other barbers up the road were you can just walk straight in and get your haircut, I only do appointments."

I thought that would move him on, but he just stood there and looked at me, and looked for just a few seconds too long.

"I'll come back" he said, and he turned and walked out of the door.

The 'driver' looked at me through the mirror "He's looks a bit of a strange one".

"Yes" I said "I know" and I had to think about it for a moment, I wasn't happy about that one.

"Do you get many like him?"

"No, not like that, but we do get one or two strange characters around here" and as I spoke I wondered whether or not he would be coming back. Some did, some didn't.

Never mind, and I decided to brighten the day.

"Hey I've a good one for you" I said to the driver "Last Friday...Friday night, I had a good one. It was be about seven o' clock in the evening and I was doing my last customer. It was dark by then and suddenly the door swung open and in walked a little Irishman. He was only about five foot tall, probably in his seventies. He came through the door and stood there for a minute, just looking around the shop.

He was wearing a full length coat that nearly touched the floor and a brown floppy cap. He looked like something out of 'Snow White'. So I stopped cutting my customer's hair for a moment and I turned to him.

"Halloo thor" he said to me in his best Irish accent, and with a grin that was a gem.

"Hello there" I replied "and what can we do for you?" I asked him.

He looked at me as he smiled, and then said "I was just wondering. Do ye sell bread?"

I looked at him "Bread?"

"Aye...Bread. Does ye have any?"

I looked at him "But...but this is a barber's"

"I know" he said.

"Well...I don't sell bread. I cut hair" I tried to explain.

"Well that's fair enough" he said "I just thought I'd give it a try" and with that he turned and shuffled out of the shop.

I turned back to my customer and I just shrugged, then my customer grinned at me and laughed, and I shook my head and we both started to laugh so much, that I couldn't cut his hair for the next ten minutes.

The driver chuckled.

"It's like that all the time" I said to him "this road's full of characters".

By then I'd finished cutting his hair.

"What do you think?" I asked as I showed him the back of his haircut through the mirror.

"Now that's brilliant. Hey, the wife won't know me" he said.

"Hey, you're dog won't know you" I said back.

And he laughed at that. "Nice one."

So I got him brushed off and as he was getting ready to leave he picked up one of my appointment cards off the reception desk.

"I'll give you a ring and tell you how I go on at the snooker club".

And he actually did, and it all went well.

I stood in the doorway as he left and I wished him good luck, and just as he was going to cross back over the road, he suddenly looked sideway and stopped for a second, and that made me look too. Walking back towards my shop was the strange young man who'd been in earlier.

The driver turned back to me and gave me a serious look.

"And good luck with that one" he said, and with that he went back to his truck.

I went back into the shop and let the 'strange' young man arrive. I didn't want to look eager, even more than that, I didn't want in any way to look compliant. There's a balance to be found when dealing with this type, and it's not wise to let them get the upper hand.

He walked straight in through the door and without a single word, he took off his jacket and hung it on the coat hook. Then he turned around to face me, neither of us spoke and I wasn't going to, I just stood there. Finally he broke.

"Am I sitting here?" he said, and there it was again, a question that was almost a threat, and once again some sort of demand.

"Yes" I said, very casually "sit yourself down and I'll get you done".

I put the gown on him in silence and I glanced at him through the mirror. It was then that I smelt the alcohol, just a whiff of it but it was there, and it wasn't just beer, this was strong alcohol, rum or whiskey or something like that. And at that moment I gave him a second look. He was thin and pale, he had dark hair that was overgrown and his face was unevenly shaved. This was a man who hadn't been living easily.

"Right" I said to him "what are we doing?" I always ask, always.

He looked straight back at me "I want it cutting...properly".

I took a deep breath and thought 'here we go'.

"I'm fussy about my hair" he then said.

As I looked down at his bedraggled locks, I considered that this certainly wasn't the hair of a 'fussy' man. In actual fact, his hair was a mess.

"Okay" I said "tell me exactly what you want doing"

And so he did, he wanted a short and very sharp haircut.

That was okay, I can do that, of course I can.

I decided that I needed to get some conversation out of this guy. I had to cut his hair, so I might as well get him talking, but it wasn't going to be easy. We weren't going to be discussing holidays or what plans he had for the family that weekend, and looking at him, he wasn't going to tell me about some nice restaurant he'd been too either.

I don't cut hair in silence, it's not my style. I always talk to my customers, but this chap, well there wasn't a lot to say. He was also starting to occasionally 'twitch'. It was all a bit strange, and every so often he would sway to one side. I put it down to the booze, maybe. But then there was something else, I noticed that his forehead had started to sweat, and it certainly wasn't 'that' hot in my shop.

So I just asked him "Are you from around here?"

He looked up "No" he said.

"You from Bolton?" I asked again.

He looked again "No" he said, and that was it.

A long minute passed, and then slowly he relented "I'm from Preston" he said.

"Oh, right" I said to him "That's a coincidence. The last customer, the guy who just left, he was from Preston too"

"Was he...oh, right" he replied slowly.

I looked at him through the mirror, his eyes had widened and he was staring into space, and then suddenly he twitched again, and he said "He'll know me then. He'll know all about me".

And that was it, nothing more.

Very curious, and a very strange thing to say.

His forehead continued to sweat, and I began to wonder if this was something more than just booze.

Out of the blue, I asked him "Where did you have your last haircut?"

And that may have been a mistake, because he told me.

"In Prison" he said, and that was that.

"Oh, right" I said. I was a bit surprised, but I tried to play it sort of casual.

"What were you in for?" I asked, and that was another mistake.

He looked straight at me.

"Murder" he said.

And suddenly I was more than surprised, I was concerned.

Those words from him, were like throwing a switch.

I've known a few lads who've been inside, who've been into prison. Mostly it's been for fighting, some for drugs. I've known a few, and when they come out they're different people.

Prison is about repetition, the same routine, the same drudgery, day after day after day.

In the end they know little else. Each day is ruled totally by the clock, repetition combined with more repetition. And in the end, it's the little things that become the highlight of their day. Mealtimes, going for a walk, getting some ciggies or scoring some drugs. All the little highlights, the little treats.

It's similar to people who've been in hospital for any length of time. With them of course it's the meals. The different meals become the entertainment of the day. It's always 'What's for lunch' and 'what's for dinner', and that becomes their whole topic of conversation.

And so it is with prison. When they're finally released, prison life is all they know and all they can talk about. People, who've spent some period in prison, permanently watch the time. And with every passing hour they'll tell you exactly what they would be doing, in prison, at that moment. And usually, all they want to talk about is prison life and that's because they've nothing else 'to' talk about. They haven't seen or done anything else for weeks or months or years. It's almost like brainwashing.

There is 'one' other topic of conversation though, and that's 'the offence' and that of course is a subject that's close to their heart. More often than not its denial and excuses and it's usually somebody else's fault.

And now as I cut his hair, I was going to find out about this guy, because he wanted to tell me. Well sort of.

So I stared at him for a moment and said "Murder?"

"Yeah" he replied "I got out last week, I served twelve months"

"Twelve months...for murder?"

"Yeah" he replied, and he seemed very casual about it.

"Is that all?" I said. I was also a bit worried. I now had a convicted murderer in my shop.

"Yeah, well there were circumstances" he said, and then suddenly, he moved in the chair.

I looked at him, and his persona was changing right in front of me. The silent man was starting to become talkative, and now suddenly, he wanted to talk. He was still sweating and he couldn't quite keep his head or his shoulders still. There was that strange gleam in his eyes that told me one thing and everything, it was drugs. He was 'live'. He must have taken something, and it was beginning to work on him. Suddenly he was 'easy' in his own body and his brain had become very, very busy.

He continued talking "Yeah...yeah, well it was all an accident really. I didn't mean it. It just...just happened".

And then suddenly, he switched, mid conversation "Hey, I'm Darren by the way, who are you, what's your name?" He was now talking quite quickly.

I told him who I was.

"Is this your shop then?"

"Yes" I said.

"Do you work here on your own then?" he continued to talk.

"Yes" I said again, and immediately regretted it.

"Best way" he said "Working on your own, I do that" and he laughed quite loudly. It was very strange.

"How come you're in Bolton?" I asked him, and changing the subject.

"Oh, to see a mate of mine, I was inside with him. He got out two weeks before me and he gave me his address. He had some...err, stuff for me. Anyway I wanted to catch up with him, he's a mate".

I was very tempted to ask him 'What stuff', but I knew what it would be, 'White powder'.

I just said "Are you going back to Preston?"

"Yeah, in a couple of days, I'm staying at my mate's at the moment. I might stay the weekend though, or longer".

And I thought to myself 'or till the drugs, or the money runs out'.

So I asked him straight out "What was with 'the murder' then?" I had to ask, I was intrigued.

"Oh yeah, yeah" he said, and he moved in the chair again and straightened himself up. Now he was going to tell me, now he wanted to talk, and the drugs were making him eager.

"I killed my stepfather" he said.

I stopped cutting his hair, and I looked at him "Your stepfather?"

"Yeah, yeah, I killed him...he deserved it".

I was more than amazed, I just looked at him "Why...how, how did that happen?"

"Coz he was a complete and utter bastard. 'Frank', that was him, always been a bastard.

Yeah, 'Frank'...'Big Frankie' that's what he liked to be called 'Big Frankie'. Well he raped and murdered my girlfriend and I caught the bastard at it. He raped and murdered her, so I killed him."

"My god" I said, I was stunned. This was hardly an everyday occurrence, not even in my shop.

"It was a long time coming" he said, and then strangely, he grinned and somewhere there I saw a glint of satisfaction.

"Why, what happened?" I asked cautiously.

He leaned back in the chair, he was confident now, the drugs making him feel like a king, he was a man who had all the answers...

"I'll tell you something" he said. "My Mam, she married 'Big Frank' when I was only a kid. I was about ten...ten years old. My dad died when I was a baby, I never knew him, cancer got him. Well she married Frank. I suppose she needed somebody to help to support us, she'd already had my two older sisters by then and with three of us to look after she must have been desperate, she had no money. So she married Frank, bad move, he was a complete 'tosser' from the word go, and she had to work while he dossed about most of the time. He spent half of his life in the pub, and spent most of her money doing it. Every so often she would complain, and they would have a row and he would end up giving her a thump, and then he'd go back to the pub. She put up with this for ten years and then the bastard walked out on us. He stole what bit of money my mother had saved and then disappeared. We were penniless. From there on, my mother had to hold down two jobs just to keep us going. We were poor. We lived on hand-me-down clothes and hand me down everything. Those years were hard, very hard.

Nearly three years ago my mother died, old before her time and worn out. We had the funeral, and would you believe it, out of the blue the bastard turned up. I wanted to kill the fucker there and then, but to my utter amazement, he went to my sisters and begged for forgiveness. He told them some bullshit about always loving my mother and that he'd always kept his eye on the family from a distance, just in case, and then he turned on the waterworks and cried like a baby, then they started hugging and there were tears all round. They forgave him and he ended up with us all in the pub after the funeral. I can see the bastard now, 'Frankie', the centre of attention and drinking for free. He was back.

Christmas arrived, and so did Frankie. We always went to my eldest sister's house every year for Christmas day. Frankie had wormed his way in, and both my sisters wanted him to come for Christmas dinner. There was nothing I could say. They all wanted 'happy families'.

So Christmas day, and me and Nicola turned up. Nicola was my girlfriend, and we were living together back then. We arrived at my sister's, and when we got there Frankie had already got his feet well under the table. There were big hugs all round and Frankie made a point of shaking my hand. And then I saw him look at Nicola, and then he took a second look and I saw the glint in his eye. He looked her up and down and stared at her, and I'd seen that look before.

We had Christmas dinner and all the family really enjoyed themselves. Christ, there must have been about twelve of us jammed in around the table. Frankie managed to get himself sat next to Nicola and by the time we'd finished the Christmas pudding he'd got his arm around her waist. Oh yes, I saw him. I knew what he was like, the bastard.

After dinner more people turned up and we had quite a party. The house was pretty full and the drink flowed. Everybody was having a good time and Frankie was in his element. He was holding court in the kitchen, telling all his stories and drinking the free booze, and he still had his arm around Nicola's waist. At one point I got hold of her as she came back from the toilet and I mentioned Frankie and his 'wandering' arm. She told me not to be stupid, he was just being 'friendly', but she'd been drinking too. It was getting late and I remember standing in the dining room on my own. Frankie had been upstairs to the toilet and as he returned to the kitchen, he passed the dining room and saw me standing there alone.

He stopped for a moment, looked at me, and then walked in.

"Can I have a word, Darren?" he said.

I turned and shot him a glance.

He came over to me "Can we have a chat?"

I nearly spat at him.

"What do you want Frankie?" I asked him.

"Well" he said to me "we've never really had time to talk have we? Darren, I've always looked upon you as being my son. I know I'm not you're real dad, I know that, but I brought you up from being a little lad, you and the girls, and they were happy times. The girls have opened their hearts to me and want me back in their lives, they want us to be a family again, like the old days", and tears started to form in his eyes as he got a bit emotional. It was probably the booze.

He came forward and reached out to shake my hand, and possibly give me a hug.

"Can we be friends Darren?" he said.

It was all so very moving, the whole drama of it. 'Father and son'...'reunited again'. What utter bullshit.

Tears are easy when you're full of alcohol. It's easy to get emotional when you're full of booze.

I took all this in for a moment, and then I put my hand up to stop him.

"Frankie, you'd better stop right there" I said to him.

He did, and he looked at my raised hand, it was a sign for him to keep his distance. "What's wrong?" he said.

"What's wrong, I'll tell you what's wrong. You're 'wrong' Frankie".

He just stood there, looking at me.

"It's like this Frankie, you fucked off. You fucked off and left us, me...my mother and my sisters, all those years ago. Now they might be up for forgiving you, but no, not me. You see Frankie, you ran off with all the money, you left us penniless and my mother had to work her fingers to the bone to keep us all going. Not once did you send us any money, you never sent us anything at Christmas, we didn't even get a birthday card from you, ever.

"You don't understand" he started to say.

"Shut your fucking mouth Frankie. I'm not a little kid anymore, get it".

And that threat stopped him in his tracks.

I glared at him "The days are gone when you could do what you want with us. My mother worked herself into an early grave to get enough money to look after us, and no fucking thanks to you".

He just stood there, not so full of himself now.

But I didn't realize that the family were all listening as I shouted at him "She struggled all her life and died too young. So it's like this 'Frankie boy', if you're ever here when I call around I'll be civil, and I won't make a fuss. But don't for one inch think that you're ever getting back into my life, no bloody way. My mother would have been alive today but for you. You're nothing more than a pathetic lying thief...you're just a fucking user!"

And suddenly I stopped, because in the doorway behind me stood my sisters, and they were both in tears and I knew that it was me who'd upset them. I couldn't say anything, couldn't apologize, I suppose I'd already said too much. I turned and walked into the kitchen, only to be met by an awkward silence from the rest of the family. Nicola was standing there, looking at me, and she shook her head.

So, I'd spoiled Christmas.

There was an awkward silence, but eventually everyone started to talk again.

I went over to Nicola.

"Very clever" she said "Nice one, you've really upset you're sisters you idiot".

I looked at her "Oh thanks for the backup"

"Well, what do you expect, shouting you're head off like that"

There wasn't a lot I could say, I took hold of her arm but she shook me off. She'd been drinking of course, and it always got the better of her.

I said to her "Get your coat, I want to go" I'd just about had enough of it all.

But then she turned on me, she was mad "Oh bloody marvellous" she said "Merry Christmas"

We left, probably to the relief of all, and to a delighted Frank.

As we walked home I spoke to Nicola and tried to explain things to her, about my mother and everything else, but she was in a right mood and all she would say was that it was 'all in the past' and that I should forget it and 'let things go'.

But we'd both been drinking and we ended up having a huge row.

In the end she just said "I'm sick of you".

And with that, we walked home in silence. Some Christmas.

The next day I got up and decided to go and see my sister, well I had to, Nicola was still giving me the cold shoulder. We'd had another row about Frankie boy having his arm around her waist. Fact was, his hand was on her backside for most of the night, and 'oh yes', I'd seen it. She called me 'pathetic' and let me know in no uncertain terms that 'she' and everybody else thought that Frankie was a great bloke.

I could have hit her.

When I got to my sister's, I walked straight into the house as I always did, and as I did I shouted the usual "Hello there...anybody home". It was always a bit of a joke.

"We're in the kitchen" called out my sister.

I walked into the kitchen, and they were all having breakfast, and who was sat there in the middle of them all, feeding his face. Yes, it was Frankie.

I was surprised, more than that I was angry and I bit my lip, hard. And suddenly I realized that nobody expected me to turn up this morning. I was a bit of an embarrassment I suppose. And sitting there in all his glory was 'Mr bloody Popular'.

He'd made himself right at home, and he actually grinned as he spoke to me.

"And how are we this morning Darren. Got a bad head?"

I couldn't believe it, he actually thought that it was the 'booze' talking last night, not the real me. I looked back at him and then around the table and I saw everyone's expression, and I knew I was outgunned. Nobody wanted an argument, and nobody wanted any bad feelings.

I just stood there and said "Yeah, something like that. Sorry everybody".

It was an apology, and I'd had to give in. There was almost a sigh of relief from everyone.   Frank smiled, and then he said "You need some grub inside you", the cheeky bastard.

"Yes" chirped in my sister "Sit yourself down and I'll get you some breakfast" and everyone moved around and made some space for me as I sat down on a spare chair. And so breakfast carried on and everybody continued to talk around me and I just faded away in silence as I ate my food.

And that was it. From then on, whenever we went around to my sister's house, Frank seemed to be there, and of course everybody loved him to bits. 'What a great bloke'.

And he was always all over Nicola like a 'rash', he used to make a right fuss over her. He was always giving her a hug and he'd never leave her alone. I should have known.

Occasionally he would call round to our house, and always when I was out. I wasn't happy about that, but Nicola just couldn't see it and that would cause another bloody row".

I looked through the mirror at Darren, he was getting a bit intense, and as I cut his hair I noticed his eyes, wide and staring into nowhere. He was almost talking to himself now. I just let him continue.

"Yeah" he said "We were having lots of rows by then, the stupid bitch. She just wouldn't listen, wouldn't listen to anything I said, stupid cow".

He was mumbling now and I began to wonder about him, and I thought that it was a bit peculiar, him calling his murdered girlfriend 'a stupid cow'.

But he carried on "She just wouldn't listen to anything I said anymore. No respect...no fucking respect. You know what I mean?"

I just nodded.

Darren went rambling on, almost incoherently now. It was the drugs of course.

"Yeah, and then I come home one afternoon, and I walked right in on it. He'd turned up and he'd raped her, as good as tried too anyway. So what the fuck, I'd caught 'em both, I fucking showed them, I did 'em both. Yeah, two for one, I sorted it. She was a lying bitch and he was a scumbag. So fucking what, and hey, guess what. I get a couple of years for doing 'Frankie' and that's reduced to twelve months for good behaviour, and now I'm out and dancing and fucking hurray".

I just kept sort of smiling and nodding in agreement, but something wasn't right here.

One minute he's telling me that he killed his stepfather for raping and murdering his girlfriend, and now he's rambling on about getting rid of both of them. What was going on?

And it struck me, not to ask.

I finished cutting his hair and asked him if it was alright, but he was 'way out' of it by then.

He never even looked in the mirror, he just kept saying "Yeah, yeah. It's okay, it's well smart" and that was that.

I got him to the till and thankfully, he paid me straightaway. Then he turned around and stared as he looked for the door handle. When he finally found it, he opened the door and walked straight out of the shop without saying another word.

I watched him go.

Then I stood there for a moment and I wondered, wondered about making a choice.

Do you take things into your own hands, take an action and do something. Or do you turn away, and simply say that 'it's nothing to do with you' and you make an excuse and you do nothing at all.

I turned and I looked at the wall opposite me and up to the top corner, and I looked at the security camera that I'd had installed there about twelve months ago. The security camera that ran all day, just as a safeguard, just in case somebody ever came in and tried to rob me, or whatever.

I looked at the camera and I knew it would have recorded everything, the whole conversation, and I just stood there for a moment. Then I turned around and I reached over and picked up the telephone, and I rang the police. I'd made my choice.

The next morning, a Detective Inspector Alan Cain arrived at the shop. He was on his own and walked into the shop very casually, he could have been a customer. He introduced himself and we shook hands. Then he asked me what the phone call was about. I had asked to speak to somebody from the C.I.D, but when he arrived, Detective Cain didn't seem to be too interested and I felt that maybe I was wasting his time. Anyway, I told him what had happened and I took out my laptop and plugged it into the hard drive from the security camera. I fast forwarded it to where the young man 'Darren' had entered the shop, and that was when Detective Inspector Cain suddenly took notice.

He looked intently at the video, and then he spoke. "I know him" he said.

He continued to study the screen "It's Darren...Darren Little".

"Yes" I said "he told me his name was Darren"

"Yes, a right piece of work that one" remarked D.I. Cain.

"Really?" I said.

"Yes really" continued D.I. Cain "He used to shunt drugs between here and Preston. We were on to him but we just couldn't nail the bugger, he was always a bit too sharp".

"Well" I said "he must be back on them, because he was as high as a kite by the time he left here"

"Right, okay" said the Detective "I thought he was still inside. He murdered somebody for attacking his girlfriend or something. It was a while ago now, a mate of mine in Preston C.I.D dealt with it. I remember it now, she'd been attacked and then murdered and Darren Little caught the murderer at it or something".

"Or something" I said "well in that case Detective, I think you need to watch this video footage and listen to what he says"

So we sat there and watched the whole of the video on my laptop.

When it had finished, D.I Cain turned and looked at me.

"Jesus Christ" he said "I don't believe it, the bastard got away with it".

He was flabbergasted "the sneaky bastard...and nobody ever knew".

"Well, no" I said "...not up till now".

D.I Cain shook his head "He obviously copped a reduced sentence because of the circumstances. He murdered his girlfriend's murderer. 'Crime of passion' and all that".

"I thought that twelve months wasn't long for murder" I said

"It probably ended up as a manslaughter charge" concluded the Detective.

"Listen" he said "I need this hardrive, and I need to get hold of my mate at Preston C.I.D and we also need to copy this".

"Yes, it's okay" I said "You can take it with you, I don't need it".

"Cheers" he said, and with that we unplugged the security recorder and D.I Cain took it to his car. I walked over with him.

He said "I'll get this back to you as soon as possible. We'll be in touch".

"No problem" I said, and I waved him goodbye.

The next afternoon I got a visit from Detective Inspector Andrew Mercer from Preston C.I.D.

 He walked into the shop carrying my security recorder and after putting it down on reception, he introduced himself, and we shook hands.

"We've recorded it all onto our own hard drive" he told me "So you can have your recorder back".

"So if I clear it now it's okay?" I asked him.

"Yes, we've got all the material we need from the drive. We've got the whole thing".

"So what happens now?" I asked.

He gave me a serious look. He was a tall, well built man, in his late forties, and I got the feeling that you would really not like to mess with Detective Inspector Andrew Mercer.

"First of all we'll try and track him down" said Detective Mercer "Like he said on the video, he's in Bolton for now, but he'll head back to Preston and he'll probably take a load of drugs with him. That's how he used to earn a living and he'll go back to that, it's like 'leopards and spots' and all that, he'll never change. He doesn't know any other way, he won't work, never did".

"Do you think you'll find him?" I asked.

"Well, D.I Cain's pulling out all the stops over here in Bolton, but if we don't get him here we'll catch him in Preston, it's only a matter of time before he pops up, his type always do. He's a bit sharp though, in the past we've never been able to catch him with the drugs on him, even though we knew he was dealing. Very clever lad is 'our Darren'. Do you know that nobody, his family, his friends...nobody at all knew what he was up to? We don't think his girlfriend even knew. Back then, he was a very sharp lad".

"And now?" I asked.

"Well, we'll see. But to tell you the truth, what we have here" and he pointed at the security recorder "What's on here should bury him. Eventually we'll get hold of him, he's just out of prison and he'll be low key but he'll have to find somewhere to live. He might even approach the council, anyway he'll end up visiting his old haunts, and we'll have an alert out for him, he'll turn up"

I was quite fascinated by it all "D.I Cain told me that you dealt with the original murder".

"Yes, it's a couple of years ago now, a right mess that was. We got a phone call, it was Darren Little himself who rang us. He told us that 'he'd thought he'd killed someone'. We all charged round there to his house, and the place was like a blood bath. I can remember Darren, he was covered in blood and the bloke that he'd killed, it was his stepfather. Well let's just say that there wasn't much left of his head".

I shuddered at the thought of it. I'd had Darren Little in my shop, and full of drugs.

Detective Mercer continued "Darren reckoned he'd come home and caught his stepfather raping his girlfriend, it was horrific, she'd had some sort of vibrator jammed into her mouth, forensics reckoned that's what actually killed her. The stepfather had choked her with it, he was on top of her when Darren walked in and caught him at it. So our Darren then grabs a baseball bat and sets sail with it, absolutely smashed his stepfather's head in, it wasn't a pretty sight. Of course we arrested Darren, and then we tried to clean up the mess. It was a nightmare for the forensic team, trying to get samples and fingerprints was near impossible because everything was covered in blood. But the facts stood up for themselves, attempted rape, murder, and then of course, retribution.

Our boy Darren goes to court and holds up his hands and admits to it. 'Yes' he did it, of course he did, he rang us up and told us didn't he? So the judge takes Darren's admission of guilt and almost commends his honesty, and of course 'your honour' can't condone the violence and the murder, but the exceptional circumstances in finding a 'loved one' being raped and murdered had to be taken into consideration.

The Judge gives him two years, obviously accepting that with good behaviour, young Darren will be out to 'rebuild' his life, in less than twelve months".

Detective Mercer gave me a cynical sort of smile, I could see where he was coming from.

He continued "Obviously Darren had thought it all through, and he threw us a smokescreen, admit to one murder to cover up the other. And we bought it, hook, line and the proverbial sinker. Yes, we bought it alright" and he shook his head. "But now this turns up, your video, and this opens up a whole new can of worms. And looking at this, well, it's an admission to a murder. What I've got to do now is get hold of him, sit him down and get the truth out of him, and that's in a perfect world. Whatever happens though, he's going to get charged with murder, well two murders actually, because the circumstances of his stepfather's death are now different. He can't have killed his stepfather for raping and murdering his girlfriend if the girlfriend was already dead, and dead by Darren's own hand. So it's back to square one."

I was overwhelmed by it all "And do you think he'll admit to it?" I asked,

"He can please himself" said Detective Mercer "but this time I'm going to nail the bastard"

It was three weeks later when I got the phone call.

"Hi there, it's me, D.I Mercer from Preston C.I.D."

"Oh hello" I replied "How's it going?"

"I'm going to come down and see you. When are you free?"

I looked at my appointment book "Err, I'm pretty booked up. I don't just know when I've got time to sit down and talk to you, this week anyway".

"I'll tell you what" he said "I could do with a haircut. Could you fit me in tomorrow and I could talk to you then?"

"Yes, no problem" I said "how does tomorrow at one suit you?"

"Nice one" and he laughed "and I've got a story for you".

Quarter to one the next day and D.I Mercer walks into the shop. I'd just finished the last customer, and so I was ready for him.

"Hi there" he said, very jovially and he sat himself down in 'the chair'.

"You okay?" he said.

"Yes, I'm fine" I wanted to get all the formalities out of the way first, so I said to him "Right, before we start. How do you want your hair cutting?"

He told me, and that was that sorted, so I started cutting his hair.

He just sat there, looking at me through the mirror with an expectant grin on his face, until I finally cracked, and I had to ask him the question.

"Well, go on then. How've you gone on?

Big smile..."Got the bugger, and a result, a 'big result'."

And that put a smile on my face too. "Nice one, so you caught him then?"

"Yes" he said "it was about ten days after I last spoke to you, there was no sign of him in Bolton so we got the feeling that he would have made his way back to Preston, and he had. We'd had some trouble with the usual low life druggies in the town, this lot are the bottom of the barrel, they just live every day to score drugs. It's their whole existence. They do a lot of petty crime, shoplifting and burglaries, that sort of thing. But when the money runs out and the drugs are thin on the ground, they start to fight amongst each other, they're like rats with a very small piece of cheese. They fight over what drugs they have left and usually somebody gets hurt or stabbed or whatever. Anyway, we'd had a call over a fight, three druggies, all of them well known to us and heavily into the white powder and more. One of them had been badly bottled, his face was all smashed in by a broken bottle, and then they'd tried to slash his neck open with the broken end, he nearly died. We'd already put out a general call that if anything drug related came in, we'd like some input, with a view to the possibility of tracking down Darren Little. So one of my lads went over to Preston Central, the two lads who'd done the attack were being held there in separate cells. Anyway he gets into their ribs, and it turns out that there's a new supplier on the scene, and with a bit of friendly persuasion they bubble him, and guess what 'Hey presto' it only turns out to be Darren Little. We got the name, and the address, and the next day we rolled up to the flat were he's living. We just knocked on the door and arrested him, simple as that. A quick search of his flat and we find a rucksack full of the 'white stuff', and there you go. We got him down to the station and put him in a cell and we got him a solicitor, 'his rights' and all that crap. Eventually the solicitor arrived and we all sat down for his first formal interview. The four of us sat in the interview room, me and another D.I, my partner Harry, along with Darren Little and his solicitor.

Now it has to be said, Darren was a little worse for wear. When we arrested him he was as high as a kite, out of his head actually, and so he was very calm about being arrested, he probably didn't even know what day it was. He came along with us no trouble, and I got the feeling all along that he thought he was just getting done for possession. Even when we sat down for the interview, he was very calm and casual about it all. He was semi blitzed of course, and I suspect that his solicitor had probably told him that he'd have him out within the hour, that's what usually happens

So we sat down, and I turned on the tape recorder and started the interview.

I stated the time and date and who was present and then I turned and spoke to Darren.

"Okay Darren" I said "You're here, firstly on a charge for the possession of drugs, but we can get back to that later. Secondly, there's also the possible charge of supplying and selling drugs, and I suppose we can get back to that one later too. Although I have to tell you, we do have enough evidence to throw the book at you for both offences. At the moment though, we want to interview you about something else.

His solicitor was now looking at me a bit strangely. So was Darren, but that was probably the drugs".

I continued "What we've actually got you in for, and what we really want to talk to you about, is your last offence, and that is the murder of your stepfather".

At that point, Darren looked up at us through his glazed eyes, this was something that he wasn't expecting, and somehow he didn't just get it".

"Excuse me" his solicitor started.

But I immediately stopped him. I just held my hand up and said "Just wait a moment please".

I turned again to Darren "Your stepfather...I want to talk about your stepfather".

"What about him?" he answered.

"His murder Darren. I want to talk about his murder".

He looked back at us and smiled stupidly "Yeah, you got me there copper. I did it okay" he said this in a silly American accent, and then he started to laugh.

I smiled back at him "Yes Darren, we know you did it".

Then he stared back at me "Fuck me 'Mr Detective', everybody knows I did it. Don't you know, I went to prison".

"My name's Detective Inspector Mercer, Darren, and yes we know you went to prison".

"Did the crime, paid the time" again in his silly American accent.

"Well yes Darren, we know you did. But you see, we want to talk to you again about the actual circumstances of his murder".

"What for?" he said, and suddenly he got annoyed "Look, I killed the bastard okay. He got what he deserved. He killed Nicola, and I killed him, and then I got what I deserved. I went to prison for it...alright".

He'd said his little speech, he'd told it 'as it is', or was. And as far as he was concerned, that was that.

"Yes, okay Darren" I said "We know you murdered your stepfather, what was he called again, 'Frank'...'Frankie'. Yes, that was it".

Darren sneered at the mention of his stepfather's name "Yeah big fucking Frankie, the piece of shit".

He looked at us "I'll tell you something copper, I'm fucking glad I killed that bastard. It's the best thing I ever did, and I mean it".

He was wide eyed and angry now, the drugs weren't letting go, and I knew it.

"Yes well, that's as maybe" I said to him "but what about Nicola?"

He gave us a sort of mystified look "What about her?"

"Her death Darren. What about 'Her' death?"

"He murdered her, that bastard. He did it, you know that".

I shook my head "No, no Darren, we don't".

He stared back at me "What do you mean?"

"We know Darren. We know it was you, you killed her".

His solicitor started to stutter, but I told him to shut up and listen. Sometimes you've got to be forceful with these people.

Darren just sat there for a second, and then his brain kicked in.

"Bollocks" he spat it out "that's bollocks, complete and utter crap. No fucking way".

"Yes Darren...Yes, I'm afraid so. You see you killed her, and 'you' know you did and 'we' know you did. You killed her, and then you killed Frank, and you blamed him to cover up Nicola's murder. It was very clever of you Darren, very clever and very sharp, and you got everybody to believe you. You even got a bit of sympathy from the Judge for your actions. Understandable I suppose, under the circumstances".

He looked back at me through his drugged filled eyes and I could see his brain going into gear. He was thinking fast, very fast. Well they don't call cocaine 'speed' for nothing.

Then suddenly he went from angry Darren, back to calm and smiling Darren.

He just said "Prove it Copper...prove it".

And he sat back in his chair and he relaxed, and he bathed in his own glory, yes prove it, prove something that happened two years ago. What had we got, some new forensic evidence, not possible? And witnesses, no way, there weren't any. So he sat there, so smug. He thought had all the answers, 'oh yes', he'd thought it all through.

So I reached into my pocket and pulled out my portable Dictaphone. It's something that I always carry, a habit.

"Darren, see this?"

Darren looked.

"This is a Dictaphone Darren, it records things. It's really handy at times, you can record all sorts of things on it".

Darren looked at me as though I was an idiot.

"Well, just let me tell you something Darren. On this Dictaphone I have a voice recording, a voice recording from a video that you're in, and it's you...you, just talking away. We can show you the video if you want, and you can watch yourself talking if you want to. It's not a problem, it's just that we'll have to get hold of a T.V monitor to show it to you, but like I said, it's not a problem."

Darren just sat there with his arms folded, and he was thinking, and I could see him thinking 'What video?'

So I put the Dictaphone on the desk in front of him and pressed the 'play' button.

The next couple of minutes were interesting.

When it had finished, I switched off the recorder. "So, what do you think Darren?"

His solicitor put his hand over his eyes.

Darren just sat there. He was trying to recollect 'where' he'd said all this, but he couldn't remember.

He suddenly twitched. He knew it was his voice, he knew it was his voice on the recorder, oh he knew that alright. And he knew that what he'd said on there was the truth, oh yes again. But it was 'where' he'd said it that was driving him mad, and the drugs weren't helping at all.

The solicitor finally spoke "And you have video footage of this conversation?"

"Yes we do, absolutely".

The solicitor sat back in his chair, there wasn't anything more he could do really. He knew it.

So, we looked back at Darren.

He just sat there, he was working out his options. It was decision time.

And I wondered if this could be the moment that we finally got the truth. Because that's what we do, we push people towards the edge of honesty, push them there and then let them jump in. It's what we're trained to do.

And they surrender to it. It's good for the soul.

Suddenly Darren sighed, and his shoulders seemed to sag slightly.

"Have you got a cigarette?" he said, and he looked a little tired, and I had the feeling that our Darren was about to surrender.

I turned to my partner "Harry...give him a ciggie".

Harry looked back at me "Smoking's not allowed in here".

I gave him the look that was next to violence "Harry, give him...a ciggie" I said quietly.

Harry knew not to argue. Harry was supposed to have given up smoking, almost religiously.

But he put his hand into his pocket and pulled out a packet of twenty and a lighter.

He gave Darren a cigarette and lit it for him.

And as our Darren inhaled in ecstasy, Harry turned to me and said "How did you know I was still smoking?"

"Coz I'm a policeman" I said. I didn't even look at him.

Back to Darren, and he took his second drag, he was almost there, jump you bastard, jump.

Then it happened. The capitulation...the final deal.

"Give us the packet of fags." he said "and I'll tell you everything".

I looked at Harry. Harry sighed.

He gave him the cigarettes.

"Harry" I said "give him the lighter too".

Harry put the lighter down in the middle of the desk, not happy, another capitulation.

Darren nodded at me and said "thanks". That was a good sign.

Now we were getting somewhere, a bit of give and take, the levelling of the playing field.

"Okay Darren" I said, tell me what happened".

He blew out some smoke, and then he looked up at the ceiling for a moment as he remembered.

"Me and Nicola, we were having a rough trip you see. We weren't getting on, and it wasn't me, it was her. Suddenly everything I did was wrong, and she was beginning to piss me off.

Don't get me wrong, I still loved her, but the constant rows were really getting me down. So I started going to the pub when she had 'one on her', and suddenly, that seemed to be most of the time. I'm sure she planned it, she knew I'd go out if we'd had a row. So I was going to the pub most nights, I got friendly with a girl who worked behind the bar, a blonde piece 'Cheryl'. Anyway, I ended up bonking Cheryl every night after last orders, it was okay. And I was on free drinks all night, so 'thanks very much', and there were no ties. Cheryl knew the score, she just wanted a shag too.

But somebody must have found out, because someone told Nicola what was going on.

I came home one night and she threw a fit, all screaming and shouting. She already had my case packed and a couple of bin bags filled with the rest of my clothes. She wanted me out and gone.

I look back now and I realize something, there were no tears, not one. No heartbreak and no crying and I know now, it was all planned. She'd wanted me to go, she just had to find an excuse, and now she had.

So I'm thrown out, and I had to go and live with my sister.

But there's something ticking away in my head, something was going on, something. And so I decide to keep my eye on things, you know how it is.

Anyway, because stupid fucking Nicola is such a dozy bitch, she completely forgets that I still have a key for the house, and I know what time she goes off to work every day, and what time she gets back. Same time, every day.

So I go round to the house every day, to check on things. To see what she's been up to. Suddenly she's going on the internet a lot, and those fucking dating sites. Can you believe it, the sad bitch, and she starts talking to different blokes on the internet, it's pathetic. Then she starts going on the odd date, and she reports back to her stupid fucking mates the next day on the internet, and she tells them all how she's gone on. And I just keep going to the house every day and read her messages.

You should have seen them, 'Jesus Christ'. Things like...'I told him all about myself, he was really interested in me' and 'He held my hand, it was so romantic'. And then a couple of days later 'the bastard's gone back to his wife' or 'he had too many commitments'...all that sort of shite. She even had one bloke e-mailing her about his undying love, and then he called her the wrong name and talked about a date that she'd never been on. Now he was 'one' stupid twat. So the silly bitch had to fire him off as well, the stupid cow".

Darren stopped talking for a moment, and he lit another cigarette. I got the feeling that he was enjoying the release. 'It's good to talk'...as they say.

He then continued "Anyway, then she starts talking to someone from Scotland, somebody called 'Chris'. And every day when I go to the house, I check her messages on the internet, and now everyday she's talking to this 'Chris'. But you're not going to believe it, I couldn't tell whether 'Chris' was another bloke or just a woman, how's that for funny? Every bloody day she's on there to this 'Chris' and long conversations about everything, 'Jesus'. Anyway in the end I had to think that it's a bloke don't I? And I have to say, that watching all the internet fucking dating going on and watching all those messages was doing my head in, and I was getting really, really jealous. In my head I kept thinking 'What the fuck is she playing at' and I kept trying to ring her at work but she would just slam the phone down on me, the bitch.

Then she went off for a weekend, off for a dirty weekend with someone to god knows where. And I was going crazy. That weekend I went over to the house and snorted coke for the whole two days. I was out of my fucking head.

Monday morning, I nearly had to crawl out of the place.

But the next day I made it back, it was in the afternoon. I went around to the house, and as usual, I went in and then clicked on her computer to read what was going on, and it was then that I finally realized that this 'Chris' was actually a woman.

Nicola had e-mailed her, e-mailed her to tell her all about some 'wonderful' man that she'd met, and according to her 'things just blossomed' and 'it was much more than just a friendship'. Christ, where did she get this stuff from. What a load of crap.

But I was mad...fucking mad.

The next day I went round again, and there were more messages on the bloody computer, but this time it went on and on. She'd been out for a meal with him, the message read 'We went out for a meal last night to an Italian Restaurant, well they do say that it's the 'food of love'.

I had a lovely time, he's so caring, and we talked, we talked all night. He ordered a bottle of the best red wine, 'Barolo' I think it was called. At the end of the meal he ordered two Liqueur coffees, and then he did something so lovely. He took hold of my hand, and then he slowly stroked each of my fingers, he never spoke a word, it was the most beautiful feeling and so erotic. Then he just looked at me and said "I love you". It was wonderful, he's so romantic. I love this man".

When I read that my head nearly exploded. I wanted to smash the fucking house to bits, I was so mad and I began shaking with anger. But I had to stop myself, stop myself and think. I just stood there shaking, and I had to think 'don't do it...don't do it, take your time and think about it'. And I stood there till I'd calmed down and the shaking finally stopped. Then my brain finally kicked in, and I picked up my coat and left, straight out and gone.

I didn't go anywhere near the house for two days, I couldn't. And then, well I went back, it was a Friday afternoon, and I let myself in as usual, and nobody was in as usual. I walked down the hallway and then I made my way upstairs to our bedroom. I walked in there, and then I stopped dead in my tracks and gasped. Because there it all was, everything, and I just stood there with my stupid mouth wide open. Her dress was thrown on the floor, along with her shoes, kicked off, and her bra and her knickers and her tights, all pulled off and dropped, and left there on the floor. And the bed, used. And the pillows used. Used by two people. And my bed, there'd been two people in my bed. My fucking bed.

I started to shake again, and my brain painted me the picture. I reached down for the sheets and pulled them back, I had to see. But then, and I couldn't believe it. As I pulled the sheets back, something had been left in the bed. I moved the sheets and a pillow and there it was. There before my very fucking eyes, was a bright purple fucking vibrator. I just looked at it and my brain went into overload. There it was, all shiny and purple and used. And I went sick, sick to my stomach. And then my brain painted me another picture, and I leant over and picked the vibrator up, and I stared at it, unbelievable.

Then I heard a sound, and I knew exactly what it was. The front door had just opened, it was Nicola. And I heard the door close behind her as she walked down the hallway and into the kitchen. So I came slowly down the stairs and I followed her in. She'd just taken off her coat and she had her back to me.

"Hello Nicola" I said.

She spun around, her face full of fear. She thought she was on her own, of course she did.

And I could see it in her eyes, the question 'How had I got in?', and in a fraction of a second she remembered that I still had my key, strange how the brain works so fast. I could see it in her eyes.

She stared at me, almost in horror. It's so strange, that you can live with someone for years, sleep, eat and drink with them, and then one little upset and it's all over and gone.

Yes, she just stood there and stared at me, and she was going to say something...something like 'What the hell are you doing here'? Something like that, it was so obvious. I knew her so well, or at least I thought I did.

But I got there before her, and I held up the shiny purple vibrator, right in front of her face. "This yours?" I said to her.

And her face twisted, from fear to furious in a single second. I'd invaded her new little world and I had hold of something personal, very personal, and she was embarrassed and angry.

But me, well I was just angry. Fuck me I was angry.

She went to snatch it out of my hand but I pulled my arm back quickly so that it was out of her reach.

"Give it to me, you bastard" she said.

But I wouldn't, I held it away from her so that she couldn't reach it.

I said to her "Is this the best you can do Nicola. A fucking vibrator, a dildo with a fucking battery, is that it?"

We stood there, just staring at one another.

And then she stopped, she stopped staring at me, and she suddenly smiled.

And then she said it..."No Darren, that's not the 'best'..." and then she laughed at me, "You just don't get it do you" and she raised her eyebrows and winked one eye sexily at me. It was a message, she was letting me know that she was having sex with somebody else, and enjoying it. And that really, really upset me.

So I smashed the vibrator right across her face, from right to left, and then with the same hand I punched her in the face. The back of her head hit the kitchen wall, it happened so fast that she was too shocked to scream. Then I back handed her, again with the vibrator, and her smashed nose started to bleed badly. This time she did scream out, so I grabbed the front of her blouse and pulled her to me. She looked up at me, terrified. She wasn't winking now, not one bit.

"Now do you like it" I yelled at her "Do you like it?", and I smashed the vibrator right into her face and her nose completely broke and splattered. She groaned and keeled over, and then I climbed on top of her. She lay there gasping, and I smacked her in the face again with the vibrator, just to get her attention. She stared up at me, trying to say something. But I spoke for her.

"So you really like a dildo do you Nicola...well you can have it" and I jammed the vibrator right into her mouth. She gagged, and then her eyes widened and she tried to move her head from side to side, but I leant over her and then put my full weight onto it, and then I pushed the vibrator right down her throat. Her legs started to kick out but she couldn't do anything.

Then I felt something crunch in her throat. I'd jammed nearly all of the vibrator into her mouth by then and suddenly she stopped moving and her very wide eyes just stared back at me.

She was dead, I knew she was.

I got up, and I can remember saying something like "Serves you right you bitch", and it did.

I went over to the sink and filled the kettle, and I washed my hands and made a cup of coffee.

I sat down in the chair and looked at her. I knew of course that I'd have to ring the police.

What was the use in doing anything else? It had to be me, didn't it?

But I just wanted a bit of time to myself to calm down, so I sat there thinking things over.

If she hadn't come home early, maybe I wouldn't have been there, maybe I would have already left. And anyway, why did she come home early. God only knew.

I'd been sitting there with a cup of coffee and a cigarette for about half an hour and it was time to make the phone call. Then suddenly, there was a knock on the front door.

And I remember thinking 'Oh hell, what now?' and I thought that it was probably one of the bloody nosey neighbours wanting something.

So I got up and went to the front door and opened it. And standing there, would you believe it...was Frank.

We just stared at each other, neither expecting the other. I looked at him and he was holding a bottle of wine in his hand. He slowly tried to hide it behind his back, and then in an instant my brain suddenly worked it all out, it was like a flash of light, and everything immediately dropped right into place. I just couldn't believe it. Nicola was having an affair with Frank. And it was Frankie boy who'd been in my bed. Yes, the bitch and the bastard.

My brain went crazy, and now I knew why she'd come home early. She'd come home early to meet up with this piece of shit.

But I was clever, 'oh yes', I was fucking brilliant. I just said to him "Oh...hi Frank" and I did the 'mock surprise' thing.

"I can't stop" I said "I'm just going out. Nicola's in the kitchen 'cooking' something or other".

"Come on through" I said and I stood aside to let him in. And he walked in. In and past me.

Hanging on the wall in our hallway was a 'New York Yankees' baseball bat. I'd always told Nicola that it was a sporting memento, and that I used to be a big fan of the 'Yankees'. But in truth, I never was. In fact, I don't know a single thing about baseball. But in my trade, dealing the drugs or whatever, it's always good insurance to have something handy by the front door, just in case someone comes a calling.

And as Frank walked past me, I lifted the bat off the wall and followed him in. I noticed that now he was holding the bottle of wine in front of him so that I still couldn't see it. What a stupid arsehole.

I called out "Hey Nicola...Frank's here".

And as I walked in behind him, I thought about what a rotten cheating bastard he was.

He'd ruined my mother's life, ruined my life as a child and even more now, he'd got his dirty little hands on Nicola and I fucking hated him for it. I looked at the back of his stupid head as we walked down the hallway. And I thought about him, sneaking in behind my back, and I thought of him in bed with Nicola, and him holding her. And suddenly I was I was so fucking mad, I was on fire.

He walked into the kitchen, or should I say 'we' walked into the kitchen.

And fuck me, he just stopped dead in his tracks.

He'd planned to walk in there and put on a big act, a 'bit of a performance', so that I wouldn't know what was going on.

But 'oh dear no'. Not today.

He just stood there, almost rigid, and it must have taken him a second or two to take it all in.

Well I suppose the sight of Nicola, bleeding and dead, with their purple love toy sticking out of her mouth, well I suppose it must have made him wonder 'What now'?

And actually, it must have done, because Frankie gave a quick little groan. I'd like to think it was a sign of resignation really, maybe he understood what was going to happen. He surely must have realized by now that I knew 'everything'. Yes, I knew everything about them, and their filthy little lies.

And I knew Frankie boy, and I knew how his mind worked. For a start, he was aware that I was standing right behind him, and he would have been frantically trying his best to think up some sort of a lie that he could use as an excuse. And I do actually think that he must have come up with something, because he was just about to turn around and speak. Yes, he was just going to turn around and say something, but I wasn't having any of that. Not today.

So I swung the baseball bat high and down, and smashed it over his head. The last thing he did was drop the bottle of wine onto the floor, and it smashed too. I think it was a bottle of 'Barolo'. Nice one Frank.

Then I bashed his brains out, I went berserk.

When I'd finished, there wasn't much left of Frankie's head, and it made me smile.

So I went over to the sink and made another cup of coffee and then lit another ciggie.

It has to be said, tobacco is good for the old brain. It calms you down and it makes you think, and it makes you somehow, reconsider things.

And then I had the brightest of ideas, and bingo!

I put down my cup and then threw my cigarette into the sink. And then I went over to Nicola and dragged her over to where Frankie lay. I reached down and ripped open her blouse and then I pulled her bra up over her breasts. Then I pulled her skirt right up to her waist and I pulled her knickers and tights down to just below her knees. I went over to the kitchen sink for a wet sponge and then went back to Nicola and wiped down the exposed bit of the vibrator, to get rid of any of my fingerprints. I looked down at my handy work, and then I carefully kicked off her shoes, so there were no fingerprints on them either.

I rolled Frankie onto his side and undid his belt and pants, then I slid them down past his arse, and then I did the same with his underpants. Christ, what a sight, I nearly got my camera out, it was the full bollocks and no head.

Once I'd done this, I ripped open the front of his shirt to make it look like there'd been a bit of a struggle. Then I went over to the kitchen drawer and took out a

tablespoon and went back over to Frankie and prised open the part that was his mouth.
I scraped some saliva from inside his mouth and then reached over and wiped the
spoon over both of Nicola's exposed nipples. Nice touch that, I knew it would keep
Forensics and the DNA boys happy. Then I rolled his body on top of Nicola, and I put
his hands all over the end of the vibrator, for the fingerprints of course. Then I sort of
arranged things so that his knee was in her crotch and that his hand was up her
backside.

I remember glancing down at them for a moment. What a great couple.

Things were looking good.

Blood was dripping nicely on and off both parties as I cleaned up. Everything else
went into the kitchen sink. Cups, ashtrays, sponges and spoons, I washed them all in
hot water and bleach. There's no history with bleach, it's timeless, it destroys all the
evidence and just runs away down the plug hole. So I washed up, left everything in the
sink and rinsed my hands with fresh running water and then 'shook' them dry, I didn't
even want to use a towel. Then I went over and picked up the baseball bat which was
covered in blood and bits of Frank, and I wiped my hands on it, a real good coating,
then I dropped it back on the floor in the blood. And finally, I went over to the phone,
and as they say 'with blood on my hands', I rang the police, and at the same time gave
the phone a good coating too."

And that was it. Darren just shrugged his shoulders as he reached over and lit
another cigarette.

"And you took the rap for Frank's murder, but of course, not Nicola's".

"That's it" said Darren "You've got it in one"

"To get the lesser charge" I said.

"Yes, that was it. I knew I was in trouble, I knew I was going to get done one way or
the other. And to tell you the truth, I hadn't got the will or the energy to run. You
would have caught me anyway, and things would only have looked worse. So I took the
'sideways' view. Okay I'd killed somebody, but that somebody was a murdering rapist,
caught in the act. So I took my chances and it worked out fairly well. In Court, the
Judge almost apologized when he sentenced me. 'There for the grace of god' and 'the
crime and the circumstances were understandable, however, we cannot condone
violence'...and all that bullshit".

"You do know Darren" I said to him "that I'm going to have to charge you with both
murders this time. The circumstances have changed now, and we'll have to retry you".

"Yeah, I know" he replied.

He sat there for a moment. Smoking and thinking.

Then he said "Do you know something, I don't really mind going back inside".

I just sat there and let him carry on talking.

"Well, life's shit on the outside. It's either work or drugs, and its permanent 'aggro' and grief. And always trying to find somewhere to live is a pain, people are on your back all the time, nobody gives a shit about you. I'll tell something about being 'inside'. I have my own cell and toilet, I have my hi-fi and a computer and there's a T.V. I get three meals a day, and I don't have to work. I tell you man, it's great. And the lads aren't that bad once you get to know them. There's plenty of ciggies to go round, and you can always score some drugs. There's loads of drugs in prison, we have a riot".

He began to laugh "It's like a home from home" and he grinned back at me "Don't worry detective. I'll go with the guilty plea, I'll make it simple".

And that basically, was that. Our job was done.

Detective Mercer looked at me. I'd finished cutting his hair.

"Nice haircut..." he said, without really giving it a second look.

"How will he go on?" I asked.

"Oh, he'll get life"

"Oh, right" I said.

"The thing is, we never actually had to use your video, he's admitted everything and he's pleading guilty".

"So I won't have to wait for him coming back for his revenge then?" I said.

Detective Mercer smiled at me "Why, will you still be here in thirty years?"

"Oh thanks very much" I said, and I laughed "Hey you never know, us barbers live a long time, hopefully".

"But seriously" he said "Thanks for your help. The likes of Darren Little need locking up, he would have just continued selling drugs, and he would have probably murdered somebody else eventually. People like him never change".

"I suppose so" I said "and well, it's been interesting"

"Yes well, that's our job. Mind you, I'll bet you can tell a story or two" he said.

"Yes" I said, I can, but none like this".

We both laughed and it was time for him to go, and he shook my hand.

"Thanks" he said. "Anything to help" I replied "I hate drugs."

"You don't know the half of it" he said "you wouldn't believe some of the things we see. I'll tell you something, there's never a happy ending with drugs. Lives are destroyed, and families are ripped apart. It's just a waste of human life".

He bid me farewell and I watched him walk over to his car, then I waved him off as he started the engine and finally drove away.

And as he left, I stood there and considered all that had happened, the murder and the violence of it all. And I gave a thought to people in general, and our relationships with one another, one minute so right and the next, all breakdown and turmoil.

And us, as human beings, we've come so far. And yet in the wrong circumstances, it seems that we can effortlessly step back into our primitive selves and have the ability to inflict violence and kill one another with an unfathomable disregard.

I just shook my head and shrugged at the stupidity of it all. And I turned around and went back into my shop, and back to work.

I suppose it was just another day. We'll see.

CHAPTER SEVEN

I've always considered that 'friendship' is perhaps one of life's greatest gifts. It's a bond that is common only to us and our fellow man, or even our fellow woman. And we always remember our friendships, even from years ago. You never lose a true friend, time and space are irrelevant...it just doesn't matter.

Yes friendship, and for me those friendships have been the oil that's made my life run a lot smoother and been made a lot happier because of the love of good friends.

Sometimes however, decisions and choices have to be made. And just occasionally, you do have to ask yourself if someone is really a true friend, or just a long standing acquaintance. And there's the question.

Time and circumstance will usually bring you the answer.

Nevertheless, unfortunately acquaintances do fall out and friendships are broken. It's strange and it's unpleasant, but it does happen. And regrettably, this is happened to a customer of mine just recently. A friendship broken irrevocably, and what transpired after is something that's just sort of stuck in my mind.

It all started five weeks ago. It was exactly three o' clock on Saturday afternoon, when into my shop walked Alan Morton, the last customer of the day, and the last customer of the week.

Big 'Al'...looking slightly jaded, and showing definite symptoms of the 'night before'

Medium in height and a bit 'round' around' the middle, 'Big Al' was a victim of too many takeaways and a fondness for beer.

"Ha" I said to him and I laughed "Friday night. Card night again?"

"Yep" he replied wearily.

"Poker with the lads?"

"Yep" he said, again.

And with that he headed for the chair and slumped himself into it.

'Big Al', he's a rotund sort of lad and usually quite jovial, but like most people when 'worse for wear', even breathing in and out can be an effort.

Alan 'Al' Morton and his legendary poker nights. A gang of mates around at his house on Friday nights, once or twice a month, drinking, gambling, and talking, all too much. They'd done it for as many years as I'd known him. Lord only knows how much money must have changed hands.

So I started to cut his hair.

"Win or lose?" I asked in passing.

"I won, I suppose" replied Al with a sort of half hearted expression.

I thought he was a bit sullen, but I put it down to the booze.

"You don't seem over impressed" I said "didn't you win much?"

Al was a man who liked to win, and when he did, it was big grins all round.

He just sighed "I don't think we'll be playing again, not for a while anyway."

"Why man, has the wife put her foot down or something?"

"No...No, it's nothing like that. It's one of the lads" and then Al looked a bit weary "one of the lads, he's got himself into a bit of trouble".

"What kind of trouble?" I asked.

"Money, money trouble, and I don't think we've helped and last night it all blew up, blew up big time".

"Really" I said. It was a useless sort of comment, and I knew it.

"Yeah, and we were having a really good time too, me and the other four lads, all of us. You know a couple of them, Jason and Pete".

I nodded, I knew them. I cut their hair.

"Yes" I said "Jason was in last week".

"Well there was Jason and Pete, and Tony and Malc, another two of my mates. We've played poker on Fridays for ages now".

"Yes I know, you've spoken about them before".

"We always kick off at about eight to eight thirty, we get the drinks sorted, always the same. A couple of cases of beer, some cider for Malc, because that's all he drinks and two or three pints of 'Jack'..."

"What's Jack?" I asked.

"Jack Daniels, its Bourbon".

"Oh yes" I said, feeling a bit naive.

Al smiled "Yeah, I know it sounds a bit stupid but we call the bottle a 'Pint of Jack', it makes it sound a bit 'American'. You know, like poker".

I smiled back "I get it".

"Well, we were having a good night. We'd had a couple of beers and got talking about some of the trips we'd been on and places we'd visited. You know the sort of thing, all the strange and the dafter things that have happened to us". " and then he laughed "God, I'm surprised some of us are still alive, me included".

He'd started to brighten up a bit "Has Pete been in?" he asked me.

"Err, yes" I said "about two or three weeks ago". I had to think.

"Did he tell you about his trip to Birmingham on his new motorbike?"

"I didn't know he had a motorbike" I replied.

"He hasn't 'now', the bloody idiot". And Al shook his head and grinned "Listen to this one, we'd had a couple of games of Poker and a few cans, and Pete starts talking about his trip to the International Motorbike Show at the Exhibition Centre in Birmingham. Pete's one of them 'born again' bikers, he used to own a little 100cc motorbike when he was about seventeen and then twenty years later, like some of his 'other' stupider mates, he goes out and buys this bright red 1000cc Honda racing machine. It can apparently outpace a Ferrari and does 160mph."

"Good god" I said "on two wheels. Lord, now that's frightening".

"Oh that's nothing" he said "Some of his mates have got bikes even faster than that, they're all bloody mad. "

I whistled, amazed.

"So on the Sunday morning of the exhibition, they all decide to meet up early, very early in some car park somewhere at about four o' clock in the morning. There's about ten of them, all leathered up and raring to go. The 'plan of attack' was to get onto the motorway early when there's hardly any traffic on the road and then really open the bikes up and see what they'll do, and so off they go. Pete follows on at the rear, he's the new boy, he's only had the bike about two weeks and I don't think he'd been above sixty miles an hour on it. Well they finally get to the motorway and they belt down the slip road and onto the empty tarmac. It's only about 4-30 am and by then its daylight and there's a whole empty motorway in front of them. The lad at the front opens up his bike with a roar and sets off like a rocket, everybody else does the same, including Pete, and before he knows it he's doing eighty miles an hour. Within ten minutes, they've all crept up to ninety and are heading for the magic '100mph' mark. Another ten minutes and they're there, '100mph' and 'easy peasy'. The bikes are almost purring, this is nothing for these high powered machines, they're only just stretching their legs. And Pete along with the others soon falls in with the pace. A 100mph and a big wide open motorway, not a problem, yes, very easy peasy, he can handle this, no problem at all and all very exciting. The mesmerizing sense of freedom, with all this effortless power, it was just like flying, ten of them all flying down the open road.

The man in front was feeling the adrenalin rush, they all were by then, and slowly but surely and with growing confidence they started to crank up the speed, gradually up to 110, and then 120, and onto 130mph.

The feeling of speed by now was unbelievable, they were eating up the road at an incredible pace and the bikes still had the power to go on even faster. Pete was on a roll, he had never been this fast in his life, he drives a Vauxhall Corsa for god's sake. He realized that the only way to stay focused was by looking straight ahead. If he glanced sideways, everything became a blur and this would throw his balance out. So on he went, head down and absolutely, absolutely straight forwards.

The bigger bikes could reach anywhere up to 170mph and the lad at the front was up for it.

He wanted to see what his bike was capable of, and of course there was also a bit of the 'macho' in all of this, simply to see whose bike was the fastest.

So, on they flew. They were eating up the road, they went up a three mile incline in a matter of minutes with a bit of extra throttle, and when they reached the crest of the incline the bikes then went even faster down the other side as they levelled out onto the long open stretch of empty motorway that lay in front of them.

Pete glanced down at the speedo to see that he was now doing nearly 140mph. He couldn't even hear the engine now he was going so fast, and on they went.

He looked up at the road in front of him, it was a ten mile raised section of motorway that looked down onto open fields, and in the distance there was a long, long curve. Whatever County they were now in it didn't matter, the empty road lay there in front of them, open and beckoning and on they flew, faster ever faster.

He hit 150 mph. It was an incredible speed, a mind bending, physical dream.

And then suddenly, things began to go wrong, very wrong.

The speedometer was just beginning to move over the 150mph mark when he felt something move in his arms, and then in his hands. A strange sensation, his arms and hands started to move of their own accord. Slowly at first, almost imperceptible even, but it was there and then it got worse, and then suddenly he felt the bike shift, and to his sudden and total horror he realized that there was something going drastically wrong.

The front wheel had begun to vibrate, and then to wobble and at over 150mph, this wasn't good.

If a wheel is out of balance, no matter how slight, at certain speeds it will vibrate and start to shake, it's called 'wheel wobble'. Cars get it, motorbikes get it, and now Pete had it.

The realization of what was happening hit him like a hammer, and though he was not the most experienced motorcyclist, he did have knowledge of motorbikes and he knew, and absolutely knew, that his gut instinct, which was to immediately hit the brakes, would simply be a disaster. At that speed, the bike would twist, jack knife and throw him off, at 150mph. He would smash onto the tarmac and then possibly be hit by his own somersaulting machine. If the fall didn't kill him, his own motorbike would cut him in two. The same thing would happen with rapid de-acceleration, cutting off the power too quickly would leave the bike in a sort of 'limbo' and possibly accentuate the wheel wobble, causing the whole bike to shake violently and then somersault, and at 150mph, the result would be the same. Not good, not good at all.

So, Pete's there, hanging on for grim death on an unstable, shaking motorbike as he very rapidly approached the long curve in the road. He knows he has to get the power down to be able to slow the bike and get rid of the imbalance in his front wheel and stop the damn thing shaking, but he has to do it slowly, and smoothly. But everything was happening too quickly.

He hit the curve, the long curve, but what would have been a long curve at 70mph is a lot different at 150mph, now it's more like a bend in the road and Pete has to bank the bike over to get round it. He's in the middle lane and leaning over to negotiate the bend, but the shaking front wheel is sending him to the left. With a terrified fascination, he watches as the shaking bike moves slowly and surely, inch by terrifying inch, into the inside lane. And he can't do a thing to stop it. He looks at his gloved hands gripped tightly on the handlebars, shaking, and he can't stop them, and for a moment he has the briefest memory of his old grandmother who suffered from 'Parkinson's Disease, her hands shook too, and she couldn't stop them shaking either, and it struck him that his own shaking hands were going to kill him. He blinked at the speedometer, he's got it down to somewhere just below 150mph, but the bikes still going like a train and the front wheel's still wobbling and it's now pulling him across the inside lane, and he realizes that if he can't get the speed down further the bike will eventually shake itself further across the inside lane and then onto the hard shoulder, and maybe even further.

It's a fact, the hard shoulder of any motorway is a nightmare for a motorcyclist. It's littered with the shrapnel and debris and spillage from the everyday traffic. There can be anything there, anything from bricks to discarded spare tyres. Hit anything and you will be off, straight over the handlebars. It's a minefield and Pete knows this and tries to lean the bike over a bit to try to somehow pull it back, but it's no good, the bike keeps on veering to the left. He's doing 140mph and the bike's now wavering onto the hard shoulder. He took a sharp look at the road looming up in front of him. It's raised motorway, twenty to thirty feet higher than the surrounding fields, which meant a twenty to thirty foot drop if he went over the edge. At 140mph though, he wouldn't drop, he would take off like a jet plane shooting off an aircraft carrier. Oh god.

He was drenched in sweat, it was all happening so quickly, all this in less than a minute.

"Cut the speed, cut the bloody speed" he was shouting to himself now, trying to get angry and stop the blind panic which was beginning to prevent his brain from working. He daren't look down at the speedometer now, he had to focus. And then suddenly, he was onto the hard shoulder. He prayed it would be clear, but at this speed would he even see anything on the road in front of him, and even if he did, what could he do? There was nothing, nothing other than try to get the speed down.

"Bloody stupid bastard, you bloody stupid bastard" he now shouted at himself, like a maniac. And in his mind he saw his kids and he gasped. It was over, he knew it was, and the bike continued to hypnotically skip across the hard shoulder towards the edge and beyond. In a few second he would be catapulted over the edge.

And then suddenly, it all stopped.

In a instant, it just stopped. The vibration, the wheel wobble, the shaking, all just stopped. At 125mph the front wheel suddenly went back into balance and the bike righted itself up and cruised down the hard shoulder as though nothing had occurred. Pete couldn't believe what had happened, what was happening, but he realized he could now stop, had to stop. He was now down to just over 100mph and even this speed was 'suicidal' and much too fast for the hard shoulder. But he knew that he could now drop a gear, and get control, and apply the brakes, apply the bloody brakes.

It took two hundred yards to get the bike to stop, and at the last minute he had to swerve around two empty milk crates, but he finally pulled it to a halt. With rattled nerves, he swung his leg over the tank and got off the bike, then let it go and watched his bright red Honda crash over on its side.

The tank scratched and dented as it hit the floor but he didn't care. He walked away from the bike as he took off his helmet and then he squatted down at the side of the road to get his breath back, and somehow try to get his nerves back in order. He tried to contain his breathing and he looked down to see his hands trembling in front of him, uncontrollable. All he could do was close his eyes and put his head into his trembling hands.

He sat down on the hard shoulder, just sat down on the tarmac, eyes closed. For ten minutes he sat there, and then he slowly opened his eyes. He was calmer now. He looked across at the bike, lying there on its side, and he suddenly hated the damn thing.

He sat there thinking about his situation, he didn't want to ride that motorbike anymore. The love affair was over, and in his mind he considered that if a taxi had magically pulled up, he would have got in it, driven away and left the bike there on the hard shoulder.

He pondered on what he should do, and then the reality of it all began to sink in. He was stuck on the motorway without any other form of transport. His mates were somewhere in the far distance, they didn't know what had happened to him and at the speed that they'd all been travelling at, nobody would have been looking through their mirrors. They would all arrive at their destination in Birmingham and then realize he was missing, and they would probably wait and hang around for a while. But eventually, they would figure out that something was wrong and then some of them would come back and look for him. The entire way back, if they had to. Finally though, and when he thought about it, there was actually nothing wrong with the bike. So in truth, he would be wasting everybody's time and effort.

Like it or not, he was going to have to get back on the damn thing and continue his journey. He walked over and lifted the Honda up off its side and pulled it onto its stand. He turned the key in the ignition to see if it would start. The engine just burst into life, he knew it would, Hondas are good bikes. He stood there looking at it, engine bubbling away, with its scarred tank. It was like owning a horse that had tried to bite you. You'd looked after it, admired it, and even loved it. But it had still tried to bite you, tried to do you harm.

Pete didn't love his bike anymore.

He slowly put his helmet back on and then walked back over to the Honda and got on it. He sat there and considered if he could do this, he put his hands back on the handlebars and then turned the throttle. The engine responded immediately of course. Could he do it, yes he could, he had too. There was no other option. He took a deep breath and put the bike into gear, revved the engine and slowly set off. He went down the hard shoulder for about three hundred yards before he felt he could get back onto the actual motorway. He was only doing thirty miles an hour.

He was ill at ease with it all, but finally he pulled onto the wide grey tarmac and slowly revved up the bike and went methodically through the gears. He got to fifty miles an hour and that was it, he just couldn't let himself go any faster, in his mind he kept thinking 'If I fall off, I'll hurt myself' and that was that, and the enjoyment had gone.

He finally arrived at Birmingham and had only just come off the motorway when he saw three of his mates coming the other way, they were coming back to look for him. He pulled over as they U turned in the road. They stopped their bikes, got off and took off their helmets. They were concerned, they had all been worried about him and had waited at the Exhibition Centre for over half an hour, and then it was decided that the three of them would go back to find him. Pete told them about the problems with the bike and they were staggered by what had happened, and could have happened.

They all rode back to the Exhibition Centre and the motorbike show, but Pete's heart wasn't really in it anymore, he kept thinking about the long ride back. It was late afternoon when they decided to leave and Pete made an announcement to the rest of the lads, he told them he would be going home at his own pace and that they shouldn't hang about waiting for him to catch up. But his mates had all spoken to each other during the day. They could see that he was visibly shaken by the experience and it had already been decided that they should all go back home as a group with Pete 'sandwiched' between them, for support and his own safety. They're a good set of lads.

They told him, and it wasn't a lie, that the trip home would be different, it would be a lot slower, and it was of course because the motorway was by then full of traffic.

So they made the long trek home. It was a hard ride because there was so much traffic on the road, and by the time Pete got home he was weary. He pushed the Honda into his garage and he knew that he'd had enough. He would get rid of the bike.

'Never again' was his final comment as he walked into his house.

The next morning he took it back to the dealer and asked him to sell it.

"Good god" I said to Al Morton "He must have been out of his tiny mind to ride at that speed".

"I know, tell me about it" Al replied.

And then a thought occurred to me and I looked at Al "Hang on a minute. Pete...Pete's job, he's a..."

"Yes" Al interrupted me "Exactly. He's a bloody ambulance driver. He's a paramedic for god's sake. He goes out to accidents all the time, he's been called out to loads car crashes and he's scraped people up off the floor and had to put the bits into plastic bags. And then the prize twerp gets onto a bloody motorbike and almost manages to kill himself"

"He's married with a couple of kids isn't he" I said.

"Yes, the bloody idiot"

"Does his wife know?"

"Well that's it" replied Al "We were all sat there drinking and playing Poker as he tells us all this, actually the poker went on hold for a while, you can imagine. But, you see his wife, Anne, and Karen my wife, are very good friends. And I just knew, if he'd told his wife what had happened, my wife would have already told me all about it. And as we sat there, Pete looked across the table at me, all wide eyed and apologetic, and I knew what he was thinking. He was worried that I was going to open my 'big mouth'.

Then suddenly "Stuff it" he said, and he reached across the table and picked up the bottle of 'Jack Daniels'. Then he unscrewed the top and poured himself a large shot. I thought that he was going to down it in one, but he leaned back and rocked on the chair and very slowly sipped his drink.

He looked across at me "I haven't told Anne" he said "I daren't, she'll go absolutely mad. She didn't want me to get the bike in the first place. She said that all that money would have been better spent on a holiday, and also our kitchen wants doing up, well above doing up really, we could do with a brand new one. We've had some massive rows about it, and of course she's never stopped nagging me".

"What did she say when you took the bike back to the dealer the morning after?"

"I told her that I'd been thinking about what she'd said, and that it made sense. I told her that I just had to get the motorbike 'thing' out of my system and that the trip all the way to Birmingham and back was dreadful, what with all the traffic and that it rained most of the time. I told her that she had been 'right' all along and that I had been 'bloody stupid' as usual. I told her that when the dealer sells the bike, I'll take the family on holiday, we've not been away for a couple of years"

"Nice one mate" I added.

"Well, we've not been getting on so well just lately. You know how it is, things were beginning to go 'off the boil' between us and I know it's probably my fault, but there it is, and then there's the kids".

He took another sip of the 'Jack' and that was it, story over.

Malc broke the moment with a belch "I'm having another can of cider" he said "Anybody want a refill?" he said as he wandered off into the kitchen.

We all shook ours heads and called out 'No' in unison.

Jason said to him "Hey Malc, that's your fourth can, what's all the rush?"

"Oops, sorry mummy" he called back, and belched again.

Pete looked at me across the table "Don't tell Karen, for god's sake"

Pete was right, if I'd spoken to Karen about it, she would be on the phone straightaway to Pete's missus, and then all hell would break loose.

"Don't worry, I won't" I said. Well I couldn't could I, he's my mate.

Malc ambled out of the kitchen and went back to his chair, then plonked himself down heavily and popped another can of cider.

"Cheers" he said, and promptly missed his mouth and managed to pour half a can of cider down his shirt.

"Oh crap" he said poetically, and we all fell about laughing.

Pete looked across at me, smiled and shook his head, discussion over.

The game carried on and we dealt the cards as the conversation continued.

"A strange thing happened to me once" said Tony, as he reached over to pick up his cards "it was on a plane, when I was in America about five or six years ago" and he sat back as he examined the hand he'd been dealt.

"I've never been out of England" dribbled Malc as he drained the now half empty can of cider.

"No" I said "You're an idiot once you've had a drink, they wouldn't let you on a plane" and with that I turned back to Tony "So go on, what happened?"

Tony started to tell us, as he continued playing his cards "Well, like I said, I went to the States, I was doing a tour of the West Coast. I'd persuaded work to let me have all of my holidays at once, it was a month, a whole month away. And so I packed my bags and got myself on a cheap flight out to San Francisco, it was absolutely brilliant, what a city that is. I spent a whole week there seeing the sights and I did the lot. I can still remember, it was about the sixth or seventh day that I'd been there, it was late morning and I'd had some breakfast in a little coffee shop that looked out onto a small park, right in the city centre.

It was a really nice day, so after I'd eaten I went outside and bought a newspaper and then went over to the park to sit out in the sun and have a read and relax, the last few days had been a bit hectic and that day I was in 'chill' mood. The newspaper was a large thick affair, a great big wad of a paper, I think it was called the 'San Francisco Times'. It had lots of different sections in it, newspapers within newspapers with all sorts of different topics, from politics to finance, along with housing and gardening and travel. I sat on a park bench and divided it up into the sections which interested me. There was even a colour photographic magazine, I can remember reading that first. Eventually I came to the 'travel section'. I skimmed through the pages and there was nothing really interesting in it, but about half way through I suddenly stopped. I'd seen something, and it was only just registering in my brain. So I turned back a couple of pages and there it was, an advertisement in the top left hand corner of the page, only a small advert, about two inches square, and it read...

'Hawaii for $150' with a telephone number and underneath 'Ring Suntime Travel'.

And I looked at it and I thought 'Hawaii...umm', and then something suddenly struck me. 'One hundred and fifty dollars' was only about a hundred pounds at the time. Hawaii for a hundred quid, what an absolute bargain!

Hawaii was never on my list of places to go, but the notion struck me, when on earth would I ever have the chance to go there again, probably never. And it's an awfully long way from England to Hawaii.

I was later to find out, that because Hawaii is an American State , flights there are actually looked upon as internal flights, and hence the price. Nice one America.

So I thought about it, got a bit excited, and then I made a decision. Straight across from me was a phone booth, so I walked over to it, picked up the phone and rang 'Suntime Travel'.

The phone was immediately answered.

"Hello there, this is Suntime Travel and this is Judy speaking. And how can I help you today" a voice sang out.

I smiled, I just loved the enthusiasm, and that's America, where the customer is king.

"Oh hello" I said "I wonder if you could help me please."

"Oh, I sure do hope so sir, and what can 'we' do for 'you' today?"

How bloody wonderful.

"Well, actually" I said "I'm thinking of booking a holiday".

"A what sir?" she sort of asked.

"A holiday"

"What's that again sir?"

"A holiday, I'm thinking of booking a 'holiday'..." I was repeating myself now.

"Oh" she suddenly exclaimed "Oh, you mean a 'Hall-i-day'. You want to book a 'Hall-i-day'. What you mean is 'a vacation'. I get it now sir" and she laughed.

"Err, yes" I said. "Well actually, I want to possibly book a flight to Hawaii, I saw your advert in the newspaper".

"No problem sir, we do have availability" at that point I thought she was going to burst into song.

I continued "Yes okay, but the thing is, I'm visiting San Francisco for the first time and I'm not sure of my bearings, so could you tell me where your offices actually are, and if I can find them, I'll call in."

She giggled "Oh, I just do love how you talk" and then she giggled again "Well sir, how about if you tell me where you are, and I'll just try to give you some directions"

"Okay, hang on a minute" I said, and I heard her giggle again as I looked around for some street signs. Then I said to her "Right, okay. I'm somewhere near the corner of Union and 6th. Yes that's it, Union and 6th."

"Well sir, you are actually standing right in front of us" and now she was laughing, probably at me.

She continued "There's a twenty storey grey building right in front of you with a silver and glass revolving door. Enter the building and catch the elevator up to the eleventh floor, our offices are right there"

"See you in a mo" I said.

"Pardon sir?"

"Never mind, I'm on my way" and off I went.

Five minutes later and I walked into the offices of 'Suntime Travel'. There were two girls in there, typing away

"Hi" I said "I've just spoken to you on the phone".

A blonde girl, thirty something, spun around with a big smile in place, she'd just been talking to her colleague.

"Hey" she said "It's 'you', you're the guy with the accent".

I laughed "Oh do you think so"?

"Yes" she said "I just love you're accent, it's 'so' funny"

I laughed again "Well no" I said "Actually, I think you'll find that 'you're' the one with the funny accent"

"And how's that sir?" she said and she glanced at her colleague who was also full of smiles and white teeth.

"Okay" I said "Tell me, where am I from? And I grinned at her.

"You're English" she replied. Good girl.

Then I asked her "And where are you from?"

"I'm American" she said.

"And what language do you speak?"

"Err...English" she replied.

"Yes" I said "and that's my language, so you're speaking 'English' with an American accent" and I pointed my finger at her "Am I right?"

Her colleague burst out laughing "He's got you there Judy. Nice one 'Englishman' and she raised her hand and gave me the 'high five'.

You just don't get this sort of banter on the high street back in Bolton.

But it was all in fun, and Judy laughed too.

"You got me there sir" she said "And yes, I'm Judy, Hi there".

So we got to the business in hand, and I produced the newspaper with their advert in it.

"There" I said pointing to the advertisement "Hawaii for 150 Dollars"

"Ah yes" she said, still with the big smile "Well sir, actually it's 'from' a hundred and fifty dollars".

"Oh" I said "It's like that is it. It doesn't say 'from' in your advert".

Judy just beamed back at me, unperturbed and a true professional. "Well let's just have a look for you sir and we'll see what we can come up with. Could you just tell me please, when do you actually want to go?"

I said "I want to go when it's one hundred and fifty dollars" and I shrugged my shoulders.

Her colleague burst out laughing "Nice one Englishman" she said and she gave me the 'high five' once more.

Fortunately for me, Judy had a sense of humour too, and with her big smile she went over to a computer and pressed some buttons, then she looked over.

"If I said there was a flight for Honolulu going out tomorrow afternoon at three, and there was just one seat left, and that seat is a hundred and fifty bucks, could you be on it?"

"I sure could" I said in my best American, and we both laughed and the deal was done.

The next day, at three, I was on a plane heading for Hawaii.

Hawaii was wonderful, absolutely.

I arrived at the airport, strolled through customs, and then amid the swaying palm trees, I jumped straight into a taxi and headed for Waikiki Beach. I asked the Taxi driver if he knew a decent hotel that was fairly central but definitely not too expensive.

"Yes sir" he said smartly "Yes I do".

About fifteen minutes or so later, we pulled up outside the 'Waikiki Circle Hotel'. We both got out of the car and I followed the driver into the lobby as he went over to the reception and spoke to the girl there behind the desk.

Then he waved me over "Yep, I've got you a reservation, sir".

I thanked him and then paid him for the taxi and his time. I gave him some money, plus a tip, plus a tip for his time, and then a 'thank you very much tip'. Well that's America, god bless 'em.

He waved the receptionist goodbye, and yes, he would probably be getting a tip from the hotel too.

I was given a room with a great view of Waikiki Beach. The climate was so good that all I wanted to do was get out there and get into the sun, so I got changed straightaway and bounced out of the hotel and onto the beach. The sun, the sand, the sea and those wonderful waves that only Hawaii can produce in such abundance.

I spent an hour or so out there and then finally decided to return to the hotel. On my way back I walked past a car and motorbike rental firm, and I stopped to look at their 'prized' rental. It was a 70's open top Cadillac, which had been sprayed bright pink with a folded back white roof. All the seats and leather work were pink and it had a large white steering wheel. There was a sign on the bonnet that read 'See the Island in Style'. I shook my head, the car was without doubt, bloody awful.

But what grabbed my attention was the row of 100cc motorbikes that were lined up at the side of the Cadillac. I stood there for a moment and thought about it as an idea popped into my head. 'Yes, what a good way to see the island'.

I walked into the showroom and saw 'the man' and twenty minutes later I was on two wheels".

Tony then looked across the card table at Pete, "a 100cc is about my limit Pete".
"And mine now" replied Pete as he raised his glass.

Tony continued with his story.

"I had the best of times ever on that little motorbike, I tell you, it was great. Every morning after breakfast I would set off around the Island. All I ever wore was a pair of shorts, a pair of sandals and a pair of sunglasses. I stuck a towel on the rear pannier and I was off, then I'd ride out of Waikiki and onto the Coast road. Every day I'd travel a bit further and find yet another beach. I would be riding along and suddenly take a turn around a bend and stop, and there in front of me was another fantastic white sandy beach with that wonderful surf just rolling in. I've never felt so free in my life.

I did that for a week, and I eventually made my way right around the whole island. I had a great time there, I visited Pearl Harbour too, and that was really memorable.

"Did you ever do any Surfing?" asked Jason "I've always fancied trying that, it looks great".

"Oh yes. I tried it, once" said Tony. He popped the can that Malc had just stuck in front of him on his way back from the fridge, again.

"I tried Surfing" continued Tony "It was my second day out on the bike. I found a wonderful beach and I rode the bike down there and parked up, then I grabbed my towel and headed for the sand. It was beautiful, and I must have sat there for over an hour watching the surfers swim out to deeper water and 'hang' there, just waiting for the next good wave. When they saw a good one coming in they would all line up and when the moment was right, they would paddle their boards to the crest of it, then topple over the edge and let the wave bring them in as they rode the wall of blue water. It was superb to watch.

In the end it got to me and I decided that I had to give it a go. I looked down the beach and saw a large open straw hut, and outside it, stacked up like dominoes were about thirty or forty surf boards. There was a big sign stuck in the sand which read 'Surfboards for Hire'.

So I walked over to the hut and looked inside. Sitting there was the biggest man I think I've ever seen.

He was a true Hawaiian, and he must have weighed somewhere around thirty stone.

He had long dark hair tied back in a ponytail and wore a pair of bright multicoloured shorts that must have been the biggest pair of shorts in the world. He was actually sitting across two wooden stools, he was so large, and he just sat there and looked at me, and never smiled.

I stood there in front of him and finally, he nodded his head in recognition.

"I wonder if could hire a surfboard please" I asked.

"You Australian?" he grunted as he tried to place my accent.

"No, I'm English" I replied.

He simply nodded and lifted up his huge arm and pointed down the line of boards...

"Half way down...yellow board"

So I went down the line and finally found the board, it was slightly taller than me, maybe that's how it works. Anyway, I picked it out and the big 'Hawaiian' guy nodded and waved me back.

"Twenty dollar" he said, and he held out his huge hand.

Who was I to argue? I paid the man.

So I'd sorted myself out and I decided to give it a go. I'd watched the other surfers all afternoon and realized that there was a tried and tested method of entering the water with a surfboard. The waves hit the shore in Hawaii with the regularity of a clock and on that particular day the waves were anywhere between fifteen to twenty foot high. It seemed that the art of entering the water was in the timing. You dive in at the base of the oncoming wave and let the full force of it wash over you. Then you pop up on the other side of it and quickly get on your board and paddle like hell before the next wave comes along. Once you get behind the swell you're okay, and you just float over the incoming waves and 'hang' there waiting to catch a good one. Well that's the theory anyway.

With that in mind, I picked up my board and headed for the surf. I stood on the water's edge with the others and when they all charged at the next incoming wave, so did I. I hit the bottom of the wave and went through it and then I held my breath as I pushed on and came up on the other side, and then along with the other surfers, I slid onto my board and paddled away. So far, so bloody good.

With a lot of effort, I got past the next oncoming wave, and I paddled on and only finally stopped when the others did. I'd got myself into safe water and I slowly got my breath back as we all floated up and down, waiting as the inbound waves passed under us and went on to turn into surf as they hit the shore. I 'hung' there in the rolling swell for about thirty minutes and I watched as the other surfer's lined up for a good wave and then they'd go for it. As the wave approached, they would lie flat on their board and paddle as fast as they could as the wave caught up with them. As the foaming swell caught them, they would go with it and let it carry them over the crest and onwards, and as soon as the wave got hold of them they would quickly get onto their knees, gain balance and then stand up and ride the wild surf.

I'd watched all this and quickly realized that I could be out of my depth here, in more ways than one. It didn't take me long to figure out, that standing up on a surfboard as it plummeted almost vertically down the side of twenty foot moving wave was going to be rather difficult. There was also the small problem, that after riding that surfboard, balancing like a ballet dancer, I was going to be carried along by the wave as it smashed me onto the shore with a phenomenal force. Well, it just wasn't going to happen. Well it wasn't going to happen to me, who was I trying to kid.

The thing was, I was now out there and I was a bit stuck. I was 'at sea' and somehow I had to get back. It could be a bit of a problem.

Well there was only one way, follow the crowd.

I realized that there was not a heaven's chance of me returning to the beach 'surfer style', but I figured that if I followed the others and I could 'catch the wave' with them, all I had to do was just hang on to the board as the wave brought me in . And hey, if it went well, I might even try kneeling up.

So there I was, and then somebody shouted something, God only knows what, but it obviously meant that 'a good wave' was coming because about ten of them set off paddling like the clappers. I never looked back. I set off after them like a bat out of hell. To my amazement I caught them up, I might not know anything about surfing, but I must be a bloody good paddler.

We were all in a line now and I still hadn't looked behind me, as far as I was concerned it was going to be 'follow my leader', so I watched the others as I felt the movement in the water under us as we all dipped and then were suddenly raised up onto the top of a huge wave. We all tipped over the edge and rolled away down into the surf, away we went.

It was like being on a liquid rollercoaster and down I went, almost vertically. I wrapped my arms around the board and clung on for dear life, I couldn't believe the momentum and the power of it all. I was being hurtled forwards at a tremendous speed, it was like being shot out of a cannon. I glanced to the side of me, and I was amazed. There to my right were five of the surfers, all standing up on their boards, arms outstretched and flying across the surf with perfect balance, and I watched in awe as they skimmed along the front of the wall of water.

That was the last I saw of them, because at that moment my board completely flipped over and instead of me riding on top it, the board was now sort of riding on top of me. The thing was, it was now me under the water, this was all the wrong way about. I remember screaming a bit as I headed for the beach, upside down and at speed, I just clung on like a bat.

This carried on for about ten very long seconds and then the board did a hand stand, dug itself into the water, and then started to summersault all the way back to the beach with me attached to it, I just hung on for grim death. Why, I don't know because it would have been simpler to let the bloody thing go.

The wave finally dumped me on the beach and withdrew. I was lying under the board, and as I lifted it off me and tried to stand up, the next monster wave hit the shore. It hit the board at a hell of a pace, and the board hit me and smashed me right in the face.

I'll tell you something, I was quickly going off surfboards.

As the wave withdrew, and took with it a reasonable amount of my blood, which was now pouring from my nose. I decided to hot foot it before wave number three arrived and beat the crap out of me again.

I slowly dragged the board up the beach and hobbled all the way back to the big Hawaiian. He was still sitting across his two stools, but was now shaking with laughter.

"You can have it back" I said to him, and I dropped the wet board at his feet. It was now yellow with red blood spatters all over it.

The Hawaiian was still laughing, with his big grin and big teeth and his huge head bobbing up and down along with his massive body.

"English" he said, and he shook his head "Man, that was the best I've ever seen"

I stood there like an idiot, a battered and bleeding idiot.

"English, I've seen all sorts of tricks done on the surfboard, 'and I thought I'd seen 'em all, but man, I ain't ever seen anybody come in like that. You crazy bastard, man"

"I didn't mean too" I stuttered.

"I 'know' that, I know you didn't mean too, but you bloody well did. And hey man, you hung on to that damn board like it was a women" and he rolled his head back and carried on laughing.

"I nearly broke my bloody neck" I said.

"Hey, you nearly broke your bloody dick" he said as he laughed "But hey, thank god the boards alright, okay?" he said as he rocked on his two stools.

The fat bastard was taking the piss.

I stared at Tony across the table "What did you do then" I asked him, I'd not even looked at my cards.

"I walked off" he said "I got on my motor bike and buggered off back to Waikiki, I needed a drink"

"Well have one now" interrupted Malc, and he dropped another can into Tony's lap as he returned from the fridge yet again.

Across the table, Jason juggled his cards "What's the night life like over there?" he asked.

Tony smiled.

"Waikiki Beach is a bit wild, well it was back then. The first night I was there, well I decided to go out, you know how it is. It would have been about eight o' clock and that's pretty early in Waikiki. I got showered and changed and out I went for a stroll. It was my first night and I wanted to have a look around. I walked out of the Hotel and down the front towards the town centre, it was beautiful there. The sun was just going under and the sky was all pink and yellow. I walked along the front and watched the sea go darker and change colour as the sun disappeared. I could feel the warm breeze rolling in off the sea, Hawaii has a wonderful climate. I crossed the road and headed along into the town centre, it's only a short walk. I strolled past some shops, glancing through the windows when suddenly I heard somebody laughing, and I looked around to see two absolutely strikingly beautiful girls walking towards me, they were both Eastern Asian or somewhere like that and they were stunning. They both wore short silk patterned dresses, split at the side, one in deep blue and the other in turquoise. Their dark hair was piled up on top of their heads in smart chignons, and both wore beautiful make-up which made their faces look absolutely exquisite. I was slightly in awe.

Then to my complete amazement, they both said "Hi" to me and giggled and smiled, and then one of them said "How 'are' you?"

I looked behind me to see who they were speaking too, there was nobody else there and I felt a right imbecile.

Both the girls burst out laughing at this.

"Are you okay" they said, well one of them said, I was past caring and they just kept on smiling.

'How friendly' I was thinking to myself, and then in horror it suddenly it struck me. They didn't actually know me, and I thought 'Oh god, they must have mistaken me for somebody else'. That sort of thing happens to me all the time. 'Oh bloody hell', how embarrassing.

So I grinned back at them like an idiot and pretended that I knew them.

"How are you doing?" I replied, trying to act cool.

The girl in turquoise put her hand on my arm.

"Hey great" she said, and then "See you later maybe" and with beautiful smiles and more laughing, off they walked.

I just stood there, still trying to figure out what had just happened, and I hadn't a clue.

Anyway, after a moment, reality kicked in and I continued to meander into town. I turned a sharp right and was suddenly walking down the main street to some sort of square, and it all looked really good, loads of restaurants on either side, along with a smattering of bars.

So on I walked, first on the right was an English Pub 'The Red Rose', and that looked okay. I decided that I would be in there later for some good English beer, yes I certainly would.

I stood there for a moment looking around the square, and there directly in front of me, about 30 yards away was a large, brightly lit bar-restaurant. The downstairs was some Chinese or Asian sort of place, but directly above, with a lovely balcony that looked out over the whole of the square, was a bar. I looked up and saw the sign, written in large fluorescent red letters, the words 'Joe's Bar'.

I stood there thinking 'That's got to be the place'.

And I was just about to cross the road and head there, when suddenly somebody shouted "Hi".

I turned around. It was a girl, she had just walked around the corner and now she was walking straight up to me. Dark hair again, and beautiful, again, she was wearing a deep red top and a black fitted skirt, high heels and beautiful legs, and it struck me that I could have possibly just spoken to two of her sisters.

"Hey, hi there" she said, with the most beautiful smile "How are you doing?"

"Err, I'm okay. I'm just having a stroll about, and how are you?" I said, trying to be more than pleasant, and again, a little bit 'cool'..."

"Hey, I'm great" she said, and then "I might see you later" and she laughed as she walked away and across the square and headed for the Red Rose Pub.

It struck me that I must have a bloody double somewhere in this town, this was weird.

With that, I walked across the square and headed for 'Joe's Bar'.

At the side of the Chinese restaurant by the main entrance were some wide marble steps that led to upstairs and another, smaller red sign above them directing you up to 'Joe's Bar'.

It was early and still quiet and so I went up the steps and walked through some swing doors and into the really, really smart bar. However, at that hour the place was completely empty and was waiting to begin the night's business. But it was one hell of a nice place.

I stood in the entrance and looked around. A silver haired man, probably in his mid sixties, was behind the bar, he was sorting out the glasses, a towel in his hand. He glanced up at me for a second, but didn't say anything. I made a snap decision, and headed for the bar.

I pulled up a tall stool and plonked myself down. At the side of me was a large open window which overlooked the square. Now that I was a confirmed customer, the barman put down his towel and came over to me.

"Hi buddy" he said "and what can I get you?"

"A bottle of Bud please" I replied in my best English accent.

He gave me a second look "You Australian?" he said.

"No, I'm English" I replied, and inwardly sighed.

"You don't sound like a Brit"

"I'm from the North, we're a bit tougher up there" I said, and then I laughed.

"Well nice to meet you pal" and he actually reached over and shook my hand.

"I'm Joe" he said "and this is my bar".

So I introduced myself too, and Joe passed me a bottle of ice cold beer.

He said "Cheers buddy" then he went back to his towel and glasses.

"Nice place" I said as I looked around.

"Yeah, well it's early yet. This place will fill up in the next couple of hours, my bar staff will arrive in" and he glanced down at his watch "in the next half an hour. I'm just sorting things out and getting the show on the road" and he smiled "When did you arrive?"

"Today" I said "It's my first night out, I'm just wandering around seeing what's happening".

"Yeah right" he said, and he started to fill up the beer fridge with shiny new bottles.

The beer tasted good and I looked out of the open window and down onto the square. People were out and milling about as the downtown started to come to life.

The Red Rose Pub was across the road and standing outside the pub where four girls, all beautifully dressed, dark hair piled high, and all stunning. And I watched as two more girls approached them, they were all chattering away and laughing. I started to look around the square and noticed that there were several other girls, all talking to each other and that they too were all beautifully dressed and made up immaculately. It struck me that there must be some party or festival on somewhere and that they must all be meeting up at the Red Rose Pub.

As I gazed out of the window, I said out loud "I'll tell you something Joe, you sure do have some beautiful women here in Hawaii".

"Ah right" he replied, and he put the four bottles of beer that he'd been holding, back down on the bar with a clunk, and then he came over to me.

He looked straight at me and said "I see I'm going to have to give you 'Uncles Joe's talk' about the girls around here".

And suddenly, of course I realized, and I said "Jesus, they're prostitutes. They're all on the game".

"Yep, they're all on the game" he replied and he smiled back at me "Hey don't get me wrong, they're allowed to. There's no law against prostitution over here, and that's how these girls make a living"

"Right" I said "Well, yes I've actually spoken to some of them already tonight, and they seem really nice girls"

"They are" he said "they're lovely, I know most of them, they wander around the town all night and the square gets really busy later, they like to hang around the pub over there" and he nodded in the direction of The Red Rose. "It's all okay as long as they don't congregate, the police don't like that, it's not good for tourism and it's not what we want Hawaii to been known for. If more than several of them stand around on a street corner, the police usually move them on, but there's never really a problem, it's all good natured. They like to sit outside the Red Rose, it's a pub and it's allowed."

I looked back out of the window and down on to the square.

"Well I'll tell you something Joe, those girls, they're all really pretty".

"Yes maybe" he said "but just let me tell you something my friend. Here on Hawaii we've got every of sexual disease going, a lot of people pass through here. We're a holiday destination and we're a port, and we're also a naval base. And what's more, 'Aids' like everywhere else at the moment has also arrived on this island."

I gulped, that was enough for me. Joe saw this and continued to enlighten me even further.

"Later tonight, you'll see those girls dragging off guys that have drunk far too much, and in the morning those same guys will wake up with 'more' than just a hangover, you get it?"

"Jesus" I replied.

"Yeah, Jesus indeed. You take care over here or you could go back home with something that you don't like, and a lot of people do. But hey, it's just like anywhere else in the world, from Vegas to Bangkok. Europe's probably the same too".

I grinned, and I said "Yes Joe, you're absolutely right. It goes on all over the world"

"World's oldest profession" he said and he shrugged, and then he went back to his glasses and his beer.

I put my cards back down on the table and took a sip of 'Jack', and looked across at Tony.

"So how did you go on?" I said with a sly grin. I was trying to get the lowdown.

Tony looked over his cards and smiled back at me "Well, I did get to know some the girls, but nothing happened."

"Yeah right, it's me you're talking to" I said, with a bit of added sarcasm.

"Seriously, nothing happened, but I did have a lot of laughs with the girls. I soon made a habit of starting off at 'Joe's bar' every night. I'd go and have a chat with him and spend an hour or so in there, he was a really great guy. Then I'd go and try a few different places around Waikiki and then later on I would head back to the bars around the square and finally head for the Red Rose Pub. By then, I'd have had a few drinks and would be quite chatty. I would go in for a drink and then go back outside and talk to the girls. They used to sit along the wall outside the pub and we would have a chat and a laugh. They all used to make fun of my accent and after a few days they were all mimicking me. It was really funny to hear them saying things like 'Ello luv' and 'Where've yer bin' in my Northern England accent. They all thought it was hilarious.

One night though, I got steamed. I'd been out early, I'd had a few drinks in the afternoon so I was on a 'bit of a roll', then I went out at night and by the time I got to the Red Rose I was 'rocking' drunk. I staggered up to the pub and to the girls, there were about ten of them there, all sat on the pub wall outside. I tripped up over the pavement, and when they saw the state I was in they all shrieked with laughter.

One of the girls shouted "Eeh Tony luv, where've yer bin" and they all fell about laughing at me.

"I'll get us all a drink" I shouted as I turned around and staggered into the pub.

Five minutes later I staggered back out again, with a large bottle of 'Jack Daniels' in my hand. I sat myself down in the middle of the girls and we 'passed' the bottle around. The girls got merry too as we drank more and more. I don't remember much, but I know we all laughed a lot.

After the best part of an hour however, I do remember making an announcement.

In a garbled voice, I slurred "Ladies, I am really, really drunk. So I am going to go back to my hotel, and so my lovelies, which one of you is coming back with me for some sex?"

I vaguely remember that they all burst out laughing.

One of the girls said "Tony, you're too drunk, you won't even remember it" and another said "Tony, you couldn't even manage it" and they all laughed even more.

I remember standing up "So I'll take that as a 'No' then" I slurred again as I swayed about.

The girls had a group discussion and chattered away between themselves for a couple of minutes, and it was decided that three of them would take me back to my hotel because I was on the verge of collapse. And off we went.

Through the drunken haze, I remember saying to them "Will we be having sex?"
The girls said "No Tony"
"Not even a kiss?"
"No Tony"
And that was the last thing that I remembered.

And so, the next morning arrived and I woke up, well bits of me did.

I lay there in bed for about five minutes before I could even open my eyes, and when I did the shock of it made me close them again immediately. Bright sunshine and a hangover just don't mix. So I lay there for another ten minutes and practised blinking. I felt awful, very ill and very dehydrated. And also, I realized that I was completely naked.

After about half an hour of just lying there, trying to remember what had happened, I made an important decision. It was coffee, that was what I needed, good, strong American coffee. I looked over the side of the bed and my clothes were all there, all nicely folded, with my sandals placed neatly at the side of them. I rolled over and off the bed and slowly and painfully got dressed. I hadn't the energy to shower or do anything else, I just put my clothes and sandals on and headed out of the door and into the lift, and I went downstairs to the breakfast bar. The lift doors glided open as I walked through the hotel reception. The girl behind the reception desk gave me a very strange look, I sort of smiled at her and she sort of smiled back, but she still stared at me. It was a bit weird really. I walked through to the breakfast bar and there was a girl behind the bar wearing a pretty floral dress with the 'Waikiki Circle Hotel' emblem embroidered on her breast pocket, she was busy serving out breakfasts and taking orders.

She looked up at me, and then abruptly glanced back and gave me a second look, and I suddenly began to wonder what exactly had happened last night.

"Hi there" I said to her "Could I have a large cup of very strong coffee please?"
She looked at me, sort of curiously and said "Yes sir."
"And could somebody bring it out to me on the terrace please?"
Again, "Yes sir, no problem"
Then I casually asked her "Did I, err. Did I see you last night at all, late on?"
She smiled back at me and said "No sir, you didn't see me at all last night".

"Oh, alright" I said, but I had a feeling that there was something was going on, maybe she'd heard about me coming back to the hotel 'in a bit of a state' and with three girls in tow.

"I'll send your coffee out to you on the terrace sir" and she smiled sweetly.

So I went outside and sat myself down at a table in the corner, in the shade. To tell the truth, I had to have my coffee served out there because my shaking hands couldn't have carried it. Within a couple of minutes the waiter arrived with my coffee, thank god, it was a great big cup of America's finest.

"Your coffee sir" said the now beaming waiter, and he put the large cup down in front of me.

"Thanks for this" I said, looking up at him wearily "I had a bit of a night of it last night".

"Oh really sir" he replied, grinning from ear to ear, again with a sort of 'knowing' look.

"Did I see you" I said to him "last night?"

"Oh no sir, I don't do the late shift, I have a family"

"Oh right" I said "Well thanks very much for the coffee"

He leaned over to me slightly "I'll bring you out another in about ten minutes" he said in a quiet voice "and if you need a refill, just give me a nod".

"Good man" I replied. He would definitely be getting a tip.

He turned and walked away, and I caught him smiling to himself and shaking his head as he headed back to the kitchen.

What the hell happened last night?

I sat there for about an hour whilst I recovered. The other guests who came down for breakfast just gave me one look and immediately turned away. And I sat there thinking 'Oh God, what on earth have I done?

An hour, and several cups of coffee later, I felt recovered enough to go back to my room to have a shower and a shave and put some fresh clothes on, and then try and do something with my day.

I stood up and slunk back through reception and headed for the lift, and again the receptionist stared at me as I walked past her. I got into the lift and sloped back to my room, by then I was feeling a bit guilt ridden. Anyway, back to my room and I went straight into the bathroom.

I turned on the shower, and then I picked up my razor to have a shave. I turned to the hand basin and turned on the hot water tap and looked into the mirror. And there, written across my forehead in bright red lipstick were the words...'Good Morning'.

That evening, I drank coke. But eventually, I added some Bacardi to it and then I finally headed back to the square and The Red Rose Pub. I had recovered by then and of course, I'd got my sense of humour back. As I approached the pub, the girls, who were all sat outside on the wall, they spotted me and started to chant "Tony...Tony...Tony..."

People walking by must have wondered who the hell I was. I walked over to them, smiling and shaking my head. One of the girls started to sing "He's a Lover Man" and then the three girls who had taken me back to the hotel started to chant "We've seen you naked".

I plonked myself down on the wall in between them.

"What happened?" I asked, like an idiot.

"Nothing" grinned one of the girls who had taken me back to the hotel.

"Nothing, really?" I said

"Yes really. You where so drunk, you didn't know what day it was" she laughed "So we carried you back to your hotel, you'd passed out by then. We had to ask the receptionist for your room number and key, she wasn't happy, she thought we were going to have some sort of orgy".

The girls all laughed out loud at that "If we'd have had an orgy Tony, you 'still' wouldn't know anything about it" and more laughter. "So we took off your clothes and tucked you up in bed"

One of the other girls said "Hey, you've got a really nice body Tony" and they all giggled.

I held up my hands in gesture "Well thank you ladies, and thanks for a great night and well 'whatever', but tonight's my last night, so I'm going to go into the pub and get us all some drinks, but not Jack Daniels".

They all cheered and clapped their hands.

I went into the Red Rose and returned a few minutes later with six bottles of cold white wine.

There was more applause and giggling from the girls as I passed the wine around. We sat on the wall for an hour or so, talking and having fun, and then I had to get up and finally leave. Hugs and kisses off all of them, and then they waved me goodbye. They were really, really lovely girls, I'll always remember them, they were good fun.

The next morning I got up and went downstairs to the terrace for a leisurely breakfast. Then I went back to my room and packed. I grabbed my bags and went down to reception, paid my bill and ordered a taxi. Within an hour I was back at the airport and a couple of hours later I was on the plane flying back to San Francisco. It was a leisurely flight and I sat there looking out of the window thinking about my time in Hawaii. It was a brilliant place, there are actually three or four islands that make up Hawaii and at some time I intend to go back there and see them all, it sure was paradise.

Hours later, the plane finally landed at San Francisco and I grabbed my bags and walked into the airport, and once again, it was decision time.

I could go back to San Francisco, but I'd seen all I wanted to see. Los Angeles was another option, but it was big and brash and I just wasn't in the mood for it. I'd just been to Hawaii and the 'beach' was still in my blood. So I went to get a cup of coffee and then I sat down in one of the lounges and took out my travel book, 'my bible'.

Half an hour later and I'd made a decision, and 'San Diego' was to be my next destination. It would be warm and sunny, and it was all the way down to the Mexican border. Yes, more sunshine and more beaches, great stuff.

I stood up and went for a walk around the airport to check out which airlines flew down to San Diego and at what time, and I finally approached one of the airline's ticket desks and bought a one way ticket for fifty dollars, which seemed incredibly cheap. The girl behind the airline desk explained to me that though there was a plane leaving in half an hour, the tickets were sold on a sort of 'first come...first served' basis and that all the tickets had numbers on them and your number would be called as the plane filled up. If I didn't get on this plane, there would be another in an hour and a half. So for ten minutes I stood in a line at the passenger gate, waiting and hoping. The plane was almost full, when suddenly they called out the last three passenger numbers...'302...303...304'. I was number '303' and I got onto the plane. 'Brilliant' I thought. Though little did I realize that things were going to get a rather entertaining.

The three of us, the last three, got onto the plane. We were shown our seats, which were all aisle seats because we were the last ones on. The engines were already running with a steady whirr and I put my bags in one of the overhead lockers and sat down and nodded to the two people sat on my left. That done, I got myself comfortable and fastened my seat belt and leaned back. It was a short flight really, I suppose about hour or so but I can't really remember. I just closed my eyes and decided to 'sleep' through the flight.

With my eyes closed, I heard the flight attendant approaching. She was checking the seat belts as another attendant went through the safety code over the intercom.

'No problem' I thought to myself.

I'd heard plenty of flight safety and emergency demonstrations on too many flights, and my safety belt was fastened correctly, so no problem, for me.

The attendant approached "seat belts...seat belts" she repeated in a mannerly and efficient voice, and she spoke so softly, I knew I didn't even have to open my eyes, and I didn't. She just checked our row and passed on, by then I was almost nodding off.

Behind us, she continued "seat belts, yes okay" she almost whispered.

And then in an almost fading voice, she checked the next row "seat belts...seat belts" and then a silence, and then "Excuse me sir, seat belts".

And the calm and the quiet of the moment was suddenly broken as I heard a man's voice say

"Hey, just leave me alone 'okay'!"

I opened my eyes with a bit of a jolt, I didn't know whether I'd heard right, and I looked at the passenger across the aisle, who was already looking behind us to see what was going on. He looked back at me and raised his eyebrows.

I heard the flight attendant say again "Excuse me sir, seat belt please".

There was a moment's silence, and then I heard "I've just told you lady, leave me alone, okay."

Oh dear me.

"Excuse me sir" repeated the flight attendant "but you've got to fasten your seat belt"

Again the reply "Listen to what I'm telling you lady, will you please just fuck off and leave me alone, coz I ain't wearing no fucking seat belt. Okay".

Oh dear me indeed, and I loosened my own seatbelt so that I could turn around and see what the hell was going on.

Two rows back, and also sat in an aisle seat, was the 'idiot'.

About nineteen years old, give or take a year, and there he sat, the original fool.

A right twerp, who was wearing a baseball cap on backwards, of course, and a red 'Che Guevara' T-shirt with old 'Che' giving the 'V' sign and the words 'fuck you all' emblazoned on the front. The 'idiot' sat in his seat with a stupid, indignant expression on his stupid face, and the expression said it all. Basically, it was that 'I'm right, and you and everybody else are wrong. And also, I can do whatever I like and you can all go and fuck yourselves, Amen'.

He had of course, also been drinking and had decided to become the 'angry young man' and the booze had made him arrogant and ignorant and very rude.

Rude and embarrassing, not only to the flight assistant, but he was also beginning to upset and cause discomfort to the surrounding passengers.

God bless her, the flight attendant remained cool and professional, she continued to talk to him.

"Please sir, you have to wear your seatbelt. It's for your own safety".

The idiot cut her off abruptly "Are you deaf or just fuckin' stupid lady, I'm not going to wear a fuckin' seatbelt and that's that. So fuck off...and take off".

Clever wording that, the rhyming of fuck off, and take off. What a clever boy.

The flight attendant stood back. This guy was going to be a problem, and a problem that she wasn't going to be able to solve. The plane's engines were beginning to rev up, and she knew that they couldn't take off until they had gone through all the passenger safety checks. She turned and started to walk back up the aisle and was met halfway along by the chief flight attendant who was coming to find out what was holding everything up. They both had a short conversation and the chief flight assistant peered over her assistant's shoulder and looked down the aisle to locate the offender.

She spoke to her assistant "Okay, let's go and see" she said.

So they both came back down the aisle, and the chief flight attendant approached the idiot.

She leaned over to him "Excuse me sir, may I have a word?"

"Oh fuck me" said the idiot in a louder voice "now the fucking cavalry's arrived".

"Excuse me sir" she said firmly "but there's no need to swear. We're just trying to do our job, and I have to tell you that International Aviation Regulations state that on take-off, everybody must wear a seatbelt".

The idiot turned to her "What 'is' your problem lady?" He was getting angry now and his voice was getting louder. He was young and drunk and was now becoming threatening.

"Watch my fuckin' lips girl, I ain't wearing a fuckin' seatbelt, for you or anybody else, get it. Now just fuck off and leave me alone".

The chief flight attendant stood upright. She looked at her assistant briefly, and then turned and strode off down the aisle, down to the flight deck. She opened the flight cabin door and went through and closed the door behind her.

A moment later the plane's engines stopped revving and went quiet as the power was turned down.

Suddenly, the flight cabin's door swung open and through it stepped the Pilot, he was the Captain and he was dressed in full uniform and hat to match. He looked across and then proceeded to walk up our aisle, closely followed by his chief flight attendant. He stopped when he got to where the idiot was sitting, and then he spoke.

"Sir, I believe we have a problem".

"Oh Christ, not again, what is wrong with 'you' people?" said the idiot.

"Well, we have a problem sir, and that is that International Aviation Regulations dictate that on take-off, for safety reasons, everyone must fasten their seat belts.

"Oh really" replied the idiot "well you can fuck your regulations".

"The problem is 'Sir', that unless you fasten your seatbelt, we can't take off. And I have to inform you 'Sir', that if we don't take off in the next ten minutes, we will lose our airspace, and if that happens, we won't allowed to take off and the plane will be grounded. And then everybody will have to get off the plane and we will not be able to fly to San Diego until tomorrow.

The idiot just snorted and folded his arms. No, he wasn't going to change his mind.

Suddenly the Captain looked over, something had caught his attention.

And I looked around too, because a couple of rows in front of me, a man had just stood up.

A big, tall man.

He was way over six feet tall and very well built. In his late fifties, with a full head of silver hair and very broad shoulders, and I remember that he wore a cream fitted suit, cool.

And I thought to myself 'my god, he's a big bloke'.

The man stepped into the aisle and walked towards us, he passed by me and continued up the aisle and stopped in front of the captain and looked down at him. Then he put his large hands onto the captain's shoulders.

"Excuse me Sir" he said to the Captain, in a soft southern drawl, and then he gently moved the Captain to one side.

Then he looked down at the idiot and said "Hey you, boy!"

The idiot looked up.

The big man then swung a punch and smashed his fist right into the idiot's face.

And it was one hell of a punch.

The idiot's head hit the back of the seat with such a force that he was catapulted forwards, and the big man caught him on the rebound and smashed him in the face again.

I heard the 'smack' this time. It was like slapping meat with a cricket bat.

And it was at this point that the idiot started to scream. The idiot's hat shot off as he bounced about and the big man then reached down and grabbed him by the hair and dragged him over the seat, and then pummelled the side of the idiot's face three or four times.

In between the screaming, the idiot started to cry and shout "Stop, stop, please stop".

The big man stopped hitting him and pulled the shocked youth upright by his hair. He held him there and looked down into a face that was no longer arrogant or ignorant, it was tearful and shocked and frightened. The idiot was now very sober and shaking.

The big man looked down at him and spoke quietly.

"Listen, you excuse for a piece of shit. I've got a business meeting in San Diego later today, an important business meeting, and I ain't got time to waste on the likes of you. You have been rude and insulting to the crew, and to every passenger on this plane, so listen to me you little bastard, don't let me have to ask you again to fasten that goddamn seat belt you dipshit ...right!"

"Yes, Yes, I'll do it. I'll fasten it now. I'm sorry, I'm sorry, I'll fasten it" spluttered the idiot. He was now more than ready to comply with the rules, and he immediately and very quickly fastened his seatbelt.

The big man let go of the idiot's hair and turned around to the startled captain, it had all happened so fast.

The big man put his hand on the captain's shoulder.

"Sorry about that captain" he said calmly and apologetically.

"That's okay sir" replied the somewhat surprised captain, and then he just shrugged.

The big man turned around and walked back to his seat.

The captain smiled, and then the flight attendants smiled. And I looked around at the other passengers, and they were all smiling too. Things were looking up.

My neighbour across the aisle looked at me and nodded towards the big man and then whispered "He's from Texas".

And that sort of said it all.

I looked back at the idiot, who was now sitting very quietly. His cap was back on his head with the brim pulled down tight so that he didn't have to look at anyone.

The Captain returned to the flight deck and within ten minutes we had taken off and were heading for San Diego. The rest of the flight was pretty uneventful, but everyone seemed to be in quite a jovial mood, especially the flight attendants.

We landed an hour or so later. The idiot was the last person to get off the plane, he just sat there with his cap pulled down over his face until everybody had gone.

And as I got off the plane a thought struck me. Of all the flights that I've ever been on, that was the one that I would definitely never forget.

And with that, Tony reached over and put his cards on the table.

"How's that then?" he said, and he laughed out loud. He'd won the game and he smiled at us all, as he reached over and scooped up all the money which lay waiting for him in the middle of the table.

Nice one Tony.

"You jammy sod" mumbled Malc. He'd lost again and he stood up and returned to the fridge, he was definitely going for it tonight. He came back with yet another can of cider and plonked himself down. The cards were being dealt around the table for another game, but he just sat there, a bit giddy, then he started to smile.

"Hey, I've got one for you" he said, and he started waving his can about.

"What's that?" I said.

"Our Works do last year" and he laughed and hiccupped at the same time "We went to Blackpool".

"The usual mayhem?" said Tony smiling.

"Oh yes, the usual antics, there were thirty of us altogether, we all met at "The Globe"

'The Globe' was the pub at the side of the Mill, which were the premises of the Mail Order Company where Malc had worked for years.

He continued to tell us his tale.

"We all met up at ten in the morning, we had a few beers for breakfast and finally the coach turned up. So we set off at about half past eleven and an hour later we arrived in Blackpool. And here's something different, our Boss came with us this year. That was a turn up for the book, he normally just sends us on our way and gives us a few quid for the drinks, but this year he brought one of his golfing mates along with him and he told us all that 'today' he was officially 'just one of the lads'.

So there you go. He was alright actually, he paid for the coach and the bar tab at 'The Globe', and also he'd organized a meal for us when we got there. So who were we to complain, eh?

Anyway, the coach pulled onto a car park in the middle of Blackpool, and before the driver let us get off the coach, he says he wants 'to have a word'. He tells us that he will be back at the car park at two o' clock in the morning and that he will be leaving at two thirty 'on the dot'. Anybody who's not on the coach by then will get left behind, and that's it.

So we all pile off the coach and into the nearest pub, and that sets the tone for the day.

We all went into the first pub and the Boss bought a round of drinks for everybody and tells us that we're booked into some place called the 'Winsford Hotel' for our Christmas dinner. We've got to be there for around five o'clock and 'if we get split up', because that's what usually happens when a gang of blokes go out, if we get split up 'Everybody' will meet outside the Blackpool Tower Ballroom at five and then we will all go from there to the Hotel. 'Okay everybody' he says. Yes okay.

And off we go.

Four hours and quite a few pubs later, we ambled back to the Tower Ballroom.

And yes we'd all split up by then, but no worries. Believe it or not, the first to get left behind was the Boss and his mate, no surprise there though. Some of our lads are big drinkers and when you get the 'gin and tonic' brigade drinking pints of lager they're always going to have a problem. Anyway we arrived at the Tower in dribs and drabs, and then the Boss and his mate finally turned up and they're both a bit 'worse for wear'. The Boss pulled out a piece of paper which had a 'print out' of a map and directions to the Hotel. It turns out that his secretary has found this place on the internet and has booked it and sorted everything out.

So off we went, and after twenty minutes and a few twists and turns, we finally arrived at

'The Winsford'. We took one look at the place and 'good god', what a hole.

If time travel exists, we were back in the sixties, which was probably the last time this place had seen a lick of paint. Faded and grey, it stood there, a monument to Blackpool's bleaker past. We all just stood there outside the place, thirty of us, and then we all turned to the Boss. Things didn't look good.

Somebody said "We could always go for a curry"

Then somebody said "We could always go for a MacDonald's"

And then somebody else said "You can't get beer in MacDonald's". So that was MacDonald's off the list.

But the Boss said we were not to worry and anyway, it was all booked and paid for, and they were expecting us.

The 'Winsford' it was then.

Inside, it didn't get any better. It was like a time warp, we should have all been wearing flared pants and wide ties. There were carpets in that place that were older than my dad. We walked into 'reception', and sat behind a desk was a fat bloke reading a newspaper.

He looked up at us over his gold rimmed glasses and folded his paper.

"Howdo" he said "Are you the 'Bolton lot?"

"Yes" said the Boss, as he looked around in disbelief.

"I'm Billy, I'm the owner" he continued "I'll just get the wife" and he pressed the buzzer on the top of his desk.

Billy made some small talk about the weather for a couple of minutes, and then his wife, the lovely 'Rona' appeared. Good lord, she could have been a man. Stocky, with bleached blonde hair piled up into some sort of a beehive, she was in her sixties and looked like something from the sixties. She was a bit of a frightener. The woman was square in stature, with bosoms like torpedoes and a face as round as a plate. We all figured that she could have been a miner in a past life.

In shock, we all stepped back a pace.

"Right, you lot" she said "Let's have you all through to the dining room. Come on, follow me, now!"

We did as we were ordered.

We entered the dining room, which was as dated as the rest of the hotel. The floor was covered with an awful red patterned carpet and there was flock wallpaper coming away from the walls at the top and the bottom of every corner of the room. The tables and chairs which were normally arranged around the room for the individual guests, had all been joined together to form one long table with the chairs placed down either side. The table was covered with an off white, floral table cloth and there was worn cutlery from another century. Placed along the centre of the table were menu's made from folded cheap white card with the word 'Menu' printed on the front in small black letters. It seems that the owners of 'The Winsford' must have owned their own printer.

As we all sat down, two teenage girls and an old woman appeared from the kitchen.

Rona then spoke "Me and the girls" and she nodded at the three of them enthusiastically...

"Me and the girls will be looking after you lot this afternoon. So have a look at the menu and we'll be back in five minutes to sort out your drinks and take your food orders. Okay?"

We all nodded and mumbled.

'The girls' disappeared somewhere after Rona gave them their instructions.

We sat down and reached for the menus and read the bill of fare, and then we stopped and looked at one another, and then at the Boss.

Somebody said "Strewth".

And why?

Well this was the Menu. Our glorious Christmas Lunch

MENU

.....Starter.....

Tomato Soup

.....Main Course.....

Fish and Chips
Or
Sausage and Mash

....Sweet....

Apple Pie and Custard

...DRINKS LIST...

Lager or Bitter

And that was it.

The Boss's face said it all. Two of the lads immediately burst out laughing, and then so did the rest of us.

Somebody piped up "Nice one Boss, touch of class".

The Boss just sat there in a sort of daze. Well he'd had a few drinks.

"The firms not going bankrupt is it Boss?" chirped in some comedian and that went down a treat.

Then the lovely Rona reappeared, notepad in hand.

The Boss seized the moment, and he stood up.

"Can I have a word?" he said.

"Yes luv" replied a smiling Rona.

He took her to one side, though why I don't know, we could all hear the conversation.

Waving the menu about, he said "What the bloody hell's this?"

"What?" said Rona, and suddenly, the smile was gone in a flash.

'Ah' I thought to myself 'there's a woman who's used to confrontation, here we go'.

"This" said the Boss "This. What the bloody hell is this load of crap, we've ordered Christmas Dinner, not sausage and 'friggin' mash".

"There 'is' a choice" said Rona coolly.

"A choice, it's Christmas Dinner. We were expecting Roast Turkey, and gravy with stuffing and all the trimmings, and Christmas Pud and Mince pies. Not fish and bloody chips and apple bloody pie"

"There's gravy with the sausage and mash" said Rona in defence.

"Stuff the sausage and mash, what about the Turkey dinner?"

"What Turkey dinner?" she said.

The Boss was now rubbing his head and getting agitated "We ordered Christmas Dinner".

"This 'is' Christmas dinner" said Rona. "This is what we do here, just plain and simple food, that's us", and with that, she gave a bit of a cocky smile which looked a lot like a threat.

"But we wanted Turkey" the Boss said.

"Oh no, we don't do anything fancy like that, and to be quite honest with you" said Rona, now folding her arms in defiance "by the time most gangs of blokes get here, they're too pissed to care".

The Boss shook his head and was about to carry on complaining when somebody shouted out

"Don't worry Boss. Just get the beer in, we'll be alright"

The Boss looked at Rona, and Rona looked at the Boss. This was a battle of wills.

"I don't suppose you have any red wine?" he asked.

"Well, give me twenty quid and I'll send Billy to the off licence across the road" she replied.

"Don't bother" said the Boss.

She shrugged her shoulders and turned to us "Right, what's everybody drinking?"

The order for the lager and bitter was given, and ten minutes later Rona and her 'girls' appeared at the table, carrying trays that were full of cans of beer.

"Who's on lager"? Shouted Rona, and the lager was doled out and then the bitter.

The Boss, who was sitting there with a cold can of lager in front of him, asked Rona "Where are the glasses?"

"Oh no, we don't do glasses" said Rona "It's the breakages, you don't get breakages with cans".

"Fuck me" said the Boss under his breath, and as he ripped the top off his can of lager, he turned to his golf buddy and said "When I get back home I'm going to sack that fucking secretary".

The beer flowed, unlike the food, and several cans later the tomato soup finally arrived.

I've never seen anything like it. It was soup that had never been near a tomato in its life. It was orange, but sort of like orange paint.

We decided to stick with the beer, they couldn't mess with that.

The Boss just stared down at his soup, and then reached for another can.

Sometime later, well much later, the main course finally arrived. We had all ordered fish and chips, and twenty four plates of fish and chips were served up. Fish and chips that looked suspiciously as though they could have come from the 'chippy' that was across the road from the hotel.

It was at that point that Rona announced that they'd run out of fish and chips and so the rest of us, and that included the Boss, would have to have the Sausage and Mash.

The Boss twitched and went a bit redder, then he took a long swig from his can and looked up at the ceiling.

A couple of minutes later the girls came out with the remaining plates of sausage and mash.

It wasn't clever, a plate of pale mash with some sort of sausage floating in a pool of gravy and fat.

The Boss looked down at it, and shook his head, and then with a bit of a sway he stood up.

"Rona!" he shouted at the top of his voice "Rona!"

Rona appeared.

He took one look at her "This is shite" he said, and then "This is shite that I wouldn't even give to a dog".

And with that, he picked up his plate full of 'shite', and threw it in her direction.

Thankfully, and due to the alcohol, his aim was off and the plate full of sausage, mash and gravy sailed off to the left of her head and smashed and splattered all over the wall behind her.

Rona went berserk. She started to shout a lot and went all abusive. She could actually swear like a miner too, she stormed off, and then immediately came back and swore at us a lot more, and then she disappeared.

Ten minutes later the police arrived.

We were thrown out of the hotel with a caution. We all stood outside as the Boss reluctantly paid for the beer and some of the damage, but we got away with it.

As the police let us go, Rona's husband, 'Fat Billy' came to the front door and shouted...

"Don't come back".

Some of the lads turned round and one of them called out "Eeh Billy, don't be like that, it's been lovely".

It's called, taking the piss.

Anyway, we all trouped back into Blackpool town centre and hit the pubs. Within a couple of hours we had to put the Boss and his mate into a Black Cab and send them both, unconscious and snoring, back home to Bolton.

We all just carried on.

Eventually of course, everybody did split up into groups and we all lost one another in the different pubs, but as the magical time of two o' clock arrived, we headed for the car park to pick up our coach and meet up with the other lads. When we got there, most of them had already arrived and were all milling about, drinks in hand. The coach driver wasn't happy. Quite a few of the lads were congregating round the back of the coach, standing in a circle. On the ground was a bloke, not one of our gang, but he was on the ground, drunk and passed out. Very soon, the combined wisdom of our addled minds came to a mutual conclusion. 'What were we going to do with him, we couldn't just leave him there, could we...no.

That wouldn't be right would it?'

Then, somebody with brains said that we should check him for I.D and then we would know who he was, what a good idea.

We opened his jacket and searched his pants and pockets and somewhere in between, we found a wallet.

One of the lads searched through it and found his name and then address on something.

"His name's Steven Carson and he live at Foundry Street in Wigan, yes, its number eleven...eleven, Foundry Street, Wigan".

"Hey, I know where that is" another of the lads suddenly said "I used to work near there, I know where he lives".

At that moment the coach driver came up to us and told us that we had to drink up and get on the coach, but we sort of ignored him because we were concentrating on what to do with the lad from Wigan.

The coach driver then told us that he would be setting off in five minutes. It seemed that he'd got a bit of a 'cob on'.

We decided we weren't happy with this, this lad was from Wigan, and Wigan folk were alright in our book. We couldn't just leave him there, so something would have to be done.

So we went over to the coach driver for a chat.

We told him that we would have to go back to Bolton...via Wigan. He flatly refused. So we told him that his coach would be going nowhere until we got this sorted out. He didn't understand what we meant, then some of the lads started to line up in front of the coach as a form of protest and the driver started getting all agitated and twitchy. Finally we offered him some money and after he'd counted it and called us a 'set of bastards', he agreed. So we carried the Wigan lad onto the coach and off we went.

An hour or so later we arrived in Wigan, and the lad 'who knew the area' stood at the front of the coach with the driver and gave him directions. After a few u-turns, we finally arrived at Foundry Street. It was now about half past three in the morning, as the coach trundled down the narrow street. The driver expertly negotiated his vehicle around the lines of parked cars and eventually stopped outside number eleven. The air brakes hissed noisily as the coach came to a halt, and then the coach door swung open and thirty drunken men, carrying one very drunken Wigan lad, all piled out. We lay him on the pavement outside his house and proceeded to knock on the door. There was no answer, so we knocked again, this time louder, but still no answer. One of the lads started to bang on the front window and somebody else began throwing coins at the upstairs bedroom window. It was all a bit of a commotion and the driver just sat behind the wheel with his head in his hands, I think he just wanted to go home and go to bed and this was all becoming a bit of a nightmare.

Suddenly the upstairs lights of the houses either side of number eleven came on and almost in tandem, each of the upstairs widows opened. A man leaned out of the window on the left, as a woman peered out of the window on the right. Other bedroom lights started to come on in the adjoining houses and then even those across the street began to light up.

The neighbour, the man on the left looked down at us all.

"What the bloody hell's going on" he shouted.

The other neighbour, the lady on the right, then popped her head out of the window.

"What do you think you're playing at?" she said angrily "You've woken up half the street. Who are you all?"

One of the lads, staggering, called up to her.

"Don't worry love, we're on an errand of mercy. We're from Bolton" and he belched loudly.

"What?" said the lady upstairs.

One of the other lads carried on the conversation for him.

"It's like this love, we've found this lad here" and he pointed at the unconscious and prostrate man who lay at his feet "It's your neighbour 'Steven'. We've rescued him, he was left in Blackpool, he's drunk and he's passed out but we've rescued him and we've brought him back home. When we found out that he was from Wigan we decided to bring him back, we weren't leaving him behind, because we like Wigan folk".

And the lad beamed up at her, with the understanding and the satisfaction of doing the 'right' thing, and a job well done.

Other neighbour's lights were now on and doors were opening on both sides of the street as the situation was being discussed.

"What do you mean, left behind?" continued the man from his bedroom window.

"Eh?" replied our lad.

"What do you mean 'left behind'?" the man repeated himself. "Where's his family"?

"Family, what family?" we asked.

"His wife and two kids, where are they?"

"Wife and kids" we asked again. "What wife and kids?"

The man stared at us "He went for a week's holiday to Blackpool with his wife and kids. They're staying at a big hotel there The 'Norbreck'..."

We all looked at one another and somebody said "Oh shit".

The lady upstairs started to shout at us.

"What the bloody hell do you think you're all playing at, kidnapping the poor lad and dragging him back here, his wife will be having a fit, she'll wonder where on earth he is.

One of the lads said "Oh bloody hell" and we decided to get back on the coach, rapidly.

The driver had already read the situation and was nervously revving up the engine.

The lady upstairs was now shouting to the neighbours across, telling them all 'what we'd done', and the neighbours who weren't impressed at being noisily woken up by our arrival, well they began to get a bit rattled.

As we all got quickly back on the coach, comments such as 'the rotten gits' and 'wankers' could be clearly heard.

Oh heck.

We retreated sharply and as the coach door slammed shut and the driver set off like a shot.

At the side of the coach, a man came running after us and he started banging on the windows, he was shouting something to us, but we just waved back at him.

Well, that was the good people of Wigan. We won't be going back there in a hurry.

And with that, Malc, who was now tipsy and laughing, finished his story.

So, more cards, more 'Jack' and more booze all round.

Malc of course continued to lose, and nothing new there then. He just didn't get it. You see, drinking Bourbon gets you drunk, but it makes you deep, it's a different kind of drunk. But beer and cider, well that's something else, it makes you giddy. And when he'd got a few ciders in him, Malc would always get giddy and you could read him like an open book, we all could, and that's why he always lost at cards. We would always let him win a few hands, just to keep the night in some sort of balance. We all knew, but nothing was ever said, we never discussed it, we just did it.

But tonight there was something about Malc, and I couldn't just put my finger on it.

Pete's mate, Jason, was the 'next' man up. It now seemed that we were all going to have to tell some strange or funny story about our various travels, it sort of went with the night, somehow an obvious progression.

Pete turned in his seat and nudged Jason.

"Tell them about that time in Chester" he said to Jason "Go on, tell them that one" and he laughed as he urged Jason on.

The cards were dealt and we filled four glasses with bourbon. Malc was in freefall with the cider by then. So we leant back and started to play.

"Go on Jason" I said "what's the story?"

Jason smiled, "Funny one really, it's a few years ago now when I think about it, probably five or six years ago, but anyway, me and my wife Sue, we used to know a couple 'Carlo and June'. They were really good friends at the time, still are really, but they live in America now, somewhere in Florida."

He took a sip of his drink and played his cards.

"Anyway" he continued "We'd first met Carlo and June at a party at a friend's house a year or two earlier, we were introduced, and got chatting, and just sort of 'hit it off'. It was a bit strange really, we were only in our early twenties and pretty naive, and they were in their late fifties and were the life and soul of the party, it seemed that they knew everybody. Like I said, we just hit it off and we eventually we became very good friends. Carlo was second generation Italian and he was always very entertaining, he'd never lost the 'Latin' spirit and also the contrariness that the Italians are famous for. He might have been born in Bolton, but his soul was still hanging in Italy, his family came from somewhere near Naples, I think.

Carlo, as they say, was 'a character'. Though he was only slightly over five foot tall, and small and square, that man would never, ever let anybody dominate him.

He would fall out with people all the time, and he'd never let anyone win an argument. But he could grab everyone's attention and hold audience at parties and be the centre of attention. He'd shoot the big men down and then woo their wives, and everyone would just laugh and say 'Hey, that's Carlo. You know what he's like'.

Carlo was a bugger.

But strange as it was, me and Carlo never had one disagreement, never a bad word, and to this day, we never have. Every couple of years, he turns up from America, and it is so good to see him. Older he may be, but the fire is still burning there.

Carlo and June, what a couple, Carlo a live wire and June, well she just loved the man, I think we all did.

So there we were, us in our twenties, and them in their fifties. They showed us another side of life, and they introduced us to restaurants and fine dining, and good wine and social etiquette.

For us they opened a door, a door that I suppose has never closed, it was an education.

Anyway, one Sunday out of the blue, they rang us up.

"What are you doing next weekend?" It was Carlo.

"Nothing" I said "Why?"

"June's found a deal, a swish hotel in Chester, its 'The Savoy', it belongs to one of the large hotel chains. She's seen a deal in one of the Sunday newspapers, it's a really top hotel and there's an offer on for next weekend. We stay Saturday night, and it includes an evening meal and then breakfasts thrown in the following morning. It's for nothing, 'peanuts', do you fancy it?"

Of course we did, and he was right, it was for 'peanuts'. I can't remember just how much it cost, but it must have been cheap because me and Sue had very little spare money in those days.

So, the following weekend, off we went. We met up with them in Chester, and it was late afternoon because I'd had to do overtime at work on the Saturday morning. So it was about four o'clock in the afternoon when we finally pulled up outside the magnificent 'Savoy Hotel' in central Chester, and oh my God, what a place. It was a huge old building, really classy and all immaculately groomed. Built in white stone, it had large oval shaped brass doors at the entrance with two shaped conifers in matching black and brass planters placed at either side. Outside stood a Porter, dressed in a burgundy uniform, he welcomed the guests and opened the hotel doors and assisted with the luggage as people came and went. He met us with an efficient smile, and once I had taken our cases out of the boot of the car, he directed me to the private car parking at the rear of the hotel. It was pretty full because the hotel was busy.

We went to reception to book in and there was a message waiting there for us, it read...

'We're in the bar...Carlo and June'.

So we were directed to our rooms and were going to unpack, but then quickly decided 'what the hell', and the bar it was.

We went down to meet them and spent a very pleasant hour on the 'gin and tonics'.

Around five thirty, Carlo announced that the 'thing to do' was to go and have a nap for an hour or so. Then get yourself sorted and unpacked, have a shower and change, and then to go round to their room for drinks.

"We've got brandy and gin and the tonics and dry ginger in our room" Carlo said.

"We always bring our own stuff, it saves paying 'full whack' at the hotel bar".

Fair enough.

And that's what we did. Just after six thirty we went round to their room and spent another pleasant hour with them both, and then went down for dinner. First of all though, we went to the bar.

It was now quite busy and so we got our drinks and sat down at a table.

"Just a quickie before we go in to eat" June told us, enthusiastically.

We sat down and were chatting away, when suddenly a couple walked into the bar. The whole room actually went a bit quieter as everybody gave them a second glance. They were that sort of couple.

He was a biggish man, late forties with thick brown hair gelled back and immaculately dressed. Pale grey slacks and a pink and black patterned sweater, he was smart and cool, all the way down to his large and obvious, gold Rolex watch and his tanned expensive leather shoes.

You could smell the wealth.

And accompanying him was his wife. She had black hair, red lipstick and a red cocktail dress with matching high, high heels. Simply stunning, she was beautiful.

Carlo took one look at her and nodded.

"She...could be hard work" he predicted.

And it turned out that he was right.

They walked up to the bar and the man ordered champagne and then they came to sit down at a corner table which also happened to be next to us. For some reason, they didn't seem to be speaking to one another, and Carlo being Carlo, caught the man's eye.

"Just arrived?" he enquired, smiling.

"Yes" replied the man and he glanced at his wife, who was fiddling in her large designer handbag. She sort of ignored him, and so he turned back to Carlo.

"And you...you arrived today too?" he asked.

"Yes" replied Carlo casually "We're just here for the weekend, and he waved his hand in some sort of 'Italian' fashion, as though this was an everyday occasion. He certainly wasn't going to mention the 'deal for peanuts' out of the newspaper. Okay, no problem.

"Ah" said the big man abruptly, as the waiter finally arrived with his bottle of champagne.

The bottle was beautifully decked out in a large silver ice bucket, which was filled with crushed ice and had a 'Savoy Hotel' anagrammed towel tastefully wrapped around it. It was brought over to them on a separate small black table and placed in front of the couple.

"Shall I pour, sir?" asked the waiter.

The man nodded.

The waiter poured the champagne into two tall and beautifully anagrammed 'Savoy' champagne flutes and then he placed the bottle back into the ice bucket, and with a discreet nod, he left.

The man picked up his glass and turned to his wife..."Happy birthday love, cheers..." he said to her.

She looked up, and then firmly closed her designer bag. It was a large black and red striped thing, she then picked up her glass and with a sort of 'vacant' expression said "Cheers", and that was it.

The man looked slightly put out, maybe even a bit embarrassed, and he turned away. He then turned back to us and nearly caught us all doing the 'wide eyed' and staring bit. We were all thinking 'What the hell's going on with those two'?

Carlo verbally stepped in "Nice hotel" he said.

"Oh, we've had a problem already" said the man.

"Oh yes, what's that?" said Carlo, enquiring, and also managing to keep a conversation going.

"The parking" said the man "We arrived earlier and the hotel car park was completely full. We've had to park the car about half a mile away and drag our cases all the way back here. There's another car park, 'a council one', just across the road and down a side street, but it has a barrier with height restrictions. We're in the Range Rover and it wouldn't fit underneath, it's ridiculous."

I felt that this wasn't the time or place to mention that our old Ford Fiesta was tucked away nicely around the back of the hotel.

He then continued "We booked this place and were told that there was ample parking. I thought that they'd reserved me a parking place but when I went to reception to complain they told me that they don't reserve spaces on the hotel car park"

Suddenly, his wife decided to speak "It's a disgrace" she said flatly "I don't 'do' walking".

The man raised his eyebrows, and then emptied his glass.

"My feet are utterly killing me" she carried on "it's just simply ridiculous".

"It wasn't full earlier" said Carlo "we arrived just after lunch and it wasn't even half full".

"Yes" said the man "When I spoke to reception, they told me they'd had a rush of last minute bookings.'Why' I don't know?"

The four of us looked at one another and all thought the same thing, 'peanuts'.

The man finally turned back to his wife and they started to talk. Within ten minutes the four of us were called into the dining room. As we left, I turned back and noticed that the man and his wife were taking delivery of their second bottle of champagne.

We were seated at our table and started to have what turned out to be a fabulous meal.

Carlo was on form and he ordered us some really nice red wine. It was 'Italian' obviously.

Half an hour, and after we'd eaten some beautiful starters, the man and his wife entered the dining room. All heads turned as usual, his wife was really good looking, smoulderingly good looking.

They sat two tables away from us at a table against the rear wall, and as soon as they were seated, more champagne arrived.

We'd finished our main course and had started on our desserts when we heard them, the man and his wife. They weren't actually arguing, but they were having a vigorous discussion and whatever it was about, it was making them talk louder. Well louder than anybody else in the dining room.

During their meal, they had polished off another two bottles of champagne, and the third one was just being delivered.

"My god" said June "that must be their fifth bottle, they had two in the bar, then two in here and now here's another".

"Seventy quid a bottle, that stuff" said Carlo. He knew these things.

I just whistled quietly.

By the time we'd had coffees and a couple of brandies, things next door but one were not getting better.

Carlo was enthralled, I'm sure he could lip read because he seemed to know everything that was going on and exactly what they were talking about. I couldn't hear a bloody thing.

June kept asking him "What's happened, and what's happening now?"

Carlo was laughing as he interpreted "Money, his ex-wife, his kids, more money, the house, a car, money, and a holiday...'Oh', and something about an opal and diamond ring that she wants and he's 'not bothered' to buy it for her yet.

Oh Christ. I looked across at my missus and she grabbed my hand and she mimicked...

"I don't do walking, and a ring's out of the question, and why? Because we've no money honey"

We all laughed, and then we stood up and left.

Carlo had it planned that we should hit the bars and nightlife of Chester. And we did, and what a good night it was. Chester is a really smart place for a good night out.

It was after midnight when we got back to the hotel and Carlo had it planned that we should have a nightcap and some supper in the 'residents bar'. It was a private bar situated on the first floor of the Hotel and Carlo had 'discovered' it whilst mooching about in the afternoon before we arrived. Good man.

We were directed upstairs by the girl on reception. So up we went in the lift, it was only one floor, but well, it had been a long night. We walked down the corridor and approached a large oak door that had dark yellow panes of glass in it. On the door was a sign in gold letters 'Private Bar – Residents Only'.

Well that was us, so in we went.

There bar was lit with subtle yellow lighting. Low and intimate and sort of calming at the end of the evening.

There were three or four other couples in the bar, we weren't really looking, so we sat down around a low coffee table and the waiter came over to serve us some drinks. We ordered and then asked for the 'supper menu'. As we sat there waiting for the drinks to arrive, we heard a bit of a commotion over in the corner, and we looked around to see that it was 'the rich couple' who we'd spoken to earlier, the husband and his glamorous wife. They were sat in the far corner of the bar, and were both pie-eyed drunk and arguing. On the table in front of them were three empty champagne bottles, one of which was upside down in the ice bucket. There were a couple of bottles of wine that 'the wife' was now drinking, and the husband had a large full brandy glass in his hand and a opened bottle of Hennessy X.O Brandy which was also on the table in front of him. He must have bought the whole bottle.

Our drinks arrived and we ordered some supper off the menu. I love hotels.

We tried to ignore 'the couple', but Carlo was further enthralled. He loved a bit of scandal and bit of trouble, or anybody having a row. In fact, any sort of confrontation and he was in his element.

And even though the four of us were sat there in conversation, I knew that Carlo's mind was somewhere else, and that somewhere else was the 'rich couple' sitting behind us.

I looked across at Carlo and I thought to myself 'here we go'.

Within a couple of minutes he was on his feet, and glass in hand, he wandered over and approached the couple as though he'd only just noticed them being there. And then he spoke to them as though they were long lost friends. Yes, I'd seen it all before.

"Well hello there" beamed Carlo, as he walked over to their table, uninvited. "How are you both, have you had a good night?" and he smiled like a cat.

The man looked up at Carlo through hazy and addled eyes, and then with a spark of recognition, he smiled and slowly laughed.

"Hey, how are you buddy?" he replied sluggishly. He couldn't remember how he knew Carlo, but somehow he recognized him.

His wife never even looked up, she was once more peering into that designer bag as though she looking for something.

"Have you had a good night then?" asked Carlo, again.

"Fuckin' terrific" said the man and he half turned to his wife, and then turned back, deciding not to bother.

"Well, you've definitely pushed the boat out tonight" continued Carlo "You've certainly got through the champagne".

"Yes, well" said the man.

"And it's the 'good stuff' too" said Carlo.

"I don't buy crap" said the man, and another smile.

"I can see that" said Carlo "and I see you like Hennessy X.O. You know, that's one of the best brandies you can get, but it's bloody expensive"

"Yes" said the man "But I can afford it" and his head swayed a bit.

I watched Carlo, flattery and agreement, it worked every time. And now he would get right into the man's ribs, perfect timing.

"What line of business are you in?" Carlo suddenly asked, straight in there.

The man almost belched as he spoke "Building and renovation, we do property speculation. We put high end properties onto the market" he said.

"Hey nice one" said Carlo smoothly "that's seems to be a good business to get into, if you're smart enough".

"Oh yes" the man agreed, of course he did. "You see, I deal with 'em all. Bankers and footballers and business men, I deal with 'em all. And they come to me".

"How's that work?" asked Carlo.

"Well what we do" the man drunkenly continued "what we do, is find exclusive properties that are a bit run down, they're 'knackered'. We sort 'em out, we even knock 'em down if need be. We redesign them and then make them smart. We build extensions, add fancy conservatories and even swimming pools, and we're bloody brilliant at interior design. And hey presto, when they're done we sell 'em for big money, to rich idiots" And with that he leant back in his chair and laughed at his own joke.

His wife suddenly looked up from her bag. She must have been listening to the conversation.

"He's a fucking dickhead" she slurred.

The man turned and shot her a glance, and it was a look that could kill.

Then he turned slowly back to face Carlo, and with his eyes now half closed with the drink, he lifted his glass and drank the contents in one, and then leant over and filled the brandy glass once more. He turned and looked at his wife and then turned back to his glass. He took another mouthful of brandy and then he picked up his bottle of Hennessy. He stood up and swayed a little, and then looked down at her.

"Goodnight...cow" he said, and he stumbled out of the bar.

Carlo watched him go, and then slid into the man's still warm seat.

"Are you alright" he then purred to the man's wife, seemingly concerned.

I told you he was good...

The woman looked at Carlo and she twitched a little.

"He's a fucking dickhead" she said again, and she leant over and picked up her glass which was full of dark red wine. Then she took a very sizeable drink.

"He's a fucking dickhead and a fucking liar" she hissed.

"Is he, why what's wrong?" asked Carlo, now with total empathy.

"Did you hear him, the bastard.'We find properties', 'we redesign them', 'we are brilliant at interior design'. Bastard, what a load of crap".

"Why's that" asked Carlo, as he refilled her glass and passed it to her.

She took another drink before she spoke.

"I'll tell you 'why's that'..." she said "I started this business, from day one. I found the properties, I redesign them, and it's me that has the eye for interior design. He knows bloody nothing."

"Really?" said Carlo, oozing sincerity.

"Really" she replied "When I first met him he was a shitty little builder, I had an affair with him and he buggered off and left his wife and kids and he moved in with me. He got a 'quickie' divorce and we got married. I should have bloody well known it, he could smell the money. And it was me who knew the wealthy and the rich. I introduced him to the 'money people', the footballers and the businessmen".

She continued to drink "He thinks he's clever, but I've found him out. He's been siphoning money out of the accounts, he's been pinching the money 'and' the bastards been seeing his ex-wife again. Yeah, I've got a private eye, I've had him followed and his phone calls traced and recorded. Oh yes, I know exactly what's going on. He's going to try and steal all the money in one big lump, and then transfer the funds to somewhere that I can't get access to, or he's going to bankrupt the company and then buy it back with the money he's already stolen from me, and he's going jump back with that fucking ex-wife of his".

Carlo poured her another glass of wine.

"You've got problems lady" he said, and this time he meant it.

"Yeah well" she said as she picked up her glass "Two can play at that game" and just as she was about to take a drink from her glass, she stopped and looked at Carlo and smiled rather drunkenly at him. It was the first time I'd seen her smile since we'd met her and her husband in the bar just before dinner. She was stunningly beautiful, and as sexy as hell. There are women in this world that just make you look, and look again, and admire. And she was one of those, a raw and exquisite beauty, even when drunk.

Smiling, she drank her wine and then said to Carlo...

"Edmonds & Co." she said softly, "Edmonds & Co." and she looked down at her wine and she laughed.

"Who's that?" said Carlo.

"A supplier, to our company, along with 'K & S Fabrics' and 'Tailor-made Fittings', oh yes and 'Canterbury and Jones Kitchens' and 'Bromley Furnishing'. They're all suppliers too".

"And what about them?" asked Carlo.

"And, they're all mine" she replied, and then she giggled "All bloody well mine".

"So you've got all these businesses as well?" asked Carlo.

"Well I've got them, and others, but there are no businesses as such. I've just got bank accounts in their names".

"And how does that work?" again asked Carlo, with ever widening eyes, he'd smelt a rat and suddenly he was intrigued.

"It's simple" she said, reaching for the wine bottle. Carlo got to it first, and poured.

She continued "I pay all these 'suppliers' out of 'our' Company business account, and the money simply comes back to me".

"Does he know about them?"

"No, he does bloody well not" she replied "They just come up as suppliers on the bank statements, if ever he looks at the bank statements, which he doesn't".

She drank her wine "Oh and there's also 'Holts painters and decorators', 'N. Nolan the plasterer' and' Pete Kelly the roofer'. They're all 'me' as well, but in their case they all get paid 'cash' so that we don't have to pay the V.A.T. And that's my excuse for employing them, because 'they' and that's 'me' again, gets the cash. 'Get it'?" and she winked at Carlo.

Carlo burst out laughing "And what about those invisible suppliers that you 'own', what about their bank accounts?"

"Their bank accounts are bursting with money" she said "and only I can access them. He may be siphoning off the money, but I'm siphoning it off twice as fast. We might just go bankrupt a whole lot faster than he expects."

"Clever girl" said Carlo slowly, he was certainly getting the picture now.

"But does he never want to meet these contractors or the suppliers?"

"Oh no" she said "No, all he wants to do these days is slope off and play golf with his buddies. He used to take an interest, but once the money came rolling in he lost his edge and started leaving all work to me. I run things now 'everything', he knows some of the people we deal with and some of the contractors, but not all of them. At night, I ask him for decisions that I've already made. He's usually full of booze and as long as I tell him the works going well and that there's other work and other projects in progress, he's happy".

She drank some more wine.

"What are you going to do?" Carlo asked her.

"Get out" she said "Get out, take the money and run"

She stared at nothing for a moment and then said "You know something. I thought we had a really good thing going, the pair of us. We used to have a great time, it was good back then, and he doesn't even realize where we could have taken this business. The sky literally 'was' the limit. But it's over, he's become distant and arrogant, and he doesn't care about me anymore. We never talk, I just look good on his arm, I'm just another thing that he thinks he owns".

She was really quite drunk, but she wasn't for stopping and she poured more wine, another full glass.

Then she said something to Carlo, and to herself really.

"But the thing is, I've got to be careful. He can be violent, especially when he's been on the Brandy, he can go a bit crazy. If he finds out what I'm up to..." and for a moment she hesitated "If he finds out what I'm up to, I think he'll kill me".

And in some way, I got the feeling that she wasn't exaggerating.

And at that point, she drank the whole glass of wine in one go and somehow managed to stand up.

"I'm going now" she said, and she struggled to lean over and pick up her designer bag, then she turned and tried carefully to walk towards the door.

As she was leaving she turned to us, and simply said "Good night all".

Carlo came back over to our table and we all sat there for a minute, a bit amazed. And then suddenly our suppers arrived and it broke the spell. We were the last people in the bar and it was really quite late, but the food was good and we decided to order some more drinks.

Out of the blue, Carlo said to me "Let's have a bottle of that Champagne".

The girls' heads suddenly shot up.

"Well" he said "we've had a great time and 'why not'...?"

I laughed "Yeah Carlo, why not indeed"

So the waiter came to us and the Champagne was ordered, it quickly arrived and was served to us in lovely 'Savoy' flute glasses, and it tasted great.

Champagne at two in the morning is definitely the 'way to go'.

We sat there eating and talking, it had been a great night. Half an hour passed and Carlo left the bar to nip to the toilets. Five minutes later he was back, wide eyed and slightly agitated. He came through the door quickly and closed it immediately behind him, then he turned and looked at us, something was definitely wrong.

"Whatever's the matter?" said June. She'd seen the expression on his face.

Carlo walked directly over to us and sat down immediatly.

I looked at him "What the hell's up?"

"Trouble" he said.

"What sort of trouble?" asked June.

"Do they have video cameras in this hotel?" he said quickly.

"Why's that" I asked.

"What's happened Carlo?" June was getting exasperated now.

"It's that woman. I've just found her in the corridor, she's naked and unconscious".

"What!" I spluttered, actually, we all spluttered.

He sat there, a bit in shock and tried to explain.

"Well I went to the toilet, I walked down the corridor and just as I was about to turn left I noticed a shoe on the floor. It was one of her red high heeled shoes and I thought 'okay she's drunk, and she's just lost her shoe'. But as I turned the corner, there was another shoe on the floor, and then further along was her bright red cocktail dress, it was just lying there on the carpet, followed by a bra, and a pair of knickers and tights. So I walked to the end of the corridor and when I turned right I found her, and you won't believe this, she was lying there completely naked and she was covered in twenty pound notes, In fact the whole of the corridor was strewn with twenty pound notes, there must be thousands of pounds there, and she's lying there in the middle of it all with not a stitch on."

I just looked at him "You're bloody kidding me" I said, this was crazy.

"No, I'm bloody well not" he continued "that designer bag thing that she carries was thrown down the corridor and it was empty. It must have been full of all the cash that she's been stashing away. I think the 'drinks' got to her and she's had a bit of a tantrum and in a moment of madness she's thrown all her money away".

"What did you do then?" asked June.

Carlo glanced at me "Well err, I tried to help her"

"Oh yes, I can imagine that" I said, giving him a smile.

"Oh Christ" he said as he put his hand over his eyes "I hope there's no bloody cameras"

"What on earth have you done Carlo?" asked a now very serious June.

"Nothing" he said quickly "It's not what you think. You see, I went to try and help her, well I couldn't just leave her there could I. So I went to try and revive her"

June nearly burst a blood vessel.

"No" he said defensively "listen to me, I just leant over and gently patted her cheek".

"Which cheek, her face or her bottom?" I said, I was laughing now. Carlo definitely wasn't.

"Sod off" he said "No, I patted her cheek to see if I could wake her up, and she 'came to' for a minute and I asked her if she was okay. But she didn't know where she was, all she kept saying was "Have your fucking money" and "bastard". So I got hold of her arms and tried to pull her up"

I considered this for a moment. Carlo is only five foot nothing, and that lady had very long legs, very long legs.

"So" he continued "I pulled her up by her arms to try to get her to sit up, and I almost managed it. But suddenly she flopped forwards, and her head fell right into my crutch"

Carlo glanced cautiously at his wife.

"Listen to me" he said "I suddenly realized what this could look like. If anybody had arrived on the scene at that moment, they're going think that I've robbed her, I've knocked her out, and now I'm trying to get a blow job".

"What did you do?" I asked him.

"I crapped myself. I'm Italian, everybody thinks we're sex mad anyway"

"Where is she now?" asked June.

"In the corridor where I left her, I just hope I'm not on video"

"Don't be ridiculous and shut up about a bloody video" snapped June, then she said "We can't just leave her there"

"Well I'm not going back" declared Carlo.

Whereupon, both our wives had a 'team discussion', and then they got hold of the barman and all of them went off to sort the poor girl out. My wife took one look at me and said...

"You stay here".

It was an order and a threat all in one. I didn't pursue it. Damn.

Twenty minutes later they all reappeared. The wives were shaking their heads, they were more than a little disgruntled, but the barman was grinning. He winked at me and Carlo as he went back behind the bar, the lucky bastard.

"How did you go on?" asked Carlo.

It's a disgrace" replied June, and my wife nodded in agreement.

"Well, we went to find her" continued June "and we turned down the corridor and there she was 'flat out', and the money was all over the place. I took off my jacket and covered her up because my god, the barman's eyes were popping out. Then we picked up all the cash and stuffed it back into her bag, and you were right, there was a hell of a lot of money there. Once we'd done that we picked her up and got her back on her feet. She was in a right state, she kept muttering and swearing but we couldn't understand what she was talking about. So we knocked on the door to her room a few times and eventually her husband appeared, he wasn't in a much better state. He just stood there in the doorway swaying, with an empty Hennessy bottle in his hand. He must have drunk the lot. All he could say was "What?"

His eyes were all bloodshot. I don't think he even recognized us. When we tried to point out to him that we were holding up his wife, he just turned and staggered back into his room and collapsed into an armchair. So we carried her in. He just sat there and watched us and then finally he told us to "leave her on the bed, the bitch", his speech was very slurred. We lifted her onto the bed, she was still muttering something.

We put the bag of money at the bottom of the bed, so as not to be too conspicuous. Then we left, I just hope she'll be okay".

"There's not a lot more you could have done" I said "they'll probably sleep it off and won't remember a thing in the morning, with any luck".

We finished off the remains of our supper and the last dregs of champagne, and then we decided to have four brandy coffees as a final nightcap. They tasted really good. It was a nice way to end an eventful evening.

And with that, we laughed about the night, and then we trundled off to bed.

So that was that, until nine o' clock the next morning, when I was woken up by a loud knocking on our door. It had been a late night and I was feeling a bit fragile, so the constant banging was a bit of a jolt.

"Who is it?" I asked, a little irritably. My wife just moaned and put her hand over her eyes.

"It's me. Open the door" it was Carlo.

I swung my legs out of the bed and stood up a bit too quickly, then toppled back onto the bed. The wife wasn't impressed. I gave it a second go, stood up a bit slower this time and straightened up. Feeling that everything was okay, I then headed for the door. I'd only half opened it when Carlo burst in, all agitated and twitchy.

"Get dressed quick" he said, he was animated and almost jumping up and down.

"You what?" I said, this was the crack of dawn for me, and things were still a bit fuzzy.

"Come on" he quickly exclaimed, and then he went all Italian and started waving his arms about.

"Hurry, come on, get dressed now. Quick...quick".

"What's going on?" I said to him.

He picked my pants up off the floor and passed them to me "Something's happened, it's that couple from last night, something's gone on. The police are here and an ambulance has just turned up, they're all in reception and the police are questioning the staff."

My wife suddenly sat upright "Oh my god, he's killed her. I'll bet he's killed her, he was in a right temper last night".

At that moment June also burst into the room, she looked at us all "Have you heard anything?"

"I think he's killed he, I'll bet she's dead" my wife continued "he'll have strangled her or something"

June quickly agreed "Yes, well he's capable of that alright" and they gave each other that 'woman's knowing look' thing. "We saw the state that he was in last night, he's got a bad temper has that one, anything could have happened"

Carlo looked at me "Come on...now" he said.

So we hurriedly left the room and went down the corridor, but when we got to the end of the corridor where 'the couple's' room was, we were stopped by two policemen who told us that "There's nothing to see here sir" and basically 'bugger off and go away'.

So we went down to the reception, were the members of the staff were gathered along with some of the guests and another couple of policemen who were also being vague.

"We don't really know what's happened" one of them said "We've just been called out to some kind of incident".

Carlo looked at me and shrugged his shoulders and I followed him as he went over to the girl behind reception.

He leaned over to her with a gleam in his eye and his best smile.

"Hey love, what's going on?" he asked in a low voice.

She melted of course, and glanced sideways for a moment, and then leaned over to him

"It happened this morning" she said quietly "one of the staff went up to their room with their breakfast, they'd pre-ordered it, breakfast in bed and all that, with orange juice and a bottle of champagne thrown in for some Bucks Fizz. The waitress arrived at their room with their breakfast all laid out on a trolley. When she got to the door, she could hear them screaming and shouting at each other, so she waited for a minute or two for them to calm down. They didn't, so finally she knocked on the door. The woman was screaming something at the top of her voice by now, and when the waitress knocked, the man shouted out to her to 'bugger off...'"

Then he started screaming and swearing loudly at his wife, and then suddenly there was the sound of smashing glass and somebody moaned out loud and then it all went quiet. The waitress knocked again and then called to them, but there was no answer. Then it struck her that if the man opened the door, he might attack her too. So she panicked and ran downstairs and here to me here on reception, and I rang the police and the ambulance."

"Good move" said Carlo "You did the right thing"

She smiled back with a hint of appreciation. It was nice to get a compliment.

Suddenly there was a noise from the balcony.

We looked up to see two of the ambulance men and two policemen at the top of the stairs with the woman on a stretcher. The four of them had to manhandle her down the steps, which were pretty steep. Her head was totally covered in bandages, but we gasped when we saw that there was blood seeping through, and by the time they'd struggled to get her to the bottom of the stairs, half of her bandaged face was covered in blood.

"God" said Carlo "he's cut her throat"

The girl behind reception gasped and put her hand to her mouth.

Once at the bottom of the stairs, the two policemen and two ambulance men each took hold of a corner of the stretcher, and proceeded to get her into the ambulance as quickly as possible.

And then, as they passed by us, Carlo suddenly said "Hey, look" and he pointed at her feet. We all looked down and then stared in amazement, because it wasn't 'her' feet sticking out from the stretcher. We looked and saw two large feet wearing men's black socks sticking out from under the sheet. It was 'his' feet, and as we realized this, we looked at the body of the person on the stretcher. It wasn't a woman...it was the body of a large man. We'd been so taken by the sight of all that blood, that we hadn't noticed the size of the body. No wonder they'd struggled down the stairs, he was a very big man. They hurried past us and got him into the back of the ambulance and shot off, all blue lights and sirens.

Carlo turned to one of the policemen "Is he dead?" he asked.

"No" said the policeman "But he's in a bad way"

Then suddenly, there was a commotion at the top of the stairs. There were two more policemen and they were having an altercation with the man's wife. They had hold of her arms and she was trying to break free as she shouted abuse at them both. Finally they got a firm grip of her and frog marched her, with great difficulty down the stairs.

Personally, I would have taken the lift.

We looked on as they marched her past. She was in a right state, her eye makeup and lipstick were all smudged and wiped, and she was obviously still very drunk, blood shot eyes and dishevelled hair. She was hardly the beauty she had been the night before, but there you go.

And as she was more or less carried past us, Carlo said to her "Are you alright love?"

The silly bugger.

She turned and then stared right through him, as though he didn't exist, totally incoherent. She was then put into a police car and driven off.

We ended up talking to the two remaining policemen.

"What on earth happened to him?" I asked them.

The policeman turned to us "Well, his face was all bashed in, and the massive bleeding is from a slashed artery in his neck, it's bad one.

"What was it" asked Carlo "a knife?"

"Oh no" said the policeman "she smashed him in the face with a Hennessy Bottle".

A smiling Jason looked across at us and shrugged, story over and we all burst out laughing.

I asked him what had happened to the woman, but he didn't know. They'd left Chester later that day and had never heard anything more about it.

So there you go, it was after midnight, and there's something special about 'the midnight hour'. Once the clock's turned twelve and you get into those late and early hours, there's a different feel to the night, I suppose it's the booze, but everyone gets mellow and the night suddenly becomes timeless.

It was then that Malc reached over for the bottle of Jack Daniels. He just said "Sod it". We all looked at him. This was different, this was strange.

"You, drinking 'Jack'..." I said?

"Yep" he replied "I'll give it a go. Why not?" And he picked up a spare glass and the bottle and poured himself a good measure. He took a sip, and then he smiled at us.

"Nice" he said, and then he drank the whole lot in one gulp.

He shook his head and slurred 'Wooh'! and reached for the bottle again.

And I realize now, that he was on a mission to get drunk. He had been all night if the truth be known, but now he was really going for it.

"You only drink cider, always cider" I said. "How come you want to drink 'Jack Daniels' all of a sudden?"

"Coz I want to" he said with a silly grin "I just want to, okay?"

His eyes were a bit hazy and by the way he was talking, he was well on his way. But there was something else, something.

I looked across at Tony, he and Malc were good mates, but Tony just stared right back at me and ever so slightly shook his head. It was a message 'Don't ask, and don't pursue it'.

I nodded back. Okay then.

Tony broke the moment. He said to me "Come on then Al, tell us a tale" and he smiled at me, and yes, the moment had passed.

"Yeah" said Jason "You've been all over the place, you must have seen some crazy things. Hey, didn't you once get locked up in Tenerife for something or other?"

"No I didn't" I said "that was two of the lads that I was with, they were fighting over some girl, stupid sods".

I looked down at my cards and threw out the five of clubs. I didn't need it.

"Yes, I've had my crazy moments, and usually it's all been down to drink and stupidity. And in that order" and I gave it some thought, and took a sip of Jack.

"Well, I've done a bit of travelling" I said to them "Mostly in Europe, and a lot of the Mediterranean and the Canaries, though for the last few years we've done a few of the Greek islands, then we went to Rhodes and we've just kept going back there. We've found a place there that we really like. We've got to know the local people, they're all so friendly, and it's a great island. I love the pace of Greek life and the food there is without doubt, second to none, good Greek food is absolutely brilliant".

Somebody played their cards, and then I carried on "Another thing about Greece. It's safe, 'as safe as houses' and by that I mean that you can walk anywhere, and go anywhere, and so can your wife and so can your kids, with no problems and no danger. And I'm only telling you this, because we once went away on holiday and it ended up being the most terrifying experience of my life, both of our lives. We were both nearly murdered, me and Karen, and that's the truth".

"When was that?" Pete asked, he was a bit taken aback "you've never said anything".

"Oh, it was before we had the kids, about ten or twelve years ago now" I said "and I've just never spoken about it. Well, we've never spoken about it, it upsets Karen, and for me, it was a nightmare".

"Where were you?"

"North Africa, that's where".

"It was in the early days of African tourism when we went there, I suppose things have changed a lot by now because these days of course it's full of polished resorts and brand new hotels, but back then there were only a handful of places in even fewer resorts. We'd decided to go there because it was going to be 'different'. It's like I said, we'd no kids back then and we were thinking that the world was 'our oyster'.

We were feeling a bit adventurous and felt like going a bit off the beaten track. In those days it was Spain every year, 'Viva Espana' and all that and we just felt that it was time for a change.

So off we went, booked and packed and off we flew. We finally arrived at some unearthly hour at an airport which looked like it was made out of corrugated tin sheets and a bit of concrete.

And we thought 'So this is Africa'.

We were then put onto a coach, it was very early morning and dark and we drove for a couple of hours before the sun began to rise. When we looked out of the coach window, we could see nothing but scrubland and an empty road in front of us, and I remember thinking 'My god, where the hell have we come to'. Anyway, eventually the coach took a sharp right and headed down a brand new black and shiny tarmac road. Within ten or fifteen minutes we finally spotted the beautiful blue sea in the distance and soon we began to pass various buildings, they were fairly shoddy, but well, it was Africa. We were nearing our resort and at last there were some signs of human life. We went over the next couple of hills and suddenly, there in the distance, we could see two hotels, side by side.

As we approached, there on the right was a brand new hotel, a sparkling palace that had just been built. There were some painters still on scaffolding giving the hotel the final touches.

On the left of it was an older hotel, a simple white oblong building and about six floors high. It was much older and showing its age, so we sat there fingers crossed and hoping, but as we came to the fork in the road, our coach turned to the left. Damn.

Anyway, our Hotel was called 'The Salamanca' and it was sort of okay, but it was definitely built in the sixties or seventies and still retained its original décor. We were soon booked in at the reception and then shown to our room, and that was sort of okay too, it wasn't the 'Ritz' but it was alright. While Karen unpacked our clothes I went for a wander, and I went downstairs and walked through the hotel and then for a stroll outside There was a pool out there with plenty of sunbeds, and a bar with a dining area. As I wandered through to the end of the gardens, I suddenly came onto the most beautiful, pristine white sandy beach, and it sort of took my breath away. At that time in the morning it was completely deserted, and I just stood there looking out to the sea, it was absolutely stunning.

Anyway, that first day we settled by the pool and got acclimatised. We just lay there all day, soaking up the sun and we only came away when the sun finally started to disappear, then we went back to our room and got showered and changed, and ready for our evening meal.

Dining at 'The Salamanca' was a bit different. We went down to the huge dining room and it full of large circular tables which seated about twelve people. You were allocated a place at your designated table on the first day and there you stayed for the duration of your holiday.

On our first evening there, we were shown to 'our' table, which was already full of guests who had started their evening meal. We were given a warm welcome by all, and the people either side of us introduced themselves and the other guests in general said 'hello'. They were a friendly bunch, and since we were the 'new guests', they proceeded to tell us about the eating arrangements and the general protocol. They also gave us instructions regarding our waiter, the one and only 'Abdul'.

Apparently, Abdul was a great bloke, very funny, and very friendly, but there was one thing you had to know, and this advice was given to all new arrivals. It seemed that Abdul would introduce himself to you and explain about how he would serve you your food and what options there were for each meal, breakfast, lunch and evening meal. And also, he would get another waiter to go for your drinks and anything else that you wanted, after that he would serve you your meal with great fuss and attention. But once your meal was at an end and as he retrieved your final plate, it was then that Abdul would 'pounce' and he try to draw you into a 'bit of business'. The guests around the table told us what to expect.

So that first evening, our waiter Abdul came to our table and introduced himself to us. Tall, slim and dark, and with a liquid voice, the other guests at our table watched on in glee.

And they were right, at the end of that first evening's meal, Abdul made his move. It was apparently known as 'Abdul's chat up'.

"Ah my new friends" he effused "You have finished, was it good. Yes, of course, very good. Abdul will look after you...you are both lovely people". And then he spoke to everyone around the table "You are all lovely people, yes". Then he spread his arms out wide "Abdul looks after you all, it is top class, yes". And everybody smiled and laughed with him, then he returned his attention to us, just us, sort of personal.

"My friends, can I have a short word with you please, it is for my brother. He has a lovely shop, it is only a short walk from here and he sells beautiful things, many, many beautiful things", and with that, he waved his arms around expansively. "Please, please, go there and you will get best prices, wonderful prices, and much, much cheaper than in the town"

And as he said the words 'in the town' he sneered with disgust. I thought he was going to spit on the floor, and then he continued "My brother, he is a very good man. I will give you a 'special' business card. You go there and give it to him and you tell him you are my 'friend' and he will give you extra super prices and discount".

Now the trick was that you would agree to go to his brother's shop at sometime during your stay. Abdul would then produce one of his brother's fancy green business cards from his top pocket and slide it across the table to you. You in turn would pick up the card, and then smile back and say something like 'no problem' and 'yes, that would be nice, you would look forward to it', and that was that. Abdul had done his bit, and you'd done your bit, it was a bit of mutual respect and everyone was happy. He would in fact, never raise the topic again and would never ask you if you'd actually been to his brother's shop.

Protocol was observed. Yes, and everybody's happy.

About four or five days later, when some of our table had left to go back home, the new guests arrived, and that evening a 'new' family of four sat themselves down.

The new family turned out to be 'Eddie' and his family, and they were from Birmingham. Eddie was a slightly stooping, thin sort of man who it seemed, found it impossible to be pleasant, in fact he couldn't even smile. And it was also a fact, that he was without doubt, truly one of the most miserable gits that I've ever met. With him were his wife, whose name I forget, and also their two children, whose names I will never forget. Tracey aged about twelve and Ryan, possibly ten. I will always remember their names, and why?

Because 'Eddie' constantly moaned, complained and criticized everything they did.

God, he was a moaning twat.

And he had the most bloody annoying way of chastising his kids. It was a 'football thing'.

Depending on what he deemed his kids had done wrong, there were two levels of threats.

Just as in football, for the first level of complaint the kids were given a 'yellow card'. And the second level, and for continuing to misbehave, it was the 'red card'. Oh dear god.

And all we heard from the word go was 'Yellow card Tracy, yellow card there Ryan, and 'I think that's a yellow card there Tracey', repeatedly and in the most bloody annoying, clawing accent in the world. But then, unbelievably it went onto "Now then, nearly a red card there Tracy" and "Any more of that and it's a red card for you Ryan"

Red card yellow card, yellow card red card, it drove us all around the bloody twist.

Everywhere they went, and it was everywhere, you could hear that pillock going on and on.

Around the pool he was driving folk to distraction. I was standing at the pool bar one afternoon and one chap, who was a bit of a drinker commented that he dared not have another pint, because if he did he would go out and find a red card and stick it up 'Eddie's rectum.

So there you go, but on that first evening when they sat down at our table, we were all blissfully unaware of Eddie's shortcomings, and as we greeted them, everyone was smiling and friendly. But as the night continued, somebody at our table mistakenly told Eddie about the 'Abdul Protocol'.

Eddie immediately sat bolt upright in his chair.

"We won't be doing any of that" he stated categorically. In fact, he was quite put out.

When it was again explained to him that he didn't actually have to go to the brother's shop, just agreed to go, well, he couldn't see the sense in it. At that moment, I should have realized that the man was a complete and utter tosser.

As usual, Abdul arrived at our table, and as usual, he was full of gusto "Ah my friends, and how are you all this evening, good, yes, very good. And tonight I will bring you some beautiful food, simply beautiful".

And then he spotted the new arrivals "Ah, we have new friends, very nice, very good. Abdul will look after you, top class service, yes V.I.P treatment". And Abdul laughed.

Eddie however didn't. He didn't laugh, he didn't even smile and you could see that the dim pillock had made up his mind to go all defensive. He must have felt sort of threatened, the idiot.

All of this went over Abdul's head of course, and he went about his work serving us all with food and organizing the drinks. We were served starters, some sort of mini kebabs on a bed of salad and couscous. And as we finished, Abdul came to clear the plates, and of course he took this opportunity to mention his brother's shop to the new arrivals.

Eddie from 'Brum' was having none of it. And he just sat there in silence, bolt upright with his arms folded, and at all costs avoiding eye contact. But it was when Abdul finally handed Eddie one of his brother's green business cards that Eddie had a bit of a 'wobbler' and started to object loudly. He started shouting "No...No...No..."

However, Eddie was from Birmingham and his accent didn't travel well, and the words 'No...No...No' actually sounded like 'Now...Now...Now', well it did to Abdul anyway. And Abdul, who was never one to miss an opportunity, was absolutely delighted. Here was an Englishman who wanted to go shopping so much, he was prepared to miss the rest of his meal, never had he known a customer so keen. However, he knew of course that English people were 'all crazy' because they drank alcohol. Abdul immediately rattled something out in Arabic to a couple of the other waiters. What he actually said to them was something on the lines of 'You two look after my table, I'm taking this idiot to my brother's shop'.

And with that, Abdul took hold of Eddies arm.

"No...No...No" shouted Eddie again, and he tried to pull away, but Abdul held on and grinned with encouragement. Once again, he thought that Eddie had said "Now...Now...Now" and Abdul was there to please.

Nodding his head profusely, Abdul replied "Yes...Now, Yes...Now". However Abdul's accent was also lost in translation to Eddie, who found himself being dragged from the table by an obsessed waiter who was shouting "Yes...No, Yes...No."

Eddie jumped up, he'd had enough of this "You're fucking mad" he shouted, and well that brought the dining room to a halt. There was a bit of a scuffle and at one point I thought Eddie was going to start boxing. What a berk.

Anyway, amid all this the Manager, a Mr Atull, came quickly strutting up to find out what on earth was going on.

"Your waiter assaulted me" exclaimed an over exited Eddie.

The manager and Abdul had a quick exchange and the Manager turned back to Eddie.

"He says you want to go shopping"

"No" said Eddie.

The Manager, also hearing the magic word 'Now' nodded his head. "So he will take you right away".

"But I don't want to go" said Eddie.

"But you just said you did" said the manager. He too was a little confused.

"Listen" stormed Eddie "I...Do...Not...Want...To go...To...His bloody shop. Get it?"

The Manager turned to Abdul to explain, but Abdul had already heard what had been said and he started to rant at Eddie in wholesale Arabic.

Eddie wasn't having any of that and in turn he started to shout at the manager.

"This man needs sacking" he ranted "He's out of order. You need to red card him, give him the red card".

"You want me to give him a red card?" said the manager.

"Yes" replied Eddie triumphantly, he now felt he was getting somewhere.

The manager spoke to Abdul, there was a quick conversation and he turned back to Eddie.

"He says he already gave you card. A green one"

Eddie groaned "I know he gave me a green card", he was now getting angry again "That's not what I meant. I want him sorting out, and when I say 'red card him', it's like giving someone a 'yellow card', and then the 'red card'".

The manager was even more confused "All these giving of cards" he said "is it an English tradition?"

"What?" said an exasperated Eddie, who was now becoming extremely agitated. He was getting nowhere, except into a deeper pile of shite, and he suddenly realized it.

"Right" he shouted loudly "That's it. Come on everybody, Tracey, Ryan" he was now shouting at his family. "I've had enough of this, we'll go and eat somewhere else" and with that, his poor wife and kids had to get up to leave.

The Manager, now also upset, asked Eddie where they were going and that they hadn't had their meal.

"We'll go and get a' bloody burger' from somewhere" shouted Eddie in reply.

An hour later, they were spotted outside at a table near the pool, with fifteen bags of crisps.

The next night, there were four empty seats at our table, and amongst the rest of us there was a mutual sense of relief.

When Abdul arrived to attend to us he was a bit on the quiet side, he was embarrassed, and so we all unanimously made a decision and then we wholeheartedly apologized to him for last night's antics.

Abdul shrugged as he spoke "It is not a problem" he said "You are all lovely people and I thank you very much, it is 'nice to be nice'. But that other man, he was difficult, yes?

"Bloody difficult" I said, and that sort of broke the ice. Everybody around the table laughed and Abdul grinned and went back to being Abdul again.

As he took our orders, two of the other waiters came over and there was a short discussion and then they removed the empty chairs.

Abdul turned to us "That man, he is sitting somewhere else, good yes? Yes good, I thought so.

We all nodded in unison.

Eddie had apparently been back to see the Manager and had demanded an apology and another table and another waiter. Since an apology was never going to happen, not from Abdul anyway, the manager moved Eddie and his family to another table at the far side of the dining room.

It was a table over in a corner, just for the four of them and away from everybody else, and of course that suited Eddie down to the ground.

However, what Eddie didn't know, and most of the other guests probably didn't know either, was that everyone who worked in the Hotel Salamanca was somehow or other related.

Brothers, brothers in law, cousins, second cousins, and third, fourth and fifth cousins, in-laws and out-laws, they were all born and raised and lived in the nearby village.

And here, the famous words 'Kick one and you kick them all' certainly came into play.

And 'word was out' in the kitchen. Our Abdul had been insulted, and therefore the 'Family' had been insulted. The hotel catering staff were not happy with Eddie, but Eddie wasn't to know that, was he?

We were half way through our starter, when Eddie and his wife and kids walked into the dining room. The Manager glanced up, blinked, and looked around nervously at his staff. Not one of them batted an eyelid. He then looked back at Eddie and politely pointed over to the Pre-arranged table. Eddie nodded and then guided his family to their new seating.

Their new waiter was 'Mussim', a slim young man with impeccable manners. He was a man of few words, and he was also Abduls second cousin.

Mussim arrived at Eddie's table, smiled curtly and handed them their menus. He then organised their drinks and disappeared, literally.

Half an hour later he returned for their order.

"I thought you'd got lost" said Eddie.

Mussim said nothing, he just gave them a curt nod and took their order, and disappeared.

Half an hour later he returned with their starters.

"Finally" said Eddie, with a deep sigh "Do you know we're all starving?"

Mussim said nothing. He just set down their starters and disappeared.

Another half an hour, and he returned to clear their plates.

As he was about to disappear again, Eddie asked him "When will we get our main course?"

Mussim turned to him "They are cooking it now, sir" he replied, and he disappeared.

Forty five minutes later he returned with their food.

By now, Eddie was tapping the table with his fork in frustration.

"Bloody hell" he said to Mussim "I thought you'd gone home". It was Eddie's attempt at sarcasm.

"I'm sorry sir, we're very busy" he replied, and he served them their food and left. Another forty five minutes, and he came back.

Eddie just stared at him, he was not a happy man.

As Mussim cleared the plates Eddie asked him "And how long is our pudding going to be?"

"It's coming now sir" replied Mussim.

"While you're at it" said Eddie curtly "bring us two coffees and two cokes for the kids"

Mussim nodded.

The drinks never arrived.

Half an hour later, Mussim finally arrived with their four sweets.

"Where the bloody hell have you been?" blazed Eddie.

Mussim looked at him "I'm sorry sir" he said "but the food ran out and the chef had to prepare fresh..."

Eddie interrupted him "And where's our drinks?"

"Drinks?" said Mussim "What drinks?"

"The drinks we bloody well ordered over half an hour ago. Two coffees and two cokes, we ordered them from you".

"And you have not had them?" Mussim asked, wide eyed.

"No we bloody well haven't" exclaimed Eddie.

"I will get them for you straightaway" said Mussim as he walked away.

The drinks never arrived.

Half an hour later Mussim wandered back to their table, it was empty, Mussim smiled.

This performance continued at every meal, on every single day. In the end Eddie and his family gave up on breakfast and lunch altogether, they would go out to the pool bar and start their day with some cheese toasties and more crisps.

Every day, we'd finished our evening meal and be leaving the dining room along with everybody else, just as Eddie and his family would be getting their starters.

Eddie was not happy with Mussim, and he complained veraciously to Mr Atull, the Manager.

Mr Atull would hold up his hands in full apology and tried to explain to Eddie that they were all extremely busy, and it was the height of season. And also, that all the food had to be freshly prepared and that his team of waiters were rushed off their feet, but he 'of course' would have a word with Mussim.

However, and unfortunately, Eddie was not aware that Mussim was actually the Manager's brother in law. He was also unaware that Abdul and the Manager were also related, they were cousins.

'Kick one, and you kick them all' as they say.

So nothing changed.

A few days later, we were sat around the pool and Eddie was standing at the bar ordering some drinks. He was talking loudly as usual, to some hapless victim that he had cornered at the bar. The poor man that he was interrogating had just arrived and he didn't know Eddie's reputation or that everyone around the pool spent their day trying to avoid him.

"Oh no, we won't be coming back here again" Eddie bleated on at the top of his voice. "Terrible service, this lot" and he rudely pointed at the poor lad who worked behind the bar. "These people are a waste of time" said Eddie loudly "they don't know the meaning of the word 'service'. You'll be waiting all night for your meal, they just don't care. No, we shan't be coming here again. It's back to Bulgaria for us. We normally go there every year, what a place, and so cheap, I can't tell you how cheap it is. I can show you a restaurant where you can feed a family of four, with beer and cokes 'and' they throw in a bottle of wine, all for under ten pounds. What about that then. The wine's awful, but it's free, so you can't complain can you?"

The 'condemned' man felt he couldn't.

"No, you won't like it here" Eddie ranted on "its rubbish, you want to go to Bulgaria, it's a beautiful country, it used to be Yugoslavia you know. The people there are really nice, not like this lot" and again he pointed at the barman.

The barman stood there silently contemplating at which point he could spit in Eddie's drink.

"Yes" continued Eddie, he was now tapping his victim on the chest "You should definitely go to Bulgaria".

Around the bar, several people heard all of this and mentally struck Bulgaria off their 'holiday wish list'. A recommendation from Eddie could unknowingly decimate the Bulgarian tourist industry.

"And I'll tell you another thing" said Eddie "we're now on the internet. Its cable, you want to try it. When we get back home, I'll be right onto the Travel advisor' website and I'll be writing a full report on this place, and it's going to get the red card"

"A red card?" said the victim.

"Yes, a red card" said Eddie "You know what I mean".

The victim didn't, but he said he did.

A few of the men sitting around the bar casually got up and wandered over to the gent's toilets. Two minutes later, there were howls of laughter from within.

Eddie however missed all this. He was back with his family and was busy giving out yellow cards to his children.

The evening entertainment at the Hotel Salamanca could be best described as 'a bit thin on the ground'. There was a snake charmer with a tame snake, and a belly dancer with a belly, there was 'Bingo' for the Brits, and finally, an Arabic version of Tom Jones. His stage name was actually 'Johnny Romano' although that made him sound rather Italian and not one bit Welsh.

The thing was, 'Johnny Romano' actually did think he 'was' Tom Jones He was in his late fifties and had a bit of a paunch, and he'd grown his curly hair and sideburns...a' la Tom.

His hair was dyed absolutely jet black, I think I've seen paler coal, but there was one thing you just had to applaud, he had 'the voice' off to a tee, there was even a touch of a Welsh accent thrown in as a bonus.

The man was as smooth as glass, and the women loved him. During his act, he would step off the stage and walk from table to table, crooning to the 'lovely' ladies, who thought he was just wonderful. Eventually he would spot a lady who was solo and he would hone in on her and look deeply into her eyes and sing only to her, or that's what she thought. After making a fuss of her he would finish his act and leave the stage. But then, ten minutes later he would re appear through a side door and make a beeline back to the woman's table. Then he would introduce himself with his best smile, almost boyish, boyo.

She of course would be bowled over. Well, he was a 'celebrity'. He was 'Tom Jones'.

He would sit down, laughing and talking, and she would be flattered. And after five or ten minutes he would click his fingers to an attentive waiter and order them both a bottle of champagne, African champagne.

They would continue to laugh and talk and he would take her onto the dance floor when the slower music was playing, so that he could put his arms around her. No gyrating to disco music for that boy, and she appreciated this, and she liked it, and liked the attention. Late into the evening he would take her to the bar and they would sit there, perched on two tall bar stools, talking intimately to each other and drinking liquor, with the certain knowledge that at some time that night they would be lovers.

At the end of the week he would wave her goodbye, and that same evening find his next love.

She would leave with a smile on her face. She'd had her fling. She'd had Tom Jones, well the next best thing. And, I suppose her family and her friends, and the neighbours, would never know.

So, 'The Salamanca', that was the entertainment, and not very entertaining. After a couple of nights of boredom we went in search of something else, and something else turned out to be the 'Cocktail Bar'.

Tucked away between the entrance to the pool and the lounge, discreet and hidden away, was the Cocktail bar, and thank god.

A little Oasis, it was filled with people who had suffered the two or three days of agony and boredom which was called 'entertainment' in the main lounge. And like us, in desperation, they'd searched for fields afresh. Another week of 'Salamanca nights' and any old pub in England would have seemed like 'little Havana'.

And so after a bit or wandering about, we found it, and we walked through the open double doors and plonked ourselves down on a couple of handy barstools next to the bar. We turned to the enthusiastic barman and gratefully ordered two large gin and tonics. Then I started to look around and could see that it was a 'sociable' sort of place, like I said 'a bit of an oasis'. Sitting next to us were another couple, who turned out to be Mark and Anne Marie. It was a chance encounter, just a matter of the time and the place, but we met and talked and we laughed together, and we became good friends.

There was a sort of 'camaraderie' in the cocktail bar, it was a gang of fairly social people who just wanted conversation, lubricated with a few drinks, and that was okay.

Mark, well he was a bit of a mystery really, but a serious mystery. Mark was in the Army and when I first met him he was a little bit vague about what he actually did, and that was fair enough, but eventually when we were into our second week's holiday and we became firm friends with him and Anne Marie, he finally told me all about his profession and what it entailed.

It turned out that Mark was an Army 'Chauffer', and that sounded a fairly tame sort of position, but when I got into deeper conversation with him, I realized that the title 'Chauffer' didn't just mean that he was a driver, he was also a personal bodyguard.

He drove exclusively for a very important Army Colonel and had done for the last several years, and by the Colonel's specific request. Mark, it seems was very good at his job and his Colonel knew it.

The Colonel held an executive position, he dealt with NATO, and his rank and standing took him all over Europe. He dealt with the heads of governments and with the very top people in their respective armed forces. Within the army, the colonel was a V.I.P.

Mark's job was the security, safety and transit of the Colonel to his varied destinations.

The Colonel's high profile meant that he would have been a significant target for any terrorist organizations worldwide, and that was an absolute fact. It was Mark's job to keep him safe and sound, and he took his job seriously. On arrival at any destination, whatever country and wherever and whenever possible, Mark would prefer to have a day's grace to check out the designated location. He preferred to have a good 24 hours to reconnoitre the area before the Colonel's meeting. During that day, he would drive all around the vicinity and familiarize himself with the roads and the side streets, and the possible escape routes. He would take note of any roadwork's, any hold ups or closed exits or blockages. He would find the quickest way in or out in the event of any adverse situation, that was his job. He told me that he always set his watch fifteen minutes ahead of time so that he was never, ever late for his Colonel. It was imperative, he must never be out of sync, and that was the protocol.

He told me that when his 'Boss', the Colonel 'left the building', he had to be there, ready and waiting to go.

Laughingly, he told me that if they were ever victim to a terrorist attack, well without doubt the both of them would be killed, so there was deal of self preservation there too. He was obviously very well trained and he could drive a car in reverse almost as easy as he could drive forwards and spin a car around on the spot.

I should have had him show my wife how to park.

He was clearly well versed in security, he actually told me about one of the guys who trained him, a Captain who had been a personal bodyguard at 'Charles and Di's wedding'. The Captain had to dress up in period costume, but under that costume, he was armed to the teeth.

I vaguely remember the scene as the 'happy couple' were trotted down Pall Mall in an open topped horse and carriage, there was a guy sat next to the driver, and I've always wondered, maybe?

So anyway that was Mark, he was a great lad, tall and dark haired, very athletic, and with the look of the 'Celtic' about him. His long time girlfriend and partner was Anne Marie. She was Irish through and through, and she too had dark hair, a head full of almost black, shiny wavy hair and skin as pale as milk, as pretty as a picture and with a personality to match.

They were nice people.

And we just hit it off, and the Cocktail Bar in 'The Salamanca' was a lively place, we were all escapees. The barman was also a strange and lively chap, small and bald, he was in his sixties and for some totally unknown reason, he told us all that his name was Patrick. Not really Arabic was it, so Anne Marie christened him Paddy. He seemed to like that.

After a few evenings in the Cocktail Bar we discovered the delights of 'Bhouka', which was the local spirit, it was some sort of brandy that was made from figs, and we discovered that if you mixed it with cola it tasted a bit like Rum and Coke. It was also half the price and was a bit lethal. So, three days in and most of the people in the cocktail bar were then drinking the stuff. Word had got around, and 'Paddy' the barman was a happy man.

"You very good man" he said to me one night "Bhouka 'eez a local drink, we make it here.

It is 'very' good for local business and you have got everybody drinking it, good eh?" and as a show of appreciation, he started to regularly top up our glasses.

Nice one Paddy.

One night we were all in the Cocktail Bar, when suddenly one of the young local lads walked past the entrance. It turned out that he was known to one and all as 'Little Ali' and he was one of the cleaners at our Hotel.

As he walked past the doorway of the bar, he stopped and peered in, probably through curiosity. And as he did, one of the guests spotted him and then called out to him.

"Ali, hey nice one, and Ali, thanks for that" and the guest, a man, raised his hand and gave Ali the 'thumbs up' sign.

Ali smiled back and waved, and then suddenly as he looked at the people around the bar, his expression changed. He stopped smiling, and his eyes gave a nervous look, and he immediately turned and scuttled off.

Strange, I thought.

But the guest, the man who had called out to Ali, had already turned back to his friends and was telling them something.

"Good lad, that Little Ali" he said to his friends "My wife lost one of her shoes and Ali found it for her. We'd searched all over the place, but he eventually found it. What a good kid, I gave him a couple of quid for his troubles".

The man opposite looked back at his friend "We lost one of our shoes too" he said slowly "and we looked everywhere, and then finally Little Ali found it. And I gave him a few quid too, as a 'thank you'.

A man, who was standing just behind them at the bar, then leant over.

"Sorry to interrupt you" he said "I couldn't help but just overhear your conversation. We also lost a shoe, and guess who found it for us?" and he smiled back at the group "Yes, Little Ali and yes, I paid up too"

The first guest then turned to all in the bar and called out loud "Has anyone here had a shoe gone missing, and had it found by little Ali, and then paid the little bugger?"

Over half of them put their hands up. There was a brief silence and then everyone suddenly erupted in laughter.

God help us, 'the English'. We fall prey to every 'con' going.

The next evening a guy came into the bar and informed us all that he had spotted little Ali at his 'broom cupboard', it was where he stored all his mops, brushes and cleaning stuff.

He told us that he had quietly walked up behind Ali and looked over his shoulder and into the broom cupboard, and inside the broom cupboard was a shelf full of shoes.

"What did you do?" we asked.

"I tapped him on the shoulder"

"And?"

"He nearly had a heart attack. He spun around and looked at me, his eyes went as big as golf balls and his mouth dropped wide open. He was caught, and he knew it, the poor little bugger nearly crapped himself".

We all chuckled at that, and you had to admit it, little Ali was certainly entrepreneurial.

"What did you say to him?" I asked.

"I put my hand on his shoulder and said to him 'Ali', if any of 'my shoes' go missing, I will find you and throw you into the pool, okay?"

Little Ali immediately started grinning and gave me a look of relief and let me know that he understood my threat. He thought he'd got away with it and that was that, but no, no, no.

"And" I continued to tell him "and you will also return all the shoes that you have stolen to their rightful owners, or I'll report you to the Hotel manager, and then I'll tell all the guests what you've done".

Ali stopped grinning, then he slowly nodded his head, and that was the deal, he had no other choice.

And so everyone around the bar had a good chuckle about it all, and more 'Bhouka' was ordered. No more shoes disappeared, well at least not for the two weeks we were there, and not until the next lot of visitors arrived.

North Africa was a curious place in those days, and I remember one day when we were taken on a trip to the local market town. Karen couldn't come with us, she had a touch of 'African stomach' and wasn't in the mood for being more than twenty feet away from a toilet. It was a red hot afternoon, very much into 40 degrees, and the coach that we were in had never even heard of air-conditioning. As we drove through the town we were struck by the obvious comparisons, between the rich and the poor. Parts of the town were constructed in marble and gold, other districts were ramshackle places with people living in complete squalor.

Anne Marie remarked on how the town was '10% gold and 90% mud'.

She was right.

Once we got off the coach we almost ran into the local market, more for the shade than the need to buy something, but it was apparently the 'thing' to do back in those days. We, along with the rest of the people on our coach were immediately set upon on by the market traders, they were relentless, it was easier to get rid of the mosquitoes. We were dragged this way and that, pestered and pulled, and in the end we daren't look at anything in case the market traders saw you and thought that you might be mildly interested. We finally escaped and went for a walk through the town with a view to sitting down somewhere in the shade and having a cold drink. We walked for quite a distance without any success and the unrelenting heat began to get to us, we were becoming dehydrated and weary. Then suddenly we turned a corner and in front of us was our saviour, an Oasis, it was a Cafe. I suppose the term 'Cafe' was probably a bit over enthusiastic, but that's what you'd have to call it. It was just a small glass fronted shop with something in Arabic written over the door. There was a battered and beaten 'Coca Cola' sign stuck to the front wall and in small worn red letters on the window was painted the words...'cold drinks'.

Well 'Hurray' for that.

We headed for an old Formica topped table which had been placed outside the shop front and we pulled out three of the four chairs there and sat ourselves down in the shade.

Eventually an old man came out to us to take our order. He was stick thin, looked seventy, and had a strange mouthful of brown teeth. He was wearing what looked like an unwashed whitish shirt, blue overall pants and very old sandals. There was no smiling, he just stood there in front of us and said "You want dreenks?"

"Yes please" I said "We'll have three cold beers please".

He looked at us with distaste and shook his head "No, no. No beers, we no sell. No sell alcohol".

For a moment I thought he was about to walk away "What have you got then?" I asked quickly.

He shrugged "coke...coffee...lemon".

After a quick discussion, I asked him for two cokes and a coffee for Anne Marie.

He nodded as he produced a cloth from his pocket, and then he leant over Anne Marie to give the table a wipe. As he did this he put his hand on her bare shoulder, only momentarily, but I saw it.

And Anne Marie felt his hand on her shoulder and pulled away. She didn't say anything, but I'd seen what had happened and I watched as she frowned and quietly shook her head. I didn't mention it and Mark seemed not to notice, so I let it go.

It had all happened in an instant, and maybe it was me, but I thought it a bit 'odd'.

Five or ten minutes later a waiter, a younger man, came out with our drinks on a tray. He was smiling and trying to be efficient. With a bit of swirl, he placed our glasses in front of us. Glasses full of ice and lemon, and then with one hand he placed the bottles of ice cold coke on the table.

Then he turned to Anne Marie "Your coffee 'Madam" he said smartly, and he carefully placed the cup of coffee in front of her.

Then, he too put his hand on her uncovered shoulder. It was almost a gesture of friendship. "Enjoy" he said, and he looked down at her.

It was a look I couldn't explain, but there was something there.

Anne Marie once again pulled away, she didn't thank or even look at the waiter. She seemed a bit uneasy, and annoyed.

She never spoke, and Mark just continued the conversation he and I had been having and we sat there talking for a while, with our drinks.

"Anne Marie" I finally said to her, she'd just been sitting there, rather quietly. She looked up.

"Is there something wrong...?" I asked her.

For a moment she didn't speak.

I asked her again "Is there a problem, with that waiter I mean?"

She just frowned "It's these men" she then said "They're always touching me, and it's getting on my nerves."

Mark listened to this and then began to laugh "What are you on about?" he sort of snorted.

She glanced at him "It's the men here, they touch you all the time. They're always doing it and I don't like it".

"Give over" Mark laughed out loud "You're imagining it"

"No I'm not" she answered him back "I've spoken to other women at the hotel about it, they've had the same thing too".

Mark grinned and shook his head, which in turn made Anne Marie rather annoyed.

Oh dear me. Not a wise move and she turned away in silence.

An awkward moment, but Mark looked at me, raised his eyes, and then carried on with our conversation as though this was all 'something and nothing'.

But I knew Anne Marie, and she had the 'Irish' in her and so I realized that this wasn't over.

About fifteen minutes later we decided to get up and go back and find our coach. We left the cafe and slowly walked back onto the still empty main street. It was fairly deserted and Anne Marie was still quiet. Suddenly on the opposite side of the street, a tall man came around the corner and came walking down the road in our direction.

Anne Marie suddenly spun around to Mark and said "Slow down, follow me, and watch", and with that she set off walking. We looked at one another, a bit mystified, and so we did as she said and followed her.

She quickly got herself about ten yards in front of us and then settled down to a leisurely pace. The tall man across the road continued to walk in our direction. He was wearing Arabic clothing, baggy black pants and a loose fitting white top and sunglasses. Suddenly, he casually crossed over the road and ambled towards us, not a care in the world, but as he approached Anne Marie, he nonchalantly lifted his arm as though to look at his watch. But as he passed by her he stopped looking at his watch and put out his hand and delicately ran it along Anne Marie's arm and bare shoulder. He then continued to walk past us as though nothing at all had happened. We watched him pass, behind his sunglasses he was expressionless, but we were a bit taken aback.

However, there in front of us stood Anne Marie. She had her hands on her hips, defiant, and point proven, and she was looking directly at Mark.

And I thought 'Now he's going to get it'.

And I was right.

"Well?" she exclaimed, loudly "What did I tell you, did you see that, it happens all the time. But 'Oh no, I'm just bloody imagining it', am I?"

Mark couldn't say a thing. He just held up his arms as a form of apology, now he understood.

"Christ" he blasphemed to his good catholic wife.

"See, I told you...and there's no need for 'that' sort of language Mark" she smartly replied and also chastised him at the same time. Only women can do that.

"I never realized " he said, and it was a good try at an apology.

I suddenly intervened "I did" I said "I saw it happen at the cafe before, that young waiter, he ran his hand along your shoulder, and so did the old guy who took our order, I saw him too".

She nodded and looked across at Mark "See, everybody else sees it" she said, she was now a bit calmer.

I turned to Mark "I did see it Mark, before at the cafe, and then just now. That man, the same thing. There is something, I just don't get it".

He reached over and put his big arm around his wife's shoulder and gave her a hug.

"I'm really sorry love" he said, and then he looked over at me and winked. "Hey, I know what it is. It's you" he said to her "It's your skin, it's because you're so pale. They all think you're bloody dead"

And then he burst out laughing "I'm married to a corpse".

"Jesus Christ, Mark" and then she punched him.

"No need for that sort of talk dear, it's ungodly" he retorted with a touch of sarcasm, and then ducked as she started to swing her handbag at him.

Sometime during the second week of our holiday, it was in the afternoon and we were lounging around by the pool, me, Karen and Anne Marie, when suddenly Mark reappeared from one of his scouting trips. He used to do this all the time, he was a man who couldn't sit still and he was always disappearing off somewhere and coming back with some tale or some useless information. But today, it seemed that he had actually struck gold.

"Listen" he said, all enthusiastic and excited "I've found us something".

We'd heard all this before, and so we sort of rolled over on our sun loungers and re adjusted our sunglasses.

"Go on 'Batman'..." I said "What have you found now?"

Anne Marie quietly groaned, this was a regular event.

"Next door" he said, all of a fidget.

"What?"I replied. I always tried to show a bit of interest.

"Next door" he repeated himself. "I've been round to the new Hotel next door, and 'strewth' you want to see it. It's unbelievable"

"How come you went over there?" I said.

"I found a hole in the fence" and he smiled.

"Oh right, very nice".

And I thought to myself 'what now'?

It turned out that there was a high fence and shrubbery between both hotels and this totally obstructed any view of the new Hotel and its grounds. And 'no wonder', I was later to find out.

Anyway, so Mark's found a hole in the fence.

"I was having a wander about" he continued, excitably "and I was walking down the side of the perimeter fence when I found a large gap, it was a break in the fence. It's sort of hidden behind a tree and some shrubs, you can hardly see it. I think the builders must have used it, maybe to get water or something from this side. Anyway for some reason, nobody's decided to brick it up or they've forgotten or whatever. So I just walked through the gap and into next door, and 'my god', you want to see it over there. It's a brand new five star hotel, it's absolutely astounding. The grounds are fantastic, and the Hotel is something else, you should see the inside".

"You've been inside?" I said.

"Yes, and I've spoken to the Hotel Manager. He's a great guy, he showed me around the place. The Hotel's called the 'Royal Taj' and isn't officially open for a couple of months.

There's no water in the outdoor swimming pool yet, but the Hotel has an indoor pool which is just great, and we can use it. We can use all of it, for free".

It was that last bit that got our attention.

"What do you mean 'all of it'?" asked Anne Marie.

"Well I spoke to the Manager. They have no guests there yet but they want to get things moving along, and they would like us to come round and check out the facilities. He told me they have a roof top cocktail bar with some American barman who's just sitting around up there with no customers to serve, and he's bored to death. And so 'folks' he said that we can go around there anytime we want and get the V.I.P treatment and all that".

And Mark gave us his best cheesy grin. 'What a clever boy'.

Karen peered over her sunglasses and looked straight at me "Why don't you go and check it out 'now' she said, and she gave me the 'go and do it' straightaway nod.

I almost saluted.

Why is it, that women find it impossible to let us men 'do nothing'? If you lie down, they want you to get up. If you get up, they want you to go somewhere. You go somewhere, and they want to know where you've been...etc, etc.

So slightly grudgingly, I got up and off we went. Mark showed me the 'hole in the wall' and through we went, and my god, I'd never seen anything like it. The Hotel was stunningly beautiful, and even with an empty swimming pool it was definitely 'something' else. The gardens were manicured, and the landscaping and the beautiful marble and mosaic tiling around the pool and dining area, was pristine. We walked through the grounds and into the Hotel itself. The interior was amassed in gold and marble. Huge chandeliers hung from the ceilings and they shone with a bright white light that the illuminated the white marble walls and pillars. The floors were laid out in an intricate pattern of ivory and gold mosaic tiles, the whole effect was fantastic, it was obvious that no expense had been spared.

Mark took me down a corridor to the indoor pool, it was huge, and the same colour scheme had been carried through. Ivory and gold tiles which contrasted with the turquoise blue water. It looked like a scene from Ancient Rome.

We just took one look at each other and Mark nodded at me and laughed, and we ran and jumped into the pool with a loud 'Yee hah'. The water was lovely and warm, it was wonderful.

There was a very smart bar in there as well, but unfortunately it was closed, and that was a shame. Because had it been open, I think we would have stayed in there all day.

About an hour later we went back to our hotel and 'spilled the beans' to the girls. They both brightened up no end when we told them that we were all going back there that night to try out the rooftop Cocktail Bar. After a week in 'The Salamanca' with its belly dancers and bingo, we were definitely ready for a change.

So after our evening meal, we met up at the Salamanca cocktail bar, had a couple of drinks and then sauntered off for an evening at the 'The Taj'.

We strolled out of our hotel and walked down through the gardens to the hidden 'hole in the wall'. It was a bit dark but we found it alright and we guided the girls through and into the 'Taj' gardens which thankfully were brightly lit up like a palace. We walked through the gardens and into the hotel. The girls were spellbound.

"See, I told you" said Mark, triumphant.

Well, they had to agree.

After a tour of the indoor pool and the resplendent lobby area, we headed for the lift.

The ornate golden door of the lift opened silently, and as we got into it Mark pressed the button for the 'rooftop'. The door slid shut and the lift hummed as it whisked us up and away to the top of the hotel

A minute later the door re-opened and we stepped out into the 'Royal Taj' rooftop bar.

We all looked at each other, and grinned. Yes, this definitely was 'the place'.

Once again the decor, it was decked out top to bottom in ivory and gold tiles. In every corner there were beautiful green tropical plants in large terracotta and gold pots. The effect was so smart, it was all really, really cool. It was also really, really empty.

We walked in and began to look around the place. We strolled past a long marbled topped bar, which to was empty, and then onto a large, open terrace which looked out sea. The terrace was lined with voluptuous cream coloured couches together with smart dark teak tables. The view out to sea was spectacular.

We'd left both the girls out there and had walked back to the bar to see if anyone was serving drinks, when suddenly the bartender arrived out of a back room. A large black man, he stood there surprised and astonished, he'd a couple of glasses in one hand and a towel in the other and he just stared back at us. Then he grinned and gave us the widest of smiles.

"Halleluiah" he said out loud "The good lord has finally sent me some customers" and then he laughed.

He walked through the bar towards us and put down the glasses and towel and reached out to shake our hands.

"Hi there" he said in a rich American accent "My names Floyd, and welcome to the 'Royal Taj Rooftop Cocktail Bar. And how are 'ya all'..."?

Well that broke the ice and we shook hands with him and introduced ourselves, and then the girls came over and there were more introductions. Floyd was a happy man, it turned out that we were his first customers. No one was staying at the hotel yet and he was stuck up there, all alone in his empty bar, polishing glasses and raring to go.

"Your first drinks have got to be on the house" he announced with a drawl and a smile.

"That's very nice of you Floyd" I said.

"Well who the hells going to know" he said back, and he raised his arms in question as he looked around the empty bar, and laughed "Hey, it's my goddamn bar. I'll do what the hell I want".

And that set the tone for the night.

He continued "I'm going to make you 'all' some cocktails, my own 'specials'. Hey, I've been stuck up here for nearly a month now, on my own. I'm going rusty and a bit crazy and I need some practice" and he laughed again.

The next thing, he was cutting up fruit and pouring drinks from different bottles, smashing crushed ice and lining up silver cocktail mixers. This guy was good.

We talked to him as he performed, and he told us that he was originally from New Orleans. He worked at a bar in a Jazz club in the French Quarter, and apparently a friend of a friend told him about this job. 'Head barman' in a brand new 5* star hotel complex in Africa', and the thought of it appealed to him. 'Broaden your horizons, travel and promotion', it all sounded good.

Floyd laughed again "Head barman, 'yeah' and head cleaner, sweeper and bottle washer. I can't wait for the season to start, I need to get busy. The management say that they'll provide me with the staff once the hotel has guests. But for now, well it's no use. I can see their point of view."

We nodded in agreement.

"Well" I said to him "you sure do have an absolutely fantastic place here".

"Yep" replied Floyd "It is isn't it, and it's all the better for you guys coming up to see me. Now then, here try out your drinks. They're 'Floyd Specials', so enjoy".

He slid four drinks across the bar. Multicoloured and in tall shaped glasses, and then topped with fruit, the drinks looked spectacular.

"Cheers" we said in unison as we lifted the glasses and drank. And 'my god', they were fantastic.

"This is beautiful Floyd" said Anne Marie approvingly "What's in it?"

Floyd tapped the side of his nose "It's a secret, it's my special drink and if I told you, I'd probably have to kill you" and he ran his finger under his throat for effect, and laughed.

We all did.

Mark wandered off, as usual, and within a couple of minutes he came bouncing back.

"Come and look at this" he said, full of enthusiasm, and he grabbed my arm.

He led me around a corner to a large alcove which was set back, and then he stood there and pointed in front of him "Look at that baby" he said.

Standing there in front of us, in all its majesty, was the most beautiful, brand spanking new Pool Table.

I looked at it, and it was a work of art, pristine. It even smelled 'new' if that's possible. Crafted in the same dark teak as the tables out on the terrace, and highly varnished and grained, it had been constructed from top quality wood, and as a finishing touch, the table itself was covered in a deep dark, red coloured felt, as opposed to the usual green.

The effect was stunning. Four small spotlights shone down on the table to give subtle illumination and on the wall opposite was a rack of brand new untouched pool cues in a variety of lengths. All new and all pristine.

Mark swooned. He loved to play pool. Over at the Salamanca there were a couple of very worn out old tables with a never ending queue of people waiting to play on them. We'd sort of given them up as a 'lost cause'. But now, well this just sealed the deal.

"We're in here every night from now on" said Mark, and it wasn't a question.

We had found sanctuary and I wasn't arguing.

So that was it. For the next four or five nights after our evening meal, we would walk down to the 'hole in the wall' and go through into the 'Taj', and then up to the rooftop bar.

It was great. The girls would sit at the bar and be entertained by Floyd, who would be mixing up cocktails like a Genie, and me and Mark, armed with a couple of large ice cold beers, could slope off to the pool table. In between games, we would wander back to the bar for refills and a chat. It was all very social.

Floyd told us that the Pool table had been 'custom built' in Chicago and had been specially flown over from the U.S.A. It certainly was a 'one off' and had been built by a firm that were without doubt, looking at their export market.

For Mark, it was 'Holy Grail'.

Finally our holiday came to an end, the two weeks were almost over and it was our last night, we were leaving the next evening. So we decided to make the most of it. As usual, we went 'through the hole' and into the' Taj' and then up to the rooftop bar. Large cocktails were the order of the day and we were determined to make the most of our last evening there. Floyd of course, knew it was our last night and was on top form. We had all had some good nights in there and he knew that after tonight he would be back on his own.

And what a good night it was. We pushed the boat out and stayed late. It was a lot later than usual and it was past two in the morning when we finally said our last goodbyes. We wished Floyd all the best and promised to keep in touch and all that rubbish, and then headed for the lift and made our way back to The Salamanca. However, as we walked through the downstairs lobby and into the gardens outside, we suddenly realized that we were walking into darkness. It was pitch black out there because all the lights had been turned off. This was going to be a problem and the girls immediately refused to go any further. I tried to get them to give it a go, but it was Mark who resolved the issue. His realized that it was impossible to see where we were going, and there was also the empty swimming pool to consider. If anybody fell into it they would seriously injure themselves, and there was also a mixture of steps and potted plants scattered all over the place. Actually the chance of 'not' falling over something was pretty slim. There was also going to be the small problem of trying to locate the 'hole in the wall', and that took some finding in broad daylight.

"We've not a chance in the dark" he said.

"Good thinking 'Caruthers" I quipped in a military fashion. He was right of course, and I'd had several Cocktails.

"We'll have to go out through the front of the hotel and onto the road and walk all the way round to The Salamanca" he explained.

It seemed a reasonable enough idea, so off we went. It was a warm night and we were in good spirits, and we had enough alcohol in us not to care or think, because we hadn't realized just how far it was. The hotels themselves were built on huge areas of land, and what we thought was a perimeter road that ran around both hotels, turned out to be an original older road and it didn't run around any perimeter at all. In fact, it meandered away from the Hotels and headed for one of the towns. It went for miles in the wrong direction, but we weren't to know that, where we?

I remember it all, as we walked along that long dark road. The road itself had been roughly laid with tarmac and it had an uneven surface that was badly cracked by heat and time. It was punctured with small potholes and looked to be half covered with windblown sand. But, it was the strange lighting that stays in my mind. On one side along the whole length of the road were street lights, they were spaced about every twenty yards and gave off a strange orange light that made the pavement and the road look almost yellow, it was all a bit surreal. The lights went off into the distance for as far as you could see, and because they were all along one side, only the road was illuminated and nothing else. On the other side of the road, there was nothing but scrubland, it was desolate and in complete darkness.

We'd set off and had been walking for maybe fifteen minutes. The girls were ahead of us, about ten or fifteen yards in front, chatting away about babies. We just shook our heads, half way through the holiday Mark and I had become consciously aware that both our women were getting broody, and after a few discussions over a few beers, he and I also realized that fatherhood was probably looming for both of us.

We walked behind them and were talking about Mark's job in the Army. He was being sent over to Brussels. His boss, the Colonel, had commandeered him for the tour.

As we walked along, a white light suddenly blinked far in the distance, and it caught my eye. I never thought much about it at the time but as we strolled along talking to each other, the light got slowly brighter and in the back of my mind I realized that it was some sort of vehicle, either a car or a van, and I still didn't give it much attention.

We walked along in procession and eventually the oncoming vehicle trundled along the road towards us. Finally I heard the engine, and it was quite distinctive. There was a 'popping' noise to it, the vehicle had a blown exhaust and you could clearly hear it in the distance. All of this just registered in the back of my mind, there was no fuss, and Mark didn't mention anything and the girls were laughing to themselves as they walked along in front of us.

We were still talking about the army as the vehicle finally came into view. It rolled around a slow bend in the road and headed directly towards us. I looked up to see that it was car, just a car, probably someone coming home from work late, or maybe somebody heading for the Royal Taj, maybe a cleaner.

It wasn't travelling particularly fast, probably to keep the engine noise down, but as the car got about a hundred yards from the girls, the engine note changed. It slowed, with a popping sound, as the vehicle suddenly changed its pace. Mark was still talking so I just didn't make anything of it. The car drove slowly past the girls, who just gave it a fleeting look and carried on chatting and giggling. It was an estate car, a battered old Renault, and as it came past us I noticed that it was a dirty burgundy colour. I also noticed that inside the car were five men, and as the car slowly rolled by I quickly glanced down at them, only to see that the five men were all staring straight back at us.

It unnerved me for a moment. The men, all in their forties, were expressionless, and they just stared back at us with dark eyes. But Mark just continued casually talking away. It was as though he hadn't even seen the car. I suppose it had only taken less than ten seconds for the vehicle to pass us and so we just walked on and I was already dismissing it as nothing.

The car carried on and so did we. Then suddenly, something happened. It was the sound, the sound of the car's engine suddenly changed, it had stopped. I turned around to look back at the car, it had stopped right in the middle of the road, and then I heard the car slowly rev up again as the driver proceeded to turn it around and come back towards us. Since the road was not very wide, the driver had manoeuvre the car to turn it about, awkwardly in forward and reverse because he couldn't manage to do a u-turn. But finally he did turn the car around and then they started to head back.

"You know what's happening" snapped Mark immediately. This was in voice that I hadn't heard before. He'd stopped talking a few minutes previously, and I hadn't really noticed.

I turned to him "What?" and that was all I said.

"Do you know what's happening, what's going to happen?" he said quickly.

I looked at him, and I looked again. This was a different Mark, this wasn't 'good old Marky', this was a suddenly different man altogether. He was starting to take in huge breaths of air and flexing his muscles, he was taking in huge breaths of air to get oxygen into his blood stream and to kick in the adrenaline. And suddenly his whole bearing had changed.

"What's going on Mark?" I asked him "What's happening?"

He quickly looked back at me "We're in trouble, big trouble. The men in that car, they're coming back for us, we've got a fight on our hands".

I was aghast, and I was mesmerized. This is what Mark was trained to do, he was a professional soldier. But I wasn't. And this was another Mark, and I could see the violence in him and the anger, and for a moment I wondered just what he was actually capable of.

"They're after the girls. They want the girls" he shouted it out.

"What?"" I said again, stupidly. It was all I could seem to say, things were happening so fast and I was completely out of my depth, I was a lost cause.

"Get with it Alan for Christ's sake" he continued to shout, and he turned on me "It's like this, these bastards are going to rape the girls. Get it. They're going to gang rape them. But first they're going to beat us senseless or worse, and then they're going to rape the girls, and kill us, and then they're going to fucking bury us. 'Now do you get it'? We're in real fucking trouble here, we're going to have to fight these fuckers and fight for our fucking lives.

"Oh Christ no" I spluttered, and the shock and the reality of what was happening made me go sick. I looked at the girls walking along in front of us, they were clueless as to what was going on.

Mark carried on speaking, hard and brutal and professional "Listen to me and listen good. We've got to go at them full on. We've got to get in there first and get the upper hand. I can take out three of them I think, can you do something with the other two until I get to you?"

"Christ Mark, I'm no fighter" I said, and I immediately felt ashamed and pathetic. I was suddenly terrified of what was happening and what was about to happen, I was so completely out of my depth.

But Mark never let up "Find yourself something, a rock or a brick. Try and find a bottle, smash it first and then stick it in the fuckers face. Look for something 'now'..!"

I was in Africa for god's sake, and could I find a bloody rock? No, nothing, no rock...no brick...no bottle. Not even a piece of wood, there was nothing but sand and bloody scrubland.

Mark saw the expression on my face, and the fear. He saw it all.

"Listen to me Alan, and listen good" he said through gritted teeth "Look at the girls, and look at your wife. These bastards are going to harm your wife. They're going to rape her and hurt her, and then they're going to kill us all and that's it. We have one chance. So forget the fear and get fucking angry, and then get mad and then get raging fucking mad. Because we're going to fight these dirty bastards and beat the shit out of them, and we're going to make them suffer, coz' they're just a set of fuckin' dogs".

And it worked. With those few words he'd got to me and he had me. I finally woke up to what was going on and some sort of anger kicked in. It was 'the adrenalin', and I gritted my teeth. I looked at Karen. I loved her, she was 'my Karen' and nobody was going to touch her, nobody. And I didn't care about myself anymore, and I hated these bastards that were coming for us. And then suddenly out of the blue, a plan came into my head, and I knew exactly what I was going to do, plain and simple.

Yes, three of them would definitely go for Mark. He was big and muscular and dangerous.

Me, I'm five foot six all day long. I'm wide but not tall and though I'm strong enough, I'm never going to be a threat. It struck me that when the car came to a stop, four of the men would jump out immediately and attack us, but not the driver. He would be slightly delayed because he was steering the car, and he would have to come to a stop and take the car out of gear. Then he would have to put on the handbrake and then finally fling the door open to get out. All little things, but they would add up. It might only be five or ten seconds at most, but it would split up the group. Instead of there being five attacking us all at once, there would be four, and yes three of them would go for Mark, he was like a raging bull, but for a short time I would be faced by only one man. If Mark could get the better of the other three, and if I could stop this one man, the driver would take off, he'd run for it. He wouldn't like the odds. After all, they were cowards.

I knew what I was going to do and how I was going to handle it. It was the only way. I would let the man come to me, his priority would be to attack me and get me out of the way so that he could go and help his friends. I was going to hold my hands up to remonstrate, I would be in 'shock' at what was happening, and I would try to plead with him, plead with him that I didn't want any trouble. I was going to be submissive and 'frightened', and I was going to keep taking a step backwards, so as to show fear.

The man would come forward, confident, and he would attack me and I would let him.

I would let him grab me, and I would let him come close, because I had two moves. My half raised hands would grab his ears and I would head butt him hard in the nose and stun him, and then in one fluid motion I would raise my head again and clamp my teeth onto his nose, and then I would bite his nose off, right off.

I have, very, very strong teeth. When I was younger my 'party piece' was to take the tops off beer bottles by biting them off, so I knew I was capable. I was just shocked that I had no qualms at all about going through with it, no remorse at all, not one bit.

Nobody was hurting my wife, nobody was hurting Karen, and I knew I would do it.

The car was now fast approaching and I looked over at Mark and nodded. He did the same back, the decision made.

I shot another glance at Mark, he was in overdrive.

At that moment he looked towards the girls and shouted "Anne Marie!"

She shot around.

He simply shouted at her, very loud "Its trouble. You both run, you get out of here!"

And then he bellowed at her in a completely different voice "That's an order...'Now'..!

They must have had some sort of code between them, something for this sort of eventuality, maybe it was because Mark worked in some strange and dangerous places. But Anne Marie never missed a beat. It was blind faith to a code that they'd worked out between themselves and practised. She grabbed Karen's arm and dragged her away, I saw her scream something to Karen and then they both took off.

The car was nearly on us now and I was ready, as ready as I was ever going to be. I knew I would have to fight and I took a deep breath. Nothing was guaranteed and I didn't know how all this was going to end.

I heard a metallic sound, and I think it was the car's doors beginning to open as they drew up behind us.

I took one last look at the girls to see how far they'd got, and I suddenly gasped in horror. They'd stopped running. They were just standing there. Another car had suddenly driven out of a hidden side road and pulled up straight in front of them and stopped.

I went sick inside, it was over, 'Oh god' what had happened. Had these men planned all this, and how, and a hundred things went through my head. Mark spun around and then he saw the girls too and he just screamed "No..!"

We were in total desperation and now everything was going wrong. We turned to face the men who were coming for us, they were only 10 yards away now and the car doors suddenly flew open as they approached. They were going to jump out and attack us, we knew what was coming. They were nearly on us and with only a couple of seconds to go everything seemed to go into slow motion. We knew what was going to happen, it was my worst nightmare, and I thought my head was going to explode.

And then unbelievably, the Renault's engine suddenly screamed into life, the exhaust popping like a machine gun. We jumped back to face them, and for a moment I thought they were going to run us over. But the car shot past us, the doors slamming shut as it tore off.

Mark and I just stood there. What the hell was going on?

The Renault sped off down the road and accelerated past the girls, who were still standing at the side of the other car. I couldn't believe it, I didn't understand.

Mark set off running towards them, and then suddenly he stopped dead, he just stood there and ran his hands over his head. Then he turned back to me.

"If there's a god, he was looking out for us tonight" he said quietly.

"What's happening Mark?" I said as I stood there.

Mark pointed towards the girls "Look" he said "That other car, it's a police car. It's the police".

And it was. And I suddenly went weak and I noticed that my hands were trembling.

Despair, anguish, I felt all of it and I gave a sigh of relief.

We both walked towards the police car. By then the policeman had got out of his car and was waving his arms about and shouting at us as we approached. He was a very angry man.

Mark tried to calm him down and kept saying "English...English". The policeman then changed language but still continued to shout.

"What are you doing here?" he screamed at us "Do you know what was going to happen, what was going to happen to you and your women, eh?" He shook his head at us "You stupid, stupid people. Why are you here?"

Mark explained to him what had happened and that we were trying to walk back to our hotel. He calmed the policeman down a bit, and then the policeman told us that the way we were going would have taken us two or three hours to finally get back to 'The Salamanca'. This road took us out of our way and we would have ended up walking miles, mostly in the wrong direction. He told us in no uncertain terms, that we would have to go back to the Royal Taj and stay there, even if we had to wait until daylight. And this was not a request, it was an order.

Then he took me and Mark to one side "Do you know what was going to happen?" he said.

We nodded, and he continued "This is not England, this is Africa. There are bad people here and those men, they would have killed you, yes. And they would have raped your women and killed them too, and then they would have taken your bodies over to that scrubland" and he pointed across the road. "They would have dug a hole there and buried you. Nobody would ever find you in that place, you would have just disappeared. They would have killed you and there would be no witnesses, nobody to point the finger, and you would all be dead".

It made me realise just how close we'd come to disaster.

Then the policeman pointed over our shoulders "Go back" he said "and don't ever come down here again". And with that he turned and strode back to his car. He gave the girls a curt nod as he passed them and then he got into his car and drove off in the same direction as the men in the Renault. Maybe he was going to try and follow them. I suppose we'd never know.

We went over to the girls, Karen was terrified and Anne Marie had put her arm around her shoulder. I took over and in silence we started to walk back to the Taj. Karen was shaking slightly and silent, and then she slowly began to cry. I kept my arm around her shoulder and tried to talk to her but she was in shock and very upset. We walked back to the Taj in silence and by the time we got there the grey of the morning had started to show. We could see now and we walked through the gardens and found the 'hole in the wall' and went through it and back into our hotel. We went to our rooms and I put Karen to bed. She was exhausted and finally she fell asleep. Me though, I still had a head full of what had happened and what very nearly happened, and I knew I couldn't sleep. I got up and quietly left our room, Karen was out for the count. I walked back downstairs, and through the hotel, it was totally deserted.

I went through to the cocktail bar, it was in darkness but I didn't care. I found the light switch which lit up the place and I then went behind the bar and took a large glass tumbler off the shelf and I opened the fridge and found a full ice bucket. Then I turned around and took a full bottle of Jack Daniels from off another shelf. I grabbed the glass, the bucket of ice and the 'Jack' and walked out of the hotel and down to the pool. There was nobody there at that hour of course, and thank god for that, because I wasn't in the mood for conversation. So I pulled up a table and chair and sat myself down. I poured some 'Jack' into some ice and just sat there, watching and waiting for the sun to finally come up and thankfully start a new day.

I sat there and contemplated the events of the night, and in the end I polished off most of the bottle, it didn't even touch my sides. It struck me that I should have gone to bed, but I was still as sober as when I'd started. Finally as I poured the last drink I almost laughed at myself. My thoughts were 'Stuff everything, it doesn't matter. We'd got through it and it was over'.

I went to bed and slept for a couple of hours, that was all, but it was enough.

I woke up, fairly fresh but restless. Karen was still asleep and so I went down to the kitchens and got somebody to make a mug of hot sweet tea and a plate of thick toast, covered in butter along with a small pot of marmalade. I went back to the room and slowly woke her. She was still not right, all this had really upset her but I managed to get some hot tea down her and a slice of toast. She didn't want to get up, and so I let her go back to sleep, it was only nine or ten o' clock. So I left the room and walked back down to the pool, I knew it would be quiet and I needed a cup of coffee. The pool area was empty. There was just one couple over in the corner who had grabbed their sun beds early. I supposed that everyone else was getting breakfast and I approached an almost empty bar. There was the barman there, who was busily sorting out glasses and re-stocking the drinks, and there was a customer, a man sitting at the bar, silently looking down into his drink. He was in his late forties, medium build, medium height, and he never even noticed me as I pulled up another bar stool, even though I was only several feet away from him. Not a good start.

The barman came over and I ordered a coffee and a brandy. The drinks arrived and I sat there in the sunshine, breathing in the heat. The coffee was divine, it was like a drug.

I drank it quickly and ordered another as I sipped the brandy. The silent customer suddenly looked up. It was as though someone had snapped their fingers and woke him up. He immediately picked up his glass and drank the contents in one go.

He looked across at the barman "Another whiskey please" he said "a large one".

A very large whiskey arrived and he picked up the glass and drank most of it in one gulp.

I glanced across at him. This wasn't a man who was drinking for pleasure.

He turned and finally noticed me. I had my brandy in my hand and I just raised it slightly, nodded to him, and said "cheers".

He simply nodded and picked up his glass and drank down the remainder of his drink, then he turned to the barman and ordered himself another large whiskey.

I thought to myself 'right, okay then'.

It was possibly time to get sociable, I don't know why, it was just the mood I was in. After the night I'd just had, I needed to talk to another human being and I needed something or someone to stop me thinking about what had happened the night before. The events kept going through my head over and over again, and it was as though I was on some sort of loop.

So I spoke to him "Are we the only one's drinking this morning?" It was an aimless sort of question, I know.

He looked across at me just as the barman arrived with his whiskey. He quietly thanked the barman and then picked up his glass and turned to me.

"I don't normally drink this early, it's just..." and his voice petered away as he picked up his glass and started to drink. His hand shook, only slightly, but I saw it.

Once again, he drank over half the glassful.

I took stock for a moment, this man didn't have the demeanour of an alcoholic but he was drinking like one.

He put his glass down and turned to me, but I spoke first.

"Are you alright"? I asked him, because I had a feeling he wasn't.

He looked at me and sighed slightly, and then shook his head, and for a moment I thought he was going to get all sort of, well sort of emotional.

"I'm sorry" he said "I've had a bad morning, I...I'm a bit confused".

I sat there and said nothing, I let the man speak.

"I...I've err, had a bit of trouble this morning. Something's happened and I just don't know what to do. I think it could be a problem".

Yes, he was a worried man, very worried.

I stuck out my arm to shake his hand, it was an introduction.

"Well umm, and what's your name again?" I asked, as though I'd already met him before.

"Peter" he replied, almost apologetically.

"Hi Peter, I'm Alan" and we shook hands.

"Listen" I said to him "I don't want to interfere or anything like that, but is there anything I can do to help. You do seem a bit upset."

He looked at me and said "I think I've been a bit stupid, or just gullible, I don't know" and then he ran his hand through his hair in agitation.

"What is it Peter?" I asked "what's wrong?"

For a moment he looked down at his glass in contemplation, and then he turned back to me and told me what had happened.

He started "In truth, I don't fully understand what's going on, it's all a bit stupid really.

I suppose, it all started when I woke up this morning. Everything was fine, and I woke up quite early, about six o' clock. I'm over here on a week's break, anyway I woke up early and I got out of bed and made a cup of coffee and then went to sit out on my balcony. The sun was up and it was fresh and not too hot, just a beautiful morning. My balcony looks out to the sea, it's a lovely view. So I drank my coffee and then decided to sort of 'seize the day'.

I grabbed my shorts, slung on a t-shirt and put my sandals on and went out. I came out of the hotel and walked through the gardens and down onto the beach. At that hour, about seven, seven thirty, it was deserted. I stood there for a while and looked at the beautiful turquoise water, and then I waded in up to my knees. The water was lovely and warm, even at that hour. I looked down the length of beach, it was all pristine white sand that backed onto tall green palm trees, it looked like paradise, so I decided to go for a walk. It wasn't too hot at that time in a morning and I was feeling good. I was in a good mood, 'on top of the world', and the start of a new day and all that. So I set off walking. It was a lovely day and I just kept going. I'd been walking along the beach, probably for over an hour really, I know I'd gone quite a way, but every so often I would look back over my shoulder and I could still see the hotel so I thought I was okay. The further out you go the quieter it gets, there are no more hotels down there and eventually you get past all the shops and cafes. I wasn't overly concerned because there's police station down there. Well it's a hut really. It's right on the beach. It's just a single storey scruffy sort of building that looks that it was once painted white. It has a 'police' sign over the door in large blue letters. I walked right past it and then I decided to stroll back down to the water's edge and stand in the sea for a while. It was getting hotter and I decided that I'd walk back to the hotel along the water's edge. Suddenly I heard a noise, it was somebody shouting, and I turned around and running down the beach towards me were two young boys. I don't know where they'd come from, they just suddenly appeared though the palm trees and were heading towards me. They were both laughing, and shouting 'Mista...Mista...' They ran right up to me, one was taller than the other, they were aged about ten and twelve, they could have been brothers, I don't know. The younger one was wearing faded white shorts that were far too big for him, they were probably 'hand me downs', and the elder and taller boy was wearing ripped denim shorts that had once been a pair of jeans and had been cut off at the knees. They both ran right up to me and started jumping up and down, still shouting 'Mista...Mista...' and then they started shouting

'Money...Money...you give us money' and they held out their hands, still jumping up and down and still laughing.

The tallest boy grabbed my hand and said "Hey Mista, come on please, you can give us some money...yes".

I took it all as a bit of a joke and I laughed along with them. "No...No" I said to them both

"I have no money". I shook my head and I thought that would be it, but no they followed me along the beach, still asking me for money. I kept telling them I had no money but they wouldn't listen. I actually did have my wallet in my pocket, but I wasn't letting on. Well you do hear tales of tourists being robbed by youths, and even though these two were very young, I was still a bit wary. If they'd snatched my wallet, I doubt if I could have chased them, let alone caught them. It was at that moment that the taller boy suddenly thrust his hand into my pocket and did try to grab my wallet. He must have somehow noticed it. It was a clumsy attempt and I grabbed hold of his arm and I shook him and started shouting at the pair of them. They must have thought that I was going to hit them or something because they then ran off. They bolted back up to the beach and onto the road. I watched them go and then decided to go back to the hotel. I felt a bit uneasy about what had just happened and so I walked a bit faster along the water's edge and back towards the 'Salamanca'. I glanced back to see if the two boys had finally gone, but to my astonishment I could still see them, they were running along the beach road and towards the police station that I had just walked past. I still carried on walking along the beach, but when I looked back again, I saw that the boys were now going into the police station, and I felt a bit uneasy. I was a bit uncomfortable about what had happened and for a moment I considered jogging back to the hotel, well running back really. But then I dismissed the thought, I hadn't done anything wrong and maybe it wouldn't look right.

And then a thought struck me 'calm down you idiot', they've probably just gone in there to annoy the police, they're probably in and out of there all day long pestering the local policeman, give over worrying, it was just a silly incident. And so I walked on, and I'd only gone about another ten yards when suddenly I heard somebody shouting, it was a man's voice.

Of course I turned around to see where the shouting was coming from, and to my horror I saw that a policeman was now running down the beach towards me, and I froze.

I suddenly thought 'Oh my god, what's happening now'?

The policeman ran straight up to me and grabbed my arm. He was a stocky man, dark and swarthy skinned, in his late forties. He forcibly grabbed my arm and then he started shouting something at me.

I didn't understand at first, so I tried to tell him that I was English and would he please let go of my arm, but he wouldn't. Then he started to jabber away at me in some sort of English, but he spoke very fast...

"You, You...You touch those boys" he said to me, and he pointed to the two boys who were stood outside the police station watching us.

"What?" I said. I couldn't believe it.

"You, You...You try to touch those young boys, and you try to give them money. You try to give them drugs".

"No...No, I've not done anything" I said "No 'they' tried to rob 'me'...". I tried to emphasize this but he wasn't listening.

"Those boys, they come to me and they tell me 'You' tried to give them money and drugs. You bad man, you must come with me. Now!" and with that he started to pull my arm and haul me back up the beach towards the police station.

"They're lying" I tried to tell him "they're lying to you". But he still wasn't listening. I couldn't believe what was happening to me.

He frog marched me into the police station were the two young boys were stood waiting in the reception. When they saw me enter they immediately started to babble away loudly to the police man. They were pointing at me and almost screaming, the whole scene was pandemonium and the policeman started to shout back at them. Eventually he threw them out of the police station and firmly shut the door, and then he turned back to me. I thought that I could possibly talk some common sense to him and that we could get all of this cleared up. But no, he then directed me into another room, it was his office. We went through and he closed the door behind him. Then he walked across his office and picked up a steel chair and put it down in front of his desk and ordered me to sit down. He walked around his desk, pulled out his own chair and sat down, and then he opened one of the top drawers in the desk and took out a black glasses case, a notebook and a pen. He opened the glasses case and took out a pair of thin gold rimmed spectacles. In silence he put them on and then picked up his pen and opened the book and began to write.

I just sat there, saying nothing, watching him write something into his notebook. He wrote about ten lines in complete silence, it was all becoming a bit unreal. Then suddenly he stopped writing and looked up at me.

Your name?" he asked me.

"Listen" I began to say.

"Your name...now!" he said firmly.

I told him.

"And where are you staying at?"

"The Hotel Salamanca", he wrote all this down.

"And when do you leave?"

I told him, and that was a mistake.

He pushed his book to one side. "Empty the contents of your pockets onto my desk please".

"What?" I said.

In single words he said "Empty...your ...pockets...and put everything onto my desk...now!"

I had to do what he said, so I stood up and emptied everything that was in my pockets onto the top of his desk. There was my brown leather wallet, my sunglasses in their case and some loose change.

"And your watch" he said.

I took off my watch and put it on the desk.

"Drugs" he said casually, it wasn't even a question.

"I don't have any drugs" I said firmly.

"Sit down" he continued, and he pointed at the chair.

I sat down and he said to me "Did you throw the drugs into the water?"

"No" I tried to explain again "Listen, I told you. There are no drugs. I've never had any drugs".

He just looked at me and then leant over and picked up my glasses case. He opened it and took out my new Ray Ban sunglasses. He looked at them appreciatively and then put them back on his desk. He did the same with my watch, it's a 'good' Seiko, he examined it and then put it back down. Then he opened my wallet. The first thing he did was take out my money, there was about a hundred and fifty pounds worth in foreign currency. He looked at the money but didn't count it. Next he took out my credit cards and looked at them like they were family photos. My driving licence was in there too, but that didn't seem to hold much interest. Then he opened the top drawer of his desk and just slid everything into it, and then he closed the drawer again.

There was a moments silence and then he looked straight at me.

"Now you had better listen to me" he said "You are in serious trouble".

My heart sunk, this was more than a warning. There was no doubt about it.

I looked back at him across the desk. What on earth was going to happen now, I had visions of him making a phone call and me being thrown in the back of a police van and taken off to some prison somewhere. And I was suddenly beginning to panic.

He continued "In my country, what you have done is regarded as a very serious offence. You tourists, you men, you come over here to find young boys and you..."

"Whoa!" I suddenly shouted back at him and I began to stand up. I'd had enough of this. It was time to say something. This was all wrong.

The policeman immediately jumped up out his chair. He slammed his hand onto the top of his desk and started to shout back at me at the top of his voice.

"You will sit down...Now! You will shut your fucking mouth or you will go to prison. Sit down right now. All I have to do is pick up the phone, do you hear me? Now sit down and shut your mouth!"

I was totally stunned, and I was scared.

I sat down and I was quiet. He'd beat me and we both knew it.

I sat there and I put my head in my hands, I was sick with worry.

"Right" he said, and he slowly sat down again.

Then he said to me "Now, let us see if we can do anything to sort out this 'Problem'..."

The tone of his voice had changed, and it took me a moment to realize it. His voice suddenly sounded slightly different, and I lifted my head up out of my hands and slowly began to straighten up in the chair.

"What do you mean?" I said.

"Maybe, we could try 'other possibilities'. Perhaps find another was to sort all this out. It would be better for you of course".

"What what sort of possibilities?" I asked.

The policeman leaned back in his chair "Well, since the children didn't actually take any drugs".

I began to speak, I had to try and make it clear that I was innocent. But he immediately raised his hand and gave me a dismissive look".

I stopped, and I realized that I had to keep my mouth shut.

He started again "As I said, since the boys didn't actually take any drugs and there's no hospital or doctor involved, and I don't have any evidence from any other witnesses that you 'touched' them or abused them."

I bit my lip, but I kept quiet.

He continued "But it's the parents you see, they will want to press charges. However, I think I could possibly speak to the families".

I spluttered "You could?" This was unbelievable, maybe and suddenly, there was a way out of this nightmare.

The policeman picked up his pen and slowly began to tap it on his desktop.

"You will have to pay them some money of course. Give some money to the family".

I just stared at him.

He kept tapping his pen "It is the way we do things here. You see, this isn't England with its English laws. This is how things are done over here...here in 'my' country.

"What will it cost?" I asked him.

He told me, and it was the equivalent of around five hundred pounds. I asked him about the money in his drawer, my money. There was a hundred and fifty pounds already there.

He looked back at me across the desk "Ah no, you see that money will have to go towards my expenses. I will have to contact the family and I will have to go over and see their people. Then I will try to sort everything out. That money is for my time in handling all this".

And that's when the 'penny' finally dropped, and I suddenly realized. This was nothing to do with those boys at all, and this was basically nothing more than robbery. And I knew that there would be no payments to the 'family', they wouldn't even be contacted. It was all a deception, and this policeman was totally corrupt.

But I had to keep my wits about me, for one stupid moment I nearly told him that I knew what he was up to, but no, no. This could still all backfire on me and I had to stay calm. I had to see this through and I had to get away from him and get away from that police station.

So I asked him how I was supposed to get all this money.

"You can get the money from your hotel" he said casually, still tapping away with that damn pen.

He was right of course. The Hotel does have a facility to draw out cash.

"I will need my cards then, to get the cash" I said "I will need my bank and credit cards" and I started to try and reason with him.

He stared back at me and I saw the look of suspicion.

"It's the only way I can get any money" I said, and it was the truth.

He slid the drawer open and took out my cards, and then he looked across at me. "Which one?" he asked.

I could see I wasn't going to win here.

"Give me the green one, it's my debit card, the money will come straight out of my bank".

He flicked through the cards and took out my debit card. He examined it and then he looked back at me. I felt like a dog being offered a bone.

He then leant forward, and this was 'the threat'.

He stared at me and said "Before I give you this, I will tell you something...something that you must understand. If you do not come back, I will come for you. If you try to leave your hotel, I will come for you. And if you try to fly out of the country without paying me, I will come for you. I know where you are staying, and I know when you are leaving, and if I have to come and find you, I will. And if that happens, I will make sure that you will go to prison. You would not like that, not in our prisons".

"Okay, right" I replied quietly. He had me.

He put the card on the desk so that I had to reach over to get it. He eyed me like a snake, because he was a snake.

"You will return here later today with the money" he almost hissed.

I picked up the card and he stood up, presumably to see me out. We left his office and walked back through the police station. When he opened the door to let me out I felt like running, but what was the use. He had me, and he knew it.

The two boys had thankfully disappeared, and the beach was still empty as I slowly walked away. I was in a complete daze.

And then suddenly, there was a shout "Stop, come back!"

I froze. What now?

I turned in the sand and saw that the policeman was once again striding towards me and I thought to myself 'Oh hell, what does he want'.

He walked up right up to me, and then all of a sudden he reached out and snatched off my glasses. I do normally wear glasses you see, and he just grabbed them off me. It was like being physically attacked.

I stepped back and gasped "What are you doing?"

"When you come with the money, you can have your glasses back. It will speed up the process I think". And he smiled in my face.

"But I can't see properly without them" I said

He simply shrugged his shoulders "In that case, hurry".

And he walked away and back to the station, swinging my glasses in his hand.

I stood there, helpless and stupefied, but what could I do. So I turned around and walked all the way back along the beach, and back here to The Salamanca. When I got here it wasn't even nine o'clock. I came and sat here at the bar, it was just opening up. I've been here ever since, I don't know what to do, if I go back with the money will that be the end of it, or will he want even more. I'm supposed to be here for another week and if he knows he's onto a good thing, I think he'll want even more money off me."

I looked at Peter. He was in trouble.

And then at that moment, I heard somebody shout "Yo". It was Mark. He strolled over as though our last night's endeavours never happened, and that was the way that he would handle it.

He came over to us with a no-nonsense grin on his face, considering the evening's events.

"How are you buddy, alright?" He gave me a nod, and I knew exactly what he meant.

"I'm okay" I said. I didn't want to talk about last night either.

So as not to get onto that particular topic, I introduced Mark to Peter. They shook hands and I started to explain to Mark just what had happened to Peter, the whole story, along with the boys and the policeman, and the money.

When I'd finished, Mark just looked at Peter and he told him straight out "No, that wouldn't be the end of it, he'll want more money" and also "that Peter was going to have to do something about it".

But in fact, it wasn't Peter that would do something about it. Mark had decided that 'We' would do something about it.

"Come on" he suddenly said to us, and he took command. Being a soldier, I suppose he could do that sort of thing.

So off we marched into the hotel and Mark found the holiday 'rep'. He was a tallish lad in his late twenties called 'Alex'. He straightaway commandeered Alex and informed him that this was an emergency and that we all needed to see the manager, and 'right away'. When Alex tried to ask what this was all about, Mark just put his big hand on the lad's shoulder and gave him 'the look'. Then he said "The Managers office. Now!"

Alex gulped, and about turned.

We quick marched to the Managers office and after a couple of solid knocks on the door, the manager, Mr Atull, called 'enter' and was a bit taken aback when the four of us paraded in.

Mr Atull had a nose for trouble and he realized that at this time in the morning, well it wasn't a social call.

He frowned slightly and said "Good morning gentlemen" his best English accent, which I've got to admit, was pretty damn good. He continued "Is there a problem?"

"There's going to be" said Mark ominously "A big problem"

Mr Atull looked across at Alex, as a possible ally, but Alex just shrugged his shoulders.

"I don't know what it's all about" he said, wide eyed and shaking his head in a show of defence.

"It's Peter here " said Mark, and he pushed Peter forward "Our friend here has had a bit of trouble and it needs to be sorted out, and sorted out right now, today".

Mark then turned to Peter and said "Peter, tell them what's happened, the whole story".

So Peter told the whole story again, word for word.

When he'd finished, Mr Atull and Alex looked at each other a little aghast, this wasn't good.

Mark took the lead "It's like this, as far as I'm concerned, you two..." and he was looking directly at Mr Atull and Alex "You two both have a responsibility towards the guests in this hotel. You Mr Atull, as the manager of the hotel, and you Alex as the holiday company representative. It is up to you two to make sure that your guests are safe and secure. If anything untoward were to happen to a guest, especially in a case like this which is nothing more than police corruption, actually its nothing more than robbery, but the repercussions for this hotel and the holiday company would be enormous".

Mark was in his stride now and was taking control of the situation.

He continued "The resulting bad press, because bad press it would be if poor Peter here were to be falsely imprisoned, well believe me, the newspapers would have a field day. And I have to tell you that if you do not act immediately and do something, Alan and myself will speak to the press personally on Peters behalf, and tell them exactly what's happened, and how you were both reluctant to be of assistance. The truth would be that if you did nothing at all to help him out of this charade, it would be seen as a disgrace".

"Whoa, wait a minute" it was Alex, now panicking a bit "What do you mean 'did nothing at all'..."

Mr Atull just sat there behind his desk, his mouth slightly open and looking slightly dumfounded.

Mark continued "It's like this boys and girls, you are either with Peter, or you are not.

There's no middle ground here, and it's up to you two to decide which camp you're in."

Mr Atull suddenly found his voice, he glanced at Alex, and whatever working relationship these two had formed in the running and management of this hotel, well it was beginning to flounder.

"But what can we do?" he spluttered "This is the police, the authorities".

"No" replied Mark "This is not the police or the authorities. This is one corrupt policeman who is trying to rob an innocent tourist. Peter here, is a guest in your country, and has also by the way, has also already been assaulted by that same corrupt policeman."

Alex interrupted "Let's just calm down a bit" and with that he glared at Mr Atull.

"Mark here's right" said Alex, he was now speaking directly to Mr Atull "We can't just let this go, we'll have to do something or this could end up being a disaster for 'all of us'. And he glared sternly at Mr Atull.

Mr Atull, who was now the bewildered and very worried manager of the 'Hotel Salamanca'.

"But what can we do?" Mr Atull was now repeating himself, and starting to twitch.

Alex turned to Mark "What do you think. Any ideas?"

"Oh yes." said Mark.

What a guy.

He looked at them both "We need to go and speak to our friend the policeman, in private.

We need to go and give a show of force. He'll want to keep this hush-hush, just between himself and Peter here. If a few of us turn up in some sort of 'public' display and start to make a commotion over the money he's demanding, and show some concern over the stuff he's stolen, Peter's belongings and money. If we start to make a fuss and start to make a bit too much noise about it all, he'll back down, he has to. If not, then Mr Atull you must inform him that you will have to contact his superiors, and you Alex must be prepared to get in touch with the British Consulate, because I'm telling you both now, this is serious shit."

Mr Atull and Alex exchanged looks. The mention of the British Consulate made Alex straightened up somewhat and he was beginning to grasp the situation.

But it was Mr Atull who finally saw the sense in it all.

He looked across his desk at everyone "You are right, we must do something. I will take steps to sort this out. We will go to the Police Station and talk to the policeman. I will go, along with Alex here, who is the representative of his holiday company. I will also take along two of my employees, they're waiters and they are good men, one of them does actually know the policeman. He will talk to him, we all will, and we will warn him off. However you three must stay here, there must not be too much intimidation. If we push this man too hard, he may try to 'lie' his way out of the situation and things could escalate and maybe get out of control. We must give this man his dignity, this is how we do things here. Nevertheless we must warn him of the repercussions, and the possibility of the huge embarrassment for all concerned."

We all looked at one another.

"Okay" said Mark. And the deal was done.

We left the office, and left Mr Atull and Alex to attempt to sort things out. Peter went back to the bar to await the outcome. Me and Mark went back to our rooms. On the way back he asked me how Karen was. I told him that she was not too good still shocked and upset.

I asked about Anne Marie?

"Same really" he said "I'm letting her sleep in"

"Me too" I told him, I was doing the same, and so he went off to his room. I quietly put my head around the door to our room to find that Karen was still asleep, so I gently closed the door again and ambled back down to the pool. Peter was there, sitting back at the bar. He looked like he needed a bit of support, so I went over and plonked myself down at the side of him.

He looked up "Hi Alan" he said, and there in front of him was another large whiskey.

"Hi buddy" I replied, and then said "Okay Peter, it's time to stop drinking" and I leant over and picked up his glass and put it to one side. Then I had a serious word with him.

"Now is not a good time to get drunk, we need to have our wits about us, so come on and let's have some breakfast."

We ordered mugs of hot tea and plenty of toast, jam and butter. And it was good, very good. We got talking and eventually I told him about what had happened to us last night, on our way back from the 'Taj'.

Peter listened, incredulous.

The whole story just came tumbling out of me. It was a sort of release. And it's a fact that until today, I've never discussed it with anyone else.

When I'd finished telling him, Peter looked at me and slowly shook his head.

"I'm going tell you something Alan" he said. "When this is all over, I'm never coming back here".

"I know Peter" I replied "and neither am I".

An hour later, Mark had joined us and we were sitting over by the pool in the shade, when Alex suddenly appeared. He strode directly over to us and stopped.

"Could you come with me to the office?" he said.

He was expressionless. So we all got up and followed him. On the way back into the hotel lobby, we tried to question him but he told us that he had to let Mr Atull clarify the situation.

I began to feel a bit uneasy about this and we all went a bit quiet, but as we reached Mr Atull's office, Alex turned to us and spoke.

"I have to let Mr Atull speak to you first. He 'is' the Manager and he's dealt with the situation".

Well at least that sounded a bit more positive.

Alex knocked on the door and we all entered. Mr Atull was sitting at his desk, stern faced.

He looked up at us "Ah gentlemen, please come in and sit down please" he said. All very professional, he was taking charge again.

We sat down.

He continued "I have been down to the station to see the officer and we have resolved the matter. There will be no further action and no further charges."

We looked at one another, and Peter sighed "Thank god for that" he said quietly.

We saw his relief, utter relief.

"Well done Mr Atull" I said "you've done really well"

Peter turned to him "I don't know how you've managed it Mr Atull, but thank you. Thank you very, very much".

Then Mark suddenly intervened "Did you manage to get Peter's belongings back?"

"Ah." said Mr Atull, and he looked just a little pensive "Some, of your property has been recovered".

"Only some" said Mark, again.

"Well" said Mr Atull "You see, we went to see 'our friend' the police officer. We arrived there and went into his office and sat down and spoke to him, then we explained about the problems that 'we all' could encounter if he pursued this action, and the repercussions if it became public. The officer thankfully saw the commonsense in this and has decided not to proceed any further. We did ask the officer for your property and he gave us these". Mr Atull then opened the drawer in his desk and produced a white plastic carrier bag that contained Peter's stuff and he then emptied it all out onto the desk.

"Here are your belongings. However, I must tell you that there is no money. The officer said that he had already given it to the family".

"I don't think so" said Mark as he shook his head.

"Ah well" Mr Atull continued "I'm afraid there is little we can do about that. We will have to call it a 'sweetener'..."

Peter leant over and picked up his property "Everything's here except for my Ray Bans, they were my new sunglasses".

Mr Atull shrugged apologetically "Things get lost".

Peter put his Seiko watch back on and looked at it, he was lucky to get that back.

"To tell you the truth" he said "I don't care. The money and the sunglasses, I'm just glad it's all over. Thank you Mr Atull" and he reached over and shook the man's hand.

And that was that. We left the office and went back outside to the bar to have a celebratory beer. Alex the 'Rep even offered to buy them. Well he was as relieved as the rest of us. We sat down at a table and he came back with four large glasses of ice cold beer on a tray. He passed the beer around and then sat down with us as we did the 'Cheers' bit.

"I'll tell you something" said Alex between swigs "That policeman was a bastard"

"Go on man, tell us what really happened" I said to him, with my best smile.

"Yeah, alright" he said as he savoured his beer "Well we all piled over there in Mr Atull's car. The policeman must have seen us coming because he was standing at the station door as the four of us got out of the car. The waiter who he knew immediately greeted him and they started to talk. Well, started to jabber away in bloody Arabic or whatever, and so that was me out of it straightaway. Anyway, the waiter introduced the policeman to Mr Atull and they shook hands. It was all very diplomatic, and next thing, we were led into his office."

"What about the fourth man, the other waiter?" I asked.

"He wasn't a waiter. He was one of the gardeners, a big ugly bloke with skin like leather. He never said a word, but Christ he was frightening, he could have been out of a horror movie. Anyway, we all went into the policeman's office and Mr Atull starts talking, then in English he introduces me, and then he goes back into the Arab lingo.

We were offered seats, but only me and Mr Atull actually sat down. The waiter and the gardener stood behind us, it's a respect thing.

Then Mr Atull kicks off, he's obviously saying to the policeman 'What the fuck do you think you're playing at' and the policeman in turn goes all indignant and starts shouting and waving his arms about. Then he points towards the beach and then he starts banging his fist on the desk. Mr Atull starts shouting back and then he jumps up out of his chair and starts pointing at the policeman, then he turns to the waiter and starts shouting at him too. The waiter then tries to say something to the policeman, but its' all mayhem at this point. The waiter's talking so fast, he sounds like a bloody machine gun going off. By now Mr Atull is going at it full tilt, he's now shouting at the policeman 'and' the waiter. Then the gardener finally started to grunt and the policeman took that as a threat and started screaming back at all three of them.

I sat there amid the bedlam, and just hoped that the policeman didn't own a gun.

Then, as quickly as it started, it stopped. It was like turning off a kettle.

Everybody stopped arguing, except for Mr Atull, who just stood there with his arms raised, he was waiting for an answer to a question. The policeman said a few more words but Mr Atull still just stood there, waiting for an answer. The policeman continued to give some excuses but you could see that Mr Atull had him. Eventually the policeman began to nod his head and then the waiter pitched in with something conciliatory. Some sort of agreement was made and the policeman opened the drawer and took out Peter's belongings and handed them over. There was a bit more talking, probably about the missing money, but everyone just shrugged and that was that. In the end we left the police station and the policeman shook hands with everyone except the gardener. Anyway, that was the end of it. We all got into Mr Atull's car and finally we drove back to the hotel. The rest you know".

As we sat around the table, we acknowledged the stupidity of it all, and drank some more beer. The sun was shining and it was a brand new day, for all of us.

"There was just one thing" said Alex, suddenly smiling, and he laughed.

He said "You know, when we were leaving the police station and we all went back outside and into the sunshine. Well, just as we were getting into the car we turned to bid the policeman farewell. The sun was really bright and I can remember the policeman putting on his sunglasses. And guess what, he was wearing a brand new pair of Ray Bans".

We ordered more beer.

After lunch, we took our cases down to reception and got on the coach to leave. Mark and Anne-Marie were on a later flight but they came to see us off. Karen was still off beat, she was still upset over what had happened. And so we came to leave, and of course we said all the usual things, like 'keep in touch' and 'come and visit'. But we never saw them again. We rang them a couple of times but there was never an answer.

I think Mark had a different agenda.

Alan finally looked up at me, I'd finished cutting his hair about half an hour back, but I'd wanted to hear his story, well stories.

"Bloody hell Alan" I said "a bit of a night"

"Yeah" he said "But unfortunately it didn't end there"

I looked at him through the mirror.

"Well it all went pear shaped" he said, and he was a bit downcast.

"Why's that?" I asked.

He looked back at me "It was Malc".

Alan took a deep breath.

"Well by the end of the night Malc was drunk out of his skull. We'd watched him drinking heavily all night and he'd put away double of what we'd had and then some. It was way past midnight, probably heading for two o' clock I suppose, when we finally threw a bag on things. We'd all had enough, but Malc was rocking. He'd stopped playing cards about an hour before, he said that he'd run out of money but he still kept drinking. Finally he passed out at the table, he just fell asleep bolt upright. We went to wake him up but by then he could hardly stand. Finally we got him to his feet and Tony rang a taxi to get them home.

It was then that Malc, all bleary eyed, turned to us and blurted out "I've nowhere to go"

"What do you mean?" said Tony.

Malc leaned back against the wall to steady himself "It's just, I've nowhere to go. Diane's kicked me out".

Diane is Malc's wife.

Tony turned to him and said "Why didn't you tell me, why didn't you say something?"

"I don't know" he slurred, and he looked back at us through half closed eyes.

"What have you done?" again asked Tony.

"Gambling, been bloody gambling" he replied.

"What, with us? I said to him "Don't tell me it's over a few games of cards with us lot".

"No...No" he was struggling now "it's more than that."

And his head lolled forwards and he nearly fell over.

The rest of us looked at one another and I said "You'd better stay here then, you can sleep on the couch" and with that we got hold of him and carried him to the couch in our front room.

His fading words were "thanks pal, you're a star" and that was it, he passed out again. So I went and got a blanket and threw it over him, but by then he was well out of it.

The taxi rolled up for the lads and they left with a wave. I went and took a last look at Malc, and wondered what the hell had gone on, and then I switched off all the lights and went up to bed.

In the morning he was gone.

I got up at about eight o' clock to make us both a mug of tea, Karen and the kids were still asleep. But when I went into the front room Malc wasn't there. I hadn't heard him leave. I hadn't heard the front door slam or anything. In fact, I don't even know what time he'd left, so he could have woken up in the middle of the night and just staggered off somewhere.

I wondered whether he'd tried to go home. Where else would he go?

I picked up the blanket that I'd put over him and there underneath it, jammed between the cushions, was a mobile phone. Malc's mobile phone.

'Okay' I thought, and I turned the phone on, it was fully charged. I went into his 'contacts' and found 'home' and I pressed the call button. The phone rang, but there was no answer.

So I went to put the kettle on and then tried it again, and again no answer. I tried ringing for the next half hour or so, and then I finally gave up.

It knew that his wife, Diane, would obviously be at home, it was Saturday morning and they had kids too. And then it struck me, if she'd thrown Malc out she would probably think that this was him ringing her on his mobile. So then I rang her on our house phone, but still nobody answered.

I began to wonder if maybe something had happened, well she had thrown him out. He could have had an accident or something, the state he was in he could have walked under a bus.

Anyway, I decided to go round to his house. I'd have a word with Diane, maybe she'd relent and let him come back home. For all I knew, he could be there already, tucked up in bed with a good hangover. And if there was nobody there, I would just push the phone through the letter box and hope for the best. I could phone him up later, or I could contact Tony, he would be up by then and he'd probably know something.

I climbed into my car and went round to his house. Whether or not I should have been driving is debatable, but anyway I got myself into the car".

Alan stopped at that point and looked up at me "Yes I know" he said "the famous last words of people who've been breathalysed. And believe you me, I got a right rollicking later off Karen for driving in the state I was in".

"Anyway I went round to Malc's, it's only about ten minutes away.

He lives in a terraced house down Glendale Street. It's quiet down there, nice place. They moved in about twelve months ago, maybe a bit longer. I parked the car and got out, and then I took a breath of fresh air and felt worse. I had to steady myself, and then I walked over to the house.

I vaguely remember wondering 'if this was a good idea', and in truth I didn't know, but by then I was there.

I walked up to the house and knocked on the door, but there was no answer. So I knocked again, still no answer, and part of me was a bit relieved but another part of me realized that maybe this wasn't so good. I took the phone out of my pocket and I was just about to push it through the letter box when I heard a noise. There was somebody inside coming down the stairs. I stood there and waited, hoping that it would be Malc, hung over and all apologetic.

But it wasn't.

Suddenly Diane swung the door open, and with some venom. She stopped and looked at me and her expression changed, she was obviously a bit surprised to see me. I wasn't who she expected.

"Oh it's you" she said. She was a bit taken aback, and then "I'm sorry Alan, I thought it was him".

"Who...Malc?"

"Yes, Malc" and her face tightened.

"He's not here then?" I said, it was a bit obvious but I had to ask.

"No, he's not, and I don't know where he is".

"I've err, I've got his mobile here, he left it at my house last night".

There was silence as she just looked at me.

"Look Diane" I tried to explain "I know you've had some sort of row".

"What did he say?" she said quickly.

"Well not much really. Just that you'd thrown him out or something".

"Or something...and that was it?"

"Well err, yes".

She stood there, just looking at me, and then she said "Alan, you look like shite" and she sighed "You'd better come in. I'll make you some coffee".

"Thanks love" I said, a truce was imminent.

We went through into the kitchen and Diane put the kettle on and then took a couple of mugs out of a cupboard. I sat down at the table.

"So what's up" I said "is this argument big time or small time?"

"It's bigger than that Alan" she said "It's over".

"What" I looked up at her "You're joking, what on earth has he done now?"

She made the coffee and put the two mugs on the table but she remained standing. Then she leant back against the kitchen sink. I looked up at her, and she was almost shaking with anger.

She said "I'll tell you what he's done. The stupid bastard's lost all our money and now we're going to lose the house".

She took out a handkerchief and started to wipe her eyes.

I looked at her and I didn't know what to do, I'm not very good at that sort of thing.

I said to her "Lose the house...how the hell has he managed that?"

She spat the words out "Gambling, bloody stupid gambling".

She saw the look on my face, and then almost apologetically "Don't worry Alan, I'm not blaming you. I know you lot only play for a couple of quid and have a few drinks, it's not that. Malc's been gambling big time, and he's even borrowed money on this house to gamble, he's gambled with our home. Do you know what it took for me to get us this house?"

I stared at her and started to shake my head, I knew they'd had hard times. In the past they'd lived in various, very rough rented properties, and they had two kids.

She was in tears now "For nearly ten years I've worked, worked to get this house. I've worked damn hard for it. Do you know that at one time I was doing three jobs at once? I've worked day and night, just to try and get us some extra money together. And let's face it Alan, Malc's always been a waste of space, he's never been a 'worker'. He's always stayed at that bloody warehouse, because it was 'easy'. But I've always wanted to do better, for the kids really, I wanted them to live in a nice house, all of us"

As I sat there listening to her, I thought about Malc, and yes, I suppose she was right, he'd never had a lot work in him. Malc worked in a mail order warehouse, nights mostly, and he'd always told us that he worked nights so that he could skive off. Just sit around with his mates and do nothing.

"How's it got to this Diane?" I asked her "You know we only play for a few quid, nothing too heavy".

"Oh no, all of this started at work, when he was on nights. I'll tell you something Alan, it's always been a problem, Malc and his gambling. I've put up with it for years. At one point I was so sick of him spending and even pinching my money that I used to give him five pounds a day to go to the bookies. Then at least I knew where my money was going. Over the years though, I thought he'd relented, he stopped heavy gambling. Well he said he had, until last Tuesday".

"Why, what happened?"

"There was a knock on the door, I was doing the dishes at the time and I just wiped my hands and went to answer it. I thought it was the postman or something, I don't know. But when I opened the door there were two very large men standing there, one was wearing a long black coat, the other a black leather jacket. They both looked like a couple of thugs and I was as bit taken aback, so I asked them what they wanted".

The man in the coat spoke for them both, he just said "We're the bailiff's love, we've come to repossess the house." and that was that. I looked at him for a moment, I was a bit stunned, and then I said to him "I think you've got the wrong address, this is 'my' house".

"No love. This is..." and he looked at the number on the door "Number twenty, Glendale Street?"

"Yes" I said.

"Well, this is the one" he said, and he just stared at me.

And then stupidly, I started to laugh and I said to him "Oh I get it, it's some sort of joke isn't it. Who sent you, Malc, or was it one of his bloody daft mates?"

But the man still just stood there and stared at me "No love, you'd better listen to me" and then he became a little bit sterner and almost aggressive "We're here to repossess this house right now" and he took out some papers from his inside pocket and started to read them to me.

"We're ordered, by the 'National Provincial Building Society' to repossess this property, due to the non payment of your mortgage. Apparently it hasn't been paid for nearly twelve months" and with that he thrust the papers at me to read.

I took the papers off him and read them, and it was all there in black and white, the Building Society, and all about the non payments. For a minute I went into a bit of a daze, I couldn't believe what was happening. And then reality kicked in. Malc took care of the mortgage, he paid it, and suddenly I got a sinking feeling and I knew that anything was possible. My next thought was the bailiffs. I had a friend who had once got herself into debt and the bailiffs came round to her house too, she told me that under no circumstances must you ever let them enter your property. If you do you, you apparently enter into some sort of verbal contract, and that means they can then take whatever they want and throw you out as well. I didn't know if this was entirely true but I knew that I'd have to have my wits about me. If I didn't make a stand, it was all over, and I'd lose everything.

"Right love" the man said suddenly, and he stepped forward "if you'll just excuse us and we'll make a start".

"Whoa" I said, and I put my hand up in front of him "Just wait a minute. I need to ring my husband to find out what's going on".

"Well while you're ringing him, we'll just take a look around" he continued.

I stepped back "No, I'll have to ring him first" and I quickly closed the door.

So I went to the phone and rang Malc at work, and somebody went to get him.

After a long enough wait on the end of that phone, Malc finally picked up the phone.

"Hi babe" he said "What's up?"

And I told him exactly what had happened, and there was just silence, he couldn't answer me.

"Well Malc, what's going on?" I asked him "Why are the bailiffs here. Why haven't you been paying the mortgage?"

Finally he said something, very slowly, and it was just "I've blown it".

"What's gone on Malc?" I asked him again, and suddenly I felt sick.

"I owe money" he said "I owe money all over the place".

"What?" I said to him.

"I owe a lot of money, I've been stupid"

"How much?" I asked, and I dreaded the answer.

There was a silence, and then the words "Its thousands"

"Oh my god, no. How?" and I knew the answer as soon as I'd asked it.

"I've been gambling again" he said, and it was as simple as that.

"I...I started playing cards at work at night, there were five of us, I thought we were mates. We got a bit of a card school going and I was doing alright, honestly I was. I was in front, I was nearly a thousand pounds in front and I kept winning. Then they started raising the stakes, they said it was the only way that they could win their money back. It was all a bit of a laugh really, they seemed to take it in good heart, but then I started to lose, and lose badly. What I didn't know was that they were cheating me, three of them were working together and they were fleecing me and the other lad, but he was hopeless at cards anyway, and he soon bowed out. But me, well you know what I'm like, I can't bloody stop can I. Before long it was me that owed them a thousand pounds, but like a fool I kept on playing. I was trying to get back the thousand pounds. They'd let me win a bit back of course, and I'd think that I was back on a winning streak, and then they'd pull the plug and take all my money. They were all in it together the bastards. So I started to have a bet at the bookies. If I won anything I would pay some of it to the lads and put the rest on another horse, or two. But I finally lost all my winnings on a dead 'cert'. It fell at the last fence, and I couldn't believe it, just my luck. Then a lad I know told me about opening a gambling account with a credit card. So I applied for one and opened an account with the bookies. Then like an idiot I applied for another credit card and opened an account with another bookie, and in the end I had five credit cards with five different bookies and it all started to spiral out of control. And then I took out a loan from the bank, I told them it was for a car, but I've gambled all that money too and now I'm in bigger debt than ever. I know should have paid off my other debts with the bank loan, but I put it on a horse, it was a 100-1. If it had come in I could have paid everything off, if it had come in I could have paid everybody and had money over. But, well it didn't, and I had no money left and I couldn't tell you, I know you would have gone mad. So I tried to save some money out of my wages. I missed a months' payment on the mortgage and gave some of that money to the lads at work. I owe them over two thousand pounds now, so I gave some money to them and the rest of it, I used as a minimum payment on the credit cards. Then the next month I did the same, and in the end it was just easier to carry on like that and not pay the mortgage. The building society started to send letters but I used to get up early and catch the post so that you wouldn't read them. I ripped them up, I know it was stupid but I didn't know what to do".

He'd told me everything, and there was a short silence, and then he started to cry on the end of the phone. He started sobbing like a child, the soft, stupid, pathetic bastard.

"I'm sorry love" he said to me "I'm really sorry".

I stood there on the phone and listened to him whimpering. In my mind I could see him crying down the other end, and I thought about him, and the kids and the house, and how hard I'd worked to get us where we were. And now the bloody idiot had thrown it all away, and now he was going to make us all homeless.

"Malc" I said to him.

"Yes love?" it was almost a whisper.

"When you come home from work tonight, there'll be a suitcase outside the door with your clothes in it. Take it and go, and never come back, ever".

And I put the phone down.

I went back to the bailiffs at the front door and told them that they weren't coming in and that I would sort it out with the Building Society. The first man stepped forward but I slammed the door in his face.

He banged on the door a few times and then he shouted "We'll be back" through the letter box. They both stood outside talking for a few minutes, and then they went.

"What are you going to do Diane?" I asked her.

"I've got an appointment to see somebody at the Building Society on Monday"

"Christ love" I said "I didn't know it was that bad. I didn't know anything about it".

"I know you didn't Alan, nobody did."

"What about Malc?"

"If he comes round here, I think I could kill him for what he's done. It's over Alan, we're finished. I should have always known that he'd never stop gambling. You don't know what it's like, one minute he's up, the next he's down and in debt. It's an addiction, and he'll never stop.

We finished our coffee and I decided that it was probably time for me to go.

As I was leaving, I said to her "I suppose gambling's like being an alcoholic, it's an illness".

"Yes" she said "Gambling's an illness, it's just like the booze. If you get hooked on it and you can't stop, it destroys lives, and I'm not having that with the kids".

I said to her "Any addiction, alcohol or gambling, it must be a disaster".

"Yes" she said "but it's gambling that's the worst".

"And how's that?" I asked her.

She turned to me "An alcoholic can only drink booze one bottle at a time, a gambler can bet ten or a hundred, or a thousand pounds all at once, and all in one go. That's how".

Al shrugged at me as he spun himself around in the chair. Haircut over, and he was ready to go. I'd taken off his cape and brushed him down and he slowly stood up.

I could see he was depressed. This thing with Malc had obviously upset him. So he paid his 'bill' and he went to leave.

"It'll work itself out Al" I said, and I tried to say the right thing.

"I don't know. I don't know whether it will or not" he replied.

And with that, he left.

So now it's five weeks later, and it's 3 o' clock in the afternoon and into the shop again walks 'Big Al' Morton. Last customer of the day, and last customer of the week.

I sat him down and we went through the usual formalities.

Then we got chatting, and before long I had to ask him.

"How did your mate go on, you know, the lad with the gambling problems, 'Malc'?"

Al looked at me through the mirror "Not so good"

"Did he get back with his wife?"

"No, she threw him out for good, and he ended up staying at Tony's house. He stayed there for a while, and then Tony found out that some of his money had gone missing, and of course, it was Malc. He'd stolen it, so Tony threw him out too. We've not heard anything of him since."

"And how did his wife go on, with the house?"

"She went to see the Building Society and told them exactly what had happened. They wouldn't do anything to help her, absolutely nothing".

Al looked up at me "She's lost the house, the Bailiffs finally got in and threw her out, the set of rotten bastards"

"What happened to her?"

"She had to go to the council and they've put her in some crappy flat. I've been round, it's bloody awful. The kids are suffering too, they all are really. I go around and so do the other lads, we drop her a few quid to help her out, she's a good kid. She always says that she doesn't want the money but we make her take it, we tell her it's for the kids, that sort of thing".

I looked at Alan through the mirror, and he wasn't comfortable talking about this.

Maybe he felt a bit guilty, I don't know.

So like any good barber, I changed the conversation, and I got on with cutting his hair.

It was time to talk about something else.

Well, there's always another story, I suppose.

CHAPTER EIGHT

So it's Saturday afternoon, the end of the week. And I've just finished cutting 'Big Al' Morton's hair. It was the last haircut of the day and of the week. Yes that's it, the weeks over.

And it's been a strange sort of week really, a week of contemplation I suppose, probably because certain events have been mulling over and over in my head. I plan to retire sometime this year, and maybe it's something to do that. But something's happened, something that has actually made me stop and think, and made me reconsider things.

In truth, it entails the story of a man's life.

You see, my customer and my friend 'Mr Jones' has just died.

It was last week, last Tuesday, he passed away peacefully and he deserved to.

At eighty nine, I suppose it's said that you've 'had a good innings', and indeed he had.

Eighty nine is certainly a good many years, and it's a lot more than most men will ever have.

So, yesterday afternoon I attended his funeral, and it was undeniably a celebration of a life.

Yes, Mr Jones has died, he was a well respected and an undeniably interesting man, and I liked him.

And now I would like to tell you his story.

Mr Jones started to come to my shop for his haircut over twenty years ago. He was not long retired back then and though he would have obviously been over sixty five at the time, he was actually still very fresh faced and full of enthusiasm, almost boyish.

Francis 'Clifton' Jones, I never did find out what the 'Clifton' bit was about, it may have been somebody's last name, it may even have been a place, I don't know. But to me he was always 'Mr Jones'.

The man was a great, great reader and his knowledge of books and their authors almost made him a walking encyclopaedia. Mention any book or author, and he could give you information on either or both. Bring up even the plot of some novel, and he would generally know its account.

It was a terrible cruelty, and it was the cruelty of old age, but in his last few years he told me that 'he was now just too old to read' and for me, that was a sadder day.

Mr Jones had always been a schoolteacher, and in later life became the Headmaster at a 'good' school in Bolton. Born in the University City of Cambridge, some of the scholastic nature of the place must have gotten into his blood, and sent him onto an academic career.

Back in the 1940's Mr Jones, along with many other young men his age, was enlisted into the army. He was around seventeen or eighteen at the time, and after seeing service in France for two or three years, he finally ended up in Paris at the end of the War. Fluent in French and with an academic background he became a junior lieutenant in the administrative section. By then France had been battered and beaten and was in disarray as the retreating Germans had wreaked havoc on the country as they ran back to their own dying nation.

The Allies were just waking up to the existence of the Nazi death camps, and the growing possibility of the Holocaust.

Within the year, and with the help of the allies, the Russian Army would chase Adolph's men all the way back to Berlin and spank them, along with the remaining Berliners, for daring to molest Mother Russia.

By 1945 it was all over. Europe was in a colossal mess and it all needed to be sorted out, and that simple fact would keep Francis Clifton Jones in Paris for the next several years.

Not that Francis Jones was bothered, in fact, he'd never been happier. Spring time, or any other time in Paris, was a damn sight better than being in dreary old England, were life was grim, all post war and poor.

So in Paris he stayed, conditionally posted. Well there was a lot to do in the administrative section. Not long after Berlin was ravished, the Allies and the Russians would eventually fall out. East and West would historically part company, and Germany would be ripped in two.

Yes, there was a lot to do.

So Mr Jones remained in Paris and lived the life, and as time went by he built up quite a circle of friends and acquaintances, both English and French. It was a natural progression really, he was young and rather charming, his biggest asset being that he was very bright and educated and clever, and he was also an exceptional and witty conversationalist. People liked him, and liked him a lot. He was an asset at any dinner party or social event because 'Young Jones' was easy on the ear. There were no awkward silences when Lieutenant Francis Jones was invited to a party. He would flit from English to French with ease, and along with his boyish enthusiasm, he was simply a joy to be with. Yes, people really did like him.

And it was at one of these dinner parties that Francis Clifton Jones would be introduced to a young Miss Catherine Beecham.

And it would change his life.

The party in question was at 'General Beaumont's' apartment. General Beaumont was in charge of 'Administrative Section' which was where Francis Jones worked. In fact he was Francis's boss.

The General liked 'young Jones' and he knew his worth. Other people at the party included a Captain Halifax and his wife. Captain Halifax was Francis's immediate senior, and he kept a wary eye on Francis, often wondering if his young asset could eventually become an adversary, rank stood for everything in the Army. Also attending the party was the secretary to the French Ambassador. He was Monsieur Delaine, who brought along his pretty but rather silly wife, Felice. There were other people there too of course, a mixture of English and French, all were involved in administration, and all were involved to a certain extent, in the uncertain future of Europe. They were principally, the people 'in the. know', and at that moment in time, they were the 'movers and shakers' in Paris. The regular circuit of evening dinner parties were not just simply social affairs, they were a method by which officialdom could keep in contact with one another without all the red tape. 'Nods and winks' and agreements and handshakes, all could be done behind closed doors and out of the public eye, and sometimes more importantly, out of the politician's ears. As with most governments, it was the civil service that did most of the work.

It was on a warm May evening when Lieutenant Francis Jones arrived at General Beaumont's fashionable apartment on the 'Avenue Silvestre de Sacy', which was only a stone's throw from the Eiffel Tower. Seniority certainly held its perks.

Several people had already arrived, most of whom Lieutenant Jones had already met on previous occasions. Drinks were already being served and some of the guests were comfortably chatting. The Lieutenant always made sure that he was never the first to arrive, it smacked of social desperation. However he was never late, he knew his place.

He was greeted warmly by General Beaumont's wife, as was usual, and he immediately looked around for the General himself, and then spotted him in the corner talking to Captain Halifax. He smiled at both of the men and they in turn acknowledged him with a nod.

A certain informality ruled on evenings such as this.

Suddenly the General's wife spoke "Could I have a quick word, Lieutenant Jones?" she said.

The Lieutenant turned back to her "Yes of course" he replied, and he smiled efficiently.

Mrs Beaumont then continued "We have a young lady staying with us, she's the daughter of close friends of ours back in England. She's over here on a scholarship at the Paris Opera Ballet School, and though she does have friends here in Paris, it's been decided that she should stay here with us. I'm afraid we've been a bit dropped on, this has all been a last minute sort of thing. Apparently the young lady who was originally chosen for the scholarship has got herself pregnant, 'silly girl', and Catherine" and here the general's wife smiled pleasantly "Catherine was offered the girl's place. The thing is, tonight we have this party to organise and I need someone to look after her, I can't just leave the poor thing standing about".

General Beaumont's wife then looked at Lieutenant Jones apologetically.

"Could you be a dear, Lieutenant Jones, and look after her?"

Lieutenant Jones inwardly grimaced as he remained smiling. The last thing he wanted to do was to have to entertain some silly dancing girl. There were people here at the party tonight that he needed to speak to. He required guidance on certain areas of local administration and some advice on a particular piece of government directive. These were difficult times and knowledge was an asset.

But, what could he do. Get on the wrong side of the General's wife and he could possibly get on the wrong side of the General. Lieutenant Jones had envisaged living and working in Paris for the next few years, and so he quickly decided not to make waves, not even ripples.

"Of course I will Mrs Beaumont, it's a pleasure" he replied, as he charmingly capitulated.

The evening progressed, and Lieutenant Jones mingled. He liked to flirt about from group to group. He'd straightaway gone over to General Beaumont and Captain Halifax, and that was almost protocol. The three of them stood and talked pleasantly about today's and tomorrow's dealings at Administrative headquarters. Lieutenant Jones carried on the banter and told them about some silliness that had happened during the day which made the General and the Captain laugh. Then the Colonel turned back to talk to his Captain, and Lieutenant Jones knew that this was the moment for him to leave. This was the way of things, nothing was ever said. It was all a matter of knowing your place, and it was a balance that the Lieutenant completely understood.

It suited him too, not to overstay his welcome. He didn't want to get stuck with the boredom of the General and the Captain all night, but neither did he want to be seen as their 'lackey'.

He was not some dogsbody that just refilled his master's drinks. He sought to be his 'own' man, well, as much as the army would allow.

So Lieutenant Jones would spend the evening hovering from persons to persons. Be it a group, or a couple, or the certain individuals who he needed to speak to. He would do the whole tour and talk to people and glean information. He'd gotten to know quite a few 'high up' individuals in the French civil service and was finding that these acquaintances were an invaluable asset, a source of knowledge. The gossip became information and that knowledge of course, was power. If possible, he would always try to give 'a bit back', a bit of inane 'tittle tattle' or some silly rumour. Once again, it was all a question of balance.

The Minister's secretaries, the local councillors, and even other lieutenants, all were worth talking to for half an hour.

Lieutenant Jones was just about to prise himself away from the French Ambassador's secretary, Monsieur Delaine. The Lieutenant couldn't deal with trying to converse with the man's stupid wife any longer, and he was also beginning to appreciate that the secretary himself was not much brighter than his spouse.

There was suddenly a light tap on his shoulder "Lieutenant Jones" a voice said.

It was General Beaumont's wife, and suddenly the Lieutenant remembered his promised chore.

He'd entirely forgotten, he had been so busy doing the 'circuit' that the promise of this annoying little task had gone completely out of his head. For a moment he closed his eyes, and considered a feasible excuse, and then he realized his position. And with that, he affixed his 'best' smile and turned around smartly.

In front of him stood General Beaumont's wife, who immediately started to say something. Lieutenant Jones listened for a second and then suddenly glanced at the young lady who standing at her side, and he suddenly stopped listening. He fleetingly looked back at the General's wife and then turned back to stare at the young lady. Then he swallowed and his mouth fell slightly open and for a split second he actually lost his bearings.

Standing there in front of him was the very lovely Miss Catherine Isabelle Beecham. And that was it. Lieutenant Francis Clifton Jones was completely smitten.

Catherine Isabelle Beecham was the only daughter to the Beecham family, who were old friends of the Beaumont's. At one time both families all originally lived out in Surrey. Catherine's father worked at a bank in London where he was fairly well connected, but nothing immense. 'Well thought of' was the term used.

Catherine had always studied ballet from being a child, and now Paris, her dream.

She had arrived in Paris at the Beaumont's apartment at what she now realized was a 'bit of an awkward time'. Mrs Beaumont had fussed a lot when Catherine had arrived, and had told the rather embarrassed young girl that they 'hadn't' expected her for another week.

"Not to worry" exclaimed the slightly put out Mrs Beaumont. She had more important things on her mind than this girl. She had a dinner party to organize.

Mrs Beaumont had no children of her own and was unaware that she lacked a certain amount of consideration to others. She then proceeded to tell Catherine about the dinner party that they were holding that evening and how there was going to be some very important people there. She instructed, almost ordered, Catherine to wear something that was 'hopefully' fashionable, and to try not to be too obvious.

That evening, as the Beaumont's got changed into their evening attire and prepared themselves for the party, Mrs Beaumont expressed her frustrations to her husband 'the General'.

"What on earth am I going to do with her?" said an exasperated Mrs Beaumont. "I've got everything to organize tonight and I haven't got the time to be looking after young Catherine, lovely girl as she is".

The General looked back at his wife through the mirror, as he attempted to knot his necktie correctly. He'd realized a long time ago, that though he could command an army, trying to command his wife was a lost cause. And he briefly considered that if she had ever been one of his staff, he would have had her court marshalled and dishonourably discharged years ago. As he struggled with his tie, the General said "I don't know why you didn't tell her to stay in her room for the evening, surely she must be tired or something of the sort".

"I can't do that" retorted his wife "the Beecham's would never forgive us. And what would she tell them? That she wasn't allowed to come to the party and that we locked her away for the night?"

Mrs Beaumont looked across at her husband, and once again, wondered 'how on earth' he had ever managed to become a General. When it came to planning and diplomacy, he was hopeless. In all of their married life, if for one moment she had left the important decisions to him, they would have been doomed to failure.

Suddenly, the General had a stroke of genius.

"I know" he said "I know what to do".

"And what that?" she said, ever sceptical.

"Young Jones, my lieutenant. Give him the job, he's an affable enough young chap, and he can talk the back legs off a horse. Give him the job. He'll look after her well enough, and he'll certainly keep her amused".

Mrs Beaumont considered her husband's words, and she smiled to herself.

"Oh 'yes' dear...you could be right there" she replied casually "I think they're both about the same age, they must have 'something' in common. And you're right about Lieutenant Jones. He's never lost for words, quite the conversationalist".

"There you go" said the General, he'd solved another crisis.

'Yes, there I go' thought Mrs Beaumont, she would now be free to circulate, and enjoy herself.

"I'll ask the Lieutenant as soon as he arrives" she announced   "Yes dear, what a good idea" she said, and she turned to the General and straightened his tie.

Catherine had sat nervously in her room. She had been ready for over an hour. She'd showered herself, and that in itself was hugely different. Most people back in England hadn't discovered the delights of a shower in those days, most English bathrooms only had a bath and a sink, and a lot more English homes didn't even have a bathroom. Back in good old England most baths were still made of tin, and taken in front of the living room fire.

Catherine had looked at herself in the mirror for the hundredth time, or at least that's what it felt like. She'd showered and had got changed into her favourite outfit, a fitted, off white cocktail dress that had a beautiful silken sheen finish. It made her look older than a teenager, she was only nineteen, and she hoped that it made her look a little bit sophisticated. She wore matching shoes that were only matching until you looked closely, and hopefully, nobody would.

A light application of makeup, just a dusting of face powder and the briefest flash of lipstick, then a dab of her favourite Chanel, and she was ready to go. That was an hour ago.

She'd sat there for over an hour and had heard the guests start to arrive. What should she do?

She didn't feel that she could just barge herself out there, she wasn't comfortable in 'making an entrance', and she also realized that she didn't know anyone. In fact, Catherine Beecham was quite a shy person who only spoke when spoken to, and she was completely out of her depth in situations such as this.

So there she sat.

Would Mrs Beaumont come for her? She was beginning to think 'not'.

She began to wonder if Mrs Beaumont had actually forgotten about her, and as the volume of noise from the ever arriving guests increased, Catherine considered that Mrs Beaumont must be very busy welcoming people and obviously had other things on her mind.

Eventually Catherine stood up and went across to the door of her room. She couldn't just sit there all night. And what if much, much later that evening, an astonished Mrs Beaumont finally remembered about her and dragged Catherine out of her room, full of apologies, and then proceeded to present her to 'all' the guests at the dinner party. She would feel totally embarrassed and ridiculous.

Why on earth had her parents insisted on her staying with the Beaumont's? She had other friends in Paris. She'd only been here a day and was already beginning to hate it.

So she stood behind the door and ever so quietly opened it a fraction. She peered through the gap and observed smart men in smart suits wandering past. Occasionally, one of the ladies would pass by, but not Mrs Beaumont. Then finally, after what seemed an age, she heard her host call out to one of the caterers. This was going to be her best chance and she opened the door and walked out as though she'd just nipped back to her room for something and was now returning to the party, all very casual. She almost walked straight into Mrs Beaumont, who was saying something caustic about the cook.

"Oh hello Mrs Beaumont" said Catherine "I've just been looking for you".

Mrs Beaumont looked at Catherine, and looked again. She was rather taken aback. Was this Catherine...'little Catherine'. Catherine who as a child had been a somewhat pain in the neck, a nattering blonde haired little girl who was always dancing about?

But now, here was Catherine, and Catherine was beautiful.

When Catherine Beecham had arrived earlier that day, Mrs Beaumont had in truth, been too busy to take much notice of her, what with the party and everything. And Catherine had been wearing a sort of floppy hat and rather large coat for the trip because it was still cold in England. So Mrs Beaumont had really just ushered the girl upstairs and out of the way.

But now, Mrs Beaumont stood back and examined her.

"My goodness Catherine, you've grown up young lady" she said "And what a beautiful dress" and as she looked at her she remembered her friends, the Beechams, and she also remembered all the happy times before the War, when life was simpler. And her heart warmed a little and she reached over to the girl and put her hands on Catherine's shoulders.

"You'll do" she said sincerely, and smiled, and actually meant it.

As she guided Catherine through the main apartment, which was now rather full of guests, Mrs Beaumont gently took her by the arm.

"There's actually someone who I would like you to meet" she said quietly "a nice young man, my husband's Lieutenant. I've asked him to look after you. I hope you don't mind Catherine, but you see, I have my other guests to attend to".

Catherine smiled sweetly "Oh no not at all, of course, I understand" she replied as she inwardly groaned and felt somewhat like the 'fatted calf' awaiting her fate.

'Oh dear god' she thought to herself 'the night's going to get worse'. And she thought about having to talk all night to some spotty lieutenant who was boring and wet behind the ears. This was certainly not her vision of the promised glamour of Paris.

So she'd dutifully followed her host through the parade of milling guests and watched miserably as Mrs Beaumont stopped and tapped on the shoulder of a young man in uniform who was talking to a young French couple.

The young man, the Lieutenant, spun around to face Mrs Beaumont, and to Catherine's surprise she saw that he was actually quite good looking, quite handsome really. And he had a sort of charming, confident smile. Suddenly the pulse in her nineteen year old body began to beat a little faster. And as she looked at him, he suddenly glanced across at her, and he stopped smiling, and that fact alone led

Catherine to assume that the Lieutenant was not impressed with her, and her heart sank a little and she felt awkward and slightly out of her depth.

"This is Lieutenant Jones" said Mrs Beaumont out loud, and she took the young Lieutenant by the arm and introduced him to Catherine.

But young Lieutenant Jones was in bit of a daze, the General's wife was still talking but he hadn't heard a word. He looked across at Catherine, with her exquisite blonde hair, pinned up in a 'chignon' style, and her beautifully featured face. She simply took his breath away.

"And this is Catherine, Catherine Beecham, Lieutenant" said Mrs Beaumont.

Lieutenant Jones heard the words Catherine 'something or other', and he began to realize what he was doing, or not doing in his case, and he suddenly snapped back into reality and the world of the living. Trying hard to regain his composure and hide his now increasingly blushing face, the Lieutenant tried to revert to his previous 'charming smiling self' and it almost worked, god bless him. But Catherine saw none of this, she was still unsure about this introduction, and now the Lieutenant seemed to be grinning at her like a lunatic.

Mrs Beaumont looked at the pair of them and wondered what the hell was going on. Wasn't anybody going to speak? And the seconds ticked past as she looked at one and then the other.

Then at last, Lieutenant Jones once again resumed self control. The confidence and charm instantly returned and as he looked into the palest blue eyes that he had ever seen.

He said "Good evening Catherine, I'm Lieutenant Jones, but please call me Francis. I'm so really pleased to meet you. Mrs Beaumont here has asked me to look after you and keep you entertained this evening" and he gave a short laugh "and it will be my absolute pleasure".

Then he turned to Mrs Beaumont "Thank you Mrs Beaumont, would it be alright if I took Catherine over for some food, and possibly a glass of wine?" and with that he quickly turned back to Catherine "If that's alright with you of course, I take it you 'are' hungry?"

Catherine smiled, and melted. The enthusiasm of this man just made her want to giggle.

She realized that she had either mistakenly read him wrong, or, he was a blatant and competent liar. She decided to go with her first instincts.

Mrs Beaumont smiled at them both and thought to herself 'job well done'. And now she could happily get on with her evening without either hindrance or guilt.

She nodded at them both and said to Catherine "Enjoy your evening" and with that she beat a hasty retreat. As she walked away from them, Mrs Beaumont looked across the large drawing room to her husband. The General looked back at her, he had been watching them all from a distance, and he smiled at his wife and winked. Mrs Beaumont just raised her eyebrows at him, and as she walked away she considered that she'd 'let him win that one'.

Lieutenant Jones took hold of Catherine's arm in a well mannered way and escorted her over to the buffet table.

"Help yourself" he said gleefully and pointed at all the food. The Beaumont's were good hosts, and the table was overflowing. Catherine was overwhelmed, and they suddenly looked at each other and started to giggle like a couple of school children. They filled two plates and Francis 'lifted' two glasses of white wine off a tray that was being passed around by the wine waiter.

He then nodded in a forward direction "Let's go over there" he said to her "we can eat, and it's a bit quieter". Catherine appreciated his suggestion, and they went over to a corner where there was a tall circular table. It was chest high, and as Francis struggled slightly to put the plates and the wine down, he quipped that they'd have to eat standing up, if that was okay with her, and of course it was.

They started to eat and there was a silence, both were aware of it, and suddenly Catherine looked up to see that Francis had stopped eating. He was just looking at her, she looked back at him and this time there was no embarrassment between them.

"You're not what I expected" he said.

"Neither are you" she said back to him.

They ate and they drank and they talked. And then they did the 'rounds'. Lieutenant Jones introduced her to most of the people there that he knew, and whenever they approached another group of guests, the Lieutenant would gently put his hand across her shoulder. It was somehow protective, and Catherine found that she quite liked that.

Later in the evening, he took her to one side and said "Come on, I'll show you a little bit of Paris" and they escaped. They went quietly down the stairs and out of the apartment building, and outside into the fresh spring air. It was still a warm night and they linked arms and felt comfortable about it. Then Francis took her down the cobbled avenue to show her the Eiffel Tower, it was only a short distance from the Beaumont's fashionable apartment. He walked her underneath the Tower and they laughed as they headed down to the River Seine. When they arrived at the river they leant against a wall and talked. Catherine told him about her 'chance' at the ballet school, and her hopes and her plans. He in turn told her about his career and his possible future. They both realized and then discussed their one common denominator, and that was that they were both hoping to stay in Paris for quite a while.

Francis suddenly looked at his watch and realized that they'd been away from the party for over an hour. He certainly didn't want to get her into trouble, or himself for that matter. Whether or not they'd be missed at all, was debatable really, they were very small players in a wide circle of political acquaintances. However, tongues could wag and he did not for one moment want to get on the wrong side of the General.

"We'll have to get back" he said, and Catherine looked at him and the disappointment showed in her face, tonight she was happy. Then suddenly Francis did something totally out of character, in his entirely organised life he planned everything with absolute precision. But not this, he reached over to her and slid his arm around her waist, and then he pulled her towards him. They were now face to face, and he looked down into those amazing pale blue eyes, this girl was remarkable. He smiled at her, and they kissed.

They walked back to the Beaumont's apartment arm in arm, and they hadn't been missed.

Food, drink and good gossip will normally keep people occupied.

At the end of the evening as the guests were slowly starting to say their 'goodnights' and were beginning to leave, Francis and Catherine 'found' Mrs Beaumont, and Francis thanked her for the party and congratulated her on how wonderful everything had been.

"Thank you so much for inviting me" he said to her. "It's been really lovely Mrs Beaumont. I've done the rounds with Catherine here" and he looked over to Catherine and smiled pleasantly "and I think she's been introduced to just about everybody" he continued, along with a good-humoured laugh "Also, I was wondering, and I've spoken to Catherine about this. Would you like me to show her around Paris and let her get her bearings? I could show her the sights, and also show her how to commute, and how to use the buses and the Metro".

Mrs Beaumont smiled, this suited her down to the ground, it was yet another chore that she could off load.

"What a splendid idea, Lieutenant" she replied, and she looked across to Catherine "You're going to have to learn all about this City my dear, and learn how to find your way around. Paris is a huge place. Yes, that would be a splendid idea Lieutenant Jones, how good of you."

And that was that.

As they walked away from Mrs Beaumont, Catherine squeezed the good Lieutenant's hand.

"Clever boy" she whispered.

So that was how the romance started. They were very much in love, well as much as they knew about love at that age, and they started calling each other 'darling', in private of course. It was fashionable at the time, but it was something that they would continue to do for the rest of their lives, well almost.

The next day Lieutenant Jones mentioned the matter of Catherine Beecham and his conversation with the General's wife, to his immediate superior, who was Captain Halifax. The Lieutenant knew that the mention of the General's wife would lend weight to the question of him having 'a little time away from the office', so that he could show Miss Beecham the sights and sounds of Paris.

The Captain was a little surprised. He would have to discuss this with the General of course, and he was again surprised, that when he did mention this request to the General, the General simply 'Okayed' the matter.

Captain Halifax was a bit put out over this. He was trying to run a very busy office and 'Administrative Section' had been undermanned, everyone was working at full stretch.

What Captain Halifax was unaware off, was that the General had already been commandeered by his good lady wife, Mrs Beaumont, and that orders had already been assigned.

So with that, Lieutenant Francis Jones got his permitted leave, and he and Miss Catherine Beecham were free to happily wander around Paris together. The very next day, they both went round to meet Catherine's friends, two similarly aged young ladies, one of whom was attending the same ballet school as Catherine and had already spent a year there. The other girl was at the University of Paris-Sorbonne and was taking a degree in French Language. Both girls lived in a small flat in the Montmartre area.

Within half an hour, the four of them had made innumerable plans, 'things that they would just have to do' and that little flat soon became the regular haunt where they all met up.

Francis and Catherine would spend their lunchtimes there together, and within a week or so when the other two girls were 'discreetly' out, Francis and Catherine became lovers.

That the two of them were deeply in love soon became evident to Mrs Beaumont, who began to sense a 'closeness' between these two young people, a closeness that was more than just a friendly acquaintance. Her suspicions were justified, when one afternoon as she was looking out of her bedroom window, she observed the couple crossing the road. They were both walking back from another day out in the City. The Lieutenant and Catherine sauntered along, intimately arm in arm, and Catherine had her head nuzzled on the young Lieutenant's shoulder in a most affectionate way.

That night, as the General and his wife were getting changed for an evening at the theatre,

Mrs Beaumont happened to mention to her husband that there may be 'something in the air' with Catherine and Young Lieutenant Jones.

The General gave it a moment's thought "He's a very bright young man" he said "Could go places. She could do worse".

Mrs Beaumont considered this for a moment, and she could see her husband's logic. "Do you think I should mention it to the Beechams?" she asked.

The General hesitated for a moment "No, I don't think so. Nothing may come of it, after all this is Paris".

Mrs Beaumont took this suggestion onboard, and possibly and unfortunately, in some way considered that if Catherine and Lieutenant Jones were eventually to become more than just an 'item', their long friendship with the Beechams would necessitate that the General and herself would also be obliged to become good friends with Lieutenant Jones. And the Lieutenant may not always remain a Lieutenant, her husband had hinted as much.

So rather inadvertently, and not by any grand design, Mrs Beaumont began to invite the Lieutenant, along with Catherine, around for tea, and then occasionally take them both along to the theatre with her and the General. And suddenly the young couple were invited to most of the social events that the Beaumont's were invited to, Mrs Beaumont saw to that.

And these two young people were very pleasant to be with, and it was almost 'quite fashionable' to be seen in the company of a younger couple, especially when one of them was a Ballerina and the other a dashing young Lieutenant.

For Lieutenant Jones too, life has suddenly become a great deal better. He had a beautiful young woman on his arm, who he was also going to bed with, and his social life had suddenly taken an upward turn. He was a regular guest at most of the social events these days, and the General and his wife were almost treating him like family, it seemed that he was never away from the Beaumont's apartment, life was good.

Lieutenant Jones was getting comfortable...too comfortable.

It was now July, and the General and his good lady wife had decided to host an evening meal for the visiting Belgian Ambassador, along with the neighbouring French Ambassador. It was to be an important evening and there were going to be quite a few 'high end' army personnel there too, top brass with a couple of colonels thrown in for good luck. Captain Halifax and his wife would be there of course, and Lieutenant Jones and Catherine were also invited, though this was more through habit, rather than their rank and standing.

Lieutenant Jones however, misguidedly took the invite as a sign of his own importance and rather rashly considered that he would be called upon for his opinion and his administrative expertise.

The evening progressed, and all the guests were served Champagne as they arrived. After an hour's light conversation it was time for everyone to be seated at the long dining table in the Beaumont's drawing room. Throughout the previous hour, the Lieutenant had flitted from guest to guest, introducing himself to one and all. Bolstered by two or three glasses of champagne, and on an empty stomach, he had become rather talkative. At one point, he actually interrupted a conversation between the French Ambassador and a Major, to give a comment on something that he had heard them both talking about as he strolled past. The astonished Major was about to reprimand him, but the Lieutenant had already moved on.

The Lieutenant continued to circulate, giving his opinions and comments. He was feeling heady, and confident...over confident.

Captain Halifax, standing in a corner with his wife, looked on in amazement. 'What on earth did Lieutenant Jones think he was playing at?' The Captain couldn't believe his eyes, or his ears. However, it had to be said that Captain James Halifax had become increasingly more and more exasperated with his young Lieutenant during the last few weeks. 'Young Jones' had been given unprecedented leave, and since then he had been more out of his office than in it. The Captain knew what was going on of course, he knew all about the young girl that 'Jones' was parading about with, and he'd inwardly sneered when he found out that she was a family friend of the Beaumont's. But more than that, he was slightly hesitant and a little perturbed when he saw how the Lieutenant had managed to get his 'feet' firmly under the General's table.

The Captain had mentioned all this to his wife one night over dinner, and she quite rightly had told him to 'watch his back', treading on the 'wrong toes' in the army could leave your path to promotion dead in its tracks. And also, she quite rightly warned him that the charming young Lieutenant, could also be charming the General, and be carving his own path to promotion. There was always more than one way to get to the top of the tree, and Lieutenant Jones was the man who was just smart enough to get there.

The Captain had thought long and hard about this. He knew that the lieutenant was a well educated and very clever young man, and it was a fact that Captain Halifax had been using the lieutenant for his own purpose. Captain Halifax had for quite a time now, taken Lieutenant Jones's reports and initialled and signed them under his own name, and then presented them to General Beaumont as his own work.

And the General had been impressed.

So back at the party, and all the guests finally sat down as the waiters filled everyone's wine glass, and kept them filled. The wine flowed, the food was served, and it was all excellent.

The Lieutenant was sitting next to Catherine of course, and on the other side of him was 'some' Colonels wife, and unfortunately the Lieutenant's wit and charm finally got the better of her, and after several humorous comments she started to giggle and so did Catherine, and this giggling, though it was not raucous laughter, it started to be heard by some of the other guests and it began to irritate slightly as those same guests were all trying to discuss the business of the day. Heads were beginning to turn to the rather forthright young Lieutenant.

Lieutenant Francis Jones was beginning to be noticed.

July...1945...and back in England, the country was preparing to go to the polls. There was going to be a general election and the Politicians were sharpening their knives as battle between the parties was about to commence. Defending his position as Prime Minister was Winston Churchill. Right-wing wartime leader, 'wartime saviour' and a man of great stature and principals, he was a legend.

On the 'left' and for the Labour party was Clement Attlee.

Back at the Beaumont's, the evening was progressing fairly agreeably, and inevitably the conversation turned to the subject of the General Election back in England. Most of the guests that night were Army, or from an Army background and were in awe of their wartime leader Mr Churchill, who himself was an Army man. The smattering of foreign politicians and Ambassadors that were there knew of 'nobody else' but Winston Churchill.

So the conversations continued and it was generally and unanimously agreed to be a 'forgone conclusion' that Mr Churchill would once again lead the Conservative Party to victory.

General Beaumont, sitting at the head of the table was nodding to the rest of 'his' men and other guests as they spoke of Churchill's wartime effort, when suddenly a voice spoke out.

It was Lieutenant Jones.

"I think you may all find that you are wrong there" he said, to everyone.

'Everyone' stopped, and heads turned to look down the table to where the young Lieutenant was sitting.

Taken aback, General Beaumont stared at the Lieutenant and said "I beg your pardon Jones, what did you just say?"

The Lieutenant, not hearing the threat in the General's voice, and actually thinking that the General was seeking information, after all, that was what he did. He took another glug of wine and continued.

"It's like this General" he said "I feel that the country is ready for a change, you see, the war is over and the population, I personally feel, is ready for change of Government. People are sick of being ordered about", and that raised a few eyebrows, but Jones continued "You see General, people are fed up with war and rationing and austerity, and being told what to do. Living here in Paris, it's very easy to forget what England's like, you lose touch".

General Beaumont nearly burst a blood vessel.

Captain Halifax felt like putting his head in his hands, and Mrs Beaumont just sat there with her knife and fork in hand, open mouthed.

The Lieutenant had quite simply, spoken down to his General. He'd forgotten his rank, and had disagreed with the General in quite a rude and arrogant manner.

The effect on the party was as though someone had opened a door and let a cold draught in.

Except for the General, he sat there and went very red and everyone saw this, everyone except Lieutenant Jones and Catherine.

Catherine just looked at her Lieutenant rather dreamily, and considered what a clever young man he was. Oh she was a lucky girl.

The General finally spoke "Oh, so that's what 'you' think then, do you Jones?"

"I think so sir" replied Lieutenant Jones carelessly, still not hearing the warning shots in the General's words.

The General sat there and realized that he had important guests at his table and that he must not make a scene. It would only cause embarrassment and he would lose a certain amount of dignity. No, that was not going to happen.

He simply picked up his glass and said to his guests "More wine everyone?"

And gradually the moment passed.

The French Ambassador, who was sitting to the right of the General, continued to eat his meal, and without looking up from his plate, he said to the General.

"Quiet outspoken, your young Lieutenant".

The evening finally came to an end, and the guests, who were all now well fed and watered, finally moved to leave. The General looked over at Captain Halifax and gave him a nod of attention, and the Captain immediately went over to his commanding office.

"Sir?" said the Captain.

The General quite casually said to him "Could you just step into my study before you leave Halifax, I have some papers for you to look at".

The Captain knew there were no papers, and he knew what this was relating to, He would keep his wits about him.

Captain Halifax informed his wife that he would have to see the General before they left, and then whispered something to her, so she made herself comfortable but scarce.

He then hovered around until he'd seen the last guests go, and then he stood discretely aside, and watched as the General went into his study. He mentally counted to thirty and then went over and knocked on the study door.

"Come" he heard the General's voice, and so he entered.

The General was leaning on his desk and eyed Captain Halifax as he entered. The Captain shuddered slightly, and walked towards him.

"Sir." he said, and saluted for good measure.

The General looked at him, and then spoke. "Can you tell me Captain, what the bloody hell that little jumped up idiot of a lieutenant thought he was playing at?"

"Exactly Sir" said the Captain, almost immediately "I was astounded sir, absolutely astounded"

"I have never been so embarrassed and insulted in my life. Do you hear me?" continued the General, his voice now rising.

"Yes sir, I do" said Captain Halifax "and I can't think what possessed Lieutenant Jones to assume that he could speak to you in such a manner sir, and embarrass us all, us and everyone else from the Army, and in front of the foreign ambassadors. It was absolutely disgraceful behaviour, sir"

The General nodded back at his Captain, almost appreciatively. 'That' was the reply that he was waiting to hear, and then slowly and deliberately he spoke again.

"Put him out in the cold, Captain" the General said "Put him out in the cold, and then pack him back off to England. Get rid of him and get him out of my sight".

"Yes sir" replied Captain Halifax "I can do that sir, leave it to me".

"Thank you Captain, that's all" concluded the General, and they saluted.

As the Captain reached the door to leave, the General called after him.

"Oh by the way Halifax"

The Captain turned around quickly "Sir?"

"Mrs Beaumont and I are going to the Opera at the end of the month, I wonder if you and your wife would like to join us?"

"Oh that would be very nice sir. Yes we would, and thank you very much sir. We'll look forward to it" and with that he left the study.

Captain Halifax closed the door behind him and smiled. He hated the Opera.

Nothing was ever said to Lieutenant Jones about his outburst at the General's dinner party,

not at first anyway. In fact the Lieutenant was blissfully unaware that he was the cause of any embarrassment at all.

However, it was Catherine who first noticed that the Beaumont's had gone a 'little distant'.

The evening invites to parties and the theatre stopped, and suddenly the General and his wife were having dinner on their own. Catherine had always been invited to dine with them of course, but there was no longer any mention of her inviting the Lieutenant.

A week or more passed before Lieutenant Jones noticed that his work load had diminished somewhat, and when he questioned Captain Halifax about this the Captain just shrugged his shoulders and told him that 'there wasn't a lot on at the moment'. Strangely, the Lieutenant thought there was.

Later that week, the Captain told him that he could have some time off, and that things were 'pretty slack just now', even though everybody else in the office seemed busy enough.

The Lieutenant wasn't complaining though, more time off meant he could have more time with Catherine. And that meant lunches at the little flat in the Montmartre, and then taking her to bed afterwards.

Winston Churchill lost the election at the end of July, 1945.

Clement Attlee, the Labour leader won in a landslide victory which bordered on humiliation for Mr Churchill.

General Beaumont couldn't believe it. Neither could any of the other high ranking army brass. What on earth were the British people thinking of.

And he thought about Lieutenant Jones's little speech and he felt the knife turn. Jones, it turned out had been right, and the General more than resented it.

Captain Halifax was summoned to the General's office.

On entering, the General informed his Captain that there would have to be spending cuts in the department. 'Apparently', they had a budget to comply to.

"We need to lose some personnel" said the General, and he looked directly at Captain Halifax "Do you know of anyone that we can get rid of Halifax?" he asked.

"Yes sir I do, it would be Lieutenant Jones sir. He's doing nothing at the moment, done nothing for quite a few weeks now sir. He really is surplus to requirements".

"Oh well, in that case" replied the General "get his transfer papers sorted out and I'll sign them straightaway. He can go back to England, they can benefit from his expertise".

The Captain and the General smiled.

"And thank you Captain" said the General.

"A pleasure, Sir" he replied, and saluted.

Two days later, Captain Halifax left a message on Lieutenant Jones's desk. It simply asked the Lieutenant to call in and see him.

It was a day later before Lieutenant Jones finally arrived at the office and read the note.

Since his new found freedom, he had discovered that he could basically come and go as he pleased. There was never a problem, and Captain Halifax had been quite easy going over his continual absenteeism. In his naivety, the Lieutenant actually considered that General Beaumont must have had a 'word' with his Captain. And that the General was quite happy for him to look after Catherine, after all, she was a family friend.

So that morning, Lieutenant Jones wandered over to the Captains office and tapped on the door.

"Come in" called the Captain.

Lieutenant Jones casually strolled into the office, these days he and the Captain didn't even bother saluting, it was all very informal.

To the Lieutenant's dismay however, Captain Halifax didn't even bother to look up. He had his head down and was scribbling away on some sort of form. The Lieutenant stood there for what seemed like several minutes and then suddenly decided to speak out.

"Did you want to see me sir?" he asked. It was almost in innocence.

"Be Quiet!" the Captain immediately barked back, in a voice that the lieutenant wasn't used to.

Lieutenant Jones went rigid. What on earth was going on?

The Captain looked up "You will stand to attention when you come into my office, and you will salute me. Do you hear me?"

The Captain was almost shouting now.

In shock, Lieutenant Jones immediately shot to attention and saluted.

He was dumbfounded and wondered 'to god', what was happening?"

"Jones" continued the Captain "You've got sloppy and lazy and arrogant above your station. We have no further use for you here at Administrative H.Q. Therefore you will be transferred back to barracks in England" and he looked down at the forms that he'd been writing on. "Tomorrow morning. We have a convoy of trucks going back home. You can travel back with them. Here is your paperwork with arrangements to get you back. You're to be barracked at Wolverley Camp, somewhere near Kidderminster, wherever that is."

Lieutenant Jones just stood there bewildered. In those couple of sentences his whole little world was about to collapse.

"But why sir?" he asked feebly.

"Why? Because Jones, you have upset the General" and the Captain sneered at him.

Lieutenant Jones was mystified for a moment. He didn't understand,. What had he done?

"There must be a mistake" he blurted out "Is there anything I can possibly do to rectify the situation, sir. Please."

Captain Halifax looked across at him and smirked.

"Yes, go and have a word with Clement Attlee" he replied.

"Sir..?" Francis didn't understand, and then all of a sudden he did. The penny dropped, and he suddenly remembered the topic of conversation and he realized what this was all about. 'Churchill...Attlee ...and the election' and he remembered the dinner party, and some of what he had said to the General, and 'Oh no', not because of that, surely?

"You're an absolute clown, Jones" said the captain with relish.

The Lieutenant stared in shock at his Captain "Sir, please".

"Get out Jones" said Captain Halifax efficiently "Get out of my sight".

And that was it, Paris was over. The good life, gone. But worst of all, Catherine, his darling Catherine. What was he going to do about Catherine? He tore out of the office and made his way to the flat in the Montmartre. They were supposed to be meeting there for lunch, as usual. He stood about outside on the pavement, pacing up and down as he waited for her. Finally she arrived and he broke the news to her, and broke her heart. Catherine was beside herself and the tears flowed. The young lovers were about to be parted. They sat in the flat that afternoon and cried and talked. In the end Francis looked at her sobbing face, her eyes now reddened by the tears, and he told her he loved her, and then he proposed to her, and she laughed and cried as she accepted.

They made their plans. Yes, Francis would have to go back. Back to England and serve out his allotted time in the army, hopefully it would be less than a year. Catherine was to stay in Paris because she had Ballet School to attend. When he was finally discharged, Francis would come back to Paris and somehow they would get married, either in Paris or in England, it would depend on how Catherine's parents took the news. Making these plans and looking to the future brightened them both up. Yes, they would have a future, and together, there was never any doubt in that.

They stayed together until around nine 'o clock that evening, and then Francis would have to leave and go back to barracks to pack and sort things out. Catherine's two friends had arrived back at the flat by then and were devastated by the news. Francis's departure was going to break up the 'gang'. They'd all enjoyed the time and the banter, the four of them, wining and dining in their little flat. All bread and cheese and cheap Bordeaux.

Francis took Catherine back to the Beaumont's for the final time. He kissed her and watched her walk away, it was an emotional moment for both of them and as she entered the apartment she turned and waved for the last time. Francis walked away, saddened and bitter.

Catherine went into the Beaumont's apartment, and she was on her way up to her room when suddenly, youth or anger got the better of her. She turned and walked through and into the lounge, where Mrs Beaumont was sitting, reading a book.

As she heard Catherine enter the room, she looked up and said "Hello dear".

Catherine walked right up to her, and stood there and asked the question "Why?"

"I beg your pardon dear" replied Mrs Beaumont. She was slightly put out by this.

Catherine just stood there with her hands on her hips, an expression of defiance.

"Why, why has Francis been sent off packing back to England? Just for expressing his political views, which actually turned out to be correct if anybody would take the time to notice?"

It was an outburst, and Mrs Beaumont didn't like outbursts. She took off her reading glasses and stood up to face Catherine. She could see that the girl was upset, but Catherine would have to be told. After all, she 'was' living under their roof and they were doing her a favour, a kindness.

"Listen to me my dear" she said sternly "At a function at this apartment, to which there attended high ranking officials from the Army, and also the Ambassadors from Belgium and France, Lieutenant Jones took it upon himself to be outspoken and arrogant. He overstepped the mark and thoroughly embarrassed the General and the other guests at our dinner party. It was unforgivable. The Lieutenant shouldn't have even been there, we only invited him because of you".

"What" said Catherine?

"Well, he was totally out of his depth. It was high ranking Army officialdom my dear, it's a bigger game, you'll see eventually. Better to let this young man go out of your life. I know he's a charmer, but he would never have made the grade. I personally found him a little weak".

Catherine was astounded, she couldn't believe what she was hearing, and Mrs Beaumont could see it in her face.

"I hope you're not going to be difficult over this dear" she added.

Catherine spoke back angrily "Mrs Beaumont, I'll tell you something right now. That 'weak charmer' is the smartest and cleverest man you'll ever know, and he is also the man that I'm going to marry. You'll regret this day".

And with that, Miss Catherine Beecham turned and left the room, leaving for once, a rather speechless and flabbergasted Mrs Beaumont.

Catherine went up to her room and cried, and packed.

In the morning she got up very early and left the apartment. She would never speak to the Beaumont's again.

When later that day, Mrs Beaumont finally discovered that Catherine had left, and left for good, she sat down in the drawing room and put pen to paper, She wrote a letter to Catherine's parents, explaining the situation. Better she let them know, and be first.

Catherine moved into the flat in the Montmartre with her two friends of course.

And Francis went back to England. After a long hard trip in a rattling old truck, he was taken across the Channel and then transported to barracks near Kidderminster in the South England. Because of his background, he was given menial office duties in the Accounts department in Purchasing Section, a position which hardly taxed his abilities.

For twelve long months he sat, watched and waited as the clock and the calendar slowly turned. It was the longest year of his life. After that, he 'bowed out' of the British Army as fast as his legs would carry him. He had of course, been in constant touch with

Catherine, letters were exchanged at least weekly, sometimes more. He decided to try his hand at teaching and Catherine had found a few possible openings at one or two of the language schools in Paris, so things were almost looking promising.

Within a week of leaving the army barracks, Francis was on his way back to Paris. He went across the Channel at Dover, and after travelling on a succession of buses and trains, he finally arrived back to the city and the girl that he loved. Knowing that Francis was about to return, Catherine realized the small flat that she shared with her friends would no longer be large enough, not for four of them, and so she'd moved out and into a larger apartment which she now shared with one of the other dancers whom she'd befriended at the ballet school. This girl had already been at the Ballet for three years and was becoming somewhat successful. She was Miss Phoebe Dupree, and she was destined to be one of the leading lights in the world of Ballet.

The apartment, located on the outskirts of the old Latin Quarter, was not ideal, but it was cheap and had a couple of bedrooms and a large open kitchen which Catherine loved.

In the evenings after the ballet, the girls would cook something on the apartment's big old stove, and sit there comfortably in front of it with whatever food they could afford, and wine that they couldn't.

Catherine fell into Francis Jones's arms as he walked out of the old Gare Saint-Lazare train station, he'd finally made it. He was back, thank god.

He looked into those pale blue eyes and ran his hand through her beautiful blonde hair, and it made him realize that this was the first time he had been happy for a year. What a waste of his life, the Army.

They made their way to the apartment in the Latin Quarter, it was lunchtime and busy and they walked arm in arm, blissful. The walk took a while but it didn't matter. When they arrived at the apartment, Francis smiled at her as he threw his bags on the floor, and then he took her to bed.

Late in the afternoon, they got up and went to sit in the large warm kitchen. They sat at the big old wooden plank table that they inherited with the apartment, and they drank good French coffee and ate the remnants of some bread and cheese and butter.

They talked for an hour, and were then interrupted when they heard a noise outside. The apartment door suddenly opened, and in walked a young woman, dark haired and vivaciously beautiful. It was Miss Phoebe Dupree.

Catherine turned to her and both girls gave a silly scream of delight. Phoebe, because she saw her friend was finally reunited with her young man, and Catherine because she saw her friend's recognition of that reality. Both girls hugged one another and Catherine immediately turned to introduce Francis to her friend. Francis stood up and shook Miss Dupree's hand.

"I'm so very pleased to meet you Miss Dupree" he said in his best English "Catherine has told me so much about you". He knew that Miss Dupree spoke decent English, but he considered that he should use his 'best' accent.

Phoebe Dupree just laughed out loud, and Francis was a little taken aback.

"Catherine" she said "You never said that 'your Francis' was such an English gentleman. So posh and so well spoken, 'very' charming and 'oh la la' and she laughed out loud again, and Catherine laughed too. Francis just stood there feeling a bit of an idiot.

Catherine stopped laughing and looked at them both "No Phoebe, he's not posh, but he is charming" and she winked at her man.

Phoebe turned to Francis "And you Francis, you will call me Phoebe, and we are all going to be very good friends". Her accent was cheekily 'clipped' with the full French lilt, and she giggled as she pouted her lips and kissed him on the cheek.

Francis smiled at the pair of them, both so very different, and both so stunningly pretty.

"Good grief" he said "I'm going to be living with the two most beautiful women in Paris".

Yes, he was.

Miss Phoebe Angeline Dupree. Now 'there' indeed, was a young lady.

Phoebe Dupree, though she was as French as good Champagne, it was a fact that she had grandparents of Portuguese descent on one side of her family tree and somewhere, an Irish grandfather on the other, and it showed.

She openly carried her 'Latino' lineage, velveteen skin the shade of the palest cappuccino. Stunningly beautiful, she had the darkest of red hair, a mixture of almost black mahogany with a tinge of deep chestnut, a calling card from her Irish grandfather no doubt. But her eyes were Portuguese, olive brown with black eyelashes and dark black eyebrows. There was something raw about her natural beauty. She was lithe and agile, again from her Portuguese blood. But she also had the strength and the force of the Irish in her, and all of this made her an incredible dancer.

Three years at the Paris Opera Ballet School had given her the skills and proficiency that would eventually lead her to dance with the best.

But she was wild, and that was another gift from her grandfather. Loud and somewhat brash and always outspoken, when Phoebe Dupree was in the room, everybody knew about it.

Once settled, the three of them, Francis, Catherine and Phoebe would all go out together. Especially at the weekends, when they would visit the local cafes and bars and meet up with other friends, sometimes dining, always drinking.

By then, Francis had got a job teaching English at a local school. The money wasn't much but it got them through.

They used to go out to the older bars in the Quarter and enjoy mixing with the locals. Phoebe would drink and shout at the men and they loved it. If there was some good music playing they would lift her onto a table and she would dance the 'Flamenco' for them in the bold Spanish style. The men would roar and clap their hands to the music, and when she'd done, she would demand money off them, and they'd have to pay.

Life was good, like bread and cheese and dark red wine, the three of them all lived well together.

On some evenings, usually after too much wine, Phoebe would pick up some capable young man and they would all go back to the apartment. Then Francis and Catherine would lie in bed laughing at the screams and demands coming from Phoebe in the next bedroom as she made love like some wild animal. They were happy, carefree days.

If there 'was' a problem, it was probably Catherine's parents. They of course had received the letter from Mrs Beaumont after Catherine had walked out. It was all one sided and painted Catherine as the 'lost child', who was completely under the spell of the 'hopeless' Lieutenant Jones.

Catherine's mother wrote two letters to her on the same day and then in frustration and worry, rang the Ballet School in Paris. Finally, and after a lot of fuss, she managed to talk to her 'wayward' daughter. Catherine of course, lied. She told her mother that her relationship with Lieutenant Jones had only been a passing friendship, nothing more. He was just an acquaintance and he had disappeared back to England to somewhere or other, she couldn't remember just where. And anyway it was Mrs Beaumont that had introduced them, and Mrs Beaumont was so busy that she couldn't manage to look after Catherine properly and that was why Catherine had moved in with friends. Because the Beaumont's social life at their apartment was so hectic all the time, she felt that she was in the way, was in the way.

Catherine then went on to tell her mother that she had actually written Mrs Beaumont a 'thank you' letter for all her time and patience, and on the morning that Catherine had left, Mrs Beaumont had gone off somewhere for the day, with her husband. Maybe the letter had been mislaid?

'Yes'. She promised her mother to call in and see Mrs Beaumont, and 'Yes' she would take some flowers round as a 'thank you'. Of course she would, not.

And that was that, for now.

Occasional letters came and went, but as long as Catherine wrote back telling her parents that Paris was lovely and the weather was nice, and that she had made good friends with the other girls, etc, etc. As long as she wrote letters along those lines and told them she was doing well at the ballet, her parents simply considered that she was doing alright and not to worry. What they didn't know however, was that there daughter was now unofficially engaged and was determined, at some point, to become Mrs Catherine Isabelle Jones.

The months passed evenly by, and then one afternoon, late in the week, Francis had finished at the school earlier than usual, and since it was a such a hot and sunny afternoon, he took the most of the opportunity and set off early to walk back 'home' to the apartment. He was tempted to stop off somewhere on route and sit outside a cafe bar and have a cool beer or a nice glass of white wine and just watch people walk by. But the further he walked, the hotter he became, and he eventually decided to go straight home and sit on their cool balcony and have a glass of wine there, which after all would cost nothing.

So he arrived home early and expected to have the apartment to himself. What he didn't know, was that Phoebe had arrived home early too.

Her dance class had been cancelled, something or other was wrong with the teacher and so Phoebe too had walked home in the full heat of the afternoon. On arriving back at their apartment, she felt that she was full of the dust and the sweat of the city, and she went to have a shower. She walked into the empty apartment and went straight into the bathroom and ran a flannel under the cold water tap and then ran the damp towel over her face and under her arms. After the fierce heat outside, it felt so, so good. She turned on the shower tap and took off her clothes and then went to stand under the wonderful stream of water.

When Francis arrived back, he too just walked straight in. His mind was on that glass of wine, and all he wanted to do was kick off his shoes and go and sit out on the balcony.

It was as he walked across the kitchen to the cupboard to get a glass that he heard the shower. He turned and thought for a moment, then called out to Catherine, maybe she had come home early too. If she had, then they could both have a glass of wine on the balcony.

There was no answer, just the sound of running water and he was cautious for a moment, it could be Phoebe of course, so he called her name too, but still no answer. So he went over to the bathroom, to knock on the door. But Phoebe hadn't closed the bathroom door, she'd just walked in and stripped off and got into the shower. So Francis walked slowly over to the open door and looked in. And he just stood there and stared.

Standing in the shower in front of him was Phoebe, totally naked. She stood there, eyes closed, as the water streamed onto her face. And Francis watched, stunned, as the water cascaded over her shoulders and down her breasts and splashed off the end of her dark nipples. He looked at her pale brown skin, wet and glistening, and he couldn't turn away.

He was gripped by the sight of her, and he looked on as the water ran down her back and over her bottom and he just stared at her body, and he became breathless as he looked at her, she so shaped, so beautiful. She had the body of an athlete, her bottom was rounded and firm and perfectly toned, and he looked at her beautiful colour and to his astonishment and wonder, he felt that he wanted to reach out and touch her, and not only touch her, more than that. He suddenly wanted to stroke her beautiful skin, stroke her and take hold of her, and run his hands over her hips, and take hold of her beautiful backside and caress those perfect breasts, and the thought of it began to take hold of him.

Then slowly, as the water flowed over her, she slowly moved and turned her back to him and now he saw the thrill of her full buttocks, so exposed, and he saw the curve in her as she suddenly stretched her arms upwards and her back arched.

Francis was breathless now. He stared at Phoebe's body, so stunningly beautiful. She was like nothing he had ever seen before, so physical, sexual, so beautiful and naked, and so close that he could just reach over...

And then suddenly he stopped. 'God'...what was he doing, and he stepped back. His head was spinning and he was aroused and shocked by the sudden awareness of how much he wanted to take hold of and make love to this woman, this physically stunning woman.

He imagined himself, slowly sliding his arms around her and putting his hands on her, and reaching over and kissing the back of her neck and her shoulders and running his hands down over her hips and round, to the softness of her stomach...and then suddenly, with a jolt of astonishment, he'd realized. 'What on earth' was he doing, and no, no he couldn't, or mustn't. And in that single moment, he suddenly thought about Catherine and that one solitary thought made him turn and step away.

He walked across the kitchen and through the glass door onto the balcony and sat down on one of the wooden chairs. He was almost vibrating with the feeling of passion that he'd just experienced, it had gotten hold of him and he was almost overcome by it. He sat there looking at nothing, but wondering what had just happened, and the guilt, of course the guilt. What was he thinking of, he loved Catherine, and then in horror he considered what if Phoebe had turned around and seen him standing there, staring at her like a pervert? She would probably have screamed.

And even worse, the thought that if he'd been stupid enough to reach over and touch her, that would have been something else, a step over the line that would have been wrong and embarrassing, and it would change things forever and ruin their friendships.

Things would never be the same.

So Francis sat there alone on the balcony and he closed his eyes, but when he did, all he could think of was Phoebe Dupree, beautiful and wet and naked.

In the bathroom and still under the shower, Phoebe leaned back on the tiles and smiled to herself.

She'd seen Francis come into the apartment. Of course she had. Their apartment had various mirrors of all shapes and sizes hung on the walls, they covered the aging wallpaper. And through these, she'd glanced up and seen the door open. And she'd watched him walk across the kitchen and seen him turn towards her, and then, through the reflection in the shiny black and white tiles in the bathroom, she'd seen his image staring at her. She could see everything.

Her first instinct had been to lean over and quickly close the bathroom door, and yes, that's what she should have done, and that's what she meant to do. But it felt so good under the shower, and it felt so good to be naked, naked in the middle of the afternoon, and then to have somebody else there with you while you were naked. And suddenly she wanted someone to lay a hand on her, to touch her. And through the tiles, she saw Francis walking towards her in the bathroom and suddenly she wanted him to see her, to see her naked body. So she took the pose, and she knew that the water would run down her body and trickle off her protruding breasts. And at the last minute she closed her eyes and stood there in the luxury of knowing that he was there and that he was looking at her and staring at her, and taking everything in. He could see every inch of her body, wet and naked, and suddenly she was aroused and she slowly turned her back to him. She wanted him to see her bottom, she wanted him to see everything, and the passion got into her and she arched her back and her buttocks and she gasped. She suddenly wanted him to reach in and take hold of her...'please do it...please, please' she said to herself, and she shook and had to catch her breath...'breathe damn you, breathe'.

Slowly she opened her eyes and in the reflection of a tile, she saw him turn and walk away.

She stood there in the shower, breathing hard as she let the running water calm her down. Then finally, she peered out of the bathroom door and saw that Francis had gone to sit on the balcony, and she looked at his face, and what she saw made her smile.

She went back under the water, and thought about what had just happened. Yes, he had come to her in the shower and he'd stood there looking at her, and she'd let him, and he was still staring at her when she turned her back to him, and he kept on staring. And Phoebe smiled again, because she knew he wouldn't forget.

Phoebe Dupree knew all about men.

She turned the water off and stepped out of the shower, she got quickly dried and then wrapped a fresh towel around herself, it went just under her arms and nearly down to her knees. She twisted and pinned up her wet hair so that it was slightly tousled and just a little messy. Then she walked out of the bathroom and across the kitchen and onto the warm and sunny balcony where she met Francis with mock surprise.

"Hello there 'you'..." she said in her lyrical tone.

Francis jolted in shock as he opened his eyes, and his head shot up. The body he was just thinking about was now standing right in front of him, in a clinging towel that was slightly split and showed too much of her pale brown beautiful thigh.

He looked up at her and started to blush, and for once, he couldn't seem to find any words.

Phoebe smiled at the blush "I didn't know you were home" she said "Did you finish early?"

"Err, yes" he replied, slightly open mouthed.

"Oh good" she said "I've just had a shower, it was wonderful, I was all hot and sticky. Hey, let's have a glass of wine. We have some white Bordeaux in the cool cupboard, it'll be lovely" and without waiting for a 'yes or no', she turned around and went back into the kitchen.

Francis sat there as he watched those legs go through the glass door. He had to steady himself and he realized that he was going to have to calm down and get a grasp on things. His body was beginning to stir again and he knew it.

Two minutes later she bounced back out of the kitchen with the promised bottle and two glasses and a corkscrew.

"Could you pull it out" she purred.

Francis just stared at her...

"The cork" she said harmlessly, and she passed him the bottle which she held by the neck and he looked at her hand and his mind thought of other things.

He took the bottle and started to open it.

"It's so hard" she said softly.

Again, he looked at her.

"The cork" she said again "It's too hard for me to do. It's a man's job, and I just can't do it myself". She was enjoying herself now.

She sat down and carefully crossed her legs, he knew she had no underwear on and the split in the towel was now enticingly high.

She cast a glance down at his groin and considered it, and yes, she had him.

He uncorked the bottle and realizing that it would be awkward for him to now stand up, he mumbled.

"Will you do the honours and pour?"

"Yes, off course" and she laughed as she realized his predicament "We women do 'everything' for you men".

And Francis watched her once again as she took hold of the bottle by the neck, firmly in her fingers and thumb. Even the way she served out the wine was sexual, poured very slowly out of the bottle, it landed in the glass with a satisfying 'glug...glug'.

This conversation, full of Phoebe's innocent innuendo, carried on for another half an hour and by then they'd finished the white Bordeaux and Phoebe had found an 'old' bottle of red from somewhere. It was actually hidden under her bed with several others, and so they carried on drinking. The wine had gone some way to relax Francis and he was now back to his old self. In fact he was quite eager, and was back to being charming and funny, very funny. And that charm was in truth working on Phoebe, who was now undeniably beginning to view Francis with a different rationale. Somehow he had gone from a friend to, well possibly something else.

And Francis, though he didn't thoroughly realize it, was actually flirting with her. He was coming on to her and the wine was making him bold, and in the back of his head he could see Phoebe naked in the shower, and in front of him 'was' Phoebe, nearly naked, as her towel somehow and occasionally kept nearly slipping off.

She knew that with another couple of bottles of red wine they would end up in bed, and she would let him ravish her. And that thought, mixed with the wine that she too had drunk, had made her headstrong and she sat there smiling and laughing with him. Every time she poured some more wine, she would somehow manage to touch his fingers as she passed him his glass, and as she moved and crossed her legs, her foot always seemed to rub against his leg. The moment was fast approaching when she knew she capable of just standing up and letting the towel slide off her, and she would let him look at her body again. And this time there would be no holding back, she knew that. She felt hot, and her legs slightly parted and he looked, and she let him look, and they both knew.

Then suddenly the cry..."Hello!" came from inside the apartment. And it was Catherine.

She'd arrived home from the ballet, and for Francis and Phoebe it was as though someone had just thrown a bucket of cold water over them both.

Phoebe immediately stood up and pulled up her towel, and then moved to the door.

"Hi Catherine" she said out loud "We're out here"

And both girls met in the doorway.

"Hi there" she said again "we're having a quick drink. I've just had a shower, here sit down with Francis and drink my wine while I get changed. How's your day been?"

And before Catherine could answer, Phoebe had disappeared through the door.

Francis sat there transfixed. The woman he wanted to bed had gone, and the woman he did bed had just arrived. He was a step behind here, and he quickly realized it. He slid the wine glass to one side and smiled brightly at Catherine.

"Hello darling" he said, trying to sound normal.

Catherine just breezed in, as ever, gabbling away as usual. Then she leant over and kissed him on the cheek "Hello darling" she replied back.

Then she went on to report all the 'in's and outs' of the day, the gossip and who said this and who'd done that and what she'd done and whatever.

She totally disregarded the empty wine bottles and the mess on the table that made it obvious that they'd not just been there five minutes and were not just having a quick drink.

Mid sentence, Catherine sat down and casually picked up Phoebe's wine and took a drink, and it was as though the two women had simply swapped places. Francis was slightly at a loss. She poured them both some more wine and just continued to talk away, and Francis just nodded back.

About ten minutes later, Phoebe popped her head around the doorway and informed them both that she was going out.

"Oh" exclaimed Catherine "I thought we were all going out together?"

"I've got to meet someone" Phoebe answered.

"A 'hot date'?" Catherine asked with a smile.

"Something like that" said Phoebe, and she winked at Catherine and clicked her tongue as she turned and went out.

Not once did she look at Francis.

They both stayed in that night and Catherine cooked a meal as Francis slept off the wine. After dinner they both read for a while, but decided to have an early night since Francis kept nodding off. At around twelve o' clock, Phoebe arrived back home, drunk. She had a bottle of wine in one hand and a man in the other. After crashing about somewhat, they finally managed to wake up Francis and Catherine.

Catherine laughed "Here we go again" she said.

Francis did not laugh. He just lay there listening to the sexual antics of their roommate.

He feigned annoyance, but what he couldn't admit to, was that he was actually jealous.

Life in the apartment changed.

Francis and Phoebe were now 'aware' of one another, though nothing was ever said. The thing being, that the both of them didn't seem to know just how the other one felt. The fact that they were both totally engrossed with one another seemed lost to them. Each thought that their own feelings and desires, were maybe only one sided.

They would watch each other, when one of them wasn't looking. Whilst reading the newspaper, Francis would watch and wait of Phoebe getting up in the morning. Catherine would be fussing over breakfast and Francis would peer over his newspaper as Phoebe would come out of her bedroom and smile at them both and say 'Good morning everybody' in her lilting accent, and she would pad over to the table and pinch a piece of toast. Then she would go over to Francis and lean over him to see what was in the newspaper, she always put her hand on his shoulder as she leant closely over him to read. The earthy smell of her early morning body, so close, made him breathless. Wearing as always, her short dressing gown, loosely tied, she would lean forward to 'share' his newspaper with him, and he would always quickly glance at her to see her open cleavage and almost all of her breasts, and breathe in her wonderful musky smell. Then his eyes would follow her as she went off to the bathroom to shower and he would look at her gorgeous brown legs and the obvious curve of her backside, tucked under her dressing gown. She would go into the bathroom and turn on the shower, undress and then slip back to close the bathroom door.

And for a brief second, every morning, he would see a greater part of her beautiful naked body, every morning...in that damn shower.

Miss Phoebe Dupree would go into the shower and stand under the water and let it calm her down. She trembled with the thought of her obsession. And she wondered why it was that she always felt so sexual first thing in the morning. She would without doubt rather make love in the morning than at night, and if she could have, she would have good sex every morning before starting her day.

So every morning when she got out of bed, she tied her dressing gown very loosely around her, and then she would come out of her bedroom to the smell of coffee and toast, and Francis. Every morning she loved to lean over him, he was always freshly showered, shaved and smelling of aftershave, always so clean.

And every morning she would almost 'offer' him her breasts from her open dressing gown and in her mind, 'her fantasy', she wished he would reach over and caress them.

She would then go to the bathroom, strip off and then go to close the door, with the hope that he was looking back at her, and remembering what her naked body was like.

All of this sexual tension went completely over Catherine's head. She simply hadn't a clue as to what was happening right in front of her. But why should she.

As the weeks progressed, the game continued, and Francis and Phoebe started to behave like a couple of 'giddy' kids, laughing and pecking at one another, and the 'touchy' thing started, and the closeness.

Whenever they were next to each other, she would touch his arm, or take hold of his hand. He in turn would continually put his hand on her shoulder or if he was moving past her he would momentarily put his hands on her back or hold her waist as he passed. And every time this happened, it was like a little electric shock of pleasure between them. Dining began to take on an altogether new meaning. Whenever they sat down to eat, they would always manage to sit next to one another. And as the meal progressed, their legs would eventually touch and neither would draw back. There was never an exchange of glances, they just carried on talking and laughing, but under the table each could feel the others every move and the feeling was absolute ecstasy, it was a kind of foreplay, as though they were caressing each other with every movement. One evening after they'd all been out for a meal and the wine had flowed, Francis had got into such a worked up state that when they'd got back to their apartment and had said their goodnights, he dragged Catherine onto the bed and made unbridled love to her.

In his mind he was having rampant sex with Phoebe, it was a cheap thing to do but he couldn't help himself. Twice more in the night he woke up in the dark and thought of Miss Phoebe Dupree and again turned to Catherine.

The next morning as he came into the kitchen for breakfast, Catherine was humming away merrily to herself as she boiled the coffee. When she saw him she stopped and gave him a wicked smile.

"Good morning Tiger" she giggled, and she went over and put her arms around him and they kissed. He looked at her, so pretty and fresh, her white blonde hair and those very blue eyes. She was beautiful, and he kissed her again. At that moment Phoebe came out of her room and saw them both embracing. She just walked straight past them without speaking, and went into the bathroom, this time closing the door rather loudly behind her.

"Is there something wrong with Phoebe?" asked Catherine.

Francis looked over her shoulder. Somehow, he'd been caught out, and he was concerned.

"Probably too much wine last night, a hangover?" he lied.

At lunch time Catherine met up with Phoebe. They sat in the grounds of the Ballet School and shared a sandwich out in the sunshine.

"Are you alright...'now'?" asked Catherine harmlessly.

Phoebe turned "Why?"

"No, we just thought you were a bit 'off' this morning that's all. Was it the wine?"

"Something like that" Phoebe replied a bit brusquely.

There was a silence.

And then "How are you and Francis doing, everything okay?" asked Phoebe, in a random sort of way.

"Oh yes, you wouldn't believe it" she said excitedly, it was the moment that Catherine had been waiting for. She had been dying to tell someone all about 'last night'. But really, it was only Phoebe that she could talk to about 'this' sort of thing.

Catherine giggled to her friend "It was Francis, it must have been the wine, or the seafood" and she giggled again "but when we got home he was like a wild animal, he 'dragged' me onto the bed Phoebe" and now Catherine clapped her hands and laughed "and again later in the night...twice."

Phoebe felt the heat in her rise with jealousy. Here was her best friend, sleeping with 'her' Francis, because that was how she thought of him now. And now he was making love to Catherine instead of her, and she was shocked. What was he playing at, what was he doing?

And for some unbelievably strange reason, she felt she was being cheated on.

"My God" she blurted out in anger, but Catherine read that outburst totally wrong as well.

"I know" she replied and laughed to her friend, who was sitting there looking incredulous.

"I don't know what got into him Phoebe.'Something' must have turned him on."

Phoebe stared back at her friend. And then she realized, and then she knew, and then suddenly, suddenly everything fitted into place. It was so obvious. Of course, Francis was so aroused because of 'her'.

All the tension and the interplay the previous night, they had been constantly touching each other, touching and brushing against one another in constant contact. Their legs had almost been intertwined under the table and the wine had made the pair of them bold, almost intimate.

And Phoebe then realized that 'she' was the reason for Francis's passion. He might have been making love to Catherine, but it was her that he was thinking of.

And she knew she was right, and she smiled back at Catherine, and laughed along with her.

It was midweek, an early Wednesday morning and Catherine had got up and showered and was back in their bedroom getting changed. The sun was barely breaking as Catherine's bustling around the bedroom finally awoke Francis.

He yawned and turned over "What are you doing?" he asked her.

"Good morning sleepyhead" she replied.

He glanced at his watch and had to focus to read the time properly. He screwed up his eyes.

"It's only six o' clock, what are you doing up so early?"

She looked down at him and smiled "It's the 'Matinee', this afternoon, I told you" And she shook her head "We're putting on an 'afternoon of dance' for our year, our troupe. We're dancing in front of the rest of the school. I 'did' tell you, I'm going in early to help with the scenery".

Francis lay there looking quizzical.

Catherine shook her head "You, Francis Jones, these days you have a memory like a sieve".

"I must have" he replied in turn, and yawned again.

She picked up her coat and her bag and she leaned over to kiss him.

"You can have another hour in bed" she said to him, and then remarked "and then you'll have to get up and make breakfast, if you leave it to 'lazy bones' next door, you'll starve".

And she laughed.

"Bye-bye" she said, and she smiled at him "See you tonight".

"Bye-bye" he replied sleepily, and as Catherine quietly closed the door, he rolled back over and went back to sleep.

An hour later, he'd got up and showered and was making breakfast. He heard the noise of a door handle and turned to see Phoebe coming out of her bedroom.

"Good morning 'sleepy'..." he said to her in a bright tone.

She looked across at him "Morning" she said, with a warm smile.

"I'm on breakfast duties this morning. Catherine's had to go in early. She's got some 'dance thing' on apparently."

"Oh has she?" said Phoebe, a bit surprised, which was strange really because she knew exactly where Catherine was.

"The coffee's nearly brewed, and I'm going to cut up some bread. We've got some butter and English marmalade left" he said.

"I'll just take a quick shower then" she replied, and she went across to the bathroom and into shower. However this time, she left the bathroom door wide open.

Francis continued to make them both breakfast as he heard the shower being turned on. He went to finish off brewing the coffee and then he took the bread out of the cupboard and began to slice it.

But, things being as they were, Francis just couldn't help himself, and as he started to cut up the bread he slowly turned to look into the bathroom, and there in the shower, was Phoebe. He just stood there and looked at her, astonishingly beautiful, undressed and naked, and under a shower of water that simply cascaded down her stunningly wonderful body. She lathered the soap under her arms and then over her breasts. And Francis momentarily stopped breathing. He just looked at her, and couldn't stop looking at her, as she rubbed the soap over the rest of her soft velvet skin.

He gasped, and then suddenly he took into account that at any moment she might turn around and see him 'spying' on her, and so he grabbed up the coffee pot and the bread knife and went over to the kitchen table. He cut a couple of slices of bread and poured himself a cup of coffee, and then he sat down and tried his best to read the newspaper.

The shower stopped, and within a minute Phoebe walked out of the bathroom.

Francis looked up at her as she came over to the table. Her hair was still wet and she had a towel wrapped around her head. She was wearing her dressing gown, which was very loosely tied at the front, and she looked at him, with an almost quizzical stare. She approached the table and leaned over as though to reach for the coffee, and then slowly, very slowly, her dressing gown fell open. And she left it open. And Francis stared at her naked body, the body he'd dreamed about, and the body that he couldn't stop thinking about, and it was now there in front of him, on display for him to look at, her full breasts, her beautiful hips and long thighs, all there in front of him. He looked up at her and she looked down at him and smiled as she reached over and put her hand to his cheek, and then she leant over and kissed him passionately. He responded immediately and blissfully kissed her too, and she put her arms around the back of his neck and drew herself forward. Her naked breasts were now pressing on his chest and he felt them, hard against him. Slowly, she pulled back and took hold of his hand and gently squeezed it.

"Touch me...please, touch me" she whispered to him, and she leant forward and kissed him again. He parted her dressing gown and gently put both of his hands onto her hips and then slowly ran them round to feel the rise of her bottom. He squeezed her and her hips involuntarily jerked. Then he slowly ran his hands back over her hips and reached up for both of her breasts. She moaned and stopped kissing him and leant her head back so that he could fully see both of her breasts. He squeezed her and caressed her nipples in his fingers and they became hard as she moaned, and he heard her breathe faster as he lifted his head and put his mouth onto her breast and sucked at her as his hands went down again to grasp her buttocks. Her legs buckled slightly and then suddenly she pulled back again.

"Over there, the settee. Come on Francis, please". She spoke with some urgency now and she pulled at his shoulders so that he stood up. She led him across the room and almost pushed him onto the settee and as he sat there she kneeled down in front of him and unbuckled his belt and undid his trousers. Francis was mesmerized as she reached into his pants and took hold of him and he gasped with pleasure as he felt her fingers on him. She moved her fingers up and down slowly and his legs quivered with the thrill of it. Phoebe knew she was now in complete control, and she suddenly let go of him and with both free hands she expertly slid his trousers off. She then stood up and quietly faced him, she let the dressing gown slowly slide off her shoulders and drop to the floor. He looked at her, fully naked in front of him, and he thought that his body was going to explode. Phoebe looked down at him, she was almost submissive, and then she moved herself on top of him, she straddled him and almost at once he was inside her. Within seconds she'd stripped off his shirt, and then they both performed breathtaking intercourse, it was simply the utter pleasure of fierce and demanding lovemaking. It was wild and it was wonderful and for both of them the inevitable had finally happened. More than the heat of the moment, this had been simmering away for weeks. They both knew that, and they almost mauled each other in raw ecstasy. In actuality, they didn't make love, because it wasn't love, it was sex. Heady and totally and immensely satisfying sex, and when they'd finished they both laughed at the madness and the audacity of it.

Yes, it had finally happened.

They both lay there on the settee, breathless and laughing. She had her legs wrapped around him and Francis looked at her, so wild with her Latin blood and her beautiful skin and he ran his hand up her hip and then up to her breast. She slowly unravelled her legs from him and stood up, then she took hold of his hand and offered him her bed, and he followed her into her bedroom and they satisfied each other in total luxury for the next couple of hours.

And so it began. The affair...and the lie.

From then on, whenever they were alone or whenever they could meet up, whenever and wherever, and anywhere and everywhere, they would have sex with each other. One evening they were all out with friends at a restaurant, and Phoebe followed Francis to the toilet and they had sex quickly in a cubicle. Then they went back to the table and carried on with the conversation as though nothing had happened.

How clever.

Nobody knew. Nobody was aware, nobody had a clue, and this deception and trickery along with the danger of the situation, simply heightened their desire for one another.

It was an infatuation.

Weeks turned into months, and their relationship had become so physical that they had almost actually stopped talking to each other to any great extent. Any communication had become almost all physical.

Touch, stroke, fondle, and then intercourse.

Francis however, didn't realize this, because he had Catherine. And of course, nothing had changed there. He could talk all night long to Catherine. They would still sit at the kitchen table, or on their balcony, with a bottle of wine and a couple of glasses and share interesting conversations.

However, there is always an imbalance.

On the evenings that Phoebe arrived home late and would see them both together, talking away and enjoying each other's company, her Latin blood would begin to boil. For the first time in her life she experienced deep and gut wrenching jealousy. She would rush in and sit with them both and somehow try to get in between them and mentally prize them apart, but she couldn't, and she felt like an intruder. So instead, she would take to sulking in her bedroom, but she could still hear them in the adjoining room and it infuriated her. She would grab her coat and storm noisily out of the apartment with some loud excuse, usually that 'she had someone to see'. Then she would walk around the Old Latin Quarter on her own, lonely and brooding.

But what really incensed her, was that Francis didn't seem to be at all bothered. He would just smile back at her and reach over to fill Catherine's wine glass, and he would make some 'nice and witty' comment, and then continue to talk away to Catherine. Never once did he question her as to where she was going, or possibly meeting.

So she punished him with sex, it was her only weapon. She thought that by having more and even wilder sex with him, she could eventually possess the man and lure him away from Catherine.

So the affair continued. Some nights, one of them would hear the other going to the bathroom and they would meet up outside the bathroom door and then have silent but passionate sex on top of the kitchen table. In the morning, it was as though nothing at all had happened. Some nights Francis would just enter her bedroom, and silently climb into her bed and kiss the back of her neck to gently wake her up. Half an hour later he was gone. But the next morning he would be fussing over Catherine again, and would simply smile at Phoebe and offer her some toast with her cup of hot coffee. She felt like throwing the coffee in his face.

Jealousy is a powerful frailty, but it's a human frailty.

One night Phoebe went out, she was miserable and on her own, and she drank too much red wine and finally picked up a man. In anger and frustration and full of alcohol, she dragged him back to the apartment and then dragged him into her bed. An hour of drunken sex took place with Phoebe screaming encouragement. Catherine and Francis could hear her, in fact, half of the apartment block could hear her.

But Miss Phoebe Dupree wanted to be heard, well not by the other residents, and not Catherine either really. But she wanted Francis to hear her, she wanted him to hear everything so that he would know exactly what she was doing, every single move.

Half awake, and in their own bedroom, Catherine just sighed "Oh my god Phoebe" and put a pillow over her head and finally drifted back to sleep.

But Francis lay there, wide awake and shaking with anger.

In his mind he could imagine her with the other man, and yes, he did know every move that was taking place and he was mad. He was mad with her for what she was doing, and mad with himself for his own jealousy, though somehow, he didn't fully understand that at the time.

In the morning Phoebe woke up alone and finally entered the kitchen when she smelt the coffee and toast. Catherine was making breakfast on her own. Francis wasn't there. Apparently he'd had to go into school early for 'something or other'.

That morning as he walked to work, Francis realized the predicament that he was in. He truly loved Catherine, she was a really, really wonderful person. But he was also having unbelievingly good sex with Phoebe, and he also 'really' wanted that to continue too.

He was at an impasse.

He was also very stupid, and very naive. And actually, he was behaving like an idiot.

For the next couple of days he and Phoebe hardly spoke, in fact they found it hard to even make eye contact. And a silent tension between them began to grow, and with it so did the sexual tension. It had become something that couldn't be dismissed, and the whole thing became extremely emotional.

They spied on each other like two cats, but neither of them was able to make a move.

Then one afternoon Francis came home from work early, and as he entered the apartment he heard the sound of the shower in the bathroom, and he knew that it would be Phoebe who was in there. He stood in the middle of the apartment and looked at the bathroom door and he thought about her, she was in there under the shower. And he thought about that, and about her, and it that one moment of weakness he didn't care anymore, he forgave her. He always knew that she was like some wild animal, yes, just like a cat, impulsive and unpredictable.

And he missed her, yes he missed her so much, and so he walked over to the bathroom and opened the door.

Inside, Phoebe was under the shower, her head down as the warm water cascaded over her shoulders. She had been crying to herself, and the tears disappeared as they fell in with the steady flowing water. She was so lonely, she missed Francis so much and she didn't know what to do about it.

Francis just there stood in the doorway watching her. She was like some kind of beautiful animal, just so beautiful.

Phoebe felt the change in the air and suddenly she looked up, and was in disbelief when she saw him standing there, looking at her.

She looked back at him, and she continued to cry. And he looked at her face and he saw the sadness there, and he knew that she was sorry. They both just stood there for the briefest moment and then, finally, he smiled.

She turned and walked out of the shower and threw her arms around him and they embraced. She kissed his cheek and then held his face in her hands and looked at him.

"I'm so sorry Francis" she said "I'm really so, so sorry. It was wrong, I was wrong".

He stared down into those deep olive brown eyes, eyes that he knew so well, and he was lost.

"It doesn't matter Phoebe" he said, and then "I've missed you so much".

She smiled back at him and they kissed, and carried on kissing, and the passion returned as they held each other, and then she began to undress him. She undid his belt and he quickly ripped off his shirt and within moments she had stripped him of his pants and he too was naked and they were laughing as she pulled him into the shower and under the running water.

She stood with her back to him, smiling to herself as he ran his hands down and around her stomach and down to the soft curly black hair between her legs, and she quivered with anticipation. Then he reached upwards to take hold her breasts, it felt so good. And so he bent her over and down, he held onto her hips, and then he took her from behind. She splayed her legs to receive him, and then his hands went back up over her buttocks and over her bottom and he gasped as he reached forward and cupped her breasts. They were in total rhythm, and in complete ecstasy. He closed his eyes under the warm running water, they were back together, and life was good again.

He leant forward and put the side of his head onto her beautiful back and felt her motion under him as they both copulated, it was an earthy, animal pleasure.

He slowly opened his eyes, and then he blinked, because they were not alone.

Standing in the bathroom doorway, someone was standing there, watching them.

Francis's eyes flickered under the water as he stopped what he was doing to Phoebe. He stood up and quickly reached over to turn off the shower and wipe the water out of his eyes as he focused. Phoebe, who suddenly wondered why her lover had stopped, and stopped doing everything, stood up and turned to him. She was just about to say something, when she saw the look of dread on his face. Francis just stood there looking at the door and she quickly turned to see what was wrong.

Standing there in the doorway was Catherine.

She just stood there looking at them both...both of them, wet and naked and guilty.

Nothing was said for a moment as Catherine looked on in shock, and Francis looked back at her in horror, and then in shame, as the tears welled up into those beautiful blue eyes and began to trickle down that pretty face.

"How could you?" It was almost a whisper, and it was a question that could have been directed at either of them, her fiancé and her best friend.

They both stood there, speechless. What could they say?

Nothing, of course.

Catherine wiped her tears and turned away. She left them both, and left the apartment.

She went back to her friend's flat in the Montmartre and the next day the three of them went to the Latin Quarter, and back to the apartment. It was late morning and there would be nobody there. They collected Catherine's belongings and left. Catherine would never return.

Francis was stupidly dumbfounded. For some strange reason, he never considered that he and Phoebe would ever be caught. He never even considered that their relationship would 'ever' be found out. And now it had, and he was in panic. What was he going to do?

He unquestionably didn't want to lose Catherine. He loved her, he had always loved her, he was going to marry Catherine, and they would have children and be a family. There would always be Catherine, surely there would always be Catherine?

But no, not now, and that thought kept turning in his head. What was he going to do, what on earth was he going to do?

Phoebe however, was not in panic. After the initial shock of being 'caught', and it wasn't the first time, she quickly regained her composure a whole lot faster than Francis did. She almost purred to herself as she realized that she now had Francis all to herself. There would be no more jealous nights for 'her'. Now she could live with him and they could be together all the time, now she would have him. At last she was happy, and she smiled to herself contentedly as she curled up in bed with him that first night.

Unfortunately, Francis didn't lie there just as contented, far from it. He lay there with a feeling of guilt and immense grief. He was almost beside himself when it finally struck him that he had lost not only the love of his life, but also his truest and best friend. He lay there in anguish, and realized his stupidity, and he wondered why? Why had he done something that would hurt Catherine so badly? It was as though it had all been some crazy sort of dream. His affair with Phoebe, he'd mistakenly considered it as something totally separate from his relationship with Catherine, he would never hurt Catherine. But he had.

At lunchtime the next day he went to the Ballet School to try and talk to her, but he was told that she was absent from classes. Nobody knew why, Francis of course, did. He figured that she must have moved back with her friends at Montmartre, so he went around to their flat and rang the downstairs doorbell. A couple of minutes later, one of the girls, the other dancer from the school came down to speak to him.

"Could you tell Catherine..." he started to say.

"Please go away" she sharply interrupted him, and she cut him dead in his tracks "Go away from here and never come back. She doesn't want to see you, ever again".

"But" was all Francis managed to say.

"You've broken her heart you rotten bastard" the girl hissed back at him "You'll never meet anyone as good as her, ever. It's over, so at least have the decency to leave her alone, you rat".

And she shut the door in his face.

Francis stood there on the pavement astounded. He couldn't believe it, the fool.

Over the next few days he tried to see her at the Ballet, but he was eventually warned off.

And then one evening he came home to find a letter that had been slid under the door, it was addressed to him and was in Catherine's handwriting. Inside was a note, it read 'Will you please leave me alone. I never want to see you again. You're a disgrace".

It was short and to the point and it said it all, and Francis sobbed because yes, he was a fool.

And he realized that, and he also realized that it was all over, and he'd lost her.

Sometimes life has a way of turning round on you and 'kicking you in the foot', and so it was for Francis and Phoebe. 'All that glitters is not gold' as the saying goes.

Quite simply, Francis went off the boil. In his anxiety over the loss of Catherine, he found that he just couldn't be bothered with Phoebe. It was the guilt, and he realized the treachery of his actions, and their actions. And now he began to implicate and blame Phoebe for all that had happened. Like most human beings, it's always easier to blame someone else for your mistakes. And suddenly, there was a change in their relationship. He soon began to realize that Phoebe really didn't have a sensible or interesting topic of conversation in her pretty head. She prattled on about mostly nothing and Francis began to just stare at her across the table and think about Catherine. And she started to aggravate him, she would never clean the apartment or think to wash up the dishes, and everything she used she would leave for Francis to move or clear away. Cooking was off limits for Phoebe, he doubted if she could even boil an egg, and at night she would complain if he didn't take her out somewhere lively to eat and drink. He began to tire of her, she was shallow and selfish, and he began to realize that though she was very beautiful, Phoebe Dupree had quite an ugly personality. And then they started to row, frequently.

From the word go, Phoebe realized that Francis was not going to be 'her' Francis, and this made her angry. She would continually catch him staring into space, and she knew that he was thinking about Catherine. Francis became miserable and she hated him for it. He was no longer charming and sharp and witty, he had become morose and in her eyes 'weak' and suddenly boring, and he began to get on her nerves. They would argue, she would scream and shout, and he would sulk.

And Francis very quickly understood that sex was not love. Sex was just sex. A pleasurable act, but it couldn't replace love, not for him. However, this knowledge came a little too late.

A month or so passed, and then one night while they were out, Phoebe drank too much red wine and took a shine to the young Spanish guitarist who played at the bar that they were in. She disappeared into the night with him, and when she stumbled back to the apartment the next morning, Francis was gone.

It was the afternoon before Phoebe woke up, and she lay in bed until she finally remembered what had happened. She thought about what she'd done, and she began to realize her mistake. But it was only when she'd gotten out of bed and started to look around the apartment that she began to grasp the situation. Everything that Francis owned had also gone. There was nothing left, it was as though he'd never lived there, and almost never existed. It took her a day to come to her senses and she began to worry that he might not come back. She understood that she'd been short tempered with him, but that was just 'her' way of rekindling their love life. It was in her personality to argue, and Phoebe thought that was the natural way of things, well it was for her. Another couple of days went by and Francis had still not reappeared. At first, she felt convinced that he would return to her for the pleasures of her bed. She missed making love to him, and now she missed him too. When they'd fallen out before, he'd come to her in the shower and forgiven her, so she was sure that he'd be back. Another two days and she wasn't so sure, and she started to fret. She wanted to find him now, but she didn't even know the name of the school where he taught, let alone where it was. She realized that she should have treated him better, and like some precocious child, now she didn't have him, the more she wanted him. Another week went by, and she was still on her own, and Phoebe Dupree hated to be on her own. There was also the small matter of money, she had none. The food had just about run out and the rent would soon be due, but her only answer to this was to drink the wine that was still left under her bed and hope that Francis would come back. And so she sat at the table and drank, and cried and cried, and eventually she realized, that the only man that she'd ever really loved, was gone.

In the small hours, and in the haze of alcohol, she considered her future. Yes, she could dance, and that's what she'd do. And she would have to go back to using men. She'd done it before, always. She'd make them all pay, and pay her well. And she realized that as she got older she'd have to look for a provider. She didn't care who he was, probably some rich old man whose bed she'd have to keep warm, but he'd only ever be a provider.

Because she'd never find another love.

'Good men become old men, and beautiful women become old women, and lives are lived.

But in truth, all the goodness and all the beauty, lies there in the heart'.

Francis moved into a small ground floor flat near to the school where he taught. It was dark and somewhat neglected, but Francis didn't care, it suited his mood. And from there, his life went into shutdown. He stopped going out. Well he had no other friends other than Catherine's, and Catherine had been his best friend. Some of the other teachers at the school occasionally invited him around to their homes for a meal, or even for a night out, but he simply turned them down, he didn't want to go out, and so the invites quickly ceased.

He took to reading avidly, and he would bury his head in his books. Reading became the only thing that he could lose himself in, completely. While he was reading he wasn't thinking.

He would read late, late into the night and soon the school and teaching and reading became his whole life. It was a poor existence.

Francis simply stopped taking care of himself, he would have coffee at breakfast, and again at lunch and very little else. Sometimes in the evening he would just drink a bottle of cheap wine as he read, promising himself that he would make something to eat later. But invariably, he would wake in the small hours to an empty bottle and an open book on his lap. Things were not going that well at the school either. The Headmaster, a Professor Mille, had begun to notice the change in young Mr Jones. Francis had lost a lot of weight and was sickly pale, and he had become unkempt and looked slightly unwashed. Up close there was the odour of stale breath, and his clothes were never ironed and were looking a bit raggedy. So Professor Mille decided to keep an eye on his young Englishman and after examining the work of some of the pupils in Francis's class, and then having a discussion with some of the other teachers, he deemed that Francis's teaching skills were no longer of a grade suitable for the school. Professor Mille decided that the end of term would be the end of Francis, and eventually the Professor called Francis into his office and informed him of the decision. Francis was not surprised. His heart had gone out of teaching. The past five months had been a dark blur for him and two weeks later at the end of term, Francis left the school, and became unemployed.

He had a month's rent paid on the flat and then it was all over, he would have to go back to England, he'd now lost everything and everyone. He sat alone in his flat one night, and he questioned himself as to how he had gone from a promising career in the army and being engaged to somebody like Catherine, to this, this complete and utter misery. He was lost.

Catherine had in some way attempted to get on with her life. The devastation of what had happened had taken a toll on her and so she threw herself into her Ballet studies, for her there was now nothing else. She tried to turn her life around and instead of living for Francis Jones she now lived for the Ballet. Unfortunately the Ballet didn't live for her. She'd somehow lost her flare, her delicate talent, and she tried to fight the art instead of embracing it. Her teacher could see it too. Catherine tried too hard, and in her efforts she ended up dancing more like an athlete than a Ballet dancer. There was no delicacy or subtleness in her movements, but Catherine just couldn't see it and it frustrated her.

The ever present talent of Phoebe Dupree did very little to help. Phoebe had a natural talent to dance. She may have had a flawed character but when it came to dancing the ballet, she could perform like an angel. And if Phoebe was around, Catherine simply couldn't concentrate on her movements. Phoebe was the dark threat, a constant reminder.

One day, Catherine left the school to go for her lunch, it was quite a warm afternoon and she was undecided whether or not to go back for the afternoon's lessons. She was also wondering whether or not she should even carry on with her ballet studies. For a while now, she'd realized that she was never going to be a supreme ballet dancer, and that had always been her wish. And now she knew that she would only ever be a 'run of the mill' dancer, always to be placed at the 'back' of the stage at performances, and that she would probably end up being just another disappointed tutor, like a lot of other young hopefuls.

The last six months had been hard on her and she was beginning to lose heart. So she walked along the streets, not in any real direction, and considered that since she wasn't in the right frame of mind to concentrate on dancing that afternoon, she may as well go back to the flat in the Montmartre and lie down and rest, and think things over.

She sauntered along, occasionally gazing into shop windows at clothes she could never afford, and eventually ended up in a small square that she didn't know or recognize.

In a corner of the square was a small cafe, it was all very pleasant and now the sun was getting a little too strong for her, so she decided to go into the cafe for at least a coffee and maybe a little lunch, although she wasn't really hungry, anything would suffice, she just wanted to get out of the hot sun. She went inside and took a welcoming seat next to the window. A young girl finally approached her and Catherine ordered "Just a coffee, for now."

She sat there and stared out of the window at the comings and goings in the square. Different people sat on different benches, an old woman throwing stale bread to the pigeons, a street cleaner going about his daily job. And she wondered, were they all happy?

The girl arrived with her coffee. It was wonderfully fresh, in a large white cup on an even larger saucer, and Catherine treated herself to a sugar cube, and then slowly stirred the milky brown liquid. She sat there sipping her coffee and once more gazed out of the window. There was a rack of clothes being delivered to a shop further down the street and she looked at the bright colours as they passed her window, bright colours for summer. Yes summer was here and the year was moving on, and she wondered about herself and whether she too should be moving on. She was lacking direction and she knew it. Her life had become a vague, and disappointing.

She turned back to the window as she sipped more of her coffee and she watched the old woman throw the last of her bread to the horde of pigeons that flocked around her feet. The woman folded up the paper bag that had contained the bread and put it into her coat pocket. Then she stood there for a moment and watched the birds feeding, and then she slowly turned and wandered away.

Catherine watched the pigeons devour the bread, there must have been fifty of them, they were so hungry that they were oblivious to anybody near them or even close by. Behind the old woman had been a man who was sitting on a bench and now the pigeons flocked around his feet searching for the last crumbs. The man never moved, he must have been watching the pigeons too, and Catherine glanced at him staring remotely down at the birds. She picked up her cup and was just about to take another sip of coffee when a spark of comprehension suddenly burst into her brain. She looked back out of the window and at the man, the last of the pigeons had just flown away, but he was still staring down at the pavement. And to Catherine's absolute disbelief, she suddenly realized that the man she was looking at, was Francis.

She went rigid, and for a moment almost paralysed. And suddenly she gasped and her hand began to shake. She had to put her cup down and she quickly looked away from the window. Then almost instinctively, she moved to the seat beside her and out of direct view.

For a moment Catherine could not bring herself to look back out of the window, she just stared down at her almost empty cup. Then suddenly there was a cough from behind her, it was the waitress, and the girl asked Catherine if she would now like to order. Catherine rather abruptly ordered another coffee and received a negative smile in return. The waitress returned a few minutes later with fresh coffee and still Catherine had not looked back out onto the square, she was almost afraid to. She stirred the coffee slowly and then it struck her that Francis might have stood up and already gone, and with that she glanced up immediately and saw that he was still there, and again she looked down. As she stirred her coffee she suddenly wondered about herself. If he'd not still been sitting there, if he'd stood up and gone, would she have regretted it? And why had she looked up immediately at the thought of him not being there. She was confused of course, but it was an unwavering moment, or maybe it was an excuse. Once more she picked up her cup and took a sip, and then again slowly looked back out of the window.

What she saw shocked her. She looked across the square at Francis Jones and was at once struck by his physical condition. Wasted and gaunt, he was almost emaciated. He was still sitting there on the bench, just looking at the floor, and for a moment, Catherine wondered if he'd suffered some kind of serious illness. She studied his face, so bleak and tired. It was a face that she'd once known so well, she used to look at that face in the mornings, when she was awake and he was still asleep. And now that face was so empty and desolate.

Ten long minutes, she sat there and watched him, and in all that time his eyes never moved from some invisible place on the floor in front of him. His head, his body, never moved an inch, and she realized that he was in deep thought, and she knew that deep thought was regret, because she knew him.

And she looked at his whole being and it suddenly struck her that Francis was going to die. He was going to shrivel away and die, because he wasn't looking after himself, he'd given up and he was just going to fade away. And as Catherine looked at him, she started to cry.

She remembered him as he was, bright and lively and funny, and now he was broken.

She felt almost guilty. Was this her fault? No of course it wasn't. Somebody had taken 'her Francis' away from her, and he had willingly gone. 'Her Francis', the sound of it was strangely trapped in her memory. 'Her Francis' and she remembered the fondness they once had. And she remembered how they'd met, and what good company he was, and his friendship and his love. And she knew too, how lonely and unhappy she herself had become. What madness had happened, and what sort of stupidity had let it happen, it was reducing them both to a nothing. They were both being destroyed and damaged and ruined, and all because of Miss Phoebe Dupree.

And suddenly Catherine was angry. This was all so futile, so foolish, they were both just a couple of idiots, and she took out a handkerchief and wiped away her own stupid tears. She picked up her handbag and took out some money and left on the table for the coffee. Then she stood up and gathered herself, and walked out of the cafe.

She stood outside in the sunlight and took a deep breath, and made up her mind.

Then she walked across to the bench where Francis was sitting. He never even looked up as she marched over and stood right in front of him.

"Francis Clifton Jones" she said robustly "What the hell do you think you're doing?"

It was the first time that she had ever sworn at him.

He suddenly jerked his head up, and he saw her. He just stared at her, and for a moment he thought he was hallucinating, he couldn't trust his eyes.

"Yes it's me" she continued "and what on earth do you think you're playing at. A fine state you've got yourself into".

He looked up at her, still in disbelief.

"When was the last time you've eaten?" she asked him, dismissing his silence completely.

"Catherine?" he finally spoke, he was one step behind.

"Yes, Catherine" she replied in a firm tone "Yes, it's me you idiot, and look at you Francis. You look awful"

"Catherine" he said again, he just couldn't believe that she was standing there in front of him. It was like some sort of illusion. He was simply staggered with emotion, and for a moment he tried to say something, but he couldn't. Then finally, his shoulders sagged and he gasped.

"Catherine...I'm so, so sorry" and tears formed in his eyes.

"Yes I know you are" she said to him, still unwavering. She had to be strong now, no tears.

"This just won't do Francis. We can't go on like this, we can't let this stupidity beat us".

He heard the word 'We' and he swallowed.

Catherine continued "We have to talk and we have to sort this out, we will sort this out. But first of all we need to get some food inside you. Where do you live?"

Francis stood up slowly and she took hold of his arm to help him, and was shocked at his frailness. There was no weight to him at all.

"I...I live near the school, a small flat, it's a bit of a mess I'm afraid".

"Nothing would surprise me Francis Jones. Your completely hopeless" and she scolded him like a child.

"Catherine" he suddenly said.

She looked at him "Yes".

"Thank you" he said, and he slowly put his arms around her shoulders and hugged her. She put her arms around his thin waist and they stood there for a moment. She smiled, it had barely taken a couple of minutes, but they were together again.

They talked as they slowly walked back to his flat. When they got there, Francis took out his key to unlock the door and they both went inside. Catherine was appalled at the squalor. How long had he been living like this?

She opened the curtains to let some light in. There were piles of books and rubbish everywhere, the whole place hadn't been tidied for months. But first of all she went into the bathroom and ran him a hot bath.

"In you go" she said to him "fill it to the top and get in it and soak, and don't come out until I call you".

She ushered him in and closed the door. Then she went out and did some shopping, twenty minutes later and she returned with some groceries. She cleared the table and then started to clean up the flat. After washing some plates and whatever knives and forks he had, she set the table and then boiled some water to brew some fresh coffee.

She went through his closet and found a clean shirt, pants and underwear, and along with a fresh towel, she went into the bathroom and laid them out for him. When he'd dried himself and changed he came out and they sat at the table and ate fresh bread and butter with some ham and cheese, along with the freshly brewed coffee, but no wine. They ate slowly, it was the first proper food that Francis had eaten for months and he had trouble digesting it in any great quantity.

They sat and talked for over two hours, it was almost like getting to know each other again. They talked about what they were doing, the present and the possible future. They did not talk about the past, they never mentioned Phoebe Dupree, and they never would ever again.

They decided to make a fresh start, and that Catherine would eventually move in with him again, once they'd cleaned up the flat. Catherine also wanted to make sure that he was eating regularly. After a couple of hours of talking and the food, Francis began to visibly tire, it was because of his physical condition. Catherine saw this and sent him to bed. Then she washed up and left him out some food for his breakfast in the morning, and then she left.

She walked back to the flat in the Montmartre and spoke to her two friends, she told them what had happened and what she was intending to do. They respected her wishes because they were her friends.

Two days and a lot of cleaning later, Catherine's flatmates helped her carry all her clothes and her belongings over to Francis's little ground floor flat. They didn't go in with her, but they kissed her and wished her well. Truth be told, the girls didn't really want to meet up with Francis, not yet. They'd both looked after Catherine when she was in despair and was inconsolable and they certainly weren't ready to forgive so easily.

Life began again for Francis and Catherine. And for the first time in a long while, they were both happy, and positive, and they quickly and 'almost' easily returned to their old way of living.

In a way, it was like being back in their old apartment, less of course, Miss Dupree.

Regular eating and the love of a good woman would eventually put Francis back on his feet, physically and mentally. Through a friend of a friend, Catherine found Francis a job at a popular city restaurant, working as a waiter. It was the best thing that could have happened to him. Suddenly he was busy again, he was thrown in at the deep end and the challenge suited him. He began to recover his charm and efficiency, and the novelty of an English waiter who could also speak fluent French, went down well with the American and English customers. And it was quickly appreciated by the owner, who soon realized the value of Francis Jones.

Catherine returned to the Ballet School and got her career back on track. She and Francis had discussed her potential, and she realized that she would never be a principal dancer, not everyone could be a 'prima' ballerina.

But there were other possibilities, and other opportunities. She had to rethink her career.

Francis had spoken to her and encouraged her and now she was ready to learn her craft to the best of her abilities.

Francis worked at the restaurant for almost two years. Time flew by, and he finally decided that it was time for him to go back into teaching He realized that he couldn't be a waiter forever, and they both appreciated that at sometime in the distant future they would eventually have to return to England, and there would be better job prospects for Francis to return as a teacher, as opposed to a waiter.

Secretly, Catherine also realized that though her family would openly accept Francis as a teacher, they would never agree to her marrying a waiter. Not the Beecham's.

Francis made an appointment and went to see his old employer Professor Mille, and he put his cards straight on the table and told the professor his honest story.

The Professor welcomed this honesty and he could see that Francis was now 'back' on his feet and had recovered from his 'malaise'. The Professor also knew of an opening at another school, and was prepared to forget the past and give Francis a chance, and a reference.

It was done, and in less than a month Francis was invited to be the new English teacher at the well respected 'Cours Moliere' Private School. The school was situated within the broad and leafy Boulevard 'Soult' in the area known as the 12th Arrondissement, a quiet and beautiful part of Paris.

Francis settled in well. The pay was more lucrative and within six months they had moved out of his little flat and into a first floor apartment in nearby Saint-Paul.

And that was it, two or three years passed, and by then Francis had met Catherine's parents on several occasions and he was deemed acceptable. The incident with Colonel Beaumont and his wife was tactfully avoided by all, and life went on.

At that time, Catherine's career was coming to an end. She had danced at various performances with different troupes and she had been happy enough, but it was time to move on. They had discussed marriage, and of course children, and they realized that central Paris was not suitable and it was time for a change. So after a lot of thought,, they decided to go back to England and marry and settle down, somewhere.

In the spring of 1952 they were both married at the Beecham's family church back in Surrey.

They rented a small house near Catherine's family home and Francis got a job teaching at the local secondary school. They managed a year, before the parochial boredom got the better of them. Paris, it certainly wasn't.

Catherine couldn't find an opening for her ballet talents anywhere, and Francis also discovered very quickly, that 'country life' in rural Surrey was definitely not for him. They started to cast their net further afield and after a few months and a lot of letters, Francis was offered a senior teaching post at a good school in a town somewhere near Manchester, up in the north of England. Manchester turned out to be in Lancashire and the town was Bolton.

Manchester itself was a growing industrial city at that time, and was starting to flex its muscles. Money was being made in Manchester, and the city elders were investing some of that money into the Arts. New Museums and Art galleries where being funded, along with the well respected 'Northern Ballet'. So Catherine applied to the Northern Ballet and her credentials were dually noted. After all, she had been taught at one of the finest ballet schools in Paris, and she was offered a position.

So, they packed their bags and headed north.

With quite a large slice of help from Catherine's parents, they put a deposit on a house. It was to be the only house that they would ever buy, they would live there all of their lives.

But more of that later.

Kings Street in Bolton, was a line of large Victorian terraces that was also situated quite close to the school were Francis was going to work. They bought number '10" Kings Street and moved in almost straightaway. The property had been vacant when they discovered it, and the previous owners had graciously left enough furnishings behind to enable 'the Jones's to move right in. Their only immediate purchase had been a bed. Once their salaries began to appear in the Bank, Catherine and Francis slowly turned their house into their home. It was a task that they enjoyed immensely, and it went nicely along with the new life they had made for themselves. Life again, was good.

All was going well. And within a couple of years, Catherine discovered she was pregnant.

In 1954 their son, Leslie was born. A happy time for one and all, and Francis and Catherine decided that they would put down 'their roots' in Bolton, they were here to stay. Several years later, and Catherine gave birth to their second child, a daughter, Emily.

They were good years, Francis was promoted to deputy head teacher at school and the children thrived.

It is a fact, that children generally do look like their parents, and in the Jones family, young Leslie was the double of his father, without doubt. A quiet, slim boy, he was studious from an early age and very soon acquired his father's love of books and reading. Little Emily had inherited her mother's features, pale blue eyes and a shock of white blonde hair. Catherine's hair was poker straight, but Emily had curls, she had a head full of beautifully white blonde curly hair that fell into perfect ringlets, she was like a little doll, and she was the apple of her daddy's eye. As in a lot of families, the second child is the more demanding, and it fell into little Emily's lap, to be the 'lively' member of the family. More vocal and more physical, that was little Emily, never precocious and never bad natured, the child was simply a joy to be with. And though they were different, both were lovely children.

The years continued to pass by and the family flourished. Francis moved on to be the deputy Headmaster of the school and Catherine continued her career of ballet tuition, though on a part time basis. Young Leslie would be around fifteen years old by then, tall and slim, he was a somewhat youthful version of his father. A quiet boy and very studious, he was academic, it was something that his father urged him on to do, perhaps a little too rigidly at times. Lesley was never enthusiastic for sport and his father had always pushed him in a different direction, and was sometimes possibly guilty of treating him more like a pupil than a son.

For Emily, life was a different cup of tea. Now eight years old and as pretty as a picture, she breathed life. Francis unashamedly spoiled her, he knew he did, and the whole family including Emily herself knew he did, but she never took advantage and her mother kept an ever watchful eye on her daughter to make sure that she never started. For Emily, being loved and spoiled was just normal. She knew her daddy adored her. He was the constant in her life.

Unlike her brother, Emily was into everything, the school choir, dancing, acting whenever possible and learning the violin, and now her latest fad, attempting to play tennis. Academia, in the form of the sciences and mathematics would pass her by, but she did inherit the 'Jones's love of reading, and to her father's utter delight, she had the unique ability to recite poetry from memory.

One Sunday morning, the whole family had to wake up early. Leslie had been given the opportunity to go London with the school. He was to be there for a week on a history trip, which included going to the Museums and seeing London's famous buildings. The whole family went down to the train station with him to meet up with the rest of the pupils and the teachers who were also going. Leslie was a bit nervous about the trip, it was his first time away from home on his own and he'd gone rather quiet about it all. Catherine had mentioned this to Francis the night before, and they decided that they'd to all go down to the station together to wave him off.

And so they did, and once the train and Leslie had gone, the three of them walked home as Emily chattered away incessantly to both of them. Francis and Catherine just smiled at one another. Their daughter was like a little bird. It was almost lunch by the time they all got back home. They had a sandwich and then Francis got himself and Emily ready for tennis. She was a member of the local tennis club, and by all accounts had been doing very, well. Emily had a junior match at the club with another girl who was of the same age.

Catherine also got ready, for a tutorial that she had to do in Manchester the next day. She would be setting off very early on the train and she had to iron Emily's uniform for school, as well as her own and Francis's clothes.

Early in the afternoon Francis and Emily set off for the golf club, it was half a mile's walk at the most. As they strolled along, Emily started to chatter away as usual, but

Francis's mind was elsewhere, because he was worried about Leslie. The boy had never been away from home and as they'd put him on the train, Leslie had looked back at them with something akin to despair, Francis had seen it in his eyes. It was because he and Leslie were so alike, that it was like his own eyes looking back at him, and for a moment Francis had wanted to take his son back off the train, he wanted to protect him, but of course he couldn't, it would be ridiculous. And so like many fathers, he'd had to dismiss this as one of those 'It'll make a man out of him' moments'. But as Francis walked on and thought about it, he had his misgivings.

When they arrived at the tennis club, it turned out that the girl who Emily was going to play had cancelled, and when Francis told Emily what had happened she was bitterly disappointed. Word went around the club and finally somebody 'volunteered' their own twelve year old son to give her a 'knock around' game. It was all sorted out and the two children started to play. Nobody took much notice of course, just two children knocking the ball about, but an hour later and those two children were both playing the game of their lives, and the club house had emptied as everyone watched on with awe. The young boy that Emily was playing was as tenacious as her, but he was stronger, and it was Emily's sheer determination and her agility and spirit that kept her in the game, she simply played to her heart out.

It took almost two hours, but finally strength and experience took its toll and the young boy finally won. Both little players got a standing ovation at the end of the game and Francis went down to his daughter and hugged her with pride, his heart nearly bursting, she was only eight.

After a lot of 'Well done's' from everybody', they finally left and walked home. Emily seemed quiet, and so Francis talked to her and told her how proud he was of her and how well she'd done against an opponent much stronger and more experienced than her, but she was still a little subdued.

Half way home she said "Daddy, I'm very tired".

So he reached down and picked her up and he carried her rest of the way home. Within minutes she was asleep in his arms. When he got home, Catherine met him at the door and they took her upstairs and put her straight to bed, she was exhausted. While Catherine cooked their dinner, Francis told her all about the tennis match, Catherine was enthralled.

"I think she's overdone it a bit" said Francis.

Catherine agreed with him "Leave her to sleep it off, she'll be alright for school tomorrow"

An hour later, Francis looked in on her, and smiled when he saw that little head of curtly hair asleep on the pillow. She had done so well today.

He then went back downstairs to Catherine, they talked, and then Francis turned to the subject of Leslie, and his hopes and fears.

After a couple of hours they went to bed. Catherine had to be up early in the morning to go to Manchester, and she looked in on Emily before they turned off the lights.

The next morning Catherine got up early and got herself ready, and just before she left she woke Francis and gently kissed him "You've got half an hour lazybones" she said brightly, and off she went.

And half an hour later Francis got up and went downstairs and made a cup of tea. He read the paper for ten minutes and then checked his watch and then went over to the fridge and took out the milk and prepared some cereal for Emily's breakfast. Then he went upstairs to wake her up. He opened the door and there she was, fast asleep, curly blonde hair all over the pillow. He looked down at her and he thought about how much the tennis had tired her out yesterday.

He sat on the edge of the bed "Wake up 'dozy Mary'..." he said, but she still slept. He reached across to her to lift her hair back and off her face, but something wasn't right, and he leant over and took hold of her shoulder, but she was somehow cool and she felt 'different'. He didn't understand, and so he reached over and he slowly turned her over, and as he looked down at her he just stared. And in utter disbelief and absolute shock, he realized that Emily was dead. His little girl, his baby, had died.

Francis would remember screaming, screaming in horror.

In despair, he screamed like a wounded animal and shrieked in agony and anguish.

He shouted the only words possible to him "No, No...No"

He pulled Emily to him and hugged her tight, as if trying to squeeze the life back into her small body. And he cried out in distress and he prayed to his god for help. But there was nothing, absolutely nothing that he could do. It was all too...too late.

He sat there with her in his arms, crying "Don't leave me darling, don't leave me, please don't leave me" and he wept because he wanted to hear her voice again, and he was struck by the terrible thought, that he would never hear her voice again. Never, ever hear that little voice again, and the laughter. He sat there and he stroked her cheek, praying that she would open those little blue eyes, and praying that this was a mistake or a dream, and that he would see those eyes sparkle again 'Just once God. Please just once'. And in his mind, the fear of the reality, he didn't want to know reality, he didn't want it. But it kept tapping on his shoulder to remind him that he would never see his little girl alive again. Not tomorrow, not the day after, not at all. There would be no tomorrows, and no more breakfasts, and no more tennis. There would be no walks, and no laughing and no hugs. It was gone. It was over, and he would never, ever see her grow up, and never see her happy again.

He sat there on the bed, sobbing and rocking slowly as he held his little girl in his arms.

He held her so close, and so tight, and he wept and cried in utter desolation.

The doctor told them that Emily had a weak heart. Nobody knew. It was one of life's cruel mysteries, and the consequence would be a lifetime of lament and regret.

The diagnosis was given a week after her death, and from there the family could start to make Emily's funeral arrangements. Francis and Catherine were in a total state of shock. Friends helped them as best they could, and the funeral company took care of everything else.

The funeral itself was a terrible, miserable finality. Many people knew the Jones family and of course attended. Emily was a popular little girl, and there were tears.

It was a wretched day, a day that you could question God for an answer, and a conclusion.

People mourn over their loved ones, the loss of a parent, a spouse or even a close friend is a terrible hurt. But the grief of losing a child is unbearable, it is unrelenting woe.

The hopes and fears, and the love for your child are dashed and broken, permanently.

There is no turning back.

And the grief in losing their little girl took its toll on Catherine and Francis. Catherine, beside herself with grief, she would sit and cry to herself for hours, for days.

The pain and the heartache was agonizing and unbearable.

But for Francis, his world collapsed.

The mind numbing anguish, and the everyday unremitting despair, had taken Francis's mind to a darker place. His only respite was sleep, and when he awoke, he only had three or four seconds of solace until he suddenly remembered his nightmare, the constant tragedy, and he was once again crushed by the awful reality of it all.

The doctor prescribed him sleeping tablets and some 'new' sort of tranquilizer. In the end Francis was either asleep or he would sit alone in some sort of daze. He began to suffer from depression, and eventually the finality of Emily's death hit home and he suffered a complete nervous breakdown.

It was a terrible time for the family. Francis was put on indefinite leave from the school.

They were very supportive, thankfully.

Catherine's ballet career understandably came to a complete halt. She would never return to it.

And in the middle of all this was young Leslie.

Catherine had immediately rung her parents, and tearfully told them about Emily's tragic death. They immediately went to London to intercept Leslie and take him out of his school trip. They then took him back to their home in Surrey and tried to explain to him what had happened. He was stricken at the news of the death of his little sister, he truly loved her and he was in shock and was very upset, he couldn't fully accept what he was being told. In hindsight, he should have been with his parents and they should have all shared their grief together, no matter how hard.

But mistakenly, the decision was made to keep 'the boy' in Surrey until things were sorted out, which meant until 'after' the funeral. Leslie was very distressed and he felt somehow 'lost'. He was a stranger in a stranger's house, and he couldn't understand or come to terms with everything that was happening. In a similar way to his father, he too shut down, but in Leslie's case he remained almost permanently shut in a bedroom where he relentlessly read his books, it was a camouflage. His grandparents misguidedly took this as a relief. They didn't really know how to deal with 'things' and in their own way considered that 'silence was golden'.

Two weeks later Leslie finally returned home, to a different world. His distraught parents simply didn't know what to say to him. And whenever they tried, they would just break down into tears. There were no explanations, no discussions, and for their young son there was only upset and loneliness and isolation. Leslie was lost, and it was nobody's fault.

It was a hard year. Francis was ill, and almost permanently in bed. Catherine just went through the motions of everyday life, but nearly in virtual silence. For Leslie, his mother cooked and ironed his clothes and smiled at the right times, but both of his parents were vacant. For him the house was like a tomb, unbearably quiet. There was no fun and no love.

Leslie came home one evening after school, he'd just finished the last of his exams and for once he had no homework and no revision. He was given his tea, and as was usual these days, he ate it on his own. And though his mother was in the kitchen with him, she just stood in the corner, repetitively and silently ironing and in far away thought. After he'd finished his meal, he went as usual, upstairs to his bedroom and within twenty minutes he'd finished the final chapter of a book that he'd been reading. The book had an unsatisfactory ending and having finished it, Leslie carelessly dropped the book to the floor. He stood up and went over to look out of his bedroom window.

It was around six o' clock and the sun was still shining, it had been a beautiful day.

Leslie was fed up with reading, in fact he was fed up with studying and if truth be known with life in general. He looked out of the bedroom window and studied the trees that were in full leaf and the flowers in bloom in the gardens across the road. He suddenly had the urge to go out, to go outside and to get out of this house.

He'd made a simple decision. It was just a simple choice. He just wanted to go out, that's all. But it was going to be a decision that would affect the rest his life.

Leslie walked straight out of his bedroom, descended the stairs and as he went out through the front door he shouted "I'm going out for a while" to anybody who may have been listening, or was vaguely interested.

He walked down Kings Street and onto the main road and he turned left. He had no idea where he was heading, he just wanted to escape from the doom and gloom of the house. The sun still shone and he perked up a little, it was actually quite nice. After several minutes of walking he came to the local park, which was straight across the road from him.

"Why not?" he thought and so he crossed the road and entered the park. It was wonderful.

All the plants and flowers were decked out in 'set' displays and were planted in contrasting colours to bring out their best. Leslie walked around in wonder, and wondered why he'd never come to the park before. It was quite busy and he watched couples walking by, hand in hand, and families all together, laughing and playing football and eating ice cream and he wondered why his life wasn't like theirs, and why it had all gone so wrong.

He knew of course that it was Emily's death that had caused the upset, but as he watched the children and their parents enjoying themselves, a thought struck him, and it wasn't jealousy, it was something else. But the thought was squarely aimed at both his parents.

Simply put, it was "Why do you never you talk to me, I'm your child too. What about me?"

And with all that floating around in his head, he went over to a bench and sat down. He tried to think things through, but there were no simple answers. So he dismissed it all, all and everything, and he went back to enjoying his surroundings.

He really liked it there in the park, it was an escape. Another ten minutes passed by and he went to get himself an ice cream from 'Mr Manfredi's' ice cream van, and then he went back to sit on his bench. As he sat there, Leslie realized that for the first time in a long while he was actually enjoying himself, and he smiled.

Finally he walked back home, and he felt at ease. He liked the feeling, it was something new. So he decided there and then, that he'd go for a walk every night, and he would go to the park, at least it would get him away from the house. He felt good and that night he slept well. And so, that's what he did, every night after his tea he would go out for a walk and go down to the park and sit on his bench, and it was on the fourth or fifth evening that he met Peter.

Leslie had been sitting enjoying his ice cream, when suddenly somebody else sat down on the bench besides him. He turned to see that it was a man, in his late thirties, and quite well dressed.

"That looks good" the man said pleasantly, and he smiled at Leslie.

"Yes, it is" said Leslie "it's from Mr Manfredi's ice cream van, over there" and he nodded in the direction of the van.

And so, they struck up a conversation.

After a while the man stood up "Just wait there a minute" he said to Leslie, and he went over to the ice cream van and came back with two cornets covered with raspberry flavouring and a chocolate flake stuck in each one.

"Here" said the man and he passed Leslie a cornet. Leslie was delighted.

"My names Peter" said the man "and your name is?"

"Leslie" replied Leslie of course, and "Thanks for the ice cream Peter".

Then they both smiled at each other.

The next evening, Leslie went to the park again and sat on his bench, and half an hour later Peter also arrived. Leslie was glad to see him, and they sat there together and talked for over an hour. The next evening they met again, and talked, and when it was time for Leslie to go home, they stood up and Peter reached over and hugged him tenderly.

For Leslie, it was the first human contact that he'd experienced in a long time and it felt good. He was comfortable with it, and in truth, he was somewhat more than comfortable. From then on they started to meet every night, and when the park got quieter Peter would put his arm around Leslie. Leslie liked that.

Three or four nights later, Peter led Leslie into the bushes and he showed Leslie how to 'stroke' him. After three nights of that, they were doing a lot more than stroking.

Then one evening, Peter brought along a friend that he wanted him to meet Leslie, his name was 'Michael'. He was a good looking man, and that night all three of them went into the bushes.

Later on, the good looking man 'Michael' gave Leslie five pounds.

That night, Leslie lay in bed with his five pound note tucked away under his pillow. He was extremely happy and he was also excited, he'd somehow found a 'new' life. It was something exhilarating that completely took him away from the dreariness and misery of home. And as he lay there that night, he also realized and understood something else. That he would never need the love of a woman.

Not long after, Peter asked Leslie if he wanted to go out 'one night'. It would be on a Friday.

So the week after, Friday came around and Leslie told his mother that he was going to a friend's house, they would be babysitting for his friend's parents. He told his mother that the friend had a 'little brother' and that he would probably be home late, but not to worry. One of the parents would drive him back home and make sure that he was okay. His mother was pleased, she was glad that he was finally going out instead of sitting in his room alone every night.

Leslie met Peter in the park at seven o 'clock, and then they both walked the mile or so into the town centre. Leslie was excited and chattered away to Peter all the way there, his was all very new for him. They walked across the town and then went down a cobbled side street that Leslie had never actually seen before, and in fact had never even known it existed. At the end of the street stood the 'Newmarket Pub', it was a grey, timber and rendered building that was supposed to be 'Mock Tudor' in style. A singular building, it stood on its own and 'was' on its own, it had unquestionably seen better days.

As they approached the pub, Peter turned to Leslie and said "If anybody asks you how old you are, tell them you're eighteen, okay?"

"Okay" replied Leslie, and then as an afterthought "Will there be a problem?"

"I very much doubt it, not in this pub" said Peter, and he laughed.

They walked in through the front door and the first thing that struck Leslie was the smell of brewed beer and cigarettes. It was a pungent mix and something that he'd always remember.

Inside, the pub was quite busy. The customers, Leslie noticed, were all men, and were stood around talking and drinking. One or two of them nodded at Peter and then looked at Leslie and smiled. Peter led Leslie over to the bar where they were greeted by the barman.

"Good evening Mr Thompson, and how are 'we' tonight?" joked the smiling barman in a lyrical tone, and it struck Leslie that it was the first time that he'd heard Peter's last name.

"And good evening to you 'Barney' my good man" replied Peter to the barman, returning the humorous gesture.

The barman 'Barney' was a tall slim man who wore a very fancy tie, gaudy was probably a better description. He had curly hair which was cut quite short at the sides but was left 'too' long on top and it gave him a sort of feminine look. The lyrical tone in his voice was nothing more than a declaration that he was 'camp', and the way he stood with his hand on his hip was an absolute giveaway.

"What'll it be boys?" said Barney, glancing at Leslie.

"A Gin and Tonic for me" said Peter "and, I think a gin and orange in a tall glass for my friend Leslie here" and he turned and grinned at Leslie.

"And good evening to you 'Leslie'..." said the ever smiling Barney as he served the drinks.

"Hi" said Leslie.

"Nice choice" said Barney, as he served their drinks, though whether he was referring to the actual drinks, or Leslie, we'll never know.

They picked up the two glasses and went to stand in a corner next to a glazed-over window. They put their drinks on the window sill and looked around the pub.

"It's nice in here" said Peter "they get a good crowd in later".

"I've never been in a pub" said Leslie.

"Well it'll be the first of many, believe me. Now try your drink out" said Peter and he lifted up his glass. Leslie picked up his glass too, and looked down at the drink.

"Cheers" said Peter and he reached over and toasted Leslie's glass with his own.

"Oh, Cheers" replied Leslie.

Peter took a sip of his drink "Well come on, try it" he said looking at Leslie.

Leslie took a drink and savoured it for a moment and then looked up with a very pleased expression "Hey, this is really nice" he said.

"First of many" said Peter again "You're not used to alcohol and the orange takes away the taste of the gin, you'll get used to it, like a lot of things" and his eyes twinkled and Leslie caught the gist and laughed at what he was really implying.

The night continued and different men came over to talk to them both. After another two glasses of 'gin and orange' Leslie began to feel the effects of the alcohol, it made him feel wonderful, and relaxed and a bit giddy.

"I need to go to the toilet" he said to Peter.

"C'mon, I'll take you" Peter replied, and he led him by the hand to the other side of the pub and down a corridor where they found a door with the 'Mens' sign on it.

They went in and Peter led Leslie into a W.C. and closed the door. They were both laughing at the audacity of it all and they continued to laugh as Peter fondled Leslie as he urinated.

"Look" said Leslie giggling. "No hands" and the pair of them burst into hysterics.

As the night and the drinking continued, Leslie went back into the toilets three or four times, along with different men who 'touched him up' and afterwards they gave him a pound for his troubles.

At around ten o' clock he went back in there with a man who required further services.

Leslie obliged and the man gave him five pounds.

At ten thirty Peter and Leslie left the pub, by then they were both quite merry. They walked back home through the park and stopped off at their bench and kissed and had sex. Then Peter walked Leslie home and waved him goodbye. Leslie let himself in, and then skipped upstairs to his bedroom and quietly got into bed. He laid there, with his money tucked under his pillow and slightly drunk. 'What a life' he thought to himself.

And a life it became. Two or three nights a week they would go down to 'The Newmarket', and drink and meet other men. And it was profitable. Lesley started to go the Post Office in the town centre where he opened a savings account. He couldn't use the local post office of course, the people who ran it knew his parents. His Mother obviously knew nothing of his double life. She was just glad to see that he was finally getting out of the house and meeting friends, she had been worried about how Emily's death was affecting him, but he seemed now to be getting on with his life and his school work and his reports were first class as usual. She had enough worries just looking after Francis, so it was a relief to her that at least Leslie was doing alright. And so she just let him get on with it.

Leslie of course 'was' doing well. One way or another he was going out nearly every other night, and his schoolwork wasn't suffering, simply because he was a natural academic. Learning was easy for him, it was one of the other things he loved to do

A couple of months of 'doing the town' passed by, and Peter and Leslie had both now become 'regulars' at the Newmarket pub. Then one evening, Peter talked to Leslie about the possibility of them both going to Manchester for a night out. The 'Newmarket' was the only 'Gay pub' in Bolton, but Peter had heard that there were plenty of them in Manchester. Manchester was a city.

Leslie was quite excited about the idea. He would go of course, but they would have to make plans. They discussed it at length and it was decided that Leslie would tell his mother that he was going to stay at a friend's house overnight, well he was really, only his mother would think that it was a friend from school. So he casually mentioned it to Catherine one morning, just as she was taking Francis's breakfast upstairs to him, as she walked out of the kitchen she called back "Yes, alright dear". It was perfect timing.

The weekend arrived, it was Saturday night and Peter and Leslie got onto the train and made their way to Manchester. Peter knew where to go once they'd arrived, there was apparently an area in Manchester were 'men' went, and they soon found it. It was a night that Leslie would always remember. This was a whole world to him, not just the one pub to hide away in. He was totally free to enjoy the company of men similar to himself. Yes, this was his world. After the pubs closed, they both ended up in a club with two other men and stayed there till daylight. They later came back home on the train the next morning and Leslie arrived home exhausted and went to bed. His mother suspected nothing.

Once again Leslie's life changed. During the week he and Peter would go to the Newmarket Pub and meet up with 'friends'. But weekends, on a Friday or Saturday night, they would both go to Manchester. They were on a roll.

Back home, and finally, finally, Francis began to get better. It was no miracle, it was Catherine. Her love and compassion were her inner strength, and she refused to let her man go. She'd seen bad times before, and she and Francis had pulled through then and they could do it again. She knew they could, she couldn't go back to living without him, not again, not ever again.

One Saturday morning, Leslie arrived home from staying at his 'friends'. Catherine had just gone to the front door to pick up the milk from the doorstep. As she opened the door she spotted Leslie further down the road on the corner talking to a man. She watched on in awe, as Leslie reached over and hugged the man, and the man hugged him back in a way that was much more than just a friendly. She stepped back into the hallway and closed the door. Leslie had always gone straight up to his bedroom after a night at his friend's house, and Catherine always considered that they'd probably been up till late talking, but now, something wasn't right. She stood back in the hallway and let him come in through the front door.

As he came in, she walked towards him and said "Hello dear, did you have a nice time?" and then she looked at him closely.

Leslie just shrugged as he passed her, but Catherine saw his red eyes and his tired face and suddenly the smell of the strong alcohol on his breath hit her, along with the odious reek of cigarettes on his clothes. Without thinking, she grabbed his arm and turned him around.

"Leslie, where on earth have you been?" she asked him.

They stared at each other.

"And who was that man you were just with?" she again asked.

Leslie looked back at her in shock. He'd been seen, he'd been caught.

All of a sudden, his attitude and even his personality changed, and without any warning he was suddenly angry, and he pulled away sharply and shook her grip from his arm.

"I'll do what I want" he said with a cursery sneer "And from now on, just leave me alone".

And with that he turned and walked down the hallway and then went upstairs to his room.

Catherine stood there in shock. What on earth had just happened? This wasn't Leslie, this wasn't him. This was somebody she didn't know, somebody she didn't know at all.

It was a turning point. And for Catherine, she would never have the same relationship with her son ever again.

Things didn't get better the next day. After Leslie had sloped off out somewhere, Catherine went up to his bedroom to tidy up and make his bed. As she fluffed up his pillows, she discovered the money hidden away in one of his pillowcases, there was nearly a hundred pounds.

In desperation, she knew that she had to get Francis back on his feet. The family was falling apart around her. She had already lost one child and she wasn't about to lose another. She had to be strong now, stronger than she'd ever been. It was time to stop mourning.

She threw away all the sleeping pills and the tranquilizers, and she got Francis out of bed and eventually out of the bedroom. She got him up and started to make him have breakfasts downstairs in the kitchen. She made him read the newspapers, and listen to the radio, and got him to help her to make the coffee and slice the bread. She had to get him back, back into his old routine. They went out walking, she took him out walking, all the time, and she talked to him and held him close. It was like waking a dead man. It was like walking him through glue. But slowly, very slowly, he began to make some improvement. It was the start of his recovery.

Two hard months, eight incredibly hard weeks later, and she had him back, sort of. He was still a bit shaky and weak, but 'Francis' was back. There were things he couldn't do, and things he wouldn't do, and he couldn't or wouldn't talk about Emily. To do this was to regress. Francis would close down, and there would be tears, and it was a step backwards. So that topic was to be avoided for the moment. There would come a time, and it would have to be the right time, but not now.

Life with Leslie too, had become much harder. He'd become more than a little estranged with his mother, and these days there wasn't much conversation between them both, no matter how hard Catherine had tried.

What Catherine didn't know however, was that on one afternoon, Leslie had met up with Peter in the local park, and as they sat on their bench, Peter had told him that he was going to go and live in Manchester. Leslie was devastated. He was going to be alone again. Peter tried to explain that he would still try to come over and see him, and that Leslie could jump on the train at weekends and stay over. But even so, Leslie felt he was being abandoned, once again he would be deserted and lost. There would be no more sitting in the park every day, talking to his only friend, and enjoying the company of the only person he'd ever loved.

Peter however had made his mind up, and within a week he'd left for the City and left behind Leslie, who was feeling forlorn and hurt.

After a period of sulking, Leslie decided that he would to go down to the Newmarket on his own. He would still meet men in there, and they would keep paying him for his company.

In fact, amazingly, he now had several hundred pounds in his post office account and it wouldn't be long before that became a thousand. Leslie was quietly taking care of business, but there wasn't the same fun in it now that Peter wasn't around. Even so, he'd given it some thought and decided that he may as well make the money.

Weekends however were different, and he couldn't wait to get on the train and be off to Manchester. He now had a steady circle of 'new' friends there, and he could always stay overnight at Peter's little flat, which was situated on the outskirts of the city.

He would return home on the train after a very wild weekend, usually still half drunk, and he would laugh and remember all the tricks and frolics. Life was good, and yes, life was certainly wild.

Because of his illness and his breakdown, Francis had been left in some sort of mental time warp. When he tried to remember his family he would start with his son Leslie, and in his mind, Leslie was still just a boy, a really lovely boy, and he was so clever, he read books and was doing so well at school, and then there was Emily...Emily...Emily...and then he remembered Emily. And then he remembered everything, and his mind would nearly explode as he realized the excruciating truth, and he would cry out 'Oh God no, no...please no. No, no...not Emily'. And then things went dark, and then black, and then disappeared.

And when he came back he would start again, and so the process continued.

Time...is the great healer, or so it's said.

And eventually, it was time for Francis to try and start his life again. Over a long period, he'd managed to get himself stronger and better, and his mind was once again working. He simply had to get himself back on track, because he had a problem, and that problem was Leslie.

Catherine had already spoken to Francis about Leslie, and had expressed her fears, and her fears were justified, Francis could see that. And he realized what was happening, and he also realized that any form of 'control' or hard tactics could possibly end in disaster.

For the last few weeks, he'd quietly sat and watched his son, and had tried to assess the situation, and he'd eventually had to come to terms with reason. Francis knew that he'd been ill for quite a while, and while he'd been ill his son had grown into a young man. He'd not been there to witness this, and he'd not been there to help and guide Leslie. And he now fully understood that this break in their relationship had damaged them both, and it was an awful fact, but they were now both strangers.

Francis had discussed the situation with Catherine. He realized that he could no longer just 'walk back in' and presume the parental roll. No, it was time to rebuild his relationship with Leslie, and to start demanding 'anything' at all was simply out of the question. He was going to try to talk to Leslie without putting any pressure on him. Communication was the only answer. He would try to work it out with his son, but he realized that whatever bond that they'd had between them, was now long gone. This was a different Leslie, he was uneasy and angry and he had stopped caring. While Francis had been ill, Leslie had changed, and though he was no longer a boy, he was not yet an adult in any sense. Yes, he'd definitely changed.

And his son, now a young man, was ill at ease.

Francis tried to get involved with his schoolwork, but Leslie didn't need him. There were no problems with his schoolwork at all, because schoolwork was effortless for Leslie.

Francis started to plan things for them to do together, but Leslie always seemed to be going out, actually he seemed to be going out all the time. There was the occasional trip to the cinema, Leslie seemed to enjoy that, but there was never a lot of conversation.

Half term at school arrived and Leslie was on holiday for a week. One night while they were having an unspectacular tea, Francis had a thought, and he turned to Leslie and asked him if he wanted to do something the next day. Leslie, as usual, just shrugged.

"Okay" said Francis enthusiastically "I'll tell you what, how's about you and I go for lunch somewhere tomorrow, anywhere you want" he said eagerly.

"I don't know" Leslie replied, half heartedly. He wasn't really interested.

"Oh come on" Francis continued "Let's do something. We can go anywhere you want, we could catch a bus somewhere, or we could even go on the train".

And that was it, Leslie suddenly heard the magic word 'the train' and it hooked him. He suddenly looked up at his father "The train?" he said quickly.

"Yes" continued Francis, still eager "if you want too?"

"Can we go to Manchester, on the train?"

"Yes, of course we could" replied Francis. He'd caught the sparkle in Leslie's eye. Finally he may have got something right with the boy.

"Okay then" said Leslie, and he smiled "I'd like that".

"Right then" said Francis "We'll have the day in Manchester tomorrow, and we'll see the sights and then have a nice lunch". Francis was almost triumphant.

"Yes, okay then" said Leslie, and he got up and went off to his bedroom.

Francis turned to Catherine, who was a bit taken aback by her son's sudden enthusiasm.

"It's a start" Francis said to her.

"I can only hope so dear, I really do" she replied.

The next morning, off they went to Manchester. They got there at around ten thirty, and in addition to having a good look around the city, Francis wanted to buy a decent pair of shoes from a particular Manchester shoemaker. Leslie, now quite chirpy, had mentioned a couple of record shops that he also wanted to visit. So they went about their business and the morning soon turned into early afternoon and eventually, it was time for lunch.

Francis mentioned a pub that he had been recommended 'The Eagle and Child', it was just off Piccadilly somewhere. He'd been told that you could get a good pub lunch there for a reasonable price. It was rather strange, but Francis had the odd feeling that somehow his son knew Manchester, and knew his way around. Leslie seemed to immediately know the direction from the train station into the city centre, and he easily found the two record shops that he wanted to visit, effortlessly in fact. He also seemed to know the direction of the shoe shop that Francis wanted to go to, and then when Francis mentioned the 'Eagle and Child' Pub, Leslie once again set off, straightaway in the right direction. Francis held back a little on the way there, and quietly noticed that his son walked right to the front door of the pub. He also noticed that his son had no problems at all in walking straight into the pub. There was no reserve, and no holding back, he didn't wait for his father to go in first. He just strolled casually through the pub door and then held it open for Francis to follow.

Francis had to gather his thoughts, there was something going on in Leslie's life that he and Catherine knew nothing about, definitely something. There was something about the boy's confidence. He was too comfortable in these surroundings. Why?

So they both went into the pub and found a table in the dining area. It was a very traditional looking place, all dark oak and brass fittings. Ornaments such as horse shoes and buckles adorned the walls in between old faded pictures, pictures painted by 'god only knew who' as Francis put it.

They picked up a couple of menus, which were handwritten on plain red card. The waitress finally arrived and Francis ordered the steak and kidney pie, Leslie had scampi and chips.

The waitress asked them if they wanted anything to drink and Francis ordered half a pint of Guinness, Leslie ordered an orange juice and smiled to himself. He was wondering what his father's expression would have been if he'd ordered himself his usual 'gin and orange'.

The drinks arrived and Francis savoured his Guinness slowly. Leslie drank some of his orange juice, and it tasted insipid and flat, much like his life at the moment. He sat there and looked at his drink on the table in front of him, and he realized that this was the first non alcoholic drink he'd ever had in this City. That thought made him cynical. He suddenly missed Peter and being here in Manchester without him put Leslie in a mood.

Francis made several attempts at conversation, but nothing came of it, and Leslie cut any topic short with just one word answers. It was 'yes' or "no' or 'maybe'.

Thankfully the food arrived and Francis ordered another half pint of Guinness. They both ate in relative silence and this started to frustrate Francis. He'd brought Leslie to Manchester for a purpose, he wanted to build a relationship with the boy, to 'build bridges', and they really did need to talk.

They both had apple crumble and custard for their pudding, and when they'd finally finished eating and the dishes had been taken away, Francis decided to take the 'bull by the horns'.

He looked across the table at his son "Leslie, I really need to talk to you" he said.

Leslie looked back at his father, he was 'trapped' and he was slightly aggrieved, and he immediately thought to himself 'Oh my god, no'.

Francis began to talk to him, and he carried on talking. He tried to give Leslie some explanations and he tried to find him some direction, anything at all. But when he tried to find out what Leslie was doing with his life, Leslie finally got angry, and that anger got the better of him and he turned on his father.

"You don't know anything about me do you? You don't know anything at all" and he spat out the words with a cold viciousness that jarred Francis.

And then he couldn't stop "You don't know what it's been like for me, do you? No, nobody does. And do you know why? Because nobody has ever bothered to ask, nobody.

Emily died and I was packed off to Surrey. My bloody grandparents just sat me down and told that Emily had died, and then they left me on my own. I was heartbroken, my little sister had died, but nobody bothered or cared to ask me how I felt. And you left me there, you left me alone. I was so upset, you'll never know how I felt.

The mention of Emily's death shook Francis, it was something he still couldn't speak about, he just couldn't. But Leslie carried on, almost brutally "Then I finally came home and you wouldn't come out of your bedroom, and my mother is running about after you all the time, and I'm left on my own again. And still nobody is bothered to find out how I feel, and how 'I'm' managing with everything".

Francis sat there open mouthed.

Leslie glared at his father "She's dead. Emily's dead, and she's never coming back, ever".

Francis trembled when he heard those words from his son, and his eyes filled with tears.

After his spate with depression, he was still not well and was not equipped for this onslaught.

He took out a handkerchief and wiped his eyes, he wasn't prepared for this, he was upset.

But Leslie took all this as a sign of weakness, he was disgusted and he was angry.

"I'm your child too you know, I'm your son, what about me. What about me?"

Leslie was so mad that there were tears in his eyes too, but these were tears of anger. He couldn't handle this any longer, not his life and everything else, not like this. Suddenly he stood up, the decision made.

Francis looked up at him and said "I'm so sorry Leslie, for everything, I never knew". But Leslie's mind was elsewhere, and he looked down at his father.

"I need to go to the toilet" he said abruptly, and he turned and left the table.

Francis just sat there, distressed. All he could do was watch him go, walk away.

It would be the last time that he ever saw his son, ever.

Francis wiped his eyes and looked around the room, at the bar he noticed the waitress staring back at him, she was obviously wondering what was going on. He held her attention and beckoned her over. He made some excuse and apologised, and he ordered a pot of tea.

He then sat there and contemplated what had just happened, and he wondered about what he could do to put things right. He'd never realized how unhappy Leslie had been, and only now he began to comprehend how badly everything had been handled. Emily's death had shaken them all, and there were no excuses really, other than the terrible shock at the death of their beloved little girl.

Even that thought made Francis gasp.

But now there was Leslie. His complex young son was having problems, and there were things going on in Leslie's life that Francis was unsure of.

He poured himself a cup of tea and slowly drank it, and he finally calmed himself down and went into deep thought. After a while he refilled his cup, and it was only when he started to drink it that it struck him that Leslie was taking his time in returning from the toilets. He began to wonder about the boy, maybe he was sulking back there, or perhaps he was feeling guilty over his outburst. Francis drank his tea. Ten more minutes passed and Francis began to worry that Leslie was unwell. He got up from the table and asked the waitress were the toilets were located. She pointed down a corridor, and Francis followed her directions and went into the Gents toilet, it was empty.

He came back out and asked the waitress if she'd seen Leslie anywhere, she hadn't.

He went back to the table and sat there for another five minutes or so, still nothing. He sat there tapping a spoon and the waitress took advantage of the moment and presented him with the bill. As he paid he asked the waitress if she'd seen which way Leslie had gone, again, she hadn't.

He went back to the toilets and checked them once more, yes, they were empty. He enquired if there were anymore toilets, upstairs perhaps, but there weren't. Then he went outside and walked around the pub a couple of times and then went back in, but still no Leslie. He stood for a while outside the pub and then went off and walked around the nearby streets and then came back to the pub again, and still nothing. Slightly perturbed, Francis stood there for a while and considered things, and then it struck him. In his temper, Leslie had probably stormed off and gone back home, he may even be at the train station waiting for him to turn up. Francis didn't know if Leslie had any money on him, but Francis didn't know a lot of things, especially about his son's finances. So he went to the train station, but Leslie wasn't there either. He then rang Catherine at home and explained the situation, she agreed that Leslie was probably on his way home, but that Francis should stay at the train station for an hour or so just in case he turned up.

He told her not to say anything to the boy, and that they would sort it all out when he got back home. He waited an hour and a half and still nothing. He rang Catherine again, and still nothing. So he got on the next train for Bolton and came home. He expected Leslie to be home by the time he got back, and hopefully the lad would apologize, hopefully.

Three quarters of an hour later, Francis walked into the house. As he closed the front door he called to Catherine. She immediately came out of the kitchen and into the hallway and had a worried look on her face that straight away told him that Leslie had not returned.

What were they to do? They considered ringing his friends, but then realized that they didn't have any telephone numbers for them. They were just names 'Jimmy and Johnny or Ben' and whatever other names Leslie had conjured up, and suddenly they realized how little they actually knew about their son's social life.

At eight o'clock in the evening, Francis made the decision to go to the Central Police Station, which was down in the town centre. He and Catherine didn't know were Leslie could be, and they were worried that he might still be stuck in Manchester. Francis considered that it would be better if the local police got in touch with the Manchester police, just in case he turned up. He went down to the station and spoke to a policeman behind the desk there. The policeman calmed him down and reassured Francis that this happened all the time, it was almost a regular occurrence. Teenagers were always falling out with their parents and going off in a huff, so not to worry. He was probably at a friend's house and probably lost track of time, no doubt he'd arrive home, if not tonight he'd most likely turn up tomorrow, and feeling sorry for himself no doubt. And of course, the children were all on school holidays so there was no school the next day, so Francis went back home to Catherine and repeated what the policeman had said.

At twelve o'clock, they realized that Leslie wasn't going to come home that night. So they went up to bed and tried to sleep.

Catherine and Francis were never to see their son ever again.
Leslie disappeared that day, never to return.
For whatever reason, they'd lost him.

But the next day, Francis returned to the police station and talked to another policeman.

Once again he was told not to worry too much, but this time the policeman took down some particulars. Another day and it took another two trips to the police station before they went into action. They contacted the Manchester police and the two forces liased. Alerts went out but nothing came of it. Thankfully, no bodies appeared and after three weeks a couple of policemen arrived at the Jones's home and sat both

Francis and Catherine down and showed them a different set of figures, and a different view on things. These were accounts of teenagers who were not lost, but had run away from home for various reasons. Catherine and Francis had already told the police about Leslie's drinking and the money hidden in his bed, and the mysterious man that Catherine had seen him hugging and all their other fears. The police then told them how hard it was to find somebody if that person didn't want to be found.

Later, back at the station and over a cup of tea, the same two policemen discussed the case.

The drinking, the men, and the money, it was all very obvious really.

For Catherine and Francis, agonizing weeks turned into heartbreaking months that slowly turned into a long year, and then years. They never really came to terms with what had happened to both of their children. For many years they wondered if one day Leslie would just turn up at their door. They had long ago decided that if he ever came home, they wouldn't ask him any questions, they would just welcome him with open arms. He was to be 'their' prodigal son. His bedroom was kept as neat and tidy as the day he'd left, nothing was ever changed. But as the years passed, they began to lose hope. Even so, they would never contemplate moving house. If Leslie ever came back, they wanted him to be able to find them, and for Francis and Catherine, the house held all the memories of both their children.

It was all they had left.

Francis eventually went back to school where he threw himself into his work. Within four years he was made the Headmaster, a position he would remain at until his retirement.

They would holiday abroad twice a year. Their first holiday would be to visit some historical city, usually somewhere in Europe and usually somewhere of great art or architectural importance. Their second holiday was always to their beloved island of Crete, were they would relax and read and walk. It was their favourite place for solace and sun.

The years passed, as did their lives.

Mr Jones got older, they both did. Catherine would ring me up at my shop to make an appointment for Francis. It was always for a Wednesday morning, and he was always the first customer. As he got older and infirm, Catherine would drive him to the shop, she always did do the driving, Francis had never wanted to learn to drive a car. They would arrive and park up and I would go outside to greet them and then help Francis to get out of their car. Then I'd hold him up and walk with him into the shop and get him seated. Catherine would then tactfully disappear. 'A bit of shopping', that was always her excuse. She would leave us to talk. She knew we both enjoyed the conversation.

I thought the world of them both. They retained an old world charm and still called each other 'Darling'. They were of an era, and I found them both a joy to be with.

One day I got a phone call from someone, a man who wanted to make an appointment for a 'Mr Jones', first thing on a Wednesday morning. I hadn't heard from Mr Jones for several weeks by then, and I did begin to wonder whether his health had taken a turn for the worse. Wednesday morning arrived and Mr Jones was helped into my shop by the man that I'd spoken to the phone. I say 'helped', he was almost carried in. Mr Jones had visibly aged, he was stooped and very fragile, and I was shocked. The man who had brought him in turned out to be his care worker, his name was 'Ian'.

"How are you Mr Jones" I said, I was concerned, and I wondered why the care worker, where was Catherine?

Mr Jones just stared up at me "We're having a terrible time of it I'm afraid" he said, in a very quivering voice "Catherine's had a stroke, she's in hospital and has been in a coma for nearly five weeks now. I haven't been able to see her for nearly a month now. I've not been fit to visit, and the doctors don't know if she'll ever come out of it. She may die" and he looked up at me "we've never been apart you see..." and the emotion of the moment made him struggle and he became tearful.

I tried to sound positive "I'm sure she'll be alright Mr Jones, you both will. Hospitals are fantastic these days".

"Young Ian here, is looking after me, it's a thankless task I'm afraid" and he gave a slight smile.

"Don't say that Francis" said the care worker "we have a great time, you and me".

Then he said to me, almost as an excuse "We play Francis's classical music, on his stereo. It's really great"

Mr Jones looked up at me and shook his head "He puts it on too loud, he thinks I'm deaf".

That haircut was the last time I saw him. I have another customer who lives just higher up the road from Mr Jones's house. He rang me up to tell me that Mr Jones had passed away. It seems that two weeks before, Catherine had died whilst still in the coma. She'd never woken up. Two days after her funeral, Mr Jones also died. They said that the shock was all too much for him, or you could say it was from a broken heart.

And so, yesterday afternoon, I attended the funeral of my customer and my friend, Mr Francis Clifton Jones, and I still don't know where the 'Clifton' bit comes from, neither did anybody else. I wish now that I'd asked him.

The weather was quite pleasant and there was a reasonably good turnout, considering Mr Jones's age. Once you reach the grand age of eighty nine, it has to be expected that a fair number of your friends and contemporaries have gone before you. There were a good many teachers and old pupils there too, and it made you realize and also respect the influence that Mr Jones must have had on their lives. The school supplied the choir and it was quite a musical service, it would have suited Mr Jones, he would have enjoyed it. Old friends and neighbours, and myself, were herded down to the front of the church. We were sat right under the pulpit. Words were spoken and hymns were sung and eventually the service ended. I sat there and I let the mourners and the rest of the congregation leave. It's something I've always liked to do, and I gave myself a few minutes of reflection as I sat there and remembered Mr Jones and his lovely wife Catherine, and my many happy times with them.

Finally I stood up, and was one of the remaining few to leave. At the rear of the church some of the elderly remained seated because of their age and mobility. And as I walked slowly up the centre aisle I looked across the pews and noticed someone sitting alone in the corner. He caught my attention because he was a vicar, and I'd spotted the 'dog collar' under his jacket. He just sat there on his own, he looked to be in his late fifties and he was wearing a dark grey chequered trilby style hat, pulled down over his head. The vicar looked cold. It was a strange mix of clothing. I had the notion that he must have been one of Mr Jones's many acquaintances, and it struck me as strange that a vicar had not said a few words at the funeral, after all, one or two other old friends had, and vicars are usually quite good at that sort of thing. Then again, I wondered if it was maybe frowned upon, it may not be church protocol for another vicar to speak on another man's patch and all that.

I inwardly shrugged as I walked past.

Then, as I walked by I looked again, and suddenly, something brought me to a standstill. Once more I glanced across at the Vicar sitting in the corner, and this time I saw his profile, and it was that image that brought me to a halt, and I couldn't believe it. I was staggered.

It was the same profile as the man whose funeral I was attending. It was the face of the man that I had looked at through the mirror and whose hair I had cut for over twenty years.

'Oh my god', it had to be, the resemblance.

Sitting there in the church was Francis and Catherine's long lost son. It was Leslie.

And for some reason, the vicar suddenly turned and looked across at me and saw me staring at him. He just turned away and stared down at the floor, and I moved on. I walked out of the church, and then walked out through the grounds and through the church gates, and then I stopped. I leant on one of the pillars that held up a pair of old wrought iron gates, and I put my hands into the pockets of my coat, and I waited. The last few mourners eventually made their way out of the church. They were mostly the older folk and the odd neighbour or two that had been sitting at the back. Finally, everybody had left. I still leant against the pillar and I waited, and I waited, and in due course I heard the sound of someone's footsteps coming though the church grounds, he was the last person, I knew he would be. The Vicar, he walked straight through the gates without even stopping, and he turned to the left and started to walk away up the road. I gave him a few seconds and then I leant away from the pillar and I called out his name "Leslie"!

He froze. He stopped dead in his tracks, and for a moment he just stood there. And as he slowly started to turn, I walked towards him. I walked right up to him, and suddenly we were facing each other.

"It is Leslie, isn't it?" I said to him.

For a moment he was shocked. He looked straight at me, but he didn't know me. He just stood there and stared back.

"Who are you?" he said, he was still startled.

"A friend of your fathers" I replied.

"You don't know me then" he said?

"Yes I do, I know all about you Leslie".

"What do you mean 'You know all about me'..." he queried "What do you actually mean?"

"I'm surprised to see you" I said, and I saw the arrogance in him. He was 'The Vicar', the man who was always looked up to, never to be questioned, never to be spoken down to.

He almost sneered at me "What do you want?" he said.

Yes, there was that arrogance there that I didn't like. And when dealing with arrogance, I've always found that to attack is better than defend, and so...

"What are you doing here?" I said to him, and it was almost a threat.

"What?" That was all he could say, and I'd caught him off guard for an instant.

"Why are you here?" I continued.

"It...It's my father's funeral".

"So where have you been?" again I snapped back at him.

"What do you mean?"

I still had him off guard, and off balance.

"Where are you living now, are you local?" I continued, and I wasn't letting go.

And he just blurted it all out "I'm in Manchester. I'm at Staple Heath. Actually, I'm the Vicar there. I'm the Vicar of St James's Church".

And there it was, he'd told me everything, and of course there was that bit of his own conceit

'I'm the vicar of St James's Church', it was a stab at his own importance.

"So you're fairly local then?" I said.

"Well...yes, of course".

"So where have you been all these years?" I asked him, and I could see that he was starting to get a bit exasperated.

"What has all this got to do with you?" he suddenly said.

"Believe it Leslie, it's a lot to do with me" I said.

He looked disturbed and then a little angry "I'm not discussing my affairs with you" he said and he started to turn away.

"Better stop right now Leslie" I said in a low voice "Walk away now, and next Sunday I'll be down at your lovely little church of St James's, in lovely little Staple Heath, and I'll be asking the same questions. But this time, I'll be sitting on the front pew of your Church, and believe me, I'll do it".

I wouldn't of course, but he wasn't to know that, was he? It was just a bluff.

But it stopped him in his tracks. He turned around again and yes, he realized that he'd told me exactly who he was and where he lived, silly man.

"So Leslie, tell me, where have you been all these years?" I asked him again, but this time I had his attention.

He stood there in silence for a moment and then he took a deep breath, and then decided to talk to me.

He started.

"Okay, I ran away from home, years ago, you obviously know that. I couldn't stand it there any longer, so I moved to Manchester. I lived in Manchester for about five or six years, and then I went down to London with a friend of mine, Peter. We found work down there, we loved London, loved the city life and we stayed. We lived down there for years, and then unfortunately, my friend Peter died. He died of 'Aids'. And with that, my world fell apart and I turned to the church. The church became my whole life, and I finally joined the ministry and at first I served as a verger. I worked hard and studied, and I took my clerical exams as I worked in different parishes over a period of several years. I eventually became a vicar.

"How long have you been back in Manchester?

"Nine years".

"Why did you never contact your parents?"

His eyes widened "I just couldn't. You don't know what my life's been like".

"No?" I said "Well tell me".

He did, and that's how I know his story. He told me about the first time he'd met Peter and his all about his life after that. He tried to make it all sound plausible, but if you picked through the bones of his story, you soon realized that he'd led a selfish and self indulgent life. And he would have carried on regardless, but for the death of his friend, and then he suddenly found that he was on his own again, and all too late. So what did he do? He grabbed religion as the next best thing, and he used the church to pay all his bills, and uses 'God' as his new best friend.

I found it all very pathetic, and so very, very obvious.

When he'd finished his little tale, I said to him "So now you're a man of God".

He gave me the look, the look of a driven man...'a man on a quest'...and it was all an act...

"I am" he replied almost devoutly, and it was all very 'holier than thou', as though through his admission, he would now be forgiven. I could have physically hit him.

"I take it that you read the Bible" I asked him.

"I do, extensively" he replied calmly, he was now wearing his 'intellectual' face, with a smattering of professional concern.

I continued "Have you read the parable 'The Prodigal Son?"

His eyes narrowed, he sensed a trap and his attitude changed again.

"Of course I have" he said, with a flash of contempt.

"You need to read it again" I said.

"What do you mean?" and now he was irritated, because he considered 'The Bible' as his own personal territory and he didn't like being given instruction on it, and the anger showed in his face.

So I carried on "The Prodigal Son went home to his father and begged forgiveness. You should have done that, you should have done the same, but you didn't. You didn't care about anyone else, and you never have and you still don't. All this religious front that you're putting on, it's all bullshit and lies, and it's all an act. All you've ever wanted was somebody to shield you from the realities of this world. Peter obviously did that for you, and now you want the same thing again, but this time you're leaning on the Church and hiding behind God. You left your mother and father without a word of warning, you were so wrapped up in your own little world that you couldn't even write them a letter telling them that you were alright. And for forty years you let them suffer, for forty years they didn't know whether you were dead or alive, and you just couldn't be bothered to send them one single letter. Not a day passed when they didn't think about you and wondered what had happened to you. For forty years they stayed in that same house, just in case you came back. They even kept your bedroom as it was, just for you. And then, unbelievably, you come back to Manchester, and you're a stone's throw away, and still you can't make your peace with them, you still let them suffer, 'You' a so called 'Man of God'. What a load of rubbish. And here's something else. You must have been back to Bolton, because you found out that they were still in the same house. You found out all about them and that they were both old and ill. And that 'my friend' is what this is all about. It's all about the bloody money".

We stood there facing each other, he was speechless and I'd caught the bastard.

"Your parent's house was paid for years ago. Your father had a very good pension and your Mother, being an only child, had inherited a large amount of money from her parents when they passed away. Your mother's parents owned a sizeable property in Surrey and her father had been a bank manager, so there was plenty of money floating about. Your parents lived very quietly, there was never any great expenditure, so Lord only knows how much money they have in the bank. And now you've realized that it could all be yours, the house, the money, everything. And once you get your greedy hands on it you'll be out of the church like a flash, and bye, bye God".

He immediately took offence "You...you don't know what you're talking about. How dare you think that this is all about money".

"Think it, and know it" I said "It's a strange thing isn't it, you wouldn't visit your father when he was alive, yet you'll go to his funeral when he's dead. You can't make your peace with a dead man, there's no last goodbyes are there, or could it just be gross hypocrisy?"

He just stood there wide eyed. But he never spoke a word.

Then I tried another bluff "And you never even went to your Mother's funeral. Why not Leslie?"

Once again, he blurted it out "I...I was very busy...and I only found out about her death a couple of days before the funeral".

And that clinched it.

I looked at him "No, No my friend. No you didn't, you didn't go to her funeral because there was no profit in it for you. There would be no money coming to you until your Father died".

I hadn't actually known whether or not he had attended his mother's funeral. It was just a good guess, but I'd a fairly good idea that he wouldn't have bothered to go.

He stared at me dumbfounded, he just stared at me. And then suddenly, like taking off a mask, his expression slowly changed. The look of bewilderment was gone, and suddenly he was all very relaxed and calm, and then he casually smiled.

"Clever little bastard, aren't you?" he said, very carefully.

And suddenly, here was a different man, it was even a different voice. Gone was all the 'offended piety' and the 'righteousness', and from behind the dog collar the real Lesley Jones finally, finally stepped out.

"So what, so what if I am here for the money" he said. "There's actually nothing anybody can do about it, so there 'you' go". And he smiled back at me, but there was also a threat there, he wanted to win 'this' argument.

"So I was right about you then?" I said "I was right all along".

"Yeah, whatever" he replied, and he didn't care now, not one bit.

"So tell me" I said to him "Why have you come to the funeral, why waste your time coming back here today?"

"Ah" he said, and he grinned "It made good sense to come to the funeral, I had to check things out, I had to see the 'lay of the land' as they say. I wanted to see just who turned up, wanted to see if any 'far flung' relatives appeared. When there's money about people get 'giddy' and you never know who's going to pop up from under the floor boards. So I just sat there in the church and kept my eye on things, and the only people that were there were old friends and work colleagues, and so 'Hallelujah' where do you think the money will go?"

And he laughed at that.

He was at ease now, and bragging at his apparent success.

"Leslie" I said. "I have to tell you, you are above contempt. You are a hypocrite and a liar, and you're possibly the cruellest person that I have ever known. Your parents were lovely people and they deserved better and better from you. They were worth more than money".

I stopped for a moment. I was so angry, and I had to think about what I had to tell him, and exactly how I was going to do it.

"Do you want to know something?" I said to him "You Leslie, will never be truly happy. It's not in you. And eventually you'll die too, and on your own, just a lonely old man".

He didn't like that remark one bit, and the truth of it suddenly angered him and his face twisted in contempt.

"Tell me about it when I get the money" he seethed at me "And I'll be selling that bloody awful house too, and with the rest of the money I'll be out of here and back to London to live the good life" and he glared at me as though he'd won something.

"Before you go Leslie" I said, slowly now "there are probably a few things that you should know".

"Oh and what's that?" he replied dismissively, and he looked away for a second, almost as if he was too busy to listen. But what he really meant was that he was that he'd had enough of this conversation and he wanted to be on his way.

"Well" I said "It's just that I know your Father's solicitor. In fact, I know him very well".

And suddenly I had his attention again, and now he looked at me closely, he realized that this could possibly be a threat.

"And...Yes?" he asked.

"Well, I actually know what's written in your fathers will" I said.

And now he went rather rigid "A Will?"

"Yes Leslie, a Will. And before you go selling the house and running off with all the money, I'd better tell you something".

And this was the moment. I'd chosen my words carefully, and I almost smiled.

"Your Father left everything, all his money and all his property, to the School and the Church. He set up two trusts funds, one for the upkeep of the Church and the other for his old School. He in particular, wanted the school to have a new Library. He was very keen on books you see. Both trust funds have been set up for quite a while. You may not know this Leslie, but your Mother was also very involved with the Church, it was her life. And your Father wanted to do the right thing. It's a very worthwhile cause."

Leslie looked like he was going to have an early death.

He started to splutter "He couldn't have", it was almost a whisper.

"Well he did" I said "He and his solicitor sat down and sorted it all out, it was quite a while ago really, and your father named his solicitor as his executor".

Leslie now became rather upset. "Oh I see" he said, he was flustered now "The solicitor, so he's the executor is he, and he'll be paying himself handsomely for his services no doubt. This was obviously all his idea and no doubt he'll try and get his hands on some of my father's money. Well, I'll contest the Will".

"No Leslie" I said "You can't. That won't work. The Trust is all above board and legal, I know that, and I know the solicitor. He's a very honest and well respected man."

Leslie was now becoming very agitated and more than slightly desperate.

"My father, he would have left me some money, I know he would. He must have known I was still alive. And why would he give it all away, somebody must have talked him into it, somebody from that school, or that Vicar at the Church, those people are always after money. Somebody's got to my father and cheated me out of my money, it's my inheritance".

I was somewhat amused that he didn't see the significance of his comment about the church.

"Well, I do see your point of view Leslie " I said "And you're right of course, somebody did get to your father, and they talked to him about giving away all of his cash".

Leslie started shouting, he was almost frantic now "Who...Who the hell was it?"

I just smiled back at him "It was me Lesley. It was me".

And with that, I turned and walked away as Leslie began to hurl abuse at me. But, they were just pathetic threats, they were only words.

And there was very little he could do.

So, Mr Jones, more than a customer, more than just a friend, he was a man that I truly admired, and a man who saw the goodness in life and the goodness in others. He was a true gentleman.

He once told me "Never lower your standards to the level of others. Always retain your dignity and your principles, and be the better man"

I once spoke to him about writing and I asked him if he'd ever considered writing a book himself, he laughed and shook his head.

He told me "No, I'm a reader, not a writer. I've nothing to say" he said with a chuckle.

I found that hard to believe, but he would have none of it.

And one time, and slightly embarrassed, I once confessed to him that I had always wanted to try to write something myself.

"And why don't you?" he said.

I gave him all the usual excuses, about being too busy, and work, and family. And then I finally admitted the real reason. It was the fear of failure, and the fear of disapproval from others. It seems that I have a pathetic concern over criticism.

"So you're a bit of a coward then" he said.

"Yes" I admitted, and knew it.

"And you're worried about 'people and their disapproval'?"

"Yes well, nobody likes being laughed at" I said, it was a sort of excuse.

"Listen to me" he said "The only people who would laugh at you are either clueless or jealous. And I don't go along with the term 'constructive criticism' either. It's 'help and assistance' that's usually needed. That's what I did as a teacher".

Then he gave me the advice that I'll always remember.

He said "In life, don't ever let anyone hold you back".

Thank you Mr Jones, thank you Francis.

And so, I'm now sat here in my Barbers shop, and its Saturday afternoon and I've finished. And Mr Jones and his story and his life keeps rolling around in my head, and it's a reminder of how quickly life passes by.

But there's something going on in my head too, and I'm beginning to wonder about my own future. Sometime in the near distance, I'm supposed to be retiring.

And essentially, the question I'm asking myself is this.

'Where am I going with my life, and what am I actually going to do with the rest of it'?

It's probably a question that a lot of people have asked themselves at one time or another.

And I sit here, and I look in the mirror and I say to myself.

"Well, what do you want to do, and what are you going to do, because life my friend is too, too short".

So I sit and I deliberate, and my brain and my imagination somehow begin to work, and I finally come to a decision. And the conclusion to that decision is that I need a change, I want a change in my life and I want to do something different. And what I want to do is travel.

It's time for me to go and see some of the 'big old world', while I can. And I lean back in the chair that I've stood behind for years, and I think about all the places that I've always wanted to see. And I'd like to spend the summer discovering the Greek Islands, and after that, go and see Seville. And I want to go to London and visit the National Gallery to see the 'Holbein's', and then go to Rome and see everything. And I want to tour Australia, and visit Tasmania, and then go to see the Giant Redwood trees over in Northern California, and have some fun in the Caribbean, and then go to Oslo, and travel back to see Hawaii and Miami again, and then a thousand other places

And when you think about it, you've got to ask yourself.

'What's the use of living to be a hundred, if the last twenty years are worthless'?

And suddenly, there's an easy answer to all my problems, the so called 'a spark of inspiration'. And I've just made up my mind.

I'm finishing, and I'm finishing right now.

I'm going to stop working today. And I'm going to close the shop, and lock the door and walk away. And then I'm going to sell the place, and it's over.

It's been a great twenty five years, and I've loved it. But repetition can blinker you, and there are certainly other things to do with your life, and working forever more doesn't have to be one of them.

I have a house, and that will always be there. I don't have to burn any bridges, I'll be okay.

I'm sitting here, and I'm smiling. And then stand I up and I head for the door.

And from there, all I have to do is to put a few things in order and get myself organized.

Then I'll pack a bag and seek adventure, and then let's see what happens.

Adieu.